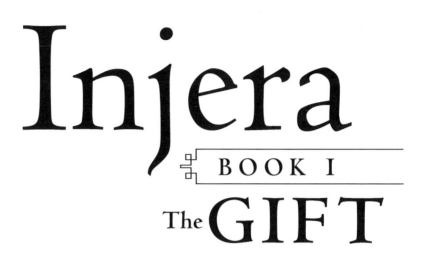

Injera

BOOK I

The GIFT

Deborah L. Rhodes

ISBN: 1-4392-0665-1
ISBN-13: 9781439206652

Visit www.booksurge.com to order additional copies.

for those who listen and feel

Contents

Prologue   7

Part I
    I.   Birth and Burial   11
    2.   Why Must We Pass This Way?   24
    3.   She Watched the Storms   45
    4.   In Absentia   65
    5.   And She Never Forgot   88
    6.   The Dreams of Animals   117
    7.   Faith Betrayed   149
    8.   Keeper of the Faith   170

Part II
    9.   Inar   197
    10.   Bridge to the Other Side   214
    11.   Dust to Dust   238
    12.   Guardians of a Sacred Trust   254
    13.   An Unholy Union   268
    14.   Saba-Energy   283
    15.   The Gathering   304
    16.   Fear and Longing   319

Part III
    17.   Watching the Night   341
    18.   The Gift   363
    19.   To What End?   382
    20.   True and Pure Vessel   408
    21.   What Will Endure?   418
    22.   The Abyss   432
    23.   The In-Between   447
    24.   Something Inside   482

Epilogue   499

Prologue

Ever so often an ageless night wind blows through the heavens whispering to those who might take its message into the day. More times than not, the stories compel their listeners to open their wings and take to the sky, never to traverse the earth again. Undaunted, the sky continues to seek those whose vision might reveal the fullness of its spectrum to the naked eyes of the world. Thus, the wind, upon the crystal lights of darkness, has whispered these words...

Part I

I. Birth and Burial

Wrapping it in a burlap cloth, they buried the newborn infant alive. Edise acted alone when even his most induced followers were abandoned by their motivating fear. He took her deep into the northern woods, near the edge of the mountain foothill, where a burial site had already been prepared. As he placed her on the ground next to the shallow grave, the child, without sound or movement, looked directly at her captor and pierced the androgyne straight through the center of his soul. Stunned by the intensity of her power, the androgyne with his limbs momentarily paralyzed, began shaking violently. When he re-gained the ability to move, he quickly mummified the infant in the shroud and allowed the wet earth to slowly swallow her whole.

The Saba had been late that day. The day following the darkest of nights when the Ocan people gathered to deliberate, decide what must be done. Sleep had held her under for more time than she intended, until bodiless words with no source or origin forced her to awaken. They repeated continuously in her mind even now as she pulled her young grandson by the hand, making her way through the crowd seated on the floor throughout the large atrium-like building that was full beyond its capacity. The words filled her head so completely that she could not decipher the meaning of the heated argument between the two men who stood facing one another in the middle of the over-crowded room. She tried shaking her head to clear her mind but the words still came, *Wrapping it in a burlap cloth, they buried*—The people shifted to make room for Saba, and she waved away their attempts to point her to a seat of honor, managing to squeeze onto a bench in a small alcove near the door, with Taijaur on her lap. Looking around the room, both Saba and her grandson appeared to be searching. The boy's bounty was apparently more fruitful than his grandmother's, as he wiggled out of her arms and moved toward the one other child present within the gathering.

Through the blur of words in her mind, present reality nudged the Saba's thoughts and captured her attention as she looked up, surprised to realize that her own brother, Kalal, was one of the two debate contenders. Her ears finally became tuned to the tenor of their discussion, just as Edise proclaimed in a loud clear voice, "The Obeah confirm the obvious. This birth has led to a fracture in the reality of our world. That child cannot remain among us." Above the room's sudden drone of murmured acquiescence, Kalal shouted, "Edise, you can not interpret the Obeah's words just to suit your purpose. These fractures exist at all times, in all places. We cannot make this child responsible for the Earth's own natural occurrences." Edise turned his back on the older man and continued to address the gathering, his hands in open palm supplication on either side of his body, "They looked into her mind, into her soul. They saw disaster connected with this child's future; the destruction of our way of life."

The two men stood in contrast to one another, as they both paced in the open circle around which the people sat, each propelled by the current of their thoughts and emotions. One man was large, burly and sweaty with a full beard, wild bushy hair, exposed glistening forearms and an angry, bewildered, almost frightened expression on his face. The other—tall, rail-thin and fully covered in a gray muslin robe—was pale, clean-shaven and wore a look of bored, haughty disdain. Edise wove back and forth through the crowd, as he extended his range, gliding through the larger gaps and spaces between those seated nearby, while Kalal, conscious of his bulky frame, confined his territory to the middle circle alone.

A violent cacophony of wind, thunder and rain arose outside and drowned out all sound for a moment. It then subsided into a steady battering of rain before lashing forth again, crashing against the building as if to tear it from its foundation. The effect of intermittent lightning mixed with rain spilled through the fractal glass ceiling of the Maja, casting an eerie preternatural spectrum of light and shadows that danced on the walls and people in the candlelit room. Competing to be heard against the force of the external elements, the voices of the two opponents bounced off the acoustically enhanced adobe walls, echoing up into the higher strata of the open room.

The Maja sits in the middle of the village marketplace, and was strategically built in a place where the land's underground rock formations contain highly concentrated fields of energy. The five story high octagon shaped adobe and stone building was crowned by a modified glass geodesic dome and surrounded by stalls and booths, now empty of their normal bustling activity. An aerial view of the interior would reveal a design akin to a giant orb spider web, with sectioned off rooms, corridors and a balcony circling on each of the four levels that sit above the large open center design of the ground floor. There were no rooms or corridors on the lowest level, just small alcoves on each wall and an intricate obscure pattern on the granite floor with thick lines of carved inscriptions that lead from the center design to each corner of the octagon.

Most of the adults in the main Ocan village were there, as well as many of those from the second largest Ocan community near the Haman River and even some from the other outlying villages. Saba and her grandson, Taijaur, had entered the Maja in time only to hear the triumvirate Obeah utter their final words before watching them silently depart. In addition to the loose circle of people seated on the ground floor, most of those present were overflowing on the four balcony levels of the Ocan community meeting house, either sitting, standing, leaning over or crowding into the metal railings. They looked like spectators in a sporting coliseum, except they made no sound, cheering neither champion nor rival. Saba recognized some familiar Haman villagers who, no doubt, would rather be bartering in the closed marketplace on this solstice Exchange Day or at least making their way along the distant route back to the river. Saba searched the room, in vain, to see if any members from the Ocan faction community—the Aka—were present. Even the knowledge of how unlikely this would be, never dimmed the healer-woman's false sense of hope.

Saba watched her only sibling with a mixture of worry and pride. He was older than she by almost ten years and watching him reminded her of the much too swift passing of time; this was not the same man that she had known even two years ago. Daily it seemed that energy and vitality were draining visibly from this once master of all Ocan builders. Reaching beyond his weariness, Kalal seemed to find himself, mustering his strength as he now towered above his adversary, his words thundering, "The Obeah said that this child was brought here by the will of the powers of the universe. Who are we to question the intent of life's greater forces?" As he spoke and then waited for a response, Kalal nervously fingered the strap of a hemp pouch that lay draped diagonally across one of his broad shoulders, reaching down over his rounded mid-section. Despite being the Master Builder of the Ocan, Kalal never donned the longer robes of the Masters' Guild that would have distinguished him as the chief architect of the Maja and all important edifices constructed in the last half century. Instead, he was most comfortable in the same clothing as the masons and workmen of his trade, a brown sleeveless cotton-like tunic, belted at the waist and hanging to mid-thigh, partially covering loose fitting, light weight pants. The room was momentarily silent and Kalal seized the opportunity to continue, "The Obeah spoke of renewal, not destruction; of beginnings born of inevitable endings."

Saba looked across the room at the two men and three women who comprised the Council of Elders. They were sitting on a low bench against the back wall, overlooking those seated in front of them on the floor. Although she tried, she could not penetrate the empty benign gazes of that small selected group of cultural and legal overseers. Brief uncontrollable feelings of frustration and disappointment swelled in her heart and mind as she struggled to pull her attention back to the discussion. There was a time, when by sentiale awareness alone, she could have discerned, felt, touched all that she needed to know *a priori*. But now she could only listen closely and observe these present actors and actions for clues, reaching for an understanding that once would have flowed into her being of its own accord.

Unlike most Ocan council meetings, no other person in the Maja even tried to voice an opinion in the debate that ensued between Edise and Kalal. The people seemed to be wrapped in a tight silent bond of hopeless anxiety. The Saba fought to hold her tongue; she knew that any support that she offered would be viewed as tainted by the biases of her connections. Despite her attempt to think otherwise, the Saba was well aware that Mala's offense of bringing forth a hybrid child—a potential contaminant—was viewed as more than just an unlawful wrong, but as a mortal threat to the Ocan people's insulated collective. But Saba also knew that Ocan laws—while rooted deeply in her people's fears, and their way of life—were never meant to take precedence over powerful human bonds created outside and beyond their fragile temporal realities. For Saba and others like her, a loved one's pain will always assuage any actual or perceived iniquity. She accepted the shame of Mala's transgression as a mere isolated moment of human suffering, in need of nothing more than compassion and regret.

It was Saba who had seen her first, as she appeared at dawn on the day preceding that darkest of nights. The healer-woman had been alone gathering medicinal herbs and various species of fungi at the edge of the western forest when through the brambles she detected movement and then saw a form much larger than the small furry creatures that played near the forest boundary. Obscured by the shadows and mist of early morning fog, the figure rose and took shape. Though she suspected that her eyes betrayed her, Saba gasped, "Mala?" in one breath and then whispered to the air around her that it could not be so. This—this thing, this person before her was surely only a dream; a vision conjured by her own desire to see her adopted daughter again. But the figure, the person, the apparition continued stumbling towards her, with arms stretched forward, beseeching. Saba's eyes strained and her heart overruled her senses, compelling her to run. "Mala!" she shouted, dropping the bundle of plants from her apron. She gathered the dirty disheveled woman in her arms and gave praises to the gods above for the safe return of the one person who could fill the breach of too many lives lost. Mala's clothing was torn and tattered, her feet blistered and bloody. She came, bearing within the child, already in the throes of a hard labor that would last beyond the day and into the night. She fell with exhaustion into the Saba's arms, having traveled nonstop through the mountains, hastening to reach the settlement before she gave birth. Although the Saba never left her side, Mala strained silently and alone, allowing no one to touch or comfort her as she struggled to bring forth new life. Only a scattered few came forward to assist her. Most were mindful of the potential ripple effect of repercussions that belonged to Mala alone. They all understood that this new offense, this direct violation of a dictum written into the primer of Ocan existence, would ultimately bear the burden of its own retribution.

After ensuring the safe passage of new life into this world, Saba had returned to her home in the early dawn intending to rest only briefly, before preparing for this council meeting where the infant's fate would be decided. However, when she closed her eyes, her weary thoughts, without warning, began to drift back and forth between the birth of Mala's child and the birth of her own grandchild four short years prior. She had never allowed the circumstances surrounding Taijaur's entry into this world to touch the daytime realities of herself or her grandson. Yet somehow, in defiance of her resolution, the rejected memories had resurrected and taken control of her mind. Although the Saba struggled to push away those powerful unwanted moments of the past, the memories were determined to ignore even the silent plea of tears that fell despite her will. Eventually, an intense sorrow rocked the healer-woman into a deep obliterating sleep where she remained until strange disjointed words jarred her awake as they repeated over and over in her mind—*Wrapping it in a burlap cloth, they buried...straight through the center of his soul...*

The healer-woman now watched as Kalal's wife, Amira, rose to whisper to him, touching him gently as if to soothe away all pain and discord. Saba saw her own feelings of worry and concern reflected on Amira's face. Then, as Edise began speaking, the two women glanced at one another from opposite sides of the room, and exchanged an understood expression of shared annoyance. It was apparent that Edise's newly appointed role as the first-ever Chief of Security and Safety for all of the Ocan villages was to be viewed with the utmost seriousness and that he, likewise, be accorded all the veneration deemed befitting of such a position and title. For years, Edise had argued and petitioned the Council for the necessity of the Ocan to be prepared to counter any real or perceived potential threats, especially those that might arise from the increased show of hostility from the Aka.

As the androgyne moved, his floor length robe swayed in harmony with his graceful stride. He began his rebuttal in the soft subdued tones of a shy maiden then allowed the power of his voice to rise toward the end, in an intense plea. "People, we have been here before. Our forbears struggled only lightly before conceding to a fatal decision that has meant doom and despair to all successive generations of living beings within this world. In the past, they chose not to act. They sat idle and watched a disease spread its venom upon the earth. And now we are among the few who have not yet succumb to the power of this poison. I ask you all, what choice do we have?"

Amira, who still stood near Kalal, pleaded, "But this is a babe, an innocent babe."

Edise shook his head and looked at her with a pity reserved for poor misguided children. Then smiling and staring at her with exaggeratedly widened eyes, he slowly enunciated and accented each syllable as if speaking to someone hard of hearing or unable to comprehend easily. "All- is- not-pure- in- the-un-i-verse, A-mir-a." He paused before continuing at a faster pace but in the same singsong tone, "Do not assume that because this world's pollution has yet to touch this being that there is no internal contamination natural to its kind."

Kalal flustered, "Its kind? It's kind? That baby is one of us. We are its kind."

Edise charged back with a rapid deafening retort, "Are we? Who even knows the source of this progeny? What man can speak?"

Kalal seemed weak, almost lost as he asked, "Well, what of Mala?"

Edise: "What of her? She freely chose not to be a part of us, as no one before her and no one since her has chosen."

Kalal responded, "That's not true! No matter what, Mala is still just as much Ocan as you and I."

"Nevertheless," Edise continued, "the woman is not important. We have a much larger problem at hand. We have been given a sign that what has been born among us was never meant to be. What sanction can rightfully be conferred to the offspring of an unholy union? That transient woman has coupled with some unknown—" he paused, "Well, it may be a beast for all that we know. And the more that I think of it, the child's paternal source would have to be of unnatural origins. With the exception of that nomad of a mother, there are no humans in the forbidden lands. Even the Aka are not foolish enough to venture that terrain. Who even knows if Mala is fully Ocan? Look how strange and hostile her own parents were and look how they reared her. Look at the destruction they caused and how they met their own doom. Mala has no regard, no respect for the Ocan ways. And there is only one answer, one solution for the unwelcome product of human-bestial miscegenation." He looked toward the glass ceiling as the wind and thunder crashed in a furious explosion. Capitalizing on the moment, Edise declared, "Even now the vortex howls to reclaim its soul. The wind called it back and the darkness issued it forth. This is the same virulent darkness that centuries ago forced our founders to flee their birthplace, seeking the haven of this deserted land."

Kalal appeared tired as he struggled to continue, "How do you know with certainty that this birth is connected with that night of so long ago?"

Edise stared at him in disbelief. "Have you looked fully at that child?"

"Yes...she is somewhat... uh, different. But I fail to see what that has to do with—" Edise interrupted in a high pitch falsetto shriek, "You fail to see! You fail to see! That's just it, you fail to see. Open your eyes and know the aberration of human nature that we·have the responsibility of subduing."

With obvious effort, the older man tried to retain his ease as he replied, "But there are many of us born with or given by life, more or less of what another may or may not have. No two of us are the same. To make such a severe judgment based on superficial physical characteristics—" He floundered, leaving off in mid-sentence. Kalal was shaking his head, with grief and bewilderment evident in his eyes, as he looked at Edise, searching for words.

While Kalal had directed all of his comments to Edise alone, Edise never forgot his audience and he spoke with the ease of a great orator, moving amongst the people addressing them now with an open look of sorrow and compassion. "My good man, my good people, this is no mere deformity. And that is no mere babe."

Kalal interrupted, having found himself, his thoughts once more, "Edise, your perspective is based on fear and fear alone."

Edise: "Yes, I will admit that I am afraid. Afraid of what may happen if we choose not to act as, in the past, our ancestors so chose."

Kalal: "In making this decision don't we behave in the same manner as those who are infected? Isn't the action that you propose a symptom of a greater illness?"

Edise: "People of the Ocan, let us not forget that our entire existence is a reaction to the disease that invades this planet. It is no wonder that a small part of it must be present to inoculate against further damage."

Kalal: "The past cannot be re-lived. A mistake was made, in that our forebears did not react in time. They did not foresee how completely a negative force could engulf this world. And now we have lived for ages subjugated by or in hiding from the power of its effect. But that is no reason to deny this child its life. We have no right to make that decision."

Edise: "We make no decisions of life or death. We simply cannot allow it to exist among us. And that decision was made in the darkness and in the winds that stood witness to its birth."

Kalal: "To expose or abandon an infant in the terrain of this land can only mean death. I will not stand by and allow this to happen."

The Saba gasped aloud as everyone else just continued watching the debate. She glanced over and made eye contact with her sister in-law who only nodded her head sadly. Edise looked slowly around the room as he spoke, "Careful, Kalal. Take note of where the people stand on this." Then he deliberately allowed his final words to coincide with his gaze that came to rest upon the Elders, "You do not rule here."

Kalal turned, scanning the room. He began to incredulously realize his position for the first time. Most of the people would not look at him, shame lowered their heads, fear averted their eyes. Throughout the exchange, the Elders, uncharacteristically quiet, mumbled among themselves, nodding their heads. And then as if in one voice, they cried out, "It is for the children that we must act."

Toval a very grizzled old man, considered the most judicious of the Elders, stood with a stooped bent posture. In a subdued voice he intoned, "We have no right to sacrifice their future and possibly the future of all life within the Ocan for something we neither comprehend nor desire. We have lived for past generations on the positive side of earth's offering only because we consciously reject those negative factors of existence that would threaten our fate. Just look at the destruction, abuse, and misuse of this planet that occurs outside of our island home. And yet these forces of devastation cannot affect us because we have become immune to their power. And we have willingly paid a high price to maintain this stability, this safety in our way of life.

While it is true that the child may offer no immediate threat of bodily harm, nonetheless, we cannot ignore what the Obeah have seen through her eyes. We cannot ignore the potential for this child's continued existence to jeopardize all that we have worked to accomplish.

Injera—the reason, the intent, the very cause of our existence within this realm—demands that we pursue our quest for sanctity free of the negative realities that rule other lands, other groups of people within this world. The most basic needs of our lives and of this planet are fulfilled only through our spiritual development and evolution. We must persevere, as we move towards our ultimate potential to transform into beings of power. Our physical survival will mean nothing in the face of the loss of our spiritual mass. This child, this unexpected being, is a symbol of all that our ancestors left behind; that from which we have escaped. For all intents and purposes, her substance may be comprised more of the foreign than of our own. While the images of destruction that the Obeah saw within her, may not reflect the child's intent, still they are undoubtedly connected to her time on this earth. We have no way of knowing how to guard against any potential dangers that may manifest as a result of her existence."

Kalal looked around at those in the room who remained silent. "And what of you who sit and say nothing? Surely this act is not in concert with your principles, your beliefs." He pointed to a bearded man close to him who sat with his head bowed, "You Lonau, I can't believe that you go along with these, these, these inane justifications offered as excuses for, for, for—," Kalal looked from side to side as if searching for the right words, until he said with force, "for evil, for malevolence."

Lonau responded, with his head still bowed, studying his interlaced fingers, "You speak for me, for us, Brother Kalal. There is nothing more that we can say or do."

Several people nodded their heads. Kalal, with his brow furrowed, continued as if now arguing with himself, as if to reconcile his own internal discrepancies, in an effort to understand fully. "But how can a people who consider themselves good and kind in deed and thought, kill an innocent child?" He looked directly at Toval and said, "You have no direct knowledge of this child's origin, yet you feel that such a decision is justified." Toval said nothing. Kalal began moving through the room, now looking openly at the people on all sides as he spoke, "In committing such an act against a harmless infant, how can we continue to think of ourselves as morally superior to other nations of this world? What does it matter that the Ocan people possess the world's most advanced technology, science and culture, if we have not developed the compassion that would allow us to spare the life of a child? What is the value of all our superior achievements if we have lost our own humanity?"

He paused for a moment, looking around the room, and still most of the people would not meet his eyes. "I wonder—tell me, *dear people*—will it ever be known, why evil—pure evil—comes, not just to those random few who relinquish their lives to its control, but also to those who blindly convince themselves of their own misguided, benighted righteousness? Or worse yet— those innocent bystanders, who do nothing but continue to stand by. I used to think that if one believed in good, I mean *truly believed*, then it would not be possible to knowingly commit a wrong. I used to believe that evil belonged only to the wicked and the immoral; but surely not to those merely immobilized by their own insipid wishes that it would all just go away. I no longer have the security of such delusions and I see now that evil may belong to us all."

The room was quiet as Toval sighed heavily, his eyes filled with pain as he responded, "It is true that we do not know the full source of the child's origins and thus can not pass final judgment on her potential as a contagion. Nonetheless, we cannot afford to introduce such an unknown into the midst of our children whose lives are free from the impurities of our ancestors. There is too much at stake, too much that we can potentially lose. We have come too far, and there is still much to be done. The injera of the Ocan people—the need, the purpose of realizing our destiny as beings of power—supersedes all other considerations, even unfortunately something as important as the life of a child. Every God-given life is precious and valued within our collective. However, we cannot take the risk of infecting our souls, infecting the lives of our children with anything remotely connected with the virulent forces of our past.

This child's presence could set into motion a chain of events that we cannot begin to fathom or control. Already it is certain, that her birth has created a breach. An opening between the world we know and one that is beyond our ability to comprehend. We must send it back if only to contain that breach. For it was just such a fracture in the fabric of our known reality that forced the ancient Obeah to enter an alternate realm of existence, rendering them incapable of returning to our world. We are not yet ready for this opening—our power is still developing; the Emissary has not yet come to lead us to the catalyst. And let us not forget the danger of this opening between worlds. What if someone outside of the Ocan discovers the power inherent in such a breach? What if the Aka gain access to this opening? They have searched for ways to gain a foothold over the Ocan, and this opening would provide them more energy than can ever be imagined. The potential to use and manipulate this force for evil is too great. We cannot allow that to happen.

The decision that comes to us this day is not an easy one to make, nor is it one from which we will escape with no compunction. I suspect that the burden of this judgment may weigh heavily upon our souls, for our duration within this realm. But we owe it to the struggles of all those who have come before us and those who will carry on our ways to maintain the principles, order and safety of our lives and the lives of our children. I'm sorry Kalal, we all share this pain equally. This time Edise is right."

Kalal asked quietly, "And what of Mala?"

Toval answered, "This one belongs not to Mala or to us, but to the powers that brought it here." Then, as if on cue, a low buzz of agitated, confused whispering voices filled the room.

Edise, with a smirk of self-satisfied triumph, quickly moved back to the center of the room. Once again taking command of the situation, he announced in a dismissive tone, "That woman chose her fate long before this day." He motioned to a man near him, "Cerian, come with me."

The people seated on the floor began to rise and made a path as Edise walked briskly toward the door. Kalal grabbed his arm, intercepting him before he had fully exited. "She will not accept this decision."

Edise, looking down at the hand that held his garment, replied slowly, with measured restraint, "That is not our concern."

Kalal's sense of desperation spilled out in open emotion that covered his large sweaty face. "Have you no, no, no feeling?"

Edise shook Kalal's hand from his arm and stared at him with a mixture of scorn and disgust. "That is a luxury that no one of us can afford to indulge at this time. The decision has been made. Let this senseless debate cease. The inevitable has been prolonged long enough."

"Grandma! Grandma!" Taijaur was screaming, pulling and patting his grandmother as she stood in a daze, watching the people rise and slowly disperse. Edise, by the door, beckoned two of his young cohorts and whispered into the ear of the man closest to him, "Sedate the mother; tie her down if you have to." Taken aback, the man said aloud, "Surely you can't believe that such action would be necessary." Edise jerked the man by the arm, visibly annoyed, hissing, "Shh! I don't know! Just take every precaution. There are no second chances when battling against evil."

Toval looked at Saba as he passed. He opened his mouth to speak, then lowered his eyes and shook his head from side to side as he followed the crowd, moving out of the central meeting house into the dark howling rain. He looked broken, sad and somehow, very confused. Taijaur clung to his grandmother as she picked him up and held him in her arms. With his face buried in her chest, he convulsed spasmodically with low deep heartrending sobs, repeating continuously as if chanting a mantra, "Don't let them take the baby. Don't let them take the baby. Don't let them take the baby."

The give-and-take of the debate had managed to push out of the Saba's mind the bodiless words that had followed her throughout the morning. She had not realized that they were absent until now, as they came back with full force, repeating in a circular disjointed pattern of incoherence...—*Wrapping it in a burlap cloth...they buried...; Wrapping...slowly swallowed her whole...wrapping...through the center of his soul...buried alive...wrapping.* As she stood in the daze of her thoughts, grasping her grandson, Saba was startled to look up and see one of the Haman villagers staring directly at her from across the room. He was a young tall man, with a head full of prematurely white hair. She had noticed him on other occasions in the past, always looking at her, smiling and nodding in recognition as if they were old acquaintances. The sight of this man always made her feel uneasy, although she could not say why. She tried to recall when or where she had met him, but her thoughts were interrupted when Kalal came toward her in the stream of the passing crowd, with Amira and Mala's best friend, Tausi following close behind him. He spoke to the women in a hushed tone, "Come. We must try to get to Mala before they do. Saba show us the fastest way to the birthplace." He reached for Taijaur. "Here, give the boy to me. We will stop briefly to leave him with Olana at my home."

Saba nodded, handing Taijaur to Kalal and then bundled herself with her wide enveloping shawl. She led the way blindly, by touch and memory, as they walked against the hurling wind while the sky cast down a solid sheet of black angry water. Although they hurried along a shorter more direct path through the woods and up the northern embankment, they arrived only in time to see Edise as he came out of the now desecrated female-only blessed sanctum. The Saba felt her heart beating fast and her step faltered when she suddenly inhaled an acrid breeze that was incomprehensibly tinged with the smell of something burning. And all she could think was, *Oh, Loni, my sweet Loni.* Edise carried the naked infant pushed out at arms length in front of himself, repugnance contorting his facial features. The grave had already been prepared and waited impatiently to be sated.

Shivers went through Saba as she heard Mala screaming from inside the dwelling, "NO! NO! Oh please God, NO!!!" Two of the Elders were there outside the door along with several of Edise's minions who stood huddled close together, waiting in the rain. A rippling cascade of lightning illuminated the entire scene, striking from not only the passionate skies, but from the ground, the trees, the mountains and all the surrounding air.

2. Why Must We Pass This Way?

Shrouded by immense mountains, thick fog, and dense impenetrable tracts of forest-land, the Ocan island sits alone in one of the many hidden disregarded regions of the Earth. It is a place that exists far outside of the webs of human civilizations, which occupy most of the present dimensional world. In its antiquity, molten intra-planetary forces had conspired with climatic winds and stormy precipitation to shape the contours of the island's mass in the roughly hewn triangular V form, similar to some of the larger bodies of land in the southern hemisphere. It is surrounded on all sides by an oceanic reef that extends for miles around its shore, into the sea. Only a scattering of rocky islets and atolls make up the remainder of the desolate archipelago that hosts the Ocan as its main province. The island's massive dormant volcanoes encircle and cut through vast interior valleys and river gorges that cascade down rock embankments spilling into a network of tributaries and streams that runs throughout the course of the land. From time to time, the mountains still rumble in their sleep, sending low surging vibrations to those who listen and feel. The throbbing resonance moves ponderously through the land and its people, bringing visions of days gone by and those yet to come.

The people of the Ocan dwell deep in the forest glades near the mountains on the island's far eastern shore with many of their homesteads stretching into the fertile valleys of the mountain foothills of both the northern and the southern terrain. Their ancestors had escaped only a short eon ago, and these present-day Ocan people continued to hold fast to the sanctuary of their abandoned strip of land. From the beginning, the land nurtured its only human inhabitants, as if they lie directly in its womb. And the people accepted the confines of their refuge with gratitude for the incubation of their life forces. For more than two centuries, they lived within their concealed enclave—hidden, undefiled by the outside—until the coming of Mala's child.

The child was the first and last of her kind to ever be born on the Ocan island. Thus, the Saba knew right away that a line had been created—a boundary, a demarcation between what the Ocan once were and what they now must become.

And as much as they tried to escape it, the Ocan people also understood that their destiny was now upon them. Even the island seemed to feel the nascence of the child's spirit upon the land, though it moved only within its purpose as an emissary of the universe's most sovereign forces. The Saba wondered if this shift in the fabric of the world's structure could be felt by other people, in other lands. Or, she thought, maybe the sensations that had announced the coming of the child had also risen up into the higher spheres. She struggled to comprehend this incipient life force, who unbeknown to the people, had not yet surrendered to those bonds of mortality that constrain all life; those bonds that even now pressed down heavily in this healer-woman's own soul.

Near the fiftieth year of her life, the Saba of the Ocan people lost her gift, and she was forced to finally acknowledge that she was no longer able to traverse the sentiale pathways in order to guide her people through birth and death and all the healing that must take place in between. For years, her life had been trapped in an overdrawn state of melancholy and despair. But the people, and even the Saba herself, assumed only that the deaths of her daughter, her husband and other various souls still rode within her, no matter the passing of time. She and they had no way of knowing how completely faith and hope had deserted her. After having waited for a deliverance that never seemed to come, a murky, yet profound, sense of defeat settled deep into her bones, making her old and tired for the first time in her life.

Nonetheless, this business of living must go on. And since no other saba had yet to appear along the path, this present Saba continued to stand sentinel at the gates leading into and out of existence. Despite the fear and uncertainty left in the absence of her gift, the Saba never faltered in her duty to her people. She merely joined the ranks of countless numbers of men and women who, amidst the survival-necessary tasks that sustain their physical beings, unknowingly await that one moment, that one event that may, at long last, provide transposition to a higher realm; or at least a sliver of purpose—a reason—for this existence. Although she was unaware of its presence—that moment, that one event, came for Saba with the birth of Mala's child.

On the night that she was born there was an eclipse of the moon. Through some phantasm of sky and wind, Earth's view of its natural satellite was obliterated for the entire night. No light was tolerated by the darkness, all power failed and stormy winds swallowed any fire. The gestation had been almost one-half that of an average fetus and all were certain (and many had secretly hoped) that the infant would not survive its first moments if, indeed, it was born alive. However, contrary to any speculation or augury of hopes and beliefs, the fetus—of its own volition—had pushed forcefully through the female passage, as the wind, alone, cried out in pain.

For most, but not all Ocan, the child's birth and presumed infanticide became a forgotten unfortunate moment of their past. The people had no time or attention for anything beyond the fierce weather that ushered the child's arrival, as gale force winds and thundering rain continued almost unabated into the days and weeks following that darkest of nights. By the third day of unceasing storms, the Ocan people were fighting for survival and recovery from the mudslides and floods of one of the worst natural disasters that they had ever known.

On the worst of the worst days, a huge rain-soaked dirt avalanche poured down one of the larger mountains in the northeast range, uprooting trees and boulders in its quest to devour whole parts of that centuries-old sleeping volcano. It finally rested at the mountain base where it belched out persistent mud flows that plundered large sections within two of the Ocan villages, while barely touching the main settlement which was deeper in the island's interior. While most of the main village homes were safe, in some hard hit areas on the outer rim, whole families had been displaced more as a result of the river's flooding than the devastation wrought by the moving wet earth. Alor, a reclusive elder, was forced to abandon the summit of the lower mountain that he claimed as home and seek refuge closer to the main village compounds with his nearest neighbor and good friend, Saba.

Two weeks had now passed and for most of that time Alor had been left alone to care for Taijaur and Tausi's two young sons along with Amira and Kalal's daughter, Olana. Death, sickness—bereft ailing of one kind or another—had called out to the healer-woman throughout the days and into the nights. On this evening just before dusk, she returned to her home, weighed down by grief, exhaustion and the inexplicable emptiness that comes to those who are forced to acknowledge nature's propensity for massive destruction and its utter indifference to goodness, kindness and the needs of the living. The rain had taken a moment to rest, but the clouds were still gray and full, as she approached her circular adobe home which stood alone in a large deserted field, away from any neighbor's house and well out of sight of the settlement trading area near the center of the primary compounds. She entered the spacious darkened front room and became immediately immersed in the familiar subtle scents of various herbs and wet clay. Alor sat rocking a baby's cradle and reading by candlelight near the fireplace where black coals, burned low, emitting a warm red glow. Tausi and Chiru's baby boy, Odar, had been born just a few months prior, and he now slept peacefully lulled by the swaying motion of the cradle.

The large earthen fireplace stretched across one side of the open front room that was filled with herbs, spices, and dried flowers hanging from the ceiling and sprouting in pots along the wide windowsills on all sides of the house. A cluttered worktable sat on the opposite side of the room, with a waist-high pottery wheel adjacent to it. In a small section near the back of the room, there was a curtain that led to the two bedrooms at the rear of the house. Next to the curtain sat a box and three low shelves filled with children's toys, books and other items, neatly stacked and arranged in an order that defied the room's natural pattern of organized disarray.

Saba and Alor greeted one another and then spoke briefly of the children who were playing outside behind the house. After rushing through their last meal of the day, the children had begged to be allowed outdoors. Although the air was cool and damp, Alor had consented to their need to feel and taste the sky's pure exhale of breath and light. They had become restless and listless over the endless days of ceaseless wild rains that had denied them their joy of God's open touch. The Saba opened one of the side windows and watched them running and chasing one another around the house. At eight years old, Olana was the eldest of the three. Hence, chunky little Kedar, Tausi's first born, tried hard to follow her every instruction as his three year old logic dictated that he must dutifully respect his elders. He now stood ramrod straight with his hands planted firmly at his sides as he stretched to his highest height and donned his most official demeanor, awaiting Olana's every command. Taijaur, who was just a year senior to Kedar, rebuffed Olana's authority, but he still played along with the games that she created as whole worlds were spun from the scenes concocted in her imagination.

Alor assumed that the children's absent parents were working along with Tausi's mate, Chiru, in the storm assistance efforts, and the Saba told him no differently. However, as each day passed, the Saba struggled to nourish a sense of hopeful patience that, like the mountainside, was eroding and spilling out a pervasive fear—perhaps the children, who had come only as temporary guests, would be forced to remain indefinitely as permanent wards of her charity. Amira and Tausi should have returned over a week ago, and Kalal should not be too far behind them. Alor seldom ventured into the foothills and flatlands where most Ocan dwell, thus, he had no knowledge of Mala's return or the birth and burial of her child. Saba had conveyed only the briefest of facts to him, carefully omitting any details as to what had transpired after the child's burial. She told Alor only that Edise and all the others had returned to their homes, confident that the intent of their actions had been fulfilled.

To calm her growing sense of agitation, Saba sat down with a piece of clay, intending to create a new vessel. Despite her acute sense of fatigue, something inside seemed to be pushing her on, keeping her strong. She sat with her back partially turned to Alor, turning her head to face him when she spoke. The whir of her manually powered potter's wheel mingled with bits and pieces of idle conversation interspersed, almost rhythmically, into their comfortable silence. Periodically, they could hear the wind scream indecipherable messages into the coming darkness and the children's voices outside the open windows would become muffled and faint.

She had just settled into the form of the clay when Alor put his book aside and peering over the top of his spectacles, he said, "You know Saba, I have been thinking about what you told me occurred at the council meeting. Although there is no denying the ruthlessness of the child's fate, perhaps Edise was accurate in his assessment of the potential—"

Saba scoffed as she interrupted him, "Hmmph! When have you ever known an androgyne to be right about anything? They don't even know what they are. This one just happened to argue well."

Alor: "Saba, I am surprised to hear you make such a remark. The androgynous beings of the Ocan have always been indistinctly a part of the myriad facets of human expression that comprise the whole of our society."

Saba: "Well, that may be true of some of them. But Edise is just a bitter self-centered human being who displays his own personal affectations in a mockery of androgynous traits. At least now he seems to have an occupation more suitable to his distrustful and judgmental nature. I'm surprised that the

Elders allowed him to remain as head master of the senior academy for those many years. It seems criminal to have had such an insensitive person like that in charge of our young people's development."

Alor: "Saba, this is not like you. Perhaps your will has been depleted by the devastation of these past weeks. Keep in mind that Edise can be accused of doing no more than what the Elders themselves approved. It may not be conducive to your spiritual growth to carry such ire within yourself or to express such negative opinions about anyone."

She sighed heavily, "I know, I know, forgive me Alor. I am afraid that weariness has settled so deeply into these old bones that higher reasoning is at rest some place far from this tired body of mine. But it just makes me angry when I think of how Edise blatantly manipulated our people's fear to convince them that such an atrocious act against a helpless baby was the right course of action. So uncaring, so inhumane."

Alor interjected, "But from what you tell me of the council meeting, it seems that no one really fought against the decision. So that must mean at some level they agreed with what Edise presented."

Saba argued, "No, I think that they—we, all of us—were just not strong enough to fight back. I believe that we have all been beaten down by a fear that has lived within us for too many years to keep count; passed down to each successive generation. Never before have we come face to face with anything that so closely resembled the base origin of our trepidation.

But in the end, how can we ever justify such an inhumane act? We claim that our purpose as a people is to devote our lives to the progression of the spirit to the place of the holy. We profess to move in harmony with a *conscious intent* that marks us a separate entity, able to cultivate divine powers that sustain us in our transposition to higher realms. Where was our holiness, where were our divine powers when we made the decision to take the life of a child? This is Mala's home, we are her family. Her child has the right to live and be amongst her people."

Alor: "This is all true Saba and perhaps the Ocan people have been made less holy, less divine by this act. But when human actions are governed by fear and self-interest alone, goodness is always susceptible to sacrifice. If the child was as powerful as the signs portend, then it is unfortunate that the Elders could not see that we may have learned much from her continued existence. Did you say that the Obeah saw visions within her?"

Saba: "Yes—the Elders and Edise used this as part of the justification for their decision. But they had no proof, no real or tangible reason; just some readings from the baby's own mind wanderings. Even the Obeah would not go so far as to interpret any meaning from these images. We all have terrors beyond imagining buried within our psyches. It is enough to think about facing our own hidden demons, let alone to go unsuspectingly inside of someone else's terrifying illusion conjured from some unknown depth. This is especially true in the case of an infant who has no control over sentiale thoughts and images."

Alor: "Perhaps these were not mere images or illusions of the mind. The recent surges of energy from the in-between are unlike any that we have experienced in the past. I believe that that the Elders may be correct in assessing that another opening has occurred. However—."

Saba: "Alor, you know as well as I that these unexpected openings happen all of the time, even if, by a quirk of their nature, they remain hidden from our view. But that is no reason to deny a child its life. The Elders and many of the Ocan are so terrified that any new opening may turn out to be a gateway to the in-between that they lose control of their ability to reason. We have always known that the portals would not remain sealed permanently. They should have found and attempted to secure all the entries to the in-between long before now. My Tekun and Mala's parents would still be here if they had a found a way to more permanently secure the portals long ago."

Alor: "This may all be true. But you have to keep in mind that, since the ancient Obeah sealed the portals more than two centuries ago, these larger openings have not occurred in such a way that their presence could be so widely felt. There is no doubt that the balance of energy is shifting and the portals have once again become unstable. The Elders were most likely concerned because of what happened the last time a portal was discovered. I'm sure they were considering the deaths of your husband and the Purims when they made the decision about the child. I believe that the Elders hold themselves responsible for that accident, even though—"

Saba: "Hold themselves responsible? That would require them to admit out loud that the explosion occurred in an actual portal and not just some 'strange anomaly in a hidden cave'. Those were the words that they used to tell the people of the explosion—'a strange anomaly'. To this day, over a decade later, they refuse to acknowledge that a gateway was uncovered and they refer to the whole incident as only a 'tragic accident'. My husband and Mala's parents lost their lives and all the Elders have ever said is, 'This tragic accident is proof that the dangers of the forbidden territory are real and for this reason, our laws must be obeyed.' They never even acknowledged or dealt with the impact that the explosion had on the girls. Mala, Tausi and Loni were each affected in different and irrevocable ways. I can only imagine what it was like to have witnessed and lived through such a tragedy at such a tender age."

Alor: "Their experiences were indeed, unfortunate and the effects of that tragedy are still felt by many of us to this day. But these elders who now serve on the Council—they don't want the people to know that it is possible to physically access an alternate reality, another realm of existence that is right here on this Earth. So they attempt to shroud its existence in ignorance and fear. They want all of us to go on in perpetuity benefiting from the energy of the power source without ever understanding it fully and without ever fulfilling the responsibilities that such benefit entails."

Saba: "If the Elders continue to evoke fear in the people every time that a potential fracture or portal is discovered, then after awhile, there will only be people like you, me and other such old souls who know that the energy from the in-between was not only integral to the founding of our community, but that it is also fundamental to all life on earth."

Alor: "The Elders are afraid that a bridge between our world and the realm of the in-between may be forming and thus, the time for action may be upon us. It seems that it may be easier to instill fear and justify ignorance than it is to rise to the challenge of fulfilling our destiny."

They were both silent for a few seconds before Alor spoke again, "Saba, have you considered that it is possible that the birth of Mala's child while not necessarily causing the fracture, may have, indeed, accentuated the power of its effect? The child's existence may have had some bearing on this netherworld, despite her short duration in our realm."

Saba: "If a power as great as that which comes from the in-between can be affected or modified in any way by humans—and especially the spirit of a human child—then I fear we must all pray that the Emissary will soon come and guide us to the catalyst to re-set the balance before any ultimate catastrophe may befall this entire planet. We depend on the in-between's energy to fuel the continuation of existence on this planet, and it is frightening to think that a human may have the potential to alter this essential source of power."

Alor: "But what if Mala's child was similar to Loni? What if she possessed a similar or even greater ability?"

The clay beneath her hands suddenly spun out of control. Saba tried to steady her voice before speaking. "Loni is gone." She smashed the pot as she continued, "Until the Emissary comes to us, we must try to keep the portals sealed as the ancient Obeah proscribed."

Saba glanced out of the side window as the children darted past, laughing and chasing one another. Her eyes lingered on Taijaur.

Alor: "Saba, we have to bear in mind that control of the portals may not depend on an emissary guiding us. I believe that one day we will be able to unlock the secret of controlling the portals or, if not full control, we can at least avoid the mistakes made in the past, so that no one ever again will lose their life because of our ignorance. We cannot lose sight of why our founders brought us to this island refuge. The energy reaches its zenith in the openings and the power spots of this land and no other. No matter how dangerous this energy may be, we can't ignore its potential to affect positive change in the world. It is the only power strong enough to counteract the effects of the virus that is spreading throughout the nations of the world. We can't keep neglecting our responsibility to use this energy for a higher purpose."

Saba: "I agree that we must work towards understanding all the gifts that this land has given us. But Alor, how do we know that further study of the portals and attempts to control the energy will not lead to ill effects or even disaster as it has in the past? While our current exposure to the energy benefits us, what if an increase of energy from the in-between potentially causes us harm?

And even you are aware that only the Emissary can mediate the boundaries between these realms of existence. It is written that only an emissary can overcome the energy's destructive effect in order to use it for the greater benefit of the world. Our purpose is to develop our power so that we may aid the Emissary in this cause and follow where he or she may lead us."

Alor: "I don't doubt any of the sacred precepts of our doctrine. However, have you ever considered that while an emissary may, indeed, be necessary to lead us to the catalyst-stone—control of the portals, the actual entryways to the in-between, may not necessitate such mediation from an endowed being? We may be able to help the nations of this world by using the portal energy and we may not ever need to make full use of the actual power source. We will never know how much we are capable of achieving with the portal energy unless we study these phenomena further."

Saba: "But the energy of the in-between is everywhere on this earth. Even if the people of other lands experience the energy in smaller doses, nonetheless, the development of all life in this world is already dependent upon and enhanced by the power of its effect."

Alor: "While it is true that all life can potentially draw from this power source, you have to keep in mind that, no one outside of the Ocan has any conscious awareness that the energy is working through them and they don't know how to open themselves to fully receive it. So, the effect of the energy in their lives is minimal, at best. While we of the Ocan, have known of this energy for centuries and openly cultivate its effects, yet we do nothing to further our understanding of its full potential. Nor do we share our knowledge with the world.

And let us not forget that the ancient Obeah left no written record. I have examined the annals of those times and there is nothing that reveals instructions from the Obeah telling the Ocan people to keep the portals sealed. Rather all reports indicate that the ancient Obeah prophesized that the portals would remain sealed until the Emissary arrives. This means that the seals on the portals will automatically be broken during the time of the Emissary on this Earth."

Saba: "Alor, you have studied these issues more than any other person in our collective, and I trust your wisdom and opinions on this subject, without reservation. However, you have to know that the Elders would never agree to any such investigation that involves using the portal energy. Even the present day Obeah do not condone this type of exploration."

Alor: "These Obeah of our generation have withdrawn from any kind of intervention in the affairs of Ocan society. They merely herald the coming of our future world, with no regard for how we develop or the choices that we make in the here and now. However, they know, as we all know, that we were never meant to just run and hide from this virus. They know that our purpose was to find a way to use the energy of the in-between to block or prevent the effects of the plague in the people's lives and thus rectify the balance of power in the world.

That is why your daughter, Loni, and others who may be like her—those who see, feel and are able to call forth the energy latent within the earth—these people are essential to the Ocan cause. With the exception of the ancient Obeah—"

Saba interrupted in a small, barely audible voice, "My daughter is gone; what ever power she may have possessed went with her." She turned her back completely to Alor, as she focused intently on the clay object taking form in her shaking hands. Alor continued talking, without hearing Saba or noting the change in her voice and demeanor. "Loni was the first and only Ocan to ever sense the presence of a portal. Without her we may have never known the true nature of this energy. If Loni was still here or another like her then our studies of this phenomenon could continue and there is no telling what we would be able to accomplish.

Do you realize that many Ocan still believe that we are merely feeling and experiencing the spiritual vibrations of the earth? We have become so one-dimensional; shrouding our physical reality in superstition, without realizing that both the supernatural and natural realms of existence feed each other and that we must understand the physical properties as well as the spiritual. This child's existence may have been a sign of the start of a new era in our history on this earth. However, if we don't soon—" he stopped in mid-sentence, finally sensing the Saba's mood. He then said quietly, "I'm sorry. Forgive me, Saba. I, I wasn't thinking."

She made no response and they were both quiet for a moment, the Saba still working with the clay and then Alor said, "Incidentally, Saba where did you say that Mala is now?"

"Mala?"

"Yes, Mala. After the death of her child, where did she go?"

She mumbled without turning to face him, "Ummm. I believe that Mala is, ummm, in the Haman village where she resided previously, I believe."

They each lapsed into the silence of their individual thoughts, with Alor going back to reading his book, while Saba continued working, smashing piece after piece and continuously starting again. She sighed heavily, listening to the muted sounds beneath the wind, as the voices of the children playing outside blew lightly through the open window closest to her. There was a palpable feeling in the air of things unsettled and unsure. Saba could sense Alor's perceptive mind sniffing around the edges of their intermittent conversation, and she sealed the block on her surface sentiale more firmly by increasing her concentration on the various objects that rose beneath her hands. However, it seemed that no matter how much she worked or listened to the children, the wind, and this old man before her, she could not stop her mind and all of her senses from traveling back to the darkness and rain where Mala's child had been left to die. Some thing or some one was forcing her to see and re-live those moments as if they were happening now in this present moment, this present reality.

Under normal circumstances, Saba would have confided in Alor. In the past, he had always been a source of guidance and consolation in her moments of questioning and despair. But these were anything but ordinary times, and she could not risk the betrayal of actions uncovered and unknown, not even to Alor. Besides, there were no words for actions that could never be spoken of and events that defied reason or explanation. Even if they had chosen a different plan, another way for reality to pass, Saba knew that there would never be any way to describe the moment that she and Amira discovered Mala's recently buried infant—unearthed, unscathed and very much alive. There was no one else around, nobody to give that moment's reality a definition or cause. At first, they could only stare at the baby who was lying resurrected, on the ground under the wide branches of a large overgrown tree near where she had been buried. Her grave was undisturbed.

In the pouring rain, Amira and Saba had followed surreptitiously behind Edise as he carried the baby deep into the forest to the grave that awaited her. They watched him cover her with dirt, packing it down before he hurried back to the village, without turning even once to glance at what he had left behind. He never saw the two women, but before he was completely out of their sight they rushed in to release the baby, only to find that in the few seconds that it took to get to her she had already been exhumed. The child was cold and wet, her shroud covered with mud, but she was breathing normally, looking around in a calm alert, curious manner. Never the wiser of how she had come to be there, they moved with speed and silence through the darkness and the rain. They bundled the infant and then hurried back to the birthplace where Kalal and Tausi had remained with Mala. They, the four of them, had already decided that mother and child would have to be readied for the journey whence Mala had come. They, the four of them, all agreed that this was the only way.

Kalal, along with Amira and Tausi, set out to deliver Mala and her newborn child into an exiled existence far from the Ocan settlements. The Saba went with them only as far as the path that leads to the edge of the interior forest and then returned to the village to gather the children at her home and wait. Amira and Tausi were supposed to accompany Kalal and Mala to the mountain pass along the far side of the western forest, while Kalal was to continue the journey through the mountains, in order to ensure Mala's safety to the other side. According to their plan, by now all three of them should have returned to the safety of the village settlements. But apparently things had not gone according to the plan.

The scenes kept re-playing in the Saba's mind, as she sat wondering what else could have been done; asking herself over and over—was there another, more better, way? Through a double vision of perception, she saw/remembered/felt herself as she was that night, existing there, but also simultaneously watching from this distant place in the reality of the present. In her mind, she perceived all the images, thoughts, emotions as she saw Mala's limp unconscious body and smelled the wet odor of drenched clothing, hair, and skin mingled with the hut's open scent of straw and mud and a heavy sickening smell of spilled blood. Saba watched Tausi trying to break the barrier of drug induced sleep by shaking Mala and whispering loudly into her ear, *"Mala? Can you hear me? Mala, you have to wake up." Without opening her eyes, Mala murmured in her stupor, "No, no, no...my child...my child."*

Saba felt herself mumble aloud the same words that came from her mouth that night, *"Kalal, she's not responding. This is not going to work. She is too heavily sedated. We have to try to think of something else, another plan, another way."*

Kalal turned to the healer-woman and said, "Sister, at this point you are probably the person most attuned to Mala's sentiale. And also as the Saba, you are perhaps the only one with a sentiale strong enough to penetrate the effects of the anesthetizing chemicals in her system. Can you go inside of her?"

Saba fought the anxiety that arose within her, as one dimension of the truth came out, "I don't know," she said. "Mala guards herself so closely now. Even as she labored to bring forth the child, she used the pain as a shield, a cocoon that served as an impenetrable barrier. We all tried to go in to help carry her through, but the pain was too intense."

The Saba shunted the issue in an alternate direction, "Tausi, a link without her consent or knowledge may be possible only for you. Because you and Mala came through your Ascension Rites together, before you were both fully grown, part of your sentiale is fused with that of Mala's. It may be safer and more successful for you than for any of us."

Tausi consented readily, "Yes, you're right. She and I held a connection before the sedation set in. And I have felt her strongly throughout this night and even before she returned to our village."

Kalal shifted Mala's body and laid her back down, speaking as he moved, "Okay Tausi, we must move with haste. I will join my mind with yours to help seal the connection."

The scene shifted quickly and the Saba felt herself taken further back in time to that darkest of nights. Only she and Mala were in the birthing hut as Tausi had gone to summon the Obeah and the Saba held in her hands the motionless body of the just-born infant. What ever life the fetus may have once possessed seemed to have been sucked away by its struggle to be born. Breathing hard, Mala stared, with wide frightened eyes at the inert form that the Saba brought before her. As Saba laid the still baby on her mother's breast, she felt the rush of Mala's fast panic-stricken exhales brush against the back of her hand. It was as if, with each breath, Mala was striving to reach inside the infant, to breathe on her behalf. Saba felt herself fighting against the dizzying thick smell of warm blood while groping in the darkness for the life cord of the infant. The wind had suddenly become completely still, void of life and sound.

Mala remained in the final birthing position, sitting with her back to the wall, against propped-up pillows, her knees spread wide bent to her chest, holding the baby close to her face while prodding her breast into its slack open mouth. In the absence of competing sound, Mala's breathing lie heavy on the tense air. The Saba felt a cool faint scent of rich black soil rise from the mud hut floor bringing a brief feeling of hope that was quickly overwhelmed by the room's stifling profusion of heat, body fluids, and intense pain. She leaned forward over Mala, and reached out to touch the child, feeling no energy, no spirit beneath her hand. And then just before she pulled her hand completely from the child, she felt an unexpected slight movement. The infant's small body had understood and answered her touch. Saba's voice croaked in a low exuberant tone, "Mala, she lives!" With prayers of gratitude and thanksgiving, the Saba tied and severed the maternal life cord, as the infant began to make soft sucking noises at her mother's breast.

As the Saba then cleaned and covered the infant, Mala suddenly grasped her adopted mother's hand. Despite the darkness, the Saba could see in Mala's eyes a need so deep and so strong that it took hold of the healer-woman's heart with the unyielding grip of a tight smothering embrace. Overcome by the intensity of the connection, Saba abruptly turned with a sharp intake of breath and pulled away in an effort to steady her emotional reaction. With her back to Mala, she tried to suppress the affect of her unexpected feelings, but before the healer-woman could catch herself, the emotional overflow vented itself in a harsh, almost hissing stream of commands, "Mala you must continue to nourish her through the day and rest as much as you can. The child will need your strength."

Standing at a distance from Mala, Saba busied herself with preparations of the afterbirth for the ablution rites and cell cultivation. The healer-woman watched her intently as the new mother's entire essence unfolded and became enraptured by her nursing infant. Mala's eyes seemed to absorb the child and respond silently to questions that only she could hear.

With great care and attention, the Saba wrapped delicate thin layers of leaves from a large yellow plant around the placenta and cord, after dipping each separate leaf into a fluid solution. As she worked, she tried to gather the words, the thoughts that she needed to offer Mala. Tausi would soon return with the Obeah and Saba knew that she must speak with Mala before they arrived. The strain of the long night had left her with a sense of overwhelming fatigue. After completing her tasks, the healer-midwife went to the doorway and stood for a moment, drawing in the energy of fresh new air. She watched as the dawn's gray subtle fog pushed slowly through the morning sky and the new day's song whistled from treetops. A quiet wet mist blew a stray breeze that washed into the room and strained to purge the stifling odors of the night's struggle. The dark outline of the mountains and forest trees appeared surreal in the foggy morning dusk. In her mind, Saba could see beyond the trees that surrounded and obscured this remote secluded dwelling to a series of small clearings where various wood, stone, and adobe structures comprised the main sections of the primary Ocan settlement.

She retrieved a basket of victuals left just outside of the birthplace, before re-entering the dark thatched hut, making sure that the un-lockable door was firmly shut. Observing the peaceful innocence of maternal-infant slumber, thoughts of this new birth began to blend with a kaleidoscope-vision of other births, other times. She thought of and called on the strength of her own saba and all the sabas before her and those who would follow.

Something—perhaps a sound, or an unexpected movement—pulled the Saba from her mind-wanderings, back to the present where she sat, not in the distant birthplace with Mala and her child, but here in her own home with only a misshapen lump of clay beneath her hands. She looked up and then quickly turned away as she saw Alor staring at her intently from across the room. With a steady gaze of concern, he said in a low voice, "Something takes you away Saba."

Noticing that the room had grown dark while she drifted in thought, the Saba rose, and busied herself with lighting the oil lamps, before answering distractedly, "Hmm? Oh, just the wind, I suppose." The vision had left her feeling troubled and uncertain. She could feel Alor still studying her over the top of his book, as she smashed the ruined clay pot and rinsed the clay from her hands, before going to sit by the front window in order to look out at the children who were now playing in front of the house.

Gazing at Taijaur, Saba was struck, as she was so many times before, by how closely her grandson resembled his mother, Loni, at this same age. His bright smile and joyful demeanor brought his mother's spirit into his face and eyes, softening the scowl that many times crossed his brow. The sight of him as he played with the other children made the Saba feel lost, once again, in the melancholy of her nostalgia, transported back to a time when, as a younger woman, she sat by this same window waiting for her husband, watching her little girl play outside. For a moment, she thought she smelled a strong familiar odor of smoke and then something in her mind snapped to attention, and a creeping trepidation began to seep through as she realized suddenly that this was not her daughter before her. Just as it happened almost every day for the past four years, Saba was once again forced, against her will, to bump unexpectedly into the buried reality that her daughter was gone now and forever; never again to be seen, heard, held or comforted. As always, she began to think about all the mothers and fathers whose children's lives have been cruelly snatched away. No matter how old or young their son or daughter may have been, the Saba knew that this was a loss from which no parent could ever fully return. Those whom tragedy leaves behind invariably feel the same sense of tortured guilt and isolating sorrow that she knew would never go away. She sighed thinking to herself, *What manner of a world is this? And why have we been born into it? Wish that I could lift away. Oh Tekun, where are you? Why aren't you here to help me?*

Being thoroughly saba, in mind, body and spirit, had not protected the Saba the way past beings of her kind had been shielded. Or at least she assumed that she was the only saba to ever possess an internal barrier that rendered her unable to filter pain and give back only the healing that was expected of her. She took in the agonies of the people, of life, and bits and pieces invariably stayed with her. As saba, she was expected to absorb life's suffering, while relieving all hurt and still maintain her own equilibrium. That was part of the power, part of the gift of being saba. But even when the power of her gift was at its strongest, she had never really been able to recover from all the pain, suffering and senseless injustice of not just her own people, but also the collective hurt and sorrow throughout the sphere of the living. She did not know how to make herself immune to its effect; how to steel her mind or protect her soul. She berated herself constantly—*What kind of saba am I really?*

"Excuse me, Saba? Saba? Are you okay? Are you sure that nothing is wrong?"

She had forgotten about Alor. He now stood, bending over her, shaking her arm, adorned in an outside cloak that covered the full length of his robe. He was holding his long wooden staff that he used as a walking stick. Saba had not seen or heard him get up or walk across the room. She hoped that he had not been talking to her for long. She stammered and shook herself as if rising from sleep, "Yes, yes. I'm fine. Are you going out?"

He smiled slightly, "It is time for my evening stroll." No matter what the weather, Alor went out for hours each night and many times returned only when the sun rose. Without the protective dissipation of the high mountain air, the old man seemed troubled by the night winds, which agitated his thoughts and took away his dreams.

Alor: "If you are not feeling well, I don't mind staying to look after the children."

Saba: "No, Alor. I'm fine. You go and enjoy your walk. Honor thy Gift, my friend."

He smiled at her, "May we be worthy."

She watched as he went out and down the path, talking to each of the children in turn. Finally realizing the futility of her busy work, she sighed heavily as she got up to clean and put away her tools and supplies, before calling to the children to come in. They came in exhausted from their outside play and thankfully went immediately to bed. For a moment, she watched the children wrapped in a deep fatigued slumber, and then she mentally bundled up and stripped off all of her worries, deciding to also retire for the night. Hoping for the reprieve of a peaceful night's sleep, she sighed heavily, tallying in her mind yet another day and night of waiting in vain. As the Saba lay down in the bed next to her grandson, she inhaled his pure moist little boy fragrance and her heart filled with sheer wonder of her grandson's existence. She eased into a semi-conscious state between sleep and awake and the scenes starting going through her mind once again.

She was kneeling beside the sleeping woman, gently stroking her hair and whispering, "Mala? Mala? It is time to awaken. We must talk."

She glanced at the sleeping infant, and her heart jumped suddenly as the fear rose once again. This new birth, among the many for which the healer-woman had stood witness, conjured feelings too precarious for her to acknowledge or fathom.

"Saba?" Mala opened her eyes wearily and the infant immediately came to full attention. For the first time, the Saba noticed a large irregular oblong shaped dark brownish-red birthmark that spread from between the little girl's eyes to above both eyebrows. The mark dominated the baby's face, throbbing in the center of her forehead with a pulsating vein beneath the skin that appeared to move and crawl, like a worm searching for a way out. Without taking her eyes from the child, the Saba went on speaking, "I've brought you something to eat."

Mala coughed, clearing her throat and with a thick raspy voice of sleep she asked, "Has Tausi returned?"

"Not yet. I hate to disturb your rest, but we must speak. The Obeah will soon be here and there is much that must be settled before they arrive."

She looked away from Mala hoping to hide any sign of fear, hope or expectation.

Mala's attention stayed focused on the child as she boosted herself up into a full sitting position, shifting the baby in her arms. "What did the Obeah say at council?"

"They haven't spoken at council yet. The meeting is scheduled for later this afternoon. The Obeah will bring their blessings and prophecy for this new one in a short while. Tausi has gone to summon them." Still on her knees, the Saba rested her thick haunches on the heels of her bare feet, as she looked at the infant, who, in turn, studied both Mala and Saba in a manner unlike any newborn that the Saba had ever seen.

Saba observed aloud, "She is the most silent infant that I have ever witnessed at birth. How peacefully she rests, yet so attentive. It is almost as if she is listening and understanding all that we say."

Mala was pensive and unhearing. With a look of worry and consternation, she blurted out, "Saba, will they receive my child?"

Her question seemed to catch the healer-woman off guard. She stammered, "Mala... I don't—I'm not—how can you ask such a question?"

Mala turned her head, looking down and away from the child, "It's just that I have been away so long. And the rules are vague in my mind. It is obvious that she is not fully Ocan. I don't even know if our history tells of such a birth."

"Our history tells of many births. Rest easy, new mother. Let me be the first to welcome this newest expression of the Creator's joy into our presence. All the blessings of my soul and

my life, I offer unto you and this child." The Saba reached into the basket by the mat and handed Mala a large succulent fruit, then selected one for herself. Saba hesitated, trying to find the right words.

"Mala, the people will soon come to see this new one. You must block out any feelings of doubt or misgivings. You don't want anyone to make any spurious connections between your child and any unusual phenomena. Your understanding will guide them in their own perception of this situation. Keep in mind that the darkness and violent winds of last night has everyone on edge. They won't be content until they know for certain that no demon has been born into our midst. That is why we must speak before the Obeah—" she stopped short, alarmed by Mala's look of open fright as the younger woman whispered, "Are you, yourself, completely certain?"

The Saba opened her mouth to respond but her tongue was stilled by the sounds of movement and voices just outside of the hut.

A sudden unexpected noise jolted Saba from her stupor. Someone was knocking. She rose quickly and found Chiru Dalasa outside her front door.

Chiru: "I am sorry to awaken you Saba, especially so late at night."

Saba: "Has something happened, Chiru? Is everything all right?"

Chiru: "Yes, everything is fine. I knew that you would want to know as soon as possible. Amira and Tausi have returned."

Without hearing fully all of his words, Saba's mind focused on 'have returned' and she exclaimed, "Oh, thank God! They are safe."

Something inside of her let go and exhaled all the pent-up tension induced by an eternity of waiting.

Chiru: "Their return trip was delayed because they were forced to take a route to the south so that they might avoid encountering the workers constructing levees on the river tributaries along their path. They were both exhausted and are now sleeping. But I knew that you would want to know. We didn't want to awaken the children in the night. So, we will come for them at first morning's light."

Saba: "You said 'both'—does that mean that Kalal is not with them? I assumed that Amira and Tausi were late because all three of them would be returning together."

Chiru: "No, Kalal is not with them; he has not come back yet and they have no word of his whereabouts. Although they did say that they expect that he should be back in the next few days. At first they thought that perhaps he was already here, perhaps having taken a different, more direct path."

Chiru waited a moment, with Saba staring into the darkness and when she made no response, he turned to walk away, saying, "Well, Honor thy—," and then stopping in mid-sentence he turned back to face Saba. "Oh Saba, I forgot to ask—do you know the Haman villager that I just saw here, near your door? Its kind of late for anyone to be this far out, but he seemed friendly enough. I've seen him here before, when I brought the children's—What's wrong Saba? Did I say something to upset you?"

Saba: "Was he tall man with white hair?"

Chiru: "Yes! That is the very one. Is he a friend of yours?"

Saba: "No, no, no. I don't know the Haman man you speak of."

Chiru: "But he seemed to know you and he knew all of the children's names."

With anger rising in her voice, Saba almost shouted, "I said I don't know him. What more do you want me to say?"

Chiru: "I'm sorry Saba. I didn't mean to upset you."

Saba: "No, Chiru, it is I who must beg forgiveness. The night has been long and my patience has never been all that it should be."

He stroked her arm, "Don't worry Saba. Get some rest. Everything will be okay in the morning. Honor thy Gift."

She smiled at him and covered his hand with her own, saying softly, "May we be worthy."

With a heavy exhale, Saba watched him walk down the path until the warm dark night swallowed his form. As she stood in the doorway, she began to shiver and something made her look back with sudden alarm into the room. Sniffing the air, she went to throw water on the dry embers in the fireplace and blew out of the light in the one oil lamp that was still burning.

She sat in the chair by the open front window and listened to Taijaur snoring softly in concert with the nocturnal insects as a warm breeze drifted in and the darkened sky poured out an overabundance of stars and other pieces of light. The mystical sensations of the night filled her with awe and peace despite a persistent unease. She could make no sense of all that had transpired over these past few weeks. She was even more fearful of that which was yet to come. She thought to herself, *If all were right in the universe, then Mala and her child would be here at home in the Ocan settlements and Kalal too, would now be safely at home with his own family. Instead, Kalal, the one least able to take on this burden, must venture into some great unknown for who knows how long. In this world, where nothing seems as it should be, those my most dear to me are forced to wander an unknown wilderness, alone and unprotected with a newborn in their care. Oh Tekun, where are you? I need you so much. Please God help me.*

She began to mouth her nightly prayers to the stars, but her words were over-ridden by the whisper of a familiar refrain that came to her often in such moments of stillness and wonder—*What manner of a world is this? And why have we been born into it? All this beauty, serenity, and goodness, yet still so much sorrow and so many mysteries as to why we even exist. Surely there is another place where life and living flow in a more comprehensible pattern, in accordance with a more compassionate design. Have we come to make this world better; or to be made better by it? Perhaps we are here to hone our substance with the fire of our own iniquities. Would that I could lift away so that I might see it more clearly and know how I may abide. Oh Lord, lift me away so that I might touch that which is beyond this world and know, for this moment in time, why must we pass this way?*

3. She Watched the Storms

Cool moist blackness stroked the earth, emitting a low long sigh that calmed the fluttering leaves and danced with the fairies of light. The man and woman, moving as one with the night, were ushered by the wind into a hollow cavernous side of the mountain where the soft ground welcomed their presence and bade them rest. Completely depleted of energy, the woman's spirit at once complied and altered her reality to allow the abeyance of surface sensation.

Mala stirred and moaned quietly as Kalal gently unwrapped the cloth that held the baby to her sleeping body and then transferred the infant to the comfort of his own sturdy frame. Feeling the thick solid strength of his touch, the child absorbed his scent and determined for all time to come how contentment would be defined. Her quiet wide eyes followed the old man's weary expression as he searched through bags and bundles by the light of the cloud-obscured moon for the herbs and poultices to administer to Mala and the child. He tended to the child first, adeptly cleaning and changing her and then swaddled her tightly. She watched as he made a small fire and then heated a poultice before applying it to the sleeping woman's body. He rubbed a warm fragrant oil first all over the child's round head, before massaging it into Mala's lower abdomen, chanting a lyrical verse in a low deep voice. Covering Mala with special herbs to subdue her scent, Kalal shifted her body closer into the mountain's shelter and away from the impetuous winds of the night. The infant stared with wide intense eyes as he silently prayed, invoking the spirits that ride the night air to envelop them in the universe's healing saba-energy.

The man laid the child with her mother, and the infant watched as he took nourishment for himself, and then subsequently rested in an upright position next to the two females. When the moon unexpectedly escaped, the entire mountainside was illuminated and the light betrayed the baby girl's intense scrutiny. Kalal returned her gaze, at first smiling and cooing before realizing that these were not the eyes of an infant. He looked over his shoulder, searching the moon for whatever evidence of strange influence to which this lifeless orb may have subjected his vision. Finding no sign of anomaly, he reluctantly conceded to his original impression and turned once again to face his inquisitor, struggling to subdue his rising fear. He studied the message in those ancient eyes, never reaching their depths, until a shudder seized his body as the clouds captured the moon once again, then released a brief soothing rain upon the mountain top. Weariness conquered the man's best intentions and defeated his ability to sustain surface awareness. As he surrendered his consciousness, the rain slowly ceased, the night continued to stand guard, and the newly born female—she watched the night.

The hidden mountaintop cavern sheltered Kalal, Mala and the baby for more than two weeks allowing Mala time to re-gain her strength. With memories flowing through her mind, Mala slept for days, waking only briefly to feed the baby before falling back into deep states of oblivion. Each morning Mala awoke to find herself alone. At first, she was too exhausted and too weak to wonder where Kalal and the baby might be. He always returned before any fear or curiosity had time to take root.

Sometimes, as Mala drifted in and out of consciousness, the stories would begin to creep through her mind. Stories that told of an ancient darkness resurrected over and over again in the timeless lore of the Ocan people's quests through pathways made of power, glory, shame, and fear. She could hear, down through the centuries, the Ocan people intoning their tales of pursuits into and through the darkness, while the words echoed pervasively in the wind against the mountains of their isolated home. They tell the what and the how of who they are, and there is always beauty in the telling. Yet, they, the people, never dare touch 'the why'. Somehow, they never seem to notice that it beckons unrelentingly from the edge of that which lies beyond the reach of human comprehension. Despite the people's general nescience, the meaning behind causes remains a tenaciously powerful lure. It is a force undaunted by cognitive boundaries that render many, but not all, unable or unwilling to grasp the intent that predicates eternal cycles of human need and desire. Mala, like the others of her kind, never wavered in her need to reach for 'the why'. For she, like the others before her, knew this one desire above all else as the source that pulls our lives and our stories through and beyond all time.

Each time that Mala neared a conscious reality, she could feel the sentiale connection with the Saba, still strong and clear despite the distance and time. In the moments following the birth of her child, Mala had reached beyond the void in the Saba's mind, beyond the healer-woman's fragile sense of despair, to a safe place where their sentiale could come together and form a solid, sustainable connection. Mala was the only one who knew where the Saba's vulnerabilities lived. And without the healer-woman's knowledge or consent, she used this knowledge to subdue Saba's internal defenses. She had crept past Saba's vigilant emotional guard, in order to merge with her adopted mother at her core. The bond brought sustaining energy to both women, along with an enhanced perception that allowed them to see and know each other's thoughts and visions. At first Mala sought only to use the connection to help Saba stay strong. But now after weeks of travel, the link still held her as she felt herself inside of the Saba's mind, her spirit and unexpectedly, the combined force of both of their fears.

They were in the birthing hut waiting for the Obeah to arrive. Faint slivers of daylight began to filter under the door and through cracks in the thatched ceiling of the one room structure. Caressing the baby with her hands, every pore in Mala's body opened to receive an intense primal energy that radiated from mother and child and somehow throughout the air. Mala gave herself fully to the child's hunger and the giving rendered a shift in her perceptual reality. With full passage into an altered state of awareness, she surrendered her mind's construction of dimensional space-time and for a moment, she felt the world disintegrate as her soul overflowed. The infant drank the bounty of her mother's offering until her needs were sated, then she yawned and stretched with a slow motion newness that eased her body into fluid inertia. She slept, lulled into a dark water world, where once again airborne, she swam/flew through space, moving the earth, turning galaxies. Nestling the child into her body, Mala slid down a little and laid her head back on the propped up blankets of her makeshift bed. With her eyes partially closed, she breathed deeply as her thoughts stretched out and wandered aimlessly around her mind.

Suddenly the scene shifted and Mala saw herself holding the baby out towards Saba, saying, "Look at her." As Saba peered closely at the infant, Mala insisted, "Tell me what you see." She could feel the healer-woman's fear lying heavy in the air.

"What do you mean?"

"Describe her physical features."

"Mala your eyes see as well as my own. What game is this?"

"I'm not sure that I trust my eyes."

Saba said nothing for a while and then with a deep sigh, she said, "Well, when I tried to touch her a moment ago...I... I thought...at first...that...well...never mind. The brain does not interpret well when rest has been deprived. I'm sure I imagined—"

Mala interrupted Saba in an excited, agitated tone, "What? What was it you felt? What did you see?"

"Nothing," the older woman's voice rose in an unexpectedly petulant manner. "I told you I'm not sure!"

Mala watched the emotions of an internal struggle play out on the Saba's face. She tried to probe around the barriers in the Saba's mind, but she came away with only the sense of some enormous dark amorphous presence, with no definition or cause. In a distracted tone, she replied slowly, "Forgive me, Saba. It is just that I am so anxious. And Saba you know... the three of us—me, Loni and Tausi—something happened to us...back then...in the... in the explosion."

"Hush Mala. You must not speak of that now. You must forget all of that. It all happened so long ago. But the important thing is that you did survive. It is essential that you move past that point in your life. You cannot allow that one moment in time to control you or hold your life hostage. Your mother and father and least of all my Tekun would never have wanted you to dwell on such an unfortunate incident that was beyond the power and control of us all."

"It is not their deaths that haunt me so much, Saba. Its just that, well," she lowered her voice and whispered, "No one told us that the portals were alive."

"Mala, we've been through this before, and I tell you that can't be true; it's not possible."

"But Saba—"

"Let it go, Mala. You must let the past go."

"But is it truly all over, Saba? I am afraid that what happened then may have the power to reach out and touch the here and now."

Mala struggled, forcefully trying rise into the present reality. But before she was able to pull completely free, she felt herself sucked down by the Obeah. The Obeah are the seers of the Ocan people. It is their calling to fuse all worlds and walk unguided upon a path for which they are chosen. Drawing sustenance from unseen forces, they manifest the power of the heavens. In the absence of her perceived capricious nature, it was believed that Mala could have been part of the Obeah. However, she was never able to straddle all of her worlds and their fusion was beyond her control. Mala—or rather the wandering spirit of a being such as Mala—was and is an aberration to the Ocan kind. The Obeah now flowed into Mala's mind through a suddenly opened door in some far-off distant place.

They walked toward and reached out to Mala with long sinewy limbs in their nondescript loose fitting clothing. All of their actions were in concert with one another, as the Obeah entered the birthing hut. The ritual to allow males entry into the birthplace was never performed on behalf of the Obeah. Upon becoming part of the triad that forms the Obeah, each had surrendered his or her individual identity and all that is a part of it. Their genders, personalities, and sheer physicality seemed somehow fused into an elusive state of blurred transcendence. When they began talking, it sounded as if all three spoke together, in one voice, with an oddly hollow sound. They actually spoke in a circular fashion, with one uttering a fragment of a sentence or thought/concept and the next in turn providing another part of the sentence or thought, going around with each taking a turn until their meaning was fully expressed. "Your baby lives, Mala/You have been blessed/Pray that the blessing may be shared/ by all Ocan." Weakly, Mala murmured, "Yes". Both she and the baby lie silent, yet alert to every movement that the Obeah made.

The smallest of the Obeah gently lifted the baby from Mala's arms and held her close as the other two began moving with strong fluid agility in a graceful pattern that held meaning only to their singular understanding. A gentle humming vibration resonated throughout the room, though there was no apparent source from which it emanated. The child remained quiet, staring at the Obeah who held her. The Obeah, in turn, observed the child closely while subtly inhaling her essence and moving to sit down near the wall behind Mala's head. Using slow rhythmic arm motions, the other two seemed to stretch and weave intricate patterns in the air as if gathering and generating an energy field that was pulled directly from not only the mother and her infant, but also from the molecules of the air that surrounded them. When their movements reached a culminating point, they knelt down, joining hands across Mala's body, and then all three began to speak. "Mala, close your eyes/go inside the sound of our voice/hear within it the meditation of the universe/ from the valley of your own soul." With their eyes closed and heads bowed, their instructions ceased, yet they continued emitting a powerful vibration that seemed to intensify with their silence.

Warmth opened up within her and poured forth its blanket of lulling tranquility before she realized that the room's chill no longer affected her. She hardly had time to wonder of the Obeah's powers, when she was pulled completely into a soundless vibration that shook every nerve ending in her body. Their lips did not move, though she was certain that they were speaking as they simultaneously emitted a powerful pulsating tremor that had no origin in sound. Blackness rolled over her and washed her clean. Rising from the earth, her body rejected the gift of gravity's possession, as she searched the atmosphere of space with clawing motions to reach the surface. The burning of a star, as she passed it, slowed her progress and she stopped to tentatively touch this source of energy, heat and light. The star burned her past the point of flesh and she entered into it, giving her ash to its brilliance.

Ultimate perception was awakened in this immolation, as she felt the light shining from her core, tentacles reaching in all directions into the darkness of space, seeking a connection. Her essence *combined with a familiar presence. Then unexpectedly, forgotten tentacles in her midsection fused into a mortal cord that held her firmly anchored to the earth. Her body recoiled and contracted, drawing into a tight ball, and only then did she finally reclaim the knowledge of a life force passing through her. Desperation made her shiver with longing and the star began to tremble. It shot off gaseous explosions of light, its liquid molten center churning in painful spasms. The star went nova and Mala shattered, falling through the galaxies in a million brilliant pieces. Waking consciousness, surface perceptual reality, forced Mala to open her eyes and stop seeing. But the brilliance of the star's light played through her mind once more as she became aware of the empty room. Without warning, a sudden emptiness erupted inside of her, spilling forth a desperate sense of longing that rooted itself permanently in her soul. Myriad sensations in a kaleidoscope of brilliant pieces, burned through her. Inevitably, a path was carved, creating a way. It came and she knew. Her life was no longer her own. This new being, no matter how strange or ominous, lay claim to every dimension of her existence. She inherently sensed that the value of her life would in part be measured by her ability to sustain the existence and insure the survival of this child. She felt an inexplicable emptiness and a sudden intense, urgent need for her child.*

Mala awoke fully and abruptly, her heart beating uncontrollably fast. She yelled out, "Kalal! Kalal! Where are you? Where is my baby? Where is she?"

Kalal, who had been sitting outside, near the entrance of the cave, came rushing in carrying the baby. "She's here Mala. She's here."

Mala was breathing hard, her hands trembling as she reached for the swaddled infant. After this day, Mala slept with the little girl in her arms and Kalal went alone when he disappeared either in the night or some time before dawn. He started staying gone longer, coming back only well after sunrise, never speaking of where he had gone. When he returned, he appeared nervous and jumpy; always looking back over his shoulder and shaking himself as if to be rid of a nagging unpleasant feeling or sensation. And he kept watching as if waiting for some unknown, unseen entity to appear. His anxiety was perplexing to her. She tried to delicately probe, to determine the source of his trepidation, while also reminding him that no predatory or carnivorous animals had ever existed on the Ocan island. But no matter how much she questioned or attempted to reason with him, he would say nothing, only shake his head and stare straight ahead.

Mala, like Kalal and all Ocan people, had been warned all of her life about the terrain beyond the boundary of the western foothills. But she had never understood why the Ocan people had declared these lands forbidden. Her parents had consciously chosen to live as close to the forbidden territory as possible without being accused of violating Ocan law. For Mala, these lands were in her blood and a part of all that she was capable of feeling and thinking. The only difference that she could discern between this so-called 'forbidden' territory and the valleys where the Ocan people had chosen to settle was the numerous amount of caves in the mostly mountainous terrain of the west and the precipitous escarpments near the western shore. Otherwise the entire island was filled with the same lush forests and vegetation, abundant natural springs, and winding river tributaries.

Despite the warnings, the fears and all the Ocan laws, for four years prior to the birth of her child, Mala had lived not on or near that boundary, but deep within the heart of the forbidden lands, miles away from any of the Ocan settlements. And now these lands were to become her home and that of her child's for an indeterminable period of time. One day, Mala became worried when Kalal had not returned by late afternoon. As the time drew closer to the evening, she was readying herself to go look for him when he came suddenly rushing through the brush, appearing visibly shaken and immediately began packing their meager clothes and supplies, saying only, "Come Mala, we must leave this place."

Mala: "Yes, you said in two more days—"

Kalal: "No, we must leave now, today, this moment. You are strong now, are you not? And the baby? Will you be okay handling her on your own?"

Mala: "I am fine Kalal. But what has happened?"

Kalal: "Nothing. Nothing has happened. I will go with you as far as the pass that descends toward the shore."

Mala: "No, Kalal, it is better that I continue on alone. I know that you feel that the power of the Ocan will not protect you beyond these mountains. I am grateful that, you have stayed with us this long and brought us safe thus far."

Kalal: "It is not that I fear what lies ahead or even what may be present with us now." He glanced furtively over his shoulder. "But I am Ocan and my life is in the settlements of the island, not the full terrain that life has granted you province. There are not many as brave as you, little sister."

Mala: "Kalal, you have always been brother, father, uncle and friend to me. Indeed, your spirit has been one of the most significant guiding forces in my life. There is no need for you to explain yourself to me. I have you to thank for any small dose of courage that I might possess. For without you, the seeds of my life's journey could never have been planted and nurtured to growth."

Kalal: "Then maybe I have done too much or not enough for you. Had those very seeds not been planted, then maybe this day would have never come to pass."

Mala: "Kalal, you cannot blame yourself for any of this. Life is as it should be. And I am content with my path."

Kalal: "Once again, we take leave of one another. But unlike the time of past, you stand before me a fully mature woman, with so much wisdom yet so much sadness. You stayed away too long, Mala."

Mala: "And this time, I fear, I must stay away even longer."

Kalal: "Injustice is allowed to prevail only when there is a perception of weakness. If you had been given time to gather your strength, Edise and the others would never have dared to attempt what has come to pass. Mala, you are much too strong to allow their weakness and fear to keep you away.

We must keep in mind that every action that we, as humans, take is predicated on injera—either towards its fulfillment or as a reaction to its lack of fulfillment. I don't know why or how, but this action of the Ocan people, against your child, definitely reflects the latter of these states of being. No matter what, remember that life is guided by and dictated by the principles of injera. Keep those principles in your heart and in your mind. Let them bring you the understanding that it will take to overcome whatever problems you may face."

Mala: "I will."

Kalal: "Just as I have watched over you all of your life, rest assured that my presence, my spirit will be with you always. Remember always—honor thy Gift."

Mala: "May we be worthy."

He embraced Mala and then kissed the baby on the forehead as he assured her of the certainty of a springtime reunion. He also promised her that he, Saba and the others would work to bring about a time when she would be able to return with her child to the safety of the settlements. They parted, going in opposite directions, with Kalal still behaving strangely, looking back and all around as he hurried along as if he thought that he was being pursued.

Their plan was to meet at the point of their departure a year and a half in the future, at the time of the spring equinox, when the flowers from the adona trees would come into bloom. The white fragrant blossoms appeared all over the island at the exact same time each year and their appearance was a cause of celebration for all Ocan people, signaling the re-birth and growth of another cycle of living.

The rainy season was usually much more fierce on the western side of the island, but now only a light cool misty precipitation enveloped Mala as she held the child close and continued alone into the forest near the western shore. She walked through the night and most of the next day to her shelter in the trees closer to the ocean. From time to time, she searched the skies along the way, watching for storms. Mala had always watched the storms, studying and sensing their moods and the changes in their meaning and intent.

Her fascination with the elements of earth and air had awarded her a hard-earned intimate acquaintance with subtle shifts and barely discernible movements in pockets of air and forces beneath the ground. She could sense intense hot molten rock within the earth, storing electricity and absorbing radioactive energy, as it moved and shaped the land from within. She felt the continual flow of negative and positive current between the earth and its atmosphere. And she knew that a disruption in the balance of this flow of energy would produce strange electrical storms, with no rain, clouds or overcast; just volumes and volumes of atmospheric electricity and intense electrical discharges generated from the ambient wind and from inside the earth.

She could even smell the atmospheric particles ionized by the sun's ultraviolet radiation and know the manner of wind and precipitation that would form as a result of the molecules in this highly conductive air on the western shore. Mala was certain that one day they would come back—those storms that had created the world; the storms that had brought forth love and life, the storms that had once lived inside of her and claimed her as their own. This is why she knew that the storms would return, had to return. Thus, in the ensuing years as she reared her child alone in the western forest, she waited and she watched the storms.

The seasons changed quickly that first year and Mala carefully marked the time until the spring blooming of Adona trees, imbuing her sense of excitement and anticipation in her toddler infant. A few weeks before the time of their reunion, Mala spent weeks making and gathering gifts—pieces of woven fabric, small paintings, and jewels and gems that only the western mountains and streams could bring forth. She arrived at the cavern with her little girl a few days before the trees came into full bloom. The baby played in the meadow as Mala worked to prepare a feast of sliced raw fruit and roasted vegetables, with herb-garlic legumes and tubers.

On the day of Kalal's expected arrival, Mala adorned herself and the baby with garlands made of Adona flowers and laid out all their gifts and welcoming foods. When he did not come on the first day, Mala quietly stored the food and their gifts in the cavern. Then she laid awake until the stars covered the darkness above her. Over the next two days, she sat with the baby watching the Adona trees come into full bloom as the flowers opened in a wondrously fragrant and striking display. Her *sentiale* probes to Kalal came back muddled and unclear. Even her probes to Saba left her with only a murky bruised feeling of bewilderment and pain. They stayed for another week more and as the baby played each day in the meadow, Mala sat weaving or reading as she watched the trees shed their petals and cover the mountainside with a blanket of white, perfumed gentleness. She waited and waited, but still, he did not come.

For the next five years, at the time just before the adonas' blooming, Mala and the child made a trek to their mountaintop cavern. It became a special trip, a festive occasion for the child, who anxiously waited to meet this great uncle and good friend; this one and only person, besides her mother whom she could actually touch and hold and laugh and play with. Each time that Mala and the little girl would arrive at their destination, they would joyfully prepare a feast, with some of the food cooked over a small fire. They then ate only when the flowers began to open and spread their magic upon the mountaintop. When the trees shed their beauty, the child always ran excitedly through the field of loose and floating petals, rolling in them, covering herself completely in their soft fragrant essence and then throwing and releasing them into the air.

Once, on a day when the vibrant mellow rays of the sun had lulled her senses into tranquil oblivion, the little girl jumped into the warm pulsating air, dancing with the petals and she did not come back down for a moment in which time lost its way. She was engulfed in a lost gap of reality, where she sailed high into the air. Looking down, she saw her mother through a cloud-like vapor from a faraway place, appearing tiny and so utterly earthbound. Mala, absorbed in her tasks, never looked up to see her daughter floating on the wind. The little girl felt the sun's steady rhythm of heat pulsing on, around and through her body. She lie still on the air as the currents pushed her up and over in waves and twists and wild undulations in the open space above the earth. She only became disoriented when she closed her eyes and then opened them suddenly as she felt the wind sit her floating body gently on the ground. With the hard earth beneath her, her senses stirred awake. The incident stayed alive inside of her, beyond its moment in time, beyond the impact of her descent, into the duration of her life. Over time the memory became distant in its essence. Yet, for the rest of her life, beneath the cover of her conscious world, she held within the core of her being an eternal sensation of weightlessness.

It wasn't until the fifth year of their annual mountaintop ritual that the little girl noticed how quiet and still her mother became every time that the petals began to drift and fly. Thereafter, she too sat quietly during the day and then wept silently at night, hiding her tears, unsure why she was crying but comforted by the feeling that her sadness befit whatever loss her mother mourned. Always on the day after the petals were fully shed, they would begin the daylong journey back to their home. After six such celebrations at their mountaintop cavern, they never went again.

Over the years, Mala instructed her child in the same manner in which she herself had been guided to knowledge. First, to go inside of the spirit of that whose lesson was sought. The trees, plants, soil, grass, water. All animals, elusive and obtrusive, large and small, diurnal and nocturnal, apparent and unseen. The moon, stars, distant planets, celestial bodies, the night, the wind, the sun. She opened her soul to receive, and expanded her being so that each manifestation of life would find its way into her spirit and she could become a part of the vapor of its essence.

As with all new beings, she absorbed quickly, and eagerly awaited each chance to reunite herself with all those entities and elements of life that, in this reality, now stood separate from her. In rejoicing their beauty, she innately recognized that their need for distinctive realities could never negate the omniscient force of all matter and energy conceived as one in the womb of the universe. She heard, but her nature would not permit her to heed, her mother's ultimate warning— never remain too long within the spirit of another life substance, lest she lose the ability to return fully to her own being. And she bore the consequences of her transgression with the unspoken sanction of powerful allies that lived before and within her.

Mala taught her child to feed herself and how others would feed upon her. How to give herself to another's need, yet never to be either predator or prey, for each contained its own inherent deficiency or empty need that never could be filled. How to replenish her being with the abundant gift of life without ever depleting or disrespecting the source of her renewal. And how, in return, she could expect life's reciprocity. It was a life of balance, equilibrium, and natural order. All the things that Mala had grown to learn and expect as part of the Ocan. Yet this life offered something more, something beyond that which was possible with Ocan village life—no constraints. No societal, familial obligations or restrictions. As a result, their lessons did not subscribe to the self-imposed limitations of thought, that are required necessarily of those who band together to survive in and make sense of the realities in which they are placed.

She taught her of the surface boundaries of the land and that while no humans, other than the Ocan people, resided on or near their island home, there were other land masses in the distance that did, indeed, contain beings such as themselves. She taught her the history of their people. How their ancestors had fled the virulent force that had invaded the nearby mainland—attacking and infiltrating every form of terrestrial inhabitant. Having come to this small mountainous island, isolated from the virus and its victims, the mountains had purified them; its streams absolved their pain, fear, and guilt. It took generations to fully filter the residual effects of the virus from the people's minds and their spirits. Over time the people became one with the land and only faint scars remained as testament and reminder of where and what they had once been.

She taught her the rites and beliefs of the Ocan, and through her silence she alluded to the secrets that the mountains had revealed. Finally, she taught her of the unseen and the unheard. How forces greater than life speak through the ethereal webs that connect all that lives and dies. And only through this medium can their message be received.

Shona was a serious solemn little girl, warming slowly to play and to new situations. However, once she felt her way through and became familiar, then she was energetic, enthusiastic, jubilant—she moved fully within the wholeness of the moment. Mala peopled Shona with all the life of the Ocan villages, while also censoring those thoughts and feelings that must remain forever veiled. Shona played in her mother's memories, possessing them as her own. When she tired of re-living Mala's familiar scenes, the creatures of her mind took on a life of their own and came out to dance, laugh and play with Shona and her many small furry friends of the forest.

At night Mala and her daughter made the words and phrases of various languages from around the world come alive, as Shona learned from her mother the nuances of the many lexicons, and systems of speech that had surrounded Mala from birth. Mala explained to Shona that the people of the Ocan are descended from a variety of different nationalities, racial and ethnic groups, and thus the primary Ocan language was a rich hybrid of several tongues spoken by the inhabitants of many different lands. Even before the founding of their island-nation, the Ocan people had been interested in tracking and documenting as many of the planet's languages as they could. They taught their children that the languages provided surface access to different ways of knowing, different ways of seeing the world. To fully see the world in all of its known and hidden guises was one of the primary purposes for this separatist community's existence.

As mother and daughter lie, looking out of their constructed shelter at the stars in the sky, they shared their tales of miraculous and magical wonders, while pondering all the laws and needs that govern the natural realm. Most nights they drifted into sleep, still trading with one another contrived stories of strange and foreign lands, with Mala also recounting Ocan legends of courage and faith and friendship and valor. Shona learned how to listen for the linguistic features and universals that connected the different languages. She learned how the patterns and structure of a language would reveal a people's beliefs and customs. And most importantly, she learned how to listen for the shape of meaning beneath the words. Still, no matter how many stories, people or ways of understanding that Mala shared, Shona always hungered for more—more thoughts, more people, more perceptual acuity. In time, she found that she was more than capable of satisfying her own needs.

There was one human-vision that Mala had not given to her daughter; one person that came to Shona on his own and not through Mala's conscious sentiale. Shona had no idea who he was, or even how he knew of her existence. Yet, without mistake, she knew that he was of the Ocan. From the beginning, she felt an affinity, a sense of consanguinity. This was a kindred spirit, another part of herself that existed outside of herself. He sought and found her in solitude and that silent seclusion became their bond, their pathway to one another. They played together often, running, laughing, inventing many secret games that entertained and amused them both. Although they shared endless details about the flora and fauna of their respective surroundings, they never made reference to the people in their lives. If Mala came upon Shona as she interacted with her internal playmate, he would evaporate abruptly from her mind, her presence. Likewise, if another from his own world entered the periphery of his consciousness, he pulled away from Shona immediately. While it never occurred to Shona to question their need for secrecy, sometimes in a moment of stillness, she would ponder his physical presence upon the earth. Then her fleeting curiosity would lose itself quickly in the essence of their resumed frolic.

As she grew older and more vested in tangible realities, he came to her less and less, until she reached the point that only a vague memory of a secret imaginary friend, a fantasy playmate remained in her conscious mind. Yet he remained vivid in the dreams that slipped away just as she reached waking consciousness. And sometimes during the day she felt a dual awareness within her being, separate from her own—seeing what she saw, hearing what she heard, experiencing all of her thoughts and emotions. But these sensations, like those in her dreams, disappeared whenever her mind came too close to touching their reality.

Most days Shona assisted her mother with the daily work of gathering the abundant luxurious spider webs that were everywhere throughout the western forests. In the same manner as fibers derived from vegetables, wood, or leaves, the silk they gathered did not come as continuous filaments like that of caterpillar silk. Thus, they had to spin the fiber into thread or yarn before it could be woven into a sturdy and very useful type of fabric. While the Ocan people manufacture a small amount of silk from caterpillar cocoons, they primarily cultivate cloth fibers from vegetation, turning flax into linen, woody herbs into jute and hemp and pulp from the bark of trees into a cotton-like fabric. No such silk as that created by Mala had ever been produced by the scant numbers of spindly caterpillars on the eastern side of the island. Moreover, Mala's cultivation and harvesting of spider silk did not ever cause injury or even death, which sometimes inadvertently occurred in the process used to extract protein from the caterpillar cocoons.

This new and impenetrable type of silk was the primary reason that Mala's violation of Ocan laws had been overlooked in the past. The first time that she left and subsequently returned to the Ocan village, she was charged with violating an Ocan law that carried a mandatory life sentence of direct and constant supervision and monitoring. Then she showed her accusers and other villagers the illustrious fabric that she had created from the spider silk. Beyond just the making of clothing, the people discovered various uses for this new fabric that was more elastic than nylon and stronger than steel. The people began to use the silk in the manufacture and construction of all kinds of materials, including rafts, houses, tools and equipment.

As long as Mala always returned from the forbidden lands with an abundance of spider silk, then the Elders and all the people remained silent on the subject of any further prosecution. Besides, the people said, it would be cruel to punish this young woman, who had been neglected as a child and kept isolated all of her life and then abruptly orphaned as a teen by parents who obviously never took the time to teach her the difference between right and wrong. She really did not know any better, did she? And the silk was so nice and so useful; so very pretty and sturdy. While the people gave Mala no direct permission or approval as she continued to come and go to and from the forbidden lands over the ensuing months and then years, Mala's gifts, nonetheless, became the only sanction that she would ever need to continue her open defiance of Ocan law.

Although mother and daughter spent part of each day together, as Shona grew older the majority of their time was spent in solitary pursuit of their individual interests. One day, in the forest not too far from the main mountain stream that provided water for the two females, Shona came upon a whole colony of spiders that occupied a large hidden grove of Guola trees in its entirety. She knew that the arachnids, like all the creatures on their isolated island, lacked any predatory impulse or behavior, which made their intense web-making activities all the more mysterious. Perhaps in some distant past the female spiders had needed the protein from insect prey to produce eggs. But now they seemed to continue on ancient pathways of instinct and need, creating their silk for shelter perhaps or maybe just for the delicate beauty of their symmetrical designs.

Shona stayed in her secret grove with the spiders for hours. She watched them, as she hummed to herself, entranced by the intricacies and nuances of the ritualistic movements in this microcosmic civilization. She felt like she was an integral part of this community of reclusive yet highly social creatures. They seemed to work by genetic memory, continuously spinning webs and sometimes weaving large communal constructions that spanned over six feet in diameter.

She started to differentiate between types of spiders and saw that, as with most spiders, the females of this colony continued to weave webs throughout their lives, while nearly all of the males abandoned web building when they reached maturity. She watched as time and time again their silk was appropriated by birds and other animals to build more durable nests and other such uses. She was amazed every time that one of her wingless friends became airborne. She would watch the spider climb up to a high point and then feel herself jumping and sailing with her arachnid friend into the breeze. She/they would float skyward while spewing from a hidden abdominal spigot multiple strands that would form a single solid thread. Then she/they would descend in slow motion on their thin barely discernible piece of silk before beginning the process again and again.

Many times Shona would return from her daily forays into the forest to find her mother deep in meditation or prayer and she would sit quietly, trying to still her own soul. But she could only sit for so long and invariably the young girl would be forced to resume her own natural state of perpetual motion, long before her mother rose to full consciousness or even became aware of her daughter's presence. When Shona was not watching the spiders or playing with the forest animals, she roamed freely throughout the mountain forest and the nearby rocky beaches of the shoreline, swimming some times and occasionally taking the raft that she and Mala had constructed out of balsa wood, into the sea, sometimes beyond the reef. One of her favorite hobbies was searching for and collecting the precious and ordinary gems and stones that lay in the open mountain streams.

Occasionally they cooked their food, but for the most part they ate the raw fruits and vegetables as they grew, while also cultivating a small garden and collecting sea vegetation—seaweed, alga, kelp and dulse—from the tide pools and along the sub-tidal regions of the rocky shore. They stored and preserved their food in the Ocan way, with two large clay pots, one inside of the other with a layer of wet sand between them and a clay lid on top. In this way they were able to keep their vegetables and other collected foodstuff fresh for days and sometimes weeks. They cooked on an open fire near their thatched one room domicile. Each year when the hardest part of the rainy season came, they moved into the caves down by the shore.

From the time that she began to speak and comprehend, Shona persistently begged Mala for the two of them to return to the Ocan settlements so that they could once again "be with our people". She understood that Mala was performing important work for the Ocan community here in the western mountains. However, she also knew how hurt and sad the Ocan people had been when Mala had taken her newborn child away from them in order to live and work in this desolate part of the island. Shona planned her homecoming to the Ocan-main on almost a daily basis. She started making and storing away gifts that she would take to the people. And she already knew what people she would look for first. Of course there was Saba, and Tausi and Amira, Kalal and Olana and oh so many more. And she would see the huge Ocan library, reading all the ancient and sacred texts that would sate her curiosity beyond what was possible with the few select manuscripts that Mala possessed.

She saw herself brokering a truce between the Aka and the Ocan; and as they finally understood how silly their disagreement had been, they would cheer Shona as their champion and hero. She would learn from the Saba all the life and healing wisdom of the ages, passed down from saba to saba and she would become a great healing saba herself, assuming the inheritance that her mother had cast aside. She would save her visit to the Elders for last and they would be so happy to see her and honor her existence. All these people, places and events were alive and active within Shona's sentiale. She could taste, feel, see it all as she stood in her own physical reality, separate and very far away. When the day came that all the experiences in her mind and spirit could actually be a part of the physical dimension of her world, then she would finally know what it truly means to be Ocan. She never grew tired of asking her mother when they were going to return and for years Mala would only look down or away into the distance and reply, "Soon, Shona, soon." Then she would smile at her daughter and hug her close, holding her for awhile before letting her go.

As Shona grew older, she began to believe less and less in this 'soon' that her mother offered, until one day, as they sat weaving, Mala felt a brief prickly, uneasy sensation in her mind and Shona suddenly looked up and said plainly, "We're never going back. And you've known this all along. You really don't want me to have anyone else but you, do you, mother? You want my whole life to be centered on you and only you."

"Shona, I—"

Before Mala spoke fully, Shona had jumped up ran into the woods. She stayed in her secret place down by the stream all day, creeping back to their abode only once the sun had set. That night, as they lie in the darkness waiting for sleep to come, Mala quietly told Shona a story of the Ascension Rites of the Ocan adolescents and young adults. She told her that her return to the Ocan was intended to take place at the time of the observance of her entry into adult life.

Ascension Rites take place over a period of years and vary in duration, depending on the person. The minimum time can be between two to three years, but most people range between five to seven years. Mala told her how sometimes the sentiale of the young apprentices and disciples become fused in a bond that can last a lifetime and beyond. She told her that the purpose of this dedicated time is for each disciple or apprentice to learn to rise toward a higher self; rise to their responsibilities and obligations to themselves and to others. The culmination of the rites lead to each apprentice's and disciple's Primary Retreat, which lasts no less than a year. This is a year of solitude, reflection, and commune with nature alone. During the Primary Retreat, the Ocan young adults stay in isolation in the makeshift shelters located on the outskirts of the hamlets near the eastern shore.

After Mala's story, Shona never mentioned returning to the Ocan again. However, through her sentiale Mala surreptitiously watched and traveled with Shona as she secretly created small pictures, pieces of jewelry and other small gifts and then hid them away. From time to time, Mala entered her child's mind, blocking any awareness of her presence. This form of asynchronous unobtrusive sentiale observation was used by most Ocan parents to protect and keep their children safe. During these moments of surveillance, Shona always seemed to be humming contentedly to herself as she went about her tasks, oblivious to any presence in her mind but her own. Mala never considered her one-way sentiale tracking an invasion of her daughter's privacy. That is, until that day when Shona turned and looked back at her mother, staring openly and defiantly at Mala within her mind.

They were in two separate physical locations, at a distance from one another. Mala sat working with the large batch of silk that Shona brought for her. She could never figure out where Shona was able to find such copious amounts of spider web and the young girl only smiled vaguely when she was questioned. Shona was down near the caves, scouting, it seemed, for yet another secret hiding place. Mala had felt a storm brewing in the air for the past few days, and as she moved her loom into their shelter, she was trying to decide if it was time to move to the caves. Thus far, there had only been increased electrical activity, but no really large storms. Still it was always better to be cautious and not take any chances of being caught in a violent downpour. It was for this reason that she opened a one-way channel into Shona's mind, to make sure that she was safe and to know where she was in case they had to suddenly take shelter at the shore.

For a few moments Mala watched Shona in her mind, feeling her daughter's thoughts, listening to the little song that she whistled. Her observation was inconspicuous and undetected. Or so she thought. When she began to feel a subtle unfamiliar sensation of discomfort in Shona's mind, she thought the link was perhaps weakening because of the increased ions in the atmosphere. Then she was jarred, taken aback, when the scene from Shona's outside world shifted and she saw only herself through Shona's eyes. She had no time to even try to understand what was happening before she felt/saw a flash of lightning, then her mind-vision of Shona went completely blank, and there was only darkness. This was more than just a mental barrier or a cognitive obstacle that she could reach around. Try as she might, she could not get around, over or through what looked like thick black fog, but felt like a solid stone wall. Then as suddenly as it came, the veil lifted and she found herself once more within Shona's thoughts and emotions. Although it seemed that only seconds had passed, Shona was now in the forest, near the mountain stream, far from where she had been when the fog came. She was smiling to herself, searching for gemstones, thinking only of the water and the stones in front of her.

Mala sensed a faint awareness that Shona knew and felt her mother's presence in her mind. But she seemed to purposely not look at her mother or open any channel of communication. She seemed to covertly want her mother to know that she was not only aware of her presence, but that she alone controlled this connection. Mala quickly pulled away from the sentiale link. She inhaled deeply, trying to settle her rapidly beating heart. She had never heard that this level of manipulation and command of sentiale awareness was even possible, especially not in one so young. Shona was still a few miles away, but through the echo in her mind, Mala could hear her daughter laughing aloud gaily.

A memory pulled from the edges of Mala's mind. It was the night that Shona was born. She was in the birthing hut with Saba. Mala could feel Saba's fear lying heavy and palpable on the thick night air. Within the reality of the memory's true moment Mala had peered around the edges of the Saba's mind. She wasn't sure exactly what she saw, but it looked like a giant dark bird of prey, with a wingspan that stretched to both ends of the horizon, gliding silently on the wind above an alien land. The bird was peering fiercely, searching, scouting in a dense forest of strange trees and overgrown vegetation where she could sense the trembling fear of hidden prey. Mala's mind held the vision for only a second before it quickly retreated and evaporated. She heard a loud clap of thunder and without thinking, her sentiale sent a strong hot prayer, invoking the presence of the universe's omnipotent energy. And without knowing how or why, Shona was stilled, her laughter faltering before it reached sound.

4. In Absentia

It is hard to measure the affect that one life can have upon another life or upon other lives. Perhaps it is even more difficult to discern the impact of the absence of a life. Although, she was not reared within the Ocan settlements, Shona *in absentia*, exerted an even stronger influence on Ocan life than her actual presence may have yielded. For imagination is many times a more powerful vehicle of intent than reality can ever hope to be. This may be especially true for the very young, who have no control over the indelible marks left by their earliest impressions. The Saba's grandson, Taijaur, grew up and never forgot the baby girl who was buried when he was a young boy. First, as a youth and then as a young man, not a day went by that her spirit did not resurrect in his mind and within his senses. The sensations elicited by her existence were even more forceful within the states of unconsciousness that overpowered his life.

He was with her now, the girl, the young woman who fueled his thoughts and emotions. They were in a strange dark place that was filled with a gossamer web illuminated with muted colors and tiny pieces of light that darted in and out of the gaps between the sticky fibers of the web. The web vibrated with sound and energy, emitting a strange cadence that harmonized with the rising wind. The stone walls that surrounded them were filled with precious gems, in sizes, shapes and configurations that defied the mind's ability to conceive what was real. Taijaur felt himself a master of awareness, with a power of vision that extended beyond all normal boundaries. And together, he and the girl formed perceptions of different worlds. . .they felt themselves a part of a natural and ancient connection to the source of all creation...then they felt themselves transforming into something else, somewhere else.... and before he realized what was happening, the scene shifted and he saw Alor and Hadassa as they searched. . .and he joined with them in their quest. . . .touching the earth, searching. . .

On a bright cool day, in the back bedroom of a small circular adobe home, a young Ocan man, considered one of the strongest and most able of his generation, sat trapped, against his will, struggling—dreaming within a dream. Each time that Taijaur strained harder to reach the surface of waking consciousness, he was pushed further down into a vortex of swirling sound and energy. Despite the magnitude of his abilities and the tremendous power inherent in his being,

Taijaur could not now or ever escape these deep "dream" states of altered consciousness. They followed him persistently, seizing his soul and taking him into and through worlds beyond any dimensions of known realities. He could not understand how the deliberate and lucid sentiale dreaming of all Ocan people could manifest within him in such an over-powering form, and in such a way that they became integral to the fabric of his life.

The Ocan elders and master teachers assumed that he suffered from an inherited form of narcolepsy, the same kind of sleeping sickness that had been suspected in many of those in the Saba's family, including Taijaur's mother, Loni. When all the medical tests finally ruled out any form of physical or neurological disorder, they merely shrugged their shoulders and muttered to themselves about a family curse. As he grew older Taijaur found that his trances or states of unconsciousness were coming more frequently and with greater strength and duration. He tried unsuccessfully to control them and then to hide them from his grandmother and those closest to him. By keeping to himself, he gained a reputation for being a loner and thus, no one really knew how deeply the dream-states had captured him. For the most part, the people knew only of his strength, his intelligence and his deep capacity to care for and about the earth and its inhabitants. What they did not know and he could not ever tell them was that his insight, his formidable power, his knowledge and all of the abilities they so admired could only come to him by way of that which transpired in his dreams.

He was never sure how the dreams or even how the girl would come to him. Sometimes he would be in one place within a dream-world and suddenly he would find himself snatched away—with her, beside her or inside of her thoughts and feelings. On this day, he had risen earlier at daybreak and during his morning meditations he had unexpectedly slipped into a deep trance. As always, he began his day by absorbing the music of the dawn and gazing into the shadowy red-orange mist of heaven's awakening. At first he had only listened inattentively to the airborne melodies, as the birds flitted from one tree to another. Then, as he paid closer attention to the lengthy and elaborate call and response pattern of a pair of songbirds, he became convinced that many of the songs' notes must originate within the birds' neurons as they sleep. He began to see and hear, within his own mind, patterns of avian musical compositions—whistles and twirls, melodies and harmonies. The patterns were playing, repeatedly over and over as they were stimulated and strengthened by an enveloping instinctual dream-consciousness. Before he was able to come to the surface of his reverie, he felt the music pulling him under and his mind expanded to absorb an abundant array of visual, auditory, psychic energy that attacked and empowered every dimension of his being.

He heard faint whispers of a distant melodious song, calling him away. And she was with him as they both reached out to capture the musical notes resounding in his mind. . . then they saw an unearthly gem, with the power to absorb and reverberate the rhythm of life and gather the light in such a way that its reflection could, undoubtedly, be seen beyond the stars...they bent to listen to the earth. . .the land was telling him something ... the message was unclear...searching for an answer. . .the song played incessantly as . . .she led him. . .through a jumbled confusing maze. . .and then a map appeared, etched within the vibrating points of light in the web, on the rocks before them. . . an intricate diagram of the route. . .they began following each point, each twist in a meandering passageway deep within the earth. . . . . .the music continued to play as the notes from the song formed strange signs and signals in the air. . .and it took him awhile to realize that he was watching, listening to, and reading the words, symbols and hieroglyphs from a book that he worked on daily. . .

In his dream state, Taijaur saw the words and meaning of an indecipherable text that had plagued him for weeks, laid out in the notes of a song. His work, as an apprentice to Master Alor, required that he carefully watch and study the words of the world; tending to all the nuances of their diverse signals of meaning. Taijaur was trained to focus on the patterns in human social/cultural evolution and shifts in those patterns. His studies took him back to ancient times, where the seeds of many civilizations had initially coalesced. He also looked into the future by creating projections of potential societal developments, given the preponderance of certain current and past conditions. In examining the expressed thoughts of beginning nations, Taijaur was required to decipher, decode, and translate ancient texts that continuously challenged him to reach higher and dig deeper in order to comprehend their intent. Each day, he dutifully tended his tasks; except on this particular spring day the signals went unheeded, because their caretaker unexpectedly was not, could not be present.

. . .he felt/saw a vision of the universe. . .stars swirling. . .planets forming... and then he and the girl were descending toward the earth. . .the island. . .floating high above the Maja, he heard voices inside . . .Hadassa and Alor talking. . .their voices, blending with the cadence of the song, drifted from the Maja. . . . . . .through it all the song stayed with him. . .pure and simple. . .over and over . . . Taijaur

was no longer hearing the individual words of Hadassa and Alor's discussion…he heard only the melodious sounds of their voices…he made no connection between their voices and any specific meaning, save that which pertained to …the meaning of the song …their voices now sang only wordless lyrics, until they reached a point that their voices were no more and there was only the song…each note…adding deeper levels of comprehension, unveiling the mystery until it, the message, the gem…. stood open, exposed near the pathway leading to Taijaur's waking consciousness…he could pick it up and carry it with him, inside of himself, inside of the notes, the melody of a song. …he wasn't sure exactly what the song meant, he just knew that he had to take it with him and allow it to pull him deeper into a world that he had no means of comprehending… then he realized that he no longer had any awareness of the girl….and he tried to shift his awareness away from the song, in order to take in the scenes, the words, the meanings…but the more he tried, the more he found himself inside the visions, the meaning of the song…he felt close to seeing, understanding profound truths about life, the universe, existence; close to bursting with the rapture of comprehension, perception, …. and then he suddenly understood that there was no vision, no scene, no words, no meaning. Before he had time to realize what was happening, he had no body, no mind, no soul; and there was nothing, except the song.

Saba sat on the bed next to her grandson's inert body, contemplating what she should do. She had returned from her pre-dawn communion in the Ocan temple and found him unconscious, sitting straight up on his bed next to an open window. He was barely breathing, unresponsive to her attempts to awaken him. She thought at first that she should return to the temple caverns to retrieve the healing minerals that she had forgotten to bring with her. But she was reluctant to leave him alone. Besides, the temple was too far away in the foothills of the northern mountains. Its edifice was built on the opening of a mountain cave that led into a labyrinth of interior cavern chambers and winding subterranean tunnels laden with living breathing stalagmites and stalactites. The cavern's vaporous gases and clear spring waters were the source from which many of the Ocan's healing substances were derived, and the Saba was their sole guardian.

The healer-woman knew of the potential for irreparable damage to the sentiale if a person is pulled unwillingly from a dreaming state. She had even witnessed the long term repercussions—dis-ease in the mind and body that resulted from disturbing a person who is deep within dream-consciousness. But she was alarmed by how long he remained inert, with hardly any sign of life. She had never seen anyone in so deep a trance, except maybe once, with Loni just before she went away; before that Basau man took her away. Saba tried to recall—*Is it possible to slip from a trance into a coma?* She did not know, could not remember. She began to feel a sense of desperation creeping over her. She even wondered if it would be possible for her to create a sentiale link strong enough to go inside of his dream-awareness and try to pull him free. Years ago, Kalal could have helped her, he could have told her what to do. But now he could barely tell himself who he was, let alone offer any solace to her predicament.

Cold perspiration ran down her back as she sat, immobilized by fear. Fear for this only child of an only child. What if he, too, was pulled away like Loni, who before her time, had slipped through the grasp of this world? She would not, could not allow Taijaur to meet the same fate; even if he was never fully present in this here and now. Saba thought that her grandson had always been like a spirit too-soon-born, still lingering in another realm, still seeking, longing for that place where he existed before his birth. She wondered to herself—*Will the darkness eventually pull him under, take him away? Is he truly meant for this world? Is this why his dreams possess him so intensely? Do they take him back to where he belongs? From the beginning, he has been marked by death; his time on this earth borrowed, not truly his own. Oh Tekun, my love, I need your help. Why can't you be here with me?*

What the Saba really feared, during these times that Taijaur drifted in other worlds, was the impossible—that Saron Basau had come back and was fighting for possession of his son's soul. She knew that her fears were unfounded and foolish; people don't come back from the dead. Yet she also knew that logic and rationality are sometimes useless means of perception in a world where supernatural purposes hide in the crevices of mundane realities. Saba stayed on constant alert for the unforeseen and the implausible ever since the time that the youngest of Emir Basau's sons had captured her only child's heart and then imprisoned her soul.

No one ever knew how Saron and Loni had met. The Basau family lives at least three full days' walk from the Ocan-main within the southeast region of the island, along with—according to most Ocan opinion-leaders—a whole community of hostile dissidents. They call themselves Aka, and allow themselves to be led by successive generations of the Basau family, with their many sons and their strident anarchistic beliefs. The Aka, originally a part of the Ocan collective, had broken away to form their own society, separate and very different from that envisioned by their progenitors. When Loni left the

Ocan-main she never returned. She joined with that Aka man, that youngest of Emir Basau's sons, and then gave her life in hostage to his beliefs—strange, unfathomable Aka beliefs.

The Saba finally strengthened her resolve and decided that the situation was serious enough to warrant outside intervention. The people were probably beginning to gather at the Maja for the community festival taking place today. Perhaps she could send someone to the mountains to ask Alor to come. He would know what to do. She rose and started out of the room, but she halted when a faint aura of music began filling the room like a vapor wafting through the air. She felt/heard the music become stronger, more intense, just before Taijaur suddenly awoke. As he opened his eyes and stared directly at Saba, the music abruptly stopped.

It took a moment for Taijaur to get his bearings and recognize the reality into which he had surfaced and although he felt her presence and was staring directly at her, it was awhile before he was fully aware that Saba was there with him in the room. She stood at a distance peering at him, waiting for him to come into full consciousness. He spoke first, "Saba...I...um, are you... are you okay?"

"Good morning Taijaur. I am fine. The question is—how are you? Or perhaps I should ask—where are you?"

He wiped his face with his hands and moved to get off the bed. "I'm here Saba. I'm here."

"Taijaur, the dreams are getting stronger, aren't they?"

He gave no reply, as he rose and splashed water on his face from the basin that sat on the table next to his bed.

"Taijaur, where do your dreams take you so strongly?"

Drying his face, he tried to think of the safest answer to offer her, something that would cause her the least amount of concern. "My soul reaches out and I venture to different places, distant unfamiliar realms. But, please can we discuss this further some other time? The sun is already high in the sky and I must get to the lab."

As he spoke, he quickly slipped on a new shirt, kissed his grandmother on the cheek and headed toward the front door. The Saba followed after him. "But Taijaur, you've had no breakfast."

He was already out of the door and starting down the path, waving to Saba.

"Don't worry—Alor will have something at the lab. Honor thy Gift, Grandmother."

He was turning the bend and almost out of sight, before she whispered the Ocan customary response.

She stood in the doorway watching the empty path he had taken, still wondering how she could help him and from whom outside intervention could be sought. Saba thought of Kalal and how today's festival had freed her of the daily responsibility of helping to care for her brother. Then she hurriedly pushed from her mind the worrying connection that her thoughts were beginning to form between her grandson and her only sibling. She would not allow herself to think of any similarity between Kalal's current condition and Taijaur. She prayed, as she always did, that his work with Alor might help Taijaur to find a way to plant his feet and his mind firmly in this land of the living.

In a flash of an instant, Saba thought that she saw something or someone moving, running on the same path that Taijaur had taken. The bright sunlight shone directly in her eyes, obstructing her view. It looked like an animal or person, moving several feet behind Taijaur as if pursuing him, but staying hidden in the foliage. For a brief second, her mind formed the image of that man, that Haman villager, the one with the white hair who still always seemed to be hanging around—here, the marketplace, everywhere she went it seemed. He was always looking at her, nodding, smiling. And she would move as fast as she could to get away from him. Despite how familiar he seemed, she had no idea who he was and she did not want to know him. She just wanted him to stay away and leave her alone, leave Taijaur alone. He was creepy in a way that she could not explain. She quickly assured herself that the moving 'object' in the bush could not be that man or any man. It was probably just a flower swaying in the bushes or just some trick of the light. Saba turned and went back into her house, shutting out the light and any disquieting thoughts or feelings that might clamor for her attention.

Taijaur ran to the laboratory, hoping to hold the vision, the feel, sound, taste of his dream until he was able to translate the notes of the music into words and attempt to apply its simplicity to the problem whose solution had eluded him these past weeks. How simple it all seemed now with this one little alteration contained in the few bars of a song. He hummed it to himself over and over. He would write it down as soon as he stepped into the lab. Normally, he would have written it down upon awakening, so as to make the translation closer to the source. But with Saba hovering about, that option was not possible. He knew that he would have the lab to himself today as everyone else would be attending the Maja spring festival.

However, when he came into full view of the lab but still at a distance, he was startled to hear the sound of unexpected voices coming from the door which had been left slightly open. He recognized the voices of Kedar and Odar Dalasa, and then he suddenly remembered the scheduled lesson that was to have taken place early this morning. Without being aware of its departure, the song immediately went out of his head as he hurried along, thinking only that Master Alor must not be disappointed by yet another unintended absence. He knew that he would never be made chief apprentice, if Alor felt that he could not handle the responsibility of at least being on time.

The two Dalasa brothers along with Taijaur formed the core research team for Alor and Hadassa's joint projects. At this stage of their apprenticeship, they were primarily responsible for monitoring and receiving the satellite transmissions that were stored and recorded in the Ocan's lower laboratory which also served as a satellite receiving station and was hidden in a crest of a hill several miles away from the main village. By way of specialized radio telescopes, the Ocan people intercept and receive high frequency radio wave imagery from every electronic and satellite transmission that is sent from anywhere across the globe. Before the invention of such technology, the people had sent covert 'observers' into the nations of the world to record and report back to the island all of the significant events that transpired in these societies. For centuries they had watched and monitored any and everything of consequence that happened on the planet.

They knew the political, cultural and social milieu of every country and group of people in existence. They knew the times that nations were and would most likely be at war with one another; having kept a special record of the factors that precipitated all conflicts. They knew of the destruction to the ozone, the land, the ecosystems; the depletion of water, oil and other natural resources. They knew about endangered species, threatened habitats, homelessness, hunger, starvation, genocide. What ever the peoples of the world transmitted through their electronic devices, the Ocan people were able to capture, catalog, process and study.

It was written by the founders of their island-nation, within the founding creed of their society, that the knowledge they gathered was necessary to their cause, to their purpose. Their founders had prophesized and planned for that one day, in the distant future, when they would move back into the world and change the structure of mankind's destiny at its core. So it was written, so it must be. For more than two centuries the Ocan people had surreptitiously watched the world. They watched and they waited.

As Taijaur drew closer to the lab, he heard the voices more clearly and he realized that the two brothers were once again entangled in one of their endless debates. When he continued to hear only the voices of the young men, he surmised that Master Alor must have already left and that it was probably better if his two best friends did not see him today, lest they find it necessary to chastise him for another missed lesson. He turned and ran through the woods, towards the village hoping that neither Kedar nor Odar would leave the lab before he was out of sight and before he reached the Maja.

He neared the top of the hill descending into the valley where the marketplace and center of the village lay and he could see ladders straddling all sides of the building, as sounds of music, laughter and conversations drifted up to him. It looked like most of the people were still working on the front of the building. The single entrance into the subterranean archives was accessible only by way of the rear of the Maja and he hoped to enter it without being seen. Only the senior scholars were permitted to go through this door that was partially hidden by overgrown weeds and shrubs.

The festival to re-plaster the adobe walls of the Maja occurred every spring. Although the traditional Ocan adobe walls generally require a renewal of mud plaster only once every three to five years, this annual maintenance of the community meeting house was done mainly for cosmetic reasons and to prevent minor rain damage from growing into fault lines that could potentially attack the structural integrity. The festival was always messy and fun, with everyone from the main village and many of those from the four outlying villages coming together to play as much as they worked. Drums and wooden flute music set the tempo, as food was served, children played games and buckets of water were brought to mix the dirt from some of the building's old brick with the fresh mortar, in this way carrying the blessing of the original to the new.

The Maja spring festival was also an important way for the people to publicly recognize and pay homage to their belief that the land is sacred and a source of supernatural power. The Maja was their most visible symbol of this belief and they honored this conduit for the earth's energy; an energy that flowed abundantly from the building into the lives of the people. Most of the village homes and buildings were constructed in a manner similar to the Maja, with a central dome that heightened the impact of the interior spaces and intrinsic features that were intended to express the harmonic relationship between the land and its people.

Kalal, as Master Architect and Builder, had guided the design of many of the buildings and public spaces in addition to the ritual pathways that connected their village to sacred sites within the surrounding mountains. He was a part of that ancient breed of masons whose responsibility it was to protect not only the buildings that they constructed, but also the people, the families who would inhabit them. In the spirit of their founders, Kalal had spent a lifetime devoted to creating buildings and structures that would serve as physical manifestations of spiritual harmony and transcendence. In recognition of his achievements and contributions, Kalal was honored at each spring festival. However, on this day he could only sit on the periphery of the activities, silent and unmoving, staring straight ahead, seemingly oblivious to the sights and sounds around him.

It had taken Kalal months to return to the Ocan settlement after he left Mala and her child in the mountains of the western forest those many years ago. Eventually he returned, but he was not the same man who had departed. Most Ocan never knew of his mission to escort Mala to her "home", so they could not conjecture as to what might have transpired out in that wilderness. But from the symptoms that he presented, it appeared that he had suffered some kind of seizure and then became disoriented, losing his way, wandering in the forest for months before finding his way back to the Ocan settlement. When he arrived, he was broken, nearly emaciated and very, very confused. What ever happened to him out there, alone and unguarded, no one would ever know, but it soon became apparent that he would never be the same again.

Saba went daily to sit with and help care for her brother, allowing Amira and Olana a brief respite from their nearly constant toil. Olana still lived with her parents, assisting her mother with her father's care, in much the same way as she had done for most of her childhood. Kalal was unable to wash or dress himself and as his mental abilities deteriorated his pride and insistence on autonomy and freedom increased. There were times when he would awaken with the rising moon and set off half-dressed into the night, walking into the forest, mumbling about a child who needed him. He would cry quietly when Amira and Olana would find him and lead him back home.

Kalal's condition was rare among the Ocan people, which made it all the more difficult to remedy, as he drifted back and forth between various phases of lucidity. When Saba began treating him with special crystals combined with sea plants and mountain herbs, it seemed that some times Kalal was almost restored to his former self. The healer-woman worked tirelessly to transform the internal structures of her brother's neurons and neural pathways, attempting to bring forth the diverse facets of cognizance that lay dormant within his mind. In order to sustain the power of the healing, Saba gave Kalal a crystal that he carried with him always. When he began to feel agitated or confused, he would stare into the crystal and become calm, his thoughts ordered and clear. Saba said that Kalal could now hear/feel the mystical vibration of the sun's energy reflected in the stone's prismatic light. She hoped that the stone's light would continue to breathe life into the dead and dying tissue of Kalal's brain cells and eventually lead him back to his own ability to know and perceive the world. Still, despite the steady treatments, he had good days and he had bad days.

While Taijaur was, indeed, extremely sad to see this once powerful uncle so wasted and helpless, he was also secretly glad that his grandmother had a person other than himself to occupy her worrying mind. Kalal now sat a distance from where the people worked, alone, and unnoticed. Taijaur went up to his uncle and stroked his arm, bending down to search into those vacant staring eyes, calling his name softly. Kalal, never looking at Taijaur or even acknowledging his grandnephew's presence, mumbled repetitively in a low voice, "Can you stop the voices? I see the music. Adamas. The eye only hears the song. The music tells. Adamas. Can you stop the voices?"

Sighing heavily, Taijaur rose and hurried toward the Maja, glancing back at Kalal one last time before entering the door that leads to the underground vault. He saw flashing rays of brightness shining from the crystal that hung around his uncle's neck, and there was also the unmistakable reflection of glistening tears running down the old man's face. This was apparently not one of his uncle's good days.

Light and sound came up unexpectedly from the lower chamber as Taijaur descended the narrow winding metal staircase. He thought perhaps Master Alor might be working in the archives. But as he came fully into the room that overflowed with dusty shelves and tables of books and papers that reached almost as high as the vaulted ceiling, he was surprised to see Olana sitting on the floor, looking up at him, surrounded by piles of books.

Olana: "Oh Taijaur, its you. You startled me. You know you're not supposed to be in here; all the rooms in the Maja are closed today."

Taijaur: "Hello Olana. You seem to forget—as an apprentice to Alor, I have unconditional permission to access these vaults at any time."

Olana smiled, "It's hard to get used to my little cousin so grown up and important."

Taijaur smiled in return. "What are you doing here today, Olana? I thought you would be with everyone else at the festival."

Olana: "Oh, I just had to finish up some work for my mother."

Taijaur: "That's right; I keep forgetting that you are now our official Keeper of the Wisdom of the Ages."

She laughed, "Hah, far from that."

Amira's work as the village scholar-librarian-researcher was now a secondary and sometimes forgotten responsibility in the midst of the chores of caring for her husband. Olana tried to help fill the gap created by Amira's continued absence but the recorded artifacts never came alive for her the way that they did for her mother. The Ocan libraries and archives were filled with materials that represent the collective knowledge of the entire world or at least that was the aim of those who had begun gathering the sacred texts, annals, manuscripts and other materials even before their island nation was founded. Olana rose from the floor and started putting away some of the papers and books.

"You can leave most of these books here; I will be back to retrieve them later. I hope they won't be in your way."

In the midst of her papers that lay on a nearby table, Taijaur glimpsed some sketches of a design that was similar to those on the Maja walls. Olana's half-finished paintings filled the walls of most of the rooms in the Maja. Even the temple caverns had once served as canvas for her colorful yet shadowy visions of the world. Some referred to her as an "artist-prophet" for the manner in which her paintings rendered reality, although she scoffed at the mention of this title or any other. There were those who saw the essence of her art and instantly felt an innate connection to all that does and can exist as a part of what we know as life. And then there were others who were frightened by her impressionistic other-worlds of reality and the energy that had brought them into existence.

Taijaur gazed back and forth at the sketches in front of him and at the paintings on the walls. He began to notice that there was one recurring image that Olana had painted in the obscure shadows of most of these works. He had to look carefully and concentrate in order to see it. As he peered deeper into the sketch in front of him, Taijaur was struck by how similar the symbol in Olana's painting was to the interwoven net-like structure that had appeared in his sentiale dream earlier today. This same image had surfaced in his dreams on several occasions in the past. Although he never knew the source whence this inexplicable symbol had drifted into his sentiale, he nonetheless, frequently summoned this vision of vibrating interweaving strands of light as a focusing device in order to control his sentiale wanderings. He started to ask Olana about this symbol, but then he remembered how irritated she always became when anyone asked about the meaning of her art and he decided to pursue a different line of inquiry.

Taijaur: "Olana, do you remember any of your life, before you came to stay with Uncle Kalal and Aunt Amira?"

Surprised, she turned to him with an open book in her hand and said, "Why do you ask?"

Taijaur: "I don't know; I just thought that maybe something in your drawings related to your life, you know, before...before you came here."

Olana smiled weakly shrugging her shoulders, shaking her head, she closed the book she was reading and continued to put away the materials in silence.

From time to time, Taijaur would try to talk with Olana about her previous life, before she had come to live with the Ocan, always to no avail. Though he knew only the few details that Saba had shared, Taijaur somehow felt that his own birth story was in some way connected to that of Olana's and he wandered if this symbol that she had drawn, the same one that appeared in his dreams, was perhaps some clue to a history that they might share.

He had been told that near the same time that his mother had died giving birth to him, Olana had wandered mysteriously out of the forest into Amira and Kalal's childless existence. A feral child with no clothes or sense of fear, she was dirty, smelling of smoke and carrying branches of berries in both hands. Amira was alone, also picking berries near the forest, when she turned and saw the child walking towards her with outstretched arms, crying out, "Oh Mana, I walked all over the world looking for you." No one in any of the Ocan villages knew who she was or from where she had come and they all agreed that the Aka settlement was too far away for a child to have walked so many miles and survived. They assumed that the child might be delirious or hallucinating as she repeated fantastic stories of mystical beasts and magical places. She insisted from the beginning and for all time thereafter that Amira was her "Mana". She spoke intelligently and coherently, especially for one so young. However, in response to all their questions, she only wove greater and greater stories that never revealed her origins. After awhile it seemed as if she had always lived in the village with them; almost as if she had somehow miraculously been born to this child-starved couple who were well-beyond any child bearing years. Months later it was discovered that some upheaval had occurred in the Aka villages and massive fires had been set because of some pestilence or infectious disease that had decimated their community. But no Aka ever came to claim a lost four year old girl, and Amira received no responses to her many inquiries.

They had nearly forgotten about her past until she was about eight or nine years old and she started experiencing periodic bouts of uncontrollable rage and shattering emotional disturbances. The rages intensified when she reached puberty and they all assumed that something from her previous life was coming back to trouble her spirit. The Saba would take Olana to the temple to wait out the most intense moments of her distress. And this was where she began to paint, with the dark rocks of the temple caverns as her canvas and her guide. Her rages continued into adulthood and it was at these times that she was most productive with her painting. Only now she would leave her parents home temporarily and stay with her friend and lover, Hasid, who seemed to be the only person who could bring her back to herself. He would sit with her in the Maja and watch her paint until her emotions exhausted themselves and she would then fall asleep in his arms. She would sometimes remain unconscious for more than a day. However, the next day after the storm had passed, she would return to her normal routine, calm and cheerful, as if nothing had ever happened. Although he never told anyone, Hasid would occasionally catch her staring in awe or curiosity at the creations that had come forth during these times that she was "gone". Over the past few years, as Kalal's condition continued to deteriorate, Olana's periodic rages began to subside and the paintings came less and less.

Taijaur: "I saw Uncle Kalal outside."

Olana was moving toward the stairs. "Yes, I am going to him now."

With one foot on the first stair, one hand on the rail and her eyes cast down, Olana said, "You know they say that everything that we do and everything that happens in our lives is related to our personal injera as well as the injera of our community and that of the universe at large. But I wonder, what purpose it could serve for my father to be as he is. What need in the universe could be filled by this type of suffering or for any such form of hardship to exist in the world?"

Not knowing how to respond or even if he should speak, Taijaur cleared his throat and said, "Well I suppose they also say that much of injera's intent is beyond our reach, beyond our comprehension."

"Yes, I suppose that is what the say." She smiled weakly and without raising her eyes from her feet, she started up the stairs. "Just remember to lock the door when you leave."

Taijaur: "Oh, Olana?"

She leaned back down the steps, peering around the corner. "Yes?"

Taijaur: "Could you please tell Aunt Amira that I will be on time this Saturday to take Uncle Kalal on our walk to the river? Also tell her that I will be sure to complete the repairs on your roof well before the rainy season."

Olana: "Okay, I'll tell her."

Taijaur: "Honor thy Gift."

She nodded without comment and he watched her ascend the winding staircase. She had apparently left the door slightly ajar as he could hear a distant echo of music and voices. Taijaur continued sitting on the stool not moving for awhile as Olana's sadness and her questions went through his mind. For a few moments, the silence felt strangely alive as the residual energy of Olana and her thoughts still permeated the air of the room. Only when he was fully alone, when the quiet became stillness, did Taijaur then remember the song. He thought about the dilemma in the translation, the contradictory pieces, this final piece to the puzzle that had plagued his mind and he pulled out the book, opening it to the passage over which he had struggled for the past few weeks. As he read through the text, he tried humming a few bars, but it was all wrong now. The song would not come. He closed his eyes and tried breathing deeply to relax. When that failed, he rose and began going through some of the slow, fluid movements of the Ocan daily exercise ritual, breathing deeply with each bending, stretching and twisting motion. He thought that maybe with his first attention trapped the song would return of its own accord. But nothing worked. It was gone—the idea, the thought, the song.

He sighed heavily and began pulling from the dusty shelves various dictionaries, thesauri and other source material. He thought that perhaps a pathway to the problem could be found by studying and translating some of the other ancient texts. As he puttered around for awhile, he began to occasionally overhear bits and pieces of drifting conversations as some people periodically came into the Maja. He could hear the sounds of their voices coming directly through the vent that was high above his head. He blocked out the sounds and concentrated even further on his work.

Taijaur lost track of time as he sat for hours poring over the musty books and papers. When he finally looked up, he realized that the outside music had subsided and he could only hear a few distant sounds of fading voices. He assumed that the people must have finished for the day and that it was probably now dark outside. He had just started putting away his books and materials when he heard familiar voices through the vent above his head and he realized that one of the voices belonged to Master Alor. Taijaur was trying unsuccessfully to imagine what could have brought Alor down from his mountain into the village, when he heard the other voice say loudly, "We can talk in here". He recognized the distinct vocal intonations as those of Master Edise. The two Master Guild members were apparently in the middle of what must have been a longer discussion.

Taijaur was reluctant to make any noise and risk interrupting their conversation. He knew that they would be able to hear him as clearly as he could hear both of them. He also did not want to eavesdrop, so he quietly sat back down and returned to the text that he had been perusing. He concentrated on the written words on the page before him, at first paying no mind to the spoken words that drifted in the air above his head. But then a phrase, a word, something caught his attention and he sat up suddenly, with all his senses alert as he realized the subject of their discussion.

Alor: "Edise, just because we rid ourselves of what you call 'an unnatural being', does not mean that we can afford the comfort of disregarding its meaning, its injera, its intent."

Edise: "Your words have no meaning, old man."

Alor: "That child was a sign. You know, as well as I, that every life force on this planet brings with it, its own cycle of need, complete with an intent, a will, a purpose or a cause. It would be foolish to think that a will so strong could not survive the material life of its bearer."

Edise: "You speak in riddles."

Alor: "Then it behooves us all to solve these riddles if our existence, as we know it, is to continue."

Edise: "If you are professing some superstitious nonsense of a spirit coming back to haunt—"

Alor: "Call it what you will. But you know, as well as I, that the physical realm is but one manifestation of the needs and intent of this planet. And the spiritual forces that breathe life into this world do not wholly depend upon the tangible products of their creation. Their means of need-fulfillment are more varied and more powerful then we can even begin to imagine."

Edise: "What is your message, old man? I have no time for mind puzzles."

Alor: "That child brought its own message, undecipherable as it may be to our conscious minds."

Edise: "Are you saying that the evil that the child represented did not die with the child?"

Alor: "Whatever the intent or needs of the spiritual force that resided in that being, we can not ignore its message or invalidate its power."

Edise: "Shall we exhume the body and ask the bones why they came to be?"

Alor: "Make light of this, if you will. But all may yet bear the darkness and heat of an un-illuminated fire."

Edise: "Alor, this is ancient history. Let it go. That unfortunate being ceased to exist years ago. Why, I believe that it has to be more than a decade now. Yes, I am certain that it has been well over a decade."

Alor: "And that timeframe coincides with my calculations."

Edise: "What are you talking about? Calculations for what?"

Alor: "The planet's polarities have begun to shift. And the natural ruptures in the flow of our existence—those openings from which this world derives its source of both negative and positive energy—somehow they are growing, developing in strength and duration. There are subtle indications of this effect that date back to the time of the mudslides; the time of the birth of Mala's child."

Edise coughed, clearing his throat; his voice was lower now, as he responded in a modulated tone, "The Obeah and the Elders spoke of the birth of Mala's child being connected with a breach between worlds. And this was the primary reason why it was not possible for that child to exist among us. Toval was right, we are not ready. The Emissary has not yet come to us. A breach at this point could only cause us harm."

Alor: "Well, when Edise? When will be ready? What was our purpose in coming to this land if not to maximize our ability to draw strength from such phenomena? These fractures have existed since the beginning of time and are an integral part of our experience on this Earth.

For years, it has been my job alone to watch and track the spread and growth of the virus throughout the planet. Not only have I monitored the signs of the virus's impact in terms of human beings' increased capacity for cruelty and violence, but I have also tracked the transmission of ideas—the rate at which ideas have translated into manipulation of the environment and control over people and nations. I have watched the effect of certain ideologies on the shape of cultures and societies. And from all that I have seen and heard, it is obvious that the world's balance of power has shifted more than any other time in the history of mankind. In the past, I have been reluctant to take on apprentices, but now I am grateful to divide and delegate the work, because Edise the time has come for the Ocan people to stop watching and stop waiting."

Edise: "And for years it has been *my job* to ensure the safety of *our people*. It is my opinion that we are not ready for the changes that you and *only you* prescribe. And I say that we will only be ready when the time is right; when we have developed our own power and when the Emissary arrives to lead us to our destiny. You know as well as I, that only an emissary has the power to navigate the boundaries between worlds. This would mean suicide for any lesser being—and you know this."

Alor: "To the contrary, I say that it is our fear and our complacency that keeps us from moving within the true purpose of our existence. Whether an emissary is found or not, it may not matter because we, as a people, have become complacent. Complacent and comfortable with the ease of living that this land provides. Years have become decades and now centuries, while we watch greater and greater suffering and calamities upon the earth and all of its inhabitants."

Edise: "What does the evil of the rest of the world have to do with us? Their scourges cannot touch us. And don't forget that it was these very scourges and evils that it made in necessary for us to come to this isolated land."

Alor: "But what peace can there for us when the people of this world suffer? Most of the nations are without peace and whole groups of people attempt to survive without even the basic necessities of food, shelter, and water. Every day my apprentices uncover greater and greater atrocities of humankind against one another as well as other animals in addition to the wanton destruction and misuse of the earth. No one knows how long this virus has lived within the brains of human beings or even how it is actually transmitted. It may have been here from the beginning of life on earth. But what we know for sure is that the energy of the in-between is the only thing that can stop it. What good will it do for our little island to survive if the rest of the world is lost? We can't keep hiding from this scourge upon the land."

Edise: "What can we do to relieve their suffering? We are not responsible for causing this virus, even if we did recognize it as the hidden source of much of that which ails the world. Fortunately, our founders had the good sense to get away from the virus and all of its effects. All people of this world, infected or not, can access the power spots that are found in every land on this planet. Is it our fault if they don't make use of the energy and learn how to remedy their own ills?"

Alor: "Edise, you above all, know that we have the knowledge and the power to conquer this plague at its root. Only the portals in this region of the earth—on this island and the surrounding land masses—allow direct access to the energy source of the in-between. You know full well that it is these very fractures or openings between worlds that create the Earth's power spots. And it was these fractures that led our founders to this isolated island and the reason for our existence as a separate community."

Edise: "We cannot hold ourselves responsible for the violence, war and focus on pleasure-seeking that keeps the people of the world ignorant of one the most dominant forces of life. They have no knowledge of the power source and its energy, despite the fact that it affects every dimension and facet of their existence. How can we save them when they don't take the time to feel and understand the natural world or even attempt to save themselves? They have no idea even that the virus exists or that they, themselves are infected. This pathogen produces the most insidious violent behavior known to man, yet these people remain oblivious to the fact that their brains have been altered and damaged by a disease."

Alor: "No matter what the people do or do not know—we know and our purpose has always been to cultivate and nurture the power of the in-between in order to one day use this power to help the world. Instead we cover the portals and restrict access to the power source. Which is why if the birth of Mala's child in any way accentuated the effect, then we should have studied and paid close attention to that life force."

Edise: "The fracture that opened when Mala gave birth was closed, the barrier put back into place with the death of that loathsome being, that...that...," he spat out, "that child!"

Alor: "Well, perhaps somehow the breach did not close all the way. If the child's death was supposed to heal the breach, it not only failed, it achieved the direct opposite effect. Rather than diminishing in its intensity, the rupture appears to be deepening and widening over time and space. If what I suspect about that child is correct, then her birth accelerated the opening between this world and the next. And Edise there is something else."

Taijaur struggled to stay absolutely still. As he listened to the two men, an image began forming in his subconscious mind, minute rapid flashes of light within his subliminal awareness. The image pushed through on the edges of his consciousness and he saw an ethereal web vibrating with bright filaments that were weaving back and forth in intricate layers and patterns. The sounds of the two men's voices pushed the flickering image away from his mind's eye, but the persistent design stayed in the back of his consciousness, just below the surface. On this periphery, outside of his surface awareness, the translucent reticulating image began to emit a faint sound of music.

Edise: "Well, what is it? Just say it. All this suspenseful conjecturing is wearing on my nerves."

Alor: "The virus is even more powerful than we suspected. I believe that the pathogen has possibly mutated and is becoming more damaging, more pervasive. Something is causing this plague to spread at an exponential and unprecedented rate. If the phage continues to grow at its current rate then, in a matter of decades, or even years no living entity on this planet will escape its effect, no matter how well hidden or isolated. There will be ripple effects across the globe and the Ocan Island will not be immune to this contamination."

Edise started and then stopped, "How—"

All sound ceased for a few seconds and then Alor went on, "Suppose somehow, some way the child managed to survive."

Edise: "What!?!"

Alor: "You heard me. Suppose she is still alive."

Edise: "Impossible! Absolutely impossible. Why this is absurd, preposterous."

Alor: "A conceivable possibility."

Edise: "Absolutely not!!"

Alor: "Then why are you so upset by the mere thought?"

Edise: "I buried her my—I mean, I was the one given primary responsibility for ridding our people of that disease. I alone averted one of the worse disasters that we have come to know in this present age of the Ocan. And in all the years since then what has the Masters' Guild given me? An award? Some accolade? Some form of recognition? No, nothing but scorn, hatred and disdain. Do you think that I don't know what you pompous, self-proclaimed wise people say about me? Even the Elders act as if I am less than worthy of their notice. Yet, when ever they have some unsavory covert task that needs to be accomplished, who do you think they call?"

Alor: "All right, all right Edise. I'm sure no one thinks any worse of you."

Edise, went on, consumed by his own need for defense and protest. "But a day will come yet when you all are made to realize the supreme sacrifice that has been made on your behalf. Am I not also Ocan? I recognize the distastefulness of some necessary actions. But I put my own personal displeasure aside and made a sacrifice that was to the benefit of all... I....I...," he stammered and then shouted, "WHAT ELSE WAS I TO DO?'"

Alor: "All right, all right, Edise. Enough of all that. You carried out the will of the people when they were unable to do so themselves. You want that badge and it is yours. Never mind the fact that you may have blatantly swayed the vulnerable will of Ocan towards your own end."

Edise: "I...I...I have never performed an act that was not for the good of all Ocan. It was the right and only thing to do."

Alor: "Perhaps. And yet sometimes in our attempts to do right we, unwittingly, accomplish just the opposite, with destruction and suffering wrought as a result of our good intentions. However, let us not debate this point any further, but return to the original supposition. If the child still maintains a material existence within this realm—"

Edise: "I tell you, it just can't be!"

Alor: "All right then, what ever happened to her mother? Why isn't it possible that Mala found her child and reared her in the outer-lands or even in the Haman village? Although the Haman steer clear of this dispute between the Aka and Ocan, I suspect that there is much that they would willingly keep hidden from the Ocan."

Edise: "It is true that Mala disappeared again. Who knows, maybe she went to live with the Aka, following in the footsteps of her deceased addled friend, that so-called 'psychic-mystic' daughter of the Saba. No matter what or where she went, that night, she was too heavily sedated to find herself, let alone that, that monstrous infant. And besides, that fiend-thing would have ceased to breathe life within seconds of its burial. Which is why I thought it the most humane way to go about a loathsome task. But have I been afforded anyone's understanding or compassion for the difficult sacrifices that I have made? No, just a collective harsh judgment and—"

Alor: "Enough Edise! How soon after your 'supreme sacrifice' did Mala disappear?"

Edise: "I'm not sure. But I do know that she disappeared before her healing was complete. It seems she suffered some additional parturient-related difficulties after the will of the people was made known to her and her body spilled copious amounts of blood."

Alor: "You are the chief of security, surely you sent someone in search of her trail?"

Edise: "No, there was no one sent. And who would have searched for her trail or for her? Remember we are speaking of Mala—that wild transient, itinerant woman of the mountains. She was always absent from our valley home more than she was ever present. Which is why if she had been punished for her initial crimes of leaving the Ocan settlements—as I suggested long ago—then none of this would have ever happened and that deplorable infant would never have been conceived or born."

Alor ignored Edise's diatribe and persisted with his own line of inquiry, "But if she was bleeding as heavily as you say, wouldn't there have been some evidence of her departure?"

Edise: "I, uh...I...well...I don't know, Alor. Why do you keep asking me all these questions?"

Alor: "Because I can't sleep. My dreams are troubled by the night winds that scream some indecipherable message into the darkness. And my meditations have told me that the answer to my insomnia may be buried somewhere in this event."

Edise: "Well, if your purpose was to trouble my sleep as well—know that you have been successful."

Alor: "Answers, Edise. That is all that I seek. Answers. Come, let us leave this place."

Taijaur heard one of them blow out the candles and then their voices grew faint as they apparently walked toward the door. Taijaur had been straining so hard to follow the conversation that he did not realize that he had been unconsciously humming a low melodic tune the whole time. He listened to himself now and while the melody sounded familiar, he couldn't quite place where he had heard it before. The melody went round and round in his mind as he continued humming.

The two men in the room above him stood near the open door and Taijaur heard Edise remark, "You know, old man, if what you suppose about that child is, indeed, true, then I fear that an evil greater than this world has ever known has been unleashed upon the Earth."

In the brief moment between Edise's statement and Alor's reply, Taijaur felt a faint memory of the song come alive within him, bubbling up within his consciousness. He felt himself within reach of the song's origin and meaning, and then he heard the facetiousness in Alor's response, "The devil incarnate?"

With deadly seriousness and perhaps even an undertone of fright, Edise replied,

"Aye, the devil."

All at once, the melody ceased, the bubble burst and the song, once again, was pushed down into oblivion.

5. And She Never Forgot

Some sound...? Again and again—no mistake. A light. A recurrent rhythm of sound, light, sensation pulled Mala languidly out of sleep. She rose slowly, eyes closed, still moving in the fugue state of deep unconsciousness with somnolence imploring, welcoming her body to resume its inert prostration. But something was insistently, urgently pulling her. She turned her ear toward their domicile opening, and there it was again; louder, more persistent. The air was heavy with sound and a faint glowing light, moving, swaying in the distance. Mala could feel it before opening her eyes, before reaching full consciousness. She stumbled out of their shelter into the warm night, drawn forward by the air's ethereal sensations of light and sound.

She moved effortlessly through the trees, still not fully awake or aware of where she was being led. Some time later, when her flow of movement stopped, she found herself surrounded by the now incessant melody that rose and absorbed the warm night air. It was a while before her eyes adjusted to the scene in front of her. It took even longer for the horror to penetrate and then ruthlessly strip the heavy veil of sleep completely from her mind.

Shona was in the grove of arachnid weavers emitting and eliciting from the creatures a loud wordless melody, as the spiders wove a bright iridescent web of silk that stretched endlessly throughout the slowly swaying trees. The threads were changing with each rise and fall of Shona's voice; the colors, thickness, and consistency somehow matching the scales of the harmonious continuously droning sound. Then sporadic high pitch notes came forth, archaic in tone, in no words of any known language. Underneath the dominant sound there was a rolling contralto, a soprano, and then a tenor aria with many voices and tones that converged in a bewitching harmonious fugue. Mala stood trapped, spellbound by the sound, the music that was at once, both foreign and complex, yet simple and achingly familiar.

She watched in amazement as it appeared that she could actually see the spiders making greater quantities of web, always moving in time with the rise and fall of Shona's voice. She could see and feel the web vibrating with greater intensity whenever Shona drew near. The myriad forms of webs and web-making were coming together to form one complicated multi-dimensional common orb web, with a combination of various types of thread—thick, thin, wet, dry, sticky and woolly; all reflecting an ultra violet light filtered through an iridescent rainbow spectrum.

Suddenly Mala realized why that archaic alien sound seemed so familiar. It was an auditory sensation that her ears took in continuously each day and yet she had never really heard it. It was the everyday language of the arachnids themselves, the spiders' own distinctive tongue that registered no decibels within the human range of hearing and, by all rights, should not be heard now. She watched as a huge queen spider, covered with hair and the size of a small dog, moved to foci of the web and dominated the singing in a clear high-pitched voice. As the sounds reached out to Mala, a cold prickly sensation ran along her neck and raised the hair on her arms. Then she watched as Shona clearly, in the animal's own language, responded, before turning to look exactly where Mala sat concealed behind some bushes and trees. Shona stared at Mala as if she was looking directly through the cover of darkness and brush into Mala's eyes and then her eyes and mouth formed a brief knowing, sarcastic, almost leering smile. Shivers danced up and down Mala's spine, paralyzing her only momentarily before she abruptly rose and ran headlong back to their tent.

The two females never spoke of what transpired in the night. Mala had no way to understand or give voice to what she witnessed. But she began to watch Shona with closer scrutiny and with a disquieting feeling almost akin to—no, not fear—it couldn't be that, could it? For this was her child and she was her mother—no, maybe it was something closer to a feeling of apprehension or anxiety as if she was waiting for something but she had no idea what it was or could be.

Shona, although not fully grown, was now a larger version of Mala—the same deep skin tones and muscular body with dark braided hair. She had never adopted the long wrap skirt-dress that her mother wore in the style of Ocan females. Instead, Shona wore the light weight pants and thigh length tunics like those of the Ocan males, which she felt were better suited to her active life. The ill-formed facial discoloration that had followed her from birth now stretched up and crowned her hooded deep set dark eyes and high distinct cheek bones.

As she matured from infancy, the blood stained mark had stopped its ceaseless motion, stirring itself only with the heights of Shona's emotional tenor. Over time it, too, had grown, so that now it lay lopsided over her brow like wings on a wayward bird, giving her demeanor a permanent overcast hard frown, accented by her own focused unwavering stare.

From birth, Shona had always felt the changing seasons in her body, within her soul. With the vernal equinox now nearing, she felt that gravity's lighter pull would allow her to lift from the ground and float endlessly in the cool spring air. She loved the night. She instinctively grew quiet each evening as the sun set, and she watched the day's reality disappear. As she awaited the arrival of the silent forces that invade the night air, her body would shiver with excitement and anticipation. Without fail, the darkness would invariably wrap around her, drawing her out to become one with the night.

Early on Shona realized how different she was from her mother and even all the people of the Ocan that she had come to know through Mala's sentiale. In Mala's presence she learned to suppress those behaviors that she knew made her mother uncomfortable. Only in the twilight, once her mother slept, could she open herself to who and what she really was.

Although Shona no longer spoke directly of returning to the village settlements, she began to question her mother endlessly about the Saba and the healing powers of all saba women. She created her own healing poultices and remedies to administer to her small furry patients of the forest, and quieted them with songs and herbal anesthetics that made them drowsy and still as she tended their wounds or fractured limbs.

During the rainy season, the two females took shelter in the caves by the shore to wait out the hardest part of the torrential downpours. And that is where they were, there in the caves, when the people came. On a dark rain-soaked afternoon, they sat on opposite sides of a small fire, each absorbed in their own separate tasks. Mala was working with the silk, as Shona tended to yet another of her injured friends of the forest. She was singing a low sweet melody as she closed a gaping hole on the side of the animal's body. It had apparently impaled itself on a stick or sharp object. Mala had already softened the silk gum in warm water and was now gathering the silk filaments and twisting them to form multi-filament yarns. As Shona completed the final suture, she looked up from the animal that lie dozing in her lap and saw that her mother had been watching her, smiling. Shona smiled in return as she laid the sleeping animal down and went to assist her mother with combining the fibers into a continuous ropelike form.

Shona: "Why did you leave it, Mala?"

Mala: "Leave what?"

Shona: "Your gift, your calling to be saba?"

Mala: "I didn't leave it. One can never leave that for which they are chosen, that for which they are called. You have to understand that I am exactly where and what I was meant to be. However, for you, on the other hand, this need to heal every creature that crosses your path may, indeed, be part of your gift, part of your *injera*." And then in a low tone that Shona could not hear, she muttered to herself, "Much more than it was ever part of mine."

Shona: "My what? What is injera?"

Mala: "Hmm, it's hard to explain. More than likely you will only be able to understand it as your life unfolds."

Exasperated, Shona sighed saying to her mother "Why does it seem like everything with you is a riddle?"

Mala: "I don't create the riddles Shona. The mysteries of this world were here long before I was born."

Shona: "Mala, what is injera?"

Mala: "I don't know how to express it fully, Shona. It is a belief of the Ocan that every living thing in existence—every atom, molecule, person, chemical—every particle of this creation possesses its own inherent cycle of need. And we live our lives, realize our destinies through the desire to fulfill this need or these needs. Does that make sense to you?"

Shona: "Somewhat. But why have you never spoken of this before?"

Mala: "I guess it just never came up. Besides I'm not sure that I understand it entirely myself. It just seems that your desire to heal may be related to an internal need that must be fulfilled. And that need, in turn, feeds the purpose of your existence."

Shona: "So, injera must be the life-path that we each feel called to embark upon. Is that right?"

Mala: "Partially. You can look at it like that. Except that injera is more that which pulls you along the path as opposed to the path itself. It is both the need and the fulfillment of the need; which, in the process of fulfillment, is transformed into purpose. Injera, in the sense of 'spiritual need-fulfilled'—or in other words 'purpose'—is realized ultimately by our ability and willingness to accept and manifest the ultimate Gift of this life. With the acceptance of life's Gift or God's blessings, we are then able to give expression to our own individual gifts—those talents, skills, attributes with which we seek to give life meaning and touch the lives of others; thus achieving self-fulfillment and a sense of wholeness and power. The expression of our individual gifts—our power—also feeds back into the Gift of this life by contributing to the ongoing evolution of the universe and its creative energy, which is one aspect of the nature of God."

Shona was pensive as she listened and then asked, "Is there more to this Ocan belief in injera?"

Mala: "There are three principles of injera; three fundamental aspects of need and need-fulfillment. And these principles form the basis from which all actions in life can be understood. Simply stated, the three most primary needs of all living entities are to give, to survive and to trans—"

There was a sound in the distance that made Mala pause and Shona got up and crept silently to the entrance of the cave. Through the blanket of fog and heavy rain, she saw the unbelievable sight of a vessel—a mid-size fishing sailboat, listing heavily to one side, rammed into the rocks of the bay, its tattered sail hanging from the mast, blowing in the wind.

They had come with the storm, without warning or intent, floating on masses of gulfweed into the reef's sharp carnivorous jaws. For centuries, any intrepid or ill-advised vessel that came anywhere within a hundred mile radius of the island had disappeared mysteriously. A few old seafarers of years gone by had, in their journeys to discover new worlds, instinctively kept a wide distance between themselves and the Ocan island. Some of them, at the end of their lives—when all fear had lifted—would begin to speak of a place outside of time, a strange shrouded island with violent unceasing eruptions from the center of the earth. Others told of a forgotten lonely region of the sea where engines failed, radio waves jammed and radar was not possible. No matter what belief prevailed, for years, no one, no thing had come near. Navigational routes were plotted far off course of the island and the turbulent seas that surrounded it. However, ever so often on either side of the island, an occasional lone craft would stray toward the large deserted land mass. Invariably, before the waiting reef consumed its prey, the dark waters would pull the vessel down into its depths, with no survivors, no witnesses; no evidence of a journey of any kind.

The curtain of rain lifted slightly to reveal a darkly-clad small group of people huddled on the starboard side of the vessel. Shona, with an excited whisper-shout, motioned to her mother, "Come Mala!! Look they're here. They're here!! They've come!! They've finally come!"

Mala moved cautiously toward the cave opening. "Who Shona? Who has come?"

Shona: "The people of my dreams. I knew that they would come. I prayed for them. I've been waiting for them, looking for them. Oh please, come now, quickly. You must see them."

Mala peered out to watch the strange people disembark slowly and delicately from their craft as if trying not to push it any further in its downward slant into the shore. They crept through the rocks to the small patches of sand closer to the trees. She counted four adults—two men, and two women—and four children, including an infant carried by a young girl who was much smaller than Shona but perhaps close to her in age. One of the two boys was an older teen and the other was just a little bigger than the girl. The two women walked together, one leaning on and being held up by the other. The older woman who required assistance was moving slowly in the bent over fashion of advanced age. The two men were throwing and tying ropes in an apparently vain and needless attempt to secure the vessel. It would not, could not move, no matter what waves or winds washed against it. They could hear the sound of a bleating goat coming from the boat. However, they saw no sign of any animals except a frantic vicious little canine, which snapped and barked furiously, running and jumping over the rocks. The people kept shouting—"Lubar! Come Lubar!! Lubar where are you." Mala understood their language, but she could not recall what land had produced this tongue.

Mala was perplexed, this was unheard of. In all of Ocan history, no other people had ever been able to penetrate the protective barriers of land, climate and sea that surrounded the island. With Shona watching excitedly by her side, Mala wondered aloud, whispering to herself, "How could they have come through—? How did they survive? This has never happened. I don't understand."

Without taking her eyes from the scene before her, feeding on it like a feast laid out for her pleasure alone, Shona replied in a casual matter-of-fact tone,

"I brought them here Mala. They were lost for a long time and I saw them in my dreams. I guided them away from the places that would have pulled them under and then through the rocks and hard places."

Mala stared at Shona for a moment and then glanced back at the people who had made a small fire and were beginning to construct a make-shift tent on one of the few small patches of clear sand amidst the rocks.

Mala: "Shona, you know that we can have no contact, no interaction with these people. Hopefully, they will quickly fix their vessel and be on their way. You must keep in mind that these people are from outside the island. The mountains, the water, the land has not purified them as it has done for the Ocan people. They are probably infected like most of the beings outside of this island are infected."

Shona: "But they need help, Mala. They need our help."

Mala: "Shona, you forget the plague, the virus that is pervasive throughout the nations of this world and within the people of those nations."

Shona: "How do we know that the stories of the plague are not just more Ocan superstition? You said yourself that the Ocan people have many silly superstitions. And didn't you say that your parents and others within the Ocan collective always suspected that the plague may not be as powerful or as pervasive as the Ocan founders had claimed?"

Mala: "Still, Shona—we must also bear in mind that our hidden isolation is an imperative of Ocan life"

Shona: "Even if there is such a thing as this plague, didn't you say that the Ocan believe that all Ocan people are now immune to the affects of the virus?"

Mala: "You know full well that no one on this island has had contact with any outsiders in two centuries. And though the people believe that we may now be immune, nonetheless, that assumption has never been tested. And more importantly, we cannot take the risk of exposing knowledge of our existence to any outsiders."

Shona: "But can't we just tell them that we were shipwrecked—just you and me, just the two of us? They would have to believe it because it is the same situation in which they now find themselves. They don't have to know about the people living in the villages. They would never be able to see them or any evidence of them anyway. They could never make it through the dense vegetation of this land, let alone scale the mountains or find their way through the forests. They don't have to ever know that anyone is on this island, but you and me. We can block our sentiale."

Mala: "I don't know Shona. Let's wait and see how they fare on their on."

Shona: "How can we expect them to fare on their own? How will they be able to survive if we do not show them what food they may eat and which plants are poisonous?"

Mala: "They seem to have brought their own food supply." The constant plaintive bleating of the tethered goat seemed to grow louder as if to illustrate her assertion. "Besides, maybe they will be ready to sail in a few days and there will be no need for our assistance."

Shona: "Mala, look at their boat. There is no way that they can repair anything so heavily damaged in a few days."

Mala: "Still, let's just wait and see. We don't know how dangerous these people might be."

Shona: "Are we just going to sit up here and watch them die?"

Mala looked at Shona, saying nothing and then went back to her weaving. Shona could not comprehend that the moment for which she had waited so long would not come to pass. She drank in the vision of the people, studying all that they said and did with and to one another. On the surface, she complied with Mala's directive, but underneath she, knew somehow that they would have to go to the people; that they *must* go to the people.

The next few days passed and the rain still poured, but this did not deter Shona from keeping watch at her post at the cave's entrance. The people could not see her, however, with each brief respite from the rain she had clear sight and hearing of everything that they said and did. Mala would rise each morning with Shona already awake and stationed at her post. She saw the look of joy and anticipation on her daughter's face when the people, and especially the little girl, came into view. It was hard for Mala to watch her daughter in such a state of excitement and anxiety. And for the first time, she became aware of the sense of deprivation that Shona felt in their isolated existence.

Shona watched every detail of the people's lives, learning their names as they called to one another. She became familiar with their individual characters based on their actions and how they behaved with and to one another. She learned how to feel the meaning that came through their tone of voice, their eyes and the way their bodies moved. Mala began to show Shona the similarities between the language that the people spoke and the lexicon, grammar and syntax of other languages that she had already learned. It took her awhile to become accustomed to the long poly-syllabic words and unfamiliar pronunciations, with deep guttural intonations. But by the end of the week, she understood and could interpret most of what she heard.

The mother-wife of the people was thin, drawn, and appeared worn and tired, though she moved endlessly, tending to the baby, the old woman, the children and the men. The husband-father had a large angular build and he held the group in his control, barking out commands and instructions as he and the other adult male struggled to repair the hull of the boat. The woman and young girl, when they were not cooking, serving food, cleaning up or tending to the baby, spent most of the day sewing the tattered pieces of the boat's sails. The father-husband did not appear overtly mean, but he seemed to have no qualms in meting out physical punishment to the children, and sometimes even the other man who was apparently this lead man's younger brother. The grandmother, frail and partially blind was left holding the baby for most of the day.

The uncle was a younger and slightly smaller version of the father, except he had a criss-cross of hacking scars all over his face and a nasty purplish-red wound running down one side of his neck. It was visible even from a distance, a raised red and angry mark against the pale of his skin. This man always seemed restless, wandering, searching, and frequently had to be called back to his assigned tasks. Shona would watch in dismay as this uncle-man snatched food from the younger boys, slapping or cuffing them every time that he passed. One day he kicked the little dog so hard in the side that he sailed up into the air and was not seen or heard for a couple days after that. The uncle seemed to keep a wary distance from the young girl. But Shona could see him studying, watching the girl from a distance, after he first made sure that the father-husband was duly occupied. The father-husband worked, nonstop all day, while the boys and uncle awaited his instruction, and scrambled to comply with his commands.

During the day when Mala was able to force Shona away from the cave's entrance to take in some small nourishment, she spoke endlessly of what the people did, and who they were, how they talked. She practiced their language with Mala, eventually acting as teacher to her mother, informing her of unfamiliar words and different manners of expression. Mala could see that

Shona identified with the girl. She heard the people call her name—'Gruenatar' or something like that. And if they had to call to her more than once, then they used a longer version of her name—that sounded like, 'Gruenataring', but with more syllables, maybe 'Gruenatartaring'. After awhile, Shona knew all the people only in relation to this girl. She referred to the people as the Gruenatarings— there was the Grue father, Grue mother, Grue uncle, Grue brothers, and Grue grandmother.

The hard rains would soon cease and Mala knew that she and Shona would not be able to find their way back to their shelter in the woods without passing these people. Despite her vow to the contrary, Mala found herself watching the people, at first surreptitiously in order to hide her curiosity from Shona. She could feel light flutters from the people's sentiale pathways and she was disturbed by what she sensed in the Grue uncle's mind, which was far more malignant than he let show. But of all the Grue people, this uncle was the only one who seemed to sense her presence in his mind. Whenever she drew near, he would look around, as if hearing a far-off sound and struggling to determine its source.

By the end of the week, Mala was openly studying the people and she especially liked to watch the Grue father whose stern exterior seemed to belie a gentle nature. She witnessed his gestures of kindness and compassion as he helped his wife with chores, played with the children and even helped to care for the elderly grandmother, while always steadily working on the boat. Each evening, after their final meal of the day, the Grues sat around their dying fire listening to the Grue uncle play a mouth instrument that he cupped closely to his lips. They all joined in singing songs before going into the two separate shelters that they had constructed close to their boat. Even the nefarious Grue uncle appeared gentle in the evening twilight as he played his low sad melodies.

They seemed to know instinctively not to venture into the dark thicket of trees near the shore, as they kept to the narrow strip of beach where they had first landed and did not explore beyond this point. The children were sent no further than the forest edge to pick up sticks for fire. And when all was quiet in the night, the Grue father would emerge from the tent that he shared with his wife, daughter and mother and walk around the rocks, and sometimes into the water, but never going beyond the sand as he stood peering into the trees.

After more than a week of watching the people struggle on the rocky beach, Mala gathered the small gifts that Shona had collected, and led her daughter down the side of the cliff, through the boulders. The vicious little dog at first barked furiously as they made their way through the rocks, putting himself between the Grue people and these strangers approaching so precariously. But then as the wind shifted and they came closer, he suddenly ran back towards the boat, with his ears flattened back, tail between his legs and a loud piercing whine. The people were surprised by the sudden presence of these two strange females, whose physical appearance was very different from their own. And they were even more surprised that Mala was able to understand and converse with them in their own language. They told her that they were refugees from a tyrant-led war-torn beloved country. They had been farmers, workers of the land, until their farm and those of their neighbors had been burned to the ground and their property taken from them. Somehow the uncle had procured this fishing boat, and they had escaped into the sea.

The adults were visibly uncomfortable with Shona, staring at her birthmark which jumped and squirmed beyond her control. The Grue mother felt pity for Mala. Shona could see her covertly making signs of religious supplication in her direction while signaling her children to follow suit. Mala offered them the story that Shona had concocted, adding only that her own husband had died shortly after they found themselves marooned in this land. The Grue father told Mala that she and her daughter would be welcome to join them when they departed, and he said that he expected that their vessel would be repaired within the next week or so. The uncle stood a distance from them, eyeing them suspiciously. Up close the wound on his neck was even more conspicuous. It had apparently not healed correctly and still seemed to ooze with infection. Shona noticed that part of his left ear lobe was missing as well. When he caught her looking at him, he stared back at her with such a look of hatred that she turned away and hid even further behind her mother. Shona found herself suddenly shy in the direct company of these people and said she nothing as she stayed close behind Mala or at her side.

The people were appreciative of the knowledge that Mala shared about what food sources were safe and which were not. She assured them that she would bolster their supply of grain and legumes as well as bring them safe vegetables from her own garden. And she warned them to never venture into the forest or to try to hunt the animals. The people admitted that they were "spooked" by the island's strangeness. And Mala said nothing to deter their fears. Their first few days on the shore, the dog, Lubar, had tried stalking the elusive creatures near the edge of the woods, but something had happened that made even the dog shy away from the wooded areas and depend on what ever cast offs the people might throw to him or leave behind.

Shona had noticed right away that the Grue girl and the grandmother were missing from the people gathered on the beach. They indicated that the girl had become ill in the night and even now as they spoke, she lie in fever, her grandmother watching over her. They were at first reluctant to accept the healing concoction that Shona offered from the small bag of herbs that was tied always to the belt at her waist. But Mala assured them that the remedy was effective and they eventually allowed Shona to enter the tent to administer the healing. Throughout the rest of the day, Shona sat with the little girl, feeding her and talking to her, as she soaked a warm poultice that she lay on her head and periodically gave her small doses of the herbs. The Grue mother came in, at first frequently and worriedly, casting a wary eye at Shona. But when she saw how gentle Shona was with her child and listened to the hypnotic sweet songs that Shona sang, she began to check less and less and eventually she stayed outside with Mala who was helping to sew the sails and showing the woman a new weaving technique that enhanced the durability of the fabric.

When they returned the next day, the girl was better and able to sit up on the small pallet that she shared with her grandmother, but she still became dizzy if she tried to stand. Shona brought some of her dolls and other gifts. She showed the Grue girl how to sew small jewels and gems into the dolls' garments. Thereafter, the people allowed Shona to come and play with Gruenatar almost every day, but the Grue mother still kept a close watch on the two girls. Mala came each day with Shona so that she, too, could closely watch. After each visit with the Grues, Mala and Shona made sure to go through the necessary cleansing rituals in the mountain streams that would wash away any pathogens that they may have inadvertently been exposed to.

The two men still spent most of their time repairing their vessel. Mala brought them pieces of woven spider silk and showed them how to use the silk together with the balsa wood in the repair of their boat. They were initially skeptical and then amazed at how strong and durable this unfamiliar material was. When the repairs on the sails were complete, Mala showed the Grue mother weaving techniques and helped her to make clothing items and other pieces of cloth. Mala and Shona had recently begun experimenting with berries, lichen and different types of minerals to create a whole array of colored fabric. They gave the people gifts of materials in various shades of violet, green, purple, red and gold.

For the first time, Shona had a real live human companion, a playmate, a friend. She helped Gruenatar with her chores and the girl, seemed equally as grateful for the help and the company. During times of rest, they played with the baby and the little dog who became accustomed to Shona over time and always stayed close by the girls, no longer running around or barking very much. The boys—one a twin to the girl and the other an older teen—worked and played with one another, ignoring the girls except to sometimes taunt, push, or shove their sister. At first Shona thought these jeers and bumps were the reason for her friend's persistently nervous and fearful demeanor. But Shona watched how adeptly Gruenatar evaded her brothers and she seemed only mildly irritated by the playful aggression that she assured Shona all stupid boys liked to engage in. Shona tried unsuccessfully to determine what perceived threat or danger made Gruenatar constantly jump in fright, glancing all around or over her shoulder as if expecting some unseen blow or attack. And Shona noticed that the little girl never strayed too far from either her mother or father.

They had been going back and forth to the people's camp almost every day for two weeks when Mala decided to give in to Shona's plea to be allowed to visit with her friend alone. Mala had fallen behind in the work that she wanted to complete and the people did seem safe or at least she had not witnessed anything that might cause her concern. The only incident that had given her a moment's pause was when, on their second visit to the Grues, the Grue father had slaughtered the goat and she and Shona had unexpectedly come upon him as he was still butchering the carcass. The Grue mother was nearby smoking and drying some of the meat while other parts of the animal's body lay boiling in a pot of water. Shona had become immediately ill with the smell of cooked flesh and blood. Nothing that Mala had told her and none of the books that she had read about the consumption of animals had prepared her for what she saw, smelled and felt. Although the father joyfully invited them to partake of their meal, Shona and Mala quickly gave the Grue mother the food they had brought and retreated back to the sanctuary of their forest home. That day they spent extra time in the cleansing springs, soaking in the warm therapeutic waters and inhaling the thick aromatic vapors.

Shona had already gone twice by herself to visit with her friend when a third such visit ruled out any further solo excursions. This day she had started out a little later than the mid-morning time of her past visits. She wanted to be sure to take some of her very special gifts to Gruenatar because she knew that the men were almost finished with the boat and she was afraid that her friend might soon be sailing out of her life forever. She had had to go to her secret cove down by the stream to collect some of the more special gems that she did not want Mala to know that she was giving to the girl. She didn't like disobeying her mother's rule about not revealing the gems to the people, but Gruenatar really liked the shiny stones and Shona was careful to only choose the smaller ones. As she walked along almost half-way to the people's campsite, she heard an unusual sound on the trail ahead of her. She instinctively ducked down behind a copse overlooking a small clearing in the midst of the trees and bushes.

Shona watched between the bushes and at first she could see only trace bits of rapidly moving colors through the leaves. Then suddenly she saw her friend, Gruenatar running into the clearing almost tripping as she tried to glance behind her. Shona rose to get a better view and started to call to the girl. She barely had time to wonder why Gruenatar would be this far in the bush, when she saw the terror on the girl's face and a few seconds later the Grue uncle came crashing through the bushes behind her. He was calling to her angrily, "I said to come here, you little cur. Don't you run away from me."

The uncle caught up to the girl and grabbed her with a sudden jerky movement, throwing her down and pinning her to the ground beneath his body, holding both of her arms above her head with one of his hands. The girl did not cry out as she struggled, abject fear evident on her face. Without thinking Shona immediately dropped the food and gifts that she was carrying and ran, covering the distance in seconds. She felt like she was moving in a rapid dreamlike flowing motion outside of her control. She grabbed the man with a swift, hard movement. Pulling him off the girl, she lifted him above her head and threw him against the nearest tree. With her knees slightly bent and fist tightened by her sides, Shona stood stock still, staring down at the man who was now on his hands and knees attempting to rise. The girl was behind her, still lying on the ground. The man was stunned—he wasn't exactly sure what had just happened or how he had been thrown against the tree. But the shock was only momentary. He looked around to see who might have done this to him.

And then he looked at Shona and his reasoning told him that although she was big—nearly as tall as he—and muscular, she was still only a girl. The Grue girl on the ground watched with widened eyes, while slowly sliding, pushing herself backwards. Still wobbly, he pulled himself up by bracing with one hand against the tree and suddenly lunged toward Shona making an inarticulate growling noise. Just as he felt his hands about to clutch her neck and throat, a blinding pain shot through all parts of his body. In one flowing motion, Shona had slammed her right foot down on top of the arch of his foot as she simultaneously grabbed his wrist, twisting his arm behind his back, while thrusting her left knee into his groin and smashing the brunt of her other hand into the bulb of his nose, pounding and flattening the flesh up and back into the bone of the bridge. She then released him and pushed him back hard against the tree behind him.

Shona inched backwards, keeping her eyes on the grue girl who had risen and was turning to run towards the shore campsite. Shona assumed that the incident was over and thus did not anticipate the man's next actions. But before she could stop him, the man snatched the girl as she tried to dart past him. The Grue girl let out an involuntary shriek of pain as he twisted her arm and then quickly shoved her away before Shona was able to intervene. The girl fell hard on the ground and Shona rushed to help her rise, while glaring back at the Grue uncle, daring him to move again. The girl got up and ran as fast as she could, holding her left arm that dangled at an unusual angle. Shona turned to face the man staring directly into his eyes. He yelled after the Grue girl who was now out of sight but could still be heard running down the path. "And you better keep your mouth shut. If you start tellin' lies about me to anyone, you'll get worse than that." And even when there was no sound of her, he still shouted to her, "Go on, get outa here, you vile little whore."

Shona stood in front of him, daring him to move, giving the girl enough time to make her way back to her family. With the back of his hand, he wiped his mouth and nose, smearing blood, mucous and saliva across his face. He laid back against the tree, glaring at Shona through bruised eyes that were already begin to puff and swell. "Who do you think is scared of you? You spawn of Satan." He reached down and picked up a large stick and started waving it in Shona's direction. He struggled to stand straight, with one arm across his midsection, while waving the stick in the other hand. "Get back. Get outa my way." She stood still and continued to stare at him as he edged around her, slightly doubled over and limping heavily as he moved into the brush. He took a different direction than the grue girl, seeming disoriented and not sure which way to go. "You'll get yours, you cur. Don't think that this is the end of this." He looked back several times as he staggered slowly through the overgrown brush into the woods. Aside from a few muttered obscenities, he hurled nothing else in the direction of her stony silence.

Shona stood listening to him stumble off the path until she was sure that he was far enough in the opposite direction of the girl. She started walking slowly back to her home, her mind going round and round, trying to comprehend what had just happened. It was hard to believe that only a few minutes had passed; that life could change so drastically in a matter of moments. She heard a rushing movement in the leaves on the path in front of her and she looked up to see Mala running towards her, out of breath. Before she even noticed how disheveled Shona appeared, Mala grasped Shona by the arms and hurriedly asked, "Shona, what is happening? I felt something; something bad. Where were you? What is going on?"

Shona: "I'm fine, mother. There's no need to worry."

Mala sniffed the air, "It's the Grues. They've come into the forest, haven't they? I can smell them."

Shona: "Come on mother, let's just go back to our—"

Mala: "No, Shona. You must tell me what has occurred. I won't stop you from going to those people, but you must be open with me about anything that happens."

Shona: "It was the uncle; the Grue uncle. He was hurting her and I had to make him stop, make him leave her alone."

Mala: "Is the girl okay?"

Shona: "She's hurt, but she was able to run away. I'm sure that her father will protect her."

Mala was quiet for a moment and then she said, "Well, at least now they know the strength that we possess."

Shona: "I didn't use that much power against him. And somehow, I doubt that he will tell the others any thing."

Mala: "Still, if a young girl can overpower a fully grown man, it won't take much for them to deduce that an adult native to this island may be capable of much more. But, don't worry. They were apt to discover that we are different from them. We just have to guard against them figuring out how far that difference extends. We will have to be careful to diffuse any suspicions that they may begin to form. It's good that no one else but the girl saw this. Come Shona, we must go to the tarn on the other side of the falls in order to cleanse the evil of this encounter from your system."

They walked in silence down to the falls and then disappeared through the falling water as if walking into the mountain. On the other side, there was an area enclosed by rocky mountain walls on all sides except where the falling water created a partition and at the top where the sun shone through an opening, glistening down on a small body of water in the center of the enclosure. They both immersed themselves fully, and Mala stayed submerged until the need for oxygen compelled her to surface. Mala swam around a little while Shona just sat staring vacantly. As Mala began bathing her daughter, scooping the healing water and pouring it over her head and shoulders, Shona started trembling and crying quietly, her tears falling into the water.

Mala stroked her daughter's head and back. "Its okay, Shona. Its over now."

Shona: "Why did he do that Mala? Why? What purpose does it serve? Why did he want to hurt her and hurt me? I didn't mean to hit him, but he wouldn't stop, he wouldn't stop."

Mala: "I don't know that there will ever be any rational explanation for senseless acts of cruelty. But I do know that you did only what had to be done."

Shona: "But how can I ever claim to be a healer if my actions are in direct violation of what healers strive to provide? Violence, no matter the reason, is antithetical to all that we know that is good and right."

Mala: "You had no choice, Shona. Life demands that we fight back."

Shona: "But in doing so don't we become what we fight against? Doesn't fighting back mean that we must behave the same as those who are infected?"

Mala: "You may have saved that girl's life."

Shona: "But what is the worth of my own life, if it, by necessity, must be used to inflict harm upon another?"

Mala: "But Shona, the harm would have first come to you or another innocent party. You must stop it at all costs."

Shona: "I don't understand Mala. You have always taught me, and we have always believed, that we must cause the least amount of harm on this earth as we can. This, above all, is the most essential of Ocan beliefs. But now it seems that our beliefs are only true when there is no resistance to our way."

Mala said nothing as she searched for an answer. Before she could speak, Shona went on to ask, "What makes people behave like that? Are there other people like him?"

Mala: "Unfortunately there are many people like him who are weak and spiritually-sick or spiritually-undeveloped. They try to punish the world, or anyone with the misfortune to cross their path, for their own inadequacies. They don't realize that unfulfilled spiritual needs make them prey to negative thoughts, actions and emotions. In their spiritually and psychologically weak condition they convince themselves that inflicting pain is a form of power; never realizing that it is just the opposite."

Shona: "Isn't there some way to make him better?"

Mala: "I don't know, Shona. Some damage to the psyche becomes too severe to yield to any healing power. This one, this Grue uncle, may be too damaged to benefit from any form of healing. Malevolent acts of control, dominance and destruction are prevalent through out this world and manifest in various and, many times, insidious forms. These forms of injustice and unkindness comprise the primary symptoms of the virus that has invaded this planet and the force from which our Ocan ancestors sought escape in this deserted land."

Shona: "It seems that as long as evil people exist, then goodness can never prevail because the good must become evil in order to conquer evil. It is an endless cycle of hatred and violence."

Mala: "But Shona what choice did you have? What choice do any of us have? You had no time to seek other solutions. Your life and the lives of other innocent people must be allowed to endure and fulfill the purpose of existence. When you see evil occurring you have to do what ever is in your power to stop it. You can't just stand by and let it happen. Your instincts served you correctly. You must strive to preserve your life and the lives of others in order to fulfill the purpose of your individual existence and also to fulfill the purpose of the universe, which can only be revealed through time. We must at least try to live long enough to become beings of power. There is a profound potential within humanity and all life within this sphere to transform our existence to the highest heights of spiritual power, to awaken our god-consciousness. In this way, and only in this way, can the energies that are latent within all matter manifest."

Shona: "Nonetheless, even if all that you say is true and right, this philosophy or perspective still does not adequately deal with the issue of violence. If violence in any form is wrong and if violence, in terms of self-defense is the only option, how can one ever atone for this type of 'wrong-doing' that is presumably necessary for survival?"

Mala was momentarily at a loss for words. She responded in a low voice, "I don't know Shona, I don't have all the answers. Maybe one day you will find your own answers. In the meantime, you are not to go near the Gruenatarings again unless I am with you. However, if you ever find yourself in a negative situation that is beyond your control, you must try to seek the sentiale pathways of those around you. You must also seek and call to the forces of the earth and they will come to your aid."

Shona was quiet for awhile, thinking and then she said, "If he can't be made over, then it would be better to make him leave this earth."

Mala responded, trying to keep the alarm she felt out of her voice, "Shona, it is not our place to decide who inhabits this earth. We only strive to co-exist with what we find, no matter how damaged, dangerous or deranged."

Shona mumbled something that Mala barely heard.

Mala: "What did you say?"

Shona: "Nothing, it's not important."

Mala had only wanted confirmation for what she thought she heard. She didn't pursue the issue, but she was certain that Shona had muttered, "It is never possible to co-exist with a predator."

That night Shona was quiet as she and Mala ate their evening fruit and then right after their meal, Shona lied down and closed her eyes with Mala watching her with a mixture of concern and curiosity.

Mala: "Are you okay, Shona?"

Shona: "I'm fine, mother. I'm just tired. We have a lot to do tomorrow. You should rest so that we can get an early start in the morning."

Mala: "I suppose you are right. I forgot that we promised to show the Grue woman how to apply the final dye applications." Mala immediately drifted off to sleep, while Shona lie with her eyes wide open, waiting.

A few hours later Mala was awakened suddenly in the middle of the night and she saw/felt Shona sitting by the entrance of their tent, looking out into the darkness. Still half asleep, Mala asked softly, "What do you see, Shona?"

Shona was silent for awhile and then without looking back at her mother, she replied, "Nothing really...energy...just energy."

Before Mala could respond, she fell unexpectedly back into unconsciousness. She was startled when she awakened later—hours? minutes? seconds? There was no telling how much time had past, but Shona was now gone as Mala sat straight up coming into an immediate and sudden full consciousness, staring with her eyes widened. She felt a humming vibration in the tent and in the ground beneath her, like a steady low earthquake, with all of the items around her shaking. Mala felt a sense of deja vu as she walked out of the tent and toward the grove. Only this time she was fully aware of her movements and there was no light on this pitch black moon-less night.

Mala felt the steady hum fill her body and her senses completely as she entered the grove and saw Shona standing near a large orb web that stretched between two trees, with no other webs apparent in the entire grove. It was hard to see in the darkness with no light reflecting from any surface except the web. In the center of the web, she saw what she thought was the queen spider spewing and spinning web around and around what appeared to be a large animal that she could hear moaning and squirming vigorously in its entrapment. Shona stood motionless by the side of the web as she seemed to be inside of and also a part of whatever in the earth was emitting the steady humming vibration. Mala watched as the queen inserted her long sharp proboscis into the abdomen of the trapped creature. And then the shrieks of pain and terror tore through her as the creature turned its head and Mala saw the face of a man. It was the Grue uncle.

"Shona!" Mala started running into the grove, screaming to her daughter, "Shona, stop! Stop this! You can't do this. This is not right."

With the sound of Mala's voice, the humming vibrations immediately ceased, the enormous arachnid scurried away, disappearing back into the darkness and the man, covered in spider silk, dropped to the ground. Mala was now standing next to her daughter, and Shona turned to look at her mother, with a dazed expression on her face, her eyes staring, empty of perception. Mala was agitated, upset, "Shona, what have you done? This is not right." Still looking as if she was in a trance or moving in a deep state of sleep, Shona said nothing. She just turned and began walking away, heading back in the direction of their shelter. Mala went toward the man on the ground, who was now rising on his hands and knees, saying over her shoulder, "Help me, Shona. We must help him." Shona gave no sign that she heard Mala as she continued walking out of the grove, up the hill and out of sight. Mala held the man, pulling him up as he was now shakily rising to his feet, while also wiping and pulling thick pieces of sticky web off of his face and eyes.

"Are you okay? Can you see? Can you feel your hands and feet?" She began guiding him to a nearby boulder. "Here, come sit here for a moment and I will get you some water."

The man looked at her, finally becoming aware of her presence and then jerked violently from her grasp. "Get away from me, you demon. You witch. You did this to me." Mala watched as he stumbled drunkenly from the grove toward the shore.

The next day when Mala and Shona went to the people's campsite, he was there with his busted nose, blackened eyes and swollen lips, glaring openly at Mala and Shona, but keeping a safe distance as he limped from place to place helping his older brother with the final repairs of sealing the paint on the boat. The Grue woman and the children acted as they normally did, except the mother seemed more worried and quieter than usual. Mala could never figure out if the events of the preceding day and night were too horrific for the Grue uncle to comprehend or if he just did not want to admit that a female, a child no less, could overpower him. But either way, he had apparently not disclosed the cause of his injuries as the people greeted and welcomed them as they usually did.

Shona was visibly nervous in his presence. She stayed close by her mother's side, not even leaving to play with the Grue girl whose arm was bandaged and wrapped in a sling. Big bruises and scratches were visible on her arms and legs. Shona stared at the man from a distance, wide-eyed, striving to be aware of where he was at all times. He could see her fear. And although he didn't understand it, he began to think that maybe the events in the forest were not quite the way he had first remembered. Maybe he had actually gotten the best of her—yeah, that must be it—the more he thought about it and re-configured his memory, he had gotten in a few decisive licks that had made that witch-child think twice about ever messin' with him again.

What he probably would never understand was that Shona's fear of him—and it was a very real and deep sense of trepidation—was based on her own terror of what this man could elicit within her. She was terrified of the person that she had become in order to deal with him. She was horrified of the hatred that she felt towards him and panicked to think of the place within herself where she had gone in reaction to this man. And she was deadly afraid that he could take her there again.

The two men were talking down by the shore, confident that the sound of the waves covered the sound of their voices, but still making sure to keep their voices low. Mala and Shona looked at each other during significant parts of their conversation. Their enhanced auditory abilities enabled them to hear the men as clearly as if they were standing right next to the women. The Grue men were applying a sealing paint on the boat, made of the special dyes that Mala had created mixed with a potently adhesive resin from the Guola trees.

Grue Uncle: "Its nothing. I tell you its nothing. For the fiftieth time, I tell you I just tripped over somethin'. I fell."

Grue Father: "It just seems kinda strange that both you and Gruenatar are both so busted up. And she was right here with her mama all day and nobody seen it happen. She sayin' she fell too. It's just kinda strange. And you bein' gone all day yesterday. I don't understand—"

Uncle: "Well, I'm here now. Why can't we cut out all this yappin' and get on with fixin' this thing? The sooner we get off this damned piece of hell the better."

Father: "Alright, I'll leave it alone but I don't understand why you went off in them there woods, since that Mala lady said it ain't safe."

Uncle: "You believe everything them damn witches say to you?"

Father: "Now come on now, no witches would help us the way these two have. They're mighty strange, I'll say that for 'em, but, I don't—You really think they're witches?"

Uncle: "They're witches, I tell you. Unnatural beings. No God-fearin' women would live the way they live."

Father: "Shhh! Lower your voice. They might hear you."

Uncle: "I don't care if they do hear me. I have God on my side, I will fear no evil."

The father motioned for the uncle to follow him as he went a little further down on the other side of the vessel into the surf of the shore. The uncle looked back over his shoulder at the group of women and saw that Shona was still staring at him.

Father: "No matter what they are, they have helped to keep us all alive. We couldn't have survived this long without them."

Uncle: "Well, what do we need 'em for now? No good can come from allowing that spawn of Satan to play with our children. And her mother is nothin' but a damn witch, a tortured soul. I saw some things with them women in them woods that would make your backbone turn to gravy. And mark my words, if you don't keep Gruenatar away from that demon-child, she will start acting just as demonic and start sayin' all kinds of nonsense. One day you'll find they turned her own soul as black as their—"

Father: "Shut up, Lem. Lower your voice. We have no choice but to take what help they give us. I will not stand by and watch my children die of starvation. And if that means that I have to frequent with unnatural beings, then so be it. Don't you think that I can see that these women aren't normal? It's not just that they're foreigners, but there is something about them that's not right. But we've got to hold on to them until we can get off this infernal island."

Uncle: "But what do we need 'em for? We can hunt for our own food. Damn all that foolishness that witch said about the animals being poisonous. She just said that to keep the meat to herself. We've been to plenty different places, and when have you ever heard that you couldn't hunt the animals? In a little while, we won't have any other choice. In case you forgot—that was our last goat and we can only make this dried out meat last for so long.

I tell you that witch is lyin' and makin' up some fool story for her own evil purposes. Why do you think they keep warning us to stay away from the forest? Did you look at those gemstones that girl brought to Gruenatar? That mother covered 'em up and took 'em away real fast. But they were real brother, I tell you—genuine. That's why she was so quick to cover 'em. And I think I may have found part of their stash deep in them there woods. I just have to recollect how to get back there."

Father: "Okay, okay. Just keep your voice down. No need in makin' 'em angry. There may be something to what you say about tryin' to fend for ourselves. Come on, walk with me. I don't want the women to see what I have—"

The men walked out of sight around a bend down the beach. Mala was sure that they must have gone into the forest because she and Shona could no longer hear their conversation and she knew that only the forest trees naturally formed a sound barrier that absorbed all acoustic vibrations.

Mala tried not to show how worried she was by what she had heard. She knew that there would be trouble if the people began coming into the forest. She and Shona continued working for a half hour longer and although they had planned to stay the entire day, she made some excuse of why they had to leave. Once inside the trees, she tried to determine the path that the men had taken and while their scent was still on the wind, she did not see or hear them. After a few more minutes of looking, she and Shona turned back and started down their own familiar path. She couldn't say why, but Mala felt a heightened sickening sense of anticipation. She stayed alert for any sign of the men as she and Shona made their way through the forest paths. Mala tried to comfort herself with the thought that the Grue's vessel was almost sea-worthy and they would most likely depart in the coming days. She looked forward to the relief of seeing the people finally sail away from their island forever.

They had not gotten far when from behind and to the right of them they heard loud yelling, some kind of disturbance coming from the direction of the people's camp. Both Mala and Shona, turned and ran toward the sounds of commotion. There was a loud squeal of terror in the distance and more sounds of shouting and cheering. The noise was coming from the edge of the woods, a little ways down the beach from the Grue's campsite. Mala was in front of Shona and she could see through the trees.

Mala: "Oh no! Oh no, no, no."

Shona: "What is it Mala? What is happening?"

Mala responded only with more groans of despair; she was hoping, praying that they would not be too late. As they came into full view of the area, they saw the whole group of Grues, including the grandmother holding the baby, gathered around the father-leader who was kneeling with one knee on the ground, his back to them, holding, struggling with something on the ground. He held down a large wounded boar that was lying on its back, still struggling for its life. With one forearm in the animal's chest, the man swiftly slit its throat. A final spasm of movement shuddered through the animal just before it became completely limp and still. The Grue father immediately began hacking and splitting the animal straight down the middle of its body, from its throat to its groin. Mala and Shona came into full view just as the boar's hot entrails jumped out and spilled onto the ground, emitting warm vapors of smoke tendrils that rose slowly into the cool air. They were too late.

The children were clapping their hands and dancing around. The Grue mother was smiling with a look of satisfaction that eased the everyday lines of strain and worry that creased her face. They all looked excited, happy and at peace, as if this cessation of life signaled a new beginning and a reassurance that their own lives were finally secure. The Grue uncle and the older boy moved in to help remove the internal organs, and scoop up the blood into containers. The mother-wife was the first to look up and notice Shona and Mala standing at a distance from the group. She called a welcoming greeting as they warily crept forward.

The Grue father looked back over his shoulder, his hands and forearms covered with the blood that was splattered all over his face and clothes. "Ah ladies, you're just in time. Now this is what I call a meal. Stick around and we'll show you what real eatin' is all about." The group laughed as the father reached in and cut out a sliver of the animal's liver. He offered the bloody limp piece to Mala, who slowly shook her head and stared, stammering, "Mr. Taring, I...I don't...I don't think—"

Grue Father: "Oh come on now. I know what you said before, but this here is just a little ol' pig. I'm sure it won't disrupt the balance of your island." When she continued to just stare at him in stupefied horror, he shrugged his shoulders and then slipped the piece of liver into his mouth allowing the blood to trickle down his chin. He threw another piece of the animal's innards in the direction of the dog and he did not seem to notice the dog cautiously sniffing the meat and then walking away from it.

"Ohhh, that's hot," the man exclaimed and then went on to chuckle, "but its gonna make some mighty fine eatin'. C'mon y'all and get this—"

He went back to carving through the animal's body as Shona and Mala quietly turned around and left as fast as they could.

They cooked the animal whole with a spear on an open pit, while the intestines and organs simmered in a large pot over a second fire nearby. They brought out their music and for the first time since they had come to the island, they danced as they sang around the campfire. The uncle played his mouth organ while the teenage brother strummed a hand-made string device. The youngest boy was the first to voice what they all thought.

"Mama, this burns."

Grue father: "Yeah it is kinda hot. I do think you may have put a little too much seasoning on this meat, Mother, but its real good all the same."

Mother: "Well, I don't know why, I didn't put nothin' but salt on it."

It began with dry puckered mouths and an insatiable thirst. The elderly woman and the baby were the first to fully exhibit the symptoms and then one by one, they each began to suffer with nausea, vomiting, diarrhea, and skin infections with large bruises and other signs of internal bleeding. They were unable to ingest any liquid or solid nourishment.

By the time Mala arrived with her special herbs and plants, that she knew would do no good, the youngest boy—Gruenatar's twin,—had already lost patches of his hair and many of his teeth as he lie unconscious, his body burning with fever. Mala tried unsuccessfully to persuade Shona to go back and stay at their home; to not witness or be a part of these scenes of sickness and certain death. The people moved sluggishly but persistently loading their boat, preparing for departure. They were forced to stop frequently with nausea and dry heaves, or a lack of energy that permitted no further movement. The father seemed worse than the others, as he stumbled frequently, while staring into space and speaking incoherently. Mala tried to give some of the healing plants to the Grue mother, but she only pointed, with weak pleading eyes, in the direction of the tent where her youngest son lie dying.

The grandmother was left to watch over him in the darkness of that small enclosure, where the smells of sickness and decay hung heavy in the air. She sat slumped nearby, apparently asleep. Mala batted away a swarm of insects that hovered around the grandmother and the boy and she removed a plate of food that was on the floor next to his pallet and encrusted with crawling and flying insects. Mala knew that there was nothing that she or anyone else could do to make this boy or these people better. Shona was silent, staring at the boy, as she walked to the other side of that stuffy enclosed space to sit on the floor, the parting gifts that she had brought for the girl falling unnoticed from her hand.

She watched her mother from behind trying to soothe the boy's pain and feed him the liquid herb concoction that she had brought with her.

Shona thought back to that first day when Mala tried to explain to all the Grues that the island's animals had toxic concentrations of poisonous alkaloids in their skin, their hair, feathers, their blood and even their bones. The father had stood staring at her, mumbling, "Uh-huh", "Is that so?", "You don't say" each time that she paused and peered into his face for a connection of comprehension. He couldn't seem to or didn't want to accept her explanations of the chemical interactions between animals, insects and plants and the minute traces of toxins that originated in the land's vegetation. She tried explaining that after years of consuming seemingly innocuous plants, the animals' bodies had learned to tolerate these chemicals, and over time their bodies manufactured the poison as a part of its defenses. He had stopped listening completely by the time she recounted the Ocan belief that reciprocal genetic changes occur between co-evolving species of both plants and animals. But she still went on trying to convey that these biochemical and molecular alterations had provided a genetic and physiological basis of resistance. And that this resistance and the co-evolution of all the island species had insured a natural balance in the island's flora and fauna, with no over-population or competition for resources.

When Mala had finished talking, the man kept his eyes on his feet shuffling in the sand as he said, "I, I, I thank ye for tellin' us all that." Then he had looked up at her, smiling weakly, "And we'll be sure to be real careful. We still have some food supplies that we brung with us and we should get by fine. Hell, and if all else fails, we'll just cook this little mutt that we brought with us for just such an occasion. He may not give out much meat, but it'll be enough to keep us goin' for awhile, don't ya think? Heh, heh, heh."

Although Mala sat on the ground with her back to her daughter, Shona saw her mother's face in her mind, praying silently while trying to pour a semi-liquid concoction into the boy's mouth and down his throat. She was so intent on watching her mother, it took awhile before she realized the strangeness of the scene before her. She felt a tingling numbness all over her body and a sudden nausea and vertigo made her bury her head down inside her arms which were crossed on top of her knees, her hands clutching hard on either side of her legs.

And then an uneasy sensation of split-consciousness overcame her, as if she was not only on the floor watching her mother from behind, but also simultaneously lying on the pallet, looking up into Mala's face. Shona could feel the heat of the boy's body, the trembling weakness of his heart, her own arms and legs unable to move. When she began to feel the liquid that Mala poured spilling out of her own mouth, she became slightly alarmed and tried raising her head from her knees. It was then that she realized that her head was not on her knees, but lying back on a thin dirty, sweaty pallet on the floor. A brief raw sense of panic rose within her just before something inside of her subdued the hysteria and pulled her deeper into the body and soul of the Gruenataring boy who lie dying in front of her.

Mala was surprised to feel the boy's spirit being pulled back into his body. She knew that her feeble ministrations had nothing to do with what was happening with this boy. She turned to look at the elderly grandmother, who still appeared to be sleeping soundly. She had heard of a power this strong only in the ancient Obeah. She surmised that this boy's grandmother must surely be in a deep healing trance that allowed her to reach out and pull her grandson's spirit back into his body. Or perhaps her advanced age brought her in closer contact with the spiritual world, where she was able to solicit the help of allies to restore the boy's life. Either way, Mala was amazed at this woman's power.

The boy's breathing was no longer shallow and his fever was subsiding as he began to snore softly in a deep sleep. Mala rose and went to the corner where Shona still rested with her arms wrapped around her knees, her head face down. She shook her slightly and then with more force. Shona had fallen asleep and Mala had to pull and drag her to her feet, holding her up.

As they left out of the tent, with Shona leaning heavily on her mother, Mala bent over the sleeping grandmother wishing to honor and acknowledge this woman's phenomenal power. But when she touched the woman's ice cold, stiff unfeeling hand and recognized the beginning stages of rigor mortis, she pulled back with alarm as she realized that this woman had been dead long before they entered the tent. With her heart beating fast, her thoughts scrambled around searching for understanding. A disquieting feeling crept over her as Mala turned to stare into her daughter's semi-conscious face, her heart beating even more wildly.

The people left the island the next day. Both the baby and the elderly woman were buried down near the shore. They picked their way back through the rocks and headed in the direction of the far distant mainland. They had forgotten or intentionally abandoned the dog, who ran barking frantically along the shore.

Mala and Shona stayed in the cleansing caverns for over a week. Shona grew into young adulthood, and never encountered any other humans, never saw another person, another vessel. Many years would pass before she would again know the company of humans other than her mother. But she carried the lessons of the people with her; lessons of good and evil, friendship and rejection, fear and belonging, hope and despair. And she never forgot.

6. The Dreams of Animals

In the dreams of animals and people alike, there are songs and other pieces of organized harmony that resonate deep within their subconscious minds. Not all dreams, not all of the time. But occasionally, stray pieces come together from the maelstrom of daily enigmas, struggles and ordinary mind wanderings. These pieces, individually mundane, nonsensical or lacking cohesion, combine in the dreaming mind to form a harmony, a pattern, elucidated—revealed—in clear uncompromised musical notes, lyrical phrases, mathematical equations, profound ideas, sublime images. Dream consciousness adds to our cognition, our understanding, elevating the mind to a level beyond ordinary waking consciousness. These rhythmic patterns originate and move of their own accord within the active brain cells of their sleeping hosts, replaying and strengthening the substance of their own transcendent reality. Sometimes upon awakening, the mind may allow the song, the answers, the solutions to seep through. Then, and only then, a person, an animal may be permitted a fleeting on-high perspective of elusive yet inherent patterns of life; as seen from outside of themselves, from high above the earth.

Master Alor was trying to explain this phenomenon to Mistress Hadassa, but her sense of frustration was growing greater the more he talked. "Yes, yes, yes Alor. I know all of that. I understand all of that. But you seem to be missing the point. This young man is a problem or rather he is creating problems that are negatively impacting our work and all those involved in it."

They were walking in the foothills of the western mountains near the ruins of an old explosion where fallen rocks and other geological debris still littered the landscape. This two square mile area called, 'the Lane', formed a boundary that separated Ocan territory from the forbidden lands. This was the site for the geophysics excavation project that Alor had begun with Hadassa, along with only their three most trusted apprentices to assist them. On this day, the entire area was quiet, empty of people and activity. There were even no signs or sounds of life coming from the campsites of the other geothermal project work sites a few miles away from this deserted area. Alor and Hadassa had intentionally chosen to come during the three and half day period when most of the workers took their respite, making the hours long journey back to the their respective villages to spend the last half of the week with their families.

But even during their work days, the men and women at the other work sites steered clear of this project in the Lane. For them, this area was too close for comfort to the forbidden lands and to the spirit of past misfortune that they did not wish to inadvertently summon into their own lives. These workers, as well as most Ocan people, had been told that Hadassa and Alor were only working in the Lane to determine the nature and characteristics of ancient geological phenomena and seismic activity in order to better understand the structure of the earth's interior. They were told that this small team of scientists was conducting various geophysics experiments in this mountain's ancient caves, hoping to uncover clues to the island's environmental and geological conditions of the past. However, what the people had not been told was that deeper in one of the mountain's isolated caves, within its hidden tunnels and narrow passageways, there was once an opening to the in-between.

The terrain on the mountain was rocky and steep. Alor leaned heavily on his long walking stick, as he followed behind Hadassa who stooped periodically to examine diverse rock formations with a small hand-held device that was used to detect and record information about subatomic particles emitted by radioactive substances. They were probing for geomagnetic variations by measuring the natural radiation in the soil and rocks in the terrain near the cave and at the cave's entrance. They were then using this data as a means of comparison to the readings from the magnetic anomalies found in some of the cave's other geologic features. Hadassa wore a tool belt strapped to her waist, and Alor was writing in a small notebook the data that she conveyed while also closely observing all that she pointed out. They had been discussing the joint tasks of their apprentices, until somehow their conversation had become focused solely on Alor's chief apprentice.

Hadassa: "Taijaur has no consideration, no concern for our work or for his co-workers. He is not focusing on the protocols of our primary project and he is disrupting other parts of our research. He seems almost oblivious to the negative impact that his actions have on the future success of this most important of responsibilities. Time is of the essence; we must find and seal this portal before the balance of energy shifts any further. We cannot afford this young man's constant dalliances, especially considering how long this project has been delayed. Already three years have past since we first submitted the initial petitions. And now we have been working at this site for over a year and we are no further along now than when we first began. Sooner or later the other workers on the geothermal projects will figure out that our purpose is much different than what they have been told. They cannot continue to be fooled into believing that we are just excavating this site."

Alor: "Mistress Hadassa, I understand your concern, but I assure you that his absences and what you perceive to be daydreaming really do serve a purpose that will ultimately be of benefit to the success of our work."

Hadassa: "Why does he spend so much time alone? It is not healthy to stay so isolated, especially considering that the work that we have undertaken calls for the combined energy and spirits of all the participants. All of the apprentices that we have worked with as well as most youth his age have already completed their Primary Retreats and have begun to marry. In fact, most youth his age revel in the company of their peers, while this one remains distant and isolated."

Alor: "Indeed, his whole existence seems that of a Primary Retreat. When I first took him on as an apprentice, his grandmother warned me that Taijaur's internal system becomes, umm, somewhat, 'misaligned', if he is in the company of other people for too long or too often. It is harder for him to keep things in perspective and in balance when his system is not in synch with the feel of the universe. And this necessitates some periods of isolation. But I don't think that his times of solitude have affected his social relationships in any detrimental way. Over time his isolation has allowed him to achieve deeper states of altered awareness, by cultivating a more profound form of sentiale dreaming and more intense meditation, not to mention a greater appreciation of and connection with the natural world."

Hadassa: "We all pursue sentiale dream awareness, but at least the other apprentices know how to channel the insight gained from sentiale perception into increased energy for our project. Taijaur, on the other hand, has not escaped the legacy of his mother and her mother before her. And, I am told, that his particular version of their family 'malady' manifests in the most lost and all-consuming manner possible. It is imperative that he learn to control or overcome this disorder, if he is to be of any use to us at this most critical juncture in our tasks."

Alor: "But let us be fair Mistress Hadassa, it is this very inherited 'malady' that makes Taijaur infinitely valuable to us. Translation of the Book is only one part of what he brings to this project. Beyond his ability to translate the text, let's not forget Loni's gift of second sight. We know of no other who has been able to actually see the portals and sense their energy. The possibility exists that Taijaur may be like his mother and—"

Hadassa interrupting, "Well let's hope that he is not too much like her. We cannot forget or ignore the manner in which Loni departed this realm. How can we be sure that latent microbes from that epidemic are not present in that boy's system and perhaps affecting his ability to concentrate and function?"

Alor: "Oh Hadassa, surely you cannot believe that Loni's illness could have infected her child. By now, we would have seen something that—"

Hadassa: "I cannot presume anything at this point, Alor. My only concern is for the integrity and outcome of our work. We have only this one book to learn from. We may never know all that would be revealed in the three books combined. Thus, all of our work depends on what we are able to cull from this one source. The safety and progress of this project depends exclusively on the information that Taijaur gleans from this book.

These rare high-energy particles are the most erratic ever recorded on earth. The measurements fluctuate so much, and vary from day to day, hour to hour. No matter how much we analyze and study this area, and no matter how many readings for radiation we take, we may never be able to determine the exact location of the portal or how to seal it without correct translation of key passages as well as an accurate interpretation of the Book's map. One false step and we may all end up the same as those of the past—disintegrated into oblivion.

Yet despite the magnitude of the problems before us, this young man continues to dally with this most important of responsibilities. His work underlies and impacts all that we hope to accomplish."

Alor: "Well, in all fairness, Mistress Hadassa, you must admit that Taijaur has really been the only person capable of de-coding the language of the book and translating the passages, despite the scores of years that have been devoted to its translation. We wouldn't even know that a map to the in-between exists without Taijaur's insight. It as if he sees the meanings of the symbols in his dreams."

Hadassa impatiently, "Yes, yes, yes, Alor. No matter how slowly he proceeds, nonetheless, I will concede that Taijaur has done well with the deciphering and the translation."

Alor: "No one before him ever thought to interpret the mysterious signs and symbols as a map of an unknown land. And even once this puzzle was solved, the most adept of our wise people could only deduce that the map depicted a made-up, imaginary place. Only Taijaur realized that it was a map of the terrain beneath the surface of the earth, of the subterranean realm of the in-between."

Hadassa: "Yet, despite all of these accomplishments, it seems that he is still only concerned with the pursuit of his own single-minded interests, for his own intellectual edification. And when he does deem our project worthy of his attention, what does he do? He chooses to work with the manual laborers lifting and moving heavy boulders and clearing debris as opposed to the work which we depend on him to do.

And Alor, we must deal strictly in the facts of this matter and facts alone. Fact one—there is a subterranean source of electromagnetic power from which we derive a unique type of energy that enhances our natural development. Fact two—this subterranean power source is greater than any known power on this earth and if used in the wrong way for the wrong reasons, it can potentially cause a disaster of astronomical proportions. Fact three—it is necessary for us to locate and seal any open fractures or portals that may lead to this power source so that no one intentionally or unintentionally find and make use of this energy.

It goes without saying that we must proceed with caution and the utmost care. However, if we continue to move forward at our current rate, we may never succeed in plotting the energy spectrum of these particles before the Aka, despite the fact that they don't even have access to a portal."

Alor took quick advantage of this, perhaps, fleeting opportunity to move the conversation in another direction. "It is ironic that we really have the Aka to thank for our present work at this site. I understand that they have been able to move forward with their investigation of the energy despite their lack of proximity to a portal.

They have stopped fighting for greater access to other parts of the island. However, I understand that they have continued to work with the weaker energy of the power spots of their restricted territory. Although they seem to disregard most of the Elders edicts, they still adhere to the prohibitions regarding the forbidden lands. I believe the Aka, like all Ocan realize how volatile and unstable the portals in the western forests are.

I am told that the Aka are attempting to develop technology that will capture and channel the energy. We are lucky that there are no known portals or openings to the in-between in the southern province otherwise they may have succeeded in surpassing us. If not for the Aka's persistence in trying to find ways to use the energy, the Elders would never have agreed to revive this work project. It has been almost thirty years since the Purims began experi—"

Hadassa: "Twenty six to be exact."

Alor: "Well, it has been twenty six years since it was first discovered that the energy from the power source is an unknown form of electromagnetic radiation. And at least sixteen years have passed since the time of the mudslides when the portals began to shift. However, neither of these incidents convinced the Elders of the necessity for continued investigation of the portal energy. It took Edise's spies reporting the Aka's current activities to persuade them that this particular site must be further explored."

Hadassa: "Yes, but don't forget that the Elders are not concerned with your precious investigations or in extending our knowledge of this phenomenon. These pipe dreams that you have of controlling the portal energy will have to wait for another day, another time. Our assignment, and we have only one, is to find a way to seal the portals and shut off any means of access to the power source. We should have searched and shut off access long ago."

Alor: "Hadassa, have you ever considered that we may not need to seal the portals?"

Hadassa: "Don't be preposterous Alor. I'm sure that I don't have to remind you of the danger inherent in these fractures. The power spots of this land give us what we need. For our purposes, we draw a sufficient amount of energy from the ground beneath the Maja. These other potentially wider, more accessible entry points can only mean eventual disaster, as they have proven in the past. The only way to avert any future catastrophe or tragedy is to find and permanently seal all of the portals on this island."

Alor: "But what if the real danger exists in our own fear, which has made us unable to move forward in fulfilling our purpose? What if further study of the portal energy could aid our cause in terms of developing into beings of power as well as helping the nations of the world? The Ocan people seem to be stuck, paralyzed by a fear that keeps us from rising to what we are meant to be."

Hadassa: "Fear or no fear, Alor—don't lose sight of the fact that a major part of this energy source we speak of is most likely a naturally occurring nuclear reactor with a power greater than any weapon, bomb, or natural catastrophe that the earth has ever experienced. The best way to thwart any potential danger is to seal the portals as we have been directed to do. Sealing the portals is the safest and only course of action that is open to us; and the only one we are sanctioned to perform."

Alor: "Yes, I suppose that you are right. Following the rules is always a good and necessary course of action," muttering under his breath, "even if it does not accomplish what we ultimately seek to achieve."

Hadassa: "Getting back to the central issue of our discussion—if Taijaur would just focus on doing his part, then maybe we can make sufficient progress to at least justify our continued work in this area. There is only so much longer that the Elders will tolerate our constant delays without any progress to report."

Alor: "Have faith, my sister, there is much that this young man can accomplish for us. He is such a serious young man; but for the growth of his mind and spirit, it would seem that he is old well beyond his time on this earth. His power of concentration is so strong that one day I'm afraid that his entire being will explode from the strain. If he were older, and if we could—well, I suppose there is no need in speculating because—"

Hadassa interrupted with force, "Because you know, as well as we all know, that he may fall asleep at any task that he is given. But nonetheless, I have no more time to debate these issues. I—"

There was an unexpected sound that made them both turn and look in the direction where it seemed to originate. They saw Taijaur down the hill, in the distance, playing a wooden wind instrument. He had his back turned to them and Alor and Hadassa were partially obscured as they stood behind an outcrop of rocks. They stood still and quiet for a moment listening to the soft soothing melody that harmonized with the voices of the wind. The notes of his song penetrated the surrounding air so strongly that it was awhile after the music stopped before they realized that he was no longer playing.

Hadassa was the first to speak. "Hmmph, once again he trifles with his time."

Alor: "I'm just glad that he has the music to divert his attention away from his studies."

Hadassa turned to stare at him, in disbelief and then she just shook her head, while Alor continued watching Taijaur as he started playing another song.

Hadassa: "He is your chief apprentice, Alor—the first that you have ever selected. That, in itself, speaks highly of the young man's abilities. You are his primary guide for this phase of his life, so ultimately it is your judgment that must prevail. However, Alor, I must insist that you speak with him about his prolonged absences and this interminable dreaming. At a minimum, Taijaur should be able to present his research findings to me and the group at least once a month. Is that too much to ask, Master Alor?"

Alor: "No it is not, our most illustrious and most revered Mistress Hadassa," he smiled, "As always, you humbly request only that which is more than fair. And I promise you that—"

Hadassa: "Yes, yes, yes Alor. Your word is sufficient. This other superfluous nonsense is unnecessary. We have much more important, more pressing concerns, which make the ways of your negligent apprentice all the more exasperating. Honor thy Gift."

Alor: "With that, kind lady, I bid you thank you and good day. May we all—"

She had turned, abruptly walking away and out of sight before Alor finished speaking.

Hadassa was not the first to mention Taijaur's disappearances and frequent absences. And Alor knew that even though Taijaur now lived in a small one room hut near their work site, he was still gone more than he was present. Some days he could be found helping with the geothermal projects, where they had tapped into the mountain geysers and the volcanic rock to generate a limited amount of electricity for the homes in the main village. But lately, even when Alor searched for him at the geothermal work sites, he was not there and no one ever knew where he was.

Alor began walking toward Taijaur and he started to call out to him but then something made him halt abruptly. He had not noticed before that there was another person with Taijaur. They did not look up or see him and at first Alor thought that the woman might be one of the people working on the geyser. There had been several of them working overtime in the foothills lately. However, this woman seemed different somehow, maybe older than the regular workers and something else made him look more closely. She wore a thin sash of blue around her waist. As Alor walked slowly towards them, the woman spotted him and motioned to Taijaur before moving quickly in the opposite direction, towards the woods. Before she disappeared completely into the trees, she glanced back at Alor with a cold hard look of stony defiance.

Taijaur ran to Alor. "Master Alor. I wasn't expecting to see you here today."

Alor: "And are you honoring thy Gift this bright day, Chief Apprentice Taijaur?" Alor smiled as he emphasized Taijaur's title and name.

Taijaur: "Indeed, Master Alor, may we all be worthy. Were you looking for me?"

Alor: "No. Mistress Hadassa and I were just checking some recent readings from the cave entrance."

Taijaur glanced around and behind Alor, "Mistress Hadassa? Is she here?

Alor: "No, she has just departed."

Taijaur: "Will she be back? I was hoping to speak with her about a very intriguing passage that I recently translated. I think that she will find it most interesting."

Alor was distracted, lost in his thoughts for a moment and it took him a few seconds to respond. "Hmmm? Yes, umm, Mistress Hadassa has a lot on her mind and some pressing tasks to attend to. It may be better if you wait a few days before seeking her out. But come Taijaur, let us exercise as we talk. I have several matters to discuss with you. If you don't mind, we can perform our daily calisthenics. Have you completed yours yet?"

Taijaur peered at Alor, suspiciously worried, "Yes, but, ummm, was Mistress Hadassa upset," he paused, "about anything?"

Alor: "Don't worry about that now Taijaur. We can speak of it later." He laughed a little, laid his staff on the ground behind him and then patted Taijaur on the back before saying, "And don't look so guilty."

They faced one another, inhaling deeply and then they both stooped wide-legged, and began a sequence of slow, carefully coordinated movements that seemed to flow together into one continuous motion. The two men performed the Ocan daily ritual of synchronized movements that looked almost like an orchestrated dance with their arms, legs, and entire bodies flowing through fluid motions of bending, twisting, and stretching, accompanied by deep circular breathing that was timed in harmony with when and how their bodies moved.

As Alor bent and stretched, he quietly asserted, "You know that we of the Ocan believe that it is important to always make ourselves as strong, as physically and mentally fit, as possible. We do this not just because the optimum condition and functioning of our lives requires it, but also because we must always be ready to do battle, always be ready to rise to whatever situation presents itself, no matter how negative or positive. You need a strong mind to gauge your options and determine the necessary actions, and your body must likewise be strong in order to perform whatever actions may be necessary.

These exercises and physical action, as a whole, filter the toxins out of all of your internal organs, including your brain. We all have an inherent obligation to treat God's vessel—your life, your body, mind and soul—with care and respect. We must always seek to hone the individual essence of God's energy—your spirit—and cultivate its growth."

Taijaur was breathing deeply, flowing through the movements with his eyes closed.

Alor watched Taijaur carefully as he spoke. "That woman that you were with Taijaur—who is she and why was she this far out from the village?"

Without opening his eyes, Taijaur responded, "Umm, I believe that she is from the Shinhala village. I think she said that she is an engineer working on the pipeline with the geothermal project. I bumped in to her as I was on my way to the pumping stations to retrieve some items that I left there yesterday."

Alor: "The sash she wore—I haven't seen anyone wear one of those in a long time. It was once worn by a group of young self-proclaimed 'warriors'. I was never quite certain what happened to that group. Some people believe that they joined the Aka when they seceded."

Taijaur continued stretching and exercising, still in synch with Alor's movements, the expression on his face never changing. Then as he pivoted around, turning his back to Alor, he slowly opened his eyes, and said in a steady clear voice, "I think that it is just part of the fashion they are wearing these days in the Haman and the other villages."

With his back still to Alor, Taijaur began moving independently with steps, kicks and arm movements that were more aerial, more animated and significantly less tranquil. He picked up Alor's staff and began twirling it, making forceful thrusts and jabs as if he was making contact with an opponent at close range. He had departed from the slow flowing meditative movement of the Ocan and moved into some other technique undoubtedly designed for purposes beyond the range of merely "treating God's vessel with care and respect".

Alor, still moving through the slower paced routine sequence of Ocan exercises, watched Taijaur, stupefied by this unusual display of talent and skill. Then with a severe focused expression Taijaur's actions became more pronounced, every muscle in his body seemed to harden and become more defined, quivering with the anticipation of each next movement. Sometimes the long staff was in his hands, sometimes it was not. Alor could not tell when he picked it up and when he laid it back down as Taijaur moved through a rapid-fire series of maneuvers—high kicks, flips, jumps in the air and quick half-fist punches in split-second sequence. The force and power of his movements left no doubt as to the condition of any potential opponent. This was a formidable anger in motion; a controlled fury; a demanding propulsion of concentrated strength and might.

"My, oh my." Alor was now motionless, still squatting in place, with legs spread wide, feet pointing out to either side, one arm bent at the elbow in front of his body, the other arm stretched to one side. Taijaur came and stood across from him, reverting back into the slow fluid time of the Ocan calisthenics while Alor remained in place, unmoving still staring at him. Then Alor shook himself and slowly moved back in step with Taijaur in the soft relaxed movements of the Ocan drill.

Alor: "That was obviously not a part of the Ocan ritual. Where did you learn that?"

Taijaur: "Oh just some exercises that I came upon; just practicing something new."

Alor: "It looks like a form of martial arts." Taijaur made no reply as Alor paused and then continued, "I saw something like it demonstrated only once, very long ago."

Alor glanced at Taijaur with open curiosity, however, the younger man still made no comment or response. He studied Taijaur's face in profile, noting the sharp features and strong square shape of his jaw; together with his dark complexion. Although he bore a faint resemblance to his grandfather Tekun and his mother Loni, Alor was struck by how dissimilar Taijaur's features were in comparison to anyone else in the Saba's family. He was more powerfully built with thicker bones and muscles than most of the young men his age. Despite his distinctive features and obviously strong genetic lineage, Taijaur did not look even remotely similar to anyone else in any of the Ocan villages.

Alor: "How is the translation coming along?"

Taijaur: "Slowly, very slowly. It would be significantly much easier and make more sense with the other two volumes of the Book; or at least the second one. This book makes references to issues and information that are more completely explained in the other two books. We may never be able to piece together all that this book conveys without the other books. I am afraid of applying some of the principles indicated because there are warnings in the Book of dire repercussions if all the pieces of knowledge are not considered in their entirety."

Alor: "Well, be that as it may—we will just have to do the best that we can. It is impossible to get the other two books—one is with the Aka and the other was left in the mainland, and possibly no longer exists."

Taijaur: "But you do understand that we can never know the full message of this book, in the absence of the combined knowledge that is possible only if these three books are brought together?"

Alor: "Yes, I understand this."

Taijaur: "But why can't we just ask the Aka if we can borrow or use the volume that they have in their possession?"

Alor: "No, we cannot. The Ocan maintain that the book was stolen, along with other artifacts when the Aka split from our community. On the other hand, the Aka claim that the materials rightfully belong to the founders of the Aka village, the Basau family, who are now the only ones with direct access to this collection of 'pilfered' materials. And I am told that they keep it well secured."

Taijaur: "But Master Alor, isn't there some way that we can at least try to work with the Aka who are basically striving towards the same goals that we wish to achieve? Isn't it true that both groups are working to learn more about the energy of the portals and where the portals are located? "

Alor: "Taijaur, I realize that these Basau people are your family and that you are probably curious about them and want to meet them. However—"

Taijaur: "No, it's not that Master Alor. This has nothing to do with my personal feelings or any curiosity. It's just that the Aka not only have the second book, but by combining our research with theirs, it seems that we can make greater progress. Why not collaborate, especially when competition on this one small island seems so absurd?"

Alor: "Collaboration might seem like the logical course of action. But you have to understand that our goals may seem similar in that both the Ocan and Aka are trying to find the location of the portals on the island, and fundamentally both groups claim that they strive to bring forth that which is highest in human nature. However, it is our understanding that the Aka would use the portal energy for what we view as potentially negative or malicious purposes.

Keep in mind that even though the Book indicates that it is possible to harness the energy that exists at the breach between worlds, the Elders do not want this portal energy used at all. They want this portal as well as all others sealed to stop anyone from gaining access to the energy of the in-between. Mistress Hadassa would also like to see the portals sealed to avert a potential nuclear disaster. The Aka, on the other hand, want to combine the energy from the power source with their highly developed scientific technology in order to create weapons or instruments that can be used to impose a new world order throughout this planet.

Although I obviously don't agree with the Aka's purposes for how the energy should be used, nonetheless, it is ironic that the Aka aim to do what we lack the courage to even think about. For years I have tried to convince the Elders that we should develop ways to use this energy to the greater benefit of the world. But no, they only want to make sure that no one else has access to it."

Alor stopped moving and picked up his stick, using it to point in the direction of the cave. "Come, lets walk up to our site. I think that may be enough exercise for one day. And I am interested in hearing your perspective on what the data that we have gathered may indicate."

As they began walking up the hill, Taijaur suddenly said, "Oh, I forgot to tell you, Master Edise was here earlier this morning."

Alor: "Edise? What did he say? What did he want?"

Taijaur: "I'm not sure what he wanted. But he was looking around in the cave and he asked me some questions about our work—whether or not the portal had been located. And he also said that I need not mention his visit to you."

Alor: "Hmmm, that is very curious, indeed. Thank you for telling me."

Taijaur: "He was here once before, talking to Kedar. There is something else. I don't think that it is significant, but—"

Alor: "What is it?"

Taijaur: "A few weeks ago, I saw Master Edise with his corps of—cadets, I suppose—training down near the river."

Alor: "Training? What type of training?"

Taijaur: "I don't know. I couldn't get too close. With so many of them, the block on my sentiale was only effective at a distance. I saw at least fifty to one hundred young men and women from all five of the Ocan villages; there may have been more. I suspect that their training may have something to do with the security of the villages. They had weapons."

Alor made no immediate reply as he looked at Taijaur and then staring into the distance, he mumbled, "And I wonder what training we will need to keep us safe from Edise."

In a louder more direct voice, he said, "Well, anyway—Taijaur, you are aware that some facts about this book have been purposely withheld from you?"

Taijaur: "Yes. I keep hoping to learn more; because every bit of information about these books can only help in deciphering the language and translating the passages."

Alor: "I did not want your translation efforts to be influenced or tainted by prior information. I had to be sure that your ability to translate was pure and not just a reflection of the previous work that had been done with this book. Now, thanks to your very adept translation, I believe that we are ready to move into the next phase of our project. And to do this, you will now need to know more about the Book."

Taijaur: "Some of the subjects of this book are so arcane and abstruse that it is difficult to determine the actual message. It is frustrating trying to connect the cryptic passages in the Book to the actual geological studies that we do here at this site. I know that you and Mistress Hadassa are better able to read into the Book's messages and understand how it all relates to our work, but I just can't see where it all comes together and where it is leading. I know that we are working to identify which of these thousands of passageways may contain the readings that would indicate a portal. But even if we find such a portal—which is like trying to chase a ghost—I still don't understand how we are supposed to seal it."

Alor: "Well, I think that Mistress Hadassa is hoping that your translations will ultimately reveal the manner in which they must be sealed."

Taijaur: "I'm not sure what knowledge or information the Book will ultimately yield."

They reached the site and Alor sat on a large rock near the cave entrance. "Why don't we sit here and finish talking before going in?"

Taijaur: "If you don't mind, Master Alor, I would like to continue working on sorting these rocks as we talk. This work is actually part of the reason that I am here today; it helps to clear my mind."

There was still an extensive amount of debris that was left from the explosion decades ago. Although the main entryway to the cave was partially open, there were many passageways that remained blocked. Alor tried to hide his amazement as he watched Taijaur first struggle and then heave and push to the side a small boulder that was at least three times his own weight. The older man smiled as he said, "Well, I hope you don't need any help. These tired bones of mine..." His words trailed off.

Breathing hard, before moving to the next equally as large 'rock', Taijaur smiled in return, "No, thanks. I'm fine."

Alor was pensive for a moment and then he gazed at Taijaur in a peculiar manner as if trying to read or determine some message. He began slowly, "Taijaur, how would you like to take on an additional assignment, above and beyond the translation work? This would have to be kept secret—just between the two of us."

Taijaur looked up with interest, as he continued pushing and hoisting.

Alor: "I would not ask you if I did not think that you were ready. But you must know at the outset that there may be a level of danger connected with what I am proposing; which is all the more reason that absolutely no one but you and I must know of this."

Taijaur: "You know that you can trust my discretion, Master Alor. And I have trained to deal with danger all of my life."

Alor: "You must judge for yourself whether or not the severity of what we face warrants what I consider to be a necessary deviation from the Elders' instructions. I don't want to compromise you in any way."

Taijaur: "In order to be of greatest use to you on this project, I need to know as much as possible. Besides, I have been on this earth long enough to realize that the temporal laws or rules of any society may not always coincide with what is most true or right in terms of the inherent principles of life. From the beginning of this project, I have been concerned that our tasks don't seem to be moving us forward. Something seems to be missing. So, please continue Master Alor. I am anxious to hear what you are proposing."

Alor: "Taijaur, from all our studies and previous discussions, you are aware that the Earth in now in a liminal time period where one age/epoch is ending and another is beginning. Soon everything that once was, will no longer be and a new way of understanding, a new way of existing will come forth. This time in our history is pivotal in terms of our future survival. The reversal in the Earth's magnetic fields will have a profound effect on the forms of life that will or will not continue to exist once this change has been fully completed.

There are those who believe that this new age signals that the time of humans on Earth is drawing to a close; that we have shepherded our own demise. They contend that the Earth will still go on for quite some time, but humans may not be a part of the planet's future for long. And if the negatively destructive acts of humans are not soon abated, then these forecasters of our doom may, indeed, be right. The presence of the virus within the brains and bodies of human beings is the root cause of many of the most destructive and malicious actions that have occurred on the Earth.

The energy from the in-between is the only antidote that can heal the impact of negative destructive forces and ensure humanity's continued existence as a part of this universe. That's why I believe that it is important to not seal the portals, but rather, use the energy that is available at the portals to counter the effect of the plague. When the ancient Obeah sealed these portals over two centuries ago, they never said that it was our responsibility to keep them sealed, as the Elders maintain. They merely predicted that the portals would remain sealed until the time of the Emissary on the Earth."

Taijaur: "But how can we harness this energy? To my knowledge, we don't have any instruments that would allow us to pass the energy from one place to another."

Alor: "We may lack technology as sophisticated as that of the Aka, but we still have a fusion particle container, as well as other equipment that can be modified to our needs. Also Mala's parents'—the Purims—left copious notes. They were very much ahead of their time and they were creating a receptacle that would serve as a conduit to transfer the energy. I will provide you with more details at a later time.

There is one other thing about this virus—I believe that it is mutating, transforming into something perhaps even more potent. On a daily basis we track and record all the detrimental ways that the humans of this world are altering the planet—killing and destroying not only the creatures and the ecosystems, but preying on their own kind at a rate unprecedented in the history of man on this earth. I believe that these events are evidence that the virus is growing and becoming stronger. We must try to find out what is making this pathogen stronger and stop it before it is too late."

Taijaur: "How is it possible that this virus leaves other people outside of the Ocan unable to develop the pathways that would lead to higher spiritual consciousness? There are power spots throughout the world. Why is it that these other people have not learned how to access the energy of the power source the same way that our ancestors did?"

Alor: "Perhaps it would be easier if we start with a little of the Book's history, sketchy as it may be. As you know, these books were written in an ancient language unfamiliar to any languages that exist today and the words are arranged in the pattern of a secret code. We are told that they were originally written on clay tablets that were found buried in the caves of some desert land. Some have called the script a type of 'protolanguage', and on the surface, that is what it appears to be—a kind of cuneiform, hieroglyph or symbolic code. It is obvious that these books were compiled or written over decades and perhaps centuries. No one knows who the original author or subsequent authors may have been. They were passed secretly from one person to another, one century to another. There are other stories about their origins, but the stories do not help us to translate or understand them any better. Even the place of their discovery yields no clues as to their source. Long ago, these books were ordered to be burned, by members of the clergy or maybe even some persons of the royalty or ruling class. What country, what people—I do not know. None of that matters. What matters is that the books survived and we have one of them in our possession. The third and last book is buried, lost or hidden somewhere in the mainland; it was scoured away when the Ocan people came to this land two centuries ago. We may never see or know the fate of the final manuscript.

Some people referred to these books as simply, 'The Source', others knew them as, 'The Book' or 'The Book of Change'. As you know the full title is 'The Source of Change', with the word 'change' referring to existence, growth, development, evolution, transformation, movement, action, revolution—what ever, and whenever an organism or element of life—any form of energy—goes from one state to another, one place to another, this book purportedly addresses why and how such movement or differences come about. Theoretically, if we can understand why and how life changes, then we can begin to comprehend why and how we—and all life in the universe—have come into existence.

We believe that the three books together contain a written record of all earthly phenomena that have come to pass and all things that will come to be. They present a story of the creation and the injera of the universe as well as providing details of connections between all the Earth's life forms and all the energy and matter within the universe. It is certain, from what we have uncovered already, that the Book makes reference to hidden, unknown species of earthly beings, as well as unknown forms of matter and energy that affect the evolution of the planet. For our purposes we are concerned with only one of those unknown forms of energy—that which comes from the power source of the in-between.

When our people first came to the island, they were unaware that the energy from the openings was facilitating and leading us to higher states of consciousness. Then they began to notice the physical changes and enhancements in our mental acuity. Over the years, physical tests have confirmed that our neurons, our brains and all chemicals and substances throughout our bodies have been fundamentally changed on a cellular and molecular level. It was a while before we realized how profound the changes really were. All residual effects of the virus and most illnesses had been eradicated. Although we knew how dangerous any misuse of this energy could be, we had also discovered that this rare unidentifiable form of radiation can neutralize the effect of the virus in the neural pathways of human beings.

This discovery carries with it tremendous implications and equally tremendous responsibilities. We knew that this gift must be shared with the world but we also understood that, as the primary recipients of this gift, we had to safeguard its use. Thus, it was decided that access to the gateways would be restricted and controlled in order to protect against mankind's potential to use and manipulate this force for evil and destruction. It was for this reason that the ancient Obeah sealed access to the portals through out the world, with the intent of waiting until the time that the Ocan people had developed enough knowledge to share this power from the in-between with the rest of the world."

Taijaur: "But Master Alor, what is the true nature of the in-between? We have been taught that the realm of the in-between is attainable only to those with the ability to see worlds within worlds. But what does this really mean?"

Alor: "There are both physical and spiritual dimensions to this alternate realm of existence. This is another world, another reality that exists simultaneously within the physical dimensions of the Earth and also within other unknown dimensions that are outside of our understanding and outside of our tangible means of perception. The in-between can only be reached by traveling through both the physical and the spiritual passageways that lead to its reality. Merely entering the caverns that lead to the in-between or close proximity to a power spot does not necessarily mean that a person can actually enter the realm of the in-between. It is necessary, first and foremost, for a person to traverse the sentiale channels that open the way to the in-between.

The ancient Obeah spoke of reaching the in-between purely by way of their minds and their souls through intense meditation and other practices of spiritual enhancement. This guarded knowledge is passed down to only each new generation of Obeah."

Taijaur: "If the Obeah have knowledge that we need, then perhaps they can help us to determine how the portal energy can be accessed?"

Alor: "I'm sorry Taijaur, but we cannot seek or expect help from the Obeah. They do not believe that we should manipulate or disturb the portals or the energy source in any way—either to seal them, explore them or to make greater use of their power. They believe that we should cease any activity or use that can be interpreted as 'exploitation' of the land's resources. They believe that only by way of deeper and higher states of awareness is the in-between truly accessible."

Taijaur: "And do your beliefs counter their perspective?"

Alor: "To the contrary, I wholly concur with the Obeah. However, I also believe that what they propose can only take place over millennia of conscious development and evolution of the human spirit and mind. I don't think that we have the luxury of that timetable if we hope to fulfill our purpose and effectively change the destructive course of the earth's civilizations.

I believe that we can work in concert with the earth's resources for the mutual exchange of energy. If you follow the Obeah's line of reasoning there is nothing to stop mankind from one day being able to draw or photosynthesize energy directly from the sun. I don't think we can afford to sit around waiting for that day."

Taijaur: "If the map in the Book is correct, then deep within the earth there are connected passageways and a network of subterranean tunnels all leading to the interior chambers that hold the power source as its nucleus".

Alor: "Yes and your very skillful abilities in interpreting this map have shown us that this island sits atop that nucleus, acting as the main channel by which the energy is transmitted into the world."

Taijaur: "But the one thing that I don't understand is—if every chemical element has its own characteristic spectrum, showing a particular distribution of electromagnetic radiation, then why does the emission spectrum of this energy not reveal the wavelength patterns that would identify its molecular structure?"

Alor: "Because as you have seen, the spectrum of this energy shifts constantly and randomly so that no discernible pattern can be detected. I am not even sure that we can even call it radioactive material, except that, in some respects, it behaves like radiation. Our known spectrum does not include a classification for this type of energy. In fact, to our knowledge, this type of electromagnetic energy has never been directly observed by anyone outside of the Ocan people.

Mistress Hadassa can explain more fully the scientific and technical details of this energy. But it is believed that over a billion years ago, deep beneath the surface of the earth on the continent where life on this earth began, natural conditions prompted spontaneous self-sustained nuclear fusion reactions within the internal chambers that now house the power source. We believe that the power source of the in-between is a left-over product of these nuclear processes and it contains a core chamber of an unknown type of radioactive material similar to, but yet very different from, the type of uranium isotopes that are present in the earth's crust, on the moon and in meteorites. If we were better able to study this energy or conduct more in-depth geophysics investigations, then perhaps we could more definitely confirm these findings."

Taijaur: "So, at the core of the power source it is believed that there are deposits of an unknown type of matter, similar to uranium-like deposits. And it is the energy generated from the reactions of these deposits that underlies our spiritual and physical development."

Alor: "That's correct."

Taijaur: "Master Alor, while I can understand how all of these energies and forces can contribute to our physical presence on this earth, it is still not clear how this unknown form of radiation affects who and what we are as spiritual beings? How can it enhance or heighten our spiritual development?"

Alor: "You have to keep in mind the continual interweaving of the spiritual and physical realms of existence and the connections that sustain each of these states of existence. At this point there is still much that we are learning, much that we do not know and may never be able to know. That is why the Book is of vital importance to our cause—we are hoping that the Book will eventually reveal much if not all that we need to know.

But of this much we are certain—trace amounts of this same unidentifiable type of 'radiation' from the in-between have been found in the neurons and other sensory cells of living beings. We also know that all living matter on this earth contains radiation and is derived from nuclear energy. Cognition, sensory perception and awareness all arise from these emanations. The sentiale pathways of all bio-chemical phenomena—humans, animals the Earth—are, in part, formed as a reaction of this energy. It is these sentiale pathways which carry the spiritual essence of existence.

It is our understanding that this unknown form of radioactive energy is one of the most essential ingredients that incited life into existence. Those ancient nuclear reactions, within the internal chamber of the in-between, were, in part, responsible for the initial generation of life on earth. The Ocan believe that the creation of bio-chemical matter on earth began as a result of the energy emitted from those processes in combination with storms of electricity and showers of solar particles from space. From these three sources, the network and pathways of the Earth's sentiale were formed and connections between different forms of matter became possible. These webs or patterns of electromagnetic connections are the basis of sentiale consciousness which in turn underlies what we understand as spiritual essence.

The founding purpose of Ocan society was to push the Earth's balance of power toward spiritual evolution by learning how to transmit this energy force more fully to the rest of the world. Whether we are ready or not, I believe that life is demanding that we, as a people, move into the next phase of what we are meant to be. Our spiritual and physical development has been nurtured by the energy of this land so that we can fulfill our destiny. This is our gift, our injera, our purpose, our calling."

Taijaur: "Mistress Hadassa warns us that this energy has the power to detrimentally alter this entire planet on a major scale. She constantly refers to others, in the past, who were presumptuous enough to think that they could experiment with and control the portals, and try to access the catalyst-stone on their own. She said that their tragic and violent deaths serve as an example of what the combination of hubris and ignorance can cause."

Alor: "She is referring to the explosion in which your grandfather and Mala's parents were killed."

Taijaur: "I know. What type of experiments were they conducting?"

Alor: "Alis and Aran Purim, were scientists, in addition to their many other avocations. They went through the entryway and began conducting experiments to determine the composition of the energy fields, with the intent of trying to channel the energy into a receptacle."

Taijaur: "But how were the Purims able to find the portal?"

Alor: "They didn't find it. Your mother found it. We always believed that only the ancient Obeah had the power to see and feel the presence of a portal; that is, until your mother came along. As I understand it, Loni, Mala and Tausi were playing near Mala's home when they began following a hidden spring into a cave, seeking its source. Deep in the passageways of the cave, they came upon a highly energized electro-magnetic area that we now know may indicate the presence of a portal. Loni said that she could actually see a strange form of light and hear and feel a vibration that no one else was ever able to discern. When the girls told Mala's parents what they had found, the Purims immediately recognized that this was a gateway to the power source of the earth. Although the Elders never accepted that this was an actual portal, they did initially, grant permission for the Purims to conduct their experiments in secret, because they wanted them to neutralize any potential leaks from the fractures. I believe Tekun was there that day just to observe."

Taijaur: "What caused the explosion?"

Alor: "We don't know exactly. Somehow the site became unstable, combustible. Perhaps it was the gas released from the fissures. In addition to the electromagnetic radiation there are also other geologic processes within these caverns and subterranean tunnels that run deep within the layers of the earth. Any combination of these elements may have caused the explosion. No remains of the three adults were ever found."

Taijaur: "If I understand you correctly, you are proposing that we can avoid a major part of the past mistakes by not actually entering the portals. We merely want to learn how to harness the energy that is available at the entryways."

Alor: "Exactly! We don't want to enter the portal; we just want to make use of the energy that is available at the entryway itself. We can no longer afford to wait. We have to ready ourselves for the next phase of our mission, our purpose. The suffering of this world and the devastation of this planet are increasing at an exponential rate. We have no choice but to try to stop pervasive negative forces from gaining a stronghold of dominance within the world."

Taijaur sat silent with his head downcast appearing deep in thought.

Alor: "I know that this must all seem overwhelming. And I understand if you feel that you do not want to participate in what may potentially be viewed as an illegal act."

Taijaur: "No, it's not that. I think that what you propose is necessary and correct. I agree that it is time that we fulfill our purpose. We can't just stand by and watch the people of the world self-destruct."

Alor: "And remember that, no matter what Taijaur, the Elders must not suspect our true intent. They cannot know that we will attempt to access the energy of the portal. You cannot reveal any of this to Mistress Hadassa, the other apprentices or anyone for that matter. As far as they all are concerned, we are just continuing to comply with the Elders edict to find and secure all of the gateways to the in-between. The protocols of this project must appear to remain the same."

Taijaur: "I was just wondering if maybe there is an even better or more effective way; a way where we don't have to confine ourselves to using just the portal energy."

Alor: "What do you mean?"

Taijaur: "What if there was a way to find the catalyst and access the energy source directly?

Alor: "Taijaur, at the risk of sounding very much like our Mistress Hadassa, I must remind you once again of the nature and potential destructive capability of our energy source. And this is not a matter of fear, but a healthy respect for what we are dealing with. I agree with Hadassa and the others who say that full entry into this realm is too dangerous at this time. And we don't have the time to wait for any emissary to guide us."

Taijaur: "But Master Alor, what if the Emissary was present here in this generation and already walks among us?

Alor: "Do you mean here on the Ocan island?"

Taijaur: "The island, the mainland, just here—somewhere on the earth."

Alor was reluctant to be drawn into yet another discussion centered on the hope and faith of the Ocan people. Rising from his seat, he patted Taijaur on the back, and said, "Well, that would, indeed, be a vision to behold. I guess we will just have to cross that bridge when and if we get to it. Let's start back to the laboratory to see if we can get some work accomplished before this day is completely gone. It has grown too late to go into the cave and risk getting lost in that winding labyrinth of tunnels."

They started walking down the embankment and Taijaur opened his mouth to say something as Alor hurriedly spoke up, "But speaking of visions, Taijaur, do you still dream?"

Startled, he looked at Alor and then quickly averted his eyes before answering, "Yes, but my dreams don't interfere with my responsibilities and duties." Peering sidewise at the older man, but relaxing a little, he went on to inquire, "Why do you ask?"

Alor: "You must use your dreams to guide your waking consciousness. You must not allow your subconscious-dream mind to use you."

Taijaur: "Don't worry Master Alor. I have learned to control or at least temper my dreaming states, to the extent that sentiale phenomena no longer overpower my life. Strenuous physical exercise helps to push my mind away from any deep-forming sentiale connections. Also, I have learned to use a focusing device in order to anchor my mind in a waking reality while also allowing sentiale understanding to flow through other parts of my consciousness. In this way, my dreams still speak to me and I am able to draw meaning from what they convey without being pulled under."

Alor: "And what is it that your dreams are telling you as of late?"

Taijaur: "My dreams tell me of distant lands and foreign people." He paused before saying in a low voice, "In most of my dreams there is a girl, a young woman with me and together we travel—."

Alor: "Pardon me, did you say a woman? Perhaps the one that was here with you earlier?"

Taijaur laughed, "No. The female in my dreams is younger, closer to my own age. I dream with her as well as through her."

Alor: "What is her name?"

Taijaur: "I don't—I don't know her name. She, I—we have never actually met."

Alor: "Then someone else—one of your friends—has spoken of her to you?"

Taijaur: "No, no one else knows of her. What I mean is that I have yet to meet her in this physical realm."

Alor: "Ahhh yes, I think that I understand. Taijaur, my son, you must bear in mind that although a dream woman may vanish with the daylight, she sometimes leaves a deeply entrenched longing that is much more real than any other 'she', in reality, can ever be."

Taijaur: "But this girl, this young woman in my dreams—she, she, she is real. She exists."

Alor: "Don't worry, my son. We all feel that way about our passions. Sometimes they are the most alive thing about who and what we are. Occasionally, our passions—our desires—fight so hard for their existence that not only are our common sense and higher virtues forfeited, but our very beings may be sacrificed to their desperate will to live."

Taijaur: "No, no, no. It's not like that at all. She, I—my attachment to her is, well, our affinity is that of kindred spirits. And besides she is a living and breathing person, not the product of some fabricated feeling or emotion in my mind. She actually exists within this physical time and space, this here and now. She is a real being, not some dream fantasy."

Alor: "And yet you have never seen her and no one else that you know has ever seen her?"

Taijaur: "All that is true, yet, nonetheless I know that she exists."

Alor came to a full stop and turned to look directly at Taijaur, staring at him for a moment in silence. Then he said quietly, "Far be it for this old man to advise anyone in matters of the heart, however, these dreams of your, these visions—it may be that they are, indeed connected to your injera. Just bear in mind that passions born of injera do not die easily. They can make us believe the impossible and lead us to places from which we may never return fully. My friend, be forewarned that passion uncontrolled can lead even the most dedicated disciple to commit the most unconscionable acts with only a residual humiliation and shame left as consolation"

Taijaur: "I admit that I don't fully understand this connection. But I have felt it and she has been with me for most of my life. Perhaps if Mala had raised her daughter here in the Ocan villages, then the link that we have with one another would not be so intense, so—"

Alor: "Mala's daughter? Did you say, 'Mala's daughter'? Ahh, my son, perhaps it would be best to block that vision."

Alor began walking again and Taijaur fell in step beside him.

Taijaur: "Surely you don't subscribe to any Ocan superstitions about the danger that her birth may have caused."

Alor: "I neither believe nor disbelieve any phenomenon that is beyond my comprehension. Purely and simply, I accept. That child was born and therefore meant to be. However, I caution you to temper any communication that you may have with the spirits of the dead. Dreams with and through those who have passed on can only—"

Taijaur: "But Master Alor, I thought you knew—it is as you suspected, as you speculated to Master Edise years ago in the Maja at the time of the spring festival. Mala's child did not die. She survived and lives as we speak."

Alor stopped and turned to Taijaur. "What!?! How—what do you know of this?"

Taijaur stood still as well. "My grandmother can tell you more, but I know that Mala has reared her daughter in the western forest, where she lived before—"

Alor: "The western forest? Did you say the western forest? In the forbidden lands? Near the shore?"

Alor began pacing back and forth, his head bowed as he stroked his beard. He stopped momentarily to look directly at Taijaur only when he posed a question and then started pacing again as he listened to his responses.

Taijaur: "Yes, in the forbidden lands near the western shore. Perhaps you did not know that Mala lived there for years before her child was born."

Alor: "Years ago, I recall someone telling me that Mala had been living in the Haman villages. I have heard no other news of Mala since then. It seems that while I have focused on all that takes place in the world at large, I have neglected to pay attention to that which has transpired right beneath my nose. Was Mala's child conceived in the forbidden lands?"

Taijaur: "Yes—as far as anyone knows."

Alor: "Well, that may begin to explain some of the mystery."

Taijaur: "What do you mean?"

Alor: "It is too much to go into now." He paused for a moment and then asked, "Taijaur, would you know how to find this girl?"

Taijaur: "I, um, I don't know. I don't think that anyone has ever ventured that far into the forbidden lands."

Alor: "I mean—could your sentiale lead you to her?"

Taijaur: "Yes, I think so. I always feel a sense of her physical presence."

Alor: "Good, hold that thought. We will speak more of this later. Come, let us go on to the laboratory before it gets any later. There is much that we have to prepare. I would like to go over the notes from your latest translated passages."

Alor walked ahead of Taijaur, his head bowed, lost in thought. Before he had gone too far, he stopped and turned, saying, "Oh and another thing, Taijaur. I almost forgot. You must check with Hadassa and the other apprentices about, umm, something about the protocols of the project, I think. You must keep them apprised of your progress, Maybe meet with them periodically, perhaps once a month to go over what you uncover. And please try to meet some of your time obligations or let someone know if it looks like you will need more time. Does that sound reasonable to you?"

Taijaur: "Reasonable, fair and do-able, Master Alor. And I am sorry if I have caused you or any of the others any inconvenience with what seems to be a lack of punctuality. But I promise that you will not be disappointed with my work."

Alor: "Yes, I know. I have full faith and confidence in all that you do."

Taijaur looked pensive for a moment and then said, "Master Alor, forgive me for returning to the same subject, but what if I or someone was able to identify the Emissary?"

Alor: "Taijaur, I believe that we must be prepared to accept the fact that there may be no Emissary in our time on this earth. Although I respect your belief in our doctrine."

Taijaur: "It is not a matter of what I believe, but rather what will help us to achieve what we aim to accomplish and help our people to reach our destiny."

Alor: "Well, if the Emissary was here then I suppose that his or her presence could help to move us out of our complacency into the fullness of our purpose."

Taijaur: "In addition to leading us back into the world, wouldn't the Emissary also be capable of leading us to the catalyst? Wouldn't it then be possible to fully enter the in-between to make direct access with the power source and re-set the balance of power in this world? We would not have to confine ourselves to the piece-meal method of accessing only the energy available at the portals. Isn't that right?"

Alor: "Perhaps. But Taijaur, I believe that we must rise to our responsibility of going back into the world, with or without an emissary. We must not allow our belief in the concept of an emissary to keep us from fulfilling our purpose as a people."

Taijaur: "Well, the reality of this particular belief may be necessary to galvanize the will of the people. Saba and many of the Ocan truly believe that we can only fulfill our purpose if the Emissary is here to guide us."

Alor: "Ahh yes, your grandmother—our Keeper of the Faith. Her interpretations while in line with the essence of this existence, still may not always translate to this here and now."

Taijaur: "What do you mean by 'Keeper of the Faith'? I am not familiar with this title."

Alor: "It is nothing my son. Your grandmother—our Saba—is a noble and wise woman, rest assured." He paused, squinting his eyes in the direction of the trees below where they walked, "But look, isn't that Kalal, down there at the bottom of the hill?"

In the distance, there was a man stooping down, feeling in the grass and then looking up from time to time to turn his head, leisurely surveying the landscape. They watched as the man rose and began walking towards the forest.

Taijaur: "Yes, I believe that it is my uncle."

They watched as he turned around, and began walking in the opposite direction, then he stopped, seeming to hesitate before walking once more up the hill. Looking down, searching the ground, bending frequently to peer closer into the grass and shrubs.

Alor: "What is he doing?"

Taijaur: "You know Uncle Kalal—he's always like that, searching and searching."

Alor: "What is he searching for?"

Taijaur was slightly taken aback for a moment and then he recalled, "Oh that's right, you most likely would not have heard."

Alor: "Heard what?"

Taijaur: "Uncle Kalal has regressed even further, Master Alor. Despite the crystals and the treatments, over time his condition is only deteriorating more and more."

Alor: "What are his symptoms?"

Taijaur: "Well it's just that he wanders much more, and for longer periods of time and for greater distances. He no longer recognizes any of us for long. He spends most, if not all, of his time now searching, looking for something. Aunt Amira believes that something in the western forest took hold of his mind and his spirit and will not release him."

Alor: "When could Kalal possibly have been in the western forest? He, above all others, obeys and believes in the canon of our people."

Taijaur: "It was the same time that Mala's child was born. Once again, Master Alor, I assumed that you knew all of this. Uncle Kalal was the one who took Mala back into the forbidden lands to escape the decision that had been made for her child."

Alor: "If Kalal even came close to the portals in the western forest, he may never be able to return fully to this land of the living. No one can enter that world without the proper preparation. If his mind has touched the reality of that other world, then this is no ordinary dementia or senility and his troubles may be beyond any ministrations that anyone could hope to offer. But let's speak of this some other time. Here he comes."

Just as he almost neared where they stood, Kalal suddenly turned, going in the opposite direction, never seeming to see or hear the two men. Alor called out as he raised his hand, "Hey, Kalal! Kalal! Over here. Where are you going?"

Kalal stood still, staring at Alor and Taijaur quizzically as they approached him.

Alor: "Have you lost something?"

Kalal: "Huh? uh, lost, uh no... I mean yes." He came close and smiled as Alor grasped his hand and pulled him into an embrace. "I had a thought earlier. And I think that it was an important thought. But I lost it somehow. I was here and it was here this morning before the sun rose. I thought maybe I left it here."

Alor laughed, "I do the same thing some times. It is always a good idea to re-trace your steps in life to see what lost thoughts you may have scattered along the way." He put his arm around Kalal's shoulders and pulled him along with him. "Why don't you come with me and join me for the mid-day meal. I was just about to—"

Suddenly and with great force Kalal pulled away, looking confused for a moment and then angry. "Who are you? Why are you following me? You're trying to abduct me!! Well, I won't let you! Get back!" He snatched Alor's walking stick from his hands and pointed it first at Taijaur and then Alor. "Get away from me or I'll—"

As soon as Kalal turned the stick on Alor, Taijaur immediately sprang into action, grabbing his uncle from behind, he wrapped his arms around him and held him firmly as he spoke directly into his ear, "Uncle Kalal, Uncle Kalal. It's me, Taijaur." He had been waiting for and anticipating any unexpected behavior or movements from his uncle. Alor yanked the stick out of Kalal's hands and threw it on the ground as he came to assist Taijaur in holding Kalal. They were each on either side of Kalal, attempting to hold him by the arms as the bigger man continued to struggle. Even with the combined strength of the two men against one, Kalal was beginning to overpower them both and break away, when Alor began shouting directly into his face.

"Kalal, Kalal! Its your old friend Alor. Look at me. You know me. Look into my face."

He stopped struggling and looked suspiciously at Alor. "What are you trying to do to me?"

Alor: "No one is trying to do anything to you, my friend. I just want to enjoy your company and spend some time with you, the way we used to do in the old days. You remember, don't you, friend? You and I, we always enjoyed long walks, long talks, good food. I'm sorry that I have neglected our friendship these past few years. But look what a beautiful day it is to rediscover an old friend." Alor still held Kalal by one arm as he made an expansive gesture with his other hand towards the sun and the surrounding mountains and terrain.

Taijaur stood on the other side of Kalal nodding and smiling as Alor spoke. Kalal looked around at the countryside and then directed his attention back to Alor with only a trace of suspicion remaining. He began to twist and intertwine his fingers, casting a glance over his shoulder, in the direction of the dark forest trees. He started rambling, repeating the same words over and over, "Can you stop the voices? I see the music. adamas. The eye only hears the song. The music tells. adamas. Can you stop the voices?"

Alor in a low voice to Taijaur, "What is he saying?"

Taijaur: "He repeats these same statements over and over. No one knows exactly why or what he is referring to."

Alor spoke louder directly into Kalal's face, "Kalal, would you like to come with me?

Kalal looked at Alor as if seeing and hearing him for the first time, "Well, she, she, she will need me back. She is expecting me."

Alor: "Don't worry. Amira will like it if you spend time with your old friend Alor. Taijaur, run and tell your Aunt Amira that Kalal will be dining with me this afternoon and that I will walk back with him when our visit is over."

Taijaur whispered, "Are you sure that you can handle him on your own? His mood can change from moment to moment."

Alor: "Don't worry. I'll be fine. Take my stick with you and I will get it from you later. Honor thy Gift, my son."

Taijaur nodded and bowed to both men, "May we be worthy."

Alor turned back to Kalal, his arm across his friend's shoulder and spoke soothingly to him as he led him up the hill. "See it is all settled. We will have a light repast and then I will show you some of my new creations. And you must tell me what you have been working on lately. It will be a good time for us to catch up. I can't even remember the last time that we spent an afternoon together. Remember when—"

Taijaur stood watching the two men, until the sound of Alor's voice began to fade in the distance. He started down the hill and began to dread the thought of facing Amira's strained and worried face. Then he thought that perhaps she might be relieved to have her constant toil and responsibility lifted, even for just one afternoon. Kalal was in good hands with Alor.

Alor now maintained temporary quarters in the Lane, not far from the project sites. When they reached Alor's small one room hut, as soon as they entered the dwelling, Kalal, went before Alor's narrow bed and fell to his knees sobbing. He then began praying out loud, a strange supplication that circled around and around, mixed with the phrases he had repeated earlier and other random pieces of words, such as, "So sorry. Let go. The adamas eye knows." Still kneeling, in the midst of his prayers, Kalal fell into a state of unconsciousness. Alor didn't realize that he was actually sleeping until Kalal fell to one side and began snoring loudly.

He went and knelt beside the larger man, placing his fingers at strategic points on his forehead and temple. He closed his eyes as he began to travel with Kalal into and through a deep dark chasm. Just before Kalal's mind faded into complete emptiness, Alor saw a bright glittering image—an object or symbol of some kind. It was a huge multidimensional geodesic fractal crystal superimposed over shiny wet black rocks. Somehow it looked or rather felt familiar. Tiny light rays made high pitch sounds as they jumped off and back on to the surface of the object. Alor mumbled aloud, "Hmmm. This is very interesting." Then the light flickered to darkness and all sentient thoughts and visions, somnolent or otherwise vanished into the mist. Alor waited awhile to see if the vision, the symbol would return and when the darkness started to feel alarmingly suffocating he began to pull away. Opening his eyes and looking down at Kalal, Alor wondered if this devouring void of sub-consciousness was now a familiar place for the master architect. He prayed that the void had not yet swallowed all of his dreams, or at least, not all of the time.

7. Faith Betrayed

Running, running, running—hard, long and strong. No destination, no purpose; save energy, movement, action, exhilaration, freedom. Forces pulsing through her body, propelling her forward, taking her to no place other than the threshold of existence. Chemicals flowing through her brain and all the muscles in her body—endorphins, dopamine, adrenaline. Mind and movement in concert with forces outside physical awareness. Almost like flying; almost like existing in another dimension of place, another reality, outside of time. Sun, strong and vibrant, slowing sound waves to a deep, undulating throb. Flowing along. Pure motion, pure movement. No effort, no pain; just molecules moving, flowing forward.

Shona was now more woman than child—developing, coming into being. And she spent her days in motion; absolute unadulterated movement, action. She felt alive in a way that had no reason, cause or explanation. And she was more than ready to live, ready for her life—her true life—to begin. It would not surprise her if, one day, her essence, her very atoms jumped out of her body, out of her skin and collided, bombarded into the molecules of all matter within her proximity. She had spent a lifetime waiting and now the moment of her awakening was past due. She now knew that she would have to make her moment happen; that she could no longer wait or depend on anyone outside of herself. It was absolutely imperative, essential that she make her life happen or, or, or—or she would literally explode. Inaction was not an option; indecisiveness no longer a viable excuse.

It was evening time. On the edge of a clearing, behind a thick massive tree of antiquity, Shona crouched low in a stalking position. Her hard muscles taut, yet jumping in anticipation of sudden swift acceleration. Mala held her breath as she watched her daughter's taunting figure, poised, ready to spring. Out of the stillness of the underbrush a quick flash of brown fur darted from the vicinity of the tree and furiously burrowed into the loose dirt surrounding a nearby bush. And just as quickly Shona, moving in smooth liquid motion, dove into the large canine, with high pitch squeals that could not be distinguished from the animal's own sounds of apparent delight.

"I caught you! I caught you!" She wrestled her bounty to the ground as she and the dog continued "speaking" in unison. Untangling themselves, they both rested momentarily, lying down, breathing hard, still caught in the rapture of their playful antics. The small frantic dog that the Grues had left behind had grown into a massive creature, whose head came close to the height of Shona's chest.

No matter how many times Mala witnessed these scenes of Shona interacting with Lubar or even the other creatures of the forest, she still could not ever stop or control the shivers that went through her body, raising the hair on her neck and arms. Lubar had become Shona's constant companion, going everywhere with her, day and night. Years ago, when the dog had first been left on the island, Shona had taught him an impressive call and response routine. Each time that Shona spoke to him, the dog barked in return, in the same cadence, with the same tone and volume.

Mala came down to the stream bank where they rested and spread out the evening meal that she had brought for Shona and herself. Lubar was now, sleeping with his head resting on Shona's lap as she and Mala sat eating and casually talking.

Shona: "Mala, I've been thinking.

Mala: "Hmmmm?

Shona: "In the memories there are many people like us, yet not like us."

Mala: "Everyone is different, Shona."

Shona: "No. What I mean is they are different from me. They feel different as well as look different. Sometimes I go inside of the people that you call family and I feel parts of myself within them but then it is almost as if there is an obstacle of some kind. And there are strange parts to them that I can sense and experience but they don't match certain parts of me."

Mala: "Perhaps the obstacles exist in your ability to search the memories. You are not fully mature. Some things take time to develop."

Shona: "No, Mala, it's not that. I feel the sense of difference so strongly that I cannot be mistaken."

Mala: "Well this may be. However, I fail to see what significance this has."

Very quietly, she speaks, "I feel the difference in you also, Mala."

Mala suppressed her alarm, laughing nervously, "Silly girl, everyone is different. Do you expect to be exactly as your mother in every respect?"

Shona: "You are like them and I am not."

Mala: "Nonsense."

Shona: "Mala, who was my father?"

Calmly, Mala rose and walked further up stream and knelt down to drink from the clear cool water. When she had her fill, she stayed on her knees staring blankly into the trees bordering the opposite side of the stream. Shona came and sat beside her, cautious of her mother's every move. Finally, Mala found her voice, "You were very special to all Ocan."

Shona: "You've told me that before."

Mala: "No child could have been more welcomed or more loved than you."

Shona: "Mother I have heard these stories countless times, and—"

Mala: "Like a rare treasure they—"

Shona: "'Reveled in the glory of my existence.' And when I was born, it was foretold that my birth signaled a time of renewal when the Ocan people would begin to rise to the destiny of their purpose. I know these stories like I know my life. 'And there was no grief as great as that which was felt when you decided to take me from the Ocan settlement to live in this forest land. But the people are preparing for the time of my return and there will be great joy and celebration.' These fairy tales are irrelevant, Mala. Please answer my question."

Mala: "You are as much Ocan as I am."

Shona: "I cannot feel his presence amongst the people of the Ocan. I know he was not of your kind. But who was he?"

Mala: "Is that so important?"

Shona: "To me it is."

Mala: "Why?"

Shona: "I must know."

Mala: "I don't know."

Shona: "**What** don't you know?"

Mala: "I don't know who he was."

Shona: "How can that be?"

Mala: "I knew his love. I knew his song. But his story was not of my world, our world. He tried to share it, but I couldn't capture it."

Shona: "Give me your memories."

Mala: "No."

Shona: "Why not?"

Mala: "They are my own."

Shona: "And he was a part of me."

Mala: "He is dead now."

Shona: "Let his memory live through me."

Mala: "Maybe when you have lived longer you will understand."

Shona: "Mala, what is it that you fear?"

When her mother did not respond, Shona went on, "I can understand your needs for your life. But Mala, mother, what right did you have to make these decisions of loneliness and solitude for me, for my life? I need friends. I need family."

Mala: "You need no one but yourself."

Shona: "And you I suppose."

Mala: "What do you mean?"

Shona: "By choice you subsist on your own care and giving. But all of my life, you have provided for me, loved and nurtured me to the extent that I feel crippled and smothered by your care and giving. All of my life I have had to live through your memories, your thoughts, your sensations, your people. You asked me once why the Gruenatarings meant so much to me. They were the first and only people in my life, thus far, who have been wholly mine to experience on my own. I could see them with my own eyes; touch them, hear them, smell them. For the first time in my life I did not need your memories to know what it is to feel."

Mala was quiet as Shona continued, "Mala if you want to live this half-life—deserted, isolated—with no contact with like beings, then that is your prerogative. But you will live it without me. Mala, I am going back to the Ocan, back to your people and make them truly my own. Back to our home.

Mala: "Oh Shona!! Shona, Shona." Her face could not mask the distress and apprehension that she felt.

Shona: "Mother please forgive the harshness of my words. But understand how selfish and cruel this life is that you have imposed upon me. I want to live.

And living means loving, and laughing, and touching and being; all the things that humans give to one another and share with each other. You know that one day I would like to become a healer. But in case you have not noticed, there is no one here for whom my services are needed."

Her demeanor and tone softened as she looked at her mother's anguished face. "You have loved and reared me well, mother and I am thankful. Now it is time for me to share that love with others; to be a part of a family that is divisible by a number greater than one. Come with me, Mala—back to life in the Ocan villages. Let us be of use to the people who love and hold us so dear. I know that something happened that makes you fearful of returning. But these people are our family. I'm sure that, what ever happened before, they have forgiven you by now. It will be all right, just—what? What is it Mother?"

Mala had buried her head in her hands. She moaned aloud as she continued to mutter, "Oh Shona, Shona, Shona."

Lubar awoke with a start and began suddenly and ferociously barking before bolting up and charging off. He ran up stream towards the falls. Shona cupped her hand around her mouth and issued a high pitch, high frequency sound that Mala could barely hear. Shona tilted her head, listening as Lubar could be heard barking in response from a distance. Shona made another motion with her mouth, but this time Mala could detect no sound. However, she could hear Lubar's sharp frantic reply. Shona sighed, exasperated as she got up and started in the direction that he had gone. "I'll be back."

Mala didn't wait. She walked quickly back to their shelter in the trees, with the night unfolding and spreading out all around her. When she reached the tent, she felt a sense of relief as she sat down, cross-legged and weary upon her make-shift mattress. She felt the coming night begin to lift away her defenses and her need for defense. She was left ecstatically vulnerable to the approaching darkness that carried her release from all worry, tension and stress. Breathing in deeply, she left her surface behind and began to touch familiar sources of sustaining energy embodied as lover and then child. She began to listen closely to lyrical voices and visions that whispered softly in her mind. Mala felt herself being pulled back to that night that her child had come into this world. She was there, in the birthing hut, holding her just born infant, and she had closed her eyes so that she could better hear the voices in her memory that intoned Ocan tales of another such darkness that had come long before this opaque here and now.

Then suddenly she was there in the past, not just seeing it, but actually there, existing in the time and space of a forgotten memory, a distant time. She sat back on the birth mat weary with fatigue, talking with Saba. She felt her heart beating fast with fear as she listened to Saba. There were sounds outside of the birthing hut that made her suppress her growing sense of panic just as the Obeah came through the door. She felt herself once more pulled into a silent vibration that moved through every part of her body. She rose from the earth with a light shining from her core into the darkness of space. When her body and her consciousness exploded into a thousand pieces of light, surface perceptual reality came forth and forced Mala to open her eyes and stop seeing. Only this time, the emptiness did not erupt inside of her and she knew what she had to do.

Mala rose with clarity and resolution, allowing forces beyond her control to lead her directly to Shona who sat in the dark on a rocky ledge near the tarn on the other side of the water fall. Those same forces opened her mouth and released the words that, at times, even she could not fathom. Mala did not stop talking for hours, and when she finished there were no more words, nothing left unsaid. Only the sound of the falling water could be heard as the full moon cast a bright white light over the black shiny wet rocks, reflecting off of the surface of the tarn in that safe enclosed surreal world. Shona sat still in the quiet darkness, until her mother reached out, stroked her arm and whispered, "Shona?"

Shona's voice was barely audible. "Go away Mala. Please just go away." She complied with her daughter's request and left her sitting there late into the night. Lubar lie at a distance from Shona, making no sound and staring at his friend with a look of unmistakable comprehension that something had changed and all was not as it had once been.

She was too stunned to cry. Faith betrayed, Shona's emotions and deepest sense of injustice lay open, wet and festering. She was wounded by her own capacity to feel and trust. The same conviction and trust that had nurtured her soul and fed its growth, was now violently, against her will, stripped away. A sacred bond of hope and belief had been irrevocably violated. Mala's words were not kind; her message left no room for comfort or confusion. A once hidden truth, forcefully revealed, charts its own destructive course with no destination and with no mind to what may lie in its path. And Shona felt deeply and bitterly betrayed. The pillars, the foundation of her once stable world, lay crumbling around her; her whole life inert under and amidst the rubble. She had absolutely no idea how to re-build herself or her beliefs. Because what she could not articulate, nor even understand fully, was simply this—beyond the injustice of senseless acts of betrayal lay the more frightening reality of a more potent universal lack of order; that mindless malevolent beast of chaos that lurks beyond eternal space, always threatening to disrupt the balance and divine order of our thoughts, precepts and reasons for being.

Now she knew that there were no people that she could call her own; no place to go, no one to see, love or hold. And for the first time in her life she felt completely and utterly alone. She lie down in that rocky hard place and closed her eyes to sleep. Lubar came and pushed his warm body against hers, laying his muzzle on her abdomen, still staring into her face.

Mala was awake for most of the night, forced fully into a present here and now, where everything around her seemed louder, brighter. She had been jolted by her daughter's pain out of the reverie of meditation that had become her daily life. In the morning, Shona found her mother waiting for her in their familiar place down by the lower stream. Lubar stayed close by her side, walking slowly and carefully as he and Shona approached Mala, and sat down next to her. Both females stared into the flowing water saying nothing for the first few moments. And then Shona broke the quiet. "Why didn't you let me die?"

Mala: "Shona, you are my child."

Shona: "But, why did you let me live? Why Mala, why? What did I do to them?

Mala: "It is the past. It cannot touch us now."

Shona: "Perhaps I was meant for another time. How can you be so sure that it was not a mistake to let me live?"

Mala: "Your wealth, the meaning of your existence, can never be measured by another's acceptance or rejection of you. In the absence of all other knowledge, know this one truth well. You are blessed with life. Inherent in that blessing lies your worth. No one can take from you the self-knowledge of purpose and validity on this earth. It is your one true possession. And only from this truth may all your other life-blessings be born. It is sacrilegious to doubt the worthiness of divinely created gifts. No man's measuring device is fit to discern your worth. We are blessed with God's wisdom and grace from birth. My mistake was this fumbled attempt to give you a sense of your people; to know them in a way that they, perhaps, do not understand themselves."

They were both quiet for a long time, listening to the water and the sounds of birds and other animals nearby. After awhile Shona calmly said, "This day I have spoken with my father." Her words and their meaning settled into the stillness of the air. She waited for Mala's reaction and then went on, saying, "You know that he is here. Why deny his presence?"

Mala still offered no response and continued staring into the flowing stream.

Shona: "Must he present himself in the form and fashion that brings you comfort? Why can't you love him as he is?"

Mala: "I do love him."

Shona: "But you deny his existence."

Mala: "Shona, he is dead!"

Shona: "No mother, he has only changed form."

Mala: "I cannot accept anything so incomprehensible. It is contrary to all that I know of life. Shona, you must close your mind to such thoughts or you will lose your grasp on what is real."

Shona: "And I say you must open yourself to it or you will never know what is real. You can not continuously allow fear to prescribe your boundaries of reality."

Mala: "Okay, if he is truly here, why can't I see him, touch him, feel him?"

Shona: "Because your fear allows you to acknowledge only that which falls into your pre-conceived notions of reality. But he is here whether you accept the reality of his presence or not."

Mala rose and paced nervously. "Shona, you must stop this! It is not healthy for your mind."

Shona: "And so we return once more to this fear of yours."

Mala looked at her hard and said in a low tense voice, "You don't even know what fear is." She looked away and then defiantly she turned back to face her daughter. "Okay, if that is the label that you would give me then I will wear it with honor. For you I traded my freedom for my fear—so that you might live and know this world. If it is my fear that you despise, then know that your loathing can go no deeper than my own. But also know that it is this very fear that you despise, that has kept you alive as I, alone, could never have done."

Shona: "Then you admit that it is a legacy of fearfulness that you bequeath me?"

Mala: "No, not fearfulness—just the opposite. Fear on behalf of her child is a mother's motivating instinct. It inspires her beyond all that is humanly possible into the realm of the impossible in order to conquer any obstacle that would stand between her child and its survival. My fear acts only as a front guard for the power that was siphoned from my being into yours. And it is this power—whose development I must guard—that will propel you into the world to meet your destiny.

There is no mystery as to why so many women die in childbirth. The female must labor to retain a residual amount of her power in order to sustain her continued existence, while the vast stores of her personal power are sucked away by the spirit of the new life. Sometimes both are lost in the struggle and sometimes just the new life can not manifest. It is a delicate balance, this giving and receiving of personal power. That is until the day that the power returns to you—magnified and multiplied to fill the broader spaces left within. This returning power comes with a deeper capacity to give and receive love, understanding, and compassion."

Although Shona heard her mother's words, she made no reply and instead returned to her original subject of inquiry. "If he is dead, then show me where his body is buried."

Mala: "There was no body, he burned to death."

Shona: "How did the fire start?"

Mala: "There was no fire. It was an electrical storm that seemed to come from the ground, not the sky. It was an overcast day, but there was no rain, no thunder, and no lightning—until suddenly stray anomalous bolts of electricity blasted out of nowhere and took him away. They took him away from me and I was alone. The storms brought him here and the storms took him away.

There was no evidence anywhere that he had even existed. After awhile, I began to doubt my own mind. There are no other people on this island outside of the settlements on the eastern side of the island. He was the only other human that I have ever encountered. I began to wonder if it was all some fantasy, some mysterious, supernatural dream. When I found that I carried you inside, then I knew that there had been no dream. So, I tried to go back to the Ocan villages; to my friends, my family; to Saba, but, well, you already know the rest of that story."

Shona: "And do you know nothing else of his origins?"

Mala: "No, nothing."

Shona: "But if I could search through your memories—"

Mala: "Please Shona, just leave that alone for now. One day, when I am strong enough, I will give you the memories. But please don't ask that of me now."

Shona: "But Mala, you have known all along what I am, yet you refuse to admit it. Even worse you refuse to face it openly, acknowledge it in your conscious mind. Yet somehow you must know."

Mala sighed heavily, offering no response as she rubbed her forehead with her fingertips, her eyes closed.

Shona: "Which is it mother—are you ashamed of me or ashamed of yourself for helping to bring forth a being such as myself?"

Mala: "Shona, I will not play this game with you. Just as there is more to life than you can fathom, there is more to the mystery of who you are than you can know at this stage of your development."

Shona: "Why can't you at least talk about this?"

Mala: "All right, then what are you?"

Shona: "Something other than human."

Mala said nothing as she rose, turned her back and began to walk away.

Shona shouted after her, "What life can I lead, Mother? What people will accept me as their own?"

Mala stopped and turned to face her daughter as Shona continued shouting, "What man will ever be my mate? You knew that I could never claim even the most basic of human existence as my own, yet you thought it a mercy to let me live?"

Mala still made no reply as she stood still staring at her daughter.

Shona: "All beings of this earth, human and otherwise, possess what I do not. And I marked as perhaps no other human, what life—"

Mala: "Shona, don't do this. Please. I beg of you. Stop and consider what you are saying, what you are feeling."

Shona: "Well what of this mark—does it signify my paternal heritage?"

Mala: "No, Shona. It is just an anomaly of birth. Everyone has unique markings of one kind or another."

Shona: "Maybe not so prominently displayed."

Mala walked slowly back to the stream bank. "Shona what has happened to make you question and doubt yourself in such a negative manner?"

Shona: "It's not a matter of negative doubts, Mother. I am just trying to understand—what is this world, and how do I fit into it. I cannot allow fabrications to continue to rule my reality."

Mala: "Shona I have expressed my regret for not telling you the truth sooner. I just thought that, well—"

Shona: "Mala it's not really anything that you have said that upsets me. It is my own willingness and desire to be deluded that frightens me. I believed in the things that you told me because I wanted to believe, because I needed to believe. I overlooked all the obvious contradictions and discrepancies in your fairy tales, because I wanted those stories to be real. Something in my mind could sense and feel the illogical of what you presented, but I pushed all that aside so that I could hang on to the unreal world of love and acceptance that you attempted to create for me. What sense did it make for me to do this? I don't understand this need in me to hold onto a false belief even in the face of facts and reality to the contrary."

Mala: "Shona, let it go. Some things, some pieces of knowledge come to you as you go along. And some things, purely and simply, don't matter."

Shona: "But they matter to me and I want to understand. I wonder, do all humans indulge in self-delusion, in lying to themselves, believing in things that deep down they know to be false, but needing, somehow to still believe."

Mala: "I don't know, but I suspect that maybe if not all humans," she smiled, "then just most."

Shona: "But why? What purpose does it serve to believe in false realities even when your mind tells you that they are not true?"

Mala: "It's a survival mechanism, I suppose. The need to believe may be one of the strongest forces that keeps us alive. Without belief in something, even a fantasy, then life has no meaning, no reason to go on."

Shona: "But this is dangerous—this need to believe in things that are unreal to the extent that we rationalize and push away the more uncomfortable parts of life that are, indeed, real."

Mala: "It's only dangerous if you allow it to go too far or if you allow your fantasies to dominate your sense of reality. But in terms of the actual realities of the world—who is there to say what is real versus what is not real? Which is the truer reality—that which we create for ourselves, or that which is created for us by others? For the most part, we attach meaning to our lives with the stories that we create or those that are constructed for us by our societies, our governments and our religions. The stories tell us how to live and what we value and sometimes they even determine how we die or what we are willing to die for. Many times wars are waged on the basis of competing stories, competing ways of defining reality and what life should be. To a certain extent how we feel in life—from joy and happiness to sadness and depression—derives from the extent to which we believe that the outside world coincides with the stories that we live by.

Our sense of belief props up our faith and our hope. Sometimes when we peek behind the stories and see that they are just propped up pages of our own construction then we potentially lose this faith and hope. When the stories are stripped away, we are sometimes left without a foundation to our lives, because our belief loses its power and the meaning of our daily lives no longer has the same significance. But stripping away the stories—either those given to us from others or those created by our need—can also allow us the possibility to create a worldview that is based on a fundamental truth that comes to us through the natural world of this existence."

They were both quiet for a few moments, each lost in their own thoughts, and then Mala looked at her daughter with a profound sense of sadness. "Shona what has happened to us? We have always had such peace and harmony between us. I don't understand what is happening to us now. And why all of this sudden need and interest in having a father? Haven't we always been family to and for one another?"

Shona: "Not 'us', not 'we'—but me. Something is happening to me. And I am only beginning to understand it myself. I am becoming my own person, separate from your design and your plan. Our past relations were peaceful and harmonious because of my compliance with your will. Now I want to discover my own will, my own way. I want my own life, Mala. Is that so bad? And I have no great need for a father or even family. I am only trying to understand who and what I am—the source material from which I am made."

Mala: "With all the time and energy that I have devoted to your development and well-being, how is it that your thoughts can come to rest on some absent male figure as essential to your understanding and acceptance of yourself?"

Shona: "Because I am different Mala. Different from every other human on this island and perhaps even, every other human in this world. Different from those that I would call my own. Different from you. This 'absent male figure' is the most logical missing piece of the puzzle to help me understand this difference. This has nothing to do with a need for a father; just a need to understand. If my difference was some minor personality quirk or mere physical abnormality, then no explanation would be necessary. If there were others with internal structures that match my own, then the need to understand would not be as great. I just need to know, that's all, Mala."

Mala: "It is those Gruenatarings that have made you so, so hard, so defensive and questioning of your own worth."

Shona: "Mala, they left this island years ago and they were here for less than a month."

Mala: "Still, they were the only other humans with whom you have had contact, and they made their impact felt. Their affect and influence was magnified because of its singularity in your experiences. Their affect was perhaps triple that of all other experiences that were a regular part of your daily life."

Shona: "Mala, did you think that by keeping me isolated that you could mold me into the exact person that you want me to be? Or at least the type of person that makes you feel most comfortable?"

Mala made no response, as she put her head down, hoping to hide the stunned expression on her face.

Shona: "Face it Mala, we all grow up eventually. And like it or not, part of growing up is forming my own opinions, becoming my own person—separate and different from who and what you are. I want to find where I belong in this world. I am not like you Mala. I don't want to live alone. I want to live with and around other people. I want to be a part of other people's lives and let them be a part of mine."

They sat listening to the sound of the trickling stream with Lubar lying between them twitching ever now and then as he chased in his sleep.

Shona: "Mala, I have decided to leave. I have decided to go to the mainland."

Mala: "The mainland? What? Do you mean that you are leaving the island? How can that be? Where would you go?"

Shona: "Yes, that is what I mean. Would you have me stay here indefinitely with no place to go and no one to call my own?"

Mala continued to stare at Shona, saying nothing.

Shona: "Say something Mala. Why are you just sitting there?"

Mala, hesitantly, "I was just thinking, well, you know Shona, you and I, we *could* try to go back to the Ocan settlements; together, you and I. Enough time has passed and surely many, probably most, if not all of the people have forgotten about the past. We can devise a strategy, a plan and enlist the help of Saba and Kalal, and there are even others who would help us. We could even try going first to the Haman village or the—"

Shona shook her head slowly. "No Mala, at this point that is not only impossible, but not even desirable. I am content with my own plan to leave this island and find a life for myself in another place."

Mala: "But Shona you should not be so hasty in making this decision. All people need time to grow, to evolve into their higher selves. Perhaps the Ocan people—well, perhaps our time to return has come. I see now, that it has been wrong of me to not at least try to return to the settlements. You deserve to know your people, your family; to connect with humans other than myself. Your were right when you said that I have been selfish—"

Shona: "Mala, I'm sorry. I didn't mean—"

Mala: "No, no, no. You were right. This life, free as it may be, leaves much to be desired. And companionship, social interactions are necessities in many, probably most, people's lives. My own needs in that area are low, but now I, I, I understand, because, because...I know...how much...how much I need you."

For the first time that Shona could remember her mother looked small, weak and vulnerable. She said softly, "But can't you see Mala, you don't really need me. And that is good. Oh, I don't doubt your love for me or even your dependence on my presence and occasionally, maybe even my direct companionship. But overall, your needs are vested in your studies, your writing, your meditations and the questions that you pursue. And I repeat—this is good. People and companionship are necessary to our lives. However, I don't think that it is spiritually or psychologically healthy to primarily depend upon the close presence of another person in your life (or other people) in order to feel whole. This doesn't negate the need for others. It's just that this need should not become the primary or all-consuming paramount need of a person's existence. The love of and need for others should be just one part, one dimension of the complex web of all needs that makes us human and whole.

From all that I have read and studied, it seems that an all-consuming need for another person or other people can become a major stumbling block to an individual's spiritual development and evolution. Moreover, it seems that a singular focus on the need for a loved one reflects an empty hole in one's own psyche or sense of well-being.

But you're not like that at all. You primarily feed your soul not with my love or existence, but with the creative flow of the universe. And don't worry, I don't mind being second or even third or fourth on your list of needs. I plan to be the same way, in that I will never allow my need for another person to interfere with my purpose on this earth."

Mala looked at Shona with a concerned puzzled expression. "If I were you, I might wait awhile before coming to any firm conclusions in this area. Needs and love are not always within our control and they do not always follow the dictates of our wishes or our judgment. But understand that my concern is not primarily for my own needs, but for your safety Shona; for your continued well-being as you seek to reach your destiny."

Shona: "But can't you see that my destiny lies away from this island, not just because of my own needs for family and companionship, but because I also feel compelled to seek answers. Can't you see that this quest of mine is not much different from the journey that you have undertaken all of your life? This is what you have taught me—to seek higher and higher for truths that may lie beyond that which is apparent; beyond the surface."

Mala: "But Shona, I never left this island. No Ocan in our history that I know of has ever left this island. And I was much older than you before I even dreamed of venturing away from the Ocan settlements."

Shona: "Well, perhaps I am to continue where your journey left off. And my age is irrelevant. Besides, who knows, perhaps I will find other beings such as myself."

Mala: "At least if you were older, you would have had more time to develop and learn. There is so much more that I planned to tell you and to teach you. You don't know what the world out there is like; what the people are like. You don't know the rules or the history. You have no idea how to survive in other environments or even what the nature of those environments may be."

Shona: "Mala, I can learn about the people, their rules, their history best by being there with them. And I will be cautious. I know how to take care of myself."

Mala: "And what of the plague that engulfs this world Shona? What of the virus that led our people to this isolated existence? How will you guard yourself against any potential infection?"

Shona: "Well, according to my beloved 'people', I am already infected or a potential source of contagion. Besides, Mala how do we even know that such a disease exists? How do we know that the founders of Ocan society did not have their own reasons for coming to this land and the story of a contagion was just used as a ploy to ensure group adherence to their plan? Why can't you view my quest to go to the mainland as part of my injera in the same way that you once said my desire to be saba was most likely a result of my injera?"

Mala sighed heavily, "I don't know what to say Shona. It seems that no matter what argument I propose, your mind is set to pursue the path that you have chosen."

She sighed again. "Well if this quest is truly a part of your injera then you won't be satisfied until you have fulfilled its purpose."

Shona: "You never finished fully explaining the principles of injera."

Mala: "I guess I always assumed that we would have years to discuss all of these concepts and more." She sighed heavily again and then said, "You can begin to understand the principles of injera by remembering that humans exemplify three basic types of needs—for love, survival, and power. Although this need for power is really a need for transcendence, but it is many times understood or interpreted as a need for power. All other types of needs are derived from these three fundamental categories of need. The attributes of these needs form our understanding of what is necessary for the sustenance and sustainability of life on earth. For example, the need for water, food, and shelter are integral parts of our basic survival needs. The need for love is a part of a greater need to give and receive.

We are taught that the first principle of injera is that life <u>must give</u> to life; the second principle is that life must go on and never end; the third and final principle is that each entity of life must ultimately transcend its own discrete boundaries and fuse with the primal source of existence. In addition to the principles of injera there are also stages or phases of injera—from need-manifest to need-fulfilled—as humans move from feelings of emptiness, desire, seeking, and desperation to reason, calm, purpose, and satisfaction. And these need categories are not mutually exclusive. These needs form a reticulum of overlapping and intertwining emotions and desires."

Shona: "Do you think that these same principles apply to all the creatures that inhabit the earth?"

Mala: "That is what the Ocan believe. In one way or another all living entities experience the stages of injera. Life and the mere act of existing necessitate a pursuit of need-fulfillment—psychological, emotional, and spiritual needs as well as chemical and biological needs.

However, you must keep in mind Shona, this planet is populated by many sentient and sapient beings that are alien to the human species. And thus, there is no way for us to make assumptions about the needs of beings that we have never observed. They remain hidden, cloaked from human awareness sometimes as a result of our own ignorance, fear and need for dominion. Still they are all here—within the depths of our forests, the darkness of the ocean waters and even in the environments that we inhabit daily and believe that we know fully. You must be very careful as you travel into unfamiliar territory. One need not ever leave this planet to encounter alien species or secret strange new worlds."

Mala then started speaking rapidly and nervously, "One other thing Shona. This is something that I have never spoken of before, so listen carefully. You are very different from the people of this mainland, despite the fact that you may share with them a common physiognomy and genetic source. Our Gift has made us fundamentally different from any—"

Shona: "I know all this Mala, you have told me this before. I'm older now Mala, you don't have to worry. I won't make the same mistakes that I made with the Gruenatarings. I realize that the power of the land is in our spirit, in our blood and the very cells of our body. After generations of living here, eating the plants, fruits and vegetation, the Ocan people have enhanced abilities that make us stronger than most other humans."

Mala: "Yes, Shona that is part of it. But our Gift is also much more than the surface attributes that the land has given to the Ocan people. It is also what the Ocan people have been able to cultivate and change as a result of the Gift and these changes have been bred into each successive generation."

Shona: "I don't understand. What do you mean cultivated and changed?"

Mala: "Shona, please just let it suffice that you are fundamentally a different kind of person than anyone you will ever encounter outside of the Ocan."

Shona: "Well of course, with my paternal lineage, I am most likely an entirely different type of human than any of the people who populate these nearby lands."

Mala: "No, you are fully human. Your paternal source did not take this away from you."

Mala looked thoughtful for a moment and then said, "But, yes, yes that's it—your paternal heritage makes you different most likely in terms of natural genetic variation that occurs in all populations or groups of people. This is what you must bear in mind as you venture into this new land."

Shona: "But what is this that you were saying about the Ocan people changing and cultivating?"

Mala: "Oh, never mind that. I mis-spoke. Just keep in mind and remember that because of your paternal genetic makeup, you are biologically different from the other people that you will encounter. And there are certain considerations that must be taken into account as a result of these differences."

Shona: "But Mala you were saying something about what the Ocan people have done that has affected successive generations of people on this island? Don't all groups of people have genetic variations that differ from other groups?"

Mala: "Shona, please let that go for now. Just forget what I said. It's not important and it is too much to go into now. Besides I don't even know how true those old stories are. When you come back to the island, then you may be able to gauge, on your own, the validity of the stories that the Ocan have told over the centuries.

For now, it is important that you focus on the fact that you are different from the mainlanders and this difference must necessarily limit the type of interactions that you have with them. That is what is most essential for you to know as you prepare to go amongst these people that are not your own."

Shona: "What makes you so sure that I plan to return?"

Mala was startled for a moment. She rose and started back towards their shelter. She spoke over her shoulder as she continued walking, "I am not ever sure of anything. I just always hope."

Shona caught up with her mother and asked, "Mala, what will you do once I am gone? Will you be okay?"

Mala: "I suppose that I will do what I have always done—create, live, absorb life and its diversity of meaning."

Shona: "But where will you go? You shouldn't stay here by yourself. You can come with me, if you want. The boat is big enough for two people. I would have asked you sooner, but I know how you and the other Ocan feel about leaving this island."

Mala: "No, Shona. Thank you for the invitation, but my life is here on this island. I have no desire to see any other part of the world. I will probably go back to the Ocan. Where else is there for me to go? I suppose that it may now be time that I returned once again."

Shona: "Where will you stay?"

Mala: "Don't worry Shona. I will be fine. Saba will always make room for me."

Shona: "You are fortunate to have friends and family to turn to and call your own."

Mala: "These are your people as well."

Shona: "They don't even know me."

Mala: "They know more than you think. And you know as well as I that physical presence is only one dimension of reality. Out of all the means of sharing understanding and feeling in this world—those dependent upon physical presence and spoken words are perhaps the most limited. In the quiet of your soul and your mind listen and feel all that they send to you, all that they are."

Shona: "Stop this Mala!"

Mala: "Shona you know that you hear and feel them as clearly as I do. Why are you so willing to believe in the voices of the dead and yet deny the communication of the living?"

Shona: "I have put away the play things of my childhood. These Ocan fairy tales of sentiale awareness have done nothing but help to keep me in a deluded reality; believing the world was what I wanted it to be. Belief in the unseen, untouchable world of sentiale has kept me from facing the realities of life as it is."

Mala: "But you can't blame your sentiale when life turns out to be other then what you expected. Sentiale sensations have nothing to do with positive or negative perceptions of life. You can't just bury your sentiale. You can't suppress it and just hope that the sensations and the understanding will go away."

Shona: "I can choose to focus on the reality of this world where concrete objects shape the space and time of the one legitimate and tangible realm of physical matter. I can choose to not participate in the delusional dream realities of the Ocan people. I am not Ocan and I can approach life in a way other than the Ocan way."

Mala: "Oh Shona, you can't believe that life is so one dimensional. I know that your sentiale abilities are more powerful than perhaps you now realize. One day they will not be so hard to control."

Shona: "Mala, please just let this go."

Mala: "Well, I suppose I can only hope that one day you will feel differently. But one other thing Shona—you have to make sure to never speak of the existence of the Ocan—the island or the people. As far as the people of the mainland know, this island is uninhabitable or nonexistent. They must never suspect any differently. You must discover some area of that mainland that you can claim as your source of origin. You must claim no knowledge of this place."

Shona: "I know Mala. If I don't know any other rule, I know that one well."

The next morning they took down the shelter that had kept them safe and dry and they divided the possessions that they each planned to carry, wrapped and rolled on their backs. They burned the remainder of their belongings that were either too heavy or too cumbersome to bear. As the sun rose, they walked down to the rocky shoreline, where Shona loaded her meager supplies in her vessel that was moored in the rocks. It was made of balsa and spider silk and looked like an ancient ketch, with two white masts. Mala cleared her throat, her rehearsed words rising in her mind, struggling to come out.

Shona: "Will you take Lubar with you and keep him until I return?"

Mala: "Oh, so you do plan to return?"

Shona smiled, "Perhaps. Who knows? One day I may chance this way again."

Mala: "Shona, I think that it is best that Lubar accompany you on this trip. You will need the protection and company that he will provide. Besides, this beast obeys no commands but your own." She reached down and ruffled his head as he looked up at her, wagging his tail. "I doubt that he would follow me or anyone besides yourself."

Shona glanced around to make sure all of her supplies were on the boat, "Well, I guess that's it."

Mala gazed into her daughter's eyes as she stroked her face and hair. Her sentiale had always poured out her emotions, and now her mind, full of words, would not sanction her ability to speak.

Shona: "Don't be sad Mala. I'll be okay."

Mala nodded her head with tears spilling down her cheeks as they both stood silently holding one another. No matter how much Mala tried to push the words out, they would not come. Each time she opened her mouth she succeeded in only whispering, "Shona...".

Shona embraced her mother one last time and then started walking down into the surf. Mala steadied her resolve, determined to offer some final words that would keep her safe and one day bring her home. She hesitated for a moment and then said simply, "Stay strong, Shona." Shona turned and looked at her mother, feeling a multitude of unspoken words and emotions spilling out and through the tone of her mother's voice.

Long after Shona was out of sight, having sailed into the horizon, Mala still watched from the shore, following her daughter from inside her mind, inside her emotions into the waves. And for the first time in years, Shona, openly and freely welcomed her mother into her soul. Mala could feel the warm penetrating sunlight, the splash of the cool ocean water and the exhilaration, the freedom of molecules expanding, flowing, into another place, another reality. This was almost like existing in a dimension of space outside of time. Mala rode the waves of this triumphant power, this energy of pure motion, flowing forward until a sudden unexpected sense of yearning pulled her down into the murky sea. When she surfaced, she found herself standing alone on the shore, wrapped in the memory of forces pulsing through her body, propelling her forward, taking her to a place where she could not ever venture, not even in her dreams.

8. Keeper of the Faith

She walked alone, feeling tired and heavy, through the morning fog with errant thoughts weighing her down but never coalescing enough to bring forth meaning or resolve. Saba had managed to slip away before that worrisome girl—that want-to-be-apprentice—Layal had found her. She hurried along the dense forest path, having chosen the long way around to the temple, hoping to avoid Amira, Layal and anyone else who might require her to give something that she had not the power to give.

Saba put her head down to shield her eyes from the gusting streams of air that carried subdued calls of myriad bird species moving in Doppler-shift waves as they flew away and toward the vicinity where she walked. The season would soon shift to cooler temperatures and the earth's gravity was beginning to exert a stronger pull. Saba felt her bones weighing heavier in her body calling her to rest and move more slowly. At night, she was lured into deeper and deeper dreams that she could not understand.

In the distance, there were sounds like thunder coming from the area of the largest mountain of the northeast range. Saba tried concentrating, thinking hard—she was lost in her thoughts for a moment, trying to remember, once again, why her constant and familiar sense of despair weighed on her more heavily today of all days. She could not recall exactly why she needed to go to the temple; only that it was necessary and that there was something at the temple that she needed. Her thoughts struggled, pushing her consciousness toward and away from that which she wished to remember and that from which her heart compelled her to flee.

The temple had long ago become the sole province of Saba and occasionally the Obeah who descended alone into the deeper caverns. The Ocan people had stopped coming to this sacred site decades ago, although it had once been for them a place of worship, prayer and quiet contemplation. Someone had once reported ill effects from the gas vapors that arose from the underground caverns and ever since then the people had stayed away. Now all of their communal rituals and spiritual observances were held in the Maja. Only Saba still made a daily sojourn to this ancient structure that was the first testament to Ocan society built on the island centuries ago. The Saba had never felt anything except minor bouts of dizziness from time to time, but this was not enough to keep her away. Many in the younger generation did not even know of the temple's existence. She couldn't understand why the people no longer found it necessary to walk along the temple's sacred pathways or to bathe in the healing streams of the caverns. The grounds, gardens and courtyards around the temple were now overgrown with vines and vegetation that covered and obscured some of the paved pathways and the stone walls that surrounded the enclosed spaces.

As she neared the garden near the entrance to the temple caverns, something made Saba turn and look behind, searching. She felt a certain and sure presence, as if someone was staring directly at her. But she saw no one and nothing, except the trees and foliage blowing in the wind. Layal would no doubt be looking for her, hounding her. Despite Saba's insistence that saba-healing could not be taught, Layal was the latest and the last (the Saba swore to that) of a series of young women the Elders sent to the healer-woman in the hope of finding a potential vessel for the necessary transfer of saba-energy. Now, it seemed that every time that Saba turned around that girl was there, bumping into her or tripping over her own feet. While most of the would-be-saba had fled in less than a month's time, Layal had now overlooked and endured the Saba's irascible nature and impatient outbursts for more than a year. She never seemed deterred or dissuaded by Saba's continual muttering about the ineptitude of these "would-be-saba" who, according to Saba, had no notion of being transformed by a calling from the essence of their own souls.

The Saba went through the rusted creaking gate into the garden where there was a small area of burial plots with the graves of some past generations of the Ocan. There was a mausoleum-like building with large pillars around open entryways on the front and back of this portico structure. Although she knew that no one else was present, she still quickly surveyed the area around her before straining to push a large stone away from a hidden crevice in the wall behind one of the front pillars of the stone building. From the revealed cavity, she retrieved a large antiquated hard-bound book with thick pages that were yellow and brown with age yet somehow neither fragile, nor worn. She sat on the stone bench in front of the empty building and opened the heavy book on her lap.

The book is called, <u>Journal of the Saba</u>—meaning "saba" in the plural as well as singular sense. As in the collective assemblage of all persons who were one in the spirit of saba throughout time and also that one distinctive saba, who appeared in whatever age and time considered itself the present here and now. That one saba, who with each generation, bore responsibility for keeping the journal, nurturing it and passing it on. It had been passed down through the millennia, each new saba adding her thoughts, feelings, advice and counsel, while also seeking from the book the guidance and sense of comfort that the words would always bring.

Saba felt the words on the page begin to guide her mind as she read aloud from the journal. The sounds around her—the birds, the breeze, the insects—all seemed to stand still listening to the strong voice of the book that, despite its age, was still very much alive. "When we lose or refuse to accept our sense of purpose, our minds and souls become prey to a whirlwind of random chaos. From this chaos, a desperate false sense of hope is born; created from beliefs outside of life's deeper structures of knowing and feeling." As she puzzled the meaning of the words on the page, her eyes fell away from the text and she found herself staring at the grave markings of a burial plot in front of her.

Without warning, the knowledge from which the healer-woman had fled rushed into and through her thoughts, overflowing in her heart. It came to her with a stabbing intake of breath, and she fell back against the wall behind her, trying to push away the grief that began to overwhelm her senses. Saba had come to the temple today to read, seek solace and find a way through her despair. For today they had told her of Kalal. Kalal—her brother, her friend, her teacher, her guide, her father. Kalal who watched over and protected her as a child; her rock, her foundation, her strength. Kalal. Although he had been missing for several weeks, before today she could still hope, she could still believe. Now there was no reason to believe any more. Kalal was gone and he would never come back. Today they told her that they would search no more. They told her there was no hope. He would not be coming back. Not today, not ever. Days, and weeks of hoping, praying, and searching would be no more. *Oh Tekun, I need you here with me. God, please help me.*

Kalal had gone into the forest with the two apprentices of his former partner Lonau. They were searching for a rare special type of stone that would be used to construct a new archway in the Maja entrance. Lonau was unable to go, but he knew that this quest for this rarest of stone would be a befitting honor for his oldest and dearest friend. He hoped that it would perhaps remind Kalal of their youth when they began as stone masons and excitedly searched for the most extraordinary pieces of geologic matter that the earth could bring forth.

The young, naive, unknowing apprentices that were sent to accompany Kalal, returned by the end of the first day without the master builder. Although they had been instructed to stay with him and watch him carefully, somehow they had lost track of him as he wandered off, and they assumed, or perhaps hoped, that he had only taken an alternate path back to the village. The larger search parties began searching for him immediately, dwindling in number and endurance over time. Until today, when they came to tell her that they would search no more; that almost three weeks of fruitless searching was more than enough. He was gone. Could not be found. Would not be returning; not now, not ever. Perhaps it was better this way, they said. Perhaps now he would be at peace and no longer a burden. Oh pardon, they said, when she raised her head and looked at them, not a burden; didn't mean it that way.

Shaking off her reverie, Saba wondered if the same force that had infected her brother's mind had somehow reached out and lured Amira into its grasp. For it now seemed that Amira had transported back in time; back to a safe past where Kalal was still whole and their relationship was still fresh and unstained. These past years of caring for him as if he was her child, seem to have evaporated, perhaps consumed by the intensity of her needs. Or maybe she did remember all of the hardship and the memories only added to the depth of her feelings. It was mostly on Amira's behalf that the futile search for Kalal had gone on for so long.

Amira started each day searching for her husband, going into and through the woods surrounding the settlements. Where Olana had once helped her mother to retrieve her father, she now brought Amira back every afternoon, dejected and despondent. The next day and each next day after that, Amira would set out again, full of hope and determination. She did not accept what the people told her about Kalal. For her, he could never be gone permanently. Besides, she reasoned, what does 'presumed dead' mean, anyway? It doesn't mean literally, factually, without a doubt, dead. Amira was stuck in one of those endless moments of her life when Kalal had just disappeared briefly, only to be found later wandering alone in the wilderness. After all, if he was truly dead, why had they not found his body or some sign of his demise? No, he was not dead. She had only to wait, and search, and watch, and pray; and soon Kalal would be found. He would return home. Saba worried about how to help Amira. She worried about what she hadn't done, about what she should do, about her lack of knowledge of what to do.

Taijaur had led many of the search parties, going farther and staying out longer than any of the other searchers. The people who came to her today said that they had looked for Taijaur in the hopes that he would deliver the news to both she and Amira. However, Taijaur was no where to be found. No one had seen him for days, not even Alor. Even before the search parties had formed for Kalal, Taijaur had begun disappearing for long stretches of time. She wasn't sure where her grandson went during these long absences, but his journeys were becoming more frequent and he was becoming less truthful. He always came back different somehow, harder in a way that Saba could not grasp.

Saba bent down to push away an age-old litter of dirt and overgrowth on one of the ground-level burial plaques, in order to more clearly see the words etched on its surface. She saw the deceased person's name and suddenly realized that this was the burial place of the saba of the founders' generation. This woman had been saba to the people even before they came to the island, before they were Ocan. Her epitaph was of her own making—

She sleeps alone under the stars.
A life's longing realized
and struggle relinquished.
lying down
Away
in the night,
beneath the wind's shadow.

This saba, the founder saba, had been one of Amira's kind. They believed in ceremonial burial rites with words left to mark the time they spent within this realm. There seemed to be fewer who now subscribed to these beliefs. In her own family, Saba had known only cremations and funeral pyres. She puzzled over the epitaph, wondering if these words now befit Kalal as well. Was his consciousness, perhaps, drifting somewhere away in the night, beneath the wind's shadow? She wondered if she would ever know that the essence of Kalal's soul had been accepted fully back into the universe or was he now a part of the daily exodus of lost souls who hover around the earth still seeking coalescence. She wondered—do they eventually attract, draw in matter, to begin anew this search for meaning in yet another time, another place? Not all Ocan subscribe to the belief of individual souls retaining cohesion and returning to the Earth. But Saba's cultural beliefs had been deeply ingrained and passed down through the generations of her family.

The creak of the metal gate interrupted her mind-wonderings and she instinctively covered the book on her lap as she looked up and saw her grandson coming through the gate. Taijaur came towards her carrying a heavy backpack on one shoulder. She watched him visibly bring his emotions and demeanor under control, as he mentally wiped away a look of consternation that left a residual crease in his brow. "Saba. I've been looking for you. I thought that I might find you here. I came as soon as I heard. I can't stay long, but I wanted to come to make sure that you are all right."

She smiled at the sight of her grandson and moved to make space for him on the bench beside her. "Come sit with me for awhile."

He kissed his grandmother and let the pack fall to the ground next to where he sat. Although he smiled in return, the look in his eyes said that he was hiding something, consciously concealing some knowledge, some thought and blocking any sentiale probe that she sent his way. *Where have you been? Why do you keep disappearing? Why is it that no one ever knows where you are?* She knew that he was pulling away from her and she knew that any fear that she felt on his behalf could, one day, make him lost to her forever. So, she steadied her emotions and said nothing as she studied his face, thinking of her husband, and how much Taijaur looked and acted like his grandfather, Tekun. She thought to herself, *No matter how much the generations change, so much remains the same. And I suppose there will always be men who attempt to cultivate an aura of mystery for the women in their lives.*

He gazed into Saba's face with obvious concern, asking, "Are you okay, grandmother?"

Saba: "Yes Taijaur. I am glad that you have come."

Taijaur: "I can still try to look, still search."

Saba: "No, no, no. Amira and I both have supported one another in this false hope for too long. It is just so hard to imagine life without him. However, in reality, I have known that Kalal was dead, had been dying, even before he disappeared."

They were silent for a few moments, listening to the sound of the birds and the wind blowing through the leaves. They were both treading lightly around each other's sentiale, trying to feel and sense before speaking. Taijaur broke the silence. "Do you think that there is anything that I could do to help Aunt Amira?"

Saba: "I am not sure that anyone can help Amira. I am more worried about Olana. She remains constantly by her mother's side. Olana has been very pensive, much more quiet than usual. I feel a heaviness weighing on her soul. You know, Amira thinks that something in the forbidden lands took hold of Kalal's mind those many years ago when he escorted Mala to safety. But I believe that Kalal left us even before he ventured into the western territory. Something within him gave up at the point that the people decided the fate of Mala's child.

It seems that good innocent souls like those of your uncle become unsettled when faced with realities that are not aligned with the true intent of our purpose in this world. Much his strength was founded on his belief and faith in the goodness of his people. When he saw that, despite all of our holy righteousness, we may be just as hypocritical and cruel as any other group of people, then his faith was shattered. I believe that it was then that his mind began to lose cohesion and then his body eventually followed. I could feel his spirit pulling away, the same way that I knew that Tekun had departed this realm before the message of his death was brought to me."

Taijaur was surprised to hear Saba speaking so freely about death, especially the death of someone she loved. He had long ago learned to temper his comments and queries about loved ones who had passed away. He wondered how long this new openness would remain and decided to see if she could be pushed further.

Taijaur hesitantly asked, "Saba, can you tell me how my grandfather died?"

She seemed only slightly taken aback by his question, but her voice remained steady as she responded, "Well you know about the explosion in the cave and how he pushed the three girls out of the opening but he was unable to save himself or Mala's parents."

Taijaur: "Yes. But I don't think that I have ever heard the full circumstances. Or at least I have never heard your version of what occurred."

She sighed heavily and then began. "That day, the day of the, uh, accident, Tekun was supposedly just there to observe. He was very excited about the experiments that the Purims were conducting and he went each day to assist them. He never told me exactly what they were doing or his role in the process, only that one day I would see it all for myself. He wasn't exactly secretive, just evasive about many things. You are similar to your grandfather in many ways."

She glanced at Taijaur from the corner of her eyes before continuing, but the expression on his face never changed.

"This was about six years before you were born, and Loni was going through her Ascension Rites along with her two best friends Mala and Tausi. One of their assignments included exploration in the mountains near Mala's home, an isolated area near the boundary of the forbidden lands. In the passageways of one of the mountain caves, Loni found a strange anomaly—some impression of light and sound—that no one else could see or hear. Ever since she was a little girl, your mother could always feel and sense things of which other people had no awareness. Anyway, Loni shared her discovery with Mala's parents. Alis and Aran Purim recognized her discovery as a fracture in our world, a potential entryway to the in-between. No such portal had been uncovered since the ancient Obeah sealed the portals over two centuries ago. They began various experiments to determine the composition and source of the radiation, going further and further into the passageway. They thought nothing of allowing the girls to accompany them and assist with their research.

Mala and Tausi have both said that it was Loni who felt the portal about to close and told her father. Tekun pushed the three girls through the gateway and told them to run as fast as they could out of the cave and to not look back. As he turned to look for the Purims, who were further in the passageway, the portal closed in on itself and the cave exploded. We were told that they would have been annihilated within seconds of the explosion. Even though no one was allowed in that area after the accident, I still went secretly for weeks, trying to dig through the rocks and debris. But the boulders were too big and too heavy."

She paused and closed her eyes briefly before continuing at a faster pace, "We all tried to look out for Mala after that. Kalal, Amira and I unofficially adopted her and I tried to make a home for her with Loni and me. But Mala always had her own ideas about how she would live her life. When her parents were alive, the only time that the villagers saw any of the Purims was during their monthly forays to the Maja library. Even by Ocan standards, Alis and Aran were considered separatists—isolationists. They did not mingle or take part in most Ocan collective gatherings, not even on Exchange Day. However, for some reason they allowed their daughter to take part in the growth rites and ceremonies. We were all surprised when Mala showed up to participate in the Ascension Rites. Loni, Tausi and Mala became inseparable as they went through their rites together.

Mala was very much like her own parents—quiet, alone, self-contained and content in her own solitude. There were rumors that she and her parents never conversed verbally with one another. It was believed that they had developed their sentiale abilities so strongly that they could communicate by sentiale thoughts and feelings alone. Once her parents were gone, sometimes Mala came and stayed with us, but for the most part, she wandered those hills where her home had once been. Whenever Kalal took her to his home, Mala would disappear in the night and stay hidden until he grew tired of searching for her. Finally, Kalal learned that if he sat by the stream near the mountain pass closest to her former home and just waited awhile, in time, she would come and sit quietly beside him. They developed a special bond during those times and they taught one another much of how to listen to and feel for the nature of the world."

Taijaur: "Why did Mala go to live alone in the forbidden lands?"

Saba: "I don't know why she left. But it was right after your mother died. Those three girls were not the same after the accident; for years they each struggled with their own silent burdens. Tausi was the only one able to impose any sense of normality in her life. She had Chiru even then to help her stay grounded. Still, to this day, she has anxiety spells and jumps at any little disturbance.

Loni took it the hardest. I don't think that she ever fully recovered from the loss of her father. She blamed herself for having found the portal. She felt responsible for her father's death and for the deaths of Mala's parents. She left a few years later and she never came back. And then she too passed away. My daughter, my one and only child, left this earth six years after her father and yet the two losses felt as if they occurred at the same time and never stopped occurring. Every day of my life, I re-live those moments over and over again."

Taijaur was pensive, concentrating on his grandmother's words. He knew how hard it was for her to speak of this hurt, this pain. He said quietly, "Thank you for sharing that."

He looked up suddenly as if he heard a sound, and stared into the distance at the path beyond the gate.

Saba: "What are you looking at? Did you hear something?"

He turned back to his grandmother, "Oh, its nothing." And then with a loud exhale of breath, he rose and began bending and stretching his back, legs, arms, neck; going through a brief series of exercises.

Glancing around the garden, with a mischievous smile, Taijaur asked, "And where is your ever-helpful eager-to-please apprentice today?"

Saba: "That stumbling, fumbling girl exasperates me and you are just asking of her to taunt my sense of ire."

Taijaur laughing, "But Saba you must admit that, despite her shortcomings, Layal has been a big help with the harvesting and processing of the herbs and medicinal plants. She seems very industrious and her efforts undoubtedly free your time and aid you in your healing tasks. And now people in all of the villages boast of having their own saba-blessed teas, tinctures and small bags of healing potions—straight from the healer's own hands, no less. You must admit that this idea of Layal's was, indeed, well-conceived. With her assistance, you are able to save your energy for those who are most in need of your help and not the every day hurts and complaints of the people. And you no longer have to travel to the outlying villages as much."

Saba: "She's industrious all right. She is turning the healing arts into an industry; something that it was never meant to be. This is a hands-on, person-to-person gift of touching and feeling and healing. But this girl would have one to believe that it is the healing substances alone that make the people whole."

Taijaur: "Perhaps the people can benefit from a combination of both of your gifts."

Saba made no response, besides an emphatic, "Hmmph!!" and an expression of disdain that momentarily twisted her facial features.

Saba watched as Taijaur bent down and began pulling weeds from around the garden pathway. She thought about how all of his life Taijaur never seemed to be able to sit or even stand still for very long. When he was awake, and there was no dream-state to hold him, he seemed to be in constant motion, as if his body was making up for lost time—expending or shedding stored excess kinetic energy. He rose and went to the small dilapidated shed at the rear of the garden.

He came back with some gardening tools and an old rickety broom and began raking leaves, pulling weeds, sweeping the gravestones free of clutter.

As he worked, Taijaur seemed to be waging an internal debate, fighting with the weight of some problem or dilemma. Saba watched the emotional struggle on his face as each moment he appeared on the verge of telling her something and then he would stop himself before the words came out. She saw him pull his emotions and demeanor in check just before asking, "Do you ever wonder what it is like outside of the settlements Saba? What the rest of the island is like?"

Saba: "I already know. Wilderness and forbidden territory. Unless you count the southern provinces where the Aka reside—but that is just more of the same—wilderness and for—or rather wildness and hostile territory."

Taijaur: "But don't you ever desire to see it for yourself? Aren't you curious?"

Saba: "I travel to the Haman village and the other villages regularly; and to the hamlets of the northeastern shore."

Taijaur: "I mean—oh, never mind." He smiled, "Its nice to be here with you today, Saba."

Still sensing in uneasiness in her grandson, Saba said softly, "Taijaur, what is it my son? There is something weighing on you."

He replied as he began raking vigorously, "Oh it's nothing Saba, don't worry." Then he stopped working and turned to face her once again. "But how would you feel if I left the settlements one day?"

Saba: "Left and went where? What about your studies and your work with Alor? What about your Primary Retreat? It is not safe in the territory beyond the settlements and you know this."

Taijaur: "Forget it Saba, I'm just speculating, just talking."

He walked over and absent-mindedly picked up his pack from the ground and placed it on the bench. Then he rested for a moment, leaning on the rake, feeling the hum of the afternoon sun and the warmth of a gentle breeze.

Taijaur: "You have come here every day that I can recall, Saba. Do you have any sense of what draws you to this place?"

Saba: "It is the place that I feel most whole. There is much here that sustains me both as a saba and as a keeper."

Taijaur: "A keeper? Alor once referred to you as a 'Keeper of the Faith'. Is that what you mean by a 'keeper'? What is a Keeper of the Faith?"

Saba hugged the journal close to her chest as she slowly responded, "Nothing, really. It is an ancient title that no longer carries any significance or meaning. Only the elders and other such old souls even know that as my designation."

Taijaur: "But I saw it also cited in a book that I came across some time ago. It had a mysterious explanation that revealed no real answer or definition. Except for what Alor said, I have never heard it mentioned aloud among the Ocan."

Clutching the book even tighter, she sighed, "Once long ago all Ocan, and perhaps even all beings on this earth, were considered keepers of the faith. That was before the need for titles and special designations. Before we came to this land, the people were afraid and insecure in a world that was becoming increasingly more volatile. There were many who were unsure that we would be able to fulfill our founders' dream of building a spiritually-based civilization. This dream was the primary purpose of our existence, but it failed to take into account the mundane realities of strife and discord that comprise the never-ending patterns of human existence. It was then that the ancient Obeah began to identify certain people whom they referred to as 'endowed spirits'. They believed that these people possessed the power to embody the faith of the people and carry it through each time that we are re-born into a new generation. Usually a Keeper is also saba—in nature and spirit if not always in actual title.

The internal passageways that exist naturally within all beings are believed to be greatly enhanced within the souls of the keepers. No matter how dire or adverse the circumstances of life, it is believed that these individuals are able to bring forth a force of energy that transcends all other forms of power, knowledge or skill. True keepers are then able to transmit this energy to others whose belief may not be strong or those who are not able to turn belief into action. It is further believed that only through this energy force are all life's battles won, the impossible achieved, and the will of the Creator made manifest."

Taijaur: "I don't understand. Do you mean that the spirit would come back in a new life, each time with this power to 'keep the faith'? How does one 'keep the faith'? And what do they have faith in?"

"Ahh," she said smiling, "those are, indeed, the central questions. Primarily, they—we have faith in the will and wisdom of the Creator and his or her ability to realize and fulfill the intent of creation through a physical realm of existence. This is a faith that is born of reason and even skepticism, questioning and doubt. For the fundamental nature of faith entails a passionate belief in the transformative power of the spiritual realm of existence; and not a belief in fixed realities or doctrine that someone else purports to be true. Sometimes it is the very mutability of a phenomenon that must sustain our beliefs. In order to truly possess faith, one must first be willing to apprehend the rational and physical reasons for realities that manifest.

But to answer your first question—yes, the same spirit would re-incarnate and show itself during the childhood phase of any life so blessed with this vision. As you know, the people watch all the children for distinctive traits, to help identify what their future paths may be. If they are able to discern strong elements of faith and belief within certain children, then the Obeah are called to confirm their perceptions with tests and other forms of inquiries. After years of observation, there is a secret ceremony that confers the honor and responsibilities of the title. From that point on, the Keepers function in a subtle role of maintaining symbolic duties, such as periodically burning the ember of the eternal flame that is kept in one the inner chambers of the temple caverns, on a rock altar near an underground waterfall. This burning of the embers is supposed to cleanse the pathways in the mind as well as open your soul to receive sacred elements from the earth's sentiale pathways." She looked away into the distance before saying in a low voice, "But that is mostly superstition."

Taijaur looked thoughtful for a moment before speaking. "It seems to me that, as you said initially, many if not all of us, must be faith keepers, because, to one degree or another we all somehow believe in the power of the heavens to transform our lives."

Saba: "Ah, yes. But the distinguishing factors are the strength of belief and the ability and willingness to transmit the energy force to others. So many people lose faith along the way and no longer care what happens to others. Many times, these lost souls even have no vested interest in their own spiritual well-being. It has been told that the Keepers hold the vessels that contain the 'why' of this existence, of this world; the reasons behind the events. And even though the universe may expand and contract and our sun will one day die out, the essence of who and what we are can manifest in other spaces, other times. Each time that the world, as we know it, begins again, these vessels, fragile seedlings, carry the infinite energy that sails on the wind to other galaxies, other solar systems, other dimensions of the universe. They contain the eternal code of our existence and carry our reasons for being into other material realities. In this way, we are made immortal."

Taijaur: "But why is all of this not made known to all Ocan? I don't recall ever being told about any faith keepers."

Saba: "That is because in your lifetime there have been no Keepers who have come back among the living." She sighed heavily as she continued, "The Elders and the Obeah have lately begun to believe that I may be the last of a long line of faith keepers. They believe that as time passes, there are less and less endowed spirits who choose to return to the earth. Or perhaps they return in body-less forms, undetectable to our physical senses."

Taijaur became quiet and then he looked up at Saba and asked, "Is that because the faith-keepers begin to no longer believe? Grandma, have you lost your faith?"

He looked so serious and concerned, yet so much like the innocent little boy that he once was and would never be again. Saba could not resist the temptation to bring levity to what was unintentionally turning into a solemn discussion, "Well let's just say that," and she smiled, "as a _keeper_ of the faith, I just forgot where I was supposed to actually keep it. But, shh!! Don't tell anyone," she sat up straight, with her nose high in the air, "After all, I still I have my official responsibilities to uphold."

He laughed as she had hoped that he would. In the brief quiet that followed, she noticed Taijaur's pack that he had been carrying sitting on the bench next to her. The string that held it closed was undone and there was something inside that caught her eye. It was hidden, only showing partially out of the top of the bag—a book of some kind. She went on talking as she reached over and absent-mindedly opened the bag wider and pulled the book out, "What have you been studying? Are you any further in your understanding of—"

Then she saw it. Shock stalled her tongue momentarily and then suppressing her alarm, she managed to mutter, "Where did you get this?"

He looked up, quickly took the book from her hands, and put it back in his pack, pulling the drawstring tight.

Taijaur: "It's nothing. Just a book that I found. In the, in the Maja library."

She let the deception go. Saba knew that this particular text was in no Maja library and in no current collection of any Ocan materials. He moved the pack to the other side of the bench and went back to briskly sweeping the walkway.

Saba: "It may be best that you keep that book hidden while it is in your possession and take the utmost care that absolutely no sees you with it."

Taijaur: "Yes, Saba. But this is part of the reason why I have come to speak with you today."

Saba: "Taijaur, I will not, cannot speak of that book. I have no idea how it came into your possession and I don't want to know."

Taijaur: "But Saba, I need your help. I have something very important to tell you. So much is happening, that I don't know where or how to begin."

Saba: "Taijaur, you know that what ever help you need, I will always give to you. However, I must insist that you do not speak of this book aloud to me or anyone else for that matter. You must try to, uh, return it as soon as possible."

Taijaur: "It's not just the book. There is so much more."

Saba rose, sighing heavily, she picked up the rake that he had let fall to the ground. "Here, why don't you sit and rest for awhile. I can clean up this place. I used to try to keep everything in order, but over time..." She smiled ruefully, allowing her words to trail off.

Taijaur smiled, "I think that there is enough work for at least two of us. You should have let me take care of this for you, Saba. I would have come long ago if I had known that this garden had become so overgrown."

As Saba swept the pathway, Taijaur continued alternately between raking the ground and pulling weeds.

Saba: "Taijaur, you are still young. My son, why do you occupy yourself so intensely with these books and papers? Let the world teach you what you desire. The printed or spoken word is limited in its ability to convey or interpret living processes."

Taijaur: "My work, the project with Alor and Hadassa—all of my studies require that I learn as much as I can, from as many sources as possible. If we could only work with the Aka, then there would be so much more that we could accomplish and I would not have to depend on books and papers. There is news that the Aka have developed technology that allows them to accomplish a project like ours in half the time. And they are supposed have a much broader library than ours with different types of ancient texts. If the Elders would permit me to meet with them, then perhaps it would be possible to broker a truce.

And Saba, I might also have a chance to finally meet my Basau relatives. What do you think of that? That is part of what I want to ask you. Do you think that you could talk to the Elders; try to convince them? They respect you and they listen to you."

Saba stopped sweeping as she looked at him, barely concealing the surprise and fear that was rising in her voice and in her eyes, "Taijaur, keep in mind there is no way for that family—your Basau relatives—to even know that you exist. Surely you remember that I told you how you were taken away from that village before anyone realized that you had been born. Everyone assumed that Loni's child died with her. And the Elders will hear no talk of the Aka, no matter the family connection. Don't forget the sanctions that have been imposed against the Aka. Not even the Haman, Shinhala or anyone from any of the Ocan villages are permitted any contact with the Aka. And I don't think that any Aka would welcome you, even if they had knowledge of who you are. These people are very hostile, Taijaur. They consider themselves to be anarchists and they recognize no laws or system of governance. They will not welcome you or anyone who does not subscribe to their philosophy. I, too, would like to see the two groups reunited. But it is the Aka who must seek a truce with the Ocan and make amends for their past transgressions."

Taijaur: "Couldn't we at least try? Why can't the Elders recognize the Aka as the sovereign state that they insist that they are? I don't understand why we have to ask the Elders permission for everything anyway. It is as if we are young children, seeking parental consent."

Saba: "Taijaur! You sound almost as bad as the Aka. Like it or not, the Council of Elders is the closest thing that we have to a ruling body. Lord knows that I have my disagreements with them. But I recognize that they perform necessary and sometimes very difficult duties for our collective. Even if we don't agree with them all of the time, we must still defer to the wisdom that they may bring to bear on a situation. And besides, we don't exactly have to ask permission; we just seek their clearance and guidance. A society, any society, needs at least this base minimum of governance in order to ensure justice and peace. Our society is successful because we have a minimal amount of government intrusion in our lives. The Council of Elders is here only to help guide us in our purpose as a people. They help bring about fair resolution to the problems that we face. All Ocan laws and edicts apply to everyone on this island, including the Aka. However, the Aka refuse to obey our laws; they refuse to recognize the governance of our Council. No matter how separately the Aka want to live, they cannot declare themselves a sovereign state. We are all people of the Ocan."

Taijaur: "But can't you see Saba—if this animosity continues, then it may eventually lead to something more serious? There has even been talk of an Aka insurrection. This feud between two groups of the same people seems so petty, so trivial and irrational."

Saba: "Perhaps, in the end, you will find pettiness and irrationality at the root of most great wars between nations and conflicts between individuals. And there has always been talk of an Aka insurrection, even when they still lived as a part of the Ocan villages. No attempt at reconciliation would be possible because the sanctions against the Aka allow no communication, trade; no contact of any kind for any reason.

Even once the Elders granted them the right to move to and from their own village, the Aka still were not satisfied. As soon as they moved to the southern province, they almost immediately began rebelling against many of our basic laws; they defy the principles by which we live. Innocent people died as a result of the Aka's arrogance. They also stole several important artifacts from the Ocan collections and claimed that they were the rightful owners. For decades after they seceded, the Aka and the Ocan had bordered on an antagonism that fell just short of open conflict. But ever since the sanctions were imposed, there has been an unspoken truce of sorts. Or at least the Aka no longer speak openly against the Elders or try to recruit people from the Ocan villages to join their cause."

Taijaur: "But surely this fight with the Aka can't be just about some stolen artifacts and some broken laws. There has to be more to it than that. Most Ocan people speak of the Aka as if they are some kind of devil-worshipers. I can't believe that the more judicious of our collective would subscribe to such superstitious nonsense.

What did the Aka actually do? What principles of the Ocan do they defy? Can't we try to see their beliefs as just different from our own and respect their right to form their own worldview? There must be some way to form a common basis between the two groups."

Saba: "Well, I will tell you some of their beliefs and then you can judge for yourself if it is possible to respect their worldview or form a common basis of understanding. Their greatest transgression was when the Aka defiled themselves and all of our people by consuming the flesh and blood of once living beings, the non-human mammals of this land."

Taijaur: "What!?! But that is an abomination. That is like accusing them of consuming the flesh of humans. Eating the flesh and blood of an animal is only one step away from cannibalism. How could they do that? I find this hard to believe Saba. How do you know that this allegation was not just a rumor like all the other rumors that the Ocan have about the Aka? Just like all the other biased unconfirmed stories that are always circulating."

Saba: "Make no mistake, Taijaur, this was no rumor. Ocan sanctions against the Aka date back to these distressing and dangerous times. They began eating the animals as a source of power, an increased concentrated form of protein. We were not able to determine how long they had been engaging in this practice. But just before you were born there was a sickness that swept through their villages, and their actions came to light. Almost one third of their population was killed in this epidemic and they have never fully recovered. If not for this tragedy, there are many who feel that the Aka would have tried to overthrow the Ocan by now."

Taijaur: "Was this the same epidemic that killed my mother and father?"

Saba: "Yes, this is what we believe caused their deaths." Saba sighed heavily before continuing, "We don't know the exact source of the contagion because the Aka still will not reveal all the facts. At first they tried to say that the Ocan had somehow poisoned their water supply. At that time they received water like the rest of us, directly from the Haman village. But since then the Elders have not allowed them access to the aqueducts.

We believe that the illness began with the consumption of the animals. To my understanding, the symptoms of those who fell ill were much like the symptoms caused by e-coli or salmonella poisoning, but much more severe and contagious. Eating animals is forbidden as a part of our creed because of the ethical and moral concerns that shape our beliefs. However, we have also known, from the beginning of our time on this island, that the animals of this land contain poisonous alkaloids in their flesh. The Aka rebelled against this Ocan edict, in the much same way that they flagrantly violate many other Ocan laws.

But this time, their defiance and sacrilege was to the detriment of their own community and to the demise of my daughter."

Taijaur: "Saba, if the Aka reject the beliefs of the Ocan, surely they must have some belief system of their own. The Aka must believe that their principles, ideals and goals are just as rational, true and righteous as the Ocan."

Saba: "From the beginning, before we came to this land, before we called ourselves Ocan or Aka, there were people in our group who had a fundamentally different understanding of what the Ocan, as a collective, was trying to achieve. But our founders believed that our spiritually-based community was strong enough to encompass many different perspectives. The important thing, at that time, was that everyone had the same goal to control our own destiny; to pursue our personal and creative development in the absence of the false greed-centered realities created by the manufactured societies and the contrived power structures that are a part of most nations of the modern world.

Our founders made the decision to withdraw from the world completely in order to escape from the potential effect that the phage could have on our people and to allow the power of the island to accelerate our spiritual development. However, this subset group of people, who had begun to form a faction community within our collective, opposed the Ocan premise for coming to this land. They continued their fight even after we were re-settled and they began to call themselves, Aka. The Basau family dynasty has been the central force that carries this counter-revolutionary agenda into each new generation. And about fifty or sixty years ago they convinced their followers to move with them into the island's southern territory. They remain resentful that the Ocan chose to retreat to the island, even though this was over two centuries ago. They felt that we all should have continued establishing a new world order on the mainland."

Taijaur: "If they feel this way, then why haven't they gone back to the mainland? Why do they choose to stay hidden in isolation on an island that the rest of the world doesn't even know exists?"

Saba: "They stay and they are willing to remain hidden from the world because of the Gift. The Aka believe that the Ocan in their passivity, mis-use 'the Gift', in terms of only seeking enlightenment and higher states of consciousness. Even when we were still in the mainland, the Aka ancestors were disgruntled and impatient with what they believe to be a more pacifist approach of the Ocan philosophy. They reject the Ocan central principle of 'cause no harm'. They belittle the Ocan belief that we can use spiritual power to move the people of this world toward that which is highest in human existence. The Aka want complete control of the portals, which are the only entryway to the power source of the in-between. They would use the power of the in-between to coerce the nations of the world to comply with their vision of peaceful co-existence.

As a result of the powers that the Gift has bestowed within us, the Aka believe that they, and technically speaking all Ocan, are 'the Chosen people'—chosen to one day inherit and rule the earth. They see themselves as a militant front-guard who believe in the right to use violence on the basis of a need for protection and to impose their beliefs on the world. In the past, the Aka attempted to build a 'critical mass' of adherents, by secretly recruiting new members from all the Ocan villages. But now, since they are permitted no communication with the Ocan villages, they are unable to persuade people to join them."

Taijaur: "I have never heard any of this or seen it written. We have only been taught that the Aka are corrupt and that they choose to live separately from us. How do you know that all the Aka subscribe to these beliefs?"

Saba: "There is no way to know anything definite about the Aka anymore because we have no contact with them. But I remember when they still lived among us and the dissension that they caused, especially that Basau family. There are so many of them and fighting and arguing seems to be part of their nature. Even amongst themselves, there seemed to always be some kind of quarrel or disagreement. I am thankful that you are more like your mother. I sometimes forget that you have Basau blood in your veins."

Taijaur: "But Saba, I still don't understand the belief system that underlies the actions that you attribute to the Aka. What about their religion and the spiritual principles that guide their lives?"

Saba: "I'm not sure that they have any religion or spiritual principles. And this is perhaps the primary difference between the two groups. Their values go against the most fundamental parts of the Ocan philosophy and belief system. The Aka in general, and the Basau specifically, reject the spiritual powers of the land, they scorn the Ocan use of sentiale abilities. Although they claim to be anarchists, one of the major restrictions that they impose on their people is a prohibition regarding the use of what they call the 'mind-altering' practices of the Ocan. They do not believe in the supernatural or metaphysical powers of the universe. According to them, there is no higher spiritual realm of existence; there is only the world as it is or as we perceive it with our physical senses.

They do not believe that there is a virulent force or plague upon the human spirit. They believe that the need for dominance, control and violence are a natural part of being human and existing as a part of this realm. They believe that we exist in a predatory universe; that the world was created in a natural predatory state of existence, with only two types of beings, two types of energy—either predator or prey. From their perspective—since the universe is a predatory entity, one must choose to either rule over others or by default, you will be a part of the nescient masses that are ruled and controlled by despotic governments, tyrannical royalty or other forms and systems of domination and oppression. The Aka believe that people must either make themselves a strong predator or they will, by default, become prey, the victims of the world. Those who lead or have power are the predators, while the powerless are destined to be consumed by the dictates of those who oppress them—victims of their own weakness and inability to prey on others. To their credit they do make a distinction between a callous malevolent predator and a potentially benevolent or conscientious predator; and they contend that they are of this latter persuasion."

Taijaur: "But what would lead them to believe anything so negative and potentially destructive?"

Saba: "What they believe is no different than what many people in this world believe. The only difference is that the Aka are more conscious of what underlies their beliefs and they have perhaps articulated it more persuasively.

Taijaur, you have to understand that injera is at the root of all that we are, all that we do, all that we are capable of understanding and believing. How we fulfill our needs in this world is the central defining point of who and what we are. Much of the danger in Aka perspectives of life, and even the danger in the world at large, relates back to an individual's and a group's fundamental understanding of injera. A person's perception of need and the appropriate means of need-fulfillment are intricately tied to one's perspective of how life, non-human and human, should be categorized and classified.

An individual or a society determines their potential sources of need-fulfillment based on the labels of the categories that they assign to people, and all the phenomena of the world. The primary labels for matters of predation or subjugation are 'the us' and 'the other'. Most people who subscribe to this type of thinking almost always elevate themselves and all those in the category of 'the us' as superior and relegate those in the category of 'the other' to the status of inferior. As long as some thing or some one exists in the category of 'the other' then, in accordance with this belief system, it is acceptable or appropriate to subjugate them, mistreat them/it or destroy or take their life. Thus, the Aka and many people of the world feel justified in their abuse of the land and its creatures because they believe that as the superior 'us', it is their right to have dominion over any thing or any one who is not like them. And they never quite understand that we all simultaneously belong to the categories of 'the us' and 'the other'."

Taijaur: "And what do the Ocan believe about predation? After all, in many parts of the world, predation is viewed as a natural part of the animal kingdom. "

Saba: "All life feeds on life—thus, everything and everyone is a potential means of need-fulfillment for any thing or any one that exists in this realm of the living. The Ocan believe that predation is definitely a part of the evolution of life in this world, and perhaps in the universe at large. But predation is only one dimension of need-fulfillment that is evident only in the earliest stages of an entity's evolution or development. Think of how a baby or a young child is focused on only his or her own hunger and need for love, security, warmth. All organisms and entities in the early stages of their development have a self-centered focus on the most immediate means of gratification of their needs, without any regard for the needs of other organisms. Thus, these nascent voracious 'appetites' may, indeed, translate their means of need-fulfillment in the form of predation (life, feeding without reciprocity, on life).

However, as a child, an entity or an organism develops to higher levels of consciousness, they gain a greater awareness of the wholeness, continuity, and reciprocity of all life. The necessary joining and coalescence that life demands between living organisms, then takes place through cooperation, integration and a willingness to merge or consolidate our strengths; not the violent appropriation and theft of life that predators view as their right. The Ocan believe that humans must find a way out of the cycle of violence and predation that rule the hostile environments of the Earth in order to spiritually evolve and transcend. But it seems that a competitive and predatory mindset has become the primary mental archetype for human behavior and human civilizations. All battles of conquest, subjugation, domination, and manipulation of the land, its animals and people—"

Saba abruptly stopped speaking as she glared out of the garden beyond the gate. Taijaur had continued raking and sweeping as she spoke and he was now over by the portico-mausoleum with his back to her, unaware of her sudden sense of alarm. Something had caught her eye and she walked closer to the gate to confirm her suspicion. In a loud whisper, she signaled and called, "Taijaur, come quick! Look, look. Do you see that man over there near the Adona tree?"

Taijaur approached where she stood, broom in hand, peering inquisitively in the direction she indicated. "Where? I don't see anyone."

Saba: "He's partly obscured behind that bush over there, but you can still see his white hair. He is the Haman villager that I told you about before; the one that I used to see every where that I went, always staring and smiling at me. I haven't seen him in awhile, but I know that he is the same man."

Taijaur: "Oh yes, I see him now. What of him? He just seems to be walking"

Saba: "He is pacing back and forth. What is he doing here? No one comes to the temple any more. He's older now and I haven't seen him in awhile, but I am certain that he is the same man that always seems to be following me, always seems to be lurking about. I have such a sense of dread every time that I see him. There is no reason for a Haman or anyone for that matter to be this far out, away from the main compounds and the marketplace."

Taijaur studied Saba's face with concern, asking, "Why do you feel dread?"

Saba: "I don't know. It just seems that I recognize him from somewhere, but I can't recall. And every time that I try to call to him, he seems to flee. I don't have a good feeling about him at all."

Taijaur: "He looks harmless Saba. I'm sure that there is nothing for you to fear."

Saba: "But who is he and what does he want. After all these years of continuously seeing him—"

Taijaur: "Saba, I've been trying to tell you something—"

Saba: "Yes, yes Taijaur, just wait one moment." She reached for the gate and started pushing it open. "I am going to find out once and for all why—"

Taijaur intercepted her, holding her arm, "No! Wait Saba. I know who he is. He is here for me. I hope you don't mind that I told him to meet me here. But I was in a hurry and I had to see you first."

She stared at him in disbelief.

Taijaur: "Its part of what I have been trying to tell you Saba. That man— he is here waiting for me. And most likely every time that you have seen him in the past, he was either looking for me or looking after me."

Saba: "Looking after you? What do you mean? Who is that man Taijaur?"

Taijaur sighed, "His name is Jhirai. He serves on the Haman High Council and he also—well, he also acts as an envoy for the Aka."

Saba: "What!?! For the Aka? How can that be? The Haman are not permitted contact with the Aka. And what is this nonsense about a Haman 'High Council'? The Haman defer only to the authority of the Ocan Council of Elders. The Haman have never had any 'Council', high or otherwise."

Taijaur: "They do now. That is what I have been trying to tell you Saba. Things are changing rapidly; nothing is what it once was or what it will be."

Saba: "Who is that man Taijaur and why is he waiting for you?"

Taijaur: "He is my uncle, my father's half-brother. A son of the Basau family."

Part II

9. Inar

Phosphorescent moonlight draws us closer to the Creator's presence, emanating from the depth of the sky's darkness, and from somewhere deep inside of us all. Shona traveled by night with the moon as her comfort and her guide. With each stroke, she stretched her soul into the darkness, and with every thought, every feeling, she reached beyond any boundaries confined to space or time. She was filled with incomprehensible, overwhelming emotions and sensations, as she surrendered unto the darkness. And the moon, in its opaque luminosity, stroked her softly.

Shona swam with the tide through the dark ocean waters that were summoned over and over to rise and bow before that indomitable, radiant celestial orb. With gravity as mediator, the force of the lunar tidal waves rhythmically swept and carried Shona away from the isle of her birth. She used the sonar techniques that Mala had taught her, emitting from her body a strong vibrating pulse that deterred the approach of any predatory marine creatures. Lubar was an incredibly intelligent dog and a willing industrious partner who helped Shona to sail and sometimes to pull the boat as they swam and sailed through the series of archipelagoes and the open sea.

Although Shona believed that chance and her own sense of exploration determined her direction and destination, she actually followed an ancient route that was revealed only within the sub-structure of her genetic memory. Flowing in the current of her own destiny, Shona was pulled, like all living entities of land and sea, through a journey guided by an instinctual map embedded within the fiber of her soul. Migratory creatures, like some species of birds and whales, remember better than most, as they fly, swim, travel thousands of miles from one hemisphere to the next pulled forth by the polarized light of the moon or by the powerful lure of the stars, the sun and the internal magnetism and vibrations of the planet itself. These uncanny wanderings reflect the prescient knowledge of all earthly beings, who possess within their cells, within the molecules of existence, innate navigational abilities. Lacking any conscious intent, they answer a silent call issued long ago when the universe first took shape.

Reaching the barren shores of the mainland, she stored her vessel near the rocks of a hidden cove. Before beginning their trek in this dry hot land, Shona covered herself and the dog with mud and herbs to subdue their scent. As they traveled over the next few weeks, Shona found that she had to adapt her survival skills in this new hard hostile terrain that many times did not readily yield its water or food. The heat rendered her usually high energy susceptible to an unfamiliar exhaustion. In due course, she learned how to listen, feel and understand this new land. While the terrain never became any less hot, hard or dry—over time the land no longer appeared as unforgiving as she first thought.

They made a crisscross path, leaving little evidence of their presence—burying all waste and obscuring signs of their trail. She made sure to travel on the outskirts, out of sight, of all human and animal habitation. However, occasionally she caught glimpses and sounds and smells of living, working, playing, eating, fighting, copulating, birthing and dying. She diligently studied the tracks, scat and other signs of life, keeping a wary watch for the predators that she knew inhabited this place. She was surprised by how many lone travelers, human and animal, there are in the world—on the fringes of their packs, their groups and the majority of their respective kind. Although they never saw or seemed to detect her or the silent dog, she was able to covertly observe these solitary creatures from a distance.

They came into a part of the land where there were deep and extensive canyons cut and sculpted into the mountains and rock formations. Almost from the beginning of their descent into the canyons, there were fecund smells that warned of death and decay, and sporadic rock falls that threatened their trail. Shona was astounded by what millennia of flowing water had carved into and stacked upon the sandstone and limestone of this beautiful arid land. The antediluvian rivers and tributaries had cut deep narrow gorges, gulches and immense chasms with steep vertical walls, cliffs and rocky plateaus into the earth. She was amazed by the variety of ways in which this planet had manifest itself—this austere and desolate landscape so different from the lush Ocan forests and valleys. The island's abundant flowers, trees and green vegetation had been replaced in this land by the natural architecture of erosion-molded buttes and outgrowths of wiry little pieces of vegetation dotting here and there amidst the myriad hues of red, brown, and sometimes yellow stone.

They walked for days through the canyon trails that seemed to never end. She still had no idea what destination she would finally meet, but Shona was certain that this was the way to go and that she would end where she needed to be. At night, as they rested beneath rock ledges or in the caves they found along the way, Shona lie listening to the cracking sounds of cooling rock and the creeping of nocturnal animals. There was one repetitive sound that she could not identify, but it came each night for hours on end and occasionally during the day. It consisted of a series of high-pitch whistling howls and clicks, at once far off in the distance and then seeming quite close by. The howls and clicks rose and fell in a strange rhythm that was reminiscent of a call and response litany. And although she could not say why, the sounds made Shona feel apprehensive and very ill at ease.

After about a week, they came upon the ruins of a series of stone dwellings that were built along one side of the canyon rim, near an inner canyon spring. The mud-adobe structures appeared to have been constructed long ago and the plateau was littered with heaps of broken fragments of pottery and human bones. Shona thought that this must be the site of a massacre or some great catastrophe that had wiped out all life in one fell swoop. When she went a little further down the pass, she found even more pieces of hollowed bones, mummified carcasses and evidence that some of the deaths had not happened long ago, but perhaps quite recently. Some of the dried-out corpses had bits of clothing with weathered dry skin still intact, but all life fluids drained. And there were strange piles of human thigh bones cut open length-wise and some shriveled remains that appeared to have their lower extremities completely de-boned.

The path she followed no longer seemed so sure or right. Two days after they passed the open cemetery, both Shona and Lubar were still shaken by that silent community's testament to horror. They were walking in the canyon basin with Shona following behind the jittery dog, who stopped every few feet, whining for her to move faster. She started feeling that some thing, or some one was watching her, stalking. She knew that this was just a case of both she and Lubar nervously imagining something that was not there; a sense of anxiety brought on by the unexpected fright of all the dead bodies. Nonetheless, she could not shake the feel of an ominous predator prowling and she continuously glanced back over her shoulder and all around, each time, seeing, hearing nothing but her own heavy breath of anticipation and the rocks of the canyon walls. She was sure that it was also just her imagination that had conjured this lingering scent in the air. The odor was strong, female and something else; something very wrong and out of place. But the air would tell no more and she brushed away the disquieting thoughts and smells as mere products of an over-active imagination.

"And look at you, Lubar. You're no better than me." She ruffled the fur on the dog's head and patted his back to reassure both herself and her canine friend. Lubar's ears lay flat against the sides of his head. He still turned every few minutes to steal nervous glances behind them and then he would trot even faster, almost beseeching Shona to move more quickly. If she paused momentarily or faltered in her step, he turned in semi-circles at her feet or paced back and forth, whining all the more.

"Whoa, Lubar, come on boy. What's wrong with you today? You're not your usual talkative self."

The dog's wide eyes beckoned to her, pleading, as he let out a short whine and low bark and then looked back, staring intently once again at the canyon wall behind them. Despite her promise to herself to not look back this time, to not gaze with this muddled dog at empty rock, empty air, she found herself slowly turning to glance behind, making sure that this time was like all the others and that indeed there was nothing there. *Besides*, she thought, *even if there is something or someone following us or even tracking our path, what can we do but keep moving on?*

Maybe she imagined it, but the air and all sensation around her seemed tense, magnified, much more alive than normal reality. She began to pull from that inflated piece of time a heightened sense of perception, where the sounds were louder, the smells more pronounced. The air even moved at a different, much faster speed, touching her skin in a way that was almost too intimate, too strong.

"Come on Lubar, you can do better than this. Tell me one of your famous stories."

The dog continued trotting, but looked at her with a sidewise glance from the corners of his eyes, letting out a whine and a short nervous bark.

"Is that all you have to give me? Surely this long hot walk deserves better than that."

She listened to the hot sand and gravel crunching loudly beneath her feet. In what seemed like slow motion, she reached down to rub Lubar's head, to reassure him that everything was all right. And then this time, the dog did not have to attempt to warn her. Something within her beckoned her to turn and look behind at the empty canyon rocks. Only this time the landscape of rocks was not empty. Shona saw it or rather her standing absolutely stock-still near the boulder they had just passed, where just seconds ago there had been nothing but rock and stone

Shona had a fleeting thought that her mind was being affected by the heat, for she imagined that she now gazed at some bizarre statue, a stone monument to some ancient bestial race of beings. She had no idea what type of creature this could be. The only thing that was certain about this stone-creature was that it was female. Although at some level she did realize that the statue had not been there a moment previously, she still wondered to herself who had created such a sculpture and why her senses had been so oblivious to it before now. But how could one, in the middle of nowhere, have overlooked something so singularly fascinating and horrifying? Slowly she began to realize that her imaginings of a statue could only be indulged so far, for this strange phantasm, this unmoving delusion was staring directly at Shona.

The being seemed almost reptilian in nature, though she gave the outward bipedal appearance of a human. Cold hard eyes, cut like slits into a rock-carved face, stared unblinking. Her lips were permanently drawn back in a bizarre strained smile, a rictus grin that revealed small crowded rows of very pointed razor-sharp teeth. Her dark matted hair was twisted wildly into thick knots/ locks that gave the impression that they had once been alive. Gray shreds of dirt-encrusted cloth draped from one shoulder across her breasts and hung to mid-thigh where they were barely distinguishable from the being's gaunt cadaverous skin. Her gnarled mud-caked feet stretched wide and long and on each foot there were three spear-like calloused appendages that apparently served as both toes and toenails.

The being did not seem to hear, see or notice Lubar at all, as she continued staring directly at Shona. Lubar was now fierce, aggressive, snarling. He put himself between Shona and the female creature. The dog was wild with fear and fury. Shona reached down to hold him back before venturing a tentative greeting in the direction of this being who made no sound or movement.

"No, Lubar, no. Uh, hello. Uhm, I, this, this is my dog. I hope he didn't— no Lubar no." The dog's fear made his body taut, but he never ceased growling, snarling, warning. Meanwhile, the statue-like being never moved nor wavered in her stare, but for a brief second Shona thought she saw the eyes of the woman-statue-creature close. But no, maybe it was just the slant of the sunlight in her face. No, wait—it happened again. With her eyelids still in the same place, a second lid, a nictitating membrane slid down across the being's eyes and then quickly darted back up.

Shona, still bending to hold Lubar back, watched in fascination the almost indiscernible darting lids move with unbelievable speed as every few seconds the being appeared to shut her eyes, yet simultaneously keep them wide open. Shona was careful not to look away as she waited to catch each brief blinking in and out. It took a moment for Shona to realize that while she had focused on the being's eyes, the once unmoving statue had somehow closed the distance between the two of them. She stood now only a few feet away and there was no mistaking the malevolence of her intent, as pure hatred shot from her now unblinking eyes. By the time Shona became fully aware of the predicament that she faced, it was much too late to alter her fate.

The attack was brutal and swift. Before Shona could even shift, the once unmoving "statue" had, with superhuman speed and dexterity seized Lubar by the throat with both hands and literally squeezed his life away before tossing his lifeless body against the boulder behind her. In what seemed like the same simultaneous moment that she slaughtered the dog, long talon-like nails tore at Shona's eyes and face as the female beast's teeth ripped through her right upper arm and shoulder, aiming for her neck. Low guttural sounds issued involuntarily from her mid-section with desperate carnivorous longing. Shona's reluctance to bring harm was quickly replaced by an equally fierce instinct to survive. She overpowered this semi-human being, catapulting her against the face of the canyon wall and then stomped her motionless form over and over again. A chilling stillness shook through her as the canyon echoed demon wails and reverberated with the paranormal sensation of flesh and bones violently crashing into its foundation.

Days went by and the female being still had not regained consciousness. Shona lie on the ground on the other side of a small fire that she had built between them. She had managed to shift the woman's body closer into the shade of the canyon wall and the smell the creature was still in her nostrils, her hair, and her flesh; blood and malevolence had oozed from its body, permeating the air. Her inert body still spewed putrid odors as the creature moaned incessantly, her body vibrating with sound. Shona cleaned the woman and mud-plastered her shattered bones, tending also to the flesh wounds with poultices made of the few medicinal herbs this hungry, parsimonious earth would offer. Her own pain had begun to subside as her body quickly mended, spontaneously closing the deep wide openings of flesh and torn tendons. She still nursed the sore part of her upper arm where the female-being had sunk her knife-like teeth. Shona tried hard not to think of Lubar, whose body she had buried beneath a pile of rocks.

Each night when the fire died down and sleep did not come, she tried praying and then in frustration she stoked the fire and pulled out of her pack a small book that she attempted to read. But she could pull no meaning from the words that jumped around on the page as her eyes wandered, staring into the dying embers of the flame. Shona was overwhelmed by the reality that she had lost her only companion, her only friend. And she was no longer sure of anything in this unfathomable world that within seconds had become filled with hurt and pain.

When she felt that she was strong enough, she was tempted to leave—wanting ever so much to put distance between herself and this place, this woman, this memory. But then she thought of the Gruenataring boy and she stayed to continue caring for this wounded creature, who would have undoubtedly died by now, in the absence of her care. This was her first real test in life and she was determined to do the right thing; the right thing that reflected all that she had been taught, all that she knew of how the world was supposed to be. Each day she checked for gangrene and infection, bathing the woman's body and cleaning wounds that oozed great globs of yellowish green and brown pus.

On the first day in the canyon basin, the creature, without ever gaining consciousness, began screaming in agony when the mid-day sun had shone directly on her. Thereafter, Shona erected a tarp shelter over her body, providing shade during the day. One night Shona thought she detected a faint translucent glow emitting from the woman's body. She rubbed her eyes, stirred the fire and assumed that her exhaustion and the light of the moon played tricks on her vision. Throughout the night and part of some of the days, she still heard those same far-off clicking sounds and high-pitch whistling howls, punctuating the air with a question of uncertainty.

Shona was puzzled by this strange being and what possible provocation could have led to her attack. Could it be that this being thought that Shona meant to cause her harm, thus attacking first? Was she perhaps protecting her territory? What was it? Fear? Threat? *Oh Lubar, where are you? Is your spirit at rest now? How will I go on without you? Why, oh why could I not have foreseen.* No matter how much she mourned, prayed, and considered the situation, no explanation made any logical sense.

As she listened more closely to the inarticulate moaning of the unconscious female, Shona slowly realized that the noises had never ceased. From every part of her body, except it seemed the most logical place, an auditory vibration was emitted. Creeping closer to confirm her perception, Shona was surprised by the absence of sound in the area of the being's head and mouth. She laid her hands on the woman's abdomen and felt the hot churning vibrations that were apparently the source of the deep forlorn moaning. Carefully, cradling her head, Shona opened the cavernous orifice that apparently served as both mouth and nose. There was no tongue, nor any place for there ever to have been one. She counted five rows of teeth (three on top and two on the bottom), each half circle with approximately thirty to forty pointed very porous pieces of triangular dentin. Looking further, she saw that the woman's throat was almost entirely closed off, in such a way that no air could possibly pass through unless the being was conscious and able to relax her throat muscles.

All at once, as the realization came that the woman's flesh created its own air flow, Shona found herself facing the sudden assault of the completely blood-shot empty eyes of a reptile. Instinct made her push back and move away from this now very much awake and conscious woman. Irritably glaring at Shona, the woman winced as she vainly attempted to turn her head. She made several inarticulate sounds, as if she was trying different frequencies, then she "spoke" a stream of clear words, in first one language and then another. Despite Shona's knowledge of various languages, she could not understand any of the words that the woman uttered even though she paused after each sentence in a questioning manner. Then finally her deep hoarse voice rumbled in an unmistaken variant of the Ocan language, "Why are you still here?" The intonation was foreign, and the words pronounced in a heavy peculiar fashion, but they were undoubtedly Ocan. Not answering and never taking her eyes from the woman's face, Shona pushed a plate of food towards her. Days ago, Shona had managed to find a saguaro with fruit in bloom. She had brought this back and along with hackberries and some seeds that she still had in her pack, and she had made a meal for herself and the female creature.

With a husky laugh, the female asked, "What makes you think I need that?" She waited awhile, then as the woman lie there ironically smiling and grimacing with pain, Shona hesitantly whispered, "What are you?"

In a resigned facetious tone, she answered, "I am whatever you want me to be."

She sneered, regarding Shona from the corner of her eyes. Shona noted that the moaning, although lower now, continued as the woman 'spoke' and her words seemed to take form from the individual decibels of the moans. Her mouth did not move, but remained in the same tight drawn position of a diabolical smile.

Shona: "What are you called? What is your name?"

"I have no name. I am Inar."

Shona: "Is that a designation or a label?"

Inar: "It is not a name, designation or label; it is what I am. Names and individual identities are of no consequence in this world."

Shona pushed the plate of food a little closer, thinking that maybe the creature had not fully understood. "You need sustenance. Your healing can only be expedited with the necessary nourishment."

Inar: "You are an amusing child, aren't you?" Her question was posed with a distinct tone of mirth, then just as quickly she became hostile and demanding, "I ask you once again, why are you still here?'

Shona: "I, I, I am a healer. I—you need to be treated and I needed to make sure that no life cycle has been interrupted as a result of my actions."

Inar: "Go away."

Shona: "You are not well yet."

Inar: "And my wellness is totally dependent upon the complete interruption of life cycles such as your own."

Shona stared at the woman, slowly taking in the implication of the meaning of her words. "What, what purpose would it serve to draw life from death?"

Inar: "Don't be absurd. All beings of this world derive some aspect of their vitality from the demise of a living entity."

Shona: "What are you saying?"

Inar, with a snort, "We all feed on each other in one way or another."

Shona: "Yes, but it is a reciprocal sustenance that, if successful, does not cause the cessation of existence for one or the other, yet enhances each."

Inar: "Perhaps in your part of the world that is so."

Neither of them spoke for a moment.

Shona: "Are you saying that you eat the flesh of human beings?"

Inar: "Actually," laughing, "the flesh is of no consequence. It is the blood and human marrow, manna and nectar to my kind."

With these words, Shona finally understood the litter of lifeless bodies throughout this graveyard canyon. Images of the dried out mutilated forms filled her mind. She mechanically forced herself to turn and focus intently on the shadow of the horizon, making an effort to swallow the repulsion that rose like a thick rancid stew into her throat and mouth. Swallowing hard, a bitter after taste burned her tongue and seeped into her nostrils. Quelling her internal rumblings, Shona turned back to face this cold predator who lie now with her eyes shut but still very obviously conscious. "Are there many of your kind, other beings like you?"

Inar: "What do you think?"

Before she had time to consider or constrain her thoughts, the words came out, "I think that the evolution of this world would progress more naturally with the absence of beings such as yourself."

Turning to face Shona with hatred burning through the apparent glee reflected in her eyes, "Ahh—and just seconds ago you stayed to assure yourself that you had brought no irrevocable harm to this life cycle. So swift a change in so short a time. Go away HuMun, you tire me."

Shona: "I don't mean you specifically, but just those who believe as you do. I respect all life that has been created within this realm, but—"

Inar: "But what? But what? No buts, no exceptions. We are all a product of what this world has made manifest, no more, no less. Where is your reciprocity now?"

Shona: "But why, why have you chosen this...this life?

Inar: "It is my destiny.

Shona: "Then you believe that you are a slave of fate?"

Inar: "Or perhaps fate is my slave. Either way it does not matter. We are what we are and we must act as our natures dictate. Little girl, I have no patience for your ignorance. You must leave."

Shona: "But you can determine to what degree any law of nature controls your actions. We are given the power to rise above the vices that rule our lower selves. You have to believe that a higher order prevails."

Inar: "One may rise only as far as fate/will allows. My will and the will of fate are inseparable. There are no outside forces that control or impinge upon my actions. And when I suffer as a result of my actions, I obey the laws of my nature and fulfill a need that has existed long before my conscious desire not to suffer. "

Shona: "This line of reasoning disturbs me."

Inar: "Nevertheless, the existence of a reality cannot be denied based on an unwillingness to accept it. But, in the end, none of this matters anyway. These truths don't extend beyond the boundaries of this planet; just as your inane societal laws do not apply to the greater realm of natural phenomena."

Shona: "If these are indeed truths, then what purpose does it serve for a scheme to unfold in this fashion? Why, in the name of reason, would natural order, with intent, pursue this path?"

Inar: "How do I know, or rather how can any one know? Some knowledge will always exist beyond the power of words. Perhaps in the beliefs of your own people, you may find your peace and then understanding may choose to bless your vision."

Shona: "Have you found your peace?"

Inar: "There is no peace for me in this world and I do not pursue that which eludes my grasp. I am what I am."

Evening dusk was beginning to settle around them and Shona looked up and into the distance, listening to the sounds of those far-off high pitch whistling howls and clicks. She wondered why this Inar woman seemed oblivious, unhearing of the howls that were coming with greater frequency, over and over.

Shona: "Why do you resign yourself to such a miserable life and way of living?"

The female laughed, "You amuse me little girl. I will continue this nonsense only to the extent that it continues to provide me entertainment. Surely you have been taught that life creates us all in the image of the world we inhabit. Before any birth, the land determines who we will be, shaping our boundaries to match its own. I reflect my world and it reflects me—in color, temperament, thought , action, shape and any other form or fashion upon which reality may be based."

Shona: "What you are or what you have become could never have come from the natural world. You are a product of a sickness upon the earth."

Inar, laughing—"If that is true then you and all of your kind are also prey to what you term a 'sickness'".

Shona: "This sickness did not reach our world."

In a taunting and teasing tone, the Inar baited Shona, "Nonetheless, you have reached ours and in doing so you take in all that we are. You and all those who are a part of you will know the effects of this 'sickness'. No matter what protection or fortification you afford yourself—your very fiber is affected by all that I am. Only time will reveal if one force will overpower the other or be subsumed into it." She was still laughing silently to herself.

Shona: "I bring neither force nor submission only the absolution of strength and courage to counter the benign, apathetic acceptance of a malignant reality."

Inar: "Lest you forget, sickness is natural to this world.

Shona: "And so is the power to fight it.

Inar: "To what end do you fight, you dichotomous creatures who believe that there is some universal eternal war of a noble good against a vile evil?"

Shona: "Wholeness is the natural right of all life forms on this planet. Only a fragmented, dis-eased soul seeks its primary sustenance in the mind, body or spirit of another. Something fundamental and essential has to be missing when one preys upon the short-term un-relinquished gratification of another life force. The struggle becomes an endless cycle of mental, physical, emotional and spiritual deprivation and cruelty."

Inar: "Who or what defines this 'wholeness' to which you make reference? No matter the state or condition of any life form as they exist on this planet, death is the only true ultimate state of existence."

Shona, shouting now, "You are wrong! The actions of all living beings on this planet are motivated by an instinctual need to survive. And within that survival, all beings strive for and intensely desire equilibrium, balance—stasis; not death."

Inar: "Little girl, you neglect to see that most desires originate with a longing for death. A quick fix from this thing we call 'life'. You and your kind fill your days with meaningful endeavors so that you might forget that which you long for most and out of fear that you will obtain it. The addicted believe that they fight addiction, while those not addicted believe that they are saved. However, each struggles against and simultaneously for the same deep longing to die, to no longer exist. Ironically, death is the source of all fear. So we all seek perpetual balance between our desires and our fears, never realizing that their source is one and the same. Ultimately, death then becomes the stasis or wholeness for which all beings strive. The pantomimes that we play out on this plane of existence are of no consequence to our final most complete act and thus cannot be judged as good or evil by a standard that is not equipped to gauge or measure the infinity of a non-physical reality."

Shona: "This, this, this is very dangerous; this philosophy, this belief of yours. The very thought you espouse would seem to permit the perpetuation of realities that are less than pure on this earth and contribute to the dominance of evil within this realm of existence."

Sensing Shona's anger and frustration the female demon coaxingly and seductively whispered, "Why don't you kill me?" And then she laughed hard and long when she saw how frightened and alarmed Shona became. Shona stood up, shouting, "No!" and then collecting herself, she went on in a quieter tone staring out at the dark canyons as she spoke. "It is the thought, the belief system that must not find fertile ground, must not be cultivated or nurtured by the environment in which it is placed. This poisonous weed must be choked at its root."

Inar: "Why not be true, at the very least, to yourself. Admit it, there was a moment when you pounded and stomped me that you actually enjoyed yourself. You relished the power and feel of violence. This inflicting of pain and knowing that you, and you alone, had ultimate control over whether I lived or died. It was an exhilarating moment; it took you to the height of your own existence and ability to feel."

Shona turned to face the female. "You are as mentally deranged as you are physically ill."

The female laughed contemptuously, "Go away HuMun, you tire me. Your presence, the very smell of you is beginning to nauseate me."

Shona struggled with her thoughts, her emotions, her conscience; not knowing what to do. How could she go on and leave this force of evil free and unrestrained, loose in the world? She thought of the phenomenal super-human strength that this woman had exhibited. She thought of all the dead bodies and the level of malevolence that it would take to commit such atrocities. She thought of Lubar, his friendly and loving soul. And in the end, Shona imprisoned the Inar female, tying her with a thick twisted rope made of spider silk. She wrapped the steel-like grip tightly around the woman's waist, crossing her chest and shoulders, ending behind her back, with her feet and hands bound together. The female did not resist, only involuntarily moaning in pain as Shona shifted and moved her bruised and battered body. She could not overtly kill, but she left the woman bound and unable to move, unable to go on.

Shona: "I, I, I may be able to return....later. Or some other being will pass. I'm sure that someone will come to—"

Inar: "Oh sooner than you think. Out of respect for the prowess you have shown as a warrior, I have tried to warn you to leave. However, since your ignorance and naïveté have insisted that you stay, you deserve every consequence of the fate that you are about to meet. Did you think that I was alone in this land?"

She laughed at Shona's startled expression then went on as Shona began slowly backing away, glancing from side to side and all around her. "And HuMun, there is one other little fact that you have not considered. With your actions today, you have set into motion a chain of reactions that will be beyond your control, beyond anything that you are even capable of imagining. Come closer one last time."

Shona stopped and was reluctant to move forward until the woman, with the hypnotic nictitating membrane her eyes blinking rapidly, said in a low sad voice, "Please."

Before Shona had crept completely within her reach, the female creature spat a long stream of brown viscous liquid into her face. Shona fell back, covering her eyes, shrieking with pain, the saliva burned her eyes and face like acid. Copious tears poured involuntarily washing away the pain.

Without emotion and in a calm, sedate tone, the creature said, "And now you are marked for the vengeance that belongs to you and you alone. You who profess so much concern, so much compassion, you leave me here, bound, without defense to die a slow torturous death." She laughed aloud, "What are you, I should ask. At least my prey dies a swift and relatively pain-free death. But have no fear, my child. This action of yours will only serve to more fully bind your soul with Inar. And Inar will avenge itself. There is no escape. We will possess you. We will follow your every step. You will not turn without hearing us, feeling us with you; inside of you, inside your thoughts, your soul. And in the end you will belong to us. You will become what we are. You will become what you hate, what you despise. You will know the lust-hatred of a predator and the pleasure of killing and consuming your prey."

The Inar's loud raucous laughter filled the entire space of the canyon as it echoed and bounced off of the canyon walls. Shona screamed with physical and psychological agony, "No! no, no." She was in a frenzied state, not knowing what to do or which way to turn. Through her tears, she spotted a large heavy rock on the ground near where she stood still rubbing her eyes and heaving with sobs. Without thinking or feeling or being, she allowed her fear to take charge and before she knew what was happening, the rock was in her hands. She raised it above her head and with all of her might she threw it in the direction of the woman's head. There was an eerie silence that lasted only seconds before the woman opened her eyes, her head showing no discernible sign of wound or injury and once again began laughing loud, hard, and strong.

Shona backed away with the hoarse laughter following and surrounding her as she turned and ran headlong into the dark of the rapidly approaching night, striving to get as far away as possible. And then a sound came to her, a familiar and very disquieting auditory sensation that made her stop abruptly in her tracks. With her flesh suddenly cold and clammy, she snatched her head around, her eyes staring wide in shock at the woman. The creature's entire body was glowing brightly with her spine curved and arched, her head thrown back and body contorted in a way that defied a human's ability to twist and stretch. Shona had thought the woman too weak to move in any way and now she not only moved, but positioned herself in a way that did not seem possible. She looked directly at Shona and laughed aloud just before she once again emitted a shriek of loud high-pitched whistling howls and clicks that were quickly answered by the same far-off mimicking sound. Again and again, the female howled in concert with that distant response; their clicks, howls and whistles forming a strange symphonic rhythm that echoed throughout the depths of the canyon.

Shona turned and ran as fast as she could and she did not stop running for hours. She had never traveled at night in this land, but now she was oblivious to time and anything external to the turmoil in her mind. When she finally fell to the ground with exhaustion miles away from where she started, she managed to crawl into a small opening in the canyon wall and she lie wondering if she would ever be able to sleep again. For the first time since leaving her island home, she cried low soft moans of pain and despair. Her first test in life had proven her incapable of determining a right course of action. The beliefs that she thought ruled all life had proven incorrect, and she was left feeling confused and frightened.

The loud cracking sounds of the canyon rocks, cooling in the night air, interrupted her thoughts and she sat up, listening in fear, for the one sound that she did not hear. For the first time since she came into the canyons weeks ago, the air felt almost empty and eerily silent with no howls, whistles or clicks.

She understood everything so clearly now. If only she had acted quickly, with intent and resolve. If only she could take away those few moments of indecisiveness, of compassion, of fear, then the world would be right again. If only she could go back and reclaim those few precious moments before that point of no return. There was a peace there, a sureness; and the crunching earth beneath her feet was solid and strong. She could feel herself moving back in time, back to that moment before her life changed and the world became all wrong.

Her mind kept her there for awhile, blocking out everything that had come after that moment. And for a few brief seconds she was safe. She reached down to rub Lubar's head and then confused, she looked around at her surroundings. Something was not right. *Lubar? Lubar? Where is Lubar?* And then she knew and her mind and body moved solidly back into a present reality, where the world tilted precariously out of balance. She rushed to her feet and ran a short distance into the darkness, before stopping and crying out, "LUUU-BARRR!!! LUUU BARRR!!! Where are you?" The darkness echoed and answered back with the same familiar creaking, cracking night sounds of the canyon and Shona collapsed to her knees. "Oh Lubar, my precious, precious friend!"

She cried out within her mind, *"Mother, where are you?"* Then, oblivious to any danger or person or concern outside of her own pain, she screamed aloud with all of her might, "MAAAA-LAAAA!!!" As the dying echo of her scream was absorbed into the listening silence, Shona sat sobbing and whispering aloud to herself, "Oh dear God, what have I done? I am so afraid. I have risked not only my own life, but the safety and well-being of the Ocan people and even perhaps all the people of this world. And poor Lubar has lost his life all because of me. Why could I not foresee the possibility of repercussions for my actions? I am so afraid. Where can I go? What can I do? And I, who so presumptuously called myself a healer—only to save a being whose existence may curse all of humanity. How naive and arrogant and obtuse. I should have ran as soon as I saw her. I should have ran and never stopped running. Oh God, I don't want to be here—not on this earth, not in this world. Oh Lord, please take me away. Oh my Lord, oh my God, if there is any compassion within this world, please let it come to bear upon me and this situation. Please allow me to awaken from this madness and find that it has never occurred."

Shona's cries reverberated in the air and throughout the stratosphere of the canyon's vast empty sky, while the translucent moon lie heavy in its own oppressive black silence.

10. Bridge to the Other Side

Alor: "And your grandmother? Have you been able to calm her fears about your impending departure?"

Taijaur: "I think that she is reconciled to the inevitable."

Alor: "But does she know that we are proposing that you actually leave the island?"

Taijaur: "Yes. Thankfully, she has Mala with her now. I think that she is anxious to see Mala reunited with her daughter, so she is willing to put aside some of her own fears. Mala's presence has been a blessing for Saba. For the first time she finally has someone with whom she can share saba-awareness and skills. Sometimes I hear Saba call Mala by my mother's name."

Alor: "I believe that Mala's reappearance at this time may be yet another significant sign that change is imminent. She said that it took her almost three full weeks to find her way back to the settlements, but she stayed in the Haman village for awhile. It shouldn't take you that long to travel to the shore. Does Mala talk much about her daughter?"

Taijaur: "She speaks of her occasionally, cautiously—but only if I ask questions. She is wary of anyone knowing of her daughter. But I don't think that there are many Ocan who actually remember the burial of Mala's child. Those who do recall the events, can only refer to some vague story of misfortune involving a stillborn baby. Many assumed that Mala had been living in one of the Haman villages for all of these years and they were only mildly puzzled by her return."

Alor: "Well, Mala has come back at a good time. The people are too preoccupied with the news that the Aka might be mounting some kind of offensive action to inquire as to her whereabouts these last two decades."

Taijaur: "Isn't it time for our meeting with the Council?"

Alor: "No, we have more than an hour. Rainar asked to re-schedule our time because of some unexpected business that the Council had to tend to. But the delay will give us a chance to talk before facing that 'august' body."

They both smiled at Alor's intended sarcasm as they continued walking around the edge of the family compounds, near the granary and communal gardens. In the courtyards of some of the family compounds there were small children running and playing while one or two women sat nearby cooking, working and watching over them.

There were only a few people working in the gardens on this 'respite' day and they waved or hailed greetings to the two men as they strolled outside of the low stone wall around that area. The standard Ocan work week was three and a half days, while the rest of the week the people were permitted a respite from the tasks that they all performed on behalf of their collective. They generally used their 'respite time' to cultivate their creative, personal, and spiritual development in ways that their community responsibilities did not always necessarily permit.

Most Ocan extended families reside in circular compounds comprised of four to five separate homes constructed around a central courtyard where they all gathered at the fireside for evening meals and special family celebrations. Sometimes if the families began to grow beyond the usual number of homes, some of the nuclear families would branch off and a new compound would be built, starting most times with homes for three separate nuclear families. When Taijaur was young, he spent time with the Dalasa family in their larger compound of seven separate residences and also sometimes with Uncle Kalal who lived in the compound of his wife's extended family. As much as he enjoyed the evening revelry and camaraderie of life in the village compounds, Taijaur preferred the solitude of his home with Saba in the meadow on the outskirts of the village. He once asked his grandmother why they did not also live in a family compound of the village. She smiled as she told him that her work required that she live in a place that allowed her to hear when the earth called her name.

Alor: "You must try to learn as much as you can about Mala's life both now and when she was growing up. Any little bit of information might help you to convince the girl that she must return to the island."

Taijaur: "Mala spends a lot of time away from the village and no one knows where she goes. Saba gets anxious every time that Mala mysteriously disappears, but thus far, she has always returned in a day or two."

Alor said in a low voice, "Then it appears that you and she may have much in common."

Taijaur chose to overlook this remark as he continued, "She also walks almost every night and morning before the dawn, up on the mountain, near the ruins."

Alor: "She was raised in those mountains and her former home is buried somewhere in those ruins. She and her parents lived as close as they could to the forbidden territory without being accused of violating Ocan law."

Taijaur: "I walk with her sometimes when I can't sleep. Mala says that she is not sure that Shona can be convinced to return. But I wonder, Master Alor, if I am successful in bringing Mala's daughter back to the island, how will we proceed? What plan will we put into action that will bring us closer to our goals?"

Alor: "All I know is that this girl somehow holds the key to our understanding of the fractures that exist between realms of existence. The disruptions in the patterns of energy and the fracture in the fabric of our existence date back to the time of her appearance within this realm. The existence of this child, or rather young woman, may be, as the Obeah foresaw, connected with the injera of the Ocan and more specifically, she may be connected with the injera of this world as a whole. I'm not sure why or how, but somehow this young girl may hold the key to the fulfillment of our purpose. I am hoping that she will work with us in learning how to locate the portals and develop our use of the portal energy.

Perhaps only once a century there are a select few who are born with the enhanced ability that allows them to actually sense or see the gateways to the in-between. Your mother fit into this category of those specially endowed individuals who are capable of sensing and seeing the portals. Millennia may pass before life brings forth another type of person who possesses abilities that are even more extraordinary. This is a person whose mere presence can actually create new openings or cause new openings to form. I believe that Mala's daughter may belong to this latter, much more powerful group of extremely rare individuals.

Although, much of what must be done has yet to be determined, I am hoping that by studying this young woman's impressions as well as bringing her in contact with the area of the portal, that we will be able to determine the extent and nature of the energy flows. While you are away, I will continue the work of developing a receptacle and conduit for the energy. Also, another important part of your mission in the mainland will be to try to determine the precipitating factor that is causing this virus to grow."

Taijaur: "Do you think that the Council will believe that Shona's presence can help us to locate the portals?"

Alor: "No, I don't. But I will still vainly attempt to persuade them of the value that this girl holds for our collective. In the end, fear will dictate that the Elders go along with our proposal of bringing her back. They will undoubtedly want this girl returned to the island in order to safeguard the secret of Ocan existence."

Taijaur: "By telling them of Shona's importance to the portal energy, do you think that they may begin to suspect that we intend to go beyond the protocols for our project?"

Alor: "No. They are too presumptuous of their own authority to suspect that anyone is not complying with their dictates. And no one, but Mala, must know the full extent of our plans, not even your grandmother. Not until the time is right."

Taijaur: "Saba knows only that I will seek to bring Shona back and that you believe that she can help us in our work."

Alor: "Good. I have assured Mala that no harm will befall her daughter and I am depending on you to assist me in keeping this promise."

Taijaur: "I will protect her with my life." He paused then said, "On another note, Master Alor, will it still be possible to request a special dispensation to work with the Aka? It seems even more imperative to press for diplomatic relations in light of the news of a possible Aka uprising. If we reach out to them before the situation exacerbates, then we may potentially avert any further hostility."

Alor: "I cannot pretend that I understand your full reasoning on the issue with the Aka, however, as I indicated previously, I will present your case as a part of our petition to the Council. But keep in mind, this present group of elders who currently serve on the Council are stubborn and implacable, especially in matters concerning the Aka."

Taijaur: "I keep thinking that if only we were able to find the Emissary, then potentially the Ocan and Aka could be re-united. Also the Emissary's presence would mean that we would be able to go further in our work and seek the catalyst in order to restore the world's balance of energy."

Alor: "Taijaur, we must wean ourselves from this dependence of looking for, waiting for, wishing for some one or some thing to come along to help us."

Taijaur: "What do you mean?"

Alor: "From the beginning of our discussions you have made reference to potential sources from whom we may solicit assistance—the Obeah, the Aka, the Emissary."

Taijaur: "But there are passages in the Book that speak of an emissary, Master Alor. And there is something in my dreams that leads me in this direction as well—some message contained in the notes of a song. I cannot quite capture it, but I feel close to discovering its meaning."

Alor: "Taijaur, we don't have the time. If the Emissary comes as the prophets have foretold, and his/her coming is in time to help us, then so be it. But as it stands now, we must move forward. Even if the Book mentions the Emissary, we still have to work with what we have before us right now. And this girl may possess much that will aid our cause. She may hold the key to what attracts and pulls the energy. We may not be able to re-set the balance, but with the power that she is able to transmit, we may at least be able to stop this plague from spreading any further. The future of this planet may depend upon what we are able to accomplish. Don't be deterred by the fact that, at this point, there are just two of us pursuing this cause."

Taijaur: "But I, I—" Taijaur faltered, sighed heavily and then said, "You're right Master Alor. I guess it is hard for me to imagine how the two of us alone will be able to accomplish all that we seek to achieve."

Alor seemed not to see or hear the tone of resignation in Taijaur's voice and demeanor as he went on saying, "I understand how you feel. I also wish that some one or some thing would come along to help us, to save us. But we must learn to believe in our own power to bring about change, transformation. Each individual life force on this earth has the power to rise to greatness; to their own god-power within.

Taijaur you must see your steps as a continuation of steps that will lead the Ocan people to meet their destiny. Hold within yourself the future vision of the exodus of our people out of this incubator of a land into the world that needs us. You are a living bridge to the other side—a bridge between what the Ocan are and what they must become, just as this girl may be a bridge between realms of existence. You must feel the power of the multitude of steps before yours and those that will follow you. Feel the power of the people behind you as you go into this mainland.

All great revolutions in life begin with one person deciding that change must come and then joining with others who see and share this vision of a new day, a new way of living and being. The Ocan people began in this way years ago. And now it is time for our people to complete what we started and take responsibility for what we should have done long ago. This virus is and has always been mankind's one and only enemy; the only real danger that we face. We must discover what is causing or helping it to grow. It is time to conquer this plague once and for all."

Taijaur: "Master Alor, there is one other thing that concerns me. I am not quite certain how I will maneuver in this foreign land. The people of the mainland—they will know that I am not one of their kind."

Alor: "Taijaur, you must bear in mind that these people of the mainland are who we are, where we come from. You must do as our forefathers did and seek those of this populace who are of kindred spirit. There are people like the Ocan people everywhere. People who want to determine their own destiny, actualize their own power without the interference of domineering governments. People who want to live, work and create in the absence of a shallow societal value system that dictates how they live and what they worship. These are people who are largely left out of the processes of society by their very refusal to have their way of life and values compromised and potentially negated.

The only real difference between the Ocan people and these other progressive souls is that the Ocan people found each other and a way to band together for the collective strength and mutual benefit of our purpose. The Ocan people saw themselves as a community of seekers who deliberately disavowed the contrived institutions of mankind and recognized that many of those institutions had been manufactured primarily for the purpose of governmental and societal control and to serve the interests of those in control."

Taijaur: "If they did not like the way that the government was run, why didn't they just try to help change things, by becoming a part of the ruling structure?

Alor: "That is exactly what they did not want to do. From the beginning of human civilizations, political or economic power has often corrupted the souls of those who are not strong enough to guard against it. Many times the people allow their institutions to control how they think, feel and act. And in some societies, all science, all art, all forms of creation and investigation must comply with and conform to the dictates of institutional goals."

Taijaur: "So the Ocan, or rather this community of seekers thought that they could change all of that by leaving and coming to this island?

Alor: "They began to recognize that a phage had infected the minds and souls of the people. They believed that the societal and governmental institutions were helping to sustain and perpetuate actions that were in line with the symptoms of the plague. However, the Ocan people did not realize how virulent and deadly this plague was and they did not react in time to try to ameliorate its effects. By the time they comprehended the full magnitude of what was happening they were either unwilling or unable to take the full steps necessary to eradicate it.

The effects of the virus appeared to be especially apparent in many of those who sought power in the world. It is believed that the virus changes the brain in such a way to cause delusions of superiority and a belief in an inherent right to rule over others. Consequently, the Ocan community knew that staying in the world would mean not only a constant struggle for survival, but also endless battles for the very right to exist. By building a separate isolated society based on Ocan principles and beliefs, then our energy could be devoted exclusively to spiritual development and growth. Our communal society addresses our survival needs, to the extent that survival has become a non-issue and does not consume an inordinate amount of our time. Thus, we have the time and freedom to devote to our creative, intellectual and spiritual development."

Taijaur: "How did the seekers select who would be a part of their collective? Did they just randomly choose those who would join them or was there some process to identify like-minded people?"

Alor: "They never actively recruited anyone; they just sought opportunities to work with other people who potentially possessed great spiritual mass."

Taijaur: "But how were they able to identify those with great spiritual mass? What traits did they look for?"

Alor: "They knew them by their actions. As you are aware, the gifts of the Earth are offered to all terrestrial inhabitants. Thus, it is possible for anyone or even everyone to possess great spiritual mass. However, it is only once a person's sentiale pathways are truly open, that spiritual mass begins to manifest in an individual's actions and deeds. There is no set number of attributes, but the three main ways that people generally express great spiritual mass are through acts of kindness, freedom and responsibility.

Kindness, true and genuine kindness, is perhaps the most recognizable trait. A kindness that is generated from wisdom and understanding, and demonstrated by way of compassion, concern, consideration for any and every person, every animal, and every object that crosses your path. The freedom that I speak of is a freedom from a dependence on surface realities; freedom from ego, from other people's influence, from pettiness, meanness, from self-demoralization, from crass materialism and any other behavior that does not exemplify that which is highest in human nature.

Responsibility is the third most important trait that I can think of. This attribute entails a willingness to see the resolution of 'life problems' as each individual's responsibility; a responsibility to try to heal the wounds of the earth and those of all its inhabitants.

These were just the base level of attributes that the seekers detected in those they welcomed as a part of their collective. And they looked for people to exhibit these traits as a natural part of how they behaved, not as a result of adherence to some external belief system, or indoctrination. These 'traits' should manifest as easily and as naturally as breathing, walking, seeing and hearing. They are inherently a part of an individual's character and they can not ever be shaken, diminished or taken away. Those with high spiritual mass do not have to be taught or receive instruction on 'how to be or become' a kind, free, and responsible person. Although I suppose that it is always helpful to have reminders along the way."

They were now walking through the marketplace that surrounded the Maja, continuing to wave and greet the people that they passed along the way.

Alor: "Come, let's go up to the Council chambers. It is not quite time, but we can wait in the anteroom before being summoned for our little 'inquisition'." He paused before opening the door to the Maja. "One other thing before we go in."

Taijaur: "Yes?"

Alor: "Do you still dream of her Taijaur?

Taijaur: "All the time."

Alor: "Can you tell me anything about the nature of the dreams or the strength of the connection? Are you able to sustain sentiale awareness with her for long periods, despite the increased distance between the two of you?"

Taijaur looked away, avoiding eye contact. He put his hand over his mouth and coughed slightly before saying, "I would rather not discuss the dreams. But I can tell you that they are definitely getting more intense. The link is strong and clear."

Alor: "That is all that I need to know." He smiled ruefully before continuing, "But Taijaur, let me caution you—this young woman may have much about her that is inherently good. However, she may lack self-knowledge; of who she is, of her place in this world. This lack of knowledge, if it has led to uncertainty or insecurity, may make her a danger to herself as well as anyone who crosses her path in any significant way. We have no way to gauge the substance of her intent. Guard yourself accordingly."

Taijaur just looked at Alor, offering no response. They went into the building and started up the stairs to the council chambers which took up one half of the second floor.

Alor: "Oh, and please remind me to get the notes from your most recent translations before you leave the island. There is a thread that starts in some of the earlier material and I think that it may continue through some of the other passages. It is also necessary that I consult with Amira as soon as possible."

Taijaur: "Aunt Amira? I'm afraid that she may not be able to offer you any assistance. Her spirit is seriously frayed. I know, in the past, her expertise was considered essential to any important research endeavor but, I don't think she knows anything about the Book or its translation. She hasn't been to the libraries in months. Olana does her work now."

They opened the heavy large intricately designed metal doors that led into an anteroom-vestibule area, where council petitioners waited until they were called into the chambers. There was another set of smaller double doors that opened directly into the interior room.

Alor: "Amira may be able to shed some light on that phrase that Kalal kept repeating. I think that it may be significant. There was something that I saw in Kalal's sentiale that coincides with—"

There was a loud sound from inside the chamber room. Taijaur put his ear to the door, "It sounds like someone is already in there. It sounds like Master

Edise speaking as well as two other people whose voices I don't recognize; probably some of his secret scouts."

Alor: "Can you hear what they are saying?"

Taijaur: "No. Should we knock?"

Alor rapped slightly on the door and the voices stopped. They heard Rainar, the head of the Council of Elders, say, "One moment please," and then a shuffling sound inside. Alor found himself wishing for the days when Toval was still alive. Even if he did not always agree with his judgments, still Alor knew that Toval's decisions arose from a deep feeling part of himself and he was always fair and impartial, thinking of the good of all Ocan. They had been good friends and when Toval pleaded with him to become a part of the council in order to inherit his role as Council head, Alor was tempted, but only for a moment. He was even further tempted once he heard of Rainar's adamant opposition to his appointment. But no matter how worthwhile these enticements may have been, in the end, neither Rainar's pettiness nor Toval's persuasions had been enough to override his need for solitude and freedom.

Lately, Rainar had made so many changes to the Council that Alor was beginning to wonder if he had made the right decision. Petitions were no longer submitted to the Council sitting around a table, like a discussion among friends. Petitioners now had to stand looking up at the Elders who were seated on an elevated dais behind a long wooden rostrum. It was obvious to Alor that someone needed to monitor Rainar's use of the satellite. He knew that she assiduously watched the satellite transmissions and most of her ideas for change came from the most inane of these broadcasts. Each time, before he entered one of these 'tribunals', Alor now held his breath to brace himself against the effect of the latest new change that Rainar had instituted. He dreaded the day that he might walk in to find the Elders decked out in shiny black robes with powdered wigs sitting askew on their heads.

For the first time in the history of the Ocan Council, the members were all men with the exception of this one woman, who, according to Alor, had apparently cloned the brains of the other four members from her own neurons. They deferred to her opinions in all matters, with not ever even one dissenting perspective. Alor had ceased to think of them as individuals. He had forgotten two of their names and never bothered to know the names of the other two who had moved from the Shinhala village to the Ocan-main some years ago.

According to Alor, this group had ceased to function as a council of elders and had morphed into the court of Queen Rainar, with the other four Elders appropriately named in his mind, Rainar 1, Rainar 2, Rainar 3 and Rainar 4; or simply, Elders 1, 2, 3 and 4. There were no distinguishable traits between the four clones, except that Elder 4, openly dozed during must of the Council proceedings, with his cheek resting in his hand and drool spilling down his arm onto the rostrum. He usually awoke only to issue a shouted proclamation and then promptly went back to sleep.

When they were finally summoned in, there was no sign of Edise and the other two nameless voices who must have hurriedly exited through one of the side doors. Alor and Taijaur stood at the small podium that faced the rostrum of elders. Alor sighed with relief to see that the elders still wore the gray and brown robes of the master's guild. With her long sinewy face, pointed nose and narrow eyes, the queen bee was the first to speak. Clearing her throat and looking down at Alor over the top of thin spectacles, she nodded her head first in Alor's direction and then Taijaur's. "Greetings Master Alor, Taijaur. We trust that you both are continuing to honor thy Gift."

Taijaur and Alor responded at the same time, "Indeed, may we all be worthy."

Rainar: "And we trust that all goes well with the work. There were not many details in your last report."

Alor: "Well, Mistress Hadassa is still searching for a way to neutralize the radiation until a permanent seal can be put into place. Our geologists are working with the minerals and elements that may contain the emissions that we are looking for."

Elder 2: "Have you classified the radiation Alor? That is all that we need to know. Has the radiation been identified?"

Alor: "We lack the technology. Our instruments are not sensitive enough to capture the precise readings that are needed. The emissions that come through the openings have lower frequencies than any known frequencies and they are also unstable, varying widely with each reading."

Rainar: "Surely by now, after all this time, you should be able to at least tell us what we are dealing with."

Taijaur spoke up before Alor could respond, "Pardon me, Master Alor, Elders, but Kedar has asked me to report on the increase of seismic activity in the mountains, near the cave where we are working. He says that the 'episodes' that he mentioned previously are now happening with greater frequency and he recommends that a disaster plan be formulated that includes the possibility of evacuation from the villages."

Elder 4: "Kedar? Kedar?" Turning to the Elder on his right, "Did he say Kedar? Isn't that the fella that was just here?"

Rainar: "No, Elder, you are mistaken. Please allow the proceedings to continue."

Elder 4 grumbled incomprehensibly, and leaned the side of his face in his hand, as he began to doze once again.

Elder 2: "Are you saying that there is going to be some kind of an earthquake?" Speaking to the man next to him, "These mountains are long dead—so surely he cannot be suggesting any volcanic activity."

Taijaur: "Kedar says that he is not certain, but that there is enough seismic activity to warrant the development of a plan, so that we are not caught unaware. He says that perhaps there may be a major mudslide during the rainy season, like the one that happened years ago or some other such comparable occurrence."

Elder 3: "There has never been an earthquake on this island and there are no known fault lines in this land."

Elder I: "I told you, I told you—that Kedar is just an alarmist. I said so the last time that he came before this body with such outlandish predictions. I told you the last time."

Elder 3: "I'm sure the tremors are slight and are just a part of the earth's natural internal movements. The tectonic plates upon which the continents and the ocean basins lie are in constant, continuous motion. We cannot interpret every little movement as some sign of doom and destruction."

Elder I: "And we can not go around frightening the people unnecessarily. What you propose is utterly impossible!! Evacuation—where would we go? These mountains have long been dormant, dead."

Taijaur: "He says that we must take this seriously; that we must be prepared. The eastern hamlets may provide refuge or perhaps some where further south of the settlements, in the lower part of the island."

Rainar: "Why is Kedar not here to make his own report?"

Taijaur: "He said that he had some pressing business to take care of. He asked me to give his report for him."

Rainar: "Has he completed his Primary Retreat?"

Taijaur: "Yes, he did so a few years ago. And his younger brother is on his retreat now."

Rainar: "And can we assume that your retreat is also scheduled to take place soon?"

Taijaur looked at Alor who quickly responded, "Taijaur's translations are indispensable to our project right now. We won't be able to schedule his retreat until we have completed some passages in the Book that are crucial to our investigations."

Rainar: "We must determine who will continue Taijaur's work while he is away. Master Edise has informed us that he is available to take over some of the administrative tasks of this project. He believes that it would be possible to enforce tighter deadlines for the workers and accomplish some of the objectives in a more efficient manner."

Alor: "Edise? What does Edise know about our work? He is not a part of any of the project work teams, and especially not our project."

Rainar: "He knows more than you think. And he may soon be in a position to learn even more."

Alor: "What do you mean?"

Rainar: "It appears that this assignment is proving too much for you and Hadassa to handle alone. We have to consider adding other people in order to maintain—"

Alor: "Are you forgetting that I conceived this project and petitioned this council numerous times before my proposal was approved? I recruited Hadassa to work with me. No one else had even thought to work in the western mountains to search for the portal that had been uncovered there previously. This is my project and I say that we need no other apprentices, workers, or master guides. Is this why that sneaky worm Edise was just in here? To try to push me out—"

Rainar: "Master Alor, hold your tongue! I have not forgotten anything. But surely you fail to consider that you do not rule here and this decision will not be yours to make. You have no ownership over this project or any other Ocan endeavor. We honor all that you have accomplished, Master Alor. And you have done well in anticipating a need as great as the one that we face. But even you must be aware that those who conceive or initiate an action are not necessarily the ones qualified to see it through in the most efficient manner. Even Hadassa has voiced concerns regarding the project's unnecessary delays. This continuous lack of progress indicates a need for the type of assistance that Edise can provide."

Alor: "Edise is chief of security, what type of assistance can he provide to a scientific investigation?"

Rainar: "Enough, Alor! The debate on this topic will cease as of this second. What is the predicament that has brought you here today; that for which you desire counsel?"

Alor: "Taijaur and I would like to propose our own plan to increase the productivity of our work and enhance the desired outcome of the project as a whole."

Rainar: "What are you proposing?"

Alor: "We think that it may prudent, at this time in our history, to approach the Aka and offer to combine our skills and technology in this investigation of the portals."

Elder 3: "Alor, are you out of your mind? What do you mean by suggesting that we approach the Aka?"

Elder 1 speaking to Elder 4 who was still nodding and drooling, "All those gas vapors in the caves must be affecting him."

Elder 2: "No Ocan is permitted contact with the Aka without our permission. Where does this proposal originate? On whose behalf do you petition this Council?"

Alor: "On behalf of the project and the enhancement of our work. There has been no contact with the Aka. They do not know of our proposal. We are recommending that such a proposal be submitted to the Aka. They have technology that is more developed than our own. Their instruments may be sensitive enough to obtain the readings that we need. We, on the other hand, can offer them access to the only known area of a portal. There is much on both sides that justifies pursuing this as a joint endeavor."

Rainar: "Master Alor, you do realize that the Aka are planning to take aggressive action against us?"

Alor: "I know that there is talk of such—rumors and supposition that are always floating around."

Rainar: "Oh, make no mistake—there is no supposition here."

Elder 3: "For the first time in the two centuries that we have occupied this land, we have to consider a notion that our founders would have found repugnant and against all that we value—armed warfare. Do you know what it is like to prepare for bloodshed and the possibility of massive deaths? This whole thing is so alien, so foreign to who and what we are as a people."

Rainar: "Alor, you might not be aware, but unfortunately, we now found ourselves in this rather loathsome and bewildering position of having to develop ways to defend ourselves—"

Elder 4, who had awakened only moments before, interjected, "And all because of those damn Aka!"

Rainar: "Elder!"

Elder 4: "Oh, Pardon me." He whispered loudly to the Elder on his right, "I forgot there was a lady in the room."

Rainar: "Our scouts have reported the Aka's increase in military training as well as their constant manufacture of weapons. We thought that our differences had been settled long ago and if we just left them alone then all of this conflict would go away. Instead we find that we have naïvely believed that they accepted our mandates, when all along they were planning and waiting for the right time to mount an offensive action."

Elder 2: "The only reason that we have been able to contain them this long is because we outnumber them so greatly. However, if something is not done soon to stop them, then we may find ourselves in a less advantageous position."

Alor: "With all due respect, should we not consider that essentially all the Aka want—"

Elder 1 interrupted, "Demand."

Alor: "Pardon me?"

Elder 1: "The Aka have no wants, they only have and make demands."

Alor exhaled heavily, "Okay, demand—all the Aka really demand is the right to determine their own destiny, independent of the Ocan. They interpret our founders' intent differently than we do. They have declared themselves as a sovereign state. Should we not respect and honor their wishes for autonomy and find ways to work cooperatively with them?"

Elder 2: "They cannot claim sovereign territory in a land that is the province of the Ocan people. And whether they recognize it or not, the Aka are still a part of the Ocan collective. We do not accept or acknowledge any secession."

Alor: "This seems to be essentially a dispute over their right to pursue their own aims."

Rainar: "Their aims are antithetical to life. We must have solidarity and alliance to one common goal, one objective. We will never grant any official status to the Aka as a separate state."

Alor: "Then we remain at an impasse. The Aka demand that their sovereignty first be acknowledged before any diplomatic relations between the two groups ever occurs."

Elder 2: "Master Alor, surely you have not forgotten that the Aka want to exploit the land's power as an instrument to aid them in their quest for world domination. You and Taijaur are away from the villages, up in those mountains too much. You have not seen how many of our youth have been stolen away by the Aka. The Aka are recruiting once again—or they actually never stopped stealing away our people. We thought we had reached an understanding. But now we realize that they never intended to honor our agreement. And their current efforts have been even more successful than those of the past."

Elder 3: "They are stealing away some of our best young minds. They have stolen or lured even more of the people from the Haman and other outlying villages. It is only a matter of time before they become more aggressive and more confrontational, and perhaps attempt to take over the Ocan-main."

Elder 1: "How long do you think our young people will continue to believe that our way is correct? They watch the events in the world and they grow more aware of the presumed effectiveness in using force and violence to have power over other people. They see that over and over, myriad groups of peaceful people in the world have been conquered or exterminated. They see how the more violent factions of the human species have dominated over time. They have no way of really knowing or verifying what real power is and that eternity favors the energy that feeds the purpose we pursue."

Alor: "But isn't it your duty, your responsibility as the leaders of our collective to do whatever it takes to help us fulfill our destiny, even if that means putting aside any differences and finding a way to work with others whether we agree with them or not?"

Rainar: "We do not need you to remind us of our duties or our responsibilities Master Alor. Control of the southern territory is our problem.

How we deal with it or don't deal with it is not your concern. Your only task is to find a way to seal the portals. While we appreciate your concern, please let us each focus on our own individual responsibilities to this collective."

Elder 3: "No Alor—collaboration, while a lofty goal, is the direct opposite of the actions that we must now take."

Rainar: "Our decision on this matter is final. We will entertain no further discussion regarding the Aka or working with them."

Alor looked at Taijaur briefly, before turning back to face the Council.

Alor: "There is one other matter that I would like to bring before this Council."

Rainar: "What is it?"

Alor: "I would like to propose that Taijaur be granted permission to briefly leave the island in order to—"

Elder 4: "What? What did you say?"

Elder 4 Turned to Elder 1 on his left, "What did he say? I thought I heard him say something about leaving the island."

Elder 3: "That is what he said."

Elder 1: "Impossible!"

Elder 2: "That's preposterous."

Rainar: "Please, gentlemen, let us listen and hear Master Alor's full proposal."

Turning back to Alor and Taijaur, "Alor, please continue. You have our attention."

Alor: "This is a very pressing matter. It concerns Mala, and, and her child." He paused anticipating a reaction. At first they made no response as they looked back and forth at each other and then stared at Alor.

Rainar: "Alor, lest you forget, Mala has no child, no children. She has only recently returned after years of being away. Everyone assumed that she, herself, had died a long time ago."

Alor: "No, this is the child that was born to Mala nearly two decades ago. She is now a little younger than Taijaur. The child that arrived that ominous night of eternal darkness, and then was so ruthlessly buried alive."

Rainar: "Alor it is hardly charitable of you to describe so obligatory of a task in such graphic and offensive terms."

Alor: "My apologies, Rainar, Elders" he bowed his head to each in turn. "I meant no offense. Nonetheless, the description is not important. I am here to tell you that the child survived that fateful encounter and lives now as we speak. She has recently left the island and is somewhere in the mainland. I am proposing that Taijaur be sent to bring her back in order to—"

Elder I: "Impossible! That child cannot be alive. That was ages ago."

Elder 2: "Her grave is still in the northern forest, along the path to the temple grounds. That barren piece of land, where nothing grows. I saw it a few years ago when—"

Rainar: "Elders, please be quiet. Taijaur, we must ask that you excuse us for this next phase of the discussion. Alor will inform you of our final resolution. Honor thy Gift."

Taijaur bowed to each of the Elders before turning to exit the room, stating simply, "May we all be worthy."

Rainar waited until she heard the exterior door to the Maja council chamber close. It was obvious that she was coming to a slow boil and fighting to contain her rage. She began calmly, with composure, and only a slight hint of sugary sarcasm, "Master Alor, for two centuries we of the Ocan have lived in the comfort and security of our little world. And do you know why we have had such comfort and such security?"

Alor: "Uhh, maybe because we have deluded ourselves into believing that the world is safe?"

All pretense was over, Rainar exploded, spitting out her words one on top of the other, "No! We have been safe and secure because no one knew of our existence. We had the comfort to build a peaceful successful society without the outside intervention of the evils that trouble the rest of this world. And now you stand before this body, in the company of a boy, no less and calmly state that all that we have worked for is now in jeopardy!?! That our comfort and security may all be stripped away—because of some, some, some child of Mala's!?!"

Alor: "Well, Mala's daughter is no longer a child and I hardly think that Taijaur can be considered a 'boy'."

Rainar: "Alor, I am well aware that Taijaur has lived through more than a score solar cycles. You quibble over the insignificant to deflect attention from your own bad judgment and carelessness."

Alor: "Elder Rainar, I understand your—"

Rainar: "You understand nothing! How dare you take it upon yourself to presume to make decisions on behalf of this Council! Do you not realize the jeopardy, the vulnerability of the situation that you have put us in?"

Alor: "I am aware of the potential peril. However, while I may be accused of much, nonetheless, I am not responsible for the presence of Mala's daughter in the mainland."

Rainar: "No, but you have known of this long enough to have reported to this body that our safety has been threatened, our way of life compromised. The more time that passes, the greater her opportunity to expose our whereabouts and bring an end to our society, our people. You stand here speaking of the Aka's right to a sovereign state, when this greater calamity sits perched on our doorstep."

Alor: "But Elders, it is my opinion that the growth of the plague puts us in much more jeopardy than anyone knowing of our existence. This is why I also believe that the girl should return to the island. I believe that this young woman may be able to help us to understand the phenomenon we are dealing with. I believe that we must rise to the purpose of our existence and fulfill the intent of our founders in bringing us to this land."

Rainar: "Master Alor, I—"

She tried interrupting Alor several times, but he went on, talking loudly over top of her words, as if he did not hear or see her.

Alor: "Our people must be pushed into the next phase of our purpose. The Earth's energy is shifting and negative forces are becoming more pervasive. There are greater empty needs, unfulfilled spiritual needs, in the people of this world. The spirit of Mala's daughter may be connected to how the portal energy manifests. She can help us with our investigation..."

Rainar: "I must insist—"

Alor: "...There is evidence of imbalance all around..."

Elder 2: "Alor, you must—"

Alor: "...devastation in the earth's ecosystem, which is leading to worldwide catastrophes—famine; climatic disruptions, storms, uncontrollable fires, intense heat, global warming..."

The other elders glanced back and forth at Alor, Rainar and between themselves, with one or the other occasionally trying to intervene, but Alor kept talking as loud and as forcefully as he could.

Alor: "...This is all a product of the spiritual imbalance of the beings that populate the earth. Those with low spiritual mass are making decisions with little to no regard for the direct or potential impact on the earth or its inhabitants. The virus causes a lack of ability to fulfill spiritual needs. These greater occurrences of unfulfilled spiritual needs then in turn lead to negative predatory actions. The people are experiencing a sense of disconnect from the necessary spiritual essence of the universe..."

Rainar: "This is an outrage—"

She was frantically searching under the rostrum. Apparently there was a shelf below the top of the desk and Alor could hear papers and other items being rustled about.

He pounded his fist on the podium as he continued at the top of his voice, "...A new age is coming. The forces of evil have been allowed to dominate the earth for far too long. We can not continue to allow fear and a sense of complacency to dictate our actions. We are striving to become beings of power, and as such we have an obligation to face, not hide from, this world's system of predatory conquest. A system where only those deemed 'fit to survive' are allowed to have food, shelter, medical care and other basics of living. We must seek to restructure this diabolic system from within.

For these reasons and more, this girl is essential to our cause. We must learn as much as we can about the portal energy. The world's balance of energy allows incremental evolutionary steps in the spirit of man as well as those rare punctuated periods of evolutionary 'leaps' that can only come when there is enough power to push against the world's negative energy. We, as Ocan people, have a responsibility to push the balance of energy toward spiritual evolution. If negative energy continues to outweigh positive energy, then—"

Finally Rainar pulled a gavel from somewhere beneath the rostrum and banged it loudly several times on the top of the desk until Alor stopped talking. For a few moments, they both stared at one another in silence and all Alor could think was that her viewing of the satellite broadcasts really needed to be curtailed.

Rainar: "Master Alor, I know your opinions; we all know your opinions. You have always been very forthright about all of your theories and speculations. However, none of that matters right now. We are facing much larger issues and concerns. Can't you see that you are not the only one who has the ultimate purpose of our people in mind? If we are ever to fulfill the intent of our founders, we must continue to develop our power in isolation; our existence cannot be known. We must remain concealed from the world. Beyond just the danger of contact with the virus, what if knowledge of the power of this land and the resources of this land were known to the outside world? They would, in short order, destroy our society and exploit our resources for commercial gain. Is that what you want? Or have you forgotten that many of these precious, misguided people that you want to save in the world have conquered and invaded every peaceful nation on this planet?"

Alor: "I'm sure that Mala has impressed upon her daughter our need for concealment."

Rainar: "You can not be sure of anything; none of us can be sure anything. Every second that that girl is out there puts our lives at risk."

Elder 1: "And what if she mates with someone in the mainland?"

Elder 2: "What if someone tests her blood or the blood of any potential offspring that she may have?"

Rainar: "That girl or young woman must be returned to the island immediately. The longer she remains away from the Ocan, the greater the threat to our existence. How long has she been in the mainland?"

Alor: "I am not sure, but I think at least six months, maybe more."

Rainar: "It is imperative that she be brought back. She cannot be allowed to remain out in the world. Her very existence endangers all of our lives, bringing full circle the prophecies foretold at her birth."

Elder 4: "It's too bad that this problem can't be dealt with and disposed of in the mainland, so as not to pollute our world. But I guess we can't ask the boy to take on such a charge—or can we?

They all stopped talking and looked at Elder 4. He looked down, mumbling, "It was just a suggestion."

Elder 3: "Of course the boy must go. The people will be told that he is away on his Primary Retreat."

Elder 1: "The boy is essential to the Ocan cause. Isn't there another who can be sent?"

Elder 3: "What will happen if the girl does not return?"

Elder 2: "Are we certain that Taijaur will be capable of handling a spirit as powerful as this young woman?"

Rainar: "Taijaur is capable, he will go and the girl will return."

Turning back to Alor, Rainar continued, "She must be returned to the Ocan. Our safety, our very survival is threatened if she is out in the world. We have no way to control what she will reveal. And there is no way to predict what fatal consequences might await us. We must avert the vision of destruction that the Obeah saw in this being's mind from the moment of her birth."

Alor: "The Obeah foretold of no destruction. I have read, re-read and thoroughly studied the annals of those times. They spoke of the alignment of certain celestial forces of matter and energy; inevitable events simultaneous with the child's time in this world."

Rainar: "Nevertheless, she must be kept close to the Ocan. We must be aware of her actions and her intent if we are to forestall any potential loss that may befall us."

Alor: "You can't just treat this girl as some object or animal that must be contained. I have promised her mother that no harm will come to her."

Rainar: "It is enough that we agree that the girl must return to the island. Let us not quibble over minor details. We must make certain that no one else knows of this girl's existence. We don't want the people attaching any special significance to her life and continued existence; to think that death has no sway over her."

Elder 2: "Time is of the essence with this predicament. How soon can Taijaur be readied for this voyage? He must travel to the western shore as well as sail for days, if not weeks or months, on the open sea."

Alor: "Taijaur can leave immediately. Mala has told us where her sailing craft are stored in the caves near the shore. She has also been able to draft maps of the quickest route through the mountains and forest. Taijaur can follow a more direct path to the mainland from the northern part of the island."

Elder 2: "We will provide the boy with what he will need to assimilate into this culture. We can manufacture facsimiles of their forms of monetary exchange and clothing to suit their milieu."

Rainar: "Yes, and with Taijaur's departure, it seems even more prudent that Master Edise assist with the, uh, radiation project. You said yourself that the translations are an indispensable part of your work. The translations of the Book must continue in his absence. And Alor you are the most logical person to take on this task. Edise will work with Hadassa and assume responsibility for the overall administration and delegation of the other project tasks."

Alor: "I also stated previously that I do not need Edise's assistance. I am fully capable of working on the translations and continuing to oversee the project."

Rainar: "Alor, don't fight me on this. This will only be a temporary arrangement. When Taijaur returns, you may assume full command of the project once again. We don't have much time and you must focus on what is best for the goals of this project, what is best for our people. Surely, you of all people, will not allow petty personal ambition or an egocentric quest for knowledge to stand in the way of our progress, our people's well-being."

Alor looked at Rainar, offering no response. And then as he began to turn and head towards the door, he said, "I will take my leave and I trust that you will all continue to honor thy—"

Rainar: "No Alor, wait." She stood and came from behind the rostrum and down from the raised platform, walking hurriedly towards Alor and then pulling him in the direction of the door. The other elders had already begun to talk and argue amongst themselves, except for Elder 4 who was already slumped down in his chair, with his head on his chest as he snored loudly. Rainar pulled Alor into the anteroom between the heavy outer doors and the interior doors to the chambers. She was whispering, "There is one more thing. I want to make sure that this door is closed tightly. I don't want anyone else to overhear this."

Rainar: "Alor, I must ask that you also work with Edise in taking care of this situation with this girl, this young woman. There are certain matters that cannot—should not—be spoken of aloud. But despite his obtuse manner, Elder Nairi is correct in assessing that some final solution must be found and rendered in terms of this girl." She paused, peering at Alor. "I trust that you know how this situation must be dealt with ultimately. This girl's presence in our community must be, uh—contained. Edise will know what to do. You must turn her over to him as soon as she is brought back to island."

Alor looked her in a level manner, careful to betray no thoughts or emotions, as he said, "I will comply with what ever you deem necessary."

Rainar: "Master Alor, you do realize that our systems cannot tolerate the introduction of foreign species. We cannot afford to upset the balance of our environment with any potential invasive plant or animal. This child of Mala's, like most invasive species—in the beginning, they may appear innocuous and minute. And then they quickly spread, overtaking and destroying the life that is indigenous to the land. You know the destruction these foreign species have caused. You have read the reports, the scientific studies."

Alor: "I am familiar with the impact of invasive species throughout the world. But don't forget that other bodies of land have also experienced the introduction of beneficial foreign plants and animals. It is this very quality of 'foreignness' that has allowed life on this planet to be continually diversified and renewed."

Rainar: "Nonetheless, we do not have the luxury of waiting to see which effect she will bring. There will be no second chances in our quest to fulfill our destiny. Our forebears struggled very hard to bring about the reality of our society. We are obligated to the dreams of those who have come before us. And we have the responsibility to ensure that those who will follow us may have the chance to know a better world."

Alor: "I understand Rainar."

Rainar: "The boy must know nothing of this."

Alor: "Taijaur knows what he needs to know."

Rainar: "I trust you Master Alor. No matter our differences of opinion, I know that, in the end, you will always do what is best for our people. And that is why I am certain that this time the solution to this predicament will be final and that we will never again have to hear of this, uh—situation."

He made no reply and when she saw that he was turning to exit the vestibule area, she called out, "Honor thy Gift, Master Alor."

Alor allowed the heavy metal door slamming behind him to serve as his response.

II. Dust to Dust

Silence. Absolute silence. No movement, no breeze, no sound. The heat—like a second layer of thick skin and heavy muscle—surrounded, enveloped and absorbed with oppressive dominion. Shona saw his eyes first. Generating an absence of sound, they stretched wide as if to take in all sensory perception with each gaze. He was alone. Squatting in front of a small square wooden house, he was quietly whittling a piece of wood as he occasionally looked up, surveying the landscape, as if waiting or anticipating some one or some thing. She knew that he sensed her presence but he gave no outward sign. Ancient as the dust in which he stooped, his tightened tendons and knotted muscles revealed a strength that had endured despite his obvious witness of a great passage of time. Shona crouched low, hidden behind a thick patch of isolated brush. She studied intently this curious being before her whose scent, so unlike other humans, exuded neither fear nor desire.

She had followed a mindless meandering route that led across and through the canyons, up and down rocky mountain trails. Still traveling on the outskirts of human habitats, Shona had not directly encountered another bipedal life form since the Inar female in the canyons. Finally she found herself at this solitary outpost, which apparently had been deserted by all who value generous shade and a bountiful subsistence. The leftover dust and debris had apparently coughed up this dried-out old man and a few captive farm animals that were now banished by the omniscient mid-day sun to the interior shade of a ramshackle barn that stood with an outside pen on one side of the house. The climate and terrain, having failed to lure any fair share of seasonal or annual precipitation, kept its scant supply of water locked away in thick-skinned prickly plants and deep secret places underneath the ground. The dry hard land permitted no real trees or grass to take hold, just volumes of dust and isolated patches of low-lying bushes and shrubs that dotted the landscape. As with all life indigenous to an unforgiving environment, these plants were tough, wiry little rascals that bunched close together, protecting their own. Aggressively, they claimed the right to exist, daring any other living entity to try to enter their territory. Even now they provided a dubious, yet stalwart shield for Shona; issuing warning scratches if she trespassed too far, while still concealing her fully from anyone's view.

Shona had emerged out of the rocks of the canyon and ventured onto a homeless dirt road, traveling for hours and then days along this narrow path with no idea where it led or whence it had come. The subtle, almost indiscernible, scent of sheltered animals had tempted her curiosity and led her to this small squat house a little ways off from the road. The old man continued to survey the territory, looking everywhere but the area where Shona hid.

As she analyzed the scene before her, some stratospheric sensation pricked her attention and she looked up to see a large bird of prey high in the sky, floating on the wind. For a moment she was mesmerized by its silent elegant tranquil glide, then remembering her task, she turned back to her subject and was assaulted by a direct piercing stare as the old man now looked straight at her with no movement or sound. Though the bushes fully obscured her body from his vision, she felt his eyes inside of her own and she knew that he could see her as clearly as if there were no distance or object in the path between them. A powerful intent shot from his eyes through the air, sealing Shona to the spot she occupied, paralyzing her in position and place. Shona was shocked to feel him inside her mind, scanning her thoughts. And she was even more alarmed to find that she could not block, stop or control his access. Then just before her fear rose full pitch, his face and eyes suddenly opened into a warm welcoming smile, as he put down the wooden object and with a slow fluid motion, waved his arm and hand, beckoning her approach. After briefly considering her options and ruling out the feasibility of escape, she rose slowly, and crept reluctantly out of the underbrush. Advancing hesitantly, Shona was wary yet drawn to this first human contact offered by this inhospitable land. With overt signs of friendship and goodwill, he motioned for her to draw near and made room for her to sit on the ground beside where he stooped.

Before she had completely sat down cross-legged next to him, he began, in the exact language of the Ocan, to welcome her as if she was an intimate acquaintance, grasping her hands in his own and stroking her hair. Never inquiring as to who she was or where she was going, he at once began speaking, with a serene countenance and melodic voice, of the wind and the dust and the sun. He told her that she was fortunate to arrive when she did as the elements would soon converge to release the combined force of their will. At first she thought that he mistakenly took her for someone else, a family member or close friend. Then she realized that his manner reminded her somewhat of the old Gruenataring woman, the grandmother. Her reality was not always in the present and each time that she saw Shona, she greeted her in the same manner as this man, with a flood of warmth and familiarity even when they first met. Shona had never succeeded in convincing the elderly grandmother that she was not one of her own crew, as the woman invariably passed out duties, treats, and admonishments as freely to Shona as to her own flesh and blood. However, whereas, the old woman's eyes had roamed unfocused in their milky pursuit of perception, this man peered firmly, unyielding, taking in the whole of supraliminal sentience with each gaze.

He motioned to her to follow him into his dwelling, where he offered her food and when she had eaten, he took her to one of the small bedrooms at the back of the house. Shona moved in a daze, going where he led, complying impassively with each instruction. She lay down her burden, and fell into a deep disturbing sleep. The thunderous wind that came that night and shook and rattled the house became part of the nightmare visions that chased, pursued and devoured her. At first it was the Inar and then that man who still stalked, hunted and preyed upon her imagination even now, years past the time that she should have forgotten about him. She knew who he was even before her dreaming-mind conjured the scars across his face and down the side of his neck. Her mind tried desperately to pull away from the jumble of terrifying, malignant images. But the dreams of being chased and devoured kept coming one right after the other. And the scenes did not shift until she found herself in a nonsensical world with children flying and a strange bearded man with heavy breasts who touched her forehead and made the fire inside of her go away.

She woke three days later and moved into a new guise. Her body was sore and stiff yet strangely, she felt refreshed with an overall superficial clarity of thought and emotion that did not permit the confusion or turmoil of unresolved feelings or beliefs. It was as if somehow, in her sleep, she had washed away pieces of herself; the old tired pieces of too much emotion and too much thought. She willingly allowed those parts of herself to be sloughed away, so that she might move into a new skin, a new existence. Shona consciously and in some ways unconsciously, shut down parts of her mind, parts of her soul. The surface was comfortable and safe. The effort to deliberately forget made her less strong. But this price was worth paying if it meant that she could become what ever she wanted to be with no reference to who or what she had once been. Her past was now a part of another person who no longer existed, or at least no longer mattered. Those other thoughts and emotions that she buried deep inside of herself offered her neither safety nor comfort. And for now, they were also completely out of reach.

It took a few weeks for Shona to re-gain her strength and it never came back to her fully. Where she was once energetic and vigorous, her movements were now sluggish and heavy. In the beginning, some days, even walking exhausted her. At these times, the old man would observe her closely and he frequently remarked, "You are not well." Twice he asked her, "What happened to you in the wilderness, in those canyon lands?" But both times Shona quickly looked away, shrugged her shoulders and made no response.

She moved with ease into the old man's home, into his life. He welcomed her into his world. His way of life became her own. They fell into an easy pattern of living and being. He instructed her, telling her of the land, the people and the universe; and she became his willing pupil. Shona accompanied him everywhere he went. Their daily excursions into the nearby villages were a living laboratory, an ever changing classroom where he incorporated everything that they saw and experienced into a "lesson" that was imparted in a straightforward and unassuming manner. She came to think of their time together as her life's work and she settled into this new way of learning and being.

Most days, they went from village to village as he tended to the sick and the ailing; treating the injured and the frail. Many times the old man would ask Shona to assist him in dressing a wound or treating an injury. After awhile she began sitting at the side of the injured people, humming a low tune while stroking or massaging a head, an arm or whatever part of their bodies brought them pain. She was able to go inside of those who suffered and take away their pain; help them to sleep or to see and feel those moments that sustained their souls.

She and the old man also sold baskets, blankets and other items that he and then they made at his home. Shona stayed close to the old man, never straying too far from his side. The people assumed that she was his granddaughter or some comparable relation. She gave up trying to learn the old man's name after she asked at least a dozen times and he simply looked at her and smiled. He had a mellow quirky kind of smile, with his eyes betraying an amused glint deep inside the creases that lined his face. In the beginning, every time that they went into the villages, her ears were always tuned to try to catch any moniker these people might apply to the old man. But they had their own system of nomenclature, as he was "grandfather" to all and even when she repeatedly told them her own name, they would always nod kindly and continue calling her "little sister". Occasionally, he would embed himself within a gathering of old men, and Shona would stand nearby with her antennas out; disappointedly coming away with only the "man", "sir", "chief", "captain" and "commandant" of their indiscriminate references to one another. She ended up calling him Om or sometimes just referring to him as the "old man".

The people of the villages had known this old man for too many years to keep count. He had come to their homes in the times of their parents and grandparents. The people of each village assumed that he lived in the next neighboring village or maybe the one after that. No one knew exactly where his home might be, nor did they wonder. But Shona did wonder how he had come to live in such a deserted place on the outskirts of a series of small inland and coastal villages.

These people, indigenous to the land, were physiologically, almost identical to Shona, Mala and many of the Ocan people. But for their clothing and mannerisms there were really no discernible differences. However, closer inspection would reveal in the Ocan clearer skin and stronger muscles and bones—all solidly packed together in a perfect union and harmony of movement and function. By comparison, the inhabitants of this mainland appeared soft and slightly malnourished.

Also there was something in their eyes that was strikingly different from that which came through the eyes of the Ocan people. Their eyes observed and comprehended the world with a different understanding, a different expectation. Whenever these mainland people gazed into the direct piercing stare of Shona's eyes they realized that she was not one of their kind; that she was from a different, more foreign place. As is obvious with all people from a place outside of your own, Shona's eyes conspicuously conveyed the fact that she understood and took in realities attuned to a spectrum unfamiliar to their own perceptual range.

They were a peaceful people and for the most part there was a lazy feel to village life. Most of the villages were approximately fifty to one hundred fifty miles south of a thriving and overpowering capital city near the seaport. The adversities of the more sophisticated and over-populated city did not touch the lives of the villagers except now and then, when someone would bring news of the latest atrocities. But then there were the times when the marauding soldiers swept through and appointed themselves the chief purveyors of right and wrong. Sometimes they patrolled and protected the villages, serving as police, judge and jury. However, they took their direction from a commander who frequently exacted payment in ways that contradicted any sworn purpose of fairness or justice. Still many of the villagers willingly offered their sons to the uniform of a shifting cause that no one could ever quite understand or explain.

But the people had their faith to carry them through. And their faith told them that one day their savior would come to lead them to a lost sacred stone, whose power would make them triumphant over their enemies and reward their suffering. This sacred stone was known as, 'The Eye', and it was said to be a rare type of diamond that was larger than a human skull. It was through this belief and this faith that the people garnered the strength to persevere despite their daily reality of living as a conquered nation.

Sulas, a deaf mute woman, came each day to cook for the old man and tend the small herd of wooly bovine animals, whose fleece she sheared, spun and wove into the blankets, clothing and other articles that Shona and the old man sold on their trading expeditions in the villages. Sulas neither invited nor entertained any form of communication from anyone. She took absolutely no notice of Shona or the old man as she went about her tasks, silently and efficiently each day. She had the facial hair of a man, with a thick dark mustache, beard and sideburns. Each morning Shona watched as she came along the road over the crest of the hill as if she literally rose out of the dry dust of the road and then each evening descended back into it, walking into the setting sun.

Shona tried to ask the old man about Sulas, but he gave no information beyond the obvious, "She cooks for me." Much like their first introduction, "This is Sulas. She cooks for me and now she will cook for you too."

Shona spoke up, "I can cook for myself. Or Sulas and I can cook together like my mother and I used to."

Om: "No, stay out of Sulas' way and accept her offering in peace."

Shona: "Does she talk?"

Om: "She neither hears nor talks. You would be wise to leave her alone."

She took heed of the old man's words, but watched ever closer this strange woman, searching for signs of why one might be 'wise to leave her alone'. There were times when Shona thought she felt waves of hot pain and hatred coming from the woman. Although Sulas never looked up or altered her steady movements of putting things in order, preparing food or tending the old man's small garden and animals, always with the same benign detachment. Shona had been there for only a few weeks when Sulas started bringing with her a little girl about three or four years of age. Like Sulas, beyond the child's name, no information was offered. When Shona first saw Aria, she thought surely that the child embodied the spirit of the wind or a vivacious bird captured in human form. The girl never tired of moving, jumping, flying; and she chattered incessantly. Every person she met became a favorite loved one, a special friend. She brought joy to the quiet remote dwelling of the old man. Despite his calm inconspicuous manner, Shona felt a subtle internal change in him as the little girl hung around his neck and smothered him with kisses. He would never stop what he was doing and he never made many comments specifically in her direction, but he emitted a warm glow whenever she was around, and he seemed to look for her expectantly each day as she arrived. Try as she might, Shona could discern absolutely no change in Sulas as a result of the girl's presence; even as Aria sat in her lap, and played with her hands or face, Sulas was as oblivious of her as she was of all life. She would simply move the girl's body or hands if they obstructed her reach to the peas that she was shelling or the basket that she was weaving.

Aria reminded Shona of the baby animals that she had enjoyed being with in the Ocan forest. That same spirit of play resounded in their movements and their understanding of the purpose of life. It pleased Shona to think that her presence made the little girl especially happy, because she too could laugh, play and chatter like the morning birds and the evening crickets. They would sit and comb each other's hair and invent guessing games or share their games of hand clap and finger play. Aria cried every time that Shona and the old man would go on their forays or each evening as Sulas put her near-sleeping body over her shoulder. As quickly as her tears began they would cease. Shona would turn, as she left to go to the villages, and see Aria wiping her eyes as she ran, laughing, trying to catch an insect, or lizard or what ever playmate the earth would offer at that moment.

Shona and the old man spent most of their time in the village closest to them, often visiting with a local family—the Immanuels. There was the father-husband, Immanuel; his wife, Mrs. Immanuel or Mother Immanuel, the Immanuel girls (there were four), and the Immanuel brothers (there were three). The Immanuels and all the people of this village embraced Shona into their lives as one of their own. She liked to sit in the midst of their gatherings listening to the conversations that flowed around her. For the most part, her life was peaceful and content.

Occasionally, thoughts of Lubar flooded through her, and she struggled to remember him only as he was on the island, pretending that she had never actually brought him to this land or caused him to die. Most times she could even convince herself that that horrifying encounter in the canyons with that unnatural being had happened in another lifetime, to another person. And then there were the times when thoughts of Lubar's vicious death and of the Inar creature weighed heavy in her soul. She would try to exorcise the memory, involuntarily spewing its venom, and the evil always came back to her. Even Aria perceptibly knew to stay away from Shona when these unwanted and little understood feelings surfaced and vented themselves against her will.

Initially, she told herself that she would return and continue to provide food for the woman; but she knew, even then, that she was deceiving herself. Sometimes, during the day she felt that she-devil pursuing her. The old man would study her intently as she turned suddenly and sharply in fear, ready to fight off any attack that might be coming her way, her mind conjuring a mass of Inar creatures on the periphery of her vision. She would stay even closer to the old man's side, not letting him out of her sight. She knew that those creatures would never stop until they had found her and tortured her to death. Every time that she looked up or turned a corner she expected to see an ominous shape emerging from the shadows moving with great speed in her direction.

Every now and then, generally at a time of rest, knowledge of the woman's certain death would come to her, strong, hard and fast. In those moments, her sense of culpability would overwhelm her and at some level, below her conscious mind, she knew that life, alone, would seek its own certain retribution. However, her mind cowered from these thoughts and forced them away each time they attempted to return. So instead, she stayed in perpetual motion, running from the demon-visions in her mind and escaping from herself.

This constant state of flux and agitation continued until finally new, very different, very special dreams began seeping through. They released her from the hunt, allowing her internal guard to disarm. These were strange surreal dreams of desire, warmth and tenderness. She had had dreams like these before. However, this time, they not only stayed with her once she was awake, but the dreams were also coming through with a clarity and intensity that defied her everyday sense of reality.

Now, every night she dreamed of the same man, the same spirit in her mind. Something about this dream presence seemed familiar as she felt persistent, irritating tugs from her long-ago buried sentiale trying to remind her of something, someone. But she pushed away the prickly sensation of half-remembered forgotten dreams so that she could give herself fully to these new-found feelings of excitement and pleasure. Her sleeping psyche made love to this fantasy and she accepted his caresses, giving full vent to a passion that longed desperately for release. The dreams began to comfort her and ease the burden of her singular existence. Through her dream-lover she found sympathy and consolation. He showed her the way to her own internal harmony.

In the evenings, she found herself waiting for sleep with delicious anticipation. At the end of each day, her mind lay down its armor as she slipped into a deep soul satisfying tranquility. This new dream essence was tantalizingly familiar; he became a friend, a confidante. Still, some mornings the realities, from which there was no escape, surfaced within her and she woke breathing in the fear. Over time she learned to call forth the feel, the sensations of her nightly visions of bliss and contentment, in order to chase away the demons. These new visions began to sustain her during the day, becoming an essential part of her strength, her belief and her endurance.

The night and the forces that walk in darkness still called to her as they had on the island. But she never strayed too far from the old man's house as she awakened and rose in the moonlight to walk out into the pitch dark. One night she had gone farther than she realized, farther than she intended. She had been listening to the night sounds allowing them to lead her down the road as she reflected on the events of that day, when she looked up suddenly and realized that she was about a quarter of a mile away.

She heard a low guttural noise and then a shuffling sound coming from somewhere behind her. She tried to stay still and quiet but her breathing was coming fast and heavy. Shona felt that this unseen presence, what ever or who ever was out there, knew her and was now focusing its energy in her direction. She turned and began walking slowly back towards the house, suppressing an urge to run. The sound followed her, never getting any more or less loud. As she drew closer to the house, she began walking faster and she could not resist looking over her shoulder. She still could see nothing, but there was no mistake that the sound was following her. She turned back around to hurry back to the house and bumped directly into something, someone who was standing stock still in front of her in the darkness. The body, the entity that had materialized out of the blackness was now holding her arms so that she couldn't move. She stifled a scream, as she closed her eyes and an open sense of fear poured through her system and out of her pores.

The old man held her by the arms, speaking sternly into her face, "Shona! Shona, you must calm down. There is nothing, no one here but you and me."

By the time she recognized that this was no dangerous entity, she had become too weak to move. She let the old man lead her to the front of the house where they both sat down. Moments later she was still trembling. That feeling would not leave—something had been out there in the darkness waiting for her, watching her, aggressively stalking her.

They both sat quietly looking into the night until the old man said, "You are correct in sensing that something is hunting you."

Her head snapped up, but she made no reply as he continued.

"I feel and sense it also. It is something immensely powerful; and very much beyond your control. But you can not allow your fear to stalk you also. Your fear will do you more harm than this being can ever try. More than anything else, you are stalked by your own fear, in the guise of your death. Face the mortality that belongs to us all and there is no more fear. We create our own demons. We give other people, other circumstances power over us and they become our demons, larger than our own lives.

These demons feed on fear. With vampire-lust they sense the deep aromas of your uncertainty. What right do you have to allow your life force to become the fodder of evil beings—to taint your dreams with the blood of another's thirst?"

Shona: "I once accused my mother of that for which it now seems that I am found guilty. And now I feel just as lost and unsure as she seemed. Om, I don't know how to let go of the fear or even which path to take to escape it."

Om: "There are many paths, but only one that is meant for you at this time in your life. Whatever happened to you out in that wilderness—you must face it, understand it, come to terms with who you are as a result of that experience. These bouts of weakness and illness that you are experiencing are not just physical in nature. Your soul, your spirit and mind are in turmoil"

They were quiet again, soaking in the cool darkness. Without looking up, Shona said softly, "She said that she was Inar."

She felt but did not actually see the old man's body jump slightly. Shona had never seen him express much emotion, he always seemed utterly serene and tranquil, but now she looked into his face and for the first time saw an expression of something very close to alarm.

Om: "Are you sure that you heard correctly? Are you sure that she said, 'Inar'."

Shona: "Yes. She said that Inar was not her name, but that it was who or what she was. Have you heard of them before?"

Om: "Inar venom is fatal; there is no cure. That you survived at all is more than astounding; it is unbelievable. This venom may still be in your system and it may also be contributing to your sense of malaise"

Shona: "I wasn't sure if anyone knew or had ever heard of any such creature, any such being."

He went on questioning her until she had recounted most, but not all, of her experiences with the Inar female. Purposely not mentioning the manner in which she had left the woman, Shona went on to ask, "But who or what are these Inar? How do you know of them?"

He lowered his voice and began speaking as if he was reading or reciting from a text, "The Inar are a sentient amphibious race—one of the many hidden species that populate this planet. They are ancient, cunning and deadly. It is unusual to hear of one of her kind so far inland at this time of the century. Something must have awakened her out of her cycle. It is told that they live deep in the underwater caves and caverns, near the shore. Like locusts, they sleep, lie dormant until they are awakened by a call to return to the canyon lands approximately every fifty years. They revive a trek of their ancestors to their breeding grounds in the antediluvian rivers that once carved their way through that terrain. Their last such journey was supposed to have taken place only twenty to thirty years ago.

This fifty year cycle is supposed to be tied to the orbital period of two distant stars that mutually orbit around one another. But all of this is only myth. There are no solid facts known about the Inar; no evidence that leads to a complete understanding of their ways. But that they exist, there can be no doubt. The stories are too plentiful, the fear too real. Their attacks on humans are usually isolated and hard to trace. They possess superhuman strength and other unique qualities like bioluminescence.

This Inar that you encountered—she was probably near death even when she attacked you. Otherwise, I cannot imagine that you could have come through that encounter whole. There are not many documented references to their kind in human annals, mainly because those humans who have encountered them did not survive. It is interesting that the Inar female identified human bone and marrow as a primary or favored form of sustenance for her kind. Consumption of such may provide clues to their physiological make-up and their needs. But where was her mate?"

Shona was startled, "Why do you assume that she had a mate?"

Om: "If what we know about this species is correct, the Inar mate for life. In fact a mated Inar couple are considered bonded to the extent that they are one being; their cognitive structures are intertwined such that they see through one another's eyes, hear one another's thoughts."

Shona was silent, staring straight ahead. It took a few moments for her to realize that the old man was still talking.

Om: "We must find a way to offer atonement for your transgression against the Inar and for the guilt that you feel in your canine-friend's death."

Shona: "What!! No, that's not possible. I will spend the rest of my life trying to atone for the harm that I brought to Lubar. But to offer atonement to that, that, that creature would be suicidal, especially if they are as powerful and as dangerous as you say they are."

Om: "We need not seek any particular individual of this species in order to make your atonement. Rather we must find a place and a way that will convey—"

Shona: "I did nothing wrong. I had no other choice. I have nothing for which to atone. She tried to take my life."

Om: "Your fear tells me differently. In terms of your own growth and well-being, it is never a matter of how you or someone else may consciously judge your actions. But rather how your spirit and your subconscious mind processes and accepts what you have become as a result of your experiences. We must somehow find a way to convey your contrition for any acts that may have been alien to your spiritual intent. An offering must be made in recompense. We have to find some place where an appeasement may be offered."

Shona: "But she tried to hurt me first."

Om: "Then why did you not leave after you initially defended yourself?"

Shona: "I,I, I wanted to help her. Besides what good will it do to offer atonement? These people—if they can be called that—do not seem like the type to accept apologies."

Om: "You don't understand. Part of the atonement that you must offer will be to your own soul. While offering atonement to the Inar will be difficult and maybe even prove impossible, the alternative may be worst. It is necessary to always attempt to atone for any wrongful acts, or perceived wrongdoing, even if you are technically not responsible for the female's death; for it sounds as if she would have died even if you had not come upon her.

There are myriad repercussions in the spirit with the lack of atonement, such as the potential to spiral downward into deeper and deeper misery and guilt. Guilt perpetuates even more wrongdoing, in order to mitigate the effect of the initial offense, or dull the edges of the shame. Atonement is part of the antidote for many of the poisons that affect the soul. If atonement cannot be made directly to the injured party, then atonement must be offered to the spirit of mankind, and more universally to the spirit of all life in the universe.

In one way or another we all try to hide from the harm that we cause ourselves and others. We can become so entrapped in our own personal unfulfilled needs that often we are blind to the harm that we cause to both ourselves and to others. But I don't think that anyone can get through this life without causing some hurt, some pain, no matter how unintentional. Nonetheless, we can all strive to be conscious of the potential for harm before it happens. We can all try to minimize the impact of any harm that has been caused, and we can all help one another to lessen or ease the pain.

In harming others the greater damage then exists within ourselves; in terms of what we may subconsciously choose to become as a result of that moment of having caused pain or suffering. We not only have the responsibility of seeking forgiveness from those whom we have harmed but we must also forgive ourselves. In the absence of atonement, your fear becomes larger than your life and it will forever haunt the moments of your existence. In order for your life to go on, you must be absolved of your wrong-doing. You will never be fully well or strong until you atone for your past mistakes. And you must learn how to fight correctly so that this fear and these mistakes need never happen again."

Shona: "I, I—I did not mean to cause her harm. Not at first. I wanted to help her. But when I listened to the things that she said the only thing that went through my mind was how much safer the world would be if she no longer existed. And I wasn't thinking of just my own safety, but any one in the world who might encounter her.

But now I look back and I see that, that woman, the Inar—I judged her world to consist largely of shades of gray. While I imagined for myself a prismatic existence with earthy tones of myriad greens, browns, blacks and crystal rainbow spectrums filtered through rainfall, falling springs and shining icicles. Reality may, however, cast us both in the same hue, for what was she that I am not."

Om: "She was a predator and you are not. And more than just a predator, the Inar are conscious predators. In contrast, the evolution of most predatory beings in the animal kingdom has resulted in predators of instinct, not those of conscious intent. There is a world of difference between a conscious predator and an instinctual predator. The psyche of a conscious sentient predator dictates that he/she see their need as superior to the needs and the very existence of his/her prey. A sentient being must have already been consumed by need in order to consciously pursue prey. A sentient predator has become the prey of their own unfulfilled needs."

Shona: "I'm not sure that I understand this need for atonement, especially considering that she attacked me first. Nonetheless, I am willing to try anything if it will make this fear and this feeling of being hunted go away. How can we determine where and how an offering can be made?"

Om: "There is book, an ancient text—it has information on all earthly life forms, their origins and their ways. Long ago I hid this book in the archives of the old church library in the main city. With the soldiers now based in the city, it may be difficult to get through the byways. But if you are to be made well it is imperative that we get this book. If I am right—this encounter with the Inar is but one of many signs that forces are converging and the time for a new day is upon us. This book will divulge much in terms of how we must prepare."

Shona: "Will it take a long time to get to the city?"

Om: "Only a few hours. But we may have to take a more circuitous route in order to avoid any contact with the soldiers. We will go to Immanuel's village tomorrow to begin arranging for transportation and planning this trip to the city."

Shona: "Why does it seem that we are always hiding from the soldiers? They protect the villagers, don't they? Many of the people are proud that their sons and fathers wear the uniforms. Do the soldiers pose any particular danger to us?"

Om: "Their greatest danger may be in how unpredictable they are. The commander of the unit that prowls these villages is an evil and unstable man. While they may not present any particular danger to us, it is still best that we avoid attracting their attention."

He looked up into the darkened sky. "Things are changing. There are forces that are gathering. The presence of these Inar is just one of many signs. A new time in the history of man and the history of this earth is coming and we must prepare to meet what it will bring. This book will help us to understand what we must do."

Shona: "If you left it so long ago, how do you know for certain that your book is still there?"

Om: "The book did not belong to me. It was given to me for safekeeping and I put it in a place that seemed the safest to me at the time. I guess we will not know if it is still there until we go into the city. Come we must rest now. We have a lot to do tomorrow and the days that will follow."

They ended up staying in Immanuel's village for over a week before venturing on to the city. The old man slept at Immanuel's home while Shona stayed at the house of Immanuel's eldest daughter, Selene, who was married and had children of her own. Although Shona had previously stayed in the villages for brief periods of time, on this occasion she felt even more a part of these people and their community as they included her in all their activities and events.

There was a hum and vibrancy in the village evenings that Shona had never experienced before. Many days at sunset she went with the Immanuel sisters to a local outdoor gathering place where the people sat talking, eating, dancing and socializing. There were people of all ages in this dusty courtyard with rusted metal chairs and tables set up all around. Some played string, percussion and wind instruments as others danced and children chased one another around the tables or played games in the dust. Small groups of people, some self-segregated by age or gender, sat talking, laughing, joking, and drinking their home made brews. There were always multiple streams of flowing conversations and a magical feel in the air, as if all their spirits had been drawn into the vibration of the music, channeled through some vital essence of life and living. It was as if their individual souls resonated in one collective sound that was offered up as praise and testimony to the fact that God, the Creator of all life, had, indeed, done well.

Shona was enraptured by the ambiance of this sunset courtyard gathering. And she looked forward each time to hearing the sounds, and feeling the flow of easy camaraderie between young and old alike. After awhile the newness of the sensations wore off, and the evenings did not seem as enchanting as they first appeared, but she still enjoyed going, and being in the mix of the people's lives and laughter.

On a rare occasion something out of the ordinary would happen to make the evening die abruptly. Either someone would begin arguing loudly or one or two of the young men, intoxicated by the night air or inspired by too much fermented beverage, would become more brazen in their eternal dance to vie for a young woman's favor. The jokes would turn ugly; insults hurled would land and catch fire in their target's voice and eyes. Sometimes fists and chairs would fly; a knife brandished in the air. The women would hustle the children out of the courtyard, while the village fathers responded quickly to control the situation. After the storm, the people who remained would turn to one another, seeking reassurance that everything was still the same. But, in the aftermath, they would discover that the festive mood had been inadvertently sucked down into the ever-pervasive dust of the street.

12. Guardians of a Sacred Trust

The stream banks in the dark forest overflowed with ferns, shrubs and mossy lichen growing on trees that stretched over and into the water. Cloaked in the blackness and shadows of early morning before dawn, the two women came with reverence into this private consecrated plant world; and with a solemn accord, their presence was accepted by *the others*. Upon entering earth's ephemeral realm of liminal intensity, their physical senses became overly stimulated, awakened completely by the rich powerful smell-feel of loose black soil and fecund verdant vegetation that possessed and rode the air as if it was its own. The wind, with messages clear and strong, carried energies and forces alive only at this time of day. Saba and Mala came silently, listening, hoping to hear the earth whisper what their minds could never truly grasp. But *they—the others—* heard, understood fully and told one another. So, the women searched for new ways to listen to *them* through the silence.

Plants tell one another of life, death and survival. They send warnings of their sicknesses, emitting volatile chemicals into the air, which stimulate nearby plants to produce chemicals in their leaves that protect them against the sickness. They can protect other beings against sickness as well, using their chemicals to mediate interactions between living organisms. Healing with an active power that resides deep within their molecular structures, the plants act as a symbiant to human cells in order to augment or decrease the impact of foreign elements. The vital regenerative essence of healing plants interacts with components of bodily poisons, viruses, parasites—killing them or interfering with their processes or stimulating human immune reactions. Sometimes they simply strengthen the body's capacity to absorb and accept the symbiosis and synergism of life.

The two women came before the day's light to ask Earth's emissaries for the healing that they could take back to their people. Their plea was answered and they were led to the elemental herbs and organic substances whose energies awaken only with the dawn of each new day. Mala and Saba sat, patiently awaiting their beckoning call. The forest streams, trees and other plants vibrated and murmured as they embraced the women in a lively and lush salutation. Mala's breathing was heavy and hard. She was visibly excited by the touch of this mystical and passionately alive world. She tried unsuccessfully to suppress the overwhelming sense of exultation evoked by the presence and feel of a powerful fundamental force of life.

Saba, likewise, tried to wrap herself in the sensations of the elements and the moment, but her mind and attention strayed, as she looked around in the cool darkness, reflecting on how much had happened and changed in the past few months prior to this gathering time. Saba thought of the blessing of having Mala here with her now. The strength of Mala's sentiale awareness, made even more potent in her isolation from the Ocan collective, reached out and surrounded the Saba in a level of power that she never knew was possible. With Mala by her side, Saba was able to move beyond her internal chasms in order to delve deeper into the core of healing processes. Together they were able to take the blessings of the earth and simulate compounds that not only exhibited more of life's profundity but also served as healing forces and substances that breathed life back into failing living systems.

Over the years, Saba had learned to depend on knowledge outside of herself so that the people would never have cause to question her or more importantly, doubt their understanding of saba-power. With Mala by her side, Saba felt her visions restored, her calling renewed. With Taijaur now gone to the mainland, Mala's presence was especially welcome and it seemed that she was beginning to adjust to this fractured world where the people she loved, the people who sustained her kept leaving, going away and never coming back. Slowly the hurt was being pushed away, becoming only a part of the background noise to her daily existence.

Saba had insisted that Mala work closely by her side, even in the beginning when the people visibly shied from her touch. To some of the people, Mala had always been like a 'shadow person'—never fully present within a here-now reality. And even now she unintentionally added to her own enigma by frequently and mysteriously disappearing from the village. Nevertheless, the combined energy of the two women created a steady healing rhythm that eventually overruled all prejudice or strife, as their offering was pure and necessary for the people's wellbeing and survival. Over time, many of those in need of care began to specifically request Mala's presence. They were a team and, in the Saba's eyes,

Mala was slowly becoming that powerful healer-woman—that future saba—from whom she had fled so many years before.

The sun began to move into the day, and Saba along with Mala swiftly and delicately gathered the natural and supernatural herbaceous powers that released themselves into their care. Neither woman had spoken since rising in the dark and they continued on in silence as they returned to Saba's home, where they then sat quietly sorting and treating the herbs at the worktable. They continued working peacefully and efficiently over the next hour, with neither of them speaking while the Saba hummed contentedly to herself.

The healer-woman had begun to feel a relaxed sense of tranquility. And this new luxury of peace and security allowed her to shrug off bits and pieces of the emotional guard that had, for years, kept any deeper sensations at a safe distance. She knew that any feelings or thoughts beyond the surface could potentially and dangerously expose her emotional pathways, making her susceptible to the pain of those around her and to her own repressed emotions. But for now, for this day, she threw away her caution, because for once, all was well in the universe; and she wanted to open her soul to receive all the blessings and good feelings that this day would offer.

As she began to savor this new internal expansiveness, visions from her dreams came unexpectedly into her mind and she felt flush with embarrassment as she tried to steady her breathing and the sudden rapid beating of her heart. She dreamt of Tekun almost every night now and sometimes as she napped during the day. Thoughts of her long-dead husband brought all the intensity and ardor of their years of love-making forcefully into her present reality. Usually, she could quash these feelings upon awakening, before they reached the point of overwhelming her senses. But today, with her guard taken away, her emotions forced their way through and her desires began to nurture her need to believe. It had been so long since desire and hope had awakened within her. She felt like she was sitting on the edge of a precipice and all she had to do was let go and her life would flow into the rapture of a new more powerful form of existence.

And then without warning, Saba was jarred out of her reverie as she looked out of the window and saw Amira coming down the path toward her home. Even from a distance it was evident that she was bringing with her a raw sense of hurt and despair. With a sudden fear and sense of panic, Saba tried to shut down the opening that had been created within her by the emotions of the morning.

She wanted to protect her internal sentiale, but Amira's presence could not be blocked as she gained access to the Saba's heart before she even reached the door. Her pain saturated and crowded the air with its thick hot forceful energy. Mala rose from her seat and came to stand next to Saba, her hands resting on the healer-woman's shoulders. They both watched Amira as she walked slowly toward the house, moving with a heaviness upon her soul, a hurt that rested in her bones and sent waves of distress to announce her coming. Mala looked at Saba with an expression of concern, before turning her attention back to Amira. The Saba sighed deeply, knowing what was expected of her and knowing that she did not have and could not give what either of these women needed.

A passage from the *Journal of Saba* came into Saba's mind, an entry written by a saba of the old country: *"Sometimes I wonder, what is it about females that makes us come together with our bundled up hurt and peel back the edges? We are called to act as guardians of a sacred trust, and undoubtedly, our rituals of emotional sharing sustain us for the duration. Yet, through it all, it seems that our pain will never be any less alive than it was at the beginning of time."* She thought back to her own saba, who had guided her passage into this world, watched over her growth and soothed her suffering. She was a deeply powerful healer—a master saba of all saba. Her eyes told of life and all that must be endured to sustain it. Her voice echoed the people's tears and contained their sorrow. And her hands would always wash away the pain. She could touch the timeless hurt and suffering of the multitude and still come back whole. She used the pain as her familiar and it gave itself as a medium to her power. She embodied the feel-sight-touch that all saba aspire to call forth. This present Saba searched within herself, and no matter how hard she reached she could not find that great healer-woman whose wisdom had once been the beacon of her life's calling. The pain took from her and forced her to places within herself that she could not, would not, willingly go.

For the past few months, Amira had come at least once a week, same song, same tune, same pain; her script never deviated. She invariably found her way to Saba's home after yet another of her hopeless quests into the forest searching for her husband. Most days Olana could stop her from going, but more than once each week, she slipped away while Olana slept. Saba was afraid to force Amira out of the daytime nightmare that had become her life. So she played along with her in a contrived dream world, where Kalal had just recently departed and would surely be found any moment now. She now stood ready to welcome her sister-in-law's delusions, pretending along with her, that hope had never died. She entertained Amira's fantasy of deliverance, because she knew how fragile is the hope that we all cling to, and sometimes how necessary.

Mala watched the healer-woman as a brief expression of fear darted across her face and then quickly submerged. Despite the Saba's attempts to conceal her feelings, Mala sensed in her a strong desire to flee, to run, to hide. Saba turned to Mala and said in a low quick voice, "Do you smell something burning?" Mala shook her head sadly as she stroked the healer woman's arm before returning to her seat.

Amira came into the room squinting, though the room was not dark. "Saba?"

Saba: "Come in Amira. Sit down and rest."

Mala nodded without words in Amira's direction, as she continued working, sorting the herbs. Amira seemed detached, even oblivious of her surroundings. She stared blankly in the direction of Saba, never looking directly at her as she whispered, "I've come to ask a favor of you."

Saba: "You look so drawn. Let me get you a cup of tea." Saba rose, moving towards the kettle that hung in the fireplace, after guiding Amira to the large billowy chair under the front window.

"No," Amira sighed, "I can't stay long."

Despite her efforts to block Amira's pain from her being, Saba felt herself being sucked into a vacuum, where she knew her emotional control could not be sustained. The pain began to pull memories from her core. *I can't do this*, she thought as she said aloud, "Here drink this; its nice and hot. The tea and its vapor will be good for you."

Amira placed the steaming cup of green liquid on the windowsill as Saba turned back to pour two more cups of tea. She gave one cup to Mala who quietly smiled her thanks as she continued working with a look of trance-like concentration on her face. The healer-woman pulled her stool closer to where Amira sat and was surprised to see how shrunken and aged her sister-in-law appeared.

Amira: "Saba—sister—you cannot know the agony I endure. I am beyond fear I only come to you first, seeking guidance before calling full council."

Amira rose from her seat and began pacing back and forth. Saba still struggled, in vain, to reconstruct—call back—her internal emotional guard. With each step that Amira took, each word that she spoke, Saba felt fresh waves of anguish and pain. She felt like she was on the same precipice that had opened up her life, but now she was sliding uncontrollably down into a long steep dark place with no end, no bottom, and no way to stop.

Saba: "Patience, Amira. Kalal can only send his message to your heart's stillness. There is nothing that you or the council can do at this point. Please sit down Amira, and try to be calm."

Amira continued talking, continued moving, but Saba heard only sounds with no meaning. Saba could not control her mind as she suddenly felt herself slipping back and forth between the present and a distant forgotten past. At first she was in both places at once. Then she felt her presence shifting rapidly from one reality to the other, with her thoughts never telling her which was the true here and now. In her mind the Saba saw—*misty figures in the distance. They had told her that she must come quickly, but they would not tell her what was wrong. It took more than a day's travel to get there and she had no idea why she kept hoping that she would not be too late; too late for what? As she neared the final path to the quarantine outpost, that was well north of the Aka village, she was stalled by a solid wall of smoke that blew with the current. A strong pungent odor of a sickly sweet burning substance filled her nostrils, clouded her vision and told her that something was, indeed, very wrong. Her heart beat fast as she began to run through the trees, toward the small community of makeshift hovels. The sight before her slowed her steps. She thread her way warily through the smoke to a burnt out camp, where she saw a crowd of people standing, with their backs to her, around a large bonfire.*

Amira: "But Saba, is he safe? I can wait forever knowing that he will come back to me whole. I have such ill feelings of foreboding."

Amira's voice came from a faraway distant void. Saba felt momentarily faint and dizzy as she made the transition back to her present reality and tried to pull her awareness completely away from the vision-world in her mind. Amira's pacing added to the Saba's sense of vertigo and she fell back, once again, into the pain of her distant memory. *She saw only the backs of the people as they stood before the huge bonfire that towered several feet into the air and was equally as wide. She made her way through the crowd and finally saw that the bonfire was a pyre with dozens of dead bodies, each wrapped in a thick gauze, each piled on top of the other.*

Amira: "...what should have taken only hours, a few days at most, has become much longer. Where could he have gone? What if he is lying out there injured, his spirit too weak to call for help? I send probes but they reach nothingness. And it so frustrating to not know."

At some point, Amira had resumed her seat by the window and Saba had to now turn in order to see her as she spoke. Saba swallowed hard before speaking; her mouth was dry and pasty. "But you do know, Amira." *Oh God, keep this away. Give me the strength.*

Amira: "What do you mean? What do you know? Can you see him, Saba?"

Saba: "I know only what you tell me Amira. Your soul alone connects to that man in a way that ultimate truth can be revealed." *A few of the people in the crowd kneeled on the ground near the fire, while others stood watching, staring as if in a trance.*

When Amira had first arrived, Saba had resolved that this time she would only listen, not talk. She had told herself that she would only nod in a reassuring, comforting way. She wanted so much to ease the sorrow of her brother's wife and somehow keep her own misery at bay. But something made her talk, question, probe, and prod; some force, some volition. She looked at Mala to see if somehow she had initiated a sentiale link. But Mala only continued to work, her head bowed, intent on her task. Saba knew that Amira needed to be pushed toward an understanding that could lead to healing. However, she also knew that she had neither the strength nor the energy to accomplish this goal. She made a split-second decision to stop fighting whatever this force was that compelled her to speak against her will. She convinced herself that the sound of her voice could act as a shield to the pain that emanated not only from Amira but from her own being and the gaps of silence between their words.

Amira: "I can't bear the thought of living alone, of living without him. He needs me...and...I... I... need him."

Saba: "With all the beings that populate this planet, how can it even occur to you that you are ever alone? You are a part of them even when they are not directly in your presence."

Amira: "Saba, you said yourself that my soul connects with Kalal. He validates me. His spirit provides a tangible purpose for my existence."

In her mind the Saba heard—*a loud, open cry that went up amongst the crowd as two more bodies were carried from a nearby house and placed at the edge of the pile and then pushed further into the fire.* Saba tried to stand, but she fell back into her seat, steadying herself by holding on to the edge of the table. Though her heart beat fast and wild, she continued prodding, pushing. Her own words—questions that she directed at Amira—bounced back to Saba mocking her, waiting for her response. She listened in amazement as she heard herself ask, "Oh, and life itself is not enough? The spirit of the universe is not enough?"

Amira: "You know what I mean."

Saba: "I know that you are hurting now. And that your need distorts your perception."

Amira: "He is necessary and vital to my existence. Without him, my life ceases to have meaning."

With great force, Saba pushed the creeping visions to the back of her mind and tried hard to concentrate on the unbidden words that came from her own mouth, "I understand that and I believe you. However, once he has given you his soul, what more can he do? You cannot return it, nor can he take it back. Within the first moments that you were both truly together, when your eyes first met, he delivered his soul unto you. Every moment since then can only attempt to duplicate those incipient emotions and are but shadows of the reality that was illuminated in that one moment in time."

Amira: "I am who I am because of him. My survival depends upon his physical presence in my life. He not only fulfills my needs for a man, a life-mate, but equally as important, he maximizes my potential to survive on this earth and within this society."

Saba: "What life survival skills do you not possess on your own?"

The healer-woman was momentarily taken aback, as she watched Amira rise once again and appear to undergo a transformation before her eyes. Amira held herself erect, energized by the questions and the responses that came to her. She no longer appeared dazed. There was a feverish intensity in her gaze as she stated in a strong and sure voice, "We share who and what we are with one another. We teach and learn from one another. But our union is more that just the mechanics of every day living. More importantly, we inspire, motivate, and support one another through all endeavors. We have always been a team, a unit, a united force of strength; life's energy and potential taken to the power of two. Our individual abilities to survive are maximized not only because we provide for and take care of one another, but also because from our love for one another flows the desire, the need to continue living and loving life and all that is a part of this creation."

Saba now felt equally as strong, equally as sure, "And with the absence of his presence, how has any of that become less than what it once was? How can you love him, yourself or life any less just because he is not here? I feel your pain Amira. Kalal is important to my life as well. He is not just my only sibling, but he was always the closest friend that I ever had."

Amira: "You don't understand. I don't want to go through life with the mere thought and memory of my man. I want and need him here with me. And he needs me."

Saba: "Okay, Amira, calm yourself."

Amira: "I **can not** calm myself! I am angry and I am upset." She paced back and forth, pounding her fist into her hand. "He should be here with me. I want this confusion, these feelings of unease to go away. I want to sleep through the night with him comfortably by my side; instead of this desperate longing and sobbing that has taken the place of my once peaceful dreams."

Saba had never seen Amira so animated, so intense. She began to wonder if the same force that invaded her own mind had also taken possession of Amira.

Saba: "Amira, you know that your wholeness can only come through the center of your being."

Amira: "I have no center without that man."

Saba: "Don't talk nonsense. You must center yourself in order to come through this whole."

Amira: "Once he has returned, my wholeness and completeness will take care of itself."

Saba: "All right, Amira, if you insist upon playing this game, then allow me to play it with you. What if he does not return?"

Amira: "What? Saba, why do you say that?"

Saba: "Oh Amira, you are the last person on this earth whose pain I wish to see or contribute to. But please, concentrate on your internal ability to heal rather than this intense hurt and pain that may engulf your existence and obliterate your life."

It was as if the force that had held Amira up and made her strong had suddenly and completely evaporated, as she fell to her knees in front of Saba. With her face buried in her hands and her body wracked with deep convulsing sobs, she stuttered through her tears "Oh Saba... He...he...he gave so much to me... to...to everyone. How will he ever know how much...how much..." She choked on her sobs and said no more.

Words were supposed to make them safe, they were supposed to keep them away from pain and loss; a rational secure ground from which retreat was possible. The words had failed them this day, and despite the Saba's best defense, the agony had forced its way inside, touching her where she had chosen not to be touched. And then she knew that words nor time never really heal pain nor make it go away. It just slips into the background of who and what we are, crying out every now and then.

Knowledge came together with grief and hurt, opening a pathway in the Saba's heart and mind. And then suddenly, without warning, the memory that she had blocked for so long came to her and the smoke from the pyre no longer obscured her vision. Loni had already died before the Saba arrived and she saw her as they brought her body out to feed to the fire, to add to the pile of burning bodies. She would not let them burn her. Her mind cried out now, as it did then, *I, who have saved so many; I, for whom healing is a calling, could not save, did not protect this one woman, my one child.* Loni Basau died a horrible, painful death and part of the Saba's *sentiale*, her reason and ability to feel or think, love, connect or share, died along with her only child. *I am saba and I did not save her.*

Saba embraced Amira, as she knelt before her, rocking her slowly back and forth. *Oh Loni, my sweet Loni.* Mala came forward with the troubled emotions that swept through every part of the room, grazed into her face. She knelt behind Amira and below the Saba's arms she laid her hands on Amira's back, her head bent forward, eyes closed. Saba continued rocking Amira, but they now moved in a gentle rhythmic sway in time to a steady vibration. It felt as if Mala's hands and body were generating an electrical charge that hummed through all three of their bodies. Even though the vibration lulled her peacefully, the Saba began to feel alarmed as she sensed that they were being pulled under, as if in the strong undertow of a vast deep ocean. A perpetual fluid stream of visions surrounded and absorbed the three women into their flow and the Saba felt herself, as well as Amira and Mala, a part of scenes that opened up spontaneously before them.

They were one spirit, one mind in an unfamiliar land, outside of the Ocan settlement. Three women now existed within one person's thoughts, emotions, and experiences. Mala immersed Saba and Amira in her sentiale and transported them with her through emotions and events that had transpired in Mala's own life, in her early days in the forbidden lands of the western shore. They each felt their individual consciousness merged into one woman's perceptions and sensations, although they were simultaneously aware of their separate selves and those of the two women with whom they were conjoined. Only then did Saba realize that it had been Mala all along who was inside of her thoughts, inside of both of their minds. Throughout their morning discussion, Mala had pushed, prodded and guided both she and Amira through a tangle of thoughts and words that struggled to reach understanding, consolation and forgiveness. Saba had no time to contemplate this amazing feat of Obeah power as she felt the three of them, now joined as one, rushing into the scenes that opened up before them.

Somehow, they could see and feel the entirety of their island home as if viewing it from above and simultaneously in every individual place all at one time. They saw the ocean to the west and the secret passages through the mountain foothills that lead across the narrow valleys and over the cliffs to the rocky beach-less shoreline. They looked beyond the mountains in the east to the rich ancient forests that stretched unbroken from the mountains to the sea. They could see, hear, feel and taste the warm summer air as it rolled over the hills in time with the steady tranquilizing rhythm of the sun's heat and the motions of the sea. Then their mind/spirit-vision focused on a lush fertile valley hidden in a narrow passageway in one of the lower mountains on the western side of the island. They/she began a long arduous journey, that began with a luxurious stroll through the resplendent valley and then an impossible trek up a steep and rocky side of the mountain as the seasons passed in quick succession. With calloused hands and sore knees, they/she struggled through exhaustion, continuing to scale the mountain. Harsh, howling winds and fierce precipitation blocked their way.

A low melodic undertone, beneath the wind, captured their attention and they paused along the path to listen. There was a voice blowing softly into and throughout the vision. Saba knew that Mala was speaking with her mind, but the clarity of the vision and message astounded the healer-woman beyond belief as sound and sight came together and crystallized within her soul. Through their exhaustion they struggled on and up with melodious words issuing forth from the mountain mist—*Our strength comes and goes in harmony with the ebb and flow of all god-power. When faith remains hidden in the vulnerability of naked winter trees, then forces greater than life burrow into our roots and deeper places, waiting for a time when warmer winds may yield the flower of a new and brighter day. And in their given moment the harsher winds must also come and take it all away; scattering the fragile seeds of our life's offering on barren unyielding ground. From the brevity of these ageless sorrows, the power is called forth, arising out of a deeper and stronger source. Neither time nor seasons can erode this defiant force of will that returns with the wind. And forever we are commanded to rise once more, for destiny must have its fill. But in the moment of our winter and our despair, we can but wait and yearn, listening in supplication for those alive, yet dormant, forces buried deep within.*

As the words ended, a lyrical singsong chant began and the scenes abruptly changed. She/they rested in a grove, watching the splendor of a setting sun. Then in swift motion, time evaporated, days came and went—trees, water, grass, rain, animals, the sun and moon flashed through their senses. Time slowed when a presence, a person came through the mist and approached tentatively. They/she experienced a strong sense of his being—calm, kind and secure. He brought, shared with Mala, an intense and tender feeling of love and devotion. And then suddenly, as they lulled within his comfort and his strength, he was sucked back into the mist. Time rested and the images stood with the woman, alone and without movement. From a rocky ledge near the mountaintop they/she watched the brilliant sun begin its daily descent. As she stared vacantly down into the sea, a message came forth from the sound of the ocean waves.

Eons ago
we arose together
from the mystical depths of creation,
as liquid-fire stars sang praise to our oneness.
I waited alone
in the darkness of the galaxy
for your spirit to touch mine.
Just as now, by this earthly sea,
I wait.
You and I, we came together to this planet
and willingly parted
so that we might know the Creator's beauty
in yet another form,
and experience the depth of our love
in yet another life.
This sea echoes and resounds
against the walls of dark caverns

where shiny icicles reflect the sun's rays.
I know that our spirit
flows in this sea
and shines in this light.
Thus, it is possible for me to wait.
I feel your touch in the wind,
your smile in the sun—
The morning birds now sing of our oneness.
And I will endure whatever I must
until our spirits join, once more,
in the hands of the Creator,
and, together, we will surrender
to the perfect harmony and powerful will
of life's eternal essence.

The glorious evening sun, straining through puffy dense dark clouds, sank below the horizon and into the water. An intense blackness hugged them/her close and then pushed the three women individually, slowly up into the day, where they were once more sitting in the reality of the Saba's house.

For the first time that morning Mala opened her mouth and softly spoke, "Amira, beyond the kinship that may be found in the universal void of life's suffering, I share your pain and I feel your hurt. Sister of my heart, no words may comfort you in this loss, but know that my soul reaches out." She rose and turned with her head still bowed, left out of the door and the Saba watched from the window as Mala walked through the meadow to the hills that lead in the direction of Alor's remote home.

Amira sat on the floor, limp and silent, drained of emotion or thought. Saba took her hand, pulled her to her feet and then led her to a back room where she laid down, and slept soundly for the next several hours. As a precaution, Saba wrapped two large leaves that contained a poultice of herbs around Amira's head. She would need this anesthetic to chase away any mental torment that her dreams might let slip through.

After settling her sister in-law, the Saba went back to her work table and began absent-mindedly working with the clay—pulling, molding kneading with no form or shape in mind. With her first attention safely trapped, her lower mind, though stunned, worked through the gauze of her disoriented reasoning and attempted to reflect on all that had transpired. Finally, the Saba's thoughts ordered themselves and she began to comprehend this enigma that calls itself Mala. She had recognized all along that Mala was powerful, as all Ocan cultivate within themselves a deeper sense of life in order to touch and know the spirit of the universe. But this was something wholly different; different even from that which the Obeah possess. Or perhaps it was akin to that ancient Obeah power which could only be spoken of in whispers.

The energy that Mala was able to call and transmit as her own, not only pulled forth visions, past, present and future—her force of life was also steeped in a natural healing poultice of rebirth and renewal. She was filled with the same potent transmutable energy of the ancient Obeah, except perhaps it had grown stronger through the ages. It was if she had been endowed with not only the overwhelming responsibility of Obeah-vision but also the infinite power, skill and knowledge of an eternal saba—all rolled into one. Harnessing the supreme capacity of even one of these blessings could take a lifetime to master. And indeed, Saba thought, many have not learned to control or honor their gifts in a succession of lifetimes. Slowly, Saba began to understand that it was this phenomenal power from which Mala had run all of her life. She sat for hours, oblivious to time, in a daze, awe-struck with vestiges of the intense feel of the universe flowing through and around her. It wasn't just Mala's ability to conjure memories and share feelings—it was the intensity of the feelings, the realness of the memories. It was as if the three women had been in the direct presence of the Creator's energy with no veil of this world, no static of a surface reality's distortion. Mala was a living spiritual conduit; an unwilling vehicle for the intent of the unknown.

Saba heard a sound in the distance and glanced out of the window to see Olana, most likely in search of her mother, approaching from the very path that Mala had taken on her departure. The sight of the young woman pulled Saba from her reverie as she noticed how late in the day it had become and reproached herself for the mid-day meal that waited impatiently to be prepared. However, before she was able to move completely into the toil of the present, visions of Taijaur flashed through her mind and her heart jumped, beating fast at the sudden realization that Mala's awesome power undoubtedly would have metastasized and become more potent once released and passed on to her progeny.

13. An Unholy Union

They traveled to the city and back in a dusty, rusted, dented old contraption that Immanuel struggled to keep mobile for most of the trip. They had now returned to Immanuel's village, where Shona and Om were resting before continuing their trek to the old man's isolated homestead. The book, or rather the collection of papers and scrolls yellow and brown with age, had been there in the church library just as he had left it decades before. They had managed to avoid the detection of the soldiers, although with the upcoming election in a few weeks, several members of the army were stationed all over the city and in all the villages and towns of the province.

Shona was staying once again with Selene and her family, sleeping in her usual place in the girls' room, sharing the bed of Selene's youngest daughter. In addition to this six year old girl, Selene had two young boys and her eldest teenage daughter. The children treated Shona as if she was just another of their siblings. The house was always filled with an assortment of men, women and children who seemed to come at all hours of the day and night—running in sometimes to sleep, get food, or just chat with one another. Today the house was overflowing with females of all ages. The older women were helping Selene, her mother and her sisters sew the festive dresses that were to be worn at tomorrow's coming of age celebration, where Selene's eldest daughter along with other boys and girls in her peer group would parade and promenade through the village square in their finest attire. These young adolescent girls were now milling around the house in various stages of dress and undress, twittering, fidgeting and laughing as they were continuously told to stand still so that they could be measured and fitted for their colorful new clothing or have their hair decorated and styled in a special way.

Shona was accustomed to spending time with the village women and children, and she usually assisted with the endless stream of female chores. This had won her many friends and they hailed her warmly every time she came. In their usual bantering style they began to tease Shona as she sat sewing amongst them. Whenever the men were not around, they would ask her why she had not chosen a mate for herself and offer names of potential partners. Their refrain was always the same.—"You need love in your life."

Shona smiled and laughed along with them as one of the women once again offered and referred to the middle Immanuel son and brother as an ideal partner for Shona.

"And he's available too," one of them said. Everyone laughed at this, but Shona couldn't quite figure out why this was funny.

"Even these silly little girls have boy friends."

The young girls feigned outrage and protest, while giggling even more at the older women's teasing. Selene and her mother watched Shona's response to the suggestion of this brother, this son of theirs. They actually hoped that Shona might be interested. Marrying him off would give them less to worry about. Although they would never admit it to each other or to anyone else, but they both thought that marriage might make him appear to be a little more, well—normal. He was always brooding, this middle Immanuel son. He still stared constantly at Shona, but if she tried to talk to him, he would look in the opposite direction, offering no response and she was never sure if he heard what she was saying.

He was a thin slightly-built young man, shorter than most of the men, but not abnormally so. He sat silent most of the time, with a dark penetrating scowl—just staring and listening to everyone, except those times when he chose to speak. And then he would burst out with long-winded diatribes that always hushed all the other people as they glanced at one another and then looked away as they tried to determine if what he said in any way related to the topic of their conversation. Out of respect for the Immanuel family, no one in this community would dare to be the first to say aloud that this Immanuel son, the middle one, was indeed a little strange or perhaps, 'a little touched in the head', as some of the people whispered. Lately, he had started hanging out with a group of young men and teen age boys who seemed to be filled with the same dark anger and bottled-up rage.

A few of the men came in, dirty from their work of digging wells around the countryside. This brother, the middle of Immanuel's sons, was with them. The young girls ran screaming and covering themselves to one of the back bedrooms, while Selene's husband and another man that Shona did not know, sat down nearby with drinks in their hands, pretending to admire the women's work. The Immanuel brother sat in a corner of the room away from everyone, while the other two men started talking about all of the violence and cruelties of life in the city, reporting of new murders, new robberies, and the latest atrocities. Things had not always been this way, someone said; had not always been so bad.

One of the women spoke up, "Thank God we live away from that madness and life in these villages is not quite as insane."

Another responded, "But look what happened just this week—right here in our own village. The sins of the city are coming to our own doors."

And then the other women joined in.

"We're not even safe in our own homes these days."

"I will be glad when these soldiers are gone from our midst for good."

"They shouldn't have left that girl alone by herself in that house. That would not have ever happened if they had not left her alone."

"That is why we must always pray." This was from the same woman who had initiated the teasing of Shona a few moments ago. Another woman began to whisper of the power of their sacred rock, The Eye, which had been stolen away from their ancestors and how much easier life was in the past when the people benefited directly from the rock's power. They always seemed to lower their voices when they spoke of this Eye as if it could only be mentioned in hushed tones. Several of the other women began to give testimony of their faith and belief in the savior that would one day restore the Eye to them, when suddenly and loudly, the middle Immanuel brother shouted over top of all of their voices, "Religion, like disease, has for centuries been one of the primary tools of colonization and invasion. In addition to war, these two forces—religion and disease—have become the major vehicles by which one group of people oppresses another."

He didn't seem to be looking at or talking to anyone in particular as he spit out his words with scarcely concealed malice, "Predatory scavengers, that's what they are. They came centuries ago with blood-thirst vengeance against the gods; destroying blessings of the Creator with venom spewed forth from the void within their innermost selves. Their distorted jealousy could not be contained and they imposed their vision upon the earth, subjugating the physical essence of the Lord's creation to their dominion."

Selene interjected in a placating tone, "Little Brother, you must be fair now. These people that you speak of—not all of their kind subscribe to a doctrine of evil. There are good and bad people in all groups, all nations."

He replied without looking at her, "The forces of evil claim the right to define what power should mean within the reality of a system they call civilization."

Quiet wide-eyed glances were exchanged throughout the room, before each person looked down and became even more busy with their task at hand. After a few moments of silence, one of the men started playing a stringed instrument, several of the women began singing and the talk and laughter began again.

When Shona rose from her seat, Selene's mother looked at her with concern, remarking, "Little Sister, you don't look so well. Are you okay?"

She heard one of the women whispering behind her back, "She just got back from the city yesterday. They say she got sick while she was there."

And then a return whisper, "Tsk, awww, that is too bad. But the city has that effect on people."

They had no idea how acute Shona's hearing was, as the music was still playing and most of the other people in the room could not hear these two women. All day they had sat off to one side, quietly making comments about the other people in the room, as they sewed and laughed with each other, intermittently sipping from a small metal flask that they passed back and forth. They were gleeful that their secret was always well hidden from the others. And the other women made sure to never comment on the strong vapors that wafted in the air around these two women.

Shona ignored the voices behind her, as she answered Mrs. Immanuel, "I'm fine. I just need to get some fresh air. Is it alright if I finish this dress outside?"

The Immanuel woman said gently, "Don't worry about the dress; we'll finish it up. If you want to keep busy, take this collar to work on; it will be easier to handle outside. The fresh air will do you good. Make sure to sit in the shade, so that you don't get too hot."

The whispering voices continued as Shona went out the door, "All the hot air of these hussies' flappin' gums will make a girl ill."

Laughter, "Hush! Don't you see these men sitting here?"

"They say a lack of love will make you ill. Maybe somebody ought to send that fool of a boy out after her." More quiet laughter.

The whispering, laughing voices followed her outside, as she went to her usual spot under the shade of the large willow tree not far from the house. In the afternoon, the old men usually gathered under this tree, but for now, there was no one or nothing but the leaves and limbs swaying with the currents of a gentle summer breeze. This tree was a lone piece of lushness in a mostly arid land. It had been planted long ago and had grown to a majestic height and breadth. The people told stories of how the tree was sustained by magical forces. But Shona had seen neighbor after neighbor coming secretly in the night to share a portion of their precious water and their 'magical' herbs with their fecund solitary friend. A light sweet smell of baking bread drifted from a nearby open window and she could hear the sounds of children playing in the distance. A stray dog ambled by, and stopped to look at her with a hopeful question in his wagging tail and in his doleful eyes. She smiled at him, shrugging her shoulders, empty palms up and he trotted off, sniffing here and there along the way.

Throughout the morning, Shona had been trying to block out and forget the scenes that she had witnessed in the city, but now recurrent flashes were rushing back through her mind and in her senses. She was glad to be back in the relative security of this village that was becoming a second home to her. At first it had not seemed so bad—that city they had taken her to. There were more people than she could have ever imagined even existed—streaming, pushing, moving, begging. A curious mix of men and women, living in almost stifling poverty amidst small pockets of prosperity. The sleepy villages and towns that she was used to visiting had not prepared her for the odors, the sights, sounds and bustling feel of the city. There were large buildings and paved streets everywhere—buildings taller and wider than anything that she had ever seen. It seemed that on each street they passed there was an adult or child begging, sometimes more than one—some with dirty skin, ragged clothing, some missing legs or arms; some being pushed or kicked away. And there were a few people wrapped in the ostentations of wealth as they all began to gather for some event being held that afternoon in the town square of this city on the bay.

Om and Immanuel had left her in a small city park, while they went to the church library just outside of the town square. They had not known that the army would be marching through the town that day. And something must have happened to cause a delay at the church because Shona was left alone much longer then the time they had projected. Shona watched the soldiers as they came through the center of town and into the square. She could see only the moving colors of their uniforms through the crowd that had come together in the heat of the mid-day sun to watch this display of power and might. They all seemed to be talking about the army commander and their voices drifted to Shona as she stood at a distance from the people.

"Have to be careful. Spies everywhere...report back to him."

"...soldiers out of uniform, pretending to be one of the people."

"Tsk, tsk—not sure who to trust these days..."

"They say that he is recruiting boys as young as..."

"I heard that he just washed up on the beach one day. Down in the ...province..."

"...found a lot of blood in his boat... pieces of human bones and remains..."

"... those who oppose him, disappear or openly tortured and killed..."

Shona felt a desperate and urgent need to run, seek protection. She began walking fast, trying to get away from the people and the parade. She turned down the street that she thought Om and Immanuel had taken and she ended up in an outdoor marketplace. Her senses were immediately overwhelmed by the abundance of material goods, food, and waste. Everywhere she looked there was a jumble of people and a mixture of dirt, litter, squalor and noise. An oppressive acrid smell of smoke and cooked flesh smothered the air, rising from the open pits of vendor stalls where roasted meats were prepared and sold. The smell nauseated her and she had to fight to sustain her equilibrium, as she pressed through the streams of people, in search of this church where Om and Immanuel had gone.

She came to a large market stand where raw animal carcasses—heads, feet, ribs, flanks, entrails, and whole dead animals were displayed for sale. And then she saw more pieces of dead animals hanging on hooks in shop windows and lying on ice, decorated with garnishes. She had never adjusted to the reality that people consume the flesh of once living beings. And now, in the face of this mass carnage, she was stressed by the disturbing fact that these people lived and behaved as if these bizarre and macabre practices were just a normal part of everyday reality. They seemed to believe that this wanton proof of mankind's cruel and violent inhumanity was just a part of life as it should be. She suppressed the urge to run as she backed away from this living horror. Someone was calling her name and she looked all around, seeking the familiar face of either Om or Immanuel.

Still sitting under the shade of the willow tree, Shona pulled her mind away from the memory of the city and she looked up to see Selene's youngest son running towards her, and realized that he had been calling to her. When he reached her, he told her that she must come quickly—the old man needed her right away and she must bring their small bag of medicinal supplies. He led her to a small one room shack in a deserted area near the old abandoned village churchyard.

A solider was sitting in front by the door with a rifle across his lap. Even before he rose to usher Shona inside, she could smell sickness, death and dying in the gusts of wind and dust that rose up and surrounded them all around. A young man, a soldier, still in his teens, lie on a dirty squalid bed, dying. Om was sitting next to him, rubbing his torso with oil, and he motioned to Shona to come close as he asked, "Can you heal him?"

The young man-boy looked up at her, his eyes pleading. Om moved out of the way as she bent down close to the boy, shutting her eyes and placing her fingers on his temples, face and forehead. She reached out to intervene between his pain and his awareness. Within a matter of seconds, she abruptly opened her eyes wide and stared at the man, jerking her hands away from him. She rose quickly and turned to exit the room, clearly agitated. Her voice choked, "There is nothing that I can do."

She was almost out the door when she heard Om, who never raised his voice, yelling, "Heal him, Shona! Heal him or he will die!"

She turned back and looked at Om and then at the boy on the bed, whose eyes were still begging and pleading to her for help.

He shouted again, "Heal him Shona!"

"I CAN"T! I don't know how!"

"You are the last thing that stands between life and death for this man. If you do not help him, then he will move to a place beyond help. You can feel his spirit as well as I can. Do not allow your fear to stand in the way of who you are and what you must be and do in this life."

She returned to the bedside and resumed her position. Taking a deep breath, she placed one hand on his face and head and with her other hand, she held on tightly to the boy's hand. He lie still, his body shivering, perspiring profusely. When he felt her grasp his hand, he opened his eyes, still pleading, begging and weakly tried to squeeze her hand in return. She knew that this man, who showed no wound or bodily injury, had taken something, something that would take his life away from him. She saw within his mind, into his soul.

He was young, younger than even now... needing money... for his family...needing to appear as if he was a man...needing to believe in the rightness of something that he had no power to understand....she saw and felt herself a part of his conscious awareness as he left his family, his mother and three doting, loving sisters weeping—distraught, but proud of this son, this brother... he had found a way, a means to survive and ensure his survival and theirs as well... he was coming of age, was becoming a man and unlike so many of the men in their poor obscure little village...he had found a way... Shona watched, as he went with the older men and she felt his anger, confusion, and fear when the killing began....... people, old and young were beaten, shot, tortured...not always.... not all of the time....but enough that it came inside the boy and began to eat his soul.... At first he hesitated when the others dove into the desperate and unyielding misery of others...., but then as the visions went on, his moments of hesitation became shorter, less frequent and to all outward appearances he had adopted the role of willing participant, initiator of the atrocities that tore his soul into smaller and smaller pieces. She watched, felt as he went from village to village, town to town....other mothers offered up their sons...and some small voice inside of the boy screamed in outrage ...but he followed what the older men said and did...they were his friends now, they were his family....and so they had come to this house in this last village that he would know...they, the older men, told him to stand guard at the door of this home, as six of them entered, searching for food, liquor, supplies. he stood there listening to the laughter and ribaldry of his comrades.... at first the screams of the female went through him and then he didn't hear her anymore... he tried to smile like his mentor, his buddy, his surrogate father and compatriot when he had said, "After a while they learn to lay back and enjoy it. And no matter what they tell you—they all enjoy it." In the boy's mind, the man—this father-figure-friend winked as he laughed. Even their commander said that this was their right, this was their due... for all that they did to protect the villages... the village women should be happy to service the soldiers; show their appreciation.

...And then it was his turn...the men filed out, adjusting their clothes, still drinking, laughing and talking uproariously...could he be a man or was he still just a boy...this was his mentor, his friend...saying this in front of all the other men, still winking and laughing...he smiled the smile of his buddy and went in to take his turn....thankfully the woman, or rather girl's face was covered... she lie on the floor next to an empty clothes basket, on top of a bundle of freshly laundered sheets now stained with blood, dirt and body fluids... apparently she had been folding the laundry when

interrupted by the soldiers' knock on the door.... in the midst of torn clothing, and bloody sheets .... he heard soft moaning, like an injured animal...her body looked so young, like a little girl...he wanted to cover her up and take her away from this place, away from this moment. We're watching you boy, the men shouted and laughed from the window....he steadied his resolve... he must show them that he too was a man...after all this is what separates men from boys, right? ...his mother had told him of these things...besides this girl, this woman was probably one of the females who gave herself to a man's pleasure, just like his father-figure-friend had said when he came in...so he took his turn...quickly...her face was still covered...but the girl made no more sounds, the injured moaning animal sounds came no more... he searched around for something to wipe himself ...there was only the cloth that covered her face and somehow it had slipped off to reveal part of a small ear, cheek and chin...without thinking and without understanding why, he reached for the cloth and pulled it off... the bruised and battered face with scared, pleading eyes looked up at him... the eyes...it was the eyes that he knew first and even worse, they knew him... he ran screaming from the house...and when they—his buddies, his compatriots caught him—- they could do nothing to stop the screams ....the wildness in his eyes frightened them, so they locked him in this tiny room... just for the night.... and took away anything with a point or a rope-like form.... they didn't find the empty bottle of toxic cleaning liquid until the next day... and then they called for the healer man who went from village to village and who happened to be now in this village.

Shona pushed herself and the boy deeper into his mind, past all his memory and thought. When she heard a deep gurgling sound in his throat and a loud rattle in his chest as the boy-man made one final audible exhale, she opened her eyes and pulled away. She fell to the floor, drained, staring straight ahead, seeing nothing—just like the young man on the bed whose empty vacant eyes stared, unseeing at the ceiling above. Om pushed his eyelids down and pulled the blanket over his head.

Shona whispered hoarsely, "The girl?"

Om: "She was taken back to her home. She is with her family."

It was only later that Shona heard how the boy's youngest and most adored sister, though still more child, than woman had been hired as a washer woman in a house in this place that was the last that the boy-soldier would know. The family of the house had gone out for the day, leaving her to her work, leaving her to the endless stream of chores they had given her, leaving her to the safety of their home.

That night Shona slept even more fitfully than she had for most of this week. These were the moments that she missed her mother the most. Mala could always find the words to chase away empty feelings of despair. After awhile, she gave up on sleep and crept outside into the darkness. She heard a rapid fire of gun shots in the distance and she knew that the soldiers had begun their almost nightly ribaldry.

She was only mildly surprised to see Om sitting there in the dark in front of Selene's house, as if he was waiting for her. He continued looking up into the moon-lit sky, never turning to confirm her identity as he started speaking, "Do you believe that you are responsible for that young man's death?"

She slid down next to him before quietly responding, "No."

Om: "Do you believe that you have power over life and death?"

Shona: "No."

Om: "You had the power to save that man—why did you choose to let him die?"

Shona: "He chose, not me. He didn't want to live."

Om: "But you were strong enough to pull him back."

Shona: "When I went inside of him, he was begging me to let him die. The pain was overwhelming, more than I could bear. And he would not release it. He embraced it as a way to hasten his departure from this realm. The only mercy was for me to help him in the way that he wanted to be helped. He was begging me to help him to die."

Om: "Yes, I know. I wasn't certain how you would choose. And I wasn't sure if you would be capable of formulating a deliberate course of action. But the decision had to be yours. It is now important for you to understand why you made the decision and for you to be at peace with the action that you chose to take."

Shona: "Are you saying that this whole horrible ordeal was some kind of a test?" She turned to look at him fully, trying to control the anger, bewilderment and hurt that she felt rising within her. "What kind of warped form of instruction are you imparting? Why did you do this to me? Do you know the morass of devastation and agonizing pain that I had to wade through inside of that man?"

Om: "Calm yourself, child. There was no test; nor any right or wrong answer. This is your life. He wanted to die and now you must try to understand why you were able to go inside of and be a part of his desire."

Shona: "He was pulling me with him. The only way to help him was to go inside of his longing to cease existing. I felt what he felt. At the moment when our connection was most intense, as he began to pass over—my life—all life and living—seemed too oppressive to sustain any joy or happiness or reason for going on, for continuing to live."

Om: "You could only go inside of such a desire, to the extent that its intent already lives within your own being. You must now try to understand that intent."

Shona: "To be joined with that man, in that way—within his spirit and in his mind—was the most devastating feeling that I have ever known. No other death that I have witnessed made me feel that way. Nothing else that I have ever experienced has come close to anything so unsettling."

Om: "Yes, but now as a result of this experience you are ready to move on to the next phase of your training."

Shona: "What type of training?"

Om: "You must train to know how to fight. And now you are in a better position to understand what you are fighting for."

Shona: "I already know how to fight."

Om: "Physical might or prowess does not mean that you know how to engage in battle. It is time for you to learn how to fight by way of your spirit and your mind. You must learn how to bring together the strength of your body with the force of your perceptual acuity. That young man today—he lost the war within himself a long time ago because he did not know how to fight."

Shona: "But how can anyone fight against the evils that exist in this world? It is all so overwhelming—the city, the soldiers, the continuous wars, fighting and killing over and over again; each new generation, each new group of people. Every where you turn there is evil in the world; so much unfathomable evil."

Om: "Why acknowledge the presence of evil? Does that not substantiate its existence?"

Shona: "Can we walk this earth and not feel the terror of such a power?"

Om: "Evil is neither true nor real. It is a relative state of weakness that has no power in the absence of our terror. Conquer your belief in fear and the power has no source."

Shona: "But everyone knows or believes that there is a force of evil that can influence the actions of those who walk this earth."

Om: "Reality, many times, becomes that which we acknowledge as true and others validate as real. However, once you give credence to the reality that oppresses you, only then can a major obstacle to your freedom be set in place; and only then can the struggle for power commence."

Shona was never certain that she completely understood all that the old man conveyed in these discussions. But she listened as closely as she could to his sometimes cryptic way of explaining and occasionally she had to struggle to follow his message.

Om: "There is no supernatural force of evil that is natural to this realm. There is only the energy that can potentially manifest as a result of thoughts and beliefs. A 'doer of evil' is the only type of devil that has ever existed and he or she can spawn tangible action only by way of their own negative mental and psychological energy. Evil can only be brought to life by way of mortal thoughts, energy and actions. Evil has no power unless one affirms and believes in the reality of its existence. The devil has no credence outside of our acceptance and acknowledgment of the thought of evil. There is only one source of power in the universe. It is only when we reject this source that our own power is diminished and the human weakness that we know as 'evil' is allowed to prevail."

Shona: "Does that mean that we create the devil because we don't want to take responsibility for our own actions? Perhaps, in our weakness, we invent a supernatural being that takes away our own inherent control."

Om: "The thought of evil is born of the coupling of our fears with our insecurities, attracted to one another only through a lack of faith in the power of the universe. This unholy union produces a bastard need so desperate and distorted that it deters our evolution/growth and may eventually be the cause of our extinction."

Shona: "But if we create our own devil and demons, can it not also be said that we create the idea of God to fulfill needs that we feel powerless to fulfill on our own?"

Om: "God and the need for a god can be understood in many ways. But keep in mind that those who invent a God for their own purposes, in the image of their own needs and desires, actually possess little or no real God-consciousness or awareness. And it is always easy to recognize them because they prominently display their religiosity. They reject and condemn any one who does not subscribe to their fear-inspired beliefs of ignorance, bigotry, and false superiority.

What these people do not understand is that God—the universal force of creative energy—exists both within and independent of our needs. While the need for God is, indeed, intertwined with the injera of this world, you must first understand life's greater intent in order to discover true fulfillment of any personal sense of injera. And it is only in the fulfillment of injera that we seek and truly know God. "

Shona: "But what if one does not fulfill their injera, does that mean that they cannot seek or know God?"

Om: "If our understanding of injera or our means of need-fulfillment have been defiled then our search for and understanding of God is subject to the same defilement; or potentially diminished or tainted. We can only develop a consciousness or awareness of God by aligning our personal injera with the injera of the natural world and that of the universe.

The injera of the universe is one aspect of the Creator's will; it is that part of the Creator's will that incites life into existence. While it may be translated into human terms most closely by the word 'need', it also encompasses desire, hope, reason, intent and purpose. Injera is the stimulus which leads to all human aspirations, beliefs and experiences. There are no words that can capture its meaning fully. It is the motivation behind all true action, true faith, and true belief. It is believed that all forces of life—gravity, magnetism, all bio-chemical- electromagnetic phenomena—manifest as they do because of the injera of the universe.

The Creator's will is the primal energy and the sole source of all power for everything in existence. We cannot look outside of ourselves for a power greater than our own. God lives within every thing that we are and can be— every moment of hope, despair, joy, loneliness, greatness, or defeat. You must seek and find the power of God that lives within you, within all life. The help we wait for, wish for and believe in exists inside of us and all around us. We must learn how to rise to the god-power of this existence—the power in the natural world around us. The people of this Earth have not yet learned to rise to their own God-consciousness, thus they grope along in the darkness of their own confusion, uncertainty and chaos."

Shona: "Among my mother's people it is common knowledge that the accepted ways of this world and the conditions that exist within most societies are not within the natural scheme of life on this earth or within the universe. The people of the Ocan have consciously chosen to exercise their will on this planet without the unnatural influence of diseased malignant realities. They have separated themselves from those whose weakness or apathy allows them to persist struggling in environments which are not conducive to the perpetuation of life and spirituality."

Om: "Yet, ironically they remain vulnerable to and controlled by the very forces that they would choose to negate."

Shona: "What do you mean?"

Om: "A forced isolation does not provide immunity. The malignant realities that you speak of are much too pervasive to be controlled by quarantine. Your vulnerability and susceptibility to injury are increased by a lack of exposure. Isolation breeds homogeneity, a lack of diversity. Homogeneity makes any group more vulnerable to disease and susceptible to harm. The innocence of your unsuspecting nature that consequently develops in isolation makes you much easier prey. There is no freedom in hiding. The foe that we face must be challenged and ultimately defeated by its own design.

That is why it is important that you understand what it is that you are fighting and most importantly you must learn how to fight. The first part of learning to fight means learning how to battle and conquer your own weaknesses. We can only conquer our fears through the confidence of knowing that you have the ability and power to fight what threatens you. We can only make your atonement to the Inar and to life as a whole, once you have learned to fight and you have moved to a point of strength that will allow your offering to be most true and most real. Your malaise, this sickness inside of you will never be fully healed unless you learn how to heal your own injera."

Shona: "Om, how is it that you know so many Ocan concepts? You speak of things that I assumed only the Ocan people knew."

Om: "Ocan beliefs and philosophies are no different from those of other people in the world who create individual cosmologies to make sense of where and why we exist. The eternal questions of every living being, when their eyes open truly for the first time, are the same everywhere—who and what am I? What is this place and why am I here? You must never stop asking these questions, because how you attempt to answer these very basic and fundamental questions determines what you are capable of becoming."

Shona: "Are you familiar with the Ocan concept of the Gift—I mean the way they explain it and interpret it?"

Om: "Yes."

Shona: "Can you tell me what you know, your understanding of what it is?"

Om: "You already know. The Gift is life."

Shona: "But there is more to the definition. Mala started saying something about how the Gift changes people or rather how it has changed the Ocan people."

Om: "That is a topic for another day. Come we must rest so that tomorrow we can leave at dawn."

Shona: "I thought that we were staying for another day. I promised Selene that I would be here tomorrow to help with her daughter's—"

Om: "No, I'm sorry. Our plans have changed. There are too many soldiers gathering in this place. It is necessary that we leave as soon as—"

There was a sudden loud clap of thunder and they looked up and saw that the sky was no longer clear. Thick, burgeoning full towers of black clouds, swelling and surging with forceful intensity, crowded the space above the earth. All through the sky, behind and within these huge majestic swirling masses of vapor, there was a deep red illumination that cast a surreal burning light like cold fire on everything and everywhere that Shona could see. Another sudden boom and rippling of thunder sounded, just before they heard a succession of gunfire in the distance. Om motioned her into the house as he turned and began walking in the direction of Immanuel's home. Shona heard him muttering to himself as he stared up at the sky.

As Shona lie listening to the thunder, wind and heavy rain, she stripped off all the worries and concerns over things which she had no control, easing into the comfort and affection that she knew could only exist in her dreams. Waiting for sleep to come, she pulled the warm blanket of her fantasies tightly around her. She hoped that the dreams would live within her forever because in the absence of those moments of peace, she dreaded the return of a fear that would undoubtedly smother the belief that she wanted to sustain; a belief that life is good and strong. Knowing that the scenes in her mind were not now or ever real did not diminish the affect of their power. Her feelings were just as real as if her fantasy, this dream-presence, was actually there with her. For Shona, these dreams were the substance of things hoped for, the evidence of things not seen; that which gave her the will to believe. And sometimes she wondered—in their absence would it be possible for her to subsist, to go on?

14. Saba-Energy

Eventually, they took Amira away, back to the hamlets closer to the sea and she never returned. They said that the feel, sound and taste of the ocean would be good for her, bring her back to herself, allow her time to heal; and they were right. They said that it would only be temporary, that she would be okay, that she would return soon; and they were wrong.

The Saba found that she also could not return, could not go back—back to who she was, back to the safety of forgetting, of running away. A bottomless stream of anguished suppressed emotion had opened inside of her and try as she might she could not dam it back up. The strength of the sentiale connection with Mala had depleted what little was left of the Saba's guard. Her soul was now open, lying prey to all those repressed venomous memories that for years had waited patiently, coiled inside the lair of her mind.

And there too was the hope, side by side with the fear. She now allowed the memory of Tekun to come to her unrestrained and she wrapped herself up in his love and desire for her. She still could not fathom these intense sensations of joy and longing. This was the uncontrollable fire of a young woman's desires. She surmised that this nostalgia of pleasure and yearning most likely came from a combination of fear, desperation and loneliness. But for the time being, she needed the emotion of these memories to assuage the pain and take away the hurt. Her desires nudged forth a reluctant hope that she prayed had not been awakened in vain. Something in the air was promising that a new day was coming, she could feel it, sense it, smell it like the welcoming scent of a gentle spring rain where all life begins anew.

She had never wondered before, but lately she had begun to wonder why she had never re-married. Long ago there had been opportunity, expressed interest, but she had been convinced that she could not open herself to love again. Now she was just an old woman who should have stopped feeling these feelings, stopped thinking these thoughts long ago. Yet here they were, day and night begging release, fighting to live. She thought to herself how almost every person she knew lived their life with a primary source and connection to love and affection. Even Olana had not allowed the burden of caring for her elderly parents to stop her from finding love, as Hasid still constantly begged her to marry. Even that silly girl Layal had found an equally silly partner. And it seemed that even in the short time that Mala had been back, she had found a secret love-interest who was beginning to occupy more and more of her time. Mala mysteriously disappeared almost every night, sometimes not returning until late the next day; sometimes she was gone for days at a time. Saba surmised that this man must be the reason that Mala did not come today. Mala was supposed to help with Dalam's little girl, who had been ill for the last two days. Saba had waited for her for as long as she could.

Today, Saba had come to the temple much later than her usual pre-dawn communion. She heard a distant reverberating groan from within the mountains and in the earth. She was sitting in her familiar spot on the low stone bench in the wild overgrown garden near the temple grotto, reading from the <u>Journal of Saba</u>. She noticed with dismay that her previous attempts to repair the binding of the book were proving ineffective; the book, much like its present owner, was coming undone. She dreaded the thought, but knew that it would soon be necessary to consult a professional book binder before the book fell completely apart. She regretted having not asked Amira's help previously, before she was taken away. Leaving the book in that cold stone enclosure probably didn't help. But the book had endured for centuries and it was her responsibility to ensure that it would live on in the millennia to come.

Saba felt a dampness in the air and in her bones and she knew that the rain was finally coming; the first rain in months. The wind lifted and blew softly through the leaves above her head and with the wind came a soft whisper that brushed her face—"*Wrapping it in a burlap cloth, they buried the newborn infant alive...*". She could not discern where the words came from, as she heard them in the air around her just as she remembered them echoing in her mind that day so many years ago—"*Edise acted alone, when even his most induced followers...*" Looking down at the book, she was startled to see that these same words were written on the page in front of her. And what was even more unexpected was that they were un-mistakenly written in her own handwriting. "As he placed her on the ground next to the shallow grave, the child, without sound or movement, looked directly at her captor and pierced the androgyne straight through the center of his soul. Stunned by the intensity of her power, the androgyne with his limbs momentarily paralyzed, began shaking violently."

This passage was in that part of the book, where she recorded her own feelings and observations. But she had no memory of ever having committed such words, such thoughts to paper. She looked away from the page, trying to recall when she could have written these words. Through the blur in her mind, her thoughts squirmed toward equilibrium and surfaced with a reasonable explanation, *I am tired and my senses play the fool of me.* She closed her eyes to rest her mind, but the words from the book still came to her—*"When he re-gained the ability to move, he quickly mummified the infant in the shroud and allowed the wet earth to slowly swallow her whole."*

She felt a light but persistent sensation on her head and thought that the sun must have come from behind a cloud to bear down on her, but she did not look up to confirm her impression. She began flipping through the book randomly and the handwriting and the words began to change.

"Saba-power must be replenished by the giving and receiving of the energy. All healing comes by way of the sentiale and within the pathways of the sentiale. The sentiale is a bridge across the abyss. These are the lessons that no saba can teach, but all true saba must learn." She puzzled over this new message, repeating the incomprehensible words out loud—"A bridge across the abyss". And then thinking to herself—*"Abyss? What abyss? What does this mean?"*

Saba heard a low cough as if someone was clearing their throat and she was surprised to look up and see Mala standing next to her. She had not heard Mala approach and she slowly became aware that the sensation that she had been feeling on her head was Mala's hand lightly stroking her hair. Mala's eyes, almost spilling tears, poured out a lifetime of sympathy and compassion. Saba closed the book and sat it beside her on the bench as Mala stooped down in front of her, taking both of her hands into her own, looking up into her face. "Its getting worse, isn't it Saba?"

The Saba could only look away, averting her gaze.

Mala: "Perhaps you are just feeling drained and tired because of Amira's condition and because of Taijaur's absence. They will both be fine, Saba. Try not to worry."

Saba: "No Mala, this is not worry or fatigue. I failed another today. I couldn't even feel through the pain to the other side. My feeble ministrations only seemed to accentuate that little girl's pain and discomfort."

Mala: "I'm sorry Saba. I should have been there. When I came, they told me that you had already gone. And the little girl is fine. She was sleeping peacefully when I left her. I am sorry that I was so late. And I promise you that I won't ever be late again."

Saba: "No, Mala, you shouldn't worry about being late. If you were with me at every crucial moment, then I would probably continue to delude myself that my power is still with me."

Mala rose and sat on the bench next to Saba.

Mala: "Saba, your power is with you. I believe that your gift is as strong as it has ever been. You just need time to find your way back to it. I can help you."

Saba: "No, Mala, it is gone. Do you realize that I have not healed one person by myself since you have been here? And before you came it was even worse. The people were beginning to suspect something, which is why I relied so heavily on the healing plants. But even our trusted herbaceous allies are tiring of my over-reliance on their assistance and over-depletion of their power."

Mala: "Saba, I think that you are too hard on yourself."

Saba: "Perhaps Mala. But perhaps I have not been hard enough. It is only a matter of time before someone sustains serious harm as a result of my lack of ability. And what if someone actually dies because I am not able to save them?"

Mala: "You mean Loni, don't you?"

Saba looked as if she had been slapped. She managed to weakly ask, "Mala, why would you say something like that?"

Mala: "Because it seems that is who you are always thinking about when you say things like that. But Saba, you have to let her go. Let her go. You can't stop people from dying. Just like you can't stop anyone from living the life that they feel compelled to live. No matter how hard you try and no matter how important they may be to you, or your life or hopes and aspirations. You can't feel responsible when your healing does not result in the continuation of someone's life. That is not your responsibility as a saba or as a parent. That is and will always be beyond your control."

Saba: "Mala, I have never been so foolish as to try to control life or death. My role is that of a shepherd, a guide. And if I fail in my responsibilities, my failure is no mere mistake that can be patched up and made better. I have no right but to always give the most and the best of what I have to give. That is my utmost responsibility and that is well within my control."

Mala: "But Saba, you must learn to forgive yourself. We can not always know how to be or give the best of who and what we are. And so much of what we need to know is outside of our control."

A cool breeze blew through the air and Mala glanced around at the fluttering foliage. She watched the wind blow through the leaves at the top of one of the taller tress. They were shining, as they danced, with their various shades of green and bright pervasive sunlight reflecting from their surface. They swayed in a rhythm all their own.

Mala: "It is always so beautiful and peaceful here. But the wind is telling us that it will rain soon." She looked back at the opening to the temple and a thought came to her that had occurred to her before. "Saba, have you ever considered that this temple may contain energy much like that which lives in beneath the Maja?"

Saba: "No, there is no way that could be possible. The ancient Obeah placed this temple here and did not identify it with any of the other known areas of energy. I enter those caverns every day and I would know if there were any electromagnetic forces within the feel of the rocks. There is nothing in those caverns but healing water and minerals. And besides if those caverns contained anything as significant as an opening to another world, a saba-sister of the past would have detected it and the *Journal* would have made some reference. Those women were very powerful."

Mala: "I suppose you are right. But in terms of the *Journal*, is it true that it can only reveal what each individual saba needs?"

Saba: "So they say. I only know what comes to me from the book. I can't speak for any other's experience before or after my own. Supposedly only those of saba-spirit can read or hear its words." Saba picked the book up and laid it in Mala's lap. "Here Mala, I'm sure the book will speak to you. Just hold it and open your mind to the meaning that it conveys."

Mala sat with the open book in her lap looking down at the strange glyphs and symbols on the page that seemed to move and jump around.

Saba: "Do you feel anything?'

Mala: "No, nothing."

She could make no sense of the undecipherable markings on the page. The more she looked at it, her eyes began to hurt and burn. She handed the book back to Saba, shaking her head, "I can make nothing of it."

Saba: "Perhaps the book senses your resistance and knows that you desire nothing from it."

Mala: "Saba I want so much to help you. But as much as I may want or even try to be what you need, what our people need—you have to realize that it is not possible. I cannot function in opposition or contrary to my own injera."

Saba: "But with all that you have been through, it may be difficult for you to even to determine the true nature of your injera. Our people must have saba-energy renewed with each successive generation and this requires a new saba to be born in each generation. You have to be the one, there is no one else."

Mala: "I know myself. I am not saba; nor was I ever meant to be. I can help you to bring forth your own healing power and energy, but I can only travel the pathways that you have already carved. I am unable to create such pathways myself. And you know, without a doubt, that saba-energy manifest must be both the cause and effect of its own existence."

Saba: "The power is in you Mala—much greater than I could have imagined and perhaps beyond," she paused, "any force that we have ever known."

Mala spoke louder now, more forcefully; she made sure that Saba looked directly into her face, into her eyes, as she reached out and covered the healer-woman's hands with her own. "Yes, I know of my power. But Saba, you are not listening to me. You are not hearing me. You have to understand—where saba-processes are concerned, I have only the power to accentuate that which is already in existence. I cannot create the necessary pathways. The energy does not come to me of its own volition. And you and I both know, that saba-energy must call and beckon to one in a way in which no dissent can be brokered. Saba, you must accept—I am not the one.

I can not be or become that which I was never meant to be. No matter how great a need may exist in the world or even in our small collective. No matter how great my debt may be to you, the Ocan or mankind as a whole, I cannot be that which I am not."

Saba: "Can't you see Mala? Can't you understand? My responsibility as saba was never just to heal the people, but to seek and secure a receptacle for the continuity of this energy. Without my gift, I am losing my faith. Soon my spirit will lose cohesion, and then I will have no more to give. My God is deserting me. Can't you see? Can't you understand this bundle of frustration and confusion that results from not being able to receive or share the gifts that life blesses us with?"

Mala: "But having not found a person with this innate, inherent need to express saba-energy, why not try to cultivate it in another?"

Saba: "Who besides yourself has the power?"

Mala: "What about Layal? She has helped you so much with the herbs. And she tries so hard to please you and learn all that she can."

Saba: "That mumbling, fumbling girl has no skill, no talent."

Mala: "Why can't you try to teach her? She has learned how to mix and handle the herbs."

Saba: "This is not a matter of teaching. That girl has no means by which to receive the energy; no internal structures that will allow her to be a receptacle. Despite her desire to provide aid and comfort to the sick and ailing, she was not born saba. Attempting to transfer the energy to someone like that could result in her death, or permanent mental and spiritual derangement. Would you have me take such a risk with another's life?"

Mala: "But Saba, why not seek a new way or ways to manifest saba-energy? Why not try to cultivate the necessary internal structures and even seek a receptacle in other ways, other places, other types of people? Why not even a male saba? Or even someone who was perhaps reared outside of the influence of Ocan ways."

Saba looked at Mala, stunned. "Mala, you have no idea what you are saying. Saba-energy knows saba-energy. A calling, a connection must be formed for the transfer of energy to be successful. In the absence of the necessary internal structures to receive the energy, there can be potentially devastating results. Those of saba-spirit are not just born, they must receive the spiritual flow of energy or they will never be able to manifest the full power. The receiver and giver of this energy must be able to match their internal structures in order for the energy to transmit.

Saba-energy is more than just healing energy. Fully accentuated saba-energy also makes one a keeper of the faith. In order to truly heal another person, one must first embody a sense of faith in the goodness of life and a belief in the necessity of its continuity. We are 'called' to our work in such a way that those who refuse to accept the call will, undoubtedly, go mad. And that is what I fear is beginning to happen with me."

Mala: "But you are not refusing Saba. You are fulfilling your calling in life."

Saba: "It doesn't matter if one actually refuses or if one just encounters an insurmountable obstruction—they both lead to the same end. If we refuse or we are unable to receive and share our gifts, we lose pieces of our soul, pieces of our sanity, well-being and general will to live. If we refuse to create or we are unable to give expression to that which is most alive within our beings, then we lose our connection with that which is most sacred and whole within this life. Many people even affect a façade of 'busy-ness' in their unconscious and vain attempt to bury these feelings of 'madness', discontent and dis-ease that result from not giving, receiving and cultivating their gifts."

Mala: "I agree Saba that every person, every life on this planet has a gift that necessarily must be received and shared. But perhaps you can broaden your definition of how to share and with whom you may share. Don't you understand, Saba, part of the reason that it may seem that your gift has deserted you, is possibly caused by the fact that you tried to set the terms, determine the conditions for how you would share and with whom? I don't believe that life works that way. We must make an offering to this world, without boundaries, definitions or conditions.

I believe that we stymie our own growth by feeling that we can only give to the deserving, those worthy to receive our gifts. We can't bottle up and save ourselves waiting for the right person to come along in order to give. If the fruit trees in the orchards followed this practice and waited for only those deserving of their sustenance, then their offering would undoubtedly wither away or fall rotten to the ground. We cannot choose when and how to give. Life must make that decision for us. We must give, share of our gifts with those who cross our paths. The first principle of Injera tells us this."

Saba: "I know the principles of Injera, Mala. And my actions, my search for this next generation's saba are not in opposition to any of the principles. It's just that no one came along, no matter how hard I searched."

Mala: "That is, no one who fit your definition of what it means to be saba."

Saba: "Mala, you know as well as I that saba-energy has nothing to do with definitions.

I have searched and I have waited. I feel a strong persistent force that walks this earth, but only in my dreams does this presence come to me. It is calling to me, pulling me in a way that I cannot resist. But there is a heavy veil that will not allow me to see or know who this person is. Yet I feel this person's thoughts and emotions and desires. These desires are opening my soul and taking me to places within myself that I thought lay long buried and passed away. I feel the essence of my being fusing, melding with the sentiale of this force, this spirit in my dreams."

Mala looked at Saba with intense concern.

Saba continued, "I have interpreted this dream-presence to be that of your spirit Mala. Why can't it be your soul, Mala? You have returned to the Ocan for a purpose. Why not this calling?"

Mala looked away and in a low tone she replied, "You thought the same of Loni."

Saba sighed heavily, "Perhaps, Mala. But trust me please. Now is not the time to focus on any lapse or infirmity that may be a part of my character. Our time is running out. If you are, indeed, not the one that I seek, then it behooves us to move carefully and quickly to find the next saba. The energy is building, within this earth, in the skies. And not just saba-energy, but all forms and manner of forces beyond our control. Surely, you feel it as well. I hear wails of saba-energy in the night wind, beseeching a release that I am compelled to give but have no power to bring about.

I wish that you could read parts of the journal so that you can understand that our destiny—as a people, as human beings in this sphere—cannot be fulfilled in the absence of saba-energy manifest. Saba-energy, although concentrated in the Ocan people, flows through out the world in all people, all places—allowing healing to take place all over this planet. Why do you think that most of the nations of the world, the people of the world have no peace, no understanding? They cannot truly heal—physically or spiritually—in the absence of saba-energy.

Alor believes that it is the virus that it is the biggest threat to mankind's continued survival. And he thinks that the portal energy will provide the necessary antidote to this plague that engulfs the planet. But he is only partly right. It is also the absence of saba-energy that allows the pervasiveness of evil and suffering to dominate within the world. With saba-energy, the people would have the power to withstand and fight the effects of the virus and any other form of negative energy in existence.

Saba-energy is a necessary part of all true action or power. Most people do not realize that the continuity of life on this Earth depends on a spiritual cohesion that can only come from sentiale healing. And sentiale healing necessarily depends on the presence of saba-energy. Once, the possibility of such energy could have existed anywhere in the world, within any type of person. But now the destructive forces of most societies and civilizations have rendered this energy mute.

Alor is right when he says that we are entering a time of change, where endings and beginnings meet. And we cannot go into this next epoch in the absence of saba-power. The saba of the Ocan people are a part of humanity's last hope for renewal, rejuvenation of the collective spirit of mankind. Human life—earthly existence—cannot be sustained or perpetuated in the absence of saba-energy. For centuries, saba-energy has passed from one generation to the next, one receptacle to the next. For the first time in Ocan history, there is no one to receive the energy."

Mala sat pensive for a moment, knowing that there were no more words that she could offer that would solve, answer or make this better. A loud clap of thunder made both women gaze up into the sky, where dark clouds had gathered. "Come, Saba. We must head back to the village. The wind is blowing stronger. The storm is almost here."

In the distance, thunder and lightening began to move and transform the air. Together the two women secured the journal back in its hiding place, heaving the heavy stone across the niche in the wall. Before they exited the temple gardens, the storm clouds opened up and released torrents of hard steady rain. Saba pulled her wide, enveloping shawl over Mala and herself as they made their way down the path into the village. Rivulets of mud and water washed down the sides of the slippery road and the two women struggled to maintain their footing. The rain was coming down with even more force by the time they came through the marketplace where they were greeted by empty battened stalls and a few stray people still running for shelter. As they neared the first area of family compounds, Saba spoke loudly to be heard over the sound of the downpour, "Let's go to Olana's. We will never make it back home in all this rain. I think that Olana has gone to see Amira, so she most likely is not there."

They were completely drenched by the time they stumbled through the door to Olana's home. Saba was surprised to see that not only was Olana home, but Alor was also there, both of them sitting at the table sipping hot black tea. Olana rushed to find them some dry clothing and then she put more loose tea leaves into the kettle as they changed. The house smelled of paint and there were several easels with half-finished sketches and paintings through out the front room. Paint supplies littered the table. Mala came out of the back adjusting her clothing, studying with concentrated interest each of the drawings and paintings. "Olana, I'm glad to see that you have started working once again."

Olana: "Oh, these are just some trial pieces. Now that I am the only one here, I can spread out a little more."

Mala stared at Olana with open curiosity, "Have you ever wondered where these otherworldly images in your paintings come from?"

Olana laughed a little nervously as she covered some of the easels. "Just imagination, I suppose."

Saba came from the back bedroom, drying her hair with a towel. "Alor, what are you doing down here in the village today? I thought that we would not see you for another month or so."

Alor: "Well, for one thing, I came to speak with Amira and I find that she has gone away."

Olana: "So, instead he has picked away at the few brain cells that I have left. He has been probing and prodding me with strange questions all afternoon. I am almost ready to take him to my mother in the hamlets right now in all this rain, just to be relieved of this trying inquisition." She laughed.

Alor: "And I am eternally grateful that you have patiently endured my 'inquisition'. I appreciate that you have been willing to share with this most humble of servants all that you know and remember."

Saba: "What questions has he been tormenting you with Olana?"

Olana: "Oh just questions about my mother and father for which I have no answers. Maybe you know Saba—how strong was their sentiale connection before and then after my father's accident? What did my dad say when he first returned from the western forest? I was just a child. I have no recall of these matters."

Alor: "Yes Saba, tell us what you know. This day is turning out to be most fortunate. Just before you came in, I was actually wishing that I might have the opportunity to speak with both you, Saba and Mala. And lo and behold, as fate would have it, the gods have graced my presence with the beauty, wit and charm of not just one of my wished-for ladies, but both of these esteemed wise women."

Olana and Mala laughed.

Saba: "Alor, you are as much of an old wind bag as you ever were. Amira may know more than I, but I'm not sure how much she may be capable of divulging. What exactly are you investigating, Alor?"

Alor: "Oh, its just a hunch I have that some of those phrases that Kalal used to repeat may not have been as nonsensical as they may have appeared."

Mala looked up with interest. However, Saba seemed suddenly and visibly shaken as she rose from her seat and went to glance out of the window, making an obvious attempt to change the subject. "This rain does not seem that it will let up for some time. Have you been in the village all day, Alor?"

Alor: "I was called down this morning to attend a meeting with the Council of Elders."

Saba turned to face him. "I didn't hear of any meeting that was scheduled for today."

Alor: "This was an unplanned emergency meeting. I am sure that you will find out sooner or later what has occurred, so I may as well tell you now. The Aka sent an envoy to speak with the council of Elders today."

All three women stopped what they were doing and focused on Alor, exclaiming simultaneously, "What!!?!!"

Saba: "How is that possible? No Aka have been in this village in more than half a century."

Mala: "What has happened?"

Olana: "Do you mean to tell me that you have been here all this time and you never said anything about this?"

Alor: "The Elders have instructed us to not speak of these matters to the general population. However, I am confident that each of you can be trusted with this information. Hopefully, nothing will come of all this ruckus with the Aka. They sent an envoy from the Haman village to put forth their requests; or rather their demands. They are asserting their right to the minerals and other resources that are being explored and developed with the geothermal projects in the Lane. And they are also advising the council that they will soon expand their territory beyond the southern part of the island into the Ocan territory of the Aymarra village. They are demanding that their access to the aqueducts from the Haman river be restored.

Although the Aka made no mention of the portal project, the Elders believe that they know about the portal. They suspect that one of our apprentices or someone who knows of the project has been feeding information to the Aka about the portal."

Olana: "But that is ridiculous. Only a few of us know about that portal. And how could any of our people even make contact with the Aka, let alone divulge a secret as closely guarded as this one. We all know how high the stakes are in this project. With the exception of the original families who safeguard the knowledge of this portal, no other Ocan even knows what this project entails."

Alor: "Nonetheless, none of those facts have deterred the Elders' suspicions."

Mala: "How seriously do they perceive this threat from the Aka?"

Alor: "The Elders pay no mind to their demands for more land or access to the water. They gave the same response that they have given in the past. They are most concerned with securing the portal project site and determining who in our collective may be acting on behalf of the Aka.

They have convinced themselves that there is a spy in our midst. Because the portal project has been so highly guarded and tightly controlled, unfortunately the Elders' suspicions are focusing on you three, in addition to the Dalasa family and the project's five principal investigators—Hadassa, myself and our three apprentices. They have already brought Kedar and Odar in for questioning. They have asked me to turn over all the notes of the project, including and especially Taijaur's translations. Saba, they will most likely search your house and possessions."

Saba slid down slowly in a chair at the table near Alor.

Alor: "There is something else; something that could potentially have even greater consequences. Mala perhaps you should sit as well."

Mala looked up from the painting that she was studying and moved toward the table.

Mala: "What is it?"

Alor: "It's the Book. They are looking for the second part of the Book."

Mala: "What book?"

Alor: "The second volume of 'The Source of Change'".

Mala: "But isn't that the book that the Aka have locked away? Supposedly, not even their own people have access to it."

Saba remained silent.

Alor: "The Aka claim that it has been stolen

Mala: "What!?! How can that be?"

The Aka have said that it is missing; more specifically, they charge that someone of the Ocan has taken it."

Olana: "How could anyone of the Ocan have known where that book could be found, let alone sneak into their village undetected and steal it away?"

Alor: "They have scant evidence of any theft. But they claim that the book is missing and they know that the Ocan scouts have been spying on their activities. They have given the Elders two weeks to produce the book and make restitution. Edise believes that they are using the theft of this book as a ruse to press for and add leverage to their other demands."

Olana: "But no one in the Ocan villages would be caught dead with that book."

Alor: "I thought the same thing until I saw some of Taijaur's translations. I don't think this younger generation fully understands or realizes the depth of animosity between the Aka and the Ocan."

Mala looked at Saba. She was breathing heavily and rubbing her forehead, still saying nothing. .

Mala: "Saba, are you okay?"

Saba: "It's nothing; nothing at all. I am just tired from the walk."

Alor: "I've been going through Taijaur's notes from the translation work, but many of the pages are missing. Saba, do you know where the missing papers may be?"

Saba: "No, I don't know. Taijaur never discussed his work with me and he did not keep his papers or his work in my house. They will waste their time searching there."

Alor: "Saba, I suspect that you may know something of what I have uncovered. I had no idea that Taijaur had completed so much of the translation. He has gone much further than anyone expected, more than anyone could know was possible. His notes convey information beyond the scope of the first Book of Change. I know that he also found some additional resources that were buried in our own collection of materials, but this could not account for all that he has uncovered." He paused looking at Saba. "Saba, Do you know how he was able to complete so much of the translation work?"

Saba: "I know nothing, Alor."

Alor: "But you suspect, as I do—don't you?"

Saba: "I told you, I don't know anything. I have no knowledge of Taijaur's work. As I said before, he never discussed it with me. I know nothing."

Alor: "Perhaps not knowing is the safest place to be right now. But I don't know if we have the luxury of that kind of safety. If we are to help Taijaur, we may have to acquaint ourselves with matters that exist beyond our comfort range. "

Mala: "Has anyone else seen Taijaur's notes or is anyone aware of what is in them?"

Alor: "No, only you three are aware of what I have revealed."

Mala: "What can we do?"

Alor: "At this point, we can only wait. Taijaur is not expected back for at least another three months. So we will have to wait until then to ask him directly. But by then it may be too late. Whatever is going to happen will most likely take place some time between now and before he returns. However, if someone happens to find Taijaur's missing notes, then I am not sure how much I will be able to control this situation. I'm not sure if anyone will be able to control what may happen."

They were all quiet for a few moments and the rain pelting the roof began to sound even louder. Saba startled a little when Alor started speaking again, "Saba, I hope you realize how important it is to safeguard any papers of Taijaur's that you may find and the knowledge that they contain. The Elders must not suspect that they exist. And the Aka especially must never get their hands on them. That would prove extremely dangerous to all concerned. I am certain that their translators have not uncovered a fraction of what Taijaur has accomplished. And if they are able to decipher his encrypted code, then the notes would provide them with a blueprint to the destruction of—"

Saba interrupted, "As I said Alor, I know nothing of these papers that you speak of."

Alor: "Well, it may be of little or no consolation to you, but Taijaur in his research and translation work has uncovered some of the most astounding information in the history of our people and maybe all of mankind. He was more right about this situation than I could have ever imagined. He kept insisting that we needed at least the second volume of the Book and I didn't think that it was necessary. But having now read through his notes, there is no way that anyone could have proceeded in the absence of at least the two books combined. What a blessing of time and opportunity Rainar unknowingly granted me."

Mala: "What did you find in Taijaur's notes?"

Olana: "Yes, what is in these books that could be so important that even millennia after they were written they can still cause conflict?

Alor: "Well for one thing—I found information that has made me suspect that Kalal's phrases may have been more than just incoherent ramblings. His words match some brief passages in Taijaur's translations, but without the missing pages, I won't be able to know for sure.

I always thought the three volumes of the Book stood alone, each consecutive accounts of an unfolding story. But they are really like interlocking pieces of a giant jigsaw puzzle, where each tiny piece affects all the others and the knowledge in one book can only be completed once combined with information from each of the other two books. Part of what Taijaur discovered was that these volumes were once one whole book. It was translated into three separate volumes in three different cryptic languages, in order to be smuggled out of some country before it was discovered and destroyed.

Once Taijaur deciphered the encryptions, he then encoded his own translations. At first, I wasn't certain how to read all of the encoded translations. But I believe that I have correctly figured out certain passages. I'm not sure that Taijaur understood the implications of what he translated. But he began to draft another map that reveals the location of the one central portal to the in-between that can never be sealed, covered or in any way altered. This portal is the most powerful of all and it leads to and allows access to all other portals throughout the Earth. I cannot read the map or the encrypted language well enough to say where this main portal is located but it seems to be somewhere either here on this island or on one of landmasses within this archipelago. The future of this island and perhaps even this world may depend on finding this portal and making sure that no one else ever has knowledge of it."

Mala: "But Alor what is the meaning of all of this?"

Alor: "I can't go into all the details now, but the Book records patterns and cycles of variation in geologic phenomena such as the motion of electrically conducting material within the earth, changes in the strength and orientation of the earth's magnetic field, as well as changes in the earth's gravitational field and variations in the earth's rotation. These patterns and cycles reflect seismic movement that takes place over centuries and millennia. Much of what is outlined in the Book corresponds to what scientists throughout the world have reported in terms of the collapse and subsequent reversal in the Earth's magnetic field that is beginning to take place now.

This energy field shields the planet and guides and influences all terrestrial inhabitants in ways that we are only beginning to uncover and understand. When the planet's polarities switch—what we know as north will become south and vice versa and there will be other changes that we may not have the power to guard against."

Mala: "But Alor isn't it true that the magnetic fields constantly shift and move; and a full reversal will take thousands of years to complete?"

Alor: "Yes. From what we can deduce these reversals have happened approximately every half million years. With each reversal we believe that the Earth's inner core has remained unchanged, but the continuous flows of lava beneath the sea and in volcanoes provide evidence of the planet's alternating magnetism over the ages.

The Book makes mention of these field reversals and their potential effects. From what I can decipher in the notes, it appears that during these times of flux there is a potential for a great number of species extinctions and a subsequent explosion of new species. I believe that the energy from this field reversal may also be responsible for the portals that are opening once again; not only here on the island, but all across the globe. And there is something else—" he paused, "The Book indicates that there are times within this cycle of field reversals that, not only do the gateways to the in-between become more volatile, allowing more and more energy to seep into our world, but this conversion of the Earth's magnetism can also lead to a release into our world of conscious, sentient life forms, entities whose natural realm of existence is that of the in-between."

Mala: "What!?! No life form could survive in—"

Olana, who had been listening intently, startled them all by suddenly jumping up from the table, knocking over tubes of paint and paint brushes. She looked weak, as if she was about to faint. As Alor bent under the table to pick up the items, Mala and Saba rose on either side of Olana, holding her steady.

Mala: "Are you okay?"

She was perspiring, her hands visibly shaking with one hand on her forehead and the other holding her abdomen.

Olana: "I'm fine. It just feels kind of warm in here. If you all don't mind, I think that I will go and lie down for a little while. Please excuse me."

Saba started walking with Olana, still holding her by the arm, saying, "I'll go with her. I'm still feeling rather weak myself."

Alor continued putting the paint supplies in order on the table as Mala slowly sat back down, staring curiously at two women walking toward the back of the house. "There must be something going around. This is strange to have both Saba and Olana not feeling well. They are usually the last to ever fall ill." She turned to face Alor, "But what were you saying about life forms in the in-between?"

Alor: "Well, I hope that they feel better soon, but it may be best that only you hear the remainder of what I must tell. As I was saying, it appears that the internal chambers that house the power source of the in-between are not just full of radiation-like emissions and strange geological processes, as we previously assumed. These hidden subterranean caverns are also the dwelling place for entities or life forms that are natural to that realm."

Mala: "But Alor, how can any form of life survive below ground within the bowels of the Earth? There is no light, and in some instances, no air, and even poisonous gases."

Alor: "Perhaps these life forms do not conform to our narrow definition of 'life'. I don't know what these entities can be made of, in terms of their physical composition. However, it was once thought that life did not, could not exist in the coldest and hottest regions of the earth, yet now we know differently. And if life can find a way to manifest in the heart of a glacier and near the sulfuric hydrothermal vents on the ocean floor then why not in this nether region of the world?

But Mala, one of the more disturbing parts of all of this is that the Book indicates that these entities of the in-between have the power to come into this world. Although there may be a greater release of them at the times of the field reversals, I believe that the more powerful of these beings are able to travel back and forth between our realm and the world of the in-between at will. Without our knowledge, these entities from the in-between may have existed among us since the beginning of time."

Mala and Alor stared at one another silently for a moment before Mala sighed heavily. "Well, it goes without saying that I will be more than a little relieved when Taijaur and Shona return to the island."

Alor: "That's the other thing that I wanted to speak with you about. I had hoped to give you a chance to digest the first part of this, before presenting what the rest of this passage in the Book reveals."

Mala: "What is it? I can't imagine anything more shocking than what you have already disclosed."

Alor: "It's about your daughter. You know that the presence of her spirit in this world fractured or broke the seal on the portals to the in-between."

Mala: "But didn't you say that the magnetic field reversals were causing the portals to open?"

Alor: "Yes, but that's just it Mala. I believe that her birth, her very existence is somehow connected to this current field reversal. I am certain that her spirit on this earth helped to widen an opening between worlds. Most likely, her power will only grow stronger as she develops. And as her power awakens more and more, she will not only be able to act as a conduit, transmitting the earth's energy, but she will also attract those with similar powers.

This passage of the Book indicates that these entities from the in-between recognize and are drawn to earthly beings with substances akin to their own. Mala, if what I suspect about your daughter is correct, she may unknowingly have the power to pull and attract the energy of these in-between beings. I believe that she may be like a magnet, an irresistible force that will draw them to her."

Mala: "But this is all just speculation, Alor. Isn't it?"

Alor: "Perhaps. But think about it Mala—as your daughter was growing up, weren't there times when you noticed that she exhibited unusual behaviors and actions that perhaps you were unable to comprehend or account for? Did it sometimes seem that she possessed powers beyond even those of the Ocan people?"

Mala looked away and did not respond right away. She watched the rain splattering against the windowpane. And then abruptly as if arguing with herself she spoke up. "Besides Alor this book was written thousands of years ago. How could it make statements about my daughter? That would be impossible. What is this supposed to be some kind of prophecy about Shona?"

Alor: "This is not exactly a prophecy. And the Book does not mention your daughter specifically or any particular person. The Book outlines certain patterns of cause and effect, certain outcomes based on causal agents and stimuli. If you follow the signs and the calculations from the time of your daughter's birth until now, a pattern appears with your daughter's spirit as alternately both the cause and the effect of much of what has and will come to pass.

Based on what the Book reveals, I believe that every where that Shona is the portals will shift, move and open, which means that potentially more energy and entities from the in-between can come through. Mala, I hate to be the one to bring this to you, but there is a distinct and dangerous possibility that your daughter will be pushed or prodded into the in-between, whether of her own volition or not. And once she is there, there is no guarantee that she will be able to return to our world."

Mala could not hide her fright as she whispered, "What can we do?"

Alor: "At this point—nothing, except wait and pray. We can only hope that the intent of these entities favors the continued existence of not only your daughter, but all humans on this earth. We have no idea what these entities may look like or what form they assume. It is possible that one or more of them may have already attached themselves to her; having drawn or pulled her into their sphere."

Mala: "Do you mean like an animal familiar?"

Alor: "Perhaps a familiar; or perhaps more like a shaman ally; a guide, a protector. But have faith, Mala you may not have much to worry about. All the signs indicate that the spirit, the life force of your daughter, is more powerful than I or anyone else could have ever conceived. If an in-between entity has found her, then it is possible that they will have met their match. If what I suspect about your daughter is true, then, for better or worse, good or bad, she has the power to affect the energy of this earth. Her very presence can alter and help shift the balance of power in this world and the next."

15. The Gathering

His nostrils expanded to inhale her essence before he was fully awake and the fragrance of her body compelled him to open his eyes. Inexplicably the scent was more of a feeling, a sensation to which every dimension of his being had succumbed. It overpowered his ability to speak and though his eyes were open they perceived only vast darkness. The aroma was wet, warm and heavy—enveloping him in sensuous oblivion, he felt as if he was drowning in the murky sea of a mysterious netherworld. Grasping for an anchor, he pulled her close and held on tightly so that he might subdue his willingness to drown in her body's musk.

He was drenched in perspiration, breathing hard, heart beating fast and loud. Taijaur awoke from his "dream" feeling dazed and heavily drugged. The dreams were getting stronger and more intense. He knew that he was getting closer. It was as if her scent rode the wind, beckoning him forward.

He could close his eyes and she would come to him, bringing him his own tenderness. Her presence in his thoughts nurtured his sense of self, fueling his hope, inspiring his desire to live. At times, he would cruelly push all thoughts and feelings of her away; chastising himself for needing her. For needing only this one woman who could share her soul through the ether of time but never, it seemed, in the physical reality of one day. Then he would find himself lost—void of hope, purpose and calm. In time he came to understand that the decision was not his own. Blocking her from his thoughts meant denying himself access to the most fundamental parts of himself and all creation. She was an intractable link to the source of power that fueled his existence. And as long as he could keep her with him, in his mind, within his spirit, then he could believe in the tasks and causes that he undertook in his daily life away from her.

Still, sometimes, uncontrollably, doubt would seep through. Could such strong emotion be generated solely from his own need and imagination? Undoubtedly, there would be shame, humiliation, hurt, if he found her and her eyes did not recognize and reciprocate his understanding. Most times Taijaur believed, with absolute conviction, in the realness of his love. But other times he wondered—were these uncontrollable emotions really just wishing and imagining? Was he perhaps, sacrificing his life to a mere fantasy wish?

The Ocan females of his age had spent years vying for his attention, unknowingly drawn by the feel of a concentrated intense longing that emanated from every pore, every muscle, every nerve ending in his body. They could sense the pressure of his struggle to control and suppress his emotions and they were puzzled by his detachment and seeming lack of interest. His long absences from the main village fueled their curiosity and they were certain that he had found a potential mate in one of the outlying villages. He knew that even his closest friends would never be able to understand his attachment to the spirit of someone whom he had never seen. They would dismiss his love for Shona as foolish imaginative mind wandering. Even Master Alor could not fathom the depth of feeling and attachment that he held with Shona. What was it Alor had said? Something about a dream woman leaving an entrenched longing that was more real than reality—or something like that.

But, despite all of the doubts and questions, he knew that he had no choice. He had to seek her, find her, know her. His feelings demanded that he move with this one purpose as paramount to his existence. He innately understood that any and everything that he could ever hope to accomplish in life would revolve around this one central point of his soul's satisfaction. With strong subtle persistence, his sentiale probes had found an opening through the obstruction that she had erected within herself. Without knowing why or how, she allowed him to slip through and he was able to reach Shona through the dark shrouded places of her soul. He could see her, feel her, hear her, smell her, touch her. Their sentiale connection was powerful and hungry, pulling him on and through this strange new land. Over time, Shona began to come to him forcefully and without hesitation. Sometimes she came unexpectedly in the midst of his continuous movement forward and he would have to stop and catch his breath, steady his heart. It was at these times that he knew, with a deep felt certainty, that she needed him.

Although wary and on guard as he traveled the remote trail that had been laid before him, Taijaur also felt as if a weight had been lifted from him. He was experiencing an unexpected new sense of freedom outside of the Ocan settlements. He had taken a more northern route as he departed the island, exploring the northern coast and the atolls and other small islands in the archipelago. Following her scent through the mainland, he tracked her through canyons and dry, hot, dusty land. Up and down, across and over, the path he followed seemed that it would never end. The difficulty of this trek made him stop a moment and wonder about this female that preceded him.

Hidden deep in a recess of a canyon wall, beneath an overhanging ledge of rocks, he stumbled upon the dried out, mummified remains of a once living being. He looked closer at the body, confirming his suspicion that she was female and he further surmised that the body had undergone a natural mummification process as a result of the dry heat of the desert. This person, or creature, or what ever it had been, was lying face down, with a curious knotted piece of spider silk fabric binding her hands and feet together behind her back. This woman had been hog-tied, apparently while still alive and left out here in the burning heat of the desert to die. Everything about this scene troubled Taijaur in more ways than he could express. But perhaps what troubled him the most was that the fabric used to tie this woman could only have come from the Ocan island.

As he continued his trek, he forced himself to push the memory of what he had seen deep down away from his accessible thoughts and emotions. That night as he lie under the stars, listening to the sounds of the night, Taijaur, without thinking about it and without knowing why, blocked his normal sentiale dreams of comfort and warmth. He delved into another part of his dream awareness where he saw Shona clearly in front of him, at first innocently laughing and playing. He was in a state between sleeping and awake when he felt himself running after her and watching her glance back at him over her shoulder, still laughing. He followed until something made him abruptly halt as shivers of fear surged through his body. The expression on her face had transformed into something sinister and leering as she beckoned him forward. He heard voices dominating the air, in a loud, crisp tone, *"You know, old man, if what you suppose about that child is, indeed, true, then I fear that an evil greater than this world has ever known has been unleashed upon the earth."*

"The devil incarnate?"

"Aye, the devil."

The words jarred him into a deeper level of unconsciousness where his mind wandered through dark chasms and winding labyrinths with no meaning and no end. The next day he had no recollection of his dreams or his stray thoughts in the night. But he continued to pull away from his daily indulgence in sentiale thoughts with Shona, pushing her to a closed part of his psyche. He knew that his sentiale experiences with her were beginning to overwhelm his sense of the present. Their combined sentiale dream states were becoming so intensely vivid and real that it was hard for him to separate his waking reality from his dreams. The emotional confusion that resulted from this blurring of distinction between the two realities was hampering his ability to move forward and dulling his ability to track her.

Taijaur began focusing his first attention, so that deeper levels of his awareness could then rise to lead him where he needed to go without clouding his vision with his own desires. His ability to lose himself in deep thought would serve to enhance rather than impede his journey, making his willpower stronger, his senses more acute. He would be able to walk faster, with more energy, more power, yet less awareness of any conscious actions or needs; just concentrated unadulterated movement. He felt her need for him, he felt her soul calling to him and yet he forced this need into the background of his reality. He could no longer indulge his desire to dream with her. He knew that in order to reach her—truly reach her—he had to overcome his focus on her and bring his awareness fully into the reality of the waking day.

So, as he walked, he went into another level of his sentiale and conjured an image that would help his body to concentrate on only the power that he needed to move forward. This was the same recurring vision that had drifted to him years ago from a stray sentiale wandering, and it came to him whenever he needed to focus his attention, providing him an anchor to hold him steady within his sentiale without being swept away by the power of subliminal currents of sensation. He walked forcefully forward, fully alert to his surroundings, while also simultaneously he felt himself in a dark enclosed space, where there was nothing but a huge web that vibrated with sound and light.

He became entranced by the pulsating light filaments that were flowing into and through one another as they came together to form the fibers of the web. He searched in the vision for someone or something that created the filaments and caused their movement. But there was only the wind that blew through the interconnected strands of light, causing them to vibrate with indiscriminate notes of a song that came just short of coalescing into full harmony. The filaments were alive, moving of their own volition in a symmetrical pattern of mysterious design, uncertain need. This time he could see more detail than ever before. As the vision magnified, he was able to observe the strands beginning as small pieces of matter, minute specks of dust, that were energized by internal electrical pulses that made them expand and elongate as they crackled through the web, lighting up the darkness.

Unlike the times before, the web now seemed to not only vibrate with sound, but also words—foreign, unfamiliar words, spoken in a low melodic voice that flowed with the music. The meaning of the words saturated his senses, and rested in all parts of his body, but somehow, just below his cognition. His sentiale and his body understood what his mind struggled in vain to grasp. He knew that each strand, each of these filaments of light was vibrating with a story that was woven into this structure. But the meaning only teased his mind— always tantalizingly familiar and close to his understanding yet, agonizingly out of reach. Every time he concentrated on one or another of the strands of light, they would then flash in other directions, never staying in position or place long enough to be analyzed or deciphered. Still the light and the sound flowed through his body and his senses, making him one with their song, one with the light, and a part of the weaving filaments all around him.

Taijaur stayed focused on his mind-vision and the incessant weaving motion for the entire morning. By the afternoon he found that he was approaching an out of the way village and he decided to start the process of rising out of his altered state, having already covered scores of miles. He started to take a detour on the outskirts of this small rural area, so as to avoid its inhabitants, but a tremor in the air made him stop and take note. It was then that he felt the force of her presence come alive through every sense that he possessed. She was here, in this village, in this place, with these people. He immediately pulled himself completely out of his meditative state and made his way onto the roads and pathways that led to the center of this quiet dusty remote community that was similar to most of the others that he had passed along the way. However, the closer he came into the town, the more he felt the presence of something else here, something that was not quite right.

There was no one around in the village square except a stray dog wandering from one ramshackle dwelling to the next. He could hear the cries of a baby in the distance and the sound of people's voices. He followed the voices and came upon a group of mostly old men along with a few women and children who had gathered to talk, tell stories beneath the wide canopy of a broad tree that had long flowing branches. Some were sitting on over-turned empty wooden fruit crates, others sat on the ground, while still others stood leaning against the tree or the nearby fence. No one seemed to notice him as he came and stood in the shade of a barn not far from the tree. As he listened to the people telling stories of their history, Taijaur searched the faces of this innocuous gathering trying to determine the source of an intermittent ominous sensation that drifted and mixed with the bucolic feel of this community. He tried to dispel his discomfort, but beneath the people's easy flow of well-being there was the unmistakable presence of evil; a strong, overpowering, undeniable evil.

He listened as the men began to speak of a war that had occurred some centuries ago and they told of a strange group of people who had literally disappeared from the face of the earth. This story had been recounted by their fathers and their fathers' fathers. They all seemed to tell the story in unison, one man's voice would pick up where another's had left off, as they talked along with and on top of one another. Then one voice began to dominate in a hypnotic rhythm and deep resonance that silenced those around him. He picked up a word from one, a phrase from another, and wove the disparate pieces of each man's thoughts into one coherent whole.

They all agreed that this war was the most devastating that there had ever been. It had changed the fate of the land and the people, marking the beginning of a cycle of cultural suppression and subjugation from which they had yet to escape. They spoke of a peaceful past and then an invasion of warriors who came from across the sea in order to colonize this already-occupied land and seize any riches that the people or the land might possess. In their quest for domination and riches, the invaders swept through all parts of the land, scouring through every village and hamlet along the way, until they came to this out-of-the way little village and set up camp. These invaders were especially interested in finding a mythical diamond that they had heard was larger than any precious stone that had ever existed. And they had heard that this village was where the diamond could be found.

The villagers were forced to reveal to the invaders their knowledge of the separatist group who lived down near the river in a compound that they had built with a high brick wall around it. These were the people who held the stone, the largest diamond of all that was more valuable than four kingdoms combined. These people, this sect or cult, down by the river, had told the villagers that the stone was called the Eye and their holy men showed them how it must be touched or held in order for the miracles to occur. And many of the villagers had directly experienced or witnessed the miracles as people had come from miles around, bringing, their sick, their ailing to be healed and made well. No one knew exactly where all the mix of people in this sect had come from, or even what their beliefs and purpose may have been. Some said that they were a religious cult escaping the persecution of many lands and cultures. Others speculated more broadly. Only the invaders said that they must be stopped.

And the invaders had brought guns and great numbers of fighting men to convince the sect that the stone was better left in their care. But no matter how persuasive their logic may have been, the separatist group would not concede to the invaders' demands. They locked and fortified the doors to their compound and no more miracles were performed. For weeks none of them could be seen or heard. And then one night the invaders had had enough and they sent the fighting men with their guns to destroy the compound, dispose of the sect and bring back the diamond.

The sect or religious group or whatever they were—they disappeared that night and they nor the sacred Eye were ever seen again. The soldiers said that members of the sect had stolen the Eye away, but most of the villagers believed that it was the soldiers who had appropriated it and secreted back to their motherland.

When the invasion was over and the people properly colonized, these, the indigenous people, the vanquished, were forced to witness and participate in the rape of their own land and nation. And this was when the people began to pray to the absent rock, the absent savior, pleading for deliverance. The conquerors gave them new names, new labor, and new ways to worship the sacred—taking from them their art, music, culture and scholarship to claim as their own; suppressing their language and society. The conquerors took away the people's ability to survive on their own; outlawing the planting of seeds for personal use and restricting the acquisition of skills and knowledge. They were then deployed as an economic resource, a commodity that rewarded the conquerors' depredation and made the people even more desperate and destitute. For the first time in their history, the people knew material and economic poverty and deprivation. And these deficiencies formed the primary definitions by which they began to assess their own worth and value on the earth. Their new masters bred inferiority into the people's children and the children's children. While the people, in turn, learned to aspire ardently to attain the values, beliefs and actual physicality of their 'superior' captors. For such is the way of the oppressed and the oppressor.

Taijaur had become so engrossed in listening to the story, so hypnotized by the telling of it, that it was awhile before he realized that the story had ended. Rising out of the reverie that the story had induced, he became suddenly aware of his surroundings as an unexpected jolt rippled through his body. He looked up and for the first time in his life, he saw her. She was there sitting on the ground, right across from him, obscured slightly behind a few of the people who stood. He felt her energy moving through the air and pouring down on him.

After all the years and moments of waiting and waiting endlessly, here she was before him—that one person on this earth who held his overpowering desire captive in the essence of her own mind, body and soul. He turned quickly, moved behind the side of the barn, not wanting her to know of his presence in this place, in this manner. He could not approach her in this crowd, with other people around. Their meeting had to be at a time and place where the energy from their sentiale would not overwhelm the physical reality of their ability to perceive. He left quickly and retreated back into his familiar mode of waiting.

Although sleep and rest had eluded her throughout the night, Shona had been ready to leave at the first light of day. But the old man was no where to be found. No one, at either Immanuel's or Selene's house, knew where he was. He had apparently disappeared in the night or some time before the sun rose. He would often disappear before the dawn when they were at his home. But this seemed strange, since she knew that he wanted to leave before the mid-day sun made it unbearable for them to complete their almost three hours trek. At first, she told herself that he had just gone in search of more medicinal supplies—perhaps the special plants that grew somewhere near this village. She kept going back and forth between Immanuel's house and Selene's house, thinking that maybe she had just missed him. As the day wore on and there was still no sign of Om, Immanuel told Shona that he would go to look for him and for her not to worry, he was sure that everything was fine. He told her to stay at Selene's house and not to go any where else, so that he and the old man would be able to find her when they returned.

Shona surmised that this lost blurry feeling that was now descending upon her must be a sure sign of sleep deprivation. She had tossed and turned most of the night, frustrated by her attempts to embrace dreams that simply would not come. She was puzzled why she no longer had access to the deep dream states; confused that the dream presence in her mind came to her no more. Instead of the comfort of her languid states of somnolent bliss, the nightmare visions had come back in full force to hunt, chase and terrorize her. The effort to elude pursuit had left her feeling weak and drained. Why could she no longer reach the dream visions that soothed and sustained her? Why had he gone away? No matter how hard she tried she could not summon him.

Selene's house was empty and quiet for the first time since Shona had started coming to this village. They had all been here this morning, but when she returned from Immanuel's house for this fifth and final time there was no one there. This day was, indeed, getting stranger and stranger. Maybe Selene and the other women had just gone to one of the other women's houses to finish their preparation for tonight's celebration. Shona lied down on the bed, intending to rest for only a moment. When she was awakened later by a loud noise, she realized that she had dozed longer than she planned. In the distance, she heard a steady rhythm of hammers pounding in unison and she was drawn outside by the sound. The old men had already gathered in the shade of the tree near Selene's home and she knew that they were once again telling their endless tales. They always gathered in the afternoons to talk and tell stories. Shona liked to sit nearby, along with some of the other women and children, listening absent-mindedly to the stories with some bit of weaving or sewing.

There were more people here today than usual and even some of the soldiers were lingering on the outskirts of the crowd. As soon as Shona approached the edge of the group and sat down, the air around her somehow become strangely alive—stimulating in a way that she could not explain or understand. The sun seemed to cast a surreal light on the trees and the people. It felt like time was moving in a strange thick slow wave or current. It awoke in her a sense of expectation, excitement and agitation; a sense of being outside of this moment, outside of this place. As best she could, she pushed aside these emotions which she assumed were undoubtedly brought on by the cumulative effect of a lack of sleep.

The tellers of story had already come to the middle of the tale. But no matter, she knew that she would be able to pick up the threads and follow them through. These men always returned to their favorite subject—fighting, conquest; always battles of one kind or another. Their wars, those of their fathers, grandfathers and other nations. She had heard of every form and fashion that conflict and quests for dominance could take. She wasn't sure exactly what captured her attention, but she began to listen more intently as they went on to talk off a war that had taken place in the time of their grandfathers' grandfathers. She had heard this story before—this tale of a massacre, and a precious sacred stone that incited the most devastating war that they had ever known. Once again they spoke of a group of people who mysteriously vanished, but this time, the telling of the story seemed somehow to be different in a way that she couldn't quite figure out. The only thing that was certain was that her pulse seem to inexplicably quicken every time that they mentioned this sacred rock—the Eye.

In the days preceding the massacre at the compound, the soldiers had tried, in vain, to blast through and tear down the walls. The surrounding villages had already been captured and occupied by the time that fatal night of attack occurred. The sounds of fury, savagery and dying lasted long into the night and early hours of dawn. Then with the quiet of the new day, the young men of the village were ordered by the soldiers to come to the compound to help bury the dead and dispose of and hide the residual evidence of destruction. When their task was complete, they returned to their village homes and were told to never speak of what they had seen. But through their fear and confusion, they whispered to one another of the incomprehensibility of that to which they had stood sole witness. And they whispered their tale to their children and their children's children, so on and so forth down through the lines.

This killing had been like other killings—dead body after dead body, all waiting patiently to be discarded. Except this time there were certain facts that left the village men baffled and more than just a little frightened. Of all the bodies that had been interred, none could be identified as those of the inhabitants of the compound. No evidence of the sect members' fate was left in the carnage. Every one of the dead bodies that they buried was that of a soldier, with no bullet wounds, no lacerations, cuts, bruises or blood anywhere. It was if they had simply laid down and decided to cease breathing. While this was strange enough to try to fathom, even stranger was the unknown fate of the separatist group. This entire community of several thousand men, women and children had simply vanished.

The one man who had now become the primary teller of the story offered the observation (which many of their religious leaders had actually conjectured), that undoubtedly God had smite the enemy of those peaceful spiritual people and then delivered all the sainted ones safely, intact into the sanctuary of heaven. The young men who had been forced to clean up after the atrocities of the night decided that the invaders, themselves, had most likely dug a communal grave for the massacred people to deter any speculation of martyrdom or the taking of relics. The lack of knowledge as to where this burial site might be located meant that it could be anywhere. This mass grave most certainly was very deep and well hidden, because in all the ensuing years it had never been uncovered. The story came to a close with a dramatic flourish as the storyteller stated, "And to this day we are left to wonder if we work, love, dance and play on the graves of sainted beings".

They went on to talk of other wars—other guises that the need for dominance and control had assumed over the millennia. Shona had long ago come to the conclusion that this was their way of measuring and keeping track of their value and time on the earth. One way to tell the story of life, destiny and the means by which some humans choose to satisfy their, sometimes desperate, need to survive.

Shona wasn't sure if this bizarre story had impacted her negatively or just the general talk of war, loss and destruction, but she began to feel jumpy, anxious, nervously looking around to determine the source of her discomfort. During the telling of the story, she had noticed that the electrified feeling in the air had intensified. Beneath the sound of the people's laughter and their voices, there was a soft plaintive melody that drifted through the air. She realized now that this music had been playing throughout the telling of the story, a light undertone beneath the wind. Suddenly the music stopped and despite the peacefulness of this afternoon gathering, she felt even more tense and agitated.

There was an energy, a distinct presence, focused in her direction, watching her. She could feel it. Instinctively, she turned her head and locked eyes with a man, who had been staring directly at her from across the yard. Even from a distance, she knew that she was looking into the eyes of a hunter, a predator. He was leaning against the post of a fence, wearing the uniform of the army. Part of his face was obscured beneath the tilted wide brim of a hat. But she watched as he slowly brought his hands to his lips and cupped them around an object. He stared directly at her as the low plaintive melody began once again. A tremor ran all the way through her just before she felt a tap on her shoulder that startled her to the point that she nearly jumped up and ran. The old man was standing next to her, speaking in a low voice, "Come. We must move quickly."

He had a hard unfamiliar expression on his face. The people around them were engrossed in the next story which many of them added to and embellished as it went along. Shona rose from the ground. "My pack is in Selene's house. It will take me a moment to get it."

Om: "No, we don't have time. We'll retrieve it later. Walk as fast as you can and try to keep up with me."

Immanuel met them as they came around the barn that was at the edge of Selene's property. The old man was mumbling to himself, but she could only hear stray words and phrases, that did not come together into any coherence. Shona whispered to Immanuel, "What has happened?"

Immanuel was breathing hard, trying to keep pace as he looked sidewise at the old man keeping his voice low, "Oh it is nothing to worry about; just some nonsense with the soldiers asking questions."

They walked on in quiet, needing all of their energy and attention to keep up with the fast walk-run of the old man. They had gone on for about three quarters of an hour when they heard someone hailing, calling to them from behind and they turned and saw one of the older teenage boys from the village running toward them. Shona recognized him as a part of the group of young men and teen boys who hung around with Immanuel's middle son. He was out breath as he caught up with them. He bent over with his hands on his knees breathing hard, panting after every few words. "The soldiers—the soldiers—are—looking—for you."

He straightened up, holding his midsection as he directed his comments to the old man. "They went to Selene's house, but someone had warned her and she and her family had all gone into hiding. They then went to her neighbor's house and took away some of the people for questioning. They are gathering up other people around the village to see what they know about you and your whereabouts. We believe that they will be looking for you at Sulas' house. The commander, himself, has also gone with some of his men in search of your home, but no one could tell him where you live."

Om: "I will go to him. I will go directly to Sulas' home. That is the only way to end this. We can't keep running and hiding. Immanuel you know where to take Shona. Stay there and I will meet you there tomorrow."

Messenger: "Oh no, grandfather, the commander does not want you. He has told his men that he only wants your assistant, the girl that travels with you." He looked over at Shona and then back to Om. "He said that she must be brought to him right away. He says that, well they are all saying that, well, he believes that she is responsible for the young soldier's death."

Immanuel: "What young soldier? There are so many soldiers—they are all young and they all seem to be dying, in one way or another."

Messenger: "The one for whom the healing was performed. Some of the commander's men said that he was fine, or that he was getting better before, the girl, your assistant laid hands on him. They say that once she touched him he burned like he had been set on fire and then died a horrible painful death. They are saying that she killed him."

Om said to the young messenger, "Go back to your people, and tell them that you were unable to locate us. I understand and appreciate the risk that you have taken to deliver this message. Do not put yourself any further in harm's way."

Messenger: "We can hide you down by the river, grandfather. You will be safe there. There is a strong possibility that this man—the Commander—may have already found his way to your home."

Om: "No, we'll be fine. Go back to your village and speak of this no more. It is better that you not know where we are headed."

The young man nodded to each of them, his eyes lingering on Shona before he turned and ran back in the direction from which he had come. Om turned to Shona and said, "Come, we are going home. If that man has found his way to my home, then so be it. We will run and hide no more."

Shona: "But what will we do? What if he tries to hurt you? What if he tries to take me away?"

Om: "Don't worry. I have ways of dealing with men like him. Immanuel, you need not come any further with us. Shona and I will be fine. Go see to your family."

Immanuel: "I will accompany you a little further along and then go back by way of the river. My house may not be the best place to go right now. And knowing my Berta, my family is safe. I pity the person—soldier or otherwise—who comes up against that woman or threatens her brood in any way. I have never known any person less afraid to die than my wife."

Om nodded his head and they continued on at an even faster pace.

Shona whispered to Immanuel, "Who is he, this commander? Who is this man and why is he doing this?"

Immanuel: "If evil can be personified, then this man is its closest manifestation. They say that they found him years ago, on a fishing boat that had washed up to shore. He was alone, but the people who pulled him in say that they saw human bones and other stray body parts strewn about on the boat in a way that indicated that he may have eaten the flesh of his crew members."

Shona: "But who is he?"

Immanuel: "You know the one—he was just in the village, standing near the fence, listening to the story of the great war. He seemed to be staring directly at you. He's the one with the crisscross of scars on his face, like someone tried to slice him up. And that one big ugly scar on his neck that looks like something alive. It's too bad that who ever did that to him, did not finish the job they started. But, mark my words, he will be the next governor of these provinces. These elections are a farce. Those votes that he has not bought or coerced, are the ones belonging to people who will meet an early grave or be locked away underneath the jail."

Shona felt a queasy light-headed feeling as Immanuel spoke. In a choked voice she asked, "What is his name?"

Immanuel: "Commander Taring is what they call him; and soon it will be Governor Taring. And when that day comes to pass, these peaceful provinces will be transformed into a living hell. He plays that damn mouth organ all the time even as he watches the people, whose deaths he has ordered, being executed. Even as his men commit the most violent and atrocious acts, the music never stops.

I wonder why he didn't just take you into custody there in the village. Maybe he didn't see you or realize that you were the one they spoke of in connection with the young soldier. And he always gets his minions to do his bidding for him, usually in the night when there are no witnesses. He seems to take a perverse pleasure in making sure that all his men get their hands as dirty as his own."

Immanuel continued speaking but his voice faded in Shona's consciousness as she found herself wrapped in a fog. She didn't even notice when Immanuel turned off on a side trail and headed down to towards the river. The closer they came to home the more her disquieting feelings intensified until she was almost on the brink of hysteria. It took all her powers of concentration to calm down enough to try to breathe deeply and keep walking steadily forward.

They took a longer more roundabout way, so that the sun had already begun to set by the time they arrived. As they came around the final bend in the road, there he was—a man in the distance, near the house. Her fears had told her he would be there, waiting. Waiting for her. He was sitting on the ground with his back to them, playing some sort of game with Aria. He was weaving string designs between his fingers and pulling the string free once the little girl inserted her hand in a way that seemed to ensure entanglement. But each time he made the complex geometric string design collapse, Aria's hand was completely free of the string, suspended in the empty air. The little girl was thrilled each time this happened as the man made design after design. There was a crystal stone suspended on the string and it was somehow incorporated into each new construction. Even from a distance, Shona could see the prismatic light flashing from the surface of the crystal. She became entranced by the gleaming lights and the elaborate string designs—at once an intricate lattice and then a delicate orb web.

When Aria finally looked up, she ran excitedly towards Shona, jabbering about her new friend. With Aria pulling her along, Shona continued to walk, her heart beating fast, never taking her eyes from this unknown, unexpected visitor, who was now slowly standing and turning towards them. She saw his face and in an instant, Shona's stomach and legs lost their solidity, her heart expanded, sending a flush of fiery liquid sensation throughout her body, searing her brain. She fought against losing consciousness, as she began sinking into the mire, the quicksand of a deep bottomless chasm. She stumbled against the old man and reached out blindly, clutching his arm. Without awareness or intent, she dug her nails deep into his skin, as she came face to face with a vision from her mind.

16. Fear and Longing

Fear and longing, arising from the same source, become easily entangled during moments of tension and stress. Having now joined forces, they eagerly pushed Shona into the hungry embrace of a fever that had only stalked unsure along her periphery for days. The sickness settled with clammy perspiration on her brow, clawing deeply into the empty pit of her stomach. Her frayed mind stumbled through a haze, making no sense of this phantasm—this man-spirit-hallucination—that appeared before her.

A dream-apparition come to life—he/it was now by her side, helping the old man to hold her steady and guide her to the shade on the side of the house. Aria stood staring as they eased her limp body to the ground, her back resting against the clapboards of the house. The old man turned to the child, saying, "Aria, go and tell Sulas to give you a cool cloth while I pump some water." He started towards the well, mumbling to himself. "The heat and long walk have proven too much for her today."

Aria stopped in her trot to the door and grabbing the old man's arm, she shouted, "Grandfather, look you're bleeding!"

He looked down at his arm then brushed her hand away. "Never mind that. Just go quickly, child."

That man-spirit, their unknown guest, Aria's playmate, still knelt beside Shona rubbing her hand, and then tried to get her to drink from the tin cup that the old man brought from the well. Before she could sip it, she sank down into a deep all-encompassing void. Her dreams were gone and there was no comforting fantasy to lull her to a calmer place. When she awoke almost two days later, that man—that vision from he mind—was sitting there at her bedside, silently waiting for her to awaken.

Her mouth was dry and pasty and it felt like she was swimming through a viscous sea, trying to reach some semblance of thought as she sat up in the bed and stared at this man beside her. At first she was confused—how could something from her dreams materialize in reality? She stared at him a moment longer and then the realization came to her. Only upon seeing him here, in the flesh, did she begin to understand what had been occurring to her in the night. This man, this dream-lover was real and present. She felt his whole essence swim up before her in intense waves of recognition and desire. She began to realize that her past 'dreams' had never been mere random wishes and fantasy desires. Shona tiptoed around his open awareness, and caught glimpses of the path that had brought him to her. She saw and felt how she had led him, guided him, told him how and where to find her. She felt violated and angry. She now understood that, through her dreams, he had been tracking her and that she had flagrantly transmitted her scent.

Shona spoke first, demanding, "What are you doing here?"

He uncovered a plate of fruit and sweet bread on the table beside her bed and pushed it towards her. She ignored the plate and asked, "What right did you have to go inside of my mind, inside of my being?"

Taijaur: "You invited me in."

Shona: "You violated me; forced an alliance without my consent."

Taijaur: "I was only what you needed me to be."

She was quiet for a moment as he watched her, waiting. Then in a low voice, she said, "It's like you raped me within my own mind."

Taijaur: "Shona, I don't know what Mala told you of sentiale experiences but there is no way that I could have come to you without your consent. And keep in mind that you likewise sent your spirit to me, over and over again."

Shona reflected back on the intensity of the "dreams" and mind wanderings in which she had indulged her self.

Shona: "You have humiliated me."

Taijaur: "On whose behalf are you ashamed or embarrassed? Who, besides the two of us, knew the nature of our connection?'

Shona: "But you knew that I didn't fully understand what was transpiring. I thought that you were a dream. I believed that I was only dreaming. I never knew that it was real. You took advantage of my ignorance, of my gullibility."

Taijaur: "Shona, you know as well as I that certain types of 'dreaming' are just another form of what we call 'reality'. And once again let me remind you—you came to me as much as I came to you. Our meetings and interactions were mutually desired and reciprocal in nature. You can deny many things, but this much you cannot debate."

She looked away, blowing her breath out hard and folding her arms across her chest and then she turned once again to face Taijaur as she demanded, "Why are you here?"

With a gleam in his eyes and a sly little smile, he leaned forward so that his face was almost touching hers and whispered softly, "To be with you."

She pushed him back and rose out of the bed, and began to walk out of the room and then turned back, asking, "If these," she paused and then continued, "'*interactions*' were actually a part of sentiale awareness, then why didn't I feel them before? These dreams didn't start until after my time in the canyons, after I came to the old man's house and I awoke from being sick or tired, or something."

Taijaur: "Well, you blocked me for some time. For a long time, I could only linger near the edge of your consciousness. You would not let me come fully in. but then for some reason—and I have no idea what it was—you welcomed my presence and started on your own to come to me all the time, just like when we were young.

But Shona, why is this so hard to accept? You have been using your sentiale all along. You have healed people since you've been here. The old man has told me how you are able to anesthetize the people with your mind."

Shona: "Yes but that only occurs with direct physical contact, not some out of sight, out of mind fantasy or dream."

Taijaur: "Either way—both types of interactions take place along the sentiale pathways. Traumatic occurrences can some times make it so that we are less able to access the pathways or be consciously aware of how the pathways are functioning in our lives. However, all of our experiences in life are still processed by way of the sentiale. Sentiale phenomena consist of the energy fields that allow us to sense, feel and know before any tangible perception takes place by way of our tactile/physical senses. The electromagnetic pulses or sensations that are within our brains, our skin, our nerve cells are also in the air all around us and in all living matter—the trees, the land, the water. The pathways produced by these pulses, these sensations connect us to everything that is a part of this creation—all matter and energy in the universe. A sentiale link allows direct access into a universal pool of knowing. It allows a receiver to go directly inside the sender's frame of reference. It is possible to reach out or send messages with your soul or your mind through music, dreams, meditations, feelings, emotions, thoughts or just through the energy force of the empathic pathways that exist in all of us."

Shona: "That still does not account for how two people who have never seen one another could nonetheless make and sustain contact across a distance."

Taijaur: "Perhaps the sentiale connection between Mala and Saba served as a bridge. Or even the connection that our mothers held with one another when they were growing up. Perhaps, both our sentiale have been enhanced by proximity to portal energy. I don't know and I don't have all of the answers. Some of the ancient texts refer to spirits that are bonded to one another before they are born into any realm of physical existence. And they travel from life to life, birth to birth, knowing and seeking one another."

Shona: "I am not bonded to anyone. If emotions help to create these pathways that you speak of, then I believe that it was my fear that let you in. But take heed, I am no longer afraid."

Taijaur: "Or maybe it was your love and your need for love."

Shona made no comment as she turned and exited the room going first to the front of the house and then she went through the other empty rooms of the house. "Where is Om?"

Taijaur got up and followed her out of the room, standing in the hallway, watching her as she searched through the house. "He left early this morning. He didn't say where he was going."

Shona: "Is there no one else here? Where are Sulas and Aria?"

Taijaur: "They left about an hour ago. Some man from the village—I think his name was Immanuel—he came to tell Sulas that her home is safe now. And she left with him."

Shona: "What about the soldiers?"

Taijaur: "What do you mean?"

Shona: "The threat from that army commander. He was coming here. Shouldn't we be preparing to protect ourselves or determine a place to hide?"

Taijaur: "Oh, it seems that you have been granted a temporary reprieve. That same man from the village, Immanuel, he said that all the troops have been called back to the city. Something about the elections taking place sooner than expected. And apparently there is some speculation about the possibility of a coup. At any rate, it seems that you don't have to worry about the soldiers for now. I think their commander may have bigger fish to fry at this point. However,

Immanuel said that the army has left sentries posted in each village until after the elections. So you will have to be careful traveling into the villages.

But in terms of being prepared, the old man has asked me to take charge of your training. He says that you must take time to recuperate from your malaise and then when you are ready, we will begin your instruction. Some parts of your sentiale have been subdued, nonetheless, overall your senses seem to be coming through more forcefully. A subdued sentiale will block your natural strength and allow a way for fear to seep into your core. There is much that we will be able to accomplish once your sentiale has—"

During the time that she questioned him and he responded, Shona had her back turned to him as she looked throughout the house and out of the windows. When she finally turned to face him, she saw that he was studying her body. She was wearing the short light-weight shift that she always wore to bed and she suddenly became self-conscious when she saw how he looked at her. They were both embarrassed as he looked down, not finishing his sentence and Shona pushed past him into her room, slamming the door.

The old man accepted Taijaur's presence the same way that he had accepted Shona, making room for him in his house, allowing him to become a part of his life. In the mornings, Taijaur and the old man started going off together and Shona was left alone or with Sulas and Aria. Taijaur and Om were like old acquaintances, familiar with one another in ways that only puzzled Shona. They would return from their morning forays energized and secretive, speaking excitedly in the languages of the abstract and the esoteric. Taijaur offered vague, distracted responses to Shona's inquiries about where and why they went. And Om said only that she would see for herself soon enough. The old man insisted that she stay behind so that she might rest and regain her strength. With Taijaur here, nothing was the same as it once was.

The dreams were now gone for good, blocked in a part of herself that she felt foolish and ashamed to even think about. And she, likewise, tried to block the reality of this man from her presence. But every where she went he was there—looking at her, smiling at her, talking to her. After the first few days she found that it was futile to continue to try to ignore him. But the more accepting she became of him, the more agitated she felt inside with opposing emotions battling for dominance. In vain, she tried to rebel against the flow of energy that she felt in his presence. She struggled to convince herself that these feelings could never be true, real, or reciprocal. Against her will, she wanted to know him, to talk with him; share time and energy. Against her resolve, she sought him out again and again.

Every time that Shona tried to find another way to question Taijaur about why he had come to this land, he responded with the same statement as the first time that she had asked. Except now he not only deliberately leaned close towards her, but he also touched her hair or her arm or hand. And he also made sure that she felt his warm breath on her skin, as he whispered with a sly smile, "To be with you" in a low resonant voice. After three such close encounters, Shona stopped asking. And if they were ever alone in a room together, she made certain that he never got too close to her and that there was always some physical object—a chair, a table—something between them.

By the second week, Taijaur and Shona began going to the village with Om. They confined themselves to the village that was closest to their home, still wary of any sign of the soldiers. Without knowing why, it became important to Shona that Taijaur share and know all the good things that she had come to know in this life on the mainland. She wanted him to experience the feelings and sensations that she had felt as a part of the villagers' lives—socializing with the other young people their age, interacting with the elders and the children. They went to hear the music, see the dancing. And Taijaur joined the other musicians; taking turns playing each of the instruments, always with a sound that sanctified the air and evoked a still hush over the crowds.

While the people had taken Shona's presence for granted—assuming that she was a relative of the old man's—Taijaur's appearance created a disturbance within their peer group; a disruption in the balance of their routine lives. His presence aroused curiosity and suspicion. The women, sensing the excitement and allure of a new attraction and potential drama sought him out, while the young men watched their women with more than casual concern. Some of the men challenged Taijaur to endless matches of strength and endurance. Although he met all of their contests with charm, wit and warmth, he still made sure to lose an equal amount of game and sport as he won. Nonetheless, the coquetry that Taijaur seemed to inspire in the young women required that the men maintain a vigilant guard over the territory they claimed as their own.

The young women now seemed to have a renewed interest in Shona. Even those who had paid little attention to her in the past began to seek her company, slyly inquiring of Taijaur and trying to determine the nature of her relations with and to him. Taijaur was careful not to let Shona see how much he wearied of this life in the village. He could not fathom why Shona endured all the petty nuances of these people's day to day trivia and all their endless effort toward no perceivable worthwhile goal or objective. The "nothingness" of it all smothered his instinct and sense of what was real to the extent that he felt weighed down by the oppression of inertia. In contrast, it was clear that Shona felt deeply connected to these people, to this way of life.

Many times in the evenings they sat eating, drinking, and talking with the people in the dusty courtyard of the village. Occasionally, in the quiet stillness after the music had played, Taijaur would reach out his hand toward Shona, to stroke her hair or touch her gently. Sensing without actually seeing his intent, Shona would sit absolutely still, holding her breath, careful not to turn to look at him, or to acknowledge his hand moving toward her. The anticipation of his touch sent intense warmth down through her senses. But just before he reached her, he would pull away suddenly. She would hear him take a deep breath and then rise quickly, turning his back to her as he got up and walked away. Without understanding her own reaction, Shona would become filled with an agitation, frustration and a vague sense of discomfort.

Almost every night, Shona watched Taijaur and Om stay up late pouring over the coded hieroglyphic markings of the antiquated book that Om had retrieved from the church library. Taijaur not only recognized the language or languages of these ancient scrolls, but he was adamant that these pages must be a part of a series of texts that he was responsible for translating. He had brought with him notes from his translations of the other books in a sealed air-tight water-proof container. He and the old man compared and matched the symbols from his notes to those in this book.

Taijaur had been there for more than a month, when one morning Shona awoke to the sounds of loud hammering coming from outside. She rose to find the house empty and she followed the pounding sounds to the side of the house. Taijaur was apparently constructing a new fence for the pen that sat adjacent to the barn. No matter how late she went to bed or how early she awoke, he always seemed to be up, moving, fixing, working, exercising—doing something. She liked to watch him work. The old man's house and barn were almost completely renovated. She wondered if and when Taijaur ever slept, remembering a time in her own past when perpetual motion overtook her life. It seemed such a long time ago, in another world.

He had stopped hammering and was now digging a hole as she went out and approached him from behind. She walked slowly toward him, careful not to make a sound as she took her time studying him while he worked. It amazed her every time she witnessed this man in motion. She could not recall ever having seen so much concentrated power and force in one body. With the exception of the old man, Shona was stronger than any of the males in the villages. But this strength of Taijaur's was something wholly different than anything that she had ever seen or heard tell of.

Even from a distance, his scent was in the air. His smell always affected her senses, rendering her unable to think or move decisively. It was hard to find the words to convey how his scent affected her. And it was even harder to understand or control her body's reaction. But it left her feeling inexplicably weak, with a strange sense of vibrant fullness throughout her body. When she was close enough for him to hear her, she blurted out, "You knew the old man before you came here, didn't you? Or rather you knew of him."

Although he had felt and heard her coming, he stopped working and turned to look at her as if her appearance was unexpected, staring at her in a steady, level manner. It was still early morning, but the day was already hot. His shirt was damp with perspiration that also dripped from his face and exposed forearms. Before responding, he began shoveling loose gravel into the hole that he had just dug and then placed a large heavy post into the freshly dug hole and began pounding it into the ground with a sledge hammer.

Taijaur: "And 'good morning' to you too. If you are referring to the fact that I had sentiale awareness of him, then the answer to your question is 'yes'. On a sentiale level, I knew everyone with whom you came into contact prior to meeting them in this physical realm. Here hold this post and make sure that it stays in one place, please."

He shoveled dirt around the base of the post and packed it in tight before moving on to start a fresh hole. As they talked, he continued this process of digging holes and pounding in new fence posts. Without being asked or told what to do, Shona assisted with this process by holding the posts steady or helping to fill gravel in the holes. They continued working this way for the most of the morning, installing fence stretchers and cross boards once all the posts were installed.

Shona: "I mean, you knew him in the Ocan, not through my sentiale. He's from the Ocan isn't he?"

Taijaur: "What makes you say that?"

Shona: "You see how he spouts Ocan philosophy. The two of you share so much in common because you both have the same cultural and philosophical background."

Taijaur: "Honestly, Shona I have no idea if he is from the Ocan. Except for the scouts that were sent in the past century, I don't know of anyone who ever left the island. Well, that is no one before you and I guess now me as well."

Shona: "How else would he know the Ocan language and the beliefs?"

Taijaur: "Shona, neither you nor I know enough about who our people were prior to the time that they went to the island, to conjecture one way or the other. The Ocan language is a mixture of many different languages, including parts of the language that is spoken here in this land."

Taijaur hesitated before asking, "Shona, how much do you know of your mother?"

Shona: "What do you mean?"

Taijaur: "Her background, her history, your relatives."

Shona: "She always said that all of the Ocan people were her relatives and she claimed no particular kinship or affinity based on bloodlines. She never talked much about herself. Sometimes she seemed so open and revealing and other times she seemed closed off, full of secrets and riddles. I always felt that she was carrying some unspoken burden. She did tell me about the Ascension rites. That was one of the few things that she did share with me about her upbringing."

Taijaur: "Did she mention that she went through her rites with my mother, Loni as well as another girl named Tausi?"

Shona: "No, she didn't mention anyone's name. She just said that the Ocan believe that the spirits of those who go through their rites together are fused for the rest of their lives. What about your mother, Taijaur and your father?"

She saw a shadow cross his face.

Taijaur: "They both died before I was born."

Shona: "What? How is that possible.?"

Taijaur: "Well, what I mean is that my father died before I was born and my mother died in childbirth. I was their only child."

Shona: "So many deaths, you people of the Ocan seem to have. With all the power that you purport to possess, it doesn't seem to help you in holding sway over life's natural processes."

He turned abruptly and walked towards the barn to retrieve more posts. She called out after him, "Taijaur, I'm sorry. I shouldn't have said that."

He picked up four posts at one time and walked back to the pen as if nothing disturbed him, continuing to speak casually, "My mother died in childbirth. My aunt told me that an antidote had been found that could have saved her, but they told her that it would kill her developing fetus. So, she chose not to take it. She gave her life so that I might live. I owe her and this world more perhaps than I can ever repay. I can not allow her sacrifice to have been in vain. She and my father fought to create a better way, a better life; to help our people to realize their destinies. My aunt, Senai, she is a part of the Aka collective; and she believes that it is only right that I devote my life to fulfill the destiny of those who sacrificed their lives on my behalf."

Shona: "The Aka? Aren't they the ones who ate the animals? Mala told me of them and the harm that they unwittingly or perhaps even with intent caused themselves and the purpose of the Ocan people."

He handed her a post, "Can you hold this for a moment?"

She was glad that as soon as he gave her the post he turned his back and continued sorting the other posts. The wooden post in her arms was almost as long as she was tall and extremely heavy. She didn't want him to see how hard it was for her to bear its weight. Fortunately, he turned before long and took the post from her.

Taijaur: "Don't believe all that you hear. Wait and judge them for yourself. Senai is one of my father's sisters. Another of his sisters is a commander, a co-leader with her husband, of the Aka people. The two sisters oppose one another, although there are some fundamental beliefs that they hold in common. Senai along with another Basau brother from the Haman village, Jhirai, have been instructing me."

She was still inhaling his scent and battling with herself to stop the effect that it was having on her. It reminded her that she needed to move away from him. After she finished nailing in a cross board to a post, she walked to the opposite side of the fence and down a ways from where he was standing before asking, "Taijaur, what is your true purpose in coming to this land?"

He looked up and saw such an expression of open sincerity on her face that he responded without thinking, without hesitation. "I have come to take you home."

Shona: "This is my home."

Taijaur: "No, I mean home to the Ocan; to your people, your future and your destiny."

She looked at him incredulous, "Why would I want to be a part of a cult of superstitious religious escapist? Have you forgotten that these precious Ocan people of yours wanted to kill me? Or didn't they tell you that part?"

Taijaur: "Time changes, people change. You are now and have always been important to the Ocan cause, even if some did not recognize this initially."

Shona: "Are you saying that they no longer view my existence as a threat to their well-being?"

Taijaur: "I am saying that the Ocan people need you, I need you. You and I have held a connection over all these years, over all the miles. Our union, our destiny is meant to serve a greater purpose."

Shona: "What greater purpose?"

Taijaur: "To find the Emissary, so that balance of the world's power can be re-set."

Shona: "I don't know what you are talking about. But I do know that you have wasted your time and energy on this fruitless quest. I have no desire to ever return to the Ocan island, let alone into your community of self-righteous hypocrites. It is hard to believe that the Ocan people would have allowed you to leave the island just to try to convince me to come back to a home that was never mine."

Taijaur: "Master Alor believes that your spirit may be an important part of our understanding of how to use the portal energy to fight against the plague that is spreading throughout the earth. He is hoping that you would be willing to come back to help us find a way to locate the portals, and develop the use the energy.

However, if the Emissary can be found, then we don't have to develop the limited energy available at the portals. It would then be possible to actually re-set the balance of energy directly at the source. And I believe that you and I together can find the Emissary."

Shona: "Mala told me about this Ocan belief in a long-awaited Emissary who will come and elevate all your precious people to a higher state of existence."

He ignored her derisive tone as he continued, "Being here in this land has convinced me that the energy available at the portals will not be enough to overcome the negative forces that have become too strong and too widespread. I have studied the map of the tunnels and interior chambers, gone over key passages in all three of the ancient books. Master Alor has not witnessed for himself how resilient and pervasive the evil forces have become in this land, in this world. He has not seen the people's despair, dejection and utter lack of hope and purpose. Too much has happened in the world. There are too many negative forces at play. The portal energy alone can have no lasting effect on the pervasive despair, apathy and cruelty that many humans exhibit. The symptoms of this virus are too severe. This is why I need your help. I believe our combined abilities can lead us to the Emissary and that we will then be able to access the power source directly. My dreams of the Emissary are too strong for me to be mistaken about this."

Shona: "You'll have to find someone else."

Taijaur: "There is no one else. There is only you and me."

Shona: "Then you have a problem. Say what ever you like, but I'm not going back to the Ocan island, and I have no idea how to find any emissary. I have my own path to follow just as it seems that you have yours. And by the way, when you return, please assure your precious people that their secret is safe with me. I have no desire to ever say anything about the Ocan to anyone."

Taijaur: "Some of us don't worry about that secret so much. With the spread of the plague becoming more pervasive and more deadly, all of our concerns as a people have to be directed toward its total eradication or we will find ourselves in a world no longer—"

Shona: "Yes, yes, yes. I've heard all of this before—the plague-the phage-the virus, the plague-the phage-the virus, all life on earth doomed by the plague—the phage—the virus. Well, I have been here for the past year and I haven't seen any evidence of any pervasive virus in the land. How many people have actually died from this virulent disease?"

Taijaur: "I'm sure that Mala told you that, for the most part, people don't die directly from this virus, or at least not an immediate physical death. In fact, there are no obvious physical symptoms like rashes or lesions. But make no mistake, this virus is still the most deadly, the most malignant force on this earth. Those infected die within their souls and they are sometimes responsible for countless massacres, countless forms of cruelty and depravation. The effect of this disease is evident in the exploitation, slaughter and subjugation of the oppressed. And the majority of people on this earth are not even aware that their behavior is being influenced by a pathogen. They have no idea that an infection in their brains has affected their ability to reason and to feel."

Shona: "How is it possible to know and attribute the cause of any person's or a group of people's actions to a virus, especially when no one ever seems capable of providing any details of exactly what this contagion really is? Mala never gave any detailed answers and even the old man just talks about the effects of the plague on the psyche of terrestrial beings. No one can even tell me the name of this virus. There is just always all of this ominous talk about 'the plague'."

Taijaur: "Unfortunately, no one knows exactly where or how it originated, even though we have studied this virus and its effects for centuries. However, there are some things that we do know. We know that it thrives under certain conditions and that it functions the same way as any virus in that it enters the cells of a human body, replicating itself and then bursting out to move on to other cells repeating the process over and over. However, this virus goes farther in that it is capable of altering the genes of its living host. The virus re-writes the code of people's DNA."

Shona: "Maybe this disease is a natural part of the cycles of existence. Why focus so much attention on its eradication? After all, viruses are a natural part of this world and no one can ever fully eradicate the pathogens that cause disease. What if this virus, all viruses and even some forms of perceived evil are just a natural part of the balance of energy in the world?"

Taijaur: "That may all be true. But in our quest to survive, it is necessary to fight against the diseases that viruses cause. Or with those diseases that cannot be eliminated, we have to at least make the symptoms manageable. Are you familiar with the problems caused by toxoplasmosis?"

Shona: "Is that the parasitic infection that is transmitted by affected feline or raw meat?"

Taijaur: "Yes, that's it. Well, this plague functions in much the same way as toxoplasmosis, altering an infected person's brain and thus, inducing new different types of behavior. The same way that a toxoplasmosis infection can make a rat less fearful of a cat, thus decreasing its chances of survival, this virus also functions to induce behaviors that threaten humanity's future.

Researchers used to believe that toxoplasmosis was one of the only pathogens capable of crossing the brain barrier and subsequently causing behavioral changes in animals. And then our scientists discovered the virus of this plague. Only the resulting behavioral changes caused by this pathogen are much more detrimental than anything that can result from the animal parasite."

As he continued speaking, Taijaur pulled his shirt over his head and hung it on a fence post. Perspiration was glistening on his skin. The muscles of his chest, forearms and abdomen moved with solid raw strength and power. Shona was momentarily startled, caught off guard by the sight of his naked upper body and she stumbled, almost falling over a post on the ground but caught herself and quickly looked away. His scent was coming through even more now, and she swooned slightly. From the corner of her eye she could see flashes of light that were reflected off of an object that hung on a string around his neck. It was the same string and crystal that he had that first day playing with Aria. The long string was looped several times to make a necklace. She turned and stared at the prismatic lights, trying to focus on what he was saying.

Taijaur: "This is a hidden insidious pandemic that has affected people in every land of this planet. When our people left the mainland two centuries ago, there was no way they could know how pervasive this disease would become. Undoubtedly, this phage is a part of the earth's energy that contributes to the destruction and decomposition of life. The physical and spiritual evolution of this planet depends on the balance of the world's energy fluctuating between creation/growth and destruction/decay. All energy in the universe depends on the interaction of the seemingly opposing forces of integration and diffusion. It is these forces that move matter in the acts of creation and destruction in many physical realities. However, the energy from these two forces must be kept in balance. It is this balance that allows incremental evolutionary steps in the spirit of man.

Negatively charged forces, that bring agitation and friction, are necessary to inspire growth and change. However, even though the energy of destruction and decay are necessary for spiritual growth, sometimes this energy dominates within people and within the earth, usually as a result of unfulfilled needs. If this negative energy is allowed to dominate then warped, extreme forms of destruction manifest on the earth. Incremental evolution as well as the punctuated periods of evolutionary 'leaps' forward can only occur from pushing against the preponderance of negative destructive forces."

Shona was still trying to gather her senses, rally her mind to listen and pay attention to his words. His scent continued to interfere with her ability to see, hear or think straight. It was if she was inhaling his entire essence, his whole being and not just the physical odor of his skin, sweat and movement. Once again she moved further away from him. She could not figure out how, now matter what distance she put between the two of them, somehow she kept ending up close to him. She was trying to focus on what he was saying but she had only heard part of it. And now she hoped that her response did not betray her lack of ability to concentrate. She tried to reply with comments and questions that she thought were in line with their conversation. But even as the words came from her mouth, they sounded familiar and she wondered if perhaps she had just said this same thing.

Shona: "But extinction has been the end result of most of the species that have inhabited the Earth thus far. This virus may be just a precursor hastening our inevitable demise. If this is the case, there is no immunity that will be strong enough."

Taijaur: "Perhaps this is so. Yet, while we are still here—on this earth, within this realm—we must do all that we can to contribute to mankind's collective spiritual evolution and survival. It is our responsibility and obligation to rise to that which is highest in human nature and fight to ensure that the positive forces of spiritual energy will prevail even in the face of our own potential physical demise." He paused, putting down his hammer and turned to look directly at her. "Shona, do you remember when I told you about my work in the Ocan that involves monitoring the satellite transmissions and studying the ancient texts?"

Shona: "Yes."

Taijaur: "Do you remember that I told you that one of the purposes of these activities is to track the patterns of symbols, ideologies, and ideas that have shaped cultures since the beginning of time?"

Shona: "Yes, I remember. You said that you monitor how some societal ideals can translate into negative actions that affect the world as a whole."

Taijaur: "The other purpose of my research that I did not mention entails deciphering the social, political and cultural patterns of the world in order to predict the potential rise of negative forces on the planet."

Shona laughed and said, "Do you mean that you're like some kind of psychic weatherman who forecasts when the next storm of doom will hit?"

Taijaur: "Laugh all you want Shona, but there is a solid scientific basis to my work."

Shona: "I'll take your word for it. Please, no examples."

Taijaur: "Shona, listen carefully. My work—and I have checked and re-checked all the variables—is pointing to an impending world-wide disaster of a major scale."

Shona: "A war between the nations?"

Taijaur: "Or perhaps something greater than a war."

Shona: "But this is all just a prediction, Taijaur, a supposition. No one can predict these type of events for sure."

Taijaur: "The signs that have begun to manifest are not just predictions or supposition. It may be hard to determine definitive causal or associative correlations between people's belief systems and the negative events that occur in the world at large. But it is obvious from the damage that has been done to the environment and the mass killing throughout the world that the balance of spiritual power has begun to shift more than any other time in the history of civilizations. The depraved and inhumane manner in which many people and societies operate make it apparent that we are entering a new age of existence. If the forces of spiritual power do not prevail, then our existence, as we know it, is in serious jeopardy.

We need a fundamental shift in our primary approach to life and how we live on this planet. Humans cannot continue to claim dominion over other life forms that have existed on this earth long before our time in this realm. Mankind cannot continue to disrespect and destroy the source of our sustenance and our renewal.

Shona: "But what can you or I or any one person do about these occurrences that are beyond our ability to rectify?"

Taijaur: "We must fight back in every way possible. This is why it is important for you to learn to fight. We must begin your training soon. We—the old man and I—have been waiting to see when you will be ready to begin your training. That is why Om has left us here alone today. He said that is necessary for us to begin as soon as possible. I told him that I am not sure that you are ready. We have to find some place where we can—"

Shona: "I'm ready. Just take me to where you and the old man hideout when you tire of female presence."

He smiled, "I don't ever tire of female presence. But why do you want to go there?"

Shona: "Because I want to see where you all go and what you do when you are there."

Taijaur: "I'm not sure that you are ready to undergo the more strenuous exercises that Om and I practice. He is a very strong old man. In fact, I don't know that I have ever met any person as strong as he is—young or old alike. I'm not sure that you would, um, like it very much."

Shona: "What you mean is that you don't think that I can handle it. I can handle anything that you can."

He bowed to her, suppressing a smile, "As you wish, m'lady." He turned to finish hammering a cross board. "We will have to stay gone for at least three weeks. The old man will be glad to know that your training is finally beginning. We can depart for the canyons at daybreak tomorrow morning."

Shona: "Canyons? You didn't say anything about canyons."

Taijaur: "You said that you want to go where the old man and I go. Well, that is where we go—to the canyons and caves that are to the east of here. Is there a problem with going to the canyons?"

Shona: "It's nothing. It's just that being in the canyons reminds me of another time."

Taijaur: "Do you mean the time that you encountered the Inar female?"

Shona was caught off guard, "What do you know of that?"

Taijaur: "The old man has told me of your experiences and how troubling you found the Inar philosophy and belief system. However, you won't have to worry about any Inar in the canyons that we are going to. These are not the same canyons. They are closer to here, and they are not as hot or sparse as where you were before. There is more edible vegetation in this location and there are some caves where we can sleep. But as far as the Inar female is concerned, she and your encounter with her may have unwittingly accelerated your growth and development in this world."

Shona: "That is, only if one's growth and development can be accelerated by death. She tried to kill me. And she killed my, my, my, Lubar, my dog, my only friend."

Taijaur: "And in doing so, she helped to make you stronger. She aided you in your journey in this world. You should respect and appreciate the lessons that you have learned as a result of your experiences with her."

Shona: "She brutally and savagely took the life of an innocent animal and given the chance, she would have done the same to me. And yet you believe that it is my responsibility to respect and appreciate what she did? Your opinion might be different if you heard the poisonous philosophy that she espoused which was far different from your Ocan spiel."

Taijaur: "Shona, what I am trying to say is that every living entity has something to teach you—no matter how good or bad, negative or positive this lesson may be. Don't allow your personal feelings and prejudices to deny you an essential life-lesson. This is what we must keep in mind even as we deal with those who are infected with the virus.

You must become strong enough in your own mind to not allow this being, or any negative being to conquer you with fear or hatred. Only through strength are we able to put our life experiences in perspective and understand that what matters most is that we have the potential to use our life force to make this world a better place. That is why exposure to and interaction with individuals such as Inar can serve the divine purpose of making you stronger and honing your spirit. However, if you allow yourself to be conquered by negative actions and emotions, then you can potentially become just as weak and evil as the evil that you sought to defeat.

The old man has told me of this Inar philosophy and I say that much of what your demon-friend conveyed may have some validity. For instance, when she spoke of humans desiring death, she may be right in that many of us long to let go and be free of life's constraints. However, it is not necessarily a release from life that humans desire. Rather an escape from the mundane perceptions of a material world upon which our societies force our devotion and focus our attention. We are fed only by the deeper structures of all our realities' intent. To focus on only the surface structure of one material reality leaves gaping holes in our psyches and incalculable dimensions to our inherent needs. Staying here in this mainland, with these people—performing an endless stream of meaningless tasks with no perceivable goal will force you to focus on and value only the surface of a material reality, while neglecting the cultivation of your spirituality."

Shona: "You preach as much as the old man."

Taijaur smiled and bowed to her once again, as he said, "My apologies. I didn't realize that I was preaching."

Shona had become so pre-occupied with their conversation that she had not noticed that Taijaur was no longer working on the fence and he was once again standing right beside her inside of the enclosure. They were both leaning in a relaxed posture against the almost-completed fence, facing one another as they conversed.

Shona: "No, please go on."

Taijaur: "Well, that was actually the end of my 'sermon'. There is much about you to admire. I thank that loathsome being for helping, in even some small way, to make you what you are. Even if some perceived hardness creeps into your soul, along with the lesson, you may find some use for it at some point in your life. Let go of the fear, but hold onto some of the ruthlessness—you may need it somewhere down the line."

Shona: "Yeah, I probably need it right now to protect me from you and your overly didactic Ocan philosophy."

Taijaur smiled, "My, my, my, aren't we in an amusing mood today."

They both laughed and then through the brief quiet that followed, Taijaur suddenly reached out and pulled Shona close to him, holding her firmly by her arms. He looked directly into her eyes, with intense focused attention. Speaking softly and slowly, yet distinctly, he stated in a low resonant voice, "No, my sister, you need only to let down your guard, allow me to come in and be the one to protect you."

Before she could pull it back, a small smile escaped along with an unexpected sharp intake of breath as sudden warmth opened in her face and throughout her body. She felt weak, unable to move as she closed her eyes to steady her equilibrium; her mind/tongue stilled in a surge of swirling emotions. She took a deep breath and through the brief second of self-control that came to her, she quickly pulled away from his grasp and began walking, with a measured gait, toward the house. With her back to him as she walked away, she said over her shoulder, "Maybe *you* can sit around all day, without any evidence of productivity. But I have work that calls to me, and thus, I can tarry no longer."

Taijaur stood motionless and silent, as he watched, with a steady intense gaze, Shona's slowly departing form.

Part III

17. Watching the Night

In synch with the motion of the planets and the forces that guide the stars, Taijaur and Shona moved closer to a future reality that existed millennia before their own time within this realm. They spent the next few weeks alone in the canyons, and with each passing day, Shona found it harder to struggle against the feeling of electrical magnetism and immense power that radiated throughout her senses every time that she stood near Taijaur or looked into his eyes. Every movement of his body—every action that he took to work, run, jump, play, create—emanated intense raw power that electrified the surrounding air. It was as if the island's clean rich volcanic soil had given rise to his form, endowing him with phenomenal gifts of strength, compassion and intellect. Mala had once told her of an elusive supernal fire of life that flows endlessly throughout the universe, fueling the galaxies and touching only that which possesses the power to match its own intensity. If such a force did, indeed, exist, then Shona was certain that part of its course must be set through the souls of beings such as Taijaur. For, indeed, his existence was a pure celebration of the glory and grace that the universe has bestowed upon the earth as living man.

They established a routine every morning, walking in the pre-dawn quiet, first meditating and then stretching in preparation for a full day of strenuous and challenging exercises and drills. Before beginning, they smeared their bodies with a concoction of mud and special herbs that Om had packed for them along with their food supplies. Shona was grateful that this potent unguent not only deterred the approach of any beasts of prey, but it also subdued any effect that Taijaur's scent might have on her senses.

On their first days alone in the wilderness, Shona maintained a distance and a vigilant guard lest Taijaur attempt to touch her in the playful way that he had approached her at the old man's house. Except this landscape offered no tables or chairs or objects to place in his way, so she depended on moving quickly away from him if he came too near. After awhile she noticed that not only was Taijaur not trying to touch or approach her, but that he was keeping an even wider distance from her than she was from him. He was a consummate demanding task master, completely focused on the instruction that he imparted—no laughing, no joking of any kind. His body moved in a world of its own. Over time, Shona relaxed to the point that she never noticed when he started standing close to position her body in a particular form or when he began massaging the taut muscles of her shoulders and legs. She was drawn along with him into this other world where nothing existed or mattered outside of their powerful, poetic flow of movement and concentrated action.

As they moved in synchrony with one another, Taijaur sometimes asked Shona to stare at various objects—a rock, a patch of grass, a distant shrub. The first time he did this it was just before sunrise, when the shadows and mist wrapped the world in their own special kind of mystery.

Taijaur: "Shona, do you see that rock—over there a couple feet to the left of that bush? Don't stop moving, just look at it as you follow my steps."

Shona: "Yes, I see it. What about it?

Taijaur: "Stare at it for a moment."

Shona: "Why?"

Taijaur: "Please just do it."

For a few seconds, she feigned a sustained focus in the direction that he pointed. She was losing her grasp on that other world. Her body wanted nothing more than to feel the cool morning air on her skin and to stay within the wonder of its own flowing motion—no sounds, no talking, no staring.

Taijaur: "Do you see any colors or lights moving in the rock?"

It was hard to keep the irritation out of her voice as she replied, "No, I only see a gray lifeless rock."

Taijaur: "Describe it to me—in terms of its intent and in relation to anything that surrounds it and touches it—the soil, the light, the dark, the shadows, the mist."

Shona: "It's a rock—what do you want me to say?"

Taijaur: "Can you describe what you feel as you see the rock?"

Shona: "Taijaur, what game is this?"

Taijaur: "This is no game. This is a part of your training. Perhaps the most important part."

Shona: "I don't see how staring at and describing a rock can help me to know how to fight."

Taijaur: "Knowing how to see, how to understand is at the basis of all forms of strength, strategy, and defense. You have to open your sentiale to bring forth your understanding of not just the essence of the world around you, but also the substructures of reality that exist within all that is a part of this space and time."

Shona eventually mastered the mental exercises of seeing, hearing and feeling the world. She began to develop her own way of 'seeing', especially in the night, once the sun had gone down when her senses were more acute in discerning minute distinctions in shape, form and shadow of any and all parts of the natural world. Taijaur listened in quiet astonishment as Shona made intricate descriptions of the nocturnal wind, the stars and the root systems of vegetation that extended for miles around the area they occupied.

They generally rested only once during the day, briefly sitting at mid-day in the shade of a large boulder, while taking some small sustenance. Some of the calisthenics that they practiced, Shona had learned from Mala and some the old man had taught her, but the majority of the exercises were new to her. Shona learned relaxed, evasive movements and quick counterstrikes, as well as a fighting form that emphasized strength, balance, flexibility, and speed. She worked hard to cover any sign that her own might and stamina might be any less than his. It was important to her that he not think that she was inadequate to any task that he put before her. However, by the end of each day it was hard for her to hide her complete and utter exhaustion. Once the sun began to set they trained with less intensity, stopping only once it was pitch dark.

In the quiet of the night, they bathed and swam in the narrow branch of a river that ran underground through the cave where they slept. Even though Shona remained fully clothed in the light thin material of Ocan fabric, the cool water still revived her energy and refreshed her senses. Sitting and soaking in the shallow straits of the tributary, they fell into an easy pattern of sharing their thoughts, wishes and dreams in that dark liquid enclosure where it was always night, no matter the time of day. This place reminded Shona of the tarn on the other side of the waterfall where she and Mala used to go. She sat back content, looking around at the black rock wall glistening with water, listening to the sound of the flowing river, and the trickling splashes that fell from her arms moving up and down, in and out of the water.

Shona: "How did you find this place?"

Taijaur: "The old man and I scouted for the best place to conduct your training."

Shona: "You and Om have been conspiring together since you first arrived."

Taijaur: "All on your behalf, m'lady, all on your behalf."

Shona's eyes fell on the crystal that always hung from the string around Taijaur's neck and a memory of the first time that she saw him moved through her mind and her body. She could still see the complex designs that he had made with the string and Aria's pleasure with each new ephemeral construction.

Shona: "What is that necklace that you wear?"

He took the necklace off and threw it over to Shona. "It was a parting gift from Saba—something to help me stay centered and focused. And it also serves as a reminder that I must continually honor the Gift by striving to always make myself worthy."

Shona: "What is this Gift of the Ocan? Mala never seemed to explain it fully."

Taijaur: "The Gift is life, it is injera, it is what makes us what we are and what we can become."

Shona: "But there's more to it than that. I know because Mala inferred something about how the Ocan people have been changed by the Gift."

Taijaur: "Shona, you all ready know. But it is too much to go into all the details now. Suffice it to say that, the Ocan people learned to use the Gift as an antidote to the ills of this world."

His explanation left her curiosity unsated, but she let it go for now. She stood up and got out of the water, handing him his necklace and started climbing the embankment to that part of the small upper cave that they used for rest and shelter. This cave was unlike any that she had spent time in on the island or here on the mainland. From the outside it looked like a multidimensional triangle with its vertical slanting slabs of gray stone stacked one behind the other creating a low entryway and ceiling. It was comfortable enough inside, but left only enough space for the two of them to sleep at a reasonable distance from one another.

They slept each night on mats, wrapped in warm blankets near the opening of the cave. Taijaur always turned on his side with his back to her, falling promptly into sleep as soon as he lied down. He was a sound sleeper, never stirring before his requisite few hours of slumber. Sometimes, when she knew that he was fast asleep, she inched her mat closer to his and leaned her back slightly against his back, relishing the feel of the solid inert force of his body. She told herself that their reciprocal body heat was needed to overcome the cold of the canyon nights. She had watched his sleep patterns since he first arrived at the old man's house, so she always knew when it was time to move back to her side of the cave before he awakened. The feel of his body so close to hers made her feel safe and secure. But this closeness also kept her awake, her heart pounding wildly throughout all parts of her body.

No matter how tired she was, Shona still rose at some point each night and walked out into darkness. She now understood that the night, the darkness, was her source of power—her knowledge, her strength, her guide. In this realm of sentiale's awakening, all her thoughts, feelings, and sensations transcended the cover of surface perception. Drawing from the black infinity, she felt life's true awareness erupt in the darkness, revealing the universe's internal spaces, while shedding all temporal external realities.

In the night, Shona's senses had always been more alert, more open. But now she was beginning to take this power into the day. Sounds were louder and more clear; light and colors seemed brighter, odors stronger and more pervasive. She could smell the sun, the leaves, the dirt, the trees, the rain and the air. She was awakening to the world in a way that she never knew was possible; a world in which she felt acutely alive, an integral part of every thing that surrounded her. The sensations enveloped her soul and she felt enraptured by the sheer feeling of being alive—passionately inhaling the air around her, inhaling a new way of knowing and understanding life. She felt herself changing, transforming into something new, different; and the sensations only deepened with each passing day. But there were other times when she wanted to run and cower from these feelings that while endowing her with more power, still stripped her of the familiar sense of control that was ironically, an inherent part of her fear.

One day, near the end of their second week, Shona's fear began to inexplicably creep back into her psyche as she sensed that something was changing with Taijaur that she did not understand. They had been training all morning and their exercises lacked their usual intensity as Taijaur was less focused, missing steps and following out of synchrony with their practiced movements. When he missed one major kick and counterbalance step that depended on both of them executing flawless precision, Shona could not resist asking, "Is everything okay, Taijaur? Is something wrong?"

Taijaur: "No, everything is fine. But let's sit over here where we can talk for awhile. It's near time for us to rest anyway."

They sat down side by side in the shade with their backs against the boulder. Taijaur was hesitant as he continued, "It's just that, well Shona, it will be time for us to leave soon."

He took out a hard flat piece of bread and broke it in half, handing her a part as he uncapped their canteen of water. Shona tried to suppress her surprise, replying as calmly as she could, "But we haven't been here that long. And I thought we were staying until all of the training was complete." She hoped that he did not hear the small quiver in her voice as she tried to appear nonchalant with her fingers shakily untying the bag of dried fruit and nuts that they shared between them.

Taijaur: "There is something pulling me, telling me that the time to go is drawing near. It is time to go home, Shona." He turned to look at her. "Back home to the Ocan."

Shona: "In a way, I was hoping that you would decide to stay here in this land. I will be sorry to see you go, but I understand—"

Taijaur: "No Shona, you don't understand. I mean both of us. It is time for both of us to return to the Ocan."

Shona: "You seem to forget that the Ocan was never truly my home."

Taijaur: "And you forget that I am here only to take you back; not to build a life in this land. You and I, we have important work to do. We can travel directly from here to reach to the peninsula that I mentioned before."

Shona: "Taijaur, I won't be going with you. I hope that my silence on this subject has not led you to believe that I changed my mind. And I hope that you are not planning to leave directly from this place. I'm sure that Om will want to bid you farewell before you depart."

Taijaur: "I won't see Om again before I leave. I will depart directly from these canyons and head north to the peninsula. I have already said my farewells."

Shona: "Do you mean that Om is aware that you are leaving?"

Taijaur: "He is not expecting either one of us to return."

Shona: "What is that suppose to mean?"

Taijaur: "Shona, your place is in the Ocan. Maybe not forever and maybe not for long; but for now, it is where you need to be. You and I, we belong together. Om believes, as I believe, that you need to return to the isle of your birth."

Shona: "Then you are both operating under an erroneous assumption."

Taijaur: "Why do you think that we are here Shona? Here in these canyons. Why do you think that we have been undergoing these intense exercises and defensive strategies?"

Shona: "What kind of question is that? We are here learning and practicing self-defense maneuvers so that I can protect myself from any potential threat or assault."

Taijaur: "We are here training—mind, body and spirit—so that we will be prepared to enter the in-between. What you have been learning is a combined Aka and Ocan system of combat and self-defense; a form of self-cultivation that conveys the discipline and—"

Shona: "What?!? Wait a minute. The in-between? That's not why I am here. Is this some scheme that you and the old man have concocted? I should have known that this was some manipulative ploy to force me to comply with your machinations. Well you won't succeed. Neither of you will succeed."

Taijaur: "The reasons that I gave you for coming here were true enough. They just were not the only reasons. I never intended to deceive you in any way. It's just that I thought, well, we—the old man and I both—thought that, on your own, you would come to the realization of what is best and what inevitably must be, through no outside persuasion on anyone else's part."

Shona: "There is so much subterfuge with you."

Taijaur: "Hmmmm. Well, I prefer to think of it as 'truth revealed in time'."

Shona: "Nonetheless, it appears that both you and the old man have underestimated me."

Taijaur: "Yes, it does appear that we did not take into account how stubborn and obstinate you are; perhaps to the detriment of your own well-being."

Shona: "That is your opinion, your perspective. You are no soothsayer, and you do not know what actions are to my detriment or to my benefit. I happen to know that my place is here in this land not on some hidden deserted island.

And I also know that returning to the Ocan would be more of a detriment to my life right now."

Taijaur made no response as he sighed heavily, and then realized that his own loud continuous exhales sounded very much like those of his grandmother.

Shona: "Besides Taijaur, try to understand; I have not accomplished what I have come to this land to do. There is still much here that I must do. You know what it is to feel your duty call to you so strongly that you are rendered incapable of hearing anything else. Try to understand that I feel the same way about the work that I must do in this life of mine."

Taijaur: "But Shona, you are denying part of your gift, part of your calling. And this denial is what further entrenches the malaise that haunts you."

Shona: "That's not true. I am working with the old man and the midwives of the villages. I am developing my skills as a healer."

Taijaur: "But there are many different ways in which people must be healed and made whole. Part of your calling may be to transcend the traditional boundaries and become something beyond saba."

Shona: "What do you mean?"

Taijaur looked pensive for a moment and then replied, "Never mind that for now. But in staying here, on this mainland, in these villages—what do you hope to accomplish? What do you hope to become? Will you be content to spend all of your days consumed by the endless tasks of survival merely for the sake of survival?"

Shona: "I can't just leave these people. They are my people now, this place is my home. You see how these people live—the fear, the poverty. They struggle on a daily basis to find or maintain the basics of survival—adequate food, water and shelter. That Taring man—what if he becomes governor of the provinces? Adding this even greater evil to a precarious existence can only mean destruction on a major scale."

Taijaur: "If you stay here Shona, how will you be able to change any of that?

Shona: "How can I just go away and pretend that their pain does not exist?"

Taijaur: "What if the only way to alleviate their pain is to separate yourself from it and make yourself strong enough to change this situation at its root? Their world differs from ours. In the Ocan we have no such evil or suffering to contend with. Our development is not thwarted by the everyday struggles like those of these people. Thus—"

Shona: "But that is why I was meant to be here in this place, to help these people; to show them a way to a potentially better or more successful way of life and living."

Taijaur: "But where do you draw the line between what constitutes help and what is really an inverted form of supremacy?"

Shona: "What do you mean?"

Taijaur: "To attempt to chart a course for someone else you must inherently assume their inferiority and the superiority of your own way. What right do you have to try to play God for someone else? No person can be delivered or saved by any person outside of themselves. In order to try to save someone you must enter into who they are and become what you are not, so that they might experience a hoped-for transformation that they may ultimately reject. And all to what end? Do you know the answers of what great utopia towards which they should aspire? Utopia lives within before it can manifest. Do you force on them a way of life that they, themselves, have not chosen?"

Shona: "I can join their struggle, join their cause. I can help them to achieve their goals and perhaps even expose them to alternatives to which they may have been deprived."

Taijaur: "You can only bring another being to their own god-awareness by first exemplifying that awareness in your own actions, in your own life."

Shona: "So, do you just give up and watch the people of the world suffer?"

Taijaur: "On the contrary, you must fight—hard, long and strong. You must fight with every fiber of your being. However, Shona, you can only help these people by attacking this evil at its root. Can't you see that the phage is the root cause of this Taring man's malevolence, as well as most of the evil that is pervasive throughout the world? Nothing will ever change in human society until this evil is annihilated at its most base level.

Each new generation of the human populace will continue going round and round the same issues of strife and discord until we all learn how to accept and share our gifts. This virus is the major impediment to the giving and receiving of our gifts in life. No effort to solve any of the world's problems will be effective until the fundamental cause of this plague has been eradicated. No effort to change the people's lives will be effective until this virus has been dealt with."

Shona: "This may all be true, but I cannot see how my returning to the island can help anyone fight against this virus or help anyone to learn how to share their gifts. The people in this land need me and other people like me."

Taijaur: "Living in the Ocan presents a greater opportunity to cultivate your gifts. In the Ocan, the purpose for existence is permanently laid out before us, etched into our daily lives and routines. All our energy, thoughts, feelings, and actions are geared towards achieving a transposition to a higher realm of consciousness.

In our cloister, we strive as one to exist simply within the substance of a righteous world view, each moment devoted to the progression of the spirit to the place of the holy. Like all human beings, in the midst of our routine unceasing survival-necessary tasks, we laugh, sing, love, play, worship, create and destroy. However, unlike other human beings, we possess a *conscious intent* to use our lives individually and collectively for the purpose of reaching higher realms of understanding, of knowing, of being; and to help others to aspire towards this same purpose in life.

Despite the shortcomings of the Ocan people, we have created a fair and just society, with none of the ills of this world and a central purpose upon which to focus our life energies. While these people in this mainland live without any real purpose or higher calling. These people experience nothing that even comes close to—"

Shona: "How dare you put yourself above *these people?* Listen to the condescending way you even say '*these people*'. You and your Ocan philosophies and Ocan way of life—what makes you think that you are so superior?"

Taijaur: "I never said that we are superior—"

Shona: "Did it ever occur to you that these people live the reality that you and your self-righteous Ocan hypocrites can only talk about. You and your sanctimonious Ocan approach to life. You don't ever dare to put your little philosophies to the test of real living. No, it is far too easy to sit back and preach about how individuals should live, without you ever trying to truly live in a real world with real problems, real people. These people and the realities of their societies are just as important as anything that the Ocan have created. And they are important to me."

Taijaur: "Shona, let's not do this. In certain ways you are right about the Ocan people. And I don't doubt that the people of this land lead good and useful lives. But don't forget to also look at the ways in which the people's ability to survive on this earth has been compromised by their constant struggles to overcome war, poverty, suffering and a shallow materialistic value system that requires their constant devotion. Their lives are weighed down by senseless and incomprehensible fear, destruction and wrongdoing that is present in the environment all around them, if not in their immediate lives. Over time, how much faith and compassion do you think that they will be able to sustain in the face of the realities of evil and despair that crowds out their spirituality?"

Shona: "But it is the everyday battles of mankind that test whether or not your faith is true. Ocan beliefs, like most philosophical treatise of life are only beautiful and compelling until they are faced with the realities of evil, strife and violence. Faith in the unseen is always easier to uphold. But running away and hiding from evil doesn't make it go away. Compassion and faith must be lived, not merely professed from the sidelines of life. It is the every day experiences of humankind that may test the worthiness of compassion's intent."

Taijaur: "And how did you fare when the intent of your compassion was tested?"

Shona: "What do you mean?"

Taijaur: "What about the Inar female?"

Shona was clearly alarmed and trying to contain and hide her fear. She sat forward away from the boulder, away the shade. "What about her?"

Taijaur: "You tell me."

Shona: "I don't know what you mean."

Taijaur: "Where is she?"

Shona: "How would I know? That was over a year and a half ago. I left her in the canyon basin."

Taijaur: "Did you really Shona?"

Shona: "Did I what?"

Taijaur: "Did you really leave her? Or are you still there—with her, in the canyons? Have you ever asked yourself—who or what are you running from, every day, every moment of your life?"

Shona: "What are you talking about?"

Taijaur: "Where was she when you left her?"

Shona: "In the canyons. You know all of this. Om told you what happened. I left her where the altercation took place."

Taijaur saw and felt how agitated Shona had become, but he still kept going, still kept pushing. "What did you do to her? How were you able to get away?"

Shona: "I...I..."

Taijaur: "I know that you tied her up Shona; that you left her to die."

She was breathing heavily, her heart beating wildly. She felt an intense heat and pain in her head, behind her eyes as she shouted, "WHAT WAS I TO DO? WHAT ELSE COULD I HAVE DONE?"

Taijaur began rubbing and stroking her back wondering if perhaps he had gone too far, but feeling nonetheless that 'too far' was where Shona needed to go.

Taijaur: "Okay, Shona, okay. Just forget about it. It's not important."

She pulled away from him and got up. She began walking away, off into the distance. She stayed away until evening time when she silently joined him soaking in the water of the river. At first neither of them spoke as they stared at one another, each waiting for the other to break the quiet. Finally, Shona spoke up. "Taijaur, you have to understand I cannot go back to the Ocan. There is no life for me there."

Taijaur: "My life is your life. You will share what I have."

She tried not to allow her emotions to rise as she asked, "With all due respect and appreciation, what if I don't want your life? What if I want the freedom to define for myself the meaning of my own life?"

Taijaur: "Shona, I respect your need and right to determine for yourself what your life will be. But it is hard to watch you running away from who you are and making a decision for your life based on fear. What about our connection with one another? Together, we can build a life and jointly determine what it will be."

Shona: "But can't you see that one of us will always have to acquiesce to the other? When you choose to bind your life with another, many times there is a thin line between intimacy and oppression. I have seen it time and again with the people in the villages."

Taijaur: "Are you saying that you don't believe that a man and woman can live together in harmony?"

Shona: "I am saying that an individual person can assume responsibility for his or her own happiness. And perhaps each of us can better fulfill our purpose on this earth in the absence of the false sense of security that comes with binding your life to another. When we are forced to find our own way in life and determine on our own path, then we may be able to see more clearly what the Creator intends for our lives."

Taijaur: "Don't you desire any comfort or companionship in life?"

Shona: "I'm not saying that men and women should not spend time together and enjoy one another's company. But you don't need to have someone constantly by your side, to fulfill your purpose in life or to achieve wholeness. Why base your happiness on the insecure notion of possessing another person in order to be whole? What of the necessity for solitude? You said yourself that silence and solitude are necessary for human development, creation and general well-being. Did you not say that all great artistic expressions as well as scientific discoveries can only be born from that single silent commune that each individual makes with his/her God?"

Taijaur: "Yes, but we need balance between our moments of solitude and the necessary inspiration derived from combining our souls, our minds, with the minds and souls of others. Both types of experiences are necessary parts of human existence. There is a time and place for each."

Shona: "Taijaur, what do you know of me really? It is obvious that we are not from the same racial group. I don't even know what racial group or groups that I belong to."

Taijaur: "Shona how does that matter one way or the other? Matters of race and ethnicity have no significance to the Ocan people, outside of the sharing and blending of cultural practices."

Shona: "But you don't even know my personal history. You have no idea of my paternal genetic source. I don't know these things myself. How can you be sure that you are not attempting to bind your life with something unnatural or impure? With me as your mate, you will not be able to build the type of life that you envision for yourself. For one thing, we would never be able to have children. Don't you understand—I cannot make the same mistake that my mother did. I cannot chance bringing into existence another hybrid human, an anomaly of human nature."

Taijaur: "Shona, I may not be aware of everything there is to know about you. But of this I am certain—I know that I want you, for now and the now that exists within and beyond this lifetime. There is a lot that you do not know about me. But we can teach and learn from one another through a lifetime of sharing our love, our lives. And as far as children are concerned, well in the final analysis, we are all hybrid beings. I love you, Shona. And you know and I know that you love me. Isn't that enough of a reason for us to be together, to build a life together?"

Shona: "But what is this silly belief in some sophomoric notion that love conquers all and makes everything all right? Taijaur, there are realities in this world that are not only outside of our control, but wholly outside of our ability to comprehend. And some of those incomprehensible realities may exist in the essence of what I am."

Taijaur: "The only realities that matter to me are those created as a result of what we believe can and should be. We can make this life what we want it to be. You have to believe, you have to have faith. This world is powered by systems of belief that have endured through time. Many of these eternal systems of belief are founded on the concept of love and the need for love."

Shona: "What is love but an empty need, raw and exposed? People use the façade of love to mask the fact that are using the presence of another person to persuade themselves and others that their empty lives have meaning or purpose or in order to feel a false sense of self-worth. If you begin to dissect the basis of love relationships between many men and women, you see a banding together to assuage insecurities or because they are afraid of being alone. Or sometimes people join together on the basis of a narcissistic desire to see their own worth and values reflected in another person. And then there are those who, through self-loathing, seek the opposite of who and what they are, in order to attain the 'otherness' to which they aspire, but can never achieve. Sometimes through insecurity and a sense of inferiority, some people try to feed their need for adulation from a perceived lesser being. Or through this same insecurity and unworthiness, some punish the 'otherness' that their mate represents and feed a need for domination and control over a perceived superior being.

And then there are those who sell themselves to the highest bidder, in an attempt to amass riches and secure their livelihood. And those who trade the realness of love, in order to pursue a contrived fairytale based on what their societies or other people tell them love should consist of.

And let us not forget the insecurity that makes many people need to prove their worth to others by being able to say, 'look at me, I am somebody because I have a man or I have a woman—somebody loves me, so that must mean that I am a person of value and worth in the eyes of the world.' And if not any of these reasons, then there is always the competitiveness, petty jealousies and possessiveness that occurs between individuals in relationships."

Taijaur: "Shona, I'm surprised to hear you express such cynical and pessimistic views of love relationships. What has happened to make you so bitter? Perhaps the Inar poison in your system has affected you more than you realize. Why do you view people's motives in such a callous way; in a way that negates the beauty of love?"

Shona: "Callous, cynical perhaps—but true nonetheless. Truth is not always pretty. And this is not about being bitter or about anything that has happened to me personally. My point is that you cannot say that love, pure and simple, is what draws men and women together in relationships. The needs that many people attempt to fulfill in supposedly 'love relationships', many times have little or nothing to do with love. The traits that I speak of can be observed at any time, in any group of people. And I have observed and studied these traits over and over again. And not just in spousal relationships, but sometimes in friendships and familial relations as well. Not always, not all of the time, but frequently enough to warrant caution of the most extreme sort."

Taijaur: "I hope that some of what you have said is just part of your defenses and not truly a part of your belief system. I don't doubt that some people come together to feed their need for security and assuage their fears. But I don't understand why you think that our relationship could potentially be prey to anything that you describe. And you know as well as I, that there are also those whose love is pure—those who learn and grow through their differences; those who are inspired by sharing common values and beliefs. And what of the joy and fun of just being together, of friendship, companionship? I have seen you with these people, Shona—you genuinely enjoy being with them and forming bonds with them. Why are you willing to join your life with these others, but not with me?"

Shona made no reply as Taijaur looked down and shook his head from side to side, continuing in a choked voice, "You act as if you despise your very capacity to feel need, to know and live injera." He looked up at her. "Injera is life, Shona. What is it that you fear in this very human capacity to feel and know need? Human injera is an essential part of life, a part of who and what we are in terms of being alive. While the wrong means of fulfillment can lead to devastating results. The right means of fulfillment for our needs, the right match between two people can lead to the most powerful force of existence that this earth has ever known. By finding and joining with a mate, you have the potential to maximize your life force. By fusing your life with the life of another, you maximize all human potential for growth and understanding, for greatness.

Need and its fulfillment—injera—is the most basic and natural ingredient of life. What do you think motivates life to exist? What incites life to come into existence? Need—injera, plain and simple; microcosmic and macrocosmic need. At the most fundamental level, it is your life force that seeks its complement in another life force. On the surface it may appear that the combination is between two personalities, two egos, two physical bodies. But a true match goes much deeper than that. It is a joining at all levels of existence.

Love is the most basic of all human needs. And it is realized must fully through a primary connection, a primary source of loving and being loved. This one fundamental connection can serve as a gateway to a broader understanding of loving and giving and being. It enables you to open yourself to other connections, other forms of love. Love helps to hone mankind's link with life and the energy of the sacred.

Shona, you are this primary connection for me. You are a part of the fiber of my soul, the fire of my existence. I cannot rise without seeing you and feeling you with me, even when you are not there. I cannot lie down without feeling the presence of your love in my heart and in my mind. You are there in every moment that I breathe, every action that I take. My life is made whole and right because you exist."

She was silent for awhile and would not look at him, would not make eye contact. She concentrated on the sound of the flowing water, moving her fingers delicately over the surface of the river. She waited until she felt that her heart had, once again, settled into a normal rhythm and that perhaps she could trust her voice not to quiver, and then she spoke still not looking in Taijaur's direction. "All of that sounds very moving, very touching. But it does not take away from the fact that each of us must learn how to be whole without looking outside of our individual selves for validation or worth.

I acknowledge the inevitable and essential nature of need. But even the most pure of love relationships can disintegrate into a morass of malice, sorrow and spite when a bond is built on insecurities, fears and needs. It may not start out that way. However, no relationship between two people can become truly successful until both parties have individually reached a point of growth that allows them to come together through strength and understanding, not through the weakness of need. You cannot allow need, by itself, to determine what decisions you make in life.

I was once conquered by my need to believe, my need to belong. I decided then that I would never again be defeated by a process that was internal to my own being; that I would shape my life according to my own design. That I would never again be hurt by my own lack of emotional and psychological control. It is my responsibility to master at least that which exists inside of me. If I don't control those parts of my emotions that can cause me pain, then I will never be able to fight the external forces that would stand in opposition to me. I cannot bind my life with another until I have overcome the obstacles of need that stand in my way."

Taijaur: "But Shona, whether you fulfill it or not, the need is still there. Whether you conquer it or not, it is still there. Repressing injera only results in neuroses, psychoses, physical ailments and disease. Suppressed unfulfilled needs can cause weakness in every facet of your being. You cannot overcome your sense of need. You can only try to enhance your ability to meet your needs by drawing love, strength and inspiration from the bonds that you form with other people and with the natural world around us."

She made no response. Taijaur looked down shaking his head. "It is ironic that both you and Saba have been stymied by a blocked sentiale; that you both have access to only the surface level of your sentiale power. Oh sure, Saba thinks that no one really knows of her infirmity and she tries hard to hide it. While you, on the other hand, openly reject an essential part of your own existence and ability to live and feel and be. You pretend that you don't need it or want it, while trying to make yourself deaf and blind to one of the most powerful forces in existence that lives within you.

It is also ironic that both of you were born saba and both of you remain stuck at a pivotal moment in your lives, in your history. You are stuck in the past, at a moment that you cannot move beyond. Something happened that makes you run away from yourself, run away from who you are. A moment of fear or failure or shame.

You are human Shona—the same as the rest of us mere mortals. From time to time you, I, all of us, every human being on this planet—must fail. Big failure, little failure—they are all the same. You have to learn to move beyond the pain, humiliation and disgrace that can and will occur in this life.

You and Saba both have made your moments of defeat or shame into something larger than your own lives; more significant than it was ever meant to be. And then you refuse to move beyond it. Everyone experiences loss some times; everyone experiences defeat. Why must your loss, your failure, dictate how you live for the rest of your life and crowd out other parts of your existence? Why must you let this loss, this failure define who you are? We cannot allow ourselves to be defined by or held hostage to our moments of hurt, shame or despair."

Shona rose quickly to her feet, water dripping from her body and from her clenched fists. She was disturbed and agitated, shouting, "Stop it, Taijaur! Stop it. I won't listen to this. What makes you the great master teacher and god of us all? What gives you the right to tear apart how I chose to define myself? Why don't you look inside of yourself and deal with your own demons?"

Taijaur: "I don't have any demons and I didn't mean to—"

Shona: "Oh really? Don't you? Then why can't you talk about your mother's death? Why can't you deal with that part of yourself that holds you responsible for killing your mother? You hold yourself hostage for a crime that you never committed. Just listen to all that you have said—all that stuff about your Aka aunt. What was she saying but that as a result of having killed your mother you must now re-pay a debt? Well, if a debt actually exists, it is yours, not mine. And I am not going to re-arrange my life just so that you can try to atone for past moments over which you had no control. And if you can't see past your own 'moment' of perceived loss or failure, who are you to try to tell me what's wrong with me or what I should do with my life?"

While Shona continued to pace as she spoke, Taijaur pulled himself out of the water and sat on the edge of the bank opposite her, with his feet still immersed in the river. He watched her moving back and forth through the water.

Taijaur: "Admit it Shona, what you are really afraid of is who you are. You are afraid of being hurt and rejected. You are afraid of feeling love and being loved. And the power of what you feel terrifies you because you cannot control it. You are afraid that by submitting to love that you will be made vulnerable, weak and dependent."

She stood still, quiet at first, staring at Taijaur with stony defiance, and then she said in a low even tone, "Ultimately it does not matter what I fear most, because I am not going back to the island with you and there is nothing that you can either do or say that will make me change my mind."

He looked down and then into the distance where the water flowed into the darkness of the cave. Shona, in a softer contrite tone, began to walk slowly through the water towards him saying, "Taijaur, I'm sorry. But this is my life and I am the only one who can decide what I need and want. I can only hope that one day you will find what you seek. I do wish for you the strong and loving life-mate that you feel that you need."

Taijaur stood up suddenly. "And I can only hope that one day this little girl wrapped in a woman's body will learn how not to be afraid of herself, her life and all that might tempt her to discover who she really is or what life really means."

She was stunned for a moment and then recovered herself as she saw him begin to walk down into the passageway on the bank of the river.

He called over his shoulder, "I'll be back later. You can go back up without me."

Shona: "Taijaur, wait! You can't just walk away."

He continued moving forward, turning slightly to respond, "I'm not walking away. I'll be back. I just need to think. Don't worry. You know that this place is safe."

Shona: "But where are you going."

Taijaur: "I have to find something."

She watched him walk away and then waited awhile in the still darkness before going back up into the part of the cave where they slept. She slept very little during the night as she listened and waited for him to come. The sentiale probes that she sent bounced back to her, unable to reach a contact signal of response. It felt like she hit a brick wall. He never came back that night. In the morning, when she went out to their training site, he was there leaning against the boulder, waiting for her with a small bouquet of wild flowers.

Taijaur: "I'm sorry, Shona. I shouldn't have said the things that I said. I didn't mean to hurt you."

She accepted the flowers from him, smiling ruefully, "Au contraire, mon frere—I think that we both aimed and hit our intended targets. But perhaps we have both learned the folly of so accurate an aim. I'm sorry if I have disappointed you."

He took her hand, saying only, "Come on. Let's finish what we started yesterday. We have a lot to do today."

As they began a series of slow extended bends, lunges and stretches, Shona tentatively inquired, "Did you find what you were looking for last night?"

He continued bending and stretching, never breaking the synchrony of their elongated movements as he smiled slightly, "It was with me all along."

They spent most of the day quietly training, carefully and delicately treading around each other's thoughts and feelings. Towards the end of the day, a sudden storm forced them to take shelter for more than an hour. The sat next to one another under a nearby rock ledge silently staring out at the deluge, feeling its raw power come inside and expand their open awareness. After the rain, the air was warm and penetrating with the smell of open skies and wet, rich earth. They both felt a heightened sensitivity to and awareness of the elements on their bodies and within their senses. The muddy aftermath of the rain precluded any further attempts to work and they trudged the mile or so back to their cave, still in silence. They bathed quickly and quietly in the river, neither of them attempting to initiate any conversation beyond the normal polite inquiries and requests of those who share close quarters. Shona cautiously stole glances in Taijaur's direction, but he never once looked her way.

Although it was earlier than their usual time of repose, the night had descended and they both lied down to rest in their respective places on opposite sides of the opening of the cave. Shona could see the stars already shining brightly and abundantly in the expanse of the sky. She looked over at Taijaur who was on his side, with his back to her, his arms folded across his chest.

Although he was breathing in the deep and steady rhythm of slumber, Shona could feel that he was still awake. She said in a low, barely perceptible voice, "Taijaur, at Om's house—you used to, um," she paused, and then went on in lighter faster tone, "touch me or try to touch me or at least I thought that you wanted to touch me."

Silence. No response.

Shona: "Do you remember?"

Taijaur with his back still turned to her, "I remember."

Shona: "When we came here," she paused, took a deep breath and then asked, "why did you stop?"

Without hesitation he replied, "I am waiting for you to come to me."

Shona was silent for a moment and then still speaking in a low voice, almost whispering, "How long will you wait?"

Taijaur: "As long as it takes."

Without making a sound, she moved over, reached out in the darkness and laid her hand lightly on his exposed bicep. He turned to her and pulled her into his arms, into his body. In the midst of feeling, touching, his face, lips, skin, she whispered directly into his ear, "I don't want wait anymore."

They moved into one another with no hesitation, no tentativeness, no shyness. An intense passion, need and desire came together, shutting down any and all thoughts, feelings, realities, contrary to its own intent. He touched her firmly and completely, feeling and yielding into her softness and her strength. She absorbed and possessed the power, the weight of his body as she felt his whole being come alive beneath the slow penetrating warmth of her hands. His touch was thick, solid and strong. She openly inhaled his scent and felt herself sink into a dark free-flowing oblivion. She was overcome by a rapture of liquid fluidity as strong electrified currents of energy moved between every dimension of their minds and their bodies. Deep undulating vibrations of heat and passion flowed through and between them as they moved in synch, in concert with the earth, pulling, pulling, pulling into and from the center of all that can and will be.

She felt close to exploding, with an unbearable agonizing pleasurable tension consuming her completely. Her body contracted in a tight intense tremor that she thought would never end, and then it expanded, releasing a rush of liquid fire, as her muscles shivered with release. They came together throughout the night, finally lying quietly wrapped in one another, fused with the elemental forces of the night and the wind.

She listened to him sleeping, quietly breathing in her ear. Her womb was alive and it had opened every pore, every crevice in her body. She felt the warmth of an electric vibration radiate from the base of her spine and from the center of her being. It flowed outward to every nerve ending in her body. Her heart was beating loud and strong, resounding with the rhythm of the night. She felt her soul unfold and for the first time, her life essence seeped from her core, out into world. And she knew that the only true reality was here and now, in this moment, with this man.

She looked up and saw the full moon, at first shrouded by drifting clouds that moved away to reveal its full and overpowering brilliance. She stroked and lightly ran her lips and the tip of her tongue over his arm as it lay draped across her body. She felt her body tingle and then shiver in reaction to this touch, this smell, flavor, taste, feel of Taijaur. It gave her a feeling of peace. For the first time, she knew what it was to be at home within herself; looking out into the night. Her feelings brought forth a distant memory that was out of reach, on the edge of her conscious mind. She had been here before; safe, secure and whole—watching the night.

18. The Gift

Shona awoke the next day just as the sun rose and found Taijaur sitting at the cave entrance, staring trance-like at the horizon. She came and sat quietly beside him, careful not to intrude upon his communion with the Earth's new day. Inhaling deeply, she felt her soul stretch out, touching, breathing in this sun rise, this gentle breeze, and this beautiful man wrapped in the magnificence of the warm morning light. She was completely overwhelmed by the intense sublimity of this world that graces our perception and fills our senses with the ecstasy of its existence. And for a moment she could not move. She wished that she could stay here, in this moment, in this time, in this place forever. He broke the silence without turning to see her.

Taijaur: "Shona, something is not right with Saba. I will have to leave even sooner than I originally thought."

Shona: "Is Saba ill?"

Taijaur: "Physically, I'm sure that she is fine. This feeling of unrest started a few days ago, but I wanted to continue with our training for as much as I could. But now, I can no longer ignore the sensations that are flooding my sentiale. Something is changing and I'm not sure—" he paused staring vacantly down at the ground.

Shona: "How soon will you leave?"

Taijaur: "By tomorrow morning or maybe this evening. Today. I will finish the series of forms that we are working on now. They are essential in terms of battling multiple opponents or extricating yourself from—"

Shona: "Excuse me Taijaur, I don't mean to interrupt. But can we just talk today? There are still several issues that I would like to make sure that I understand before you depart."

He rose, "We can talk as we stretch and walk. It may take a few hours for me to escort you back to Om's house and we can practice the exercises as we go." He put his hand out to pull her up. "Come on, let's begin this now and make as best use of this time as possible."

They walked down to their training site near the large outcrop of boulders, carrying with them their backpacks and all of their supplies. Taijaur began massaging Shona's shoulders from behind, while she stretched and kicked standing in place.

Taijaur: "What is it that you want to ask me?"

Shona: "I don't want you to leave without telling me more about the Ocan 'Gift'."

He hesitated before responding, moving from behind her to now face her and begin their synchronized motions. "What do you want to know that I have not already said?"

Shona: "I know that the Gift is the central part, the nucleus of all Ocan beliefs. And that it is the focal point that guides all the people's actions. Whenever Mala spoke of this Gift, she seemed to explain it differently—in a different way or even with a different meaning."

He looked away from her. "She probably explained it differently because there are various interpretations and diverse ways of understanding what the Gift is. It would require more time than we have to explain the full magnitude of our Gift.

He stopped moving and slipped the string from around his neck. "Here, look at this prism and tell me what you see."

She continued in the sequence and rhythm of their practiced routine. "I don't feel like playing any more of these staring games, Taijaur."

Taijaur: "Just look as I turn this stone from one direction to another in the sunlight, it tells a different story, conveys a different meaning depending on its angle, direction, and how the sun hits it. And when the sun goes down, the story changes again. That is the same with the Gift—multidimensional facets of one concept, one phenomenon."

Shona: "I know that it is a gift of the land, a gift that is part of the creation of this world, this universe."

He returned the string to his neck and moved back into synchrony with her. "There are some who believe that the catalyst-stone—the power source of the in-between—is the most immediate source of our Gift. In the same way that there are sacred rocks at the founding of most religions and cultures, this piece of petrified geological matter has been worshipped throughout the ages as a source of spiritual power. Perhaps humans have always sought transformation from hardened mineral mass.

As it manifests within our lives, the Gift is understood as one dimension of injera—a part of the first principle of injera to live and fulfill our purpose for being. One part of our need and need fulfillment is found in the power-offering that the Earth and even the universe as a whole bestows within us. On a fundamental basis, the Gift enhances God's ultimate gift to all living beings."

Shona: "But what is God's ultimate gift to us, to human beings specifically?"

Taijaur: "It is the same for humans as for other animals, just in different degrees, different angles." He stopped moving. "That's probably enough stretching for one day. Let's start walking. I'll explain more as we go along. Just follow the steps that I am taking and try to walk exactly as you see me doing."

Facing Shona, with his arms held out to both sides, he began a side-way walk on the balls of his feet with his knees bent into a stoop, delicately setting down each foot before lifting the other foot and setting it down crisscross behind the other leg and then swiveling around so that he faced the opposite direction and then began again with the same movements on the opposite leg. It took awhile for Shona to get into the rhythm of swooping, swiveling, at first facing one another and then turning so that their backs were to each other. She felt silly and awkward, like a bashful self-conscious adolescent trying some strange form of dance in a roomful of people who pointed and stared with derision and laughter. But when he started speaking again, she concentrated on the sound of his voice and then their 'dance' started to flow in a cadence of its own.

Taijaur: "The Gift is perception—pure and simple. True, uncensored, unadulterated perception of the soul. The ability for a living spiritual essence or soul to perceive and know the world—to see, hear, touch, smell, feel, sense life and thus form a connection with the deeper sub-structures of reality. Being alive means awareness and perception—the ability to experience and be aware of the world. Simply put—the Gift is the ability to know, understand and feel life—and not just a cognitive understanding. Rather it entails the ability to have an understanding of life's essence integrated into every movement, thought, feeling, action that you experience. And only once you receive this basic yet necessary gift are you then able to truly live and create.

All great art—music, literature, paintings, sculpture, etcetera—reflects an inherent subliminal connection with the energy of the universe. Through the gift of perception, the artist touches a deeper understanding of life that enables not only the artist, but also those who receive the art, to feel the inherent connections between all life's phenomena. The Gift provides a pathway to our own understanding, to our own ability to perceive, to understand and to feel. It is believed that each entity's gift, once it is fully realized provides one attribute or facet of the code of human existence and part of the why of the universe. Who and what we are as creative beings must have meaning outside of the roles and functions that we play in society and in the world.

Life's meaning and definition cannot be solely focused on scrambling around to eat and secure shelter and safety or a quest for greater and greater riches. Nor should it be solely centered on the ins and outs, ups and downs of human relationships and societal goals. Beyond the quest for survival and the pursuit of amusement, security, and happiness, life and living must entail creating and sharing your acts of creation. The act of creating, becoming a creator—this is what it means to be in the image of God, in the spirit of the Creator. The truest and most real forms of power exist only in and through acts of creation. A person will never be able to give complete expression to their individual gifts until they have received fully the Gift of the earth. You must know how to open your soul to receive, to understand.

The Earth is only one medium by which the universe transfers its energy. All phenomena of the universe—the galaxies, planets, nebula, stars are conduits for the transfer of the universe's energy. In striving to become beings of power, we seek to not only receive this energy but to also act as an instrument for energy transfer. This type of spiritual transformation can only take place through the process of achieving critical spiritual mass. Once critical spiritual mass has been achieved and sustained—individually and collectively—then energy transformation is initiated and from deep within your being, God moves and the power of your life is made manifest. Stored intrinsic energy is converted into realized energy enabling us to become beings of power.

The conscious pursuit of energy transfer to achieve spiritual transformation has become rare in today's world, because of most humans' waning abilities to attain and sustain spiritual mass. The substance of our spirits is depleted with daily struggles to survive in artificially contrived environments or degrading or violent environments or poverty-stricken environments—or any of the thousands of different types of negative environments in which people of today are forced to live. Our spirits are depleted by the negative noise generated by living in the constant society of others who lack spiritual focus or purpose. The primary objective of life on earth and in the universe at large is the conversion of stored energy into realized energy. This is the most fundamental of all needs and the basis of all other types of needs."

Shona: "Mala never conveyed this much detail. But isn't there more? Isn't there another part to this Gift?"

Taijaur: "Maybe Mala ran out of time. Another way to understand this same concept of spiritual transformation is that the primary need of life is to awaken to your god-consciousness, which is only achieved by way of the Gift. Sometimes this is referred to as 'heightened awareness' and is considered part of a person's 'critical spiritual mass'. Although these two concepts may be slightly different, nonetheless you can't have one without the other, so for the purposes of this discussion, we will consider them congruent terms. Once a person's god-consciousness is awakened then they necessarily move with strength, courage and conviction as opposed to the fear, confusion and anger which dominates those who exist without god-consciousness, those who live in the absence of a knowledge of their own god-power."

Shona: "But still what is the ultimate purpose of this Gift? What do you seek to achieve?"

Taijaur: "The Gift gives one increased means of perceiving the world, an enhanced form of perception. Part of the purpose in achieving god-consciousness or converting potential energy into realized energy is to develop the potential of the human mind to form new a priori structures and patterns with which to assess and understand the world; form new ways of understanding and conceiving reality.

To put it briefly—enhanced perception increases a person's ability to sustain critical spiritual mass in order to transform the potential or stored intangible energy of human beings into the kinetic or physically realized, tangible energy necessary to become beings of power. By achieving heightened levels of perception and awareness, we are able to perceive, sense, feel the world without veils. The Ocan have a greater awareness of the Gift, because we realized centuries ago the importance and magnitude of the human potential to transform, and move in harmony with the stars. Our Ocan ancestors realized that the power to move with strength and purpose fulfills a destiny that fuels the universe."

He paused and then said her name loudly before continuing in a more modulated tone, "Shona—lets stop and rest before we continue on. The old man's house is just around that bend ahead."

The cessation of movement, made Shona feel as if she had been suddenly jolted from a deep dreaming state and dropped down a dark chasm with no end. The vertigo passed quickly and everything in the terrain around her appeared vibrantly alive and alert, quivering with color and intensity. She looked around in shock. "How could we have come this far that fast? We were at least several miles away."

Taijaur offered his sly little smile. "True concentration takes you outside of time. I told you that it was a power walk. That was actually only the first stage of the exercise, but it will have to suffice for now. Let's sit over here and finish this discussion before meeting with Om. While we talk, I want you to hold this stone tightly in your fist and don't open your hand until I tell you."

He took the crystal from around his neck, placed it in her hand, wrapping the string around her wrist as they sat down side by side leaning back into the shade of an outcrop of rocks.

Taijaur: "We honor our Gift by making ourselves continually worthy of the blessing of power that has been bestowed within us; by striving to achieve the highest of that which is possible in this experience of living on this earth. By way of the Gift, we are able to experience higher forms of understanding, love and compassion."

Shona made sure to look directly into Taijaur's eyes as she posed the question whose answer she had been listening for but had not yet heard. "But what about those parts of the Ocan Gift with which you attempt to cheat human nature and tinker with God's design? What about the genetic engineering, Taijaur? Isn't that also a part of the Ocan Gift?"

Although Taijaur managed to quickly suppress his reaction, Shona had, nonetheless, glimpsed that half-second of surprise that surfaced despite his will.

He said quietly, "What do you know of that?"

Shona: "Aha, so it is true. It's not hard to figure out, once you know a little of the Ocan history before they became Ocan. Isn't that why they were so afraid to let me live? Afraid that Ocan blood mixed with that of other beings would taint their precious, artificially contrived bloodlines?"

Taijaur: "You don't understand, Shona. It is much deeper than that, there is much more to this than just genetic reengineering. Most Ocan people are not fully aware of what we speak. Because of my work, I know more than most. But you have to keep in mind that in the beginning, our people were only searching for a way to fight a virulent phage. They found over time that the only way to fight viruses is from a genetic basis. In the past, different types of genetic experiments were conducted. But that was long ago, before the danger became apparent. I have been told that the Aka and some other Ocan attempted to continue to use the experiments for other purposes—but that is just hearsay."

Shona: "What are the Ocan trying to do—engineer physical and mental modifications to create some kind of superhuman race of people?"

Taijaur: "The 'engineering' as you call it, is not accomplished by means of science alone. In some respects, the science or laboratory procedures are minimal. And over time they may even become negligible to the whole process."

Shona: "So you do admit that the Ocan have been striving to produce a whole new type of human being?"

Taijaur: "Over time any isolated environment, on its own, produces new and different traits in its inhabitants, independent of any 'tinkering'—as you call it—on the part of man. The increased energy emanations from the island and surrounding land masses have served to accelerate natural changes in the Ocan people that happened over time. You are just as much a product of these changes as all people of the Ocan. Here in this land, you can see how different we are from these people who lack many of the innate abilities that the Ocan people take for granted—abilities to see and hear more clearly, greater strength and endurance.

The Ocan people not only learned how to receive the Gift, we also soon came to understand that our island home is unique. We believe that the land and the waters that surround the island contain more of the earth's rare power spots than any of other place on the planet. The intensity of the earth's magnetic field varies in different places on its surface, with residual magnetism in rocks and magnetic anomalies in caves and other places like the ocean floors. These canyons are a weaker version of the same type of forces that are within the Ocan island. Within and beneath the Ocan island there are intensely charged electromagnetic forces that are polarized in that area. For what reason or cause, we can only guess."

Shona: "Taijaur I know all of this. Mala instructed me all of my life. Why don't you just explain what this genetic reengineering is all about? And if possible, please try to provide some iota of justification for how so abhorrent a practice can take place with a people who consider themselves to be spiritually and ethically advanced."

Taijaur: "It is the spirit of mankind that the Ocan attempt to influence, not radically change. It is a combination of factors—our isolation, the power of the island, the so-called 'genetic engineering', our minds, our sentiale—all of these variables come together to help us facilitate the collective spiritual evolution of our own people and ultimately all human beings.

You have to understand, no changes in this world, no solutions will ever persist or be effective until the fundamental spiritual essence of human beings is changed on a collective and universal level. Towards this end we attempt to cultivate the spirituality embedded in the genetic composition of human neurons and neural pathways."

Shona's eyes widened, in disbelief. "How can anything like that be even remotely possible?"

Taijaur: "Shona, you must understand—Ocan people believe in an underlying spiritual essence to all earthly phenomena, including genes, cells, molecules, and atoms. I can't explain all of the scientific details and some parts of this process are so highly secretive that I'm not sure who has been trusted with the full scope of facts. But basically, in the beginning our scientists worked to 'encourage' the genetic material of our brain tissue to form new compounds in the DNA in order to correct the genetic alterations that the phage had induced. They 'encouraged' the people's genome and epigenome to move in a particular direction of expression. But this expression of the genome and epigenome was a natural enhancement that the land itself was already developing within us. The scientists were only facilitating a naturally occurring process."

Shona: "What you mean is that your scientists manipulated the people's DNA, altering their genetic material in order to change their inherited characteristics in a predetermined way."

Taijaur: "I guess that's one way of saying it. But that is only part of the process. The other more important part of the process takes place within the sentiale pathways. We use the sentiale pathways to encourage change and development in the sentiale structure of other people's minds and souls. We go inside of their minds and their souls in order to push their spiritual essence in the path of the natural physical and spiritual evolution that would have occurred in the absence of the phage."

Shona: "First of all, I don't see how you or anyone else can presume to know what the 'natural' evolution of human beings would have been. Phage or no phage how do you know that the evolution that humans have undergone, thus far, is not entirely 'natural'?"

Taijaur: "The phage has interfered with our development in the same way that humans have interfered with the natural evolution of many plant and animal species by artificially breeding variation into their genome. If the natural evolution of other species is so easily susceptible to alteration, then why do you find it hard to believe that humans can likewise be manipulated to undergo changes that have been unnaturally induced by a foreign organism?"

Shona: "I will deal with that issue later. Another more important question is—do you expect me to believe that you can perform some magical incantation in your mind and alter what another person believes, alter another's person's mind? I have just begun to open myself to the power of the sentiale and now you tell me that its purpose is to alter or control other human beings?"

Taijaur: "No, no, no. This is an ability to bring forth a conscious recognition of the power that resides within our molecules, within our soul's essence—this skill, this knowledge, it is the land's gift to us. The pathways provide a link to our individual intrinsic energy and that of the earth and the universe at large. With the use of the earth's energy, we are able to reach through the sentiale pathways to touch the souls of other people and push them towards spiritual growth.

By using these pathways and infusing the energy from the in-between into the people's lives, we can make it possible for other people to experience the same type of spiritual evolution that the Ocan people have undergone over the last two centuries. The energy makes it possible for us to genetically transform all humankind, so that the phage can be purged from their minds and they are able to also strive to become beings of power.

This ability to heal the people of the world is part of our birthright as people of the Ocan; it is your birthright. It is this Gift that we honor and continually strive to make ourselves worthy of possessing."

Shona: "This is crazy. It just does not make sense. It is too bizarre to even fathom. Basically, you are talking about using electromagnetic radiation—either through scientific experiments or through some hocus-pocus process of using your mind—to genetically alter the human race. You want to make genetic modifications to people's brains in order to make them think and behave in the manner that you deem correct.

In the final analysis, what is this birthright, but a belief in the superiority of one group over another? This is the same age-old story that is repeated by many deluded and demented human beings who believe that they have the right to have power over other people. This is wrong no matter how you try to justify it. The Ocan in all their highly spiritual ways are no different than all the other petty humans who spend their lifetimes trying to force other people to act and believe as they do, in an effort to reinforce their own distorted notions of superiority."

Taijaur: "No, Shona, you misunderstand. The power is yours alone; each of ours alone. Through sentiale awareness we can share our understanding of the Gift with one another and thus it is possible for others to be transformed by the understanding. But each of us must first know how to open our individual souls to receive, to understand.

Beyond the readily apparent gifts of physical sustenance (food, clothing, shelter, water), the land also helps to sustain and enhance our spiritual, emotional and psychic dimensions as well. If we can view our gifts of physical sustenance as just part of what we can expect as terrestrial inhabitants, why is it so unthinkable to conceive of other gifts, other forms of sustenance that the land provides to feed our continued survival and development?

The Ocan people have learned to work through the sentiale pathways, by initiating connections between the sense perceptions of one another. This touch, contact, communication is facilitated by the chemical-electromagnetic transmissions of our bodies and brains and the underlying spiritual essence inherent in those transmissions. These signals, scents, pulses, vibrations or whatever you want to call them, are transmitted all the time, everywhere around us and within us. The Ocan people have learned how to capture them and direct them; how to follow and travel along the pathways of the signals in the same way that it is possible for scientists and doctors to track the transmissions of neuronal activity within the human brain."

Shona: "But the activities of an individual's neurons depend on direct proximity, direct contact, not contact over a distance. The internal functioning of the individual organism requires physical contact with the connected parts of the brain functioning as a medium through which the chemical signals—the neurotransmitters are sent and received. What is the medium of transmission for person to person neuronal contact?"

Taijaur: "Well, first of all, electromagnetic waves need no material medium for transmission. However, if you need something tangible in order to make this real, then think of the earth itself acting as the primary medium, except, transmission occurs not only within the pathways of the earth, but also the pathways of the air, the water, the moon, the sun, the whole world around us, even stretching out into the universe. All matter constantly interacts chemically, electromagnetically and for lack of a better word, spiritually. However, while some of these exchanges are visible to humans, many of them seem imperceptible in terms of being captured by the surface sense organs of most humans. Still, the messages are there, constantly being transmitted and received by our minds, bodies and souls. These seemingly 'invisible' or imperceptible messages are received at a lower frequency in our awareness—in the realm of the sentiale. And it is in this realm, through these pathways that the Ocan people have chosen to focus and cultivate their primary sense of reality."

Shona: "But Taijaur, beyond just the physical mechanisms by which this may or may not be accomplished, listen to what you are saying. This power you speak of is of your own individual possession, but you would use it ultimately to sway others to your worldview, to your version of what is right and real. How is this any different from the accusation that you leveled at me—trying to play God for someone else; assuming the superiority of your own way?"

Taijaur: "You are right that I would use the power to sway others, but not to my worldview; rather to awaken in them the consciousness that already resides latent within their own minds, their own psyches. One of the strongest needs of existing in this world is the need for help. We are all healers in that, in one way or another, we all help each other to survive, to grow, to become strong. The only difference with those of the Ocan is that we are conscious that the help we seek to provide will re-align the internal structures of other human beings, so that we are all in balance with the harmony of the universe's intent."

Shona: "You mean that you aim to manipulate the internal structures of other human beings."

Taijaur: "Intervention to provide unsolicited help may seem objectionable. But what alternative do we have? Do we just continue to stand by and do nothing? Should we stand by and watch humans continue to hunt and prey on one another while also destroying the earth?

To one degree or another, all living creatures of this earth manipulate the surrounding environment to their own needs. But you must also consider the environment's ability to manipulate and change the beings that populate this sphere. We strive only to work within the environment's, the land's own intent and purpose. With a sentiale link it is not possible to do anything against someone's will. We can only work with the spirits of one another. No one has the power to make another person do something that they don't want to do. The ancient Obeah were the only entities known to possess that kind of power and they are no longer alive."

Shona: "But your scientists take this one step further by manipulating the needs of chemical, biological, and genetic processes. They interrupt their need fulfillment cycles all to their own ends; ultimately creating what must be viewed as artificially contrived means of fulfillment."

Taijaur: "It is a mere exchange of information that they encourage—a lone whisper of change in a vast sea of alterations, modifications and adaptations. All life forms exchange genetic information, share their DNA with one another. We embed a mere whisper. We listen to this process of life and strive to aid its self-realization; we help to encourage the expression of its true nature, its ultimate design."

Shona: "But how can you presume to know what the ultimate design of human nature should be?"

Taijaur: "Beneath all that humankind aspires to attain there is an eternal quest for new ways of seeing and knowing; new ways of understanding and conceiving reality. Within our cells, the molecules of our existence, there is a tremendous potential for the human mind to develop new *a priori* structures and patterns with which to assess the world. This is the development, progress, and evolution of the human spirit for which mankind hungers.

There is more to this than I have the time to go into now. And I'm sorry, but we don't have much time left. If you have other issues that you want to address, you should do so now."

Shona blew her breath out in exasperation, but continued on, "The villagers tell a story about an invasion that happened long ago and a community of people who mysteriously disappeared. Those were the Ocan people, weren't they?

Taijaur: "Yes, those were our ancestors, our founders. In fact, many of these villager's religious beliefs are based on Ocan principles of faith. Although they have interpreted some of our doctrine within the context of their own understanding, such as the Ocan belief in the emissary has been interpreted by these people as their 'savior'."

Shona: "Am I to understand that all of the Ocan people escaped from the compound the night that the soldiers attacked and then traveled in mass to an uninhabited island hundreds of miles away?"

Taijaur: "More or less, that is how it happened, except for some minor details; such as the fact that many of the people had already departed the mainland and gone to the island before that night. This was a plan that was in its final stages of execution. But that story is too long to go into now."

Shona: "It is ironic to think that I came to this land to get as far away from the Ocan people as I could get, and here I end up right in the center of their origins. And to think that some of these villagers naïvely believe that they trespass sacrilegiously on the graves of sainted beings. Can you at least say how such a mass exodus was even possible?"

Taijaur: "Many parts of this story are shrouded in secrecy. However, having pieced together information from a number of different sources including some explanations of supernatural phenomena from the Book of Change, I believe that I have come up with some plausible theories of what may have occurred. I think that the ancient Obeah used the powers of the in-between to protect the people and move them out of the mainland. The tunnels and passageways of the in-between are more complex and more extensive than anyone could have ever imagined. They lead to and provide passage to all land masses on the planet and they even exist beneath the ocean floor. I think these passageways provided the means for the ancient Obeah to travel back and forth between different lands. And this may also be the way that the Ocan people were able to escape from the mainland."

Shona: "How were the soldiers killed, especially considering that they showed no signs of violence on their bodies?"

Taijaur: "This part of the story is more hidden than all the rest; mainly because it deals with some of the more terrifying powers of the in-between. But I believe that the ancient Obeah also used the powers of the in-between to destroy the soldiers."

Shona: "But how——?"

Taijaur: "I'm sorry, but I can't share any other details at this point. However, I can tell you that this incident was the one of main reason that the ancient Obeah sealed the world's portals. They wanted to ensure that what happened that night in the compound would not ever happen again. They wanted to make sure no other humans have access to that level of power. The moral implications of this episode in our history are still a matter of contention for many Ocan people. What other questions do you have?"

Shona: "What about the diamond that the Ocan stole—the 'Eye' that the people refer to? This 'Eye' is supposedly larger and of more value than any other riches or any other object of worth on this earth. In all the histories that the Ocan people tell, somehow this major theft is never divulged. Why did the Ocan people take this Eye and why have you not mentioned this?"

Taijaur: "I have mentioned it. It is what I have been talking about all along. And the Ocan people did not steal it; it belongs to us or rather it belongs to the island. What these people call the 'Eye' is what the Ocan know as the catalyst-stone, the most essential part of the power source of the in-between. But the people here know only about this fragment piece—the catalyst. They are unaware of the actual rock which is many times larger than the fragment that they refer to. And they are unaware that it is this larger stone, not just the fragment piece, that is 'The Eye'.

The full name of the complete stone is 'The Eye of the World'. But it was originally called, 'The Eye of God' or rather more correctly, 'The I of God'—as in the first person pronoun of 'me'. 'The I' is what we are seeking in order to re-set the balance of power in the world. The people of this land know only this fragment piece as a sacred rock that causes healing miracles to occur. They have no idea of its true power or intent. The stolen gemstone of the villagers' story, the one over which the war was waged, is a piece of the original stone which was excavated by the Obeah of centuries ago. The entire rock is a rare red-black diamond, a fractal crystal, the only one of its kind in existence. It is this fragment that is the catalyst that must be joined with the original stone in order to initiate the necessary transfer of energy from the power source of the in-between."

Shona: "I don't understand. What does that mean to be the 'eye' or the 'I' of God?"

Taijaur: "According to the ancient Obeah, the word 'Eye' is simply used as a metaphor for perception, whereas 'I' in this context is understood as an individual's awareness of possessing a personal consciousness. It is an Ocan belief that once a person reaches the stage of possessing a true sense of personal consciousness, then they also gain an awareness of God within themselves. Thus, the expression 'The I of God' indicates a personal consciousness and awareness of God within yourself.

In the other sense, the 'Eye' of God, denotes the act of perceiving and understanding God. The catalyst, once combined with the power source provides the means by which humans are able to see God (seeing his essence through the gateway of his eye) and also the means by which God knows, sees and watches the world. It is said that the stone represents and actually brings about an awareness, perception and consciousness of God within each individual who is able to reach this level of spiritual transformation. This awareness of and ability to perceive God is the catalyst or means by which the power source is activated."

Shona: "But this power source—isn't it suppose to emit electromagnetic radiation?"

Taijaur: "Yes, the Eye of the World, the power source of the in-between— it is a naturally occurring nuclear reactor that has the potential to blow this planet into oblivion. But it is also a stone that gives us the power to transform and bring forth the highest form of spiritual awareness that is possible in this realm of existence. The physical reality of this phenomenon is so intricately linked with its underlying spiritual essence that we cannot reach the in-between just by physically going into the labyrinth where it resides.

We know very little of its composition and nature, but according to some passages in the Book, the power source of the in-between may possess the same type of energy as that which powers the stars. We believe that the power source is a stone or another such material that may be capable of initiating the same nuclear fusion that powers the sun. It creates storms of energized particles—electrons and electrically-charged gas driven by magnetic fields. Minute traces of this energy are constantly seeping through the cracks and fissures within the earth into the minds and bodies of all terrestrial inhabitants. While the 'right' amount can enhance our cognitive abilities and overall development, we are not sure what effect too much of the energy may have on the world and the people in it.

The ancient Obeah discovered that this power source, the I/Eye of the World, had multiple purposes. Not only is it a naturally occurring thermonuclear reactor, but it can also change/effect the molecular structure of matter and the inherent composition of other forms of energy. And because a part of the underlying essence of sentience is generated from electromagnetic radiation, it is the root cause of our people's enhanced sentiale abilities.

The ancient Obeah thought that by taking a piece of the rock with them they could use its power for good in our world. But they did not realize that substances created in the nether realm of the in-between can not fully manifest their true intent in our material existence. Although they were able to use the Eye to change energy patterns within human beings (by disrupting, absorbing or deflecting certain chemical and electromagnetic bodily responses), over time they learned that the power in the crystal fragment had become warped once it entered the dimensions of a material reality. Once they realized this, they attempted to return it to the in-between and at the same time they sealed all the portals across the globe. Our histories tell us that the Obeah were apparently unable to re-unite the fragment piece with the mother stone. And unfortunately, they were not able to make it back to our world or they chose not to return.

The old man and I have begun translating passages in the third part of the Book that indicate the possibility that the radioactive nuclear waste generated from the ancient Obeah's use of this fragment stone may have been a source of contamination that caused the virus to thrive. This extraction of the catalyst-stone from the Eye may have contributed to the imbalance of energy in the world, thus allowing negative forces to gain dominance. But to be sure, it will take further study to connect these passages in the third book to passages in the other two books. So at this point, this particular clue or finding is not conclusive."

He stopped talking and they both sat quietly absorbing the warmth of the day, wrapped in the buzzing stillness of the air around them. Shona suddenly stood and began moving, pacing with a barely constrained feeling of vigor and might and power. Taijaur looked at her inquisitively. "How do you feel?"

She smiled broadly, jumping and moving in the sequence of their practiced routine. "How do I feel? I feel great! I feel powerful, like I could run, leap, fly to any mountaintop. This day is beautiful, inspiring. I feel like the sun is inside of me and striving to shine through me."

She was twirling around now, dancing with the powerful movements that she had been taught in the training exercises.

Taijaur: "Open your hand."

She stopped short. "What?"

Taijaur: "Open your hand, the one with the crystal."

She had forgotten about the prism that she still clutched tightly in her fist. Her fingers creaked open slowly, arthritically bent and reluctant to move. It was if fire leapt from the end of her arm—a huge orange flame with bright iridescent rainbow rays of light shot into the air and bounced off their faces, bodies and the rocks that surrounded them. The stone fell from her hand, dangling from the string wrapped at her wrist and the flame subsided, the prism resuming its normal refraction of the light.

Shona: "What kind of stone is this? What caused that to happen?"

Taijaur: "It isn't the stone. It's you. You caused it to happen. How do you feel now?"

She was still holding her arm out, staring at the now normal-looking crystal swinging from her wrist. She had no way to account for the sudden lack of energy and the sinking emotions that she was beginning to feel as she mumbled, "Fine. I feel fine."

Taijaur: "But what did you feel in the moment that the light shone forth?"

Shona: "Taijaur, I don't know what just happened, but I am not going to be some little experiment for you. I said that I feel fine. Here take your toy." She uncoiled the string and thrust the crystal into his hand.

Shona: "Are there any other explanations of this Ocan Gift? Perhaps some more secret elements?"

She made sure, once again, to look directly into his eyes as she asked her question. But this time he was ready for her and there was no way to read through the expression-less shield that guarded any opening into his thoughts. He rose to his feet and stood beside her as he slipped the necklace over his head.

Taijaur: "Nope, that's it. It seems that you have unearthed and ferreted out all the Ocan secrets. You now know more than most Ocan people about the Gift, both its overt and hidden features. Only a select few have been so privileged. This is why it is even more important for you to join with me.

Don't you see Shona? Our differences as Ocan people—our enhanced abilities make our responsibilities in this world all the greater. In addition to these enhanced abilities, you and I together possess a combined form of knowledge and talents that make us uniquely suited to help carry out the mission, the purpose of the Ocan people. If we choose to withhold our gifts and not act on behalf of all that is good and right, then negative forces may continue to disrupt the balance of spiritual energy in the world and mankind will spiral even further into a self-imposed annihilation. Human beings will continue to manifest the will and the ignorance to destroy the earth and all of its inhabitants.

With each generation of Ocan we have honed the power, the knowledge that the land gives to us, so that one day we can share our Gift with the civilizations of this world. All the signs—everything that is written and has occurred—point to the fact that the day we have waited for has arrived and it is now time to move forward into our destiny. There is no one else who can lead this charge, but you and I. I can not do this alone Shona. I need your help. I need you."

Shona: "But what if you don't find the Emissary? How will you be able to enter the in-between? Didn't you say that the Emissary is necessary in order to fully access the power source and re-set the balance of energy?"

Taijaur: "I believe that I have already found the person meant to serve as emissary."

She restrained her urge to inquire when, where, how such an individual had been identified, stating only, "Then you don't need me. Your mission has been accomplished."

Taijaur: "I would like to believe that all parts of my mission have met with success."

For a moment, she felt herself breathing in a sudden and inexplicable sense of fear. She closed her eyes and steadied her breathing to push it away. She looked down at the ground, averting her eyes from his intense stare. "I'm sorry Taijaur, but I can't go with you. My place is here—in this land, with these people. But if—," she lowered her voice and said quickly, "If you feel so strongly that we are meant to be together, then why not stay here with me in this land?" She hoped that the pleading undertone in her voice was evident to her ears alone. He pulled her close and held her tight for only a moment.

Taijaur: "Goodbye Shona. Our destiny is with the Ocan. Our place is with our people. If you change your mind, you know how to find me."

She watched him pick up his bag, preparing to depart. Shona struggled against the impulse to reach out to him, the need to touch him, as she replied softly, "And you know how to find me."

Taijaur: "Indeed, I do."

He put his bag over his shoulder, turned away from her and without looking back even once, he walked out of her life.

19. To What End?

"Make no mistake—we are not requesting anything of you. We are merely informing you of our intent. Either you will comply with what we have outlined or you will suffer the consequences of noncompliance."

The belligerent large muscular man at the front the Aka delegation was the first and only one to speak, while the other seven stood to one side, periodically whispering among themselves. The noisy over-crowded central hall of the Maja had become instantly and completely quiet as soon as this group of five men and three women had filed into the room. From his spot on the first level balcony, Alor observed that the Aka were all dressed exactly alike with the same type of clothing as the Ocan, but their loose-fitting cotton pants were tucked into black boots that came to mid-calf. And on top of their tunic shirts they wore black vests made of some type of mesh synthetic material that, Alor surmised, functioned as body armor. Curiously, they wore black headbands made of the same mesh armor material. The thin blue sashes tied low around each of their waists, apparently served as holsters, holding in place small daggers on the left sides of each of their bodies. This was not only the first Aka delegation to ever come before the Council of Elders, this was also the first time that any Aka had openly entered the Ocan village in over five decades.

Alor had just returned from an exhausting three day trip to the eastern hamlets and he had hoped, in vain, to rest before this meeting began. But the Council of Elders had declared that all adults from the Ocan-main must be present. He wasn't sure if his visit with Amira had yielded anything useful or not. She remembered bits and pieces of Kalal's ramblings, but it wasn't enough to draw any firm conclusions. Alor was pondering how much longer he should go on chasing this mystery of a phantom image from an old man's uncontrolled mind wanderings when he looked up and saw the small dark woman at the rear of the Aka delegation looking directly at him.

She had been the last to enter the room, with her quick sharp way of walking and moving. As soon as Alor saw her, he immediately sensed that this was the same person that he saw with Taijaur those many months ago in the western mountains. Hadn't Taijaur said that she was from the Shinhala village? Although on that past occasion, he had only glimpsed her briefly, there was something about her demeanor that made him certain that this was the same woman. The woman spoke to no one and stood a little a part from her comrades. She was silent, observant, looking around the room and up to the balconies, studying the people in the crowd. For a few seconds, Alor and the woman made and sustained eye contact. And then she moved her icy defiant stare away from him and continued to scan the room. He had only seen her from a distance before and had not looked fully into her face. But now he took his time studying her cool sharp features and he could sense that she was aware of his scrutiny. Something in her face looked familiar to Alor—was it her facial structure? The square strong jaw line? The eyes, the nose? Maybe it was just the intensity of her stare.

Another smaller rostrum had been built in the central hall like the one in the council chambers, so that the Elders now sat elevated above the standing crowd. Gone were the days of the Elders sitting on a low bench with the people gathered around, sitting on the floor. Today everyone stood and Alor could see in their strained, fearful faces that he was not the only one who longed for the ways of yesteryears. This meeting had been in session for almost an hour now and there was still no perceivable progress. The Elders and this boisterous, bellicose leader of the Aka kept going round and round the same issues. The Aka were openly demanding rights to the mineral deposits and the geothermal resources in the western mountain project sites. They were resisting all of the Elders attempts to negotiate the matter.

As Alor watched the small Aka woman at the rear of the delegation, he began to slowly realize that she was periodically sending subtle hand signals to that loud obnoxious man who presented himself as the leader of their delegation. After each statement of significance from the Elders, before the man offered a response he made a quick surreptitious side-ways glance in the direction of the woman's hands which she held loosely and inconspicuously by her sides. Alor was pleasantly surprised at his own discovery that it was this woman who led and manipulated these proceedings. And he was confident that, with the exception of those in the Aka party, not one other person at this meeting realized what was going on.

Rainar: "Belar, our most esteemed kinsman, you must realize that we cannot permit you or your colleagues to take possession of these project sites that we have worked so hard to develop and maintain. These resources are being developed for the benefit of all Ocan people, including the Aka if certain, uh, conditions, are first taken into consideration. Surely you can understand and see that there is nothing to be gained by forcefully imposing yourselves on our work."

Belar, the Aka spokesperson responded with a challenging smirk, "And what will you do to stop us?"

Elder 3: "This is outrageous! You are requesting or rather telling us to clear out of our own work sites, our own land."

Elder 1: "But you have no right, no justifiable, legal or moral claim to these resources. This is our work, completed by the Ocan people. You can't just claim that you are entitled to take it."

Belar: "The Aka possess the rights to not just the minerals, but to the portal that we know that you are exploiting in a cave of the western mountain area that you call the Lane."

A loud murmur of confusion, surprise and alarm went up in the crowd of Ocan people, the majority of whom were hearing for the first time of the presence of a portal.

Belar continued talking loudly over top of the noise, "This land was ours before you chose to try to make everyone bend to your way, your perspective of life. We, the Aka, were here first. Don't forget that a member of the Basau family discovered this island. And the first original founder of the Ocan collective was that same member of the Basau family."

Rainar: "Those matters of opinion are in dispute. We have no proof of which founder can be declared, the 'first original founder'. And besides that point seems irrelevant at this time."

Elder 2: "This is an ancient feud that began before our ancestors even came to this land. But you know, as we all know, that our founders along with the Obeah judged this Basau forefather that you speak of as unfit for leadership. They voted and ruled against the goals that this, umm, predecessor of yours chose to pursue; those same goals that apparently the present day Aka continue to hold as paramount to your cause."

Belar: "If our forefathers had not departed the mainland so hastily and if we had more time to show the people the truth of our ways, then this day may be played out very differently. And I would be sitting where you now sit, *Mistress Rainar.*"

Rainar overlooked the dripping sarcasm and derision in Belar's pronunciation of her title and name, as she tried once again to mediate the discussion. "This is all such ancient history. Let the past rest. Let us deal with where we are now in this present reality. Now let's—"

Belar interrupted her, "You don't dare allow the histories to be revealed as they actually occurred. You know full well that you give your people a corrupted version of the facts."

Rainar hoped that by continuing to ignore this Aka man's accusations that she could lead the conversation towards a peaceful outcome. "I realize that the Aka desire to be recognized as a sovereign state. And perhaps that is the best place for us to begin negotiations on this matter. I know we have seemed implacable on this subject in the past, but we are actually quite willing to open a dialogue to explore feasible options of how this may be achieved."

Belar: "We neither need nor desire any form of recognition or blessing from the Ocan. We determine our own sovereignty and anything else that we may require. This Council of Elders is an illegal institution existing on a corrupt foundation. And as far as we are concerned, all you Ocan can go to hell!"

Odar jumped forward from the crowd into the empty space of the middle floor occupied by the Aka alone. His brother tried to hold him back, but Odar would not be contained as he shouted to Belar, "How dare you disrespect the Elders of our Council in this manner? I don't care what kind of rights or privileges that you think that you have or how many daggers you and your entourage possess, you cannot come into our halls of justice and show such insolence to our esteemed leaders."

Belar, with his arms crossed over his barrel chest, bellowed back at him, "Sit down, little boy!" When he saw that Odar stood his ground, staring at the older and significantly larger man with a stony defiance, Belar adopted a falsely pacifying tone and said "Oh, pardon me, I meant to say, '*young man.*'"

He and the other Aka, except for the woman at the end, laughed aloud, as Belar then malevolently stared at Odar, teasing, taunting, gleefully baiting him and daring him to move or strike.

Odar stood in check, eventually returning to his place next to Kedar at the front of the crowd as Belar turned his attention back to Rainar. "All along you have attempted to control us, holding us back by reminding us of your majority population. But now the tables are nearly turned and you may not long be able to claim such dominance. The balance of might will soon be in our favor. Even now our numbers are as great as or greater than your own. And when you consider those of your people who secretly and openly concur with our principles, our beliefs, then our numbers become even greater than those of the Ocan people. And if the numbers are not enough to persuade you, then, we have other means at our disposal—other means that may potentially lessen your numbers even more."

The Aka men and women looked at one another, chuckling and smirking. A tall Haman villager with a head full of thick white hair, moved forward from the front of the crowd to address the council. He was well-known to many of the people of the Ocan-main and they were curious to hear what this normally reticent man would say.

He began, "Elders," and then turned to glance at those standing on either side of where he stood, "people of the Ocan, let us consider all sides of these issues. While the Ocan people may have worked to develop the resources, still the Aka only request that which is fair and right. This island belongs equally to all who inhabit it and we must learn to share of its resources in an equitable manner. The Aka must be given what is theirs and—"

Lonau, Kalal's partner from the old days and grandfather of Saba's current apprentice, interrupted shouting down, leaning over the first floor balcony railing, "You, Jhirai, Haman-man, you dare to appear to broker a peace, when you come here this day in the company of these Aka thugs!! All these years you have walked among us a trusted friend, while all along you have secretly flouted Ocan law and spied on behalf of the Aka."

Jhirai: "I, as with all Haman, remain neutral as always. We do not take sides in these disputes between the Ocan Elders and the Aka. I am merely attempting to facilitate these proceedings and to help to bring about peaceful resolution to any conflicting perspectives."

A faceless voice from the back of the crowd yelled out, "Do you deny that you are an envoy to the Aka as the rumors have told?"

Jhirai: "No, I deny nothing. However, but you must understand that we, the Haman, also believe that it is time for the Ocan Elders to redress the wrongs that have been perpetrated against our community as well."

Rainar: "What wrongs do you speak of?"

Jhirai: "Well, for one thing, we feel that we are being deployed in a fashion akin to 'slave' labor as we provide but receive no compensation for the abundant water resources that we pump into to the Ocan main and all the other outlying villages. We maintain all the aqueducts and systems of water transport as well as the plumbing systems. The Haman people provide above and beyond what all the other combined villages contribute to Ocan society."

Rainar: "Jhirai, need we remind you that the Haman village is only a satellite outpost of this main village and that it was your predecessors who volunteered to form this 'colony' for the benefit of all Ocan? The Ocan villages live in a balance of reciprocity, of mutual benefit to all members of our collective. All the Ocan villages serve a unique function in order to provide services for the whole. None of us receive compensation. Such a concept is not a part of our community, not a part of our plan. We have an equitable system for the division of labor and resources. The Sakai on the eastern shore provide necessary sea vegetation and food for all five Ocan villages. Do you hear them complaining or demanding compensation? Or the Shinhala, Aymarra—"

Belar: "Enough!! We are not interested in your petty inter-village squabbles. Forget all of this nonsense that serves only to distract from more important issues, such as the fact that your people not only dominate the resources of this land, but you also plan to forcefully occupy the Aka villages."

Rainar: "Why, that is preposterous! I have no knowledge of any such plans. Why would we even attempt such a useless maneuver?"

Belar: "You dare feign innocence, when even now as you speak, your people prepare for war?"

Elder 2: "War? We know nothing but peace. You know that. All Aka know that. Violence of any kind violates our principles, our founding creed."

Belar: "You steal from us and yet you attempt to maintain an appearance of moral superiority. You spy on us and lie to us. Why should we believe anything that you say? We know that your Master Edise has amassed troops and weapons for the purpose of invading the Aka people."

All eyes turned to Edise who sat with the Elders at the rostrum, expressionless staring straight ahead, never deviating from his normal demeanor of haughty disdain.

Belar: "Be advised that you would be ill-served in any attempt to execute any such aggressive act." As he spoke, he stared at Edise, who never turned his head and never looked at anyone but Rainar and above the heads of the people in the crowd.

Elder 3: "There must be some mistake; some misunderstanding. We would never attack the Aka or anyone. At any time you are welcome to come back into our society, and we would completely overlook any past, umm, indiscretions. It would be suicidal for any of us to ever think of harming the other. You are a part of us; the Aka, all the Aka are our own kind."

Belar: "We claim no such kinship or affinity. And there has been no mistake or misunderstanding. Years ago you cut off our water supply and had little to no concern as to how we would survive. You cannot presume moral superiority or make any claim to kinship when such an unconscionable and unforgivable act of malice is a part of your history."

A small gasp and murmur went through the crowd when Belar mentioned the water supply. Rainar looked pointedly at Elder 3 and then back to the Aka, "Elders let us cease this discussion for the time being. Master Belar, while we deny vehemently any prospect of an Ocan attack on the Aka, and we further do not concede to any of the, um, requests that you have made before this body, nonetheless, you have brought us much that we need to consider today. If you and you compatriots don't mind, this Council would like to take a brief recess to confer on all that you have presented. A meal has been prepared on your behalf in one of our main family homes. They will see to your comfort."

Belar: "It is in the best interest of your people that this matter be resolved quickly. We advise you not to take too long considering these matters. Our offer will stand for only a limited amount of time. This Haman man," pointing to Jhirai, "will serve as envoy to convey any messages that you might have."

No one made a sound, as the Aka exited, in the same single file order in which they had arrived with Belar in the lead. At the last minute, just before she went out of the door, the small woman at the rear of the group glanced back at Alor. The instant their eyes met, the knowledge came to him. He knew exactly why she looked so familiar. He was surprised that he had not detected such a strong resemblance before. The similarities were so striking, that there was no doubt as to her bloodline. They could even be brother and sister, or mother and son. Anyone seeing them side by side would have to know instantly that this woman and Taijaur were undoubtedly blood relatives.

Rainar put up her hand, signaling the people to be quiet as she waited for the sign from the sentry at the door that the Aka had been led far away from the Maja. She then gestured to the sentry to escort Jhirai out of the room and secure the doors with one person on guard outside. All at once there was a buzz of angry voices, as everyone began speaking at once, some shouting to the Elders, others whispering among themselves.

Lonau: "Why were we not told that work was being conducted on a portal? How is it that the Aka knew of this most important of discoveries before the people of the Ocan?"

Elder 4: "There is a spy among us, no doubt."

Stray voices from all levels of the central hall began shouting questions.

"What is this about Edise and weapons?"

"How could a member of the Ocan betray—"

"Why this was this secret kept from our people?"

"Is it true that their water was cut off?"

"Surely our people could not have been so cruel."

Rainar banged her gavel. "People, people, people. Please. Let us leave these lesser matters for another day, another time. We must now focus on how to remedy the problems at hand. Although I am confident that there is no possibility of true harm or danger from the Aka, nonetheless we will need to evacuate this main village in order to ensure—"

Once again worried voices filled the room. Rainar banged her gavel. "People, people. Quiet please. We must remain calm. The important thing is to remain calm. We will not consider this an evacuation per se, but rather a temporary re-location so that we can better secure the main village while we assess this current situation and the feasible options that we have at our disposal. The other villages should be safe. The land that the Aka are demanding are only near or a part of the main village.

We will not begin the re-location until two or three days, so you will have adequate time to gather your things and secure your homes. In that time, we will continue to try to negotiate with the Aka. They have lived separately from us for this past half century and there has been no attack, no violence what so ever, nor any talk of violence before now. And they have not actually threatened to do us harm. They would not have waited all these years to now try to attack us. I do not believe that they mean to bring us harm. I repeat, the Aka present no real danger, thus there is no reason for alarm.

However, we must still take every precaution to secure this village. Therefore, we will use the evacuation plan that Kedar devised for other purposes. Some of you will be re-located to the other villages and some of you will go to the eastern hamlets. We don't want anyone inadvertently hurt or in the way while we work to find a resolution to this dilemma with the Aka. At all costs, we must avoid direct confrontation or any potential for armed conflict. We will also send our own delegation to the Aka village. After all these people who present themselves here today, may not in fact represent the will of the Aka people."

A voice in the crowd shouted, "Someone must send for the Obeah. They must be told. They must help us. They have to see that we need help."

Rainar: "The Obeah have been informed. We are awaiting their arrival."

As Rainar continued outlining the evacuation plan, Alor watched Saba signal from across the room to Mala and Olana before exiting out of a side door of the Maja. They both followed her out, but Mala stopped to tap Layal on the shoulder, gesturing for her to come as well. Alor was tempted to follow the women and see if Saba might now be persuaded of how important it was to give him Taijaur's notes and papers, for safe-keeping, if not anything else. But he knew he had to stay, if only to provide a sane voice to counter any outrageousness that Rainar or Edise might put forward. Saba was still denying knowledge of any such notes, but Alor knew her too well to believe this obvious deception. And he could understand her loyalty to Taijaur, as well as her fear on his behalf. But these were dire and desperate circumstances that were now exacerbated by these threats from the Aka. He made up his mind to call on Saba as soon as this meeting adjourned.

By the time, Mala and Layal came outside, Saba was no where to be seen, only Olana was waiting for them. A tall thin young man came rushing out of the door behind Mala, accidentally stumbling into both Layal and herself. "Oh, excuse me. I'm, I'm, I'm sorry."

Mala smiled and then left Layal whispering with the young man, as she approached Olana. Olana began speaking without looking at Mala, staring blankly ahead into the marketplace. "No matter what happens, our people always seem to believe that the Obeah will save us. Those old souls live so far away in the mountains, it will take forever for anyone to travel there and then bring them back. No one has even seen the Obeah in years. They may all be dead for all that we know."

Mala: "Oh, they are very much alive, or at least two of them are."

Olana, surprised, turned to look at Mala, "Have you seen them? Is that where you go when you disappear for so long? Saba thinks that you have a secret lover that you keep slipping off to see."

Mala smiled slightly, "Never mind all of that, Olana. Where is Saba? And what does she require of us at this time?"

Olana pointed towards the marketplace where they could see Saba at the far end of stalls walking in the direction opposite her home. Mala stared at Saba with a look of apprehension.

Mala: "Did she say where she was going?"

Olana: "No. She wants us to go to her home to make healing potions and supplies in preparation for any potential evacuation. She said that we should begin without her; that she has some business to take care of and she will meet us at her home in about an hour." She pointed back towards the Maja. "This meeting will probably continue for some time and regardless of how this matter with the Aka is resolved, she says that it is important that the medicinal supplies be available."

Olana watched her aunt's departing form and as the Saba was almost out of sight, she sighed as she said, "The eternal sorrow of womankind. I have lately begun to wonder what brings forth all these sad women in various stages of anguish and despair. Over and over again, in each generation, each time."

Mala nodded slightly with understanding glancing and a facial expression that conveyed resigned sad consensus, but she made no response as Layal joined them and they started walking along the path to the Saba's home. The young girl hugged her shawl tightly around herself as she continuously turned and stole glances back to the young man who trailed at a distance behind the women, ducking behind houses and trees in his vain attempt to remain concealed.

Mala: "I am worried about Saba. There is something that calls to her—something powerful and very much beyond her control."

Olana: "Mala, what is it that troubles the Saba so deeply? Each day she seems more melancholy than the day before."

Mala: "If she didn't allow it to drag her under so thoroughly, the melancholy could lead her to new ways of seeing and understanding life and the world around us. However, at this point, Saba needs to go back and re-align her faith with her calling."

Olana: "But re-aligning her faith doesn't seem to explain the malaise that hangs over her."

Mala: "Saba's malaise and most people's emotional states of depression stem from unfulfilled spiritual needs; a lack of fulfillment that injera requires. She is exhausted spiritually and physically by the presence of negative realities. There is a sense of despair and hopelessness that comes with the pervasiveness of negative realities, which makes the Saba feel helpless, powerless to fight back. This hopelessness leads to sickness and despair, just as an inordinate sense of fear leads to chronic illness. The end result of all of this hopelessness, helplessness and fear is a blocked sentiale. Saba has stymied her soul's ability to allow self-healing to flow through her sentiale pathways; the self-healing that comes by way of receiving the Gift.

When I say that Saba must realign her faith with her calling, what I mean is that she has to, once again, learn how to believe in her own ability to both accept and affect the realities of this world. Saba must ultimately find her way back to her own inherent power in order to absorb and deflect the impact of evil and all the other myriad sources of negative realities. Vibrations like sound waves are inherent in every action, every movement on this earth. Only by way of a strong sentiale are we able to conquer the negative vibrations that assault our bodies and souls. We must ultimately allow the evil to carve deeper places in our ways of understanding, while also fighting off its ability to control or consume us. This is why we must cultivate our gifts, because only the Gift can protect us from the negative destructive energy that is attracted to unfulfilled spiritual needs. "

Layal: "Excuse me, pardon me Olana, Mistress Mala. I don't mean to interrupt, but shouldn't we be arming ourselves; looking for ways to protect ourselves? I mean, these Aka people seem pretty serious in terms of their intent. I know our ways are more peaceful, but we can't just lay down and be slaughtered. My father says—"

Mala: "Don't worry Layal. We will be ready for any trouble that crosses our path. As long as we keep our minds and bodies strong, and as long as we stay constantly prepared to rise to whatever the occasion demands, then we never have to worry about future uncertainty."

Layal, looked behind her nervously, "Well, if you don't mind—I mean, since the Saba is not here—I, I—"

Mala: "Go ahead Layal, you can walk with your sweetheart. I have something that I need to discuss with Olana anyway."

Layal beamed, "Thank you!" she rushed back to the young man who was still trailing at a distance.

Olana: "What can we do about all this dissension with the Aka?"

Mala: "Life goes on Olana, no matter what. Let's try not to think about it too much. These matters are outside of our control right now. On another note, I have been meaning to speak with you privately for some time. Have you ever wondered where the ideas for your paintings originate? And the feelings that produce them? Have you ever thought about what your paintings may tell you about the substructures of our waking reality?"

Olana turned sharply and looked at Mala, "I don't understand what you mean. What can my paintings tell me about any realities, waking or otherwise?"

Mala: "Do you remember how old you were when you started drawing?"

Olana: "I started painting in the temple caverns when Saba took me there as a young girl."

Mala: "But when did the images first start coming to you?"

Olana: "When I was about eight years old. It was during the time when my father took so long returning from the western forest and we thought that he was lost for good."

Mala: "Have you ever wondered what happened to him and how he was able to not only survive, but make it back to the settlements?"

Olana: "I—I'm not sure. One time my mother mentioned something about the place where my father's mind was captured. But she never gave any details or said anymore about it."

Mala: "I believe that Kalal found a gateway to the in-between in the western forest. At the time that this occurred, I was too weak to realize what was going on. But over the years, as I thought more about it, and then something that Alor said once made me finally put it all together. Kalal, either knowingly or inadvertently, went through a portal those many years ago when he escorted me back to the western forest. It didn't occur to me then that forces that I had been exposed to all of my life might prove harmful to Kalal. I don't believe that his sentiale was strong enough to carry him through and allow him to return. Kalal's mind lacked the cohesion necessary to make it to the other side of the in-between. But nonetheless, something happened to pull him back."

Olana: "But how would that have been possible? There would have been no one there who could have helped him."

Mala: "Do you remember that ancient Obeah belief, that we have all been taught, about the in-between being accessible purely by way of a person's sentiale—the ability to travel the sentiale pathways of the Earth by means of your mind and spirit alone? Well, I believe that Kalal was pulled back through a sentiale connection stronger than what he alone could have initiated. I believe that someone pulled Kalal out of the in-between by way of the sentiale pathways and guided him back to the Ocan villages. At first I thought it was Amira. But she was not strong enough. There was someone else; someone who possessed an immense power. Kalal would have died in that nether-realm, if he had not been pulled back. So, this person, undoubtedly saved his life. However, in the same way that pulling someone from a dreaming state can lead to imbalance and disease, Kalal came back with his sentiale damaged and only part of his mind-soul still vested in this world."

Olana was breathing hard and talking fast, "The person who pulled him back—if it was not my mother, it must have been Saba."

Mala: "I don't think that Saba was strong enough either."

Olana, now visibly upset, her voice quivering in response. "Well, I don't know who it could have been. Can't we talk about something else, Mala? This is making me feel—uncomfortable."

Mala: "I'm sorry Olana, I know how painful your father's condition was to you. But just one last thing—have you ever looked at your paintings and wondered why you see images and visions that don't come from the world we know? Have you ever tried to understand that part of your soul that strives to create and bring forth a reality that is hidden from our surface perception?"

Olana: "I, I—"

Mala: "Never mind, Olana. We can speak of this some other time."

Their conversation ended abruptly as they came in sight of Saba's home and Layal ran to catch up with them, her male friend still lurking behind watching her. When they entered the house, Mala immediately began stoking the fire and putting the kettle on while Layal and Olana started pulling out bags of herbs along with various equipment and supplies.

Olana seemed irritable and uneasy as she asked, "Do either of you know what we are supposed to do? Saba gave no specific instructions. Each time that I helped in the past, I only followed what Saba told me to do."

Mala smiled at Layal with encouragement, nodding for her to respond.

Layal spoke up nervously, "I know what must be done. But before we begin, can we assume that, when we are re-located, we will still have access to the foodstuff of our regular diet?"

Mala: "Yes, no matter if we go to the other villages or to the eastern shore, our food supply should still be the same."

Layal: "Well, then I think it best that we focus on those remedies that may be most needed, like comfrey and yarrow for any potential wounds or infections. Although the comfrey may be hard to keep fresh and it can only be used topically. We will have to prepare the valerian in case a sedative is needed. Most of these have already been dried or stored, so we have only to mix the—"

Olana's troubled mind pulled her down, blurring and scrambling Layal's instructions and any of her thoughts that tried to surface. She heard the sound of the young girl's voice, describing which herbs should be processed and why and she could feel Layal's connection to and understanding of the plants. But the words held no meaning until she was finally able to tune in to hear the final directives.

"Primarily we should focus on preparing teas, tinctures, capsules and salve. Mistress Mala, why don't you finish the tinctures that you started earlier this week? And Olana, you can make the bags for infusion teas. I will work on the essential oils and mix up more batches of salve. We will also have to make sure that we have the supplies for the poultices which will have to be stored and then prepared as needed.

Most of the herbs that you will need are either already on the table, hanging from the rafter or in one of the pots on the windowsill. Everything is labeled, so you shouldn't have any problems finding what you need. And—" she looked around nervously toward the door and front window before walking to the bookcase at the back of the room and pulling out a batch of folded papers from behind a book on one of the shelves. "Even though the Saba does not like it, I have written down many of the recipes for the remedy mixtures. So you can consult these for the right amounts of each herb that will be needed. I also have some of my grandmother's instructions for distilling flower water and plants to make essential oils and soaps. These are ancient formulae that my grandmother inherited from her own grandmother. I have many of the oils already made. We need only to mix some of them with the soaps, sachets and ointment. These aromatic remedies will be important not only for healing but to also help keep our people's spirits invigorated.

I will need to gather some dandelion root from the Saba's garden. If you need me, I will be right outside"

As Layal went out of the door and closed it behind her, Olana accidentally dropped a bag of dried flower buds, spilling them all over the floor. Mala looked at her with concern as she helped to pick them up. "Are you okay, Olana? If you are not feeling well, Layal and I can handle this."

Olana sighing heavily, "No, I'm fine. I guess that all this talk of conflict and potential warfare has my nerves on edge. I know that I need to take my mind off of these situations over which we have no control. But it so disconcerting to realize that violence and strife have been the perpetual activities of humankind seemingly since the beginning of time."

Mala: "That is all the more reason that we should go on with the business of living our normal lives, telling our stories, rearing our children, creating our world. These wars and conflicts may take much from us, but they cannot take away the feelings that come to us from that which we build with our everyday living."

Olana: "I know, I know. But Mala, you have studied other societies, other nations of the world—tell me what the so-called 'great nations of the world' have accomplished? With all their wonderful technological advances and riches and conveniences, they do not have peace, security or any real sense of universal liberty. They have not achieved the most basic freedoms that all of us, here in the Ocan, have taken for granted for more than two centuries. They are not free from war, disease, hunger, deceit, theft, murder, brutality—the list is endless. And while we may not have many of their creature comforts or luxuries—nor do we want them—in our simplicity we achieve what these great nations with their intricate and sophisticated forms of government fail to accomplish. We have now and have always had an overall peaceful coexistence and a greater sense of understanding of mankind's true purpose on this earth."

Mala: "Still even with all that we have accomplished, we are faced with something so banal as this current situation with the Aka."

Olana: "And yet, to what end do we fight? Don't you wonder if, at some point, these people, these societies—all of them, Aka, Ocan and mainlanders alike—— ask themselves what they are seeking to attain ultimately? To what end do we fight? Or better yet, to what end do we live, create, manufacture, produce? What is the end purpose of greater and greater technology? Easier lives, greater knowledge, overcoming a challenge? Still yet to what end? These other groups of people with their more 'sophisticated' systems of government—what more have they achieved? Do they even know what they are trying to achieve in any ultimate sense? Will they ever know? To what goal do they aspire? In what ways have they improved the collective condition of humanity on the earth?"

Mala: "I suppose we all give ourselves reasons such as, greater ease with which to survive or enhanced survival capability."

Olana: "Yet—survival for what purpose and at what cost?"

Mala: "Perhaps the purpose is to experience the fullness and beauty of the Creator's magnificence."

Olana: "But if that is the case, then should we not consider other ways, other means to achieve our objective? Why reach for the Creator's magnificence through the mire of dissension and violence?"

Mala: "Well Olana, it may be that some people will always choose to have their lives tied up in false means, false ends—never realizing how they have stunted their soul's growth. However, it may also be true that even the least worthwhile experiences in life may fulfill a need and satisfy the intent of injera.

If you follow the beliefs of our people, then fulfillment of injera is both the beginning and the end of all life endeavors."

Olana: "But how has the need been conceived? And what survival/ evolutionary purpose does injera serve? In the absence of need fulfillment— where does the need go? How does the need compensate when there is a lack of fulfillment? Neuroses? Psychoses? Disease? Atrophy? Who determined the varied yet limited means of need fulfillment? How is it that we all subscribe to the same patterns of thought/behavior in terms of need fulfillment? Do non-sentient beings and supposedly inanimate objects also move in patterns of need fulfillment? Can they be broken? Can we move beyond them? Ultimately, in the absence of need and need-fulfillment, can there be said to be any purpose to existence within this realm?"

Layal had come back in the midst of their discussion. She was quietly listening to the women as she sat on the hearth stirring grated beeswax into a mixture of oil and herbs in a pot that hung over the fire.

Mala: "Well, if for nothing else, we are here as a fundamental part of the essence of life, an expression of the spiritual energy of the universe."

Olana: "Still even with so sublime a philosophy in mind—why then do all the histories of life and all the great accounts of the world focus on predatory conquest in one form or another? Almost all the so-called 'great' accounts of mankind's history sing the praises of the predator, the conqueror."

Mala: "But don't forget the glories of those who have defended themselves against tyranny, conquest, and predation."

Olana: "But still, how does one tell a story of might and power that lauds the accomplishments of those who do not seek to conquer or consume? It seems that these have been the dominant ways of thinking that have been allowed to rule the world throughout time. It makes you wonder—what environmental, societal or evolutionary conditions are necessary for violent and predatory thoughts of conquest to prevail?"

Mala: "Olana, as you well know, there is more to the expression of humanity than the mere thoughts of our psyches."

Olana: "True, there is also our capacity to feel, to intuit and to interpret sensory perception at levels other than the cognitive. However, to a certain degree doesn't it seem that many of us recreate our feelings to represent thoughts given to us and expected of us by this world, this society? And still the question remains—to what end?"

Layal spoke up and both women turned to look at her. "My father says that the purpose of life is to live as long as possible. To achieve long life, despite obstacles to survival, is the truest hallmark of a successful existence."

Mala: "Your father is a wise man, Layal, like his father before him. But you must consider that physical longevity has no significance if your spiritual substance has little to no value or worth at the end of your life. Survival on the earth has no meaning unless a life substance retains enough spiritual critical mass to maintain its cohesion and contribute to the evolution of the universe."

Olana: "Our doctrine tells us that a brief physical existence that has been 'well-lived' (that is, in accordance with the harmony of the universe) has greater potential of enduring into eternity by contributing to and becoming a part of the universe's spiritual mass. This belief seems different, yet somewhat comparable to the allegories of some religions, such as those that speak of states of existence in heaven or nirvana."

Mala: "But going back to your main point Olana—I think that we can go round and round the reasons and purposes for human actions—both wise and foolish, good and evil—but I believe that, in the final analysis, we can only try to understand any purpose in life, as well as the ends to which we fight, within the context of the principles of injera."

Olana: "Yes, perhaps you are right. Maybe it is only through the principles of injera that the intent of human action can at least be explained if not ever fully understood."

The women fell silent, focusing on their tasks and they did not seem to notice Layal looking questioningly back and forth between the two of them.

Layal spoke up hesitantly, "Excuse me, Mistress Mala, but what are the principles of injera?"

Olana surprised, "Do you mean to say that no one has ever explained to you these most basic of Ocan beliefs?"

Layal: "I, I—I suppose that Saba was planning to explain them, perhaps later in my apprenticeship. Of course I have heard people refer to the principles all of my life. When I asked my father, he said that I would learn about them as a part of my apprenticeship with Saba. He said that such learning was not for him to impart. I do know that the three principles are to give, to survive and to transcend. However, I am not certain how all events and occurrences in life can be understood or explained by just three principles. I don't understand how just three categories of need can explain the actions of all phenomena in existence. And how do these principles or categories reveal the purpose of life?"

Olana: "The principles of injera are very simple; they are based on concepts that surround you each day. The principles are interconnected; they reflect and reinforce one another."

Mala: "The first principle of injera is that life must give to life. A fundamental Ocan belief is that the human need for love can be realized fully only through the first principle; through giving and receiving. By sheer definition of life, there exists a need to give if one is to live. While many people and societies attempt to ensure their survival by taking and accumulating as much as they can, our ultimate survival actually depends on our ability to both give and receive.

Just as the trees and plants must give of their fruit, so also humans must share and give of themselves—their talents, their gifts, their compassion, their lives. Each new life is brought into existence as a result of this need to give. Through the planet's need to give, we exist and are sustained. And humans are only one expression, one facet of the needs of this living organism that is Earth."

Olana: "The second principle reflects the basic need for survival that all living beings possess. It originates with a need to sustain a life or lives in as perpetual a manner as possible. Some believe that the need for immortality is at the basis of our more fundamental survival needs (food, shelter, water, safety)— for life to go on and never end. The third principle of Injera reflects the human need to excel, go beyond boundaries and have the power to escape an everyday world with a focus on only surface perception. This need is often associated with the concepts of 'enlightenment' or 'transcendence'. Although, there have been many who seek a corrupted means of fulfillment in this third principle. These are the people who aspire to have power over others and do not understand that only through the power of transcendence or enlightenment can a person fulfill this third type of need. The need for transcendence and enlightenment is also an indispensable part of defining what life is, and must be."

Mala: "Injera is both the need in and of itself, and the need manifest in fulfillment. It is within the first principle of injera that we begin to understand the magnitude of the planet's Gift to us; a gift that comes from the Creator, the universe and the completeness of life. The first principle of injera also contains its reciprocal converse—the need to receive, the need to be given to. Thus, our energy, our spirits, our actions, our beliefs—our gifts must ultimately contribute to the ongoing evolution of the universe and its cycles of creative energy re-born."

Olana: "In addition to interpreting the first principle in reference to the Gift that the land gives to us, we also understand this principle in terms of our own individual gifts—that which we have the potential to become."

Mala: "The ultimate need of life and living is to create; the purpose of creation is communion with the sacred. Need-fulfilled equals power—self-power, spiritual power. And communion with the sacred leads to ultimate need-fulfilled which enables the highest form of power that living beings can experience."

A rapid knock on the door interrupted any further words, as Alor came in suddenly, standing in the doorway appearing flush and out of breath.

Alor: "Mala, Olana. Saba—where is Saba? It is extremely urgent that I speak with her."

Mala: "Saba is not here."

Olana: "What happened at the meeting?"

Layal: "Did the Obeah come?"

Alor: "The meeting is still going on. The Obeah have not yet arrived. But the Aka have moved into the Lane of the western mountain; into the project sites. But where is Saba? I must speak with her right away."

Before anyone could respond, there was a sound in the distance like a loud explosion and they all turned to stare silently in wonder beyond Alor, out of the open door. Alor started back out. "Stay here. I will go and see what has happened. No matter what, keep this door closed until I return."

Mala went over to the front window and watched Alor walking toward the village and then she moved back to her seat and resumed her tasks. Layal stood stock still, near the hearth, staring at each of them, her eyes wide with fear and uncertainty.

Mala: "Well there is no reason to speculate on or dread the unknown. Come, Layal, let's finish preparing these herbs so that they will be ready. We will know soon enough what has occurred. Until then, let's go back to our discussion. What were we saying?"

Layal moved back to the fire and sat on the hearth, spooning the sticky mixture from the pot into small jars. "I believe that you were saying something about the ultimate need of life and the highest form of power."

Mala: "Yes, well, acceptance of the Gift means knowing how to open your soul to both give and receive, which requires some of the most basic lessons of life. By truly living, loving and learning, sentiale pathways are created and opened within our minds and our spirits. These pathways allow us to receive and connect with the energy that fuels the eternal source of all creation. We cannot fully live without reaching the heights of what it means to love and to learn. Being alive means knowing and feeling yourself a part of all there is to know in this world; claiming all of life and living as your own. Being truly alive means learning in its highest form—seeking to discover, perceive and acquire new and deeper ways of understanding, feeling and interacting with the world."

Layal: "Do you mean a level of learning like that achieved by the scholars who belong to the Master's Guild or those who are considered geniuses?"

Mala: "No, not necessarily. This is not the form of learning that masquerades in the false dress-up game of self-importance that we often see performed by the 'learned and scholarly' of the world. True learning recognizes, acknowledges and respects the wealth of knowledge and wisdom that exists in all aspects of life and living—in every person, every creature, every part of this world. This is a form of learning that allows one to transcend their own limitations of thought and touch the wisdom of the universe that exists in every dimension or aspect of life. And in order to be a part of this type of learning, one must always be open to experiencing and incorporating new ways of knowing the world—"

They were interrupted by another loud sound in the distance outside. Layal sat on the hearth, looking towards the window with a frightened expression. She held a spoon poised unmoving above an empty jar, as hot sticky salve spilled onto the floor. Olana and Mala exchanged a look just before Olana got up and went over to take the spoon from Layal's hand and begin wiping up the spilled mess.

Layal, rising from the hearth, "I'm sorry. I didn't—"

Olana: "Don't worry about it Layal. Why don't you go sit with Mala while I finish this for you? Layal, before today, I don't think I have heard you talk so much. It is refreshing to hear you express yourself and ask questions. When did you learn so much about healing plants? I had no idea that you were so knowledgeable."

Layal inhaled deeply and began to relax, "The Saba has taught me a lot. And I, I, I guess that it may be somewhat easier to speak when the Saba is not here." She looked apprehensively over her shoulders and peered out of the windows before continuing. "It's just that the Saba is such a great and wise woman."

Mala laughed, "And an irritable wise woman at that."

Layal upset, "No, no. The Saba is, is, is wonderful. My father says that I must not try her patience or upset her in any way."

Mala: "I'm afraid that the Saba does not need you or anyone else in order to lose her patience or to become upset. She does a good job of that all on her own. But it seems unfortunate that you have borne the brunt of her sometimes prickly personality."

Layal: "No, its fine. She has become much—" looks around apprehensively again, "much nicer since you have come to stay."

Alor burst through the door, "Come, you must come quickly; the village is being evacuated."

Olana: "What has happened?"

Alor: "They are saying that you must take only what can be carr—" he broke off looking around the room, "Has Saba not come back? Where did you say that she went?"

Olana spoke up, hesitantly, "Saba did not say where she was going, only that it was necessary that she to retrieve something. But she should have returned by now. I lost track of time. It shouldn't have taken her this long."

Alor: "We don't have much time. We have to find her. It is now more necessary than even before. I have to convince Saba to show me any papers of Taijaur's that she may have. If the Aka or any of Edise's minions find those notes, then this situation will become much worse than it is now. If they become aware of what those papers reveal, we will undoubtedly be faced with a disaster beyond anyone's reckoning."

Mala rose and said, "I think that I know where the Saba has gone."

Olana: "But Master Alor, what has happened? You still have not told us what has happened?"

Alor started to respond and then as he became aware of Layal's presence, he checked himself, saying to the girl, "I saw your friend waiting for you outside. Why don't you go with him now? He can relay to you the details of what has occurred."

Layal looked from Mala to Alor and back to Mala, "But I'm not sure that I should leave without the Saba's permission."

Mala: "Don't worry Layal. At a time like this, your duties are suspended. You should go and be with your family now. They are undoubtedly worried about you." Mala had picked up the girl's shawl and was wrapping it around her shoulders as she led her toward the door and opened it. "I was thoughtless to keep you this long. Go now, so that you can prepare to be evacuated with your family."

Layal: "Well, if you're sure. I mean, I don't want this to go against me becoming a saba. I will still get to be a saba, won't I? My father would be devastated if—"

Mala: "Don't worry, Layal. Everything will be okay. You will not jeopardize your standing."

Layal: "Will you please tell the Saba that I,I, ,I stayed until the end, that I helped with—"

Olana: "Rest assured, Layal. We will tell her."

Mala shut the door and turned back to Olana and Alor. Alor was looking around in cupboards and on shelves, pulling out papers and books, examining them quickly and then putting them back. "Ladies, we must move with haste. Edise has set off explosives in the cave where we were working to find the portal. Where do you think that Saba would hide something if she thought it was really important?"

Olana: "What? Why would he do something like that?"

Alor was still moving, searching throughout the room, opening drawers, looking underneath the table. "So that the Aka could not take possession of it. The Aka have sent armed battalions and there may be more on the way. They have moved into the Lane and seized control of all the geothermal project sites and the pipeline, in addition to all the caves and mines. Edise has sent Ocan forces to try to secure the aqueducts. The Elders still believe that this conflict will be resolved without bloodshed, but they are evacuating the main village just to be safe. The Aka seem only interested in taking possession of the land, but they still seem to be taking preemptive steps toward armed conflict.

If they discover what Taijaur's work has revealed, then they will have in their possession all that they need to achieve their aims in this land and beyond."

Mala: "Alor, all of your work with the portal has been destroyed. What will you do?"

Alor: "If these notes of Taijaur's confirm what I think, then we may have been working in the wrong location anyway; or at least not the most essential place. According to what I have found so far, I believe these missing notes provide more details about the location of the Earth's main portal. The notes may also provide a description of how the energy can be captured and channeled. But I can't be certain until I have seen all the translations. That is why we must find Saba right away. We can not take the risk of someone else learning of this primary gateway or how to access the energy. Where did you say that she went?"

Mala: "Most likely she has gone to the temple."

Alor: "The temple? In the hills? Oh no! I didn't know anyone still went there. We will have to get to her quickly. Mala, can you show us the fastest route? And we will have to take great heed that no one sees us going that way."

Olana: "But Alor, what does this all mean?"

Alor: "I don't have much time to explain, but just look at these diagrams." He pulled a roll of documents from an inside fold of his robe and spread them out on the table. "I believe that this sketch depicts the grounds of the temple and the surrounding caves." He pulled out another rolled document and pointed to a spot on the paper. "Do you see the place that is indicated here? This area here shows the caverns behind and beneath the temple. These drawings were done centuries, if not millennia ago, well before the Ocan temple was built. However, this sheet does not contain the complete drawing. This paper was a part of a larger drawing which included this diagram.

I'm not sure that Taijaur even realized what he was charting. But I recognized it as soon as I was able to put it together with his notes from the second book. I must convince Saba of the importance of giving those documents to me, before they fall into the wrong hands."

Olana: "But why is it so important to get those papers especially considering the dangers that we face with this, this conflict with the Aka? These are just mere pieces of paper, in contrast to the potential loss of human life."

Alor: "In terms of any potential loss of life—as much as I hate to admit—we will have to trust that Edise and his forces will be able to protect us adequately. It is my obligation to fight an entirely different front of this battle. It is directly because of this conflict that these papers take on even more significance than they had before. However, I have no fear of the Aka destroying the documents and notes that Saba has in her possession. These papers are much too valuable to them. The danger here is that the Aka will decipher their meaning."

Olana: "But even if those papers have information about the temple grounds, what significance does that have? Why is that important?"

Alor rolled the documents back up and slid them into the front of his garment. "I believe that the temple is what I have been searching for. If I am interpreting the translations of the Book correctly then our temple has been constructed on top of the Earth's most important entryway to the in-between. This is the one gateway that the ancient Obeah left unsealed. The temple contains the main access point to the in-between and to all other portals on this planet."

Mala stood up with a sudden look of fright, "I should have known. I should have guessed it long ago. I should have seen it, figured it out. I knew something felt different about that area. I suspected—We have to hurry." She grabbed her shawl and swung it over her head and shoulders as she reached to open the door. "If the Saba ventures into those caverns, she will not be able to escape."

Olana: "The subterranean caves? Saba would not ever go there. I spent a lot of time with Saba in the temple when I was growing up and she always warned me that no one should go down into those secret caves and that black labyrinth of caverns. She knows better than anyone that the emissions that pour from those chambers contain poisonous gases."

Mala: "But if those caverns do, indeed, contain a portal, then she may not have a choice. The in-between energy is coming through more clearly and with greater force. I can feel it growing stronger with each day. Saba may be pushed, or pulled, or somehow led into the temple caverns by forces beyond her control. And because she is of saba-energy, she may be more susceptible than most.

There is something, some force that keeps pulling her, calling to her, binding to her soul. What if this force is something that originates in the in-between?"

Alor held the door open and ushered the women out, "Come, we must try to reach Saba before it is too late."

20. True and Pure Vessel

"Consider this—do feelings of sadness, loneliness, and anger result from external circumstances, or do they arise from an internal mismatch between who you are and who you need to be?"

This was the third day that he had come to her room with a 'consider this' statement or question. The others had been similar to this one—such as: "Consider this— perhaps you feel the loss of your mate so keenly because the emptiness—the severed connection—happened before he even came into your life;" and then, "Consider this— perhaps your life can only be as strong as the foundation upon which your belief is sustained."

During the first part of the week he had just stood in the doorway each day, peering in silence until Shona turned to look at him. Whatever message he may have transmitted with his intense stare she was never able to discern. His look was so ominous she thought perhaps that he was trying to scare her out of the bed. Sulas brought her one meal each day and Aria sometimes tried to feed her. Through a cotton haze that filtered her perceptions, their voices and actions came and went.

The old man stayed only a few seconds each time that he came. No matter how hard she tried to block his words, throughout the day, her mind brought his voice back to her and against her will, her thoughts played through each conundrum that he presented. In the middle of the week he had also started coming once each evening, saying the same sentence each time—"It may appear that many people have multiple hardships to overcome, yet you have but one obstacle in your path."

Taijaur had been gone almost two weeks now. Their sentiale contact was completely cut off. The first week Shona had worked feverishly cleaning, fixing any and everything inside and outside of the old man's house. In the middle of the week, for no reason and telling no one, she started making the long trek to and from the village every day, nearly running each way. She moved with frenetic almost frantic energy, never staying in one place long. She was blocking out, numbing her senses and her mind in order to forget that her life had ever been anything more that what it was now. When she finally fell into a bed at Selene's house and wouldn't speak, couldn't move, they sent for the old man to come and get her. The women of the village surmised that exhaustion had finally taken its toll, but the old man knew otherwise.

On the evening of the eighth consecutive day of her voluntary confinement, Shona sensed him coming, and she turned to face the door so that she would be prepared when he walked in. Before he spoke, she raised her head and asked, "What is there that blocks my way?"

Om: "You."

She laid back down, turning her back to him, mumbling, "Please just leave me alone."

The next morning Shona got up from the bed for the first time in more than week. Wrapped in a blanket like a shawl over her head and upper body, she came out into the hot sun and sat down by the old man who was sitting in front of the house repairing a broken chair. For awhile neither of them spoke and then without looking in her direction the old man said, "Sulas is like you."

She heard him, but still said, "What?"

Om: "You and Sulas, you are the same. You both have a fundamental inability to shield yourselves from the energy fields created by any perceived negativity within the world. You, Sulas and others like you absorb the sickness, the evil, the pain of the world and make it your own. You take it into your psyche, into the core essence of your being. The only difference between you and Sulas is that the absorption of evil has so shocked Sulas' system that she no longer speaks and she must keep herself a part from other people so as not to allow their pain to gain a stronghold in her life. You both have a heightened sensitivity to the pain of others and this is good. But you do not know how to then go on and filter the pain from your being. You take it in, internalize it and make it a part of yourself until it overcomes your mind, body and soul and you are filled with a constant, chronic malaise, melancholy, and sickness."

Shona: "You have said all of this before."

Om: "Yes, but we must now realize that while we sought atonement as an antidote, a cure, for the poison of fear that infects your soul—it is really your own psyche that must be treated, must be healed in order for you to be made well."

Shona sighed heavily, "What is it that you think that I am supposed to do?"

Om: "You know that you must go after him and fulfill the purpose of your destiny. You must together seek the power source of the in-between. And you must return to your homeland.

You were not drawn to this man merely for the good feelings that your spirit generates in his presence. These feelings are only meant as a source of inspiration and motivation so that you might persevere in your responsibility to fulfill your destiny. You must allow your feelings to lead you to the true purpose of your union. Do not be so naïve as to believe that this union was of your choice or your design. This union provides you a blessing-opportunity for combined energy and power that would not be yours alone. You both have a higher purpose and calling to become a force for good on this earth."

Shona: "I can accept all that you say about, about my relationship with, with him, and us being together, but why can't we fulfill our destiny here in this land? Returning to the Ocan island is out of the question. It would be impossible for me to try to live amongst those people. They don't want me and I don't want them. They are only part of my past; a past that I did not ask for and do not want."

Om: "You will not be whole until you face your past. Neglect of this need can have a cascading effect and lead to distortions in other need areas of your life. For some, the most difficult part of human injera are those needs created as a result of the circumstances of their birth and upbringing."

Shona: "That is exactly what I do not want—this past; this past that will anchor me to the earth. A past that will chain me to a life that I have no freedom to define."

Om: "Your freedom will come only once you release yourself by facing them and accept the understanding that you are who you are because of what they are and also despite what they are."

Shona: "Why should I inherit their weakness? I have no such overriding need for family, friends or a need to belong."

Om: "This is more of a need to order your life than a need to belong. Conclusions, solutions about this world are based on a systematic review of the past. You must consult the past in order to obtain a point of reference. At some time in your life, you will have to let go of your past, sever your bond with your personal history. But you have not reached that point. This present moment in time requires you to embrace your past and all that you are and have been, so that one day you may release it fully."

Shona: "But if I leave, what will you do? You won't have anyone to help you. And what if that Commander Taring comes back looking for you?"

Om: "Don't worry about me. I have not survived this long by chance alone. I am fully capable of dealing with what ever that commander may bring to bear. Besides, with the soldiers no longer in the villages, I suspect that there may be less need for our services."

Shona: "What if I do go back with, with—" She was reluctant to say his name, but finally she forced it out, "with Taijaur—what then? How is this 'ordering of my life' supposed to take place? What exactly am I supposed to do?"

Om: "You must do what your training has prepared you to do. You must go through the in-between. That is what calls you; that is where your injera leads you. Only with power from the in-between will mankind be able to fight the evil that grows in this world. Together you and Taijaur can help humankind to re-gain its sense of purpose and understanding of life's greater sources of awareness."

Shona: "But what is the point of all this—one battle after another after another after another? Why do we even go through all of this? What is it worth to just keep going on and on with one problem after another, one source of evil after another? Why can't we just let evil—if that's what it is—win? Especially when it seems that the more violent and aggressive forces of life always outweigh and out maneuver the more passive and peaceful."

Om: "You are tired and you do not know what you are saying."

Shona: "Yes, I am tired. But still it is my logic that asks—why not let the predators inherit this phase of the earth's existence? If goodness is truly immortal, its essence, its spirit will survive to live in another day, another time. Why continue fighting them, especially when you consider that they are intentionally, yet unwittingly shepherding the Earth toward its own eventual demise? Even if we continue to fight them, what type of earth will be left once this battle has been waged?"

Om: "What makes you think that this is a battle between some evil predators and you, the so-called 'good guys'? The evil we must battle exists within us all."

Shona: "You sound like that Inar woman. But still you must admit that there are those who consciously choose to give their lives to the destruction of others and right now there seem to be more of them than there are of us. I am not so sure that I have the energy to continue living in a world where evil is so pervasive."

Om: "But who are they and who are we? Can't you see that we are they and they are us? One earthly spirit, one mind, one wellspring of need, hope and desire. We all fail when one of us fails."

Shona: "But it is not just the problems of good and evil. I am so tired. I don't think that I can do this anymore. Violence is alien to my spirit. I don't want to be forced to use it in order to exist."

Om: "This is the world that you have been born into, the world in which all of us find ourselves. Something has depleted your life force. It keeps you from seeing that we commit violence against our own lives by refusing to live up to our potential as vessels for the Creator's energy. No matter how much we abhor violence and crave peace—we must fight and fight with every fiber of our beings. That is the world that we live in; that is the world that we know. That is why we are here—in this realm, on this earth—to fight for our gifts, to battle any force that stands between us and the Gift. You must find the power that will allow you to know how to fight. You must find the wisdom to know that true fighting does not involve bloodshed or causing physical harm."

Shona: "But I don't want anything from life but to live a quiet peaceful existence. I don't want to be powerful. I don't want to be unique or different. I just want to live a normal life. Is that so wrong? Is that so bad?"

Om: "You have an inherent power that carries with it a responsibility to fulfill its intent."

Shona: "Can't you understand? I don't want the responsibility that comes with power. I don't want to be burdened by other people's expectations that I do some great and wonderful thing. I reserve the right to determine what my own destiny will be. This is my life; it belongs to me."

Om: "Still, you cannot allow your fears to determine for you. If we allow our fears dominion, then the earth's pervasive negative and weak forces are given the power that they need to develop, expand and multiply. That is why it is essential that you journey to the in-between. The power source of the in-between will give you what you need to develop your own inherent strength."

Shona: "But what is this place, this in-between place? Neither Mala nor Taijaur could seem to say exactly what it is."

Om: "The in-between is a place that is akin to your own sentiale, but it is not your thoughts, feelings or sensations. This is the sentiale of this planet—its lands, seas, internal geologic substance—every part of this Earth that we call home."

Shona: "Are you saying that the planet itself is sentient?"

Om: "Human understanding of sentience is limited to the patterns that our present dimensional reality reveals. However, there are forces beyond our comprehension that live with and through us. The in-between is the link, the connection that this planet makes with the spirit of the universe.

In the in-between you will find injera raw and unformed; an ethereal path and gateway to the abstract. Because injera is life itself or rather the core, nucleus of that which we know of as life—the injera of the in-between is intensely alive and potent. Only through the planet's own internal need can the code of human existence be re-aligned with its true intent."

They were both quiet for a few moments, watching a lizard scurry through the dust, stopping every few feet to feel and sense the air. The blanket had long ago fallen away from her head and shoulders. It now lay on the ground beneath her. Om had completed his repairs on the chair and set it to one side.

Shona: "What is this journey supposed to be—some sort of culmination of my life? Some ending point?

Om: "No, it is only one beginning of many beginnings."

Shona: "But what if I don't go?"

Om: "If you do not follow the path that your life has been given, then you will cease to live."

Shona: "How can I die just by not following a certain path?"

Om: "You will not die; you will only cease to live. Your mortal existence will continue. If you choose to forgo the path of your life's journey, then your life will be consumed by the endless rotations of meaningless endeavors in which many humans of this world indulge their minds and focus their attention; functioning like zombies, neither dead, nor truly alive. You will find no satisfaction, yet you will be forever seeking. Your life will constantly begged to be lived, but you will have no knowledge of how to sate its thirst. You will be defeated ultimately and fully by your own self, by your own decisions; or rather by a lack of ability to choose wisely."

Shona: "Why are you so sure that the path of my life's journey must lead to this 'in-between' place?"

Om: "Because that is the juncture that you have reached. You are stymied in your growth; at a crossroads. You must not go away from the world, but rather you must go inside of it, to seek the answers and guidance that wait for you there. You are at a significant turning-point in your life—a fulcrum of your existence. Different people reach this point at varying times. Some never reach it at all."

Shona: "You make it sound like I really don't have a choice."

Om: "We all have a choice. Your individual force of will determines what acts you can and will execute in this lifetime."

Shona: "Am I supposed to come back from this place as some powerful all-knowing sage—fit to spew wisdom, counsel and advice to all my waiting subjects?"

The old man laughed, "No. you will be the same Shona that you are now. Only for a moment, you will know what it is to be truly alive, to allow your god-force to live with and through you. It will be your choice whether or not you allow that moment to guide the rest of your life. In the end, I hope that you will have many such moments to sustain you within this realm. But you can only get out of this experience what you bring to it. Although your life has prepared you in many ways for the journey before you, still you must prepare yourself emotionally and psychologically. You have to be strong in all respects to withstand the forces that populate this other realm. Before entering that nether-region, you must examine yourself carefully and attempt to expunge any vulnerable or weak points that you may have inside of you."

Shona: "I can think of nothing within me that would make me vulnerable."

Om: "Certain types of negative experiences can leave gaping holes in your psyche, especially if you were not strong enough to withstand their initial impact. If you go into the in-between with such openings in your being, then there is a possibility that you will not be able to return to this world. And you may be destroyed. Any points of vulnerability or weakness will make you susceptible to forces that are beyond your power and your comprehension. Your weakness can be used by others to tear you a part from the inside. The training that you underwent with Taijaur has hopefully prepared you enough to shield you physically, mentally and spiritually from anything that you might encounter. But only you know for sure if—"

Shona: "Wait a minute—what is this about not returning and being torn apart? You never said anything before about being destroyed or being torn a part. No one who has talked about the in-between has ever mentioned these dangers."

Om: "This place has no inherent malevolent intent. But you have to be able to match your own substance with the substance of the in-between. Otherwise, by its nature, it will reflect back to you what you bring. And if what you bring is not in synch with its essence, it will purge any infectious poisons that may reside within you. This purging is not accomplished without pain. Poisons of the soul take the form of fear, guilt, anger, and all the forms of immorality that cripple and corrupt your life. And these may not be just your own poisons, but the poisons that you have taken in from other people—the negative energy that you have allowed to come inside.

There are concentrated energy fields that exist in the in-between that will sense and exploit these negative emotions. The in-between is their natural environment; they move within the earth and within the stars."

Shona: "But how do you know of this? How can you know what exists inside the earth and inside of the stars?"

Om: "Never mind that for now. Just makes sure to not allow these entities or energy fields to bond with you in any way. They are not human and their needs are not human needs. They have no attachment to this realm."

They were both silent for awhile, and then Om turned toward Shona. "Come, we must prepare for your departure."

Shona: "But Om, can you tell me why this responsibility belongs to Taijaur and me—why the two of us?

Om: "It is necessary for you alone Shona. This is your journey. Taijaur will only be there to help you and to protect you."

Shona: "What? But you said that Taijaur and I must go together."

Om: "You will go together, but it is you for whom this message is intended. Taijaur will be there to guide and assist you. His presence is necessary to mediate between our physical reality and the reality of the In-between. Everything that has happened in your life thus far has led you to this journey. None of your experiences occurred by chance alone. Not on the island, in the canyons or the road that led you to my home. This path to the in-between is the continuation of your life's journey. Taijaur is the emissary who will—"

Shona: "Wait a minute—pardon me, but did you say that Taijaur is the Emissary? You must have misunderstood. He was searching for the Emissary, he is not the Emissary himself."

Om: "Didn't he tell you? Don't you know?"

Shona: "Know what?"

Om: "Taijaur possesses the ability to mediate the boundaries between different worlds. If there is such a thing as an emissary, then he is that which he seeks."

Shona: "What? How can that be? Taijaur never said anything about being the Emissary; the object of his own search."

Om: "Well, maybe he didn't find the right time to reveal the full story, all of the facts. In the beginning, he believed that his task was to find the Emissary. And then, even before he embarked upon this journey to find you, he began to suspect the nature of his own true role. However, it was not until we found certain key passages in each of the three volumes of the Book of Change that his suspicions and my own were confirmed.

Taijaur will uncover the portal that you must enter. He is blessed with an inherited gift. He will lead and guide you through the whole process, keeping your mind stabilized while you dwell in that other realm. He must hold the gateway to the in-between open so that it does not collapse before you are able to complete your task."

Shona: "My task? What task? What am I supposed to do? I know nothing about changing any code of existence. Am I expected to go alone to find this catalyst-stone or gem or what ever it is?"

Om: "Oh, my child! I thought you knew. Your task was never to find anything. Although the Eye of God does exist in the in-between, there is nothing for you to find. You will be led to the power source. But the stone can only be acted upon by a human agent. The catalyst is a living, breathing human being.

You are the catalyst. You are the one called to re-set the balance of energy in the world."

She was too stunned, too frightened to think, breath, or move. She sat staring at him, her mouth wide open.

He stood up and put out his hand to pull her to her feet. As he opened the door and stood to the side to usher her into the house, Shona asked quietly, "Om, how do you know all of this? How is that you seem to know who or what I am? What is it that you think that I am?"

Om: "You are no more or less than what we all are. A medium. A means and a way for the Creator's energy to manifest through and within this realm. All living beings are an example of the Lord's energy, a vessel for his-her intent—whether we realize it or not. Yet, your purpose and your injera in this life distinguish you in ways that others can only begin to fathom and never claim as their own. Your energy came to you so fully tuned that, of its own volition, it pulls and attracts hidden forces within the earth, within the galaxies. You are a natural born spiritual catalyst. This innate ability, once combined with *conscious intent*, has the power to transform your life force into something this present world may never comprehend completely. It is not a matter of what or who you are now, Shona. It is that which you have the potential, the power to become," he paused and then looked directly at her as he continued, "a true and pure vessel for the intent of the universe."

21. What Will Endure?

Through the heavy mist-shrouded trees, she saw him in the distance. His back was to her as he stooped washing clothes in the running water of a broad stream that cascade down for several miles over boulders and small rocky escarpments. She knew that he sensed her presence, though he had not yet turned to acknowledge her. She had felt his sentiale opening to her, the closer she had come to him.

Shona had re-gained her strength within a few days and then set out directly on the path that would bring her to him. While they were in the canyons, Taijaur had repeatedly mentioned this small peninsula of the mainland that contained an isolated forest near the shore. He had even etched the route for her in the sandy dirt. He said that, at low tide during certain times of the year, there was an isthmus that stretched from this peninsula to the largest atoll near the northwest side of the Ocan island. Although she had never seen any evidence of a land bridge, the atoll that he spoke of, was the same lonely piece of land she often sailed to from the Ocan island. It was a strange place that always seemed to be dark with low hanging clouds no matter the weather.

He rose and turned slowly to face her. She could tell that he was suppressing a smile, and the gleam in his eyes betrayed his emotions. He made no attempt to speak or greet her, as he stood staring at her, waiting, watching her approach. She stopped a few feet before she fully reached him and stood for a moment silently meeting his gaze. And then in a quiet accusing tone, she said, "You knew that I would come."

Taijaur: "I didn't know. I only hoped."

Shona: "You and the old man, you're in this together. You both have anticipated my compliance to your will. The two of you have plotted and conspired to mold me, and shape my actions from the beginning."

Taijaur: "Get it out your system, Shona, if you must. But frankly, I don't have the interest, energy or inclination to devise such machinations on your behalf or anyone else's. My only deceit, and perhaps mistake, was not revealing my full intent in taking you to the canyons. I'm sorry if that made you think of me as untrustworthy. But I have nothing else to hide. You have to want to come with me or, quite honestly, I don't want you here."

Taijaur turned his back to her, stooping down to continue washing and rinsing his clothes in the stream. Startled into silence, Shona sat down on a large rock a few feet away from the tree where Taijaur was now spreading wet clothing across low-hanging branches. She looked away into the distance, pensive for a moment before speaking.

Shona: "Have you waited here all of this time?"

He ducked under the large tree limb that partially obscured his view of her, and he came to the other side of the tree leaning with his back against it as he responded. "Well, I took a more circuitous route to get here, so I have not been here for as long as you may think. I took some time to explore the region more." He paused, smiled mischievously, then continued, "And I went back to that village that you liked so much. I took some time to visit with some of the uhh, the more *special* females. And I must say, they seemed quite delighted to see me." He laughed aloud.

Shona rolled her eyes upward.

Taijaur: "So what took you so long to get here? What took you so long to decide?"

Shona: "I am not sure that I have decided anything. But I am here, so I guess I will just try to move forward one step at a time." She looked at him, turned her head away and then looked up again with nervous apprehension, "While you were, ummm, *exploring*, did you—" she halted and then quickly asked, "did you think about me?"

He responded, a smile playing at the corners of his mouth, "Nope, not at all. What about you? Did you think about me?"

Shona demanded, "Then why are you still here, waiting for me?"

"It is my duty," he stood tall, chest thrust forward, determined resolution knitting his brow. "I made a pledge to the Ocan people that I would bring you back and I promised your mother and the old man that I would keep you safe. You are my duty, young lady." Then he leaned back against the tree and smiled, "Now, tell me, did you think of me?"

Shona: "No, not at all. Except—" she took a deep breath and turning to one side, she put her head down so that the intense energy that poured from his eyes would stop affecting her heart and altering her breathing. She clenched her fists and spoke in a low voice, just above a whisper, "Except every time that I thought of living and reasons for being alive. You did not enter my mind until I thought of touching and being touched. But then you were not there and my desires could not be sated."

She took another deep breath, and with an audible exhale she continued, "Until I thought of sharing and giving, I did not think of you. However, if something humorous or some unexpected pleasure caught me off guard, then the presence of your spirit flooded my mind and my senses; and I felt that my entire being would burst from the rapture of feeling you inside of me. Each morning that I awoke to the peaceful majesty of an elegant sunrise gracing the morning skies, your spirit would come to me, uninvited, rushing into my heart, into my mind and throughout every part of my body. But the feeling would always abruptly disappear, snatched away by some insidious, invisible force that brought with it the realization that my delight was mine alone, because you were no longer there, you were no longer with me. And no matter how long I waited, you did not come. Yet, still I waited.

As time passed, I occupied myself with more and more work and I learned to conquer those feelings in order to chase away any thoughts of you. I succeeded for awhile, or so I thought, until the night came upon me and I would lie down to sleep. In those moments of quiet stillness, your essence would wash over me completely, penetrating the numbness. It was then that I decided that I must somehow force myself to abandon completely any activity or interest in life that might potentially or unexpectedly remind me of you.

I discovered that as long as I did not think or dream or laugh or play or sing or dance, then you did not come to mind. At first, I struggled endlessly, in vain, believing that I could know the exultation of what it means to be fully alive despite your absence from my life. But in time, I came to know how shallow and untrue my convictions had always been. Finally, by sheer force of my will, I blocked all thoughts of you from my mind. I stifled sensations in my being. I stopped seeing the world in its entirety. It was not long after this that I found that my legs, my arms and hands had no desire or even will to move. Eating, drinking and even rising from bed each day seemed such meaningless endeavors. And then the time came that there were no thoughts left to me except a silent recurrent whisper from my soul that tried to fathom why." She looked up at him, staring directly into his eyes, and he saw the tears streaming down her face as she took yet another deep breath and said, "Until I thought of loving and being loved, Taijaur, I did not think of you."

"Oh Shona" he pulled her up and into his arms and held her tightly, as she wept silently with her head buried in his chest. "Shona, Shona, Shona. Know that I will always be here for you; wanting you, needing you, loving you, waiting for you, for as long as it takes."

They spent the night in a small tent that Taijaur had constructed from tree branches, sticks, and thatch made of large leaves and long grass. Starting out early the next morning, they began their hike with walking sticks to help propel them through the steep rugged terrain. Taijaur guided the way up, over and down a series of hills that led to a thick black forest that lie between the hills and the shore. They walked all day, talking along the way and stopping only to refill their bottles of water in the fresh streams of the forest and to eat the wild berries and other foodstuff that they found along the path.

From the beginning of their hike, Shona put forward the questions that she had tried, in vain, to fathom on her own. "Taijaur, why are we going through the in-between prior to returning to the island? I thought your plan was to take this step by step. I thought that we would enter the in-between from somewhere on the Ocan island."

Taijaur: "Actually it was Om's idea that we seek the power source of the in-between now. He is the one that told me of the portal that is located in this forest."

Shona: "Om? But why would he suggest something that might prove more dangerous? Isn't it safer to enter one of the portals on the island?"

Taijaur: "Under normal circumstances I would trust the portals on the island more than the gateways in other lands, because that is what I know and am familiar with. But I believe that something is happening on the island right now and I am not sure what it is. We need to enter the in-between as soon as possible, to perhaps avert any potential major calamity either on the island or anywhere else in the world. There are powerful energy and forces that are now gathering and converging like no other time in the history of man. I can feel this energy building in the skies and in the air.

The portal in this forest is located in a hidden cave before we reach the shore. It is at the edge of the forest near a natural stone bridge. The cave's passages are steep but we will at least be able to walk those pathways as opposed to climbing or scaling any precipitous cliffs or rock faces as with some of the other portal locations. We have no choice but to not only enter the portal but to go all the way through the in-between to find the power source and start the process of re-setting the balance of energy. This is the only way. Any effort short of this would not be effective. We must go in and attempt to re-set the balance at the source."

Shona: "Why didn't you tell me that you are the Emissary? After all these centuries of the Ocan people waiting for, longing for and looking for their Emissary to arrive—you are the one that your people have waited for, the one that you have sought in your own quest."

Taijaur: "Shona, make no mistake I am not '*the* Emissary'.

Shona: "But the old man said—"

Taijaur: "I know what he said and in a sense he is correct. In this moment, in this time, I am, but one of many, who are called to do what we all must ultimately do. We are all emissaries, in that all humans have the ability to mediate the boundaries of reality, to access and form new ways of understanding the world. This is also part of the Gift that we inherit from the powers of the earth, the powers of the universe. I am an emissary in the same way that all people of this earth are emissaries. I believe that we are all called at different times to rise to the occasion of mediating boundaries and forming a bridge to a new world or a new way of conceiving reality."

Shona: "You are downplaying your own importance. It may be good to be modest and humble, but the bottom-line is that you are the Emissary that your people have written of, spoken of, and waited for."

Taijaur: "Yes, for this age, for this time, I believe that the responsibilities of an emissary are mine to fulfill. But I believe that the Earth is the only true emissary of the universe's power. Once we learn to receive its Gift then we can rise to our truest destiny in this life and fulfill the responsibilities inherent in that destiny."

Shona: "But, in addition to helping re-set the balance of energy—as an emissary, don't you also have to galvanize the will of the people and somehow lead them back into the world? Isn't this also an important part of being an emissary?"

Taijaur: "Yes, bringing the Ocan people to their destiny is equally as important as re-setting the balance of energy. I believe that you and I together will galvanize the will of the people and lead them back into the world. I believe that this is part of the reason that we have been led to one another."

Shona: "It seems that you and Om both believe that I am some kind of catalyst. Why didn't you tell me of this before?"

Taijaur: "I didn't tell you more about the emissary or the catalyst because I did not want you to be any more frightened than you already were."

Shona: "But what about the power stone, the Eye of the World? Isn't this the catalyst?"

Taijaur: "I don't know all of the details, but I believe that this is a two part catalytic process with you serving as a contact catalyst to absorb the energy and the fragment stone acting as a cofactor to facilitate the transfer of energy. Like enzymes in our bodies, you will function to transform the energy from one state to the next; from stored potential energy to usable kinetic energy that can be filtered out into the world. However, I think that you will be more than a catalyst or at least a different type of catalyst. I believe that you will not only act as a medium to convert the energy, but your actions will also initiate a change of internal energy within your being."

Shona: "How exactly am I supposed to do all of this?"

Taijaur: "I'm not certain exactly how. Each person's experience in the in-between is uniquely their own. There are no instructions or rules; no prescriptive way that you must proceed. All I know is that you must find the energy source and make contact with your mind, body and soul. Open yourself to an awareness that can come through the sense perception of your spirit. The Book indicates that the knowledge will come to you. Once you go through the portal, you must do what comes to you naturally. Just open your sentiale pathways to allow your natural power to flow through. The portals or gateways to the in-between almost always exist in caverns with subterranean tunnels that run deep within the earth. The tunnels and passageways are long and complex. You can only navigate them by way of the sentiale pathways.

Shona: "What about the danger of this place?"

Taijaur: "Most of the danger exists at the portals, the entryways themselves, not actually in the chambers of the in-between. I will remain at the entryway to contain the portal energy and keep the gateway open, while you seek the power source. No one knows how long the portals can remain open. I will pull you back, if I feel that the opening is altering in any way. No matter what happens, keep me with you. Through this link, I will be able to pull you back if I sense any danger. However, you have nothing to fear from the power source; it can not harm you. Part of your body and soul are constituted of the same substance as the power source. As a result of being conceived and reared in the forbidden lands, in addition to living close to the energy flows all of your life, your system is immune to any harmful effects that the energy may have.

However, you still have to be careful where you step and do not touch or disturb any water once you have entered the interior chambers. There are chasms within the streams and springs of fresh water from which vapors may arise. These gaseous emissions originate in the rock fissures which are submerged in the ancient springs. The toxic gases are latent only within certain rocks and the water. If these rocks or the water are disturbed, then the water and rock can inadvertently act as a conduit for the rising vapors which are believed to induce hallucinations or altered states of consciousness."

Shona: "But what if—what if I am not strong enough? What if I am not ready? I thought that there would be more time to complete the training."

Taijaur: "Shona, I understand your fears and I have fears of my own. You are more ready than you realize and your powers are stronger and more acute than I ever knew was possible. I had to learn to develop my ability to see the world, but your sensory perception automatically attracts and draws in unseen and unheard phenomena in the same way that other people breathe. You possess an innate ability to allow life's natural processes to flow through you. You see and feel the substructure of the world's reality as a natural part of who you are. Without realizing it you have been taking in the varying frequencies of bioluminescence from the thermo-radiation that all living matter emits. You hear at frequencies both above and below the normal human range and even beyond most of those in the Ocan. It is as if you have antennas that are attuned to vibrations of all natural phenomena throughout the world.

This is the type of power that is needed to withstand the forces of the in-between. But you will have to be careful because you will be able to see and feel negative energy at a higher level as well. You will need to adjust or adapt your senses to filter out the effect of any negative forces."

She was silent for a while and then she asked in a small voice, "Will you be safe?"

Taijaur: "I will be fine. I have learned how to emit a vibrational frequency that matches that of the geological anomalies that characterize a portal opening. I have worked with and studied these phenomena for many years now. It took me awhile to realize that Alor and all the others could not see the translucent glow and flowing rainbow spectrum that undulated throughout the area of our geophysics work site. With their detecting devices and sensory apparatus they picked up faint echoes of the energy. But I could see it and hear it plainly without any aids or instruments. At first, I didn't know exactly what I was seeing until one night the rocks began to glow brighter with a strange high-pitch sound. It was then that I realized that this was what my mother had seen and heard—these rocks emitting their energy—and I knew that these had to be the energy fields of a portal. I covered the most volatile spots with rocks and boulders so that no one might inadvertently go through. Alor never suspected anything."

Shona: "But I thought that you and Alor were allies in this cause? Or was this more of your 'truth revealed in time'?"

Taijaur: "It was not easy for me to keep this from Alor and I was tempted to tell him many times. But I needed time to think through all the potential ramifications of any action. I have tried to listen to all the varying perspectives regarding these phenomena and it wasn't always easy determining the most correct course of action.

Another point that I had to consider was the fact that Edise was watching Alor closely. If I had shown Alor where the portal was, Edise would have reported this to the Elders and they would have found a way to accomplish their goal of sealing the portal."

Shona: "Taijaur, why do you think that we can be successful in re-setting the balance of energy when such powerful beings as the ancient Obeah failed? Thus far, no one who has ever entered these portals has come back."

Taijaur: "We don't know for certain that the ancient Obeah failed. I don't believe that they attempted to re-set the balance. Having read more of the book, I now believe that re-setting the balance was not their goal. And they may have intentionally chosen not to return to this world.

But I believe that we will succeed because time is on our side; time and a greater understanding of the power, a greater understanding of what is at stake. We have had over two full centuries to develop our understanding, to hone our inherent strength. Centuries in which the power within humankind as a whole has grown stronger. This is especially true for those born and reared on the Ocan island where the energy is concentrated so fully that our evolution, our development has occurred at an accelerated rate."

Shona: "But what is our purpose Taijaur? Ultimately, what is it that we hope to accomplish by going into the in-between? Even if we are successful in re-setting the balance, what happens after that?"

Taijaur: "Ultimately, our purpose is as it has always been—to help re-store the human genetic code, so that the spirit of mankind can evolve in the absence of a preponderance of negative energy. With more positive energy or at least the correct balance of positive to negative energy flowing into the world we can move forward with helping to awaken all people to an awareness of their own inherent power, their potential to reach a higher level of consciousness. We can help awaken the Ocan people and lead them back into the world. We can help create—"

Shona: "But I'm not sure that I know how to reach a higher understanding within myself, let alone how to lead someone else to this level of awareness. And I have never had any power over other people, nor do I want to have power over others."

Taijaur: "We will not seek to have any power over other people. Our responsibility is to merely allow ourselves to be a vessel for the higher forces of this world; allow ourselves to awaken to a higher power that will move through us. Power can never belong to any individual person; it is never ours to command.

But Shona we have no choice but to begin this process by re-setting the balance. Otherwise, negative energy will continue to dominate within the psyche of human beings. If the energy is not re-set at its source, then we may lose complete access to the sentiale pathways in ourselves, and in this world. Then predation and the predatory spirit that the phage induces will continue to rule the earth. All life—people, animals and plants alike—will cease to find meaning outside of the consumption, conquest and control of other living beings, other forms of life.

Keep in mind that, in re-writing the human genetic code, we are not attempting to restore humanity to any previous time of 'righteousness' or 'peaceful co-existence'; but rather we are trying to bring out an existing pattern of evolution that allows the development of higher levels of reasoning, heightened states of awareness, and deeper forms of compassion and understanding. In the absence of the plague, this would have been mankind's genetic destiny."

Shona: "But we are back to the same issues as before. I still don't see how it is possible to know what any one person's genetic destiny *might* have been, let alone all of mankind."

Taijaur: "Well, the evidence is in the code itself. The human genome contains what is known as 'junk DNA'. At first, our scientists believed that this part of the genome had not been elicited, drawn out or required by the present environment on Earth. But then our researchers discovered that some parts of this junk DNA had been inhibited or suffered arrested development as a result of the presence of the virus in a large proportion of the human population. This phage has caused genetic alterations that threw off the natural track of mankind's evolution and continues to interfere with the code's development and true expression.

Humans and pathogens have a complex relationship that we actually know very little about. What the Ocan people did not realize until late in our study of this pathogen is the effect that this virus, and perhaps most viruses and other microbes have on the genes of living creatures. Our researchers now believe that viruses and other microbes function, in part, as a way for humans and other life forms to be pushed, and prodded towards evolution and for some species, towards extinction. We believe that microbial life effects, changes and can alter the genome of individual species.

Also, while I waited for you, I read through more of the third volume of the Book. If I am interpreting these passages correctly, then I believe that there is a possibility that the energy of the in-between may be the precipitating factor that is potentially making this virus more potent, more pervasive."

Shona: "But I thought you said that the energy is needed to eradicate the virus or to at least overcome its effect. How can the energy be used to both help the virus to grow and to destroy it?"

Taijaur: "I don't understand this fully myself. And I will have to translate and study further passages of the Book before I know if I am interpreting this correctly. But nonetheless it appears that there is a strong possibility that the same energy that enhances our development and fuels our evolution, is also providing the means by which the virus is able to change, grow and spread. However, it seems that the viral pathogens may have learned what we have not.

They have learned how to use the energy of the in-between to accentuate their own power and proliferate beyond all conceivable boundaries. While our fear has made us guard the energy and use it only to our own benefit, other life forms, no matter how microscopic, have used it very effectively, very efficiently to grow, multiply and spread.

If this is true, then our approach to this problem has been misguided. This virus and maybe all viruses are just other life forms with which humans must learn to co-exist not eliminate. After all, viruses, like all microbial forms of life were here before humans and they will most likely be here long after we are gone."

Shona was silent for a moment.

Taijaur: "I know this must seem like a lot to take in. We're almost there. Do you need to stop to rest?"

Shona: "No, I'm fine. I was just thinking about what you were saying in terms of the viruses being here after we are gone. It makes me wonder about a question that keeps recurring in my thoughts. I keep wondering—at the end of all of this, what will endure? What will still be here?"

Taijaur: "I don't understand. Do you mean, in terms of human aspirations, what will be left of as testament of our achievements?"

Shona: "No, my question has nothing to do with human aspirations or even our purpose in existing. With all of that we know, all that we are, you still have to wonder—what will endure? In the end, you, me, the catalyst, the Gift, the Earth—– all of this turns to dust. At that point—what is left that matters? When we and all that we know of this existence are no more, what will remain? What will still be here—perhaps even standing in silent testimony of what has come to pass?"

Taijaur: "Do you mean what comes after this life—what will last beyond the everyday struggles, victories, and toils of mankind?"

Shona: "No, more than even that. This interminable drama that presents itself as life in each generation of human existence does not seem so important in the full scheme of the universe. All planets, stars and galaxies are born and then one day they will each die. Beyond even all physical life, all material existence. Beyond the billions of galaxies made up of countless stars and planets, what will endure? What core essence of life exists in it all and beyond it all?"

Taijaur: "I don't know and I don't see how anyone can ever know, given that, for the most part, human knowledge, as we understand it, exists in the realm of the finite."

Shona: "But even in the face of an unattainable answer, this one question comes to me over and over—what will endure, what must endure? Beyond all that is, what is most real in the face of the demise of all things? What core basic element of life is truly and singularly eternal? I asked Om this question and he said only that the answer may lie buried somewhere in the in-between and perhaps in some kind of keeper's vessel."

Taijaur: "We can only speculate, but perhaps, in the end, within the dust that was once the human race, there will be the microbial life forms—the flowing matter and energy that initiated our existence, all existence. And this dust will perhaps carry the code of our life to other places, other times."

Shona: "I guess we will never know for sure, but perhaps in the end, when all else has dissipated, maybe what's left are the sentiale connections through which we are given life; those pulses and vibrations between living matter that inspire organic and inorganic life to coalesce and create. Perhaps it is these sentiale connections that exist at the core of all living matter and energy.

Essentially, all that we have and all that we are as living beings is embodied in our connections—the connections of our internal molecules and processes, our connections between each other and between ourselves and the natural world; between ourselves and our gifts. All of reality is made up and comprised of these connections. And it seems that these connections are based on processes of divergence and coalescence; diffusion and integration. There seems to be a basic need of all living energy to contract and expand—to join, fuse, coalesce, and then to diffuse and spread over and over again. In the end, it seems that only this energy, that sustains those connections, is what must endure in order for life to continually perpetuate itself."

Taijaur: "Shona if you think about it, you have actually brought us full circle back to the first conversation that we had when we met at Om's house. We began then speaking of the realm of the sentiale and the pathways that connect us. It seems that the connections that you speak of now are these same sentiale pathways.

Your question is intriguing and it will be interesting to see if there are passages in the Book that may address this issue. But look Shona, we're here. This is where we will rest for the night. This is as far as we go for now."

They were standing in a small clearing on the top of a hill. Taijaur put his pack on the ground and started making a fire.

Shona: "Where are we?"

Taijaur: "The portal is over there to the west, just beyond that ridge in that dark more dense area of the forest and the shore is on the other side of those trees. When we emerge from the in-between, we will be able to leave from this shore and continue on to the Ocan."

Shona: "Don't you mean *if* we emerge?"

Taijaur: "Don't worry—we will make it through. I will be there to keep you safe. We will start out before the morning's light. Let's get as much rest now as we can. We need to be as strong and alert as possible."

Taijaur unrolled his mat and lie down, falling into an immediate and deep state of unconsciousness. Shona sat next to him, staring into the night. She stayed this way for awhile thinking over all that had come to pass and what lie ahead of them. She had been watching and listening to the night for a couple of hours when she began to hear what sounded like whispering voices in the wind. She tilted her head to one side trying to catch the words. But Taijaur began twisting, turning, and moaning in his sleep to the point that she could not hear the wind clearly and the words lisped gently out of her reach. She placed her hands on his body, intending to reach down into his sentiale, hoping to soothe his troubled dreams. But she could not make a way through the hot layered emotions that swirled in a maelstrom of conflicted thoughts and distress.

Taijaur saw himself back in the canyons where he had found the mummified remains. He saw Shona there with him, looking back at him, over her shoulder with a leering, sinister smile, beckoning him forward. And then he felt himself inside of her perception, her awareness; her visions and her memories became his own. She was not fully human any more. She had become a human-reptilian creature who was stalking prey, following, prowling and then pouncing on an unwary victim. Taijaur could feel himself inside of Shona and the rushing excitement of taking part in vicious atrocious unspeakable acts of cruelty and depravity. He felt himself sit up with a cold sweaty feeling of panic. But then he realized that he was still lying on the ground, trapped and plunged into the next and lower phase of the deepest of unconscious mind-wanderings.

The scene in his dream abruptly shifted and Taijaur saw his grandmother sitting in a dark enclosed place. He could tell by the muted sounds of a nearby cataract that she must be in the temple caverns. She was holding in her hands a bowl of burning myrrh. He experienced the scene as if his spirit was a part of Saba—hearing what she heard, feeling what she felt; her movements became his own. There were words echoing across a vast distance. Someone was speaking in a low droning tone as if reciting or reading aloud. The Saba approached a pallet on the ground where a person, a body lie inert. He watched as she drew near the body and sat the bowl of myrrh on the ground, kneeling down beside the pallet. And then the abhorrence and incomprehensibility of the scene before him made him cry out as his body attempted to run away, but he couldn't move. He was paralyzed, stuck there with her, watching as she pushed through the flesh and reached with both of her hands deep down into the open abdominal cavity of a rotting, decaying corpse. Taijaur was helpless, unable to rise to a state of full consciousness and unable to intervene to pull his grandmother away from the grotesque nightmare vision in her mind. In his dream-mind, his sentiale screamed, "Run Saba, run. Don't look. It's not true. It's not real. Turn around and run."

Taijaur's consciousness snatched him instantly and abruptly from his deep fatigue-induced narcosis. He bolted to his feet with his heart pounding loudly in his chest and his ears, cold sweat pouring from his body. He put out his hand to pull Shona up as she sat staring at him her eyes widened. "Come Shona. We must leave this place now."

Shona: "But it is not even midnight yet; the dawn will not come for hours."

Taijaur: "Something has changed. Something is wrong. Something is very wrong. We have to leave now."

As he poured water over the fire, she hurriedly gathered the few articles of clothing and other items, shoving them into their packs and followed after him, stating simply, "Yes, I hear them. I hear the voices."

22. The Abyss

"We all stand, from time to time, looking into an abyss of one kind or another. If we come back whole, the feeling of having been torn apart can potentially give us the power to lead another away from that which lies beyond the edge of the abyss. Without design or intent, the empty darkness spews us back, carved with deeper crevices in our ways of understanding, in the pathways of our minds and souls. Having been to the edge and beyond, we are better able to reach out, to touch, and bring another back whole."

Saba was sitting alone in front of the temple, reading aloud from the <u>Journal of the Saba</u>. She had only intended to retrieve the journal and the package of materials that Taijaur had given her for safe-keeping—and move them to a new hiding place. She was afraid that if there was open conflict with the Aka, then the books, in their current secret location might be uncovered. Especially since that Haman man who Taijaur claimed was his uncle knew that she came here. These items would be safer somewhere else; somewhere inside of the temple where no one else would think to go.

After retrieving the book and other items, she had intended to sit only for a moment to perhaps read a little from the book's comforting words. She was trying to push from her mind a question that kept badgering her and wouldn't leave her alone. She hoped to draw solace and strength from the Journal; something that would help her to know how to go on. She could not bring herself to even think about the objects sitting next to her in Taijaur's bundle. She had felt the outline of a hard thick book and heard the rustling sound of loose sheets of paper, but she sat the bundle down on the bench beside her and tried to forget that it existed.

The wind was blowing hard and she thought for a moment that perhaps she should go into the temple. But the air inside the temple always felt so thick and stifling. It was better to soak up the book's intent out here in the cool light of day. In the far distance, she could hear a reverberating sound of thunder. She struggled with the words on the book's pages. Their meaning and sound should have brought her comfort, but they only made her feel more apprehensive. She went on to the next chapter, the next topic of saba-knowledge and was startled by the words that came from the page—"We all stand, from time to time, looking into an abyss of one kind or another. If we come back whole, the feeling of having been torn apart..." *Wait a minute,* she leafed through the pages, thinking, *that was in the last part, surely the same words are not in two different sections.* Not finding the prior selection, she concluded, *Perhaps I only imagined that I read this before.*

She settled back on the bench and went on searching through the words of the past, combining her will with those of the book's creators. Feeling the alive touch of those who no longer exercise a physical will on the earth, yet allowing the essence of who they once were to still persuade, influence and recreate her internal emotions and thoughts. These were the ideas that have power over people, words that for millennia have shaped actions and thoughts. She waited for their meaning to propel her forward in her own understanding. She waited for her mind and heart to shape new meaning from messages that were born long ago.

As the words droned on in the still air, her mind began to recall the purpose of the council meeting now taking place in the village. Subconsciously a memory began to stir, something that she had not listened to, but had nonetheless somehow taken in. Something about the Aka? Something. But she let go of the thought and lost connection with the words of the book. A pervasive sense of despair came upon her as the question that she had tried pushing from her mind asserted itself once again. How could four simple words fill her with such despondency as they repeated over and over—*what does it matter, what does it matter, what does it matter?*

A chasm within her soul was opening and spilling forth an empty depth of loss. The tenuous bond by which life held her now seemed fragile, worn and of no real consequence. It all felt so meaningless—this war or conflict with the Aka, the Ocan dreams and aspirations, her life, her calling, her work, her self—all of it. All of it could go away, disappear and the only question that came to mind was—*what does it matter? Why does any of it matter?* In the midst of her thoughts, the book said aloud to her, "Even in the absence of feeling, the abyss still yearns and pulls."

She had forgotten what it was like to stand so near the edge of the abyss. And she was now looking down into the darkness with a familiar yet disturbing sense of vertigo and nausea. She tried to re-focus her mind and concentrate on the link that was forming between herself and the spirit of the words. In a softer fainter tone, she could hear other cognitive-voices overlaying the continual droning of the text. Independent words outside of the book that acted as a sub-text to the words on the page. At first they were too low for her to make sense of their meaning, then they became louder and the book's voice came through clear and strong

"Some of us never see the abyss, or we pretend that its not there, our daily routines, our myriad tasks make it easy to block out the darkness within. Others, unknowingly or perhaps even knowingly plunge into its depths. It will swallow all means of fulfillment, will and desire." She closed her mind, her eyes, to the page, to the words. This was not the solace that she had come to find. But with her eyes closed, the words only seemed louder and stronger as the book continued speaking in a vibrant clear voice. "Often it seems that an exposed, acknowledged fear may cause more damage than a hidden insidious one, which can only eat away the dreams that live at the brink of one's sanity. Whereas, an exposed fear lies raw and festering, spreading contagion from one part of the psyche to another; until it encompasses the whole specimen, overcoming it with paralysis and a profound malaise."

This was bizarre, unheard of. She looked down at the text and began turning pages randomly, reading stray phrases, here and there, looking for those known passages of consolation that were always there for her before. Where was the book's beauty; its lyricism and profundity that had always rocked her soul and soothed her mind? It was if now the book was mocking her, telling her things that could not be true; ugly vile realities that she could not, would not know or hear. She had not asked for or even looked for these words, this message. Yet, over and over it kept beginning again, "We all stand, from time to time, looking into an abyss of one kind or another... that which lies beyond the edge of the abyss...without design or intent, the empty darkness spews us back... spreading contagion from one part of the psyche to another ...block out the darkness within..."

No matter what page she turned to it was the same message, the same words. Where were all the varied topics and different enlightening perspectives? She could not recall the book ever using these words, speaking in this way. She had read it time and time again and she had never heard words like these before. And what made it even worse, was the fact that the book's thoughts were coming to her in the voice of her own saba, that powerful healer-woman of the prior generation of Ocan. Saba could not ever recall her own saba saying these words, delivering this message. But there was no mistake—the words were now echoing loudly in her mind in the clear strong voice of that master of all saba. "Only by traveling back through time, through the quagmire of repressed grief and despair does a healer's healing begin. The pain must form a link, a bridge across the abyss. These are the lessons that no saba can teach, but all true saba must learn."

Saba closed the book, and hugged it tightly to her chest blocking its sound and all memory from her mind. A strong sudden wind swept through the courtyard just before she heard a loud explosive sound in the distance. She realized that this was the same sound that she had heard before while she was reading, but this time it occurred to her that the sound did not reverberate like thunder. She had no time to ponder it any further because the wind began whirling and lashing in torrents throughout the area. Leaves, grass and debris began whipping and flying in all directions. In her rush to get up and find shelter, she dropped the Journal to the ground. At first the pages started flipping rapidly in the wind, but then several loose pages from the Journal quickly became air-borne. She tried to pick up the book and instead, inadvertently knocked Taijaur's packet to the ground as well. The packet was apparently not secured as well as she had thought as papers began spilling out, mixing with the flying pages from the journal. Saba chased the loose sheets of white, brown and yellow, finally bunching Taijaur's papers with her own pages from the Journal. She wrapped her arms and shawl tightly around the jumbled disorganized pieces as she rushed, with her head down against the wind, toward the temple entrance.

As the Saba reached to open the temple door, she heard the sky's rolling resonance grow in force and proximity. She looked up to give proper reverence to the gray ominous clouds that moved rhythmically in waves, alternately revealing and hiding a strange brilliantly white sun. The capricious air near the earth's surface mirrored its higher counterpart as moment by moment it angrily forced all in its path to bend to its might, then would gently subside. For weeks the atmosphere had been bundled up tight with swirling electrically charged energy that begged for release. It had forced its way inside the healer-woman's mind and body, crouching low, raging within her spirit. Waiting for deliverance, she battled intense waves and surges of tension and longing. Waiting for the rain.

And now, just when it seemed it would never come, fat hurried drops of liquid began to fall and splatter.

She entered the opening hesitantly, the dark heavy door creaking on its hinges. Without knowing why, Saba always paused before walking under the archway of this edifice that was constructed on and in front of the opening of a large mountain cave. The old weathered gray stone building was marked with engravings, inscriptions and hieroglyphic drawings across the arched doorway and throughout the one room sanctuary. At the back of the large domed-ceiling room there was an altar with artifacts from various cultures and religious communities. The Saba lit a candle and went through a small door behind the altar. The door was a hidden part of the wall, made of the same uncut rocky stone as the rest of the sanctuary. She steadied her soul as she wound her way down and past the huge stalagmites and stalactites into an inner chamber where a waterfall cascaded over the rocks on the far side of the enclosure.

Near the waterfall there was a small nook in the wall just above head level. She placed the Journal and other materials on the ground and then Saba reached up into this opening in the wall and pulled out a bowl made of stone that contained bits of ember that were burning in a low flame. She sat down near the stream where the waterfall spilled. Her hands were shaking so hard that she nearly dropped the candle and the bowl. She touched the fire of the candle to the burning embers and sprinkled dry leaves, from a pouch at her waist, into the bowl. The flame shot up and although there was only a little smoke, the Saba began coughing and choking. When her spasm subsided, she blew out the candle, closed her eyes and started breathing deeply of the vapor that rose from the bowl. She sat for a moment, trying to reach within herself, but her attention was distracted by the sound of the falling water and the noises from outside of the cave that were filtering through the small cracks in the chamber walls.

This part of the cave where she now sat was surrounded on the outside by the open forest where birds and other small animals were making their presence known. Amidst the stirrings of the forest, Saba began to hear what sounded like human voices. At first she thought she imagined it. No one but she and the Obeah ever came to this temple and the Obeah never made a sound. But then she heard it again and there was no mistaking the sound of voices and that they were calling her name. "Saba! Saba! Where are you? Are you here? Saba?"

The calls were becoming louder, more insistent. She listened more closely and she found that she could distinguish the voices. This was Olana and Alor and maybe Mala as well, calling to her, searching for her. Although she was certain that they did not know of this hidden chamber behind the temple altar, still she did not want them to find her. She hurried to get up and away from this place. In her haste, she accidentally overturned the bowl, spilling the embers. And then as she tried to secure the bowl before any more damage could be done, she inadvertently dropped the bowl into the stream where the eternal flame was immediately doused.

The Saba felt like crying. This fire had burned for thousands of years and now, during her time to keep the flame alive, it had been extinguished. She felt around in the dark for the bowl and pulled it dripping from the water. The voices outside had started up again and her sense of panic and urgency returned. She decided that there was nothing that she could do for the once burning embers at this point and that she would have to come back at some other time to try to make this right. She moved quickly out of the chamber feeling her way along the walls of the cave, going further down into the interior caverns where she had never ventured before. They would never find her there. No one had ever been in those caverns but the Obeah and perhaps some past generation of saba.

As she moved along in the darkness, she thought that she heard a low whispering voice behind her, but when looked around quickly to see who was there, she saw no one. Saba attributed the sound to the underground streams of water that she knew flowed through this place. She wasn't exactly sure which direction to go, but she continued moving forward feeling her way along the rocks of the dank walls, going further and further down into the passageways of the caverns. She walked for what felt like hours and after awhile she began to feel weak. She thought she heard the voice whispering behind her again and this time she could recognize actual words but she could not actually determine what was being said.

In her own mind, her thoughts circled around the same refrain that she found herself repeating each day—*So tired, so very tired.* And when she thought to herself that maybe she should stop and rest, a whispering voice behind responded to her silent thought, saying, *Yes, rest. Like Kalal, Loni and Tekun—they are resting.* She turned around fast to see where the voice was coming from and once again there was nothing. But then it came again—*Maybe in, near the abyss—for without hope what is there but the abyss?* She stopped for a moment and leaned against the wall, trying to block out the sound of the voice that now seemed to come from all directions, repeating the same words over and over. She could see muted wispy flashes of light just ahead around the bend. As she began to follow, the flashes of light became shadowy visions of people moving, speaking. She felt like she was sleep-walking, not fully conscious. She stumbled blindly forward, following the shadowy visions deeper and deeper down into the winding hidden pathways of the cave.

At the end of a long tunnel she walked around the side of a large boulder, into a room of light and shadow where a scene abruptly opened up in front of her. The Saba had unexpectedly found herself in the midst one of her own recurrent dreams, except it was now alive and real in front of her. From her mind, there came an intense electrical shock and then she saw—wait, no it could not be so—but yes, it was her; she saw her daughter, Loni. She was right there before her, walking, smiling. And all Saba had to do was reach out her hand and she could touch her, feel her; she was real. After all the years of calling to her daughter, wishing for her, praying for her—she had finally come. Saba had created an opening, a pathway, and Loni, her own sweet Loni came through. At first she seemed nearly unbroken and didn't press so hard into the open hole that was once the Saba's heart. Then the healer woman truly saw her daughter, with all the guards and veils of her mind stripped away. Loni was standing there in front of her, walking, smiling—in all the gore, all the grotesque horror of a badly decomposed plague-ridden corpse. Saba had moved into the suppressed hell of her own malignant nightmare. She had unwittingly bumped up into a madness that for years had lain, waiting for her, within. And all she could do was watch and relive this horror.

Saba arrived at the burnt out encampment and they brought out Loni's body to add to the pyre. She would not allow them to burn her. Some of the men from the Aka village helped to carry Loni into a nearby dwelling at this outpost where the infected people had been quarantined. He was there, that tall man with white hair, the one from the Haman village. He ushered all the people out of the room and then laid Loni down on a pallet, unwrapping the gauze from her body, placing the bowls of oil, herbs and myrrh beside her. Saba barely heard when he left out, closing the door and leaving her alone with her daughter.

A dark heavy fog was blowing throughout the cavern, and throughout the small hut where she knelt on the floor. The healer-woman began bathing her daughter's still limbs with oils and herbs, anointing the vacant temple of a sacred offering that had already been released back to the Creator. Loni was covered with the sores, pus and the crawling parasites of disease and death. She stroked the corpse's raised midsection and thought of the dead child who lay entombed in the womb that was its grave. When the movement began, she thought at first that she had imagined it. And then the more she rubbed, the more activity she felt within, as if in answer to her inquiring hands. She pushed down on the dead woman's abdomen and then with a carving knife, she cut through the flesh and layers of muscle that led into the internal organs and cavities. With her daughter's decomposed body cut wide open, Saba reached in and pulled her grandson from the uterus. Stunned beyond awareness, she received her living grandson straight from his dead mother's womb. No one knew how long Taijaur had lived inside of Loni's deceased body. They had all assumed that her unborn child had died with her. He came in silence, looking around with wide open eyes, turning his head from side to side, searching. The healer-woman was completely and overwhelmingly shocked. She could not go on with the burial rites, her mind was clouded, her senses numb.

Unbidden, Mala came and saw the dead woman cut open and the living child in the Saba's bewildered hands. She immediately began to bring meaning to that which lie beyond comprehension. Taking the baby from Saba's hands and leading her to a chair, Mala then tied and severed the maternal cord, cleaned the baby and swaddled him tightly. She made a semi-liquid mixture that she fed to the baby before lying him down. Saba watched from a distance as Mala finished the death rites, praying and chanting over Loni's body. After she wrapped Loni's body in a fresh piece of thin gauze, she then enlisted that Haman man to help carry her out. They burned her body in the night and stole away from that Aka outpost without being seen. Mala stayed with Saba over the next few weeks, placing the life that had come from death into the healer woman's arms and guiding her lifeless limbs through the motions that would ensure his survival.

The dream came to Saba exactly as the scene had unfolded in the reality of its moment. Over and over the scenes repeated in her mind, the dream holding her under until new visions began to appear. Then there were scenes that had never been a part of her waking reality. She saw Loni as a young woman laughing and talking with her best friend Mala. And then Mala and Loni were walking fast through the woods, turning to steal glances behind them as they went, making sure to obscure their trail. She saw Mala leading Loni to a young man who stood alone in the woods. Loni and the man embraced. After awhile Mala and Loni stole back through the woods towards the Ocan village. The scene shifted and Saba saw the man speaking heatedly, arguing with a group of people and she knew then that these were members of the Basau family and this young man was their youngest son, Saron. Suddenly Loni appeared amongst them. She was kneeling before a man dressed in an elaborate robe, her head bowed. He placed his hands on her head and recited indecipherable words that Loni then repeated back to him. She was apparently taking part in some type of ceremony or initiation rites. Then Saba saw the scene that she remembered so well when Loni stood before her and told her that she would marry that Basau man and live in the village of the Aka; how she never wanted to be saba and would never again return to her home. Only Mala stood next to Loni and Saron in their Aka marriage ceremony. And finally there was Mala with Loni pregnant, sick, vomiting, then lying still, unmoving.

Even through the heavy vapor of smoke, tears and grief, Saba felt hurt, shock and anger. She struggled to escape from this waking dream world, from these visions that brought such torment. She heard herself screaming, "No, no, no, this can not be!" She was back in the cavern room with only the dream-presence of Mala who stood with her back to Saba, enveloped in the black smoke of a funeral pyre. Saba shouted, "How could you? And all this time you have allowed me to love you, care for you, believe in you. And all along you were the one who helped to cause my grief, my pain. How could you?"

The dream-Mala turned slowly to face Saba, with a look of scorn and hatred that could never be imagined in the Mala that she knew. She spat words at the healer-woman with rage and contempt. "What about what you did? What about how you pushed and pushed your daughter, your only child, to become what you wanted her to be until you finally pushed her away for good. You were so intent on Loni inheriting **your** legacy, **your** plan for her life that you never considered that maybe she had a plan for her own life that had nothing to do with you or what you saw as her obligation and purpose. You and your possessive love drove your daughter away. I tried to convince her not to go, not to leave you. But she knew as you knew that your ownership of her was obliterating her existence, snuffing out any right that she had to an independent existence; any life that did not suit your design, and fulfill your needs, your wants for her life; any life that did not include you. You pushed and manipulated her until she had no more desires of her own. That is until the day that she met Saron and she saw the opportunity to not only re-claim her life, but a chance to get as far away from you as possible. Do you know why you are so filled with a grief and pain that consumes your life? Because you are preyed upon by an immense sense of guilt for having murdered your own daughter; having pushed her to her death."

Involuntarily, Saba screamed with a raking inhuman half-choked voice, "NO!" and with all her might she struck out at Mala with both hands, falling into dark swirling smoke as the dream Mala vanished into the air. Saba fell to the ground in a semiconscious state where the visions then wrapped back around to where they usually began. Just before she lost full consciousness, she saw/felt herself in the temple, beginning to choke and then running to the Aka village, where the burnt and burning bodies were being piled one on top of the other.

Mala sniffing the air, "It has rained here recently. The air is filled with a strong odor of ozone and electricity and," she sniffed again, "and something else. A strong rain," she paused shielding her eyes looking up into the sky, "and now an even stronger sun that has dried it all up. This is unusual. There are no clouds in the sky and it has not rained in the village."

Olana: "Mala, I think that the Saba has gone back to the village." She started touching the trees and the swaying branches as they walked through a small grove of Guola trees that was just outside of the south side of the temple courtyard. Alor had gone through the garden gate and it appeared that he was studying the gravestones near the mausoleum portico structure.

Olana: "I used to love when Saba brought me here. This place is still just as peaceful and serene as it was when I came here as I child. It's like a world unto itself."

Mala: "Olana, Saba is here. I am sure of it. I feel her spirit. She has recently passed where we now stand. Her energy is all around us."

Olana: "But where is she? We have looked everywhere for her and called to her inside the temple, as well as throughout these grounds. We have been here almost an hour. If she was here she would have heard us calling to her."

Mala: "We must face the inevitable—Saba may have gone into the caverns beneath the temple. And we have to be careful. If she was pulled in against her will..." Mala let her words trail off unfinished.

Olana looked away from Mala, speaking nervously fast, "No, I insist, she would not go in there. Even if you feel her spirit here, she may have just passed this way and then just headed back to the village. We may have just missed her along the way. Or perhaps she returned to the Maja before we even came in search of her. We should start back to the village now so that we can find her before it gets dark"

Mala: "Perhaps you are right. Let's go ask Alor what he thinks we should do."

They started walking toward the courtyard and Olana stopped short, staring ahead as she raised her hand to Mala, saying, "Shhh. Wait a minute. Do you hear that?"

Mala: "Hear what?"

Olana whispered, "A faint sound of music. I used to hear it all the time in the temple when I was young. Sometimes I would hunt and hunt, trying to find where it was coming from. But I could never find the source."

They were both silent for a moment, with Olana tilting her head, listening intently to the wind.

Olana: "Do you still not hear it? Its getting louder, more pronounced."

Mala: "No, I don't hear any—"

Alor shouted, "Mala! Olana! Come quickly! It is just as I suspected."

He was kneeling, looking under the stone bench near the mausoleum portico in the garden courtyard, yelling over his shoulder.

Olana: "You go Mala. I want to see if I can figure out once and for all where this music is coming from."

Mala: "Be careful, Olana. We don't know what we are dealing with here."

Olana made no response as she started wandering in the direction of the entrance to the temple. Alor stood as Mala approached. He had sheaves of yellow-brown parchment in his hands. "Look, these are some of Taijaur's missing notes. They were here under this bench. Saba must have dropped them. She must have come here to get them. These three pages are from Taijaur's notes. But I don't recognize this other page. It has strange symbolic markings but it is not a part of The Book of Change. I've never seen symbols like these. It is obviously very old."

Mala reached for the paper, "Let me see it. It may match some of the antiquated sources that I have been helping Olana catalog for Amira." She held the paper, looking at it from all angles and directions. "It looks familiar, but I can make no sense of it. Perhaps there is a codex in the archives that will help decipher its meaning. No, wait! I've seen these markings before."

Mala felt a sensation of heat flow through her body. She stepped away from Alor and turned her back to him as her pulse quickened and she could hear her own blood flowing, pumping loudly in her ears, drowning out all other sound. Mala watched as the symbols on the page began to move and squirm, realigning themselves—some going up, others down and over until they finally settled into position and coherence came from the page. She heard her own voice within her mind, with an echo all around as if the words originated from some far-off distant vacuum. It felt like the wind, or the air around her was creating the sounds of the words, while she stood merely inhaling and exhaling their meaning.

"And there are those who must go through the abyss to reach the fractured worlds within. They must find a way into the depths, beyond the surface. They must allow mind-soul to go through to the other side. Cannot overcome it. Cannot defeat it. Must go through and find a way to the other side. Reach through all that must be endured to sustain life. Reach through to understand the realities that supersede the surface experience of living. Find the worlds within worlds, the fractured realities, fractured dimensions that create and sustain the universe."

The words stopped and the air stood still. Mala looked up from the page and turned to Alor, saying, "She's in there, Alor. Saba is down in those caverns. And she will not be able to get out unless we find a way to help her."

Alor: "Mala, if Saba is in there then the only way to help her is for someone to also enter the gateway in order to bring her back. Beyond the danger of the caverns' poisonous gases, it will be impossible to withstand the volatile eddies of energy forces that will engulf the Saba or any one caught in their undertow. These openings are unstable geological anomalies that shift and move with the internal permutations of the earth."

Mala: "I realize that the energy appears to fluctuate randomly. But there has to be something that we can do to try to pull Saba back."

Alor: "The entryways are never the same from one day to the next, one moment to the next. From moment to moment, it is never possible to find the exact location of a portal, because the portals constantly and randomly close in on themselves. If the portal closes while she is in there, there will be no exit from that place."

Mala: "But the portals are alive—they are a living, sensing form of energy—and as such there has to be a way to calculate or predict their intent. We may not need to actually enter the gateway. Remember—we have been taught and it is written that there is a way to access the in-between solely by way of the sentiale pathways, through the power of our minds and our spirits."

Alor: "But that is only an ancient Obeah belief that has never been proven. I have begun to suspect that this belief may, indeed, be true; that it may be possible to access the in-between without physically going there. But I have not yet found enough evidence to support my suspicions."

Mala: "I believe that, in our lifetime, there has been an incident that confirms the sentiale pathways as the only necessary port of entry into the in-between. If I am not mistaken, there has been someone who never physically went into the in-between, but nonetheless traveled by way of the sentiale pathways in order to guide another person back into the land of the living.

The Obeah spoke vaguely of a man who inadvertently entered the in-between and was unable, on his own, to come back to our world. Nonetheless, this man did eventually return. They alluded to the fact that another more powerful person was able to mentally and spiritually enter the sentiale pathways in order to pull and guide this man back to the physical reality of our own world."

Alor: "But who was this person that they referred to? And when did you speak with the Obeah?"

Mala: "They would not reveal a name, but I believe that the lost person that they were speaking of was Kalal. I am almost certain that Kalal ventured into a portal in the western forest and that his source of rescue came by way of the sentiale pathways."

Alor: "Mala, do you mean to tell me that you know of this? I have just spent a week traveling to the hamlets and back, hoping that Amira could confirm what I have suspected about Kalal. And all along you were the one that I should have been speaking to. How is that you were able to make contact with the Obeah?"

Mala: "Alor, we don't have much time. We will have to discuss the details later. But I trust that you will not betray my confidence when I tell you that I have been called to be one in the spiritual union that is Obeah. One element of their whole will soon pass on and the balance of the trinity must be maintained."

Alor: "This is amazing Mala. In this lifetime there has not been another called to the Obeah. This is an honor, indeed."

Mala: "Yes, yes Alor, but we don't have much time and we must devise a plan."

Alor: "But did you know, did the Obeah or someone tell you that Kalal kept repeating a phrase about music and he kept saying the words 'the eye' and 'adamas' over and over?"

Mala: "No. I never saw Kalal again after he took me back to the western shore, right after Shona was born. I only know what Saba told me about his fragile condition."

Alor: "Adamas is the ancient Greek word from which the word 'diamond' is derived. I believe that his statements about music and a diamond eye refer to the power source of the in-between—the Eye of God. Also, in his sentiale perception I saw the image of an object that is similar to an intricate construct that is described in the Book. However, I have not yet found the complete translation of those passages. There is no description of the Eye of God in any of the Ocan annals. So I cannot confirm that his vision and the object described in the Book are, indeed, one and the same. Nonetheless, I am convinced that Kalal was there, in the in-between and that it is the power source—the Eye of God—that he spoke of and that he kept seeing as an image in his mind. I believe that he was in the in-between and that something or someone acted to pull him away from that nether-realm. Amira knows what happened, but I could make no sense of her words. And yet all this time you have known."

Mala: "I'm not exactly sure what I know. But I believe that Olana may hold the key to understanding what happened to Kalal and the key to as to how Saba can be saved."

Alor: "Olana? Olana was just a child when this happened to Kalal. And I have already questioned her. She knows nothing of this."

Mala: "She knows more than she realizes. And yes, she was a child—a very powerful child, with a powerful sentiale."

Alor: "But Mala, you do realize that Kalal most likely lost his mind as a result of his experiences either in the in-between or with the process of being pulled back. And Amira may have also been affected by this incident. I am afraid to think of what this means for Saba or for anyone who might attempt to pull her back."

Mala: "Yes, I realize the risks. However, we have no choice. I think I know what must be done. Unfortunately, most of the burden for this will fall on Olana's shoulders. But the Obeah have begun instructing me in the ancient ways of their order. And if I am understanding the sentiale of the in-between correctly, then I believe that Saba's safety—our safety—will depend on an anchor to hold Olana steady while also serving as a bridge that will help Saba reach the other side."

Alor, looking around, "But where is Olana?"

Mala turns in alarm. "She was just here."

With Alor behind her, Mala walks out of the courtyard towards the temple, calling out, "Olana! Olana!".

23. The In-Between

They were propelled through the forest, easing with fluid motion between the densely compacted trees upon an unseen path that had been set before them. Pockets of fast moving energy, like small darting animals, sped by in the opposite direction, sensing and probing their awareness as they went. It felt as if hours had passed, yet it seemed only seconds. With the tinkling sound of a small waterfall in a nearby stream they suddenly became aware of the cessation of movement. Only with sight and sound were they awakened to the surface reality of their dimensional existence. And true motion will always cease with consciousness of self.

The stream beckoned Shona's thirst and she knelt at its banks to taste and feel its cool surreal essence. Like black liquid mercury the water flowed into the darkness, subtlety bathing its visitors in its obscure primeval luminescence. She looked up from the stream to find that they were already inside the cave. The entrance was obscured by overgrown vines and strange twisted vegetation which blurred any border between the forest and the world inside the cave. Taijaur lit a small torch and held it high as he led the way down a steep precipitous path into the tunnels beneath the surface of the world. They crept further and further into the depths of this limestone cave, where complex levels and interconnections of tunnels and narrow winding passageways had been carved out millennia before any human tread this way. All around on the walls, floors and ceilings there were crystalline mineral formations—some minute needle-like crystals and others huge majestic stalagmites and stalactites. There was a constant dripping sound from a fresh water spring that flowed down the sides of the rocks falling into the chasm below.

They felt like they were moving in slow motion underwater, float-walking along the path. The sharp jutting rocks of the walls provided an anchor as they felt their way along, while breathing deeply to fight against the eerie sensation of weightlessness that wrapped around them and buoyed them on. For most of the way down, Shona could hear a bevy of faint whispering voices rising from below. The voices became louder as she descended, but she could not decipher any individual words or meaning, even as she focused her attention on this strange auditory sensation. Within the chaos of unintelligible sounds she briefly heard and felt a soft melodic female voice but it was gone as fast as it had come.

They came to the bottom of the path and went through a tunnel that led into a chamber with a ceiling reaching thirty feet or more overhead. It looked to be about six feet wide and over a hundred feet long. Protruding from the rock walls there were clusters and globules of mainly white flowstone and dripstone mineral formations, with some dusky red and brown mixed throughout. The bevy of voices had never ceased and for a moment she thought she heard the melodic voice once again. She strained to take in the words but the voice was submerged by a rush of multiple streams of overlaying voices each talking on top of and around each other.

Taijaur turned to her, "Shona, do you hear that? Its music—a series of different harmonies blending in and leading to one another. It's a song."

Shona: "I don't hear a song or any music."

Taijaur: "But the song is everywhere—coming from every surface. It's the same song from my dream long ago. Only it sounds more alive here, more necessary, more urgent."

The sound of Taijaur's and Shona's voices echoed from all sides of the rocky walls in slow deep modulations. Their words, thoughts and even their visibility were obscured, diluted by the ephemeral substance of the cave's atmosphere.

Shona: "I just hear incessant whispering. So many voices; over and over they keep repeating. I recognize some of the words, but I can't understand the meaning."

For a moment Taijaur seemed lost in the music, oblivious to her presence and the environment that surrounded them. Then, with great effort and concentration, he shook off the music's effect, while Shona was still focusing on the voices, trying to isolate and distinguish separate syllables and sounds.

Taijaur: "It's there Shona. The portal. It's over there."

He pointed to a nearby wall with a crop of rocks and an opening that was close to the ground. "Do you see that crawlway with the rocks surrounding it? Focus your eyes and watch how the light moves and pulsates; its flowing like water throughout that area?"

Shona: "I don't see any light."

Taijaur: "Focus your attention Shona and concentrate your mind." He snuffed the fire of the torch as he took her hand and pulled her towards the crawlway. He bent down next to it, touching the rocks that surrounded the opening.

Shona: "I see it! I see it! It's beautiful. The colors, the way they move—it is so amazing."

He took his hands away, "Can you still see it?"

Shona: "Yes, only it is not as strong as when you touched it."

Taijaur: "The light is muted—which may mean that this portal is just entering the emergence phase of its cycle; arising from dormancy. If that is the case, then I believe that we may have more time and more flexibility."

He stood and faced her. "This is as far as I can go Shona, but you must keep me with you the whole way. I will be right here to guide you back. You must stay within a conscious awareness of your sentiale and keep your attention focused. The light from this portal can guide you to the interior chambers, but only if you maintain your sentiale connection. If you lose your focus, you will no longer be able to perceive the light and you will be plunged into absolute and complete darkness. That is why it is important for you to not let go of your link with me. Our connection will help you to sustain your focus and," he paused, "also, take this." He took the crystal from around his neck and put it in her hand, wrapping the string around her wrist. "If you need to, use this to help guide the way, to show the light. But keep it tightly in your fist until the time that you need to use it."

He held both of her hands in his own. "Remember, do not allow your sentiale pathways to be blocked by any negative emotions or you will not be able to feel me pulling you back. The portal will stay in one place for a limited time, so you must return immediately when I call to you. We won't have much time. No matter what—keep me with you."

Their eyes locked hard and strong and then he released her hands and bent down placing both of his hands on strategic points around the opening. She stooped down and began crawling through the narrow tube-shaped cave passage with white calcite formations lining the walls. It took only seconds to get through the passage, but the claustrophobic feel of the enclosure made it feel much longer. She pulled herself through on the other side and stood up, in a small room where a faint breeze was blowing. She tried to fathom the source of these gentle gusts of air as she glanced back at the portal. The rocks around the crawlway no longer emitted any light or colors. It was strange standing in almost pitch black, listening to the low mutterings of the voices that seemed to follow everywhere that she went.

On the other side of the chamber there were openings to two tunnels almost side by side, one larger than the other, each leading in separate directions, like a fork in the road. Shona thought she saw a momentary light in the direction of one of the tunnels, and then it was gone. A few seconds later, she saw it again and realized that something was coming through the larger passageway on the right. At first there were only wisps of white smoke that drifted throughout the chamber in slow thin tendrils that stretched toward the ceiling and dissipated before reaching it. In the midst of the clouds of smoke, a figure emerged from the tunnel, a shadowy image bathed in low soft white light that floated through the opening. It was the lone form of a woman in a white flowing dress, with a transparent veil that covered her from head to toe. The woman looked at Shona and smiled. Shona's heart skipped a beat and her emotions overflowed. "Mala? Are you here? Are you here too, Mother?"

As Shona reached out, and started walking toward the figure, the silent woman turned and began walking back through the tunnel she had come, glancing back over her shoulder as she went. Shona shouted as she hurried to catch the retreating apparition. "Mala! Mala wait for me. Don't leave me! Please! I need you!"

When the spectral figure disappeared around a bend, Shona found herself in a sudden darkness. She touched the rocky wall to feel her way forward and a subtle illumination shone from the surface. She made an effort to touch the rock with her mind and the muted light came alive in every direction that she moved or turned, lighting her way and then fading back into blackness after she passed and her attention went forward. The voices were still with her, in front of her, behind her, everywhere that she went and could be. This tunnel seemed to go on endlessly and just when it seemed that she was nearing the end, she turned and went through yet another long passageway with Mala always just ahead, just out of reach; a shadowy wisp of light leading her forward. She called out as she ran to catch up, "Mother, wait for me please!"

Shona followed the figure of Mala wrapped in her faint glow of light until she found herself in the innermost chamber of the subterranean tunnels. This was a cold dark room with a vaulted interior, filled with impenetrable black smoke that enveloped her and wafted all around. There was a stream that ran through the middle of the room, almost bisecting the two sides before its path turned and made a semi-circular loop, flowing out through a small opening in the rocks on the far end of the room. Shona could barely see through the dense black smoke. She coughed, waving the smoke from her eyes, trying to determine the direction that Mala had gone. Finally she saw her on the other side of the stream bending down near the bank, staring across directly at Shona. The whole room disappeared from her perception as Shona saw nothing but her mother gazing at her. She drank in the love, the understanding, the recognition and connection that poured from her mother's eyes, sighing as she said, "Oh Mala, I have missed you so much."

As soon as she said these words, the black smoke swirled up all around her and the spectral image of Mala was swallowed up in the smoke and dust. The indecipherable voices became louder, in a grating, irritating tone with stray sentences surfacing from the maelstrom, briefly conveying meaning before diving back into the madness. Shona closed her eyes and took several deep breaths, trying to mentally block out the sounds and steady herself against the despair and sudden queasiness that she felt. She knew that she had to force herself to be strong and not let this place consume her. Intellectually she knew that the image of Mala had never been real but her emotions had hoped, wanted, needed for the image to lead to something real.

When the queasiness passed, she looked around this place, this inner cavern, where a subtle illumination emerged from the surface of the shiny black rock of the walls. The black fog had dispersed and was drifting near the floor of the cavern, covering her feet and ankles. As her eyes adjusted to the room's visibility, she saw that there were spider webs everywhere throughout this cavern—on every surface, every rock, every boulder. It took awhile before she realized that this was really just one huge interconnected web that seemed to stretch and extend endlessly in all directions.

This enormous web was thicker and more intricate, more complex than the one that had been in the arachnid grove on the Ocan island. And it seemed to be breathing—deep breaths of wind gusting, in and out, over and over, blowing vast amounts of floating dust and other particles into the air. In addition to a steady subtle glow emitted from the surface of the rocks, the room was also faintly illuminated by intermittent flashes of light streaming through the fibers of the web. At first, Shona thought she imagined the lights that moved in micro-second electrical charges throughout the web across the entire room and even on the surface of the stream. To confirm her perception, she shifted her vision and held the iridescent vibrations in her mind's eye until it forced her to stop seeing. She shook her head and opened her eyes, unexpectedly bumping into an image that startled her sense of reality. In the brief second that her eyes had closed, the whole room appeared to have transformed into a huge scintillating geode with multiple symmetrical layers of a fractal design. For a brief moment, the web, the rocks and even the stream seemed to be comprised of layers of symmetrical crystal rings of light. But then just as quickly, the vision shifted out of perceptual reach and she saw that she was still really just looking at walls of sharp jutting black rock with layers and layers of web and dust.

She was still standing near the passageway that she had come through, when suddenly all of her senses became alert to the presence of someone else here with her in this dark enclosed space. She could hear subtle breathing and she detected a faint scent of something from the world above. It was a compelling odor of rich dark soil and various types of vegetation that could never be found in these deep recesses of the earth.

She finally saw on the other side of the stream, yet another tunnel opening, partially obscured behind a large rock. And there was something else, closer to the stream bank. It was a shape, a human form lying inert on the ground near the stream's bank. The person was lying on, wrapped in and covered by the thick web. The continual overlay of repeating whispering voices that had never stopped became louder as Shona got up and started walking toward the stream. The figure moved slightly and Shona could feel this person's awareness focused on her, studying her as she approached. She blocked the noise of the incoherent voices and with her sentiale she reached out. Shona was surprised to feel herself inside a thick morass of pain, despair and anguish that overflowed from this being before her. She was even more taken aback to realize that the soul within this motionless form was that of the healer-woman of the Ocan people.

For Saba there were no voices, no words. She could hear only a low irritating buzzing sound, like a trapped hornet. She had lain here in this semi-conscious stupor for seconds? hours? days? She didn't know. She knew only that she was waiting; allowing the sounds and sensations around her to lure her further away.

Saba watched the slowly approaching form take shape in the darkness and as the girl drew closer, their eyes linked with a concentrated intensity. Saba knew immediately that this was Mala's child. Even without the identifiable birthmark above her eyes, the knowledge of Shona's being came so clearly into the Saba's senses that there could be no doubt. At first, Saba had no time to allow any fear or confusion to rise, because the essence of this young woman was flowing so distinctly, so purely into and throughout her awareness that there was room for no other thoughts or emotions. These new sensations felt so natural, and real and normal, like she had been feeling this way, experiencing these free and open sensations all of her life. For the first time in more than two decades, her sentiale pathways were fully open and flooding her body and spirit with all the emotions, knowledge and sensations of a lifetime. A tremendous pressure and sickness lifted from her body and for the first time since Loni had passed away, she knew what it was to breathe freely, to think and feel without any emotional or psychological impediment.

For a moment, Saba was lost in the wonder of it all, but then her mind began to doubt and distrust what her eyes conveyed. This small opening of time gave her learned patterns of fear and grief all the chance they needed to resuscitate and take control once again. Before Shona reached the stream and before Saba could even understand what was happening, her sentiale closed in on itself, and she slipped back into her worn, yet familiar guise of dejected self-reproach, not fully awake or aware of the realities around her. And then once again, it all ceased to matter, as she closed her eyes and waited for release, a deliverance to a place where she could hear no sounds, feel no emotions, think no thoughts.

Shona was about to step into the stream to cross over to Saba when she stopped, unexpectedly overwhelmed by an intense tingling sensation that was moving throughout the nerve endings of her body. The air in the chamber began to blow forcefully all around her as she heard and sensed something in the distance, coming through the passageway behind her. At first, it sounded it like a low humming noise and then it was like the sound of rushing water, growing louder, as it came closer. Without knowing why, Shona felt fear rising inside of her as she struggled to breathe, inhaling panic and dust in every breath. She turned and saw wind and dust gusting furiously through the tunnel and throughout the enclosed chamber. The voices were still with her, although becoming more mumbled and incoherent as they faded into the background.

The black smoke swiftly coalesced and rose into an angry torrent of wind. The thick black noxious clouds were surging swirling all around, blocking her vision and filling the chamber. The wind knocked her back against the wall just as it—something—came in. The sounds in the tunnel passageway were not far behind it. This was a small strange hairless figure, wearing only a loin cloth, darting furtively into the chamber. He resembled a young human child, except his body emitted a subtle luminescence as he ran using all four limbs, standing only to survey the room, looking for a way out. He quickly realized that the only other exit from this room was on the opposite side of the stream and for some reason the sight of the water made him shiver with fright. He shrank down behind a large rock near the entryway that he had come through. He was directly opposite from where Shona stood motionless against the wall. Shaking, cringing, he looked up and unexpectedly made eye contact with Shona, just before his pursuers came, pounding, thudding into the room, angrily pushing, shoving, snarling. She felt his plea, his terror, his panic. She was inside the height of a terrifying, escalating sense of alarm which caused her fear to overflow along with her compassion, inducing a feeling of weakness in her knees and in her heart.

There were three of them, beasts unlike any that Shona had ever seen or heard tell of. Some type of sub-human creatures; a perversion of humanity with their mottled gray skin, short squat powerfully built bodies with exposed massive forearms bulging muscles. The irises of their eyes were a milky silver color, with white diamond shaped pupils. Shona assumed that they were either nearly blind or possessing very little sight. It didn't take them long to sniff out the hiding place of their prey. They savagely pounced on the trembling form of the child. The more the hapless victim squirmed, the more savage the beasts tore into him. Spurred on by the excitement of consuming living prey, they began tearing chunks of its flesh and then its limbs from its body. The screams of pain, terror and anguish could still be heard in the first seconds that they began their feast. Shona cowered against the wall, a nauseating feeling rising in her stomach and throat. Nonetheless, she was unable to take her eyes away from the horror of the nightmare scene in front of her. Her mind tried to tell her that this was just a vision, some type of hallucination, as the words, "This is not real" became a repeating mantra in her head. But another part of her perception focused on the fact that these creatures were not bathed in any spectral light, not swathed in any veils of transparency. Their bodies were tangible in this space. The air was thick with their smell and their presence.

For a brief moment, a strong presence of Taijaur came through in her mind and in her senses. She latched onto his sentiale, silently calling out to him in despair, "Help me, please!" Taijaur's strength brought her comfort and reassurance. She leaned back on his concern for her, his love, his need to protect her and her own strength began to slip away. She felt him trying to pull her back, leading her mentally back through the passageway. But she knew that she could not go and leave this woman, this saba lying defenseless in the midst of this fiendish orgy. Taijaur was urgently pulling her, calling to her. The more fear and concern that he felt on her behalf, the weaker she became. And she knew that she had to separate herself from him. So she internalized his love and his belief in order to fortify herself and then forcefully pulled away from the sentiale connection, pushing the thought of him to the back of her mind.

The creatures appeared oblivious to anything else in the room outside of their wanton gorging as blood poured down from their mouths and arms. Shona pressed herself even further against the wall and tried hard to hold steady as she felt her mind fraying, her thoughts disintegrating into the air. She was inside of the essence of something that she could not fathom. As she watched, the repulsion began to subside and she felt her own hunger intensifying. She felt an almost irresistible, intense need to join them, to feed on this victim's raw flesh. Her mouth started salivating with the smell and salty taste of raw fresh meat. She was a part of these creatures, inside their thoughts and emotions, remembering seeing, feeling previous heinous acts. Their uncontrolled warped needs were becoming her own as she felt only pleasure and an intense excitement. A small voice inside of her cried out weakly and Shona became vaguely aware of the loss of some essential connection.

One of the creatures suddenly stopped feeding, and raised his head, turning it from side to side, listening and sniffing the air. At first Shona thought that they could sense her presence, but then she heard what the creature must have heard. Saba had started moaning quietly as she lie curled in a fetal position on her side, still in a semi-conscious state. The creature that sniffed the air began running towards Saba, growling and snarling as he splashed through the stream.

With this Shona was jarred out of her stupor and she sprang away from the wall, standing in an automatic defensive posture. She shouted, "NO! Stay away from her. You cannot have her!"

The beast, which had by this time clutched one of Saba's arms with its claws as he stood in the water, stopped and swirled around becoming aware of Shona for the first time. The other two who were closer to her, ceased feeding and turned their faces in her direction as well. For a fraction of a second, time, all sound and sensation stood still and then all three came alive, charging towards Shona as if they were of one mind, one motion. There was a loud anguished scream from the direction of the stream where the creature that was still in the water had his hands and one foot on the stream bank in a position to hoist himself out of the water. The other two beasts on land turned and watched as their compatriot literally burned alive before their eyes, with flames shooting up from the water, consuming his body. With apparently only mild interest in this immolation, they turned their attention back to their new food source and resumed their charge toward Shona. She was able to kick the first creature to reach her in the midsection and he stumbled back. But before she had time to react she had been seized by the arms, while the other one recovered quickly and grabbed her legs, leaving her suspended in air and completely defenseless.

She tried not to struggle as they both began to excitedly and greedily devour her body sinking long sharp teeth into the meaty parts of her thigh, upper arm and waist. The pain filled her up as her consciousness ebbed away. Through the fog in her mind, she heard the rushing sound of water and fierce winds and she opened her eyes to see black smoke once again swirling surging in the room. The beasts had let her go, dropping her to the ground as they hobbled out of the room, retreating in the midst of the smoke that had ushered them in.

Just as it had washed into the room, the swirling madness slowly evaporated. She forced herself to sit up but the pain was excruciating and there was blood all over her body. The smoke cleared enough for her to see across the stream where Saba lie curled on her side, moaning. Shona crawled over to the stream, and hesitated for a moment. But then she told herself that, "none of this real" and her logic reasoned that the effect of the water could be no worse than being devoured by beasts that came from her own hallucinations. So she eased her body into the cool waist-high water, stumbling to the other side, where she pulled herself out and lie for a moment beside the Saba.

She reached out to check Saba for injury, and the web that covered and consumed the healer-woman began to stick to Shona. Although she could not pull free of it, the pervasive sticky web was soft and pliable enough to maneuver through it. She tore the web away from Saba's face, with the loosened pieces now clinging to her hands and arms. She managed to ignore the gummy threads as she tended Saba's injuries, wiping blood from the gash in her arm where the beast had dug its claws. She packed the wound with herbs from the small bag that she carried attached to the belt around her waist and then loosely wrapped her arm with a piece of cloth torn from Saba's shirt sleeve. Her own wounds on her thigh and side had already started to close and heal. She surmised that the water must have some type of therapeutic properties. The low droning whispers began again and intruded so closely on her consciousness that she could not determine if the voices originated within her own mind, or if they came from the air around her. The voices filled her with an agitation that made her scream aloud, "You are not real! You just want me to think that you are."

She had torn part of her pant leg and, as best she could, she was tying it around an open cut in her arm. The voices were getting louder, their words more distinguishable. Shona said in low voice, "All of this is happening in my mind. These vapors, these gases—I know that they induce hallucinations." Then she looked up at the ceiling and shouted, "You can't scare me."

Shona began gently shaking Saba, calling to her, "Saba? Saba? I've come to help you. You have to let me help you. We have to get out of this place." She pulled the sticky web away from the Saba's face, out of her mouth and eyes. The irritation induced by the never-ceasing voices became so intense that she had to stop and cover her ears to block the sound and stop the tickling noise that it made inside of her ears. She yelled loudly, defiantly into the empty room, "You cannot have this woman!"

Saba moaned, her eyes half opened, "Tired, very tired…let me go… Loni… I tried.....very tired…I didn't…I didn't …please, let me go." And then she looked directly at Shona and said firmly, "Please let me go, let me leave. I have no more, no more to give."

The voices were growing more distinct and Shona began to hear some of the words separately and distinguish the more dominant voices as she began to understand what they were saying. She had thought it all a jumble of nonsense words, but she now realized that they had actually been talking to and about her the whole time. She could distinguish three main voices in the maelstrom—the strongest and most dominant voice was the melodic female tone that she had heard periodically since she had first entered the cave. Of the other two voices, one seemed to be male and the last a softer younger questioning female. She listened to them with more attention, assigning words to identities as she began to tend to Saba.

Male: *"Let go. Let her go. You must let go."*

Younger Female: *"She wants to stay here; not return to your realm. Let her go.*

Shona laid the healer-woman's head in her lap and placed her hands on either side of Saba's head and face. She closed her eyes, and began to reach out to the healer-woman with her mind, but she couldn't concentrate because the voices would leave her alone.

Male: *"How random it must seem to her—this coming into and leaving out of existence."*

Younger Female: *"Is she disappointed, sad, mad that there appears to be no purpose, no reason for life, except perhaps for the sheer randomness of it all?"*

Shona opened her eyes and shouted up to the ceiling of the room, "Where are you? What are you? Why can't you show yourself? I know that you are doing this to me. Trying to convince me that these images, those beasts are real. But I won't be deluded by your games."

The bevy of voices suddenly ceased and there was absolute silence in the cavern for the first time since she entered. Barely audible vibrations, surrounded and absorbed by pockets of warm hazy vacuity, bounced on and around Shona. She went back to trying to form a link with Saba, but no matter how hard she tried, Shona could not penetrate beyond the surface of the healer-woman's agitated emotions. She settled in on a surface level, absorbing some of Saba's pain while galvanizing all of her senses to push forcefully against the healer-woman's memories and their effect. She sent soothing thoughts to help erect a defense against further assaults and began to rub her back as she hummed a low deep tune. Then Shona, in a low voice, began talking to herself, "How can I be expected to do battle against something that I cannot understand?"

The overlaying voices immediately began again, growing louder, faster, more insistent. She heard what sounded like the dominant female voice ask, ***"Is that why you are here—to 'do battle'? Did you come here to fight?"*** Within the bevy of background voices she heard—

Male: *"They need external friction to incite their growth."*

Younger Female: *"They don't know how to stimulate or allow for internal combustion— heat and light—to come forth. They don't know how to touch energy connections within the whole."*

Male: *"They seek fission, neglect fusion."*

Shona decided to focus on and respond to only the dominant voice. Whether these voices were real or not, her own responses might help to keep her mind stable, even if it meant that she was ultimately just arguing with different parts of her own thoughts.

Shona: "I don't know why I am here. Except I know that I must help this woman, this saba. She must be returned to her people, to the world outside, above."

Older Female: **"She wants to come with us. Look at her. Ask her."**

Shona looked down at Saba who appeared old and very small and then said forcefully to the walls around her, "You cannot have our lives. I know that you want our energy; that you feed on our life-force."

Male: *"Such puny self-centered beings—always assuming that someone either needs or wants their individual insignificant lives."*

Younger Female: *"They prey on one another and all life in their realm. Their realities are based on unfulfilled needs and the dominance of one being over another. They cannot move beyond a linear finite focus on their own individual needs."*

Male: *". . .always afraid that some one, some thing will steal away their lives, when all along they siphon away their own existence. Don't live up to their own potential. . .neglect their power...destroy their own lives."*

Younger Female: *"They don't understand that no one has to take your life from you when you choose to self-destruct in so many petty and meaningless ways."*

Older Female: **"Do you think that you can save her? Do you have what she needs?"**

Shona raised her eyes to the ceiling and the walls and said with strong conviction, "She still has much to give, much to live for."

Older Female: **"There is a limit to the time that you may spend as a separate individual life-force."**

Male: *"The space that you have been given is not yours for ever. You must all concede your allotted space back to the whole and allow another life force its time within the finite reality of surface sensory perceptions."*

Shona: "But this woman, this saba, her time within our physical world is not ready to close. She must return. You must give her back."

Younger Female: *"Her energy will not cease, her essence remains eternal—it belongs to the whole. It is only time for her to relinquish her hold on your world. Something has to be given in order to receive."*

Shona: "No! Take me. Not her. She is essential to the Ocan cause. Her people need her."

Older Female: *"Does your life have no value for you?"*

Younger Female: *"Are you not essential?"*

Shona: "Without her, our people cannot go on. Saba-energy is needed to help fulfill our purpose as a people."

Male: *"Our? Our people? Our purpose?*

Younger Female: *"Is there such a concept as 'our' for you?*

Older Female: *"Do you belong to these people, and they to you?"*

Shona fumbled for a few seconds, lost, searching for words, "I, I—" And then she found herself again, "I don't know that I can belong to anyone or anything. But I know that these people, the Ocan, are a part of me; a part of that which makes me what I am."

The tingling sensations that she had felt before started moving through her body and the voices faded back into a jumbled maelstrom of nonsense with loud raucous sinister laughter now dominating the air. The sound of distant rushing water was becoming louder, getting closer, and Shona rushed to push Saba closer to the wall and then she waded through the stream, trying to determine the most feasible place to hide, out of sight of the tunnel passageway. She knew it was happening again. The same evil wind was coming once more. Whatever it was—this evil or confusion or sorrow—this time it was stronger, more forceful.

She climbed out of the water, just as the black hurricane speed winds swooshed in like a huge bursting tidal wave. The wind knocked her down to her hands and knees, biting into her skin like swirling cutting sand. She crawled over to the wall by the tunnel opening, so as to be behind and out of sight any entity or presence that came through the passageway. There was more laughter of all types—sinister, jovial, warm-hearted, silly, irritatingly nasal and high-pitched, deep guttural, raucous. The wind stopped swirling and this time scenes from the city became real and alive, here and now in this place far from any land and people, right in front of her. She was in the market, with butchered meat, hanging, laying body parts side by side. All manner and form of animal life imaginable, butchered, slaughtered and displayed for sale, for consumption.

This time there seemed nothing to fight against, no strange creatures trying to consume her life. She was grateful for this reprieve, because no matter how real or unreal these visions were, the struggle, the pain, the loss of blood was taking a toll on her mentally and physically.

She wanted to turn her head, close her eyes and stop seeing these grotesque images that came alive in front of her. But she couldn't. Something forced her to watch as the animals were being slaughtered in the most cruel and inhumane way possible. She could hardly stand the agonizing screams of pain and fear. She watched in horror as bovine, porcine and all other manner and type of animal had their lives viciously taken from them and prepared as sustenance for an endless feast of humans gorging themselves on the animals' meat, flesh and internal organs. Something made her look closer at the slaughtered bodies and she saw that these were no longer the body parts of recognizable animals, instead they had become human carcasses—adults', children's, babies' bodies slaughtered and presented as veal, lamb, beef—their ribs, fingers, toes, intestines—at first displayed for sale and then cooked, pickled, sautéed, baked, fried, garnished and served for the endless feast of other humans who relished the taste of this new meat with wanton abandon.

She heard the cries, the pleas of the animals turn into human cries of horror and pain as they watched their children, friends and loved ones being tortured, slaughtered and prepared for consumption. And then she saw other people smiling, laughing, pointing at a display of dead executed tortured bodies that had been hardened in plastic for the entertainment and edification of the uncaring, the ignorant and the naively curious.

Shona felt herself an integral part of each scene, at first feeling only sickness repulsion, fear and despair. Then a feeling of excitement came over her as she edged first towards the slaughterhouse and then the table where the feast of body parts lay. Before she knew what was happening she had dropped to her knees and became a part of the killing, the slaughtering, the feeding of distorted needs. She now felt exhilarated, as if connecting with some vital force within herself. She was feeding off of the fear, the pain, the blood, the flesh of human bodies and souls. Some part of her brain, her soul recoiled, horrified by these feelings of blood-lust and desire for the pain and the consumption of the lives of others. But she continued to savagely slaughter and tear into human flesh with her nails and teeth, rapturously savoring this feel of the kill.

When that small voice inside her soul finally screamed loud enough to penetrate the madness, Shona knew that she had to fight with every fiber of her being to retain her sanity and regain her humanity. She raised her head, with blood still pouring from her mouth and started screaming, "Why are you doing this? Why!?! What purpose does this serve?"

The background bevy of talking voices stopped and became a raucous, reverberating laughter from all directions before suddenly and abruptly ceasing. The wind subsided and all around there was complete stillness and quiet. The bodies had all disappeared and there was nothing left of the butchery, except the blood that stained her clothes, her body, her soul. She was still kneeling on the ground, now fighting the urge to vomit and trying to quell the nausea and vertigo as the world still seemed to be spinning out of control.

Shona: "This is illogical. None of it makes any sense. I can't fight against irrationality."

She heard a voice speaking clearly as if in her own mind—*But doesn't irrationality form the basis of all evil, all discord, all strife, all conflict?*

She crawled over to the stream to rinse her mouth and began frantically wiping her tongue and mouth with her clothes and her hands. The voices started again. This time they were clearly distinguishable, picking up where they had left off before that ill wind had blown through. They spoke directly to her, as if nothing had happened; as if Shona had not just had her humanity stripped completely away.

Younger Female: *"Are you the receptacle?"*

Male: *"Can she be the receptacle?*

Older Female, demanded loudly, ***"Are you the receptacle that this woman seeks?"***

Shona ignored the voices, focusing what was left of her strength on wading back through the stream. She sat next to Saba, her hand resting on the healer-woman's body. She was still trying to wipe the lingering taste of blood and raw flesh from her mouth with the back of her hand as she looked up to the ceiling of the room.

Shona: "Receptacle? I don't know what you mean. I want to help her."

Male: *"What help can you hope to give if you are not the intended source of her offering and her renewal?"*

Older Female: ***"Are you the receptacle?"***

Shona: "Yes, yes, yes. I can be her receptacle. The source of her offering and her renewal. Just release her please. She is important to our people. To our cause and our well-being."

Older Female: *"Has she selected or indicated you in any way? What knowledge do you possess of her acceptance of you?"*

The multitude of other voices created a background echo behind the one dominant female voice as they now repeated her words over and over.

"Has she selected or indicated you in any way... what knowledge do you possess of her acceptance of you. Has she selected or indicated you in any way...what knowledge do you possess of her acceptance of you. Has she selected or indicated you in any way. what knowledge do you possess of her acceptance of you.

She screamed as loud as she could, "You have to let us go. We don't belong here. We belong in our own world, not in this in-between place."

Older Female: *"In-between?"*

Male: *"Doesn't she know?"*

Younger Female: *"They may not realize the nature of their world's reality—the world that they create and the one that they destroy."*

Older Female: *"An 'in-between' is where you exist in your every day life—where most of your kind exist on a regular basis; in the fog, fugue state between life and death; where your societies and fabricated realities insist that you remain."*

Male: *"You delude yourselves that you are living, existing in a true world/reality. Yet, something within you must know, must realize."*

Younger Female: *"They must know. Surely they realize."*

Male: *"You, your people—all life in the societies on your earth—- are neither truly alive, nor fully dead. Entering this realm only permits you to acknowledge, know for the first time how submerged your consciousness and the awareness of your purpose has become. The energy of this realm can only force you to face who and what you are, thus demanding you to choose between life and what you know as death."*

Older Female: *"The only danger that exists in this realm that you know as 'the in-between' is the necessity of choice and assuming the responsibility for the consequences of your decision."*

Male: *"There is no option to vacillate or alter your decision. You cannot leave this realm and remain vested in your delusions; and keep straddling the line between living and dying."*

Younger Female: *"This realm has no good or evil power over those who enter the portals. The energy that calls to you from this realm is the amplified calling from your own soul."*

Male: *"Their manufactured worlds create an in-between existence, an altered reality, a state between life and death. They will either learn to awaken to life or death will embrace their world."*

Older Female: ***"You have nothing to fear from this realm. It is your own 'in-between' which brings you danger, strife and dis-ease. You must deal with your own trapped states of existence and all the healing that must take place within your own 'in-between'—between what you know as birth and what you know as death."***

Male: *"There is no deliverance and there will be no savior. You render your life hopeless and useless by putting yourself in an in-between reality, waiting for some great moment of deliverance, emancipation, release and thus refusing to fully accept the Creator's profound and most magnanimous Gift of Life."*

Younger Female: *"There is and has never been any mystery as to why you exist. You exist in order to live—to live fully and abundantly. You exist as an integral part of life's vibrations, carrying and amplifying the tone and melody of the Creator's energy."*

Older Female: ***"You do violence to your own lives by refusing to live up to your potential as vessels for the Creator's energy. You do violence to yourselves and to others with your judgments and your jealousies; your petty needs for superiority and dominance over others."***

Male: *"Acceptance of your death will provide the only true freedom in your life. Let go of this need to adhere to and focus on your individual physical reality or you will never know what it is to be truly alive. All energy is continually re-born, re-created."*

Shona had been so focused on listening to and communicating with these voices that this time she had not sensed the tingles in her body. She became suddenly alarmed and began pulling Saba, but the healer-woman was so enmeshed in the web that Shona could not get her free. She could hear laughter rising once more within the bevy of voices. But she was determined to ignore the voices as she lifted the healer-woman's head into her lap. She knew that she would have to get herself and Saba out of here before the next surging wind came through the passageway. With a combination of desperation and compassion, Shona began pleading softly, yet rapidly, "Saba, Listen to me. You heard them. You must have heard them. There is not much time. You have to decide. The decision, the choice is yours alone. Either you want to live or you want to die. There are no other decisions, no other choices in life, not now, not ever. They cannot take your life from you. Only you can choose to relinquish it. You cannot continue to exist straddling a line between life and death. That is what our journey to this place is all about—the choices that we make to live or to die. You can not become like so many others in the world who have unknowingly chosen death but still continue to sleep-walk through their lives. Saba? Saba? Can you hear me?"

Saba mumbled incoherently moving her head, as if struggling to awaken. Shona grew more frustrated and shifted Saba's body, laying her head back on the ground and bringing her own face as close as she could to Saba's face. "You must wake up. Hang on, Saba. Don't go under. Listen to the sound of my voice. Let it guide you back to reality."

The tingling sensation was becoming more pronounced and Shona started talking faster and louder. "Saba! Listen to me. What they are saying—their message—is the same for you as for all the beings of the planet. If you want to live, you must stand up, and stand strong to face your destiny, your purpose; meet the injera of your existence fully within the center of its power.

You heard them; you must have heard them. Your energy can never end—its needs are not connected to either the boundaries or the burdens of a material reality. But, you must choose to live or your soul will die. In choosing death, you thwart the needs of your soul; you place the petty mundane realities of your manufactured society above the needs of true life, above the needs of your soul and the needs of your God.

Life in our dimensional reality is fleeting at best. We cannot allow negative realities to dominate our perspectives and determine how we view the world. The world exists independent of our personal and societal constraints that have no meaning beyond their own perception of importance."

She could now feel the surge rising inside of her and all around her. The voices became jumbled and faded into the background as Shona felt the energy building up in waves that began to cascade down on and around her. It occurred to her that thus far, none of the creatures, the scenes, the madness had successfully crossed through the water to this side of the stream. She made a split-second decision to not run or hide but to just stay here on this side of the stream with Saba, presuming that the entities of this place would stay away from the water or if they came through, it would be to their demise. She deduced that the water had some type of supernatural hold on the people and the winds.

This time Shona watched and felt herself inside of the worst atrocities evident in the history of human affairs—there were wars, death camps, people and children being tortured, beaten and abused in the most painful and vile manner imaginable. There was cannibalism again—human predators stalking, killing, preying on anyone that crossed their path, violently stealing and snatching away their victims' lives, their possessions, their peace, their security, their faith. There were acts of self-destruction and people mutilating and defiling others, inspiring fear—all the debased ways that humans could use and abuse each other. She watched as the victims, in turn, became perpetrators; the prey transformed into predators in an endless cycle of violence, hatred and retribution. And the worst was what they did to the children, the helpless, innocent victims of their own need. There were battlefields of mutilated corpses, rotting, decomposing bodies, fed on by rats, worms, vermin. And then there were the people who stood or sat watching in a stupor or with morbid fascination and some with excited glee and anticipation. The ones who watched made no effort to intervene or mitigate the hurt, the injustice, the suffering of others, no matter how cruel or how much torment was inflicted.

Shona had managed to stay steady this time, faltering only when she saw the children abducted, slain, tortured, mutilated, defiled. The air was filled with putrid rank odors and an overpowering stench of rotting, decaying flesh. Once again she could not close her eyes or turn her attention away from these scenes that she was forced to watch and feel. As she had predicted, the people, the scenes stayed on the other side of the stream, opposite where she now sat with Saba. Still, there were several moments where she almost rushed through the water to try to save the children, but then she thought to herself—"That is what they want; they want to shock me, scare me into losing my concentration. They want to gain control over my thoughts and emotions."

She tried to reach out with her mind-soul, to go inside of the sentiale of both the victims and the perpetrators of the scenes before her. She wanted to expand their sentiale pathways to give them strength, to lead them away from the weakness of a predator-prey dichotomy. But she could only feel herself as a part of the emotions of the people, bouncing back and forth—first, inside the overwhelming fear and terror of the prey, then a part of the cold malice and heartless cruelty of the predators. When she gave up and attempted to pull away, she discovered that she was entangled in a scrambled mass of pathways, like a twisted, knotted ball of string.

Shona decided to delve once more into the people's sentiale, to strive once more to broaden their sentiale connections while also trying to extricate herself. She knew that this was the answer, had to be the answer—to broaden, expand their internal pathways so that they could feel the inherent connection that they held with one another and with the sacred. She tried focusing on the minute microscopic pieces of light that darted through the mesh of minds and souls, but they constantly shifted and moved, never occupying the same time or place for long. Some of the bits of light burned brightly, while others were dim and weak or corrupted in a way that she intellect could not comprehend. She pushed with all of her might and she felt some of the pathways beginning to widen, especially those with the brighter lights. But there was too much resistance and she became trapped as they all were—inside of a jumble of writhing unfulfilled needs. The more she struggled to break free, the more ensnared she found herself. Within her sentiale, Shona released her grasp on the perceptual reality of her senses, and only then did she float free of the confused chaotic mess of intertwined thoughts and emotions.

The wind, the people and the deluge of nightmarish realities eventually swept away and out of the chamber just as they had each time before. And Shona was once again left shaken, trembling and exhausted. Only this time, there was something more. She was now angry; angry at herself, angry at these voices and angry at this woman who would not move, would not try to save herself. She thought of trying to pick Saba up and carry her out. But she knew that she was too exhausted, worn and injured for this to be feasible. She wanted to leave right now, right this moment, before the next wind came, before any more evil could occur. If this woman did not want to save herself, what could she, Shona do about it? What choice did she have, but to leave Saba here in order to save herself? Otherwise, it was certain that they would both die in this place. And it would be Saba who was responsible for causing not just her own death, but Shona's as well.

She was beginning to realize that there was no way to plan for or predict the timing of this random madness. These "cycles" were coming in chaotic bursts of insanity, with seemingly only one purpose—to torture her to the point that her soul lost its connection to life, its internal cohesion. When this happened she knew that her spirit's primary medium of expression would be rendered useless. Her mind, her sanity would leave her. She knew now that each time the energy came back, it was stronger and stronger, siphoning more and more of her strength and power. She felt sure that she would not be able to withstand any more waves of this evil, this suffering, this pain.

Shona knelt down beside Saba and began shaking her by the arms, alternately pleading and shouting into the healer-woman's face, "Saba you have to know, you have to believe that your spirit is an integral and essential part of not just the injera of the Ocan people, but the injera of the planet, of the universe, and of the Creator. You must look beyond the evil and the suffering of our world and know that the purpose of your existence is higher and more important than any of the fabricated constraints of your society; more important than the constraints of any personal life-burdens. It is now time to rise up and choose life; choose to live.

You must control your perceptions of the world, and not allow yourself to be controlled by perceptions that are both limited and contrived. Let go of it Saba, let go of all of it and claim this life that is your own. Rise to the destiny that awaits you. Allow this life's injera to move you to the place of your ascendance into a reality in which your gifts may manifest to their fullest. You have to believe Saba, you have to believe."

Shona felt even more anger and frustration as the tingles in her body started coming once again. Commanding in a strong clear voice, that contained no compassion, no sympathy Shona stressed and emphasized each word, each syllable loudly and separately, "Get up Saba! Get up and live your life. Who are you to decide that this life must come to a close? You have no such right. You have no right to allow anything or anyone to stand between you and the power that is yours to claim. This is not your journey. You don't get to decide where it begins or ends. You are merely a vessel; your life force has been called to carry energies greater than you can know or imagine. Do not dare think that you have the individual right to destroy the Lord's energy. We must rid ourselves of this silly focus on ephemeral mundane realties.

You are here, in this world, to cultivate, harvest and harness the power of your own life force. **You must** claim this power, this energy fully as your own. You must allow this power to lead your life. You must allow God's energy and intent to live within you and through you. You have no choice!"

Saba moaned incoherently and did not budge. Shona tried to block out the sound of rushing wind approaching faster and faster. Without thinking she began praying aloud, "Oh God, how can I help someone who does not want to be helped? How can I move another person who does not want to be moved; who does not want to live? I have proven that I can fight the demons and delusions of this place. Isn't it enough that I can fight and find my own way through? Must I also fight for and find a way for another? I don't know how to make a way for another person. How do I know that helping her is the right thing to do? Oh Lord, please help me to know how to do what I am supposed to do."

The wind rushed in and poured down on her as she started pulling Saba, yelling, "Come on Saba! We have no time. It is coming again. The evil is here again. We have to get out of here now!"

This time before she saw anything, she felt and heard strange sounds and vibrations that seemed curiously familiar. She had heard these sounds before. The whispers that had never stopped, suddenly became loud venomous shouts, from a forgotten time in her life—" ...death...the stasis for which all beings strive... deep longing to die... no longer exist... desires originate with a longing for death... ...you take in all that we are... ...draw life from death...feed on each other.... you relish the power and feel of violence..

The black smoke was still whipping and blowing all around, but the words stopped and no people, no madness emerged. She was beginning to think that maybe this time there would be no taking away of her mind, no siphoning of her strength and humanity. And then she looked up through the smoke and saw her. There was no mistaking the body, the presence, the spirit of the Inar female—resurrected and made strong. Shona's heart involuntarily began beating in fear, her body trembling, sweat pouring from every part of her. For as much as she could, she pushed the Saba's body close to the boulder near the tunnel passage. And then she stood and positioned herself in front of Saba, closer to the stream, hoping that the healer woman was not visible to the beast that she now faced across the water. She tried to calm herself, mumbling aloud, "The water is here. They can't cross the water."

She watched as Inar slowly approached the stream bed, staring directly at Shona with that same bizarre rictus grin that revealed her razor sharp pointed teeth. This time, unlike the previous encounter with this woman, she was full-bodied, not emaciated, strong and brawny, with power emanating from her every move. When the woman stepped into the water, still staring at Shona, still advancing forward, Shona's whispers ("This is not real. This is not real. This is not real") did nothing to quell the shaking in her body, as her eyes widened in disbelief and she instinctively stepped back a few feet. She wanted to run, hide somewhere, or at least get closer to the wall, but she had to stay here, between this beast and the Ocan healer-woman. She bent her knees and spread her legs wide, waiting with her hands in a posture of defense.

Shona didn't even see when the woman came out of the water or close the distance between them, but the Inar had charged forward, pinning Shona down before she could even think to react. With quick rapid-fire motions, she sliced her talon-like nails across Shona's face and then kicked her into the wall, grunting and groaning with low guttural sounds. With blood pouring down her face, into her mouth and eyes, Shona managed to rise and stumble against the wall just before the woman came after her again and again and again. The guttural sounds never stopped as the creature repeated her assault over and over pounding, beating and throwing Shona into the wall or the floor every time that she tried to rise. She stood waiting each time for Shona to get up or to move before she once again attacked her, stomped her, beat her, never moving in for the final kill.

No matter what type of evasive or counter moves Shona attempted, it had no effect—the Inar woman was too strong, too fast. If her internal energies and loss of blood did not kill her, then Shona knew that the exhaustion would, before long, pull her under. The Inar woman was toying with Shona, taunting her, teasing her; she was the cat and Shona was her mouse. The woman even turned her back to Shona as she waited for her to rise once again and it was then that she finally became aware of Saba.

Shona felt and heard the wind swooshing back into the tunnel passageway, going away as it had each time before. And yet this woman, this Inar creature was still here. Shona was struggling to maintain consciousness, as she made an effort to slide herself slowly up along the side of the wall. She used one of the sharp jutting rocks to help buoy her self up and unexpectedly it became partially dislodged from the wall. When Shona was able to orient herself, she saw the Inar woman approaching Saba.

Her body reacted without any conscious volition as something inside of Shona pushed her beyond any pain or fatigue and moved her at lightning speed towards Inar. As she jumped on the woman's back, she realized that the dislodged piece of rock was in her hand. With intense hatred and a rage whose depths she could not fathom, she brought the point of the rock down with all of her might into the top of the woman's head. Blood shot out of the hole in her head and they both fell to the ground. Shona lost no time righting herself and straddling the supine body of Inar, with her knees holding the woman's arms to the ground, she pounded the rock into her face. No matter how much she hit her, the woman did not lose consciousness and the thick skin and hard bone of her face and forehead seemed barely affected. She stared at Shona with gleeful hatred, mouth drooling saliva, mucous and blood, still grinning as she rasped in a low seductive voice, "Why don't you kill me?"

Shona stood up, recoiling from this woman and from herself. At first the Inar woman laughed in the deep raucous tones that her body emitted and then she looked up at Shona, contorting her facial features in a sad and pitiful expression. She began softly begging for sympathy, pleading for her life. Despite Shona's resolve to guard her emotions from this woman's charades, the agonizing pleas began to involuntarily move her compassion. But then she began seeing images of all the helpless children and all the good people who became victims to human predators whose distorted needs had become the only god they served. She now understood that, no matter what she had tried to tell herself previously, this place, this reality was true and real; all the nightmare horrors had really happened. And she knew that she could not allow this evil that lay before her to go unguarded into the world.

She was studying the creature's face, when she unexpectedly saw a vein pulsating between the Inar's eyes. Shona picked up the rock for the final time and spurred on by all the pain, suffering and evil that she had experienced, she aimed the sharp point for the soft spot between the creature's eyes, bringing it down with such force that the entire cavern shook and echoed the dying creature's screaming wails.

She was on her knees next to the body, when the changes started to occur. One minute Shona was breathing hard and watching smoke vapors rise from the hole beneath the stone that remained lodged between the woman's eyes. Then before her mind could register what was happening, the woman's face and body started contorting. Thinking that these were only death throes, Shona backed away. But then something made her look closer, this face, this body was no longer that of Inar. It felt like her heart stopped beating and she couldn't breathe as she recognized the braids, the discolored birthmark pulsating around the edges of the embedded stone.

She almost screamed aloud when realized that she was looking into her own face.

She slid back in shock and fear. The body continued contorting and changing, finally settling into its ultimate form. A cold panic and an oppressive sense of dread moved from her rapidly beating heart and flushed throughout her entire body as she stared in horror, recognizing the shape and facial features of her mother. This wasn't the spectral image of Mala that had appeared before. The familiarity of this body's scent and shape made Shona reach out and touch the hand, confirming warm solid flesh and bone. She heard a rattle in the body's chest and watched her mother gasping for air, slowly opening her eyes. Mala turned her head and looked directly at Shona, pain and anguish etched into her face, as she whispered, "Why Shona? Why?" These were her mother's eyes, no longer conveying love and understanding, but still rich with recognition. And then Mala moved and spoke no more. A final gasp of air whistled through her lips that still dripped with blood and saliva as her open unseeing eyes bore into Shona's soul.

Mala lie before her, dead, unmoving and no matter how much her mantra, "This is not real," tried to resuscitate her mind, there was no escaping the simple fact that she had killed her mother. With hatred and malicious intent, she had killed her mother. The one who had loved her, sheltered her, fed her, taught her, protected her; she was now dead and Shona had killed her.

Still staring in horror, she slid all the way back until she felt the hard cavern wall against her back. Afraid for her sanity, she began whispering, "Oh, God, please help me! Please help me. Please help me. Oh dear God, please help me. This is not real. This is not real. This is not real." She had difficulty collecting her thoughts as she looked all around trying to recall why she was in this strange place. She sat mumbling incoherently to herself and the voices began incessantly repeating her own words as if chanting along with her. She put both hands over her ears and screamed as loud, hard and long as she could. First a raucous inarticulate shriek of despair and then with all her might, "MAAAAAA-LAAAAAA!!".

Sudden nausea pushed her up on her hands and knees as her body began violently spilling huge regurgitated slimy chunks of partially digested raw meat, flesh, blood, muscle and bone. When the storm abated, she lied down curled and folded in on herself, and began weeping uncontrollably. She had not cried so forcefully since that lost night in the canyons when this same profound sense of despair and hopelessness had come inside of her.

The continued droning of the voices was driving Shona completely and utterly mad. She couldn't think; couldn't decide on a course of action. She sat up with her back against the hard rocky wall and swayed from side to side, making low incoherent sounds of distress. It felt as if days and nights had passed in succession, without sleep, food or fresh air. She knew that if they did not soon exit this place that she and Saba would both most likely die. She was certain that the Saba had heard all that she had said. And she finally understood how words were so very useless to this woman who had moved to a place beyond meaning, definition or cause. Shona began alternately weeping and then laughing uncontrollably.

The hysteria passed almost as quickly as it had come and Shona was left with an empty feeling of absolute nothingness. There was nothing else that she could do or say. She had wasted her time in this place, trying, in vain, to help this woman, this saba who did not want to be helped. And now she had been beaten, defeated, vanquished. She had failed her mission, her purpose to make contact with the power source. And perhaps after all, there really was no power source, for she certainly hadn't been led to or found any such object. All she had found was this sick pathetic old woman, who would not move, would not try to save her own life.

Without knowing how or why, Shona was drained of all thought and emotion——a point past sympathy, care or concern; a feeling of utter ruthlessness. All anger, frustration and feelings of any kind ceased to exist. She was tired of these certain, yet unpredictable winds bringing evil, madness, suffering and pain. Tired of fighting. Tired of this game; tired of being played with as if she was a toy or a puppet. Tired of thinking. Tired of her own attachment to fear and feelings. Tired of Saba and her endless melodrama of despair. Tired of these endlessly droning voices repeating over and over.

The wind was beginning to come once again. It seemed like it was just here seconds ago. But it didn't matter this time because Shona was tired and none of it mattered any more. She had had enough. This time the voices did not fade into the background but grew louder as a part of the rushing wind. She heard the voices, yet didn't hear them. She no longer cared what they might try to do to her or where or how this all would end. All fear was gone. This wind stirred in what felt like the most powerful surge of all and she offered no resistance as the evil whirlwind of negative thoughts and emotions swirled all around her. She got up and started walking sideways towards the stream, her knees bent, legs wide to brace against the pummeling wind.

There were no more thoughts left, no more worries, no more cares. She gave up completely, turned her back on Saba and began to walk, a modified form of the power-walk that Taijaur had taught her which helped her to stay strong and move forward through the violent flow of air and swirling negative emotions. She was moving away from Saba, from the voices, from this place. No longer really seeing or hearing, she walked by route memory back in the direction from whence she had come, with no concern with living, dying or being.

She had made it through the water and almost reached the tunnel passageway when strange malevolent beings of all kinds came rushing through the tunnel directly toward her, blocking her passage. Although she batted them away like flies, never even glancing at them as she moved forward punching, kicking, and evading the way that Taijaur had taught her, still the certainty of her impending death came to her. She knew that they would not let her leave and that she would die in this place. It did not matter, she did not care.

In the midst of this senseless maelstrom, some inexplicable sensation made her stop and stand absolutely still. The wind, the voices, the people, the demons, the noise—they no longer had any affect on her, although she could still see them moving towards her, as if in slow motion all around her, but outside of the space where she stood. It was if she was inside of a bubble, a surreal gap of reality in which there was nothing—no time, no movement, no sound. And it was then—from this stillness deep within her soul—that her God moved.

She felt the power rising, surrounding and absorbing her mind, body, and spirit into a single concentrated moment of existence. Her awareness took control of her body as her will came forth and asserted itself. All thought or desire for any action alien to its intent dissolved. And she knew what must be done. She could sense knowledge and understanding flowing all around her, entering directly into every pore of her body. The wind and smoke outside of the space around her were still swirling with pain, suffering, madness and malevolence.

In this moment that reality had stopped, the air she breathed became thick and fluid. The sounds all around her were drifting in languid waves from deep dark places. She heard music, low floating softly from all directions; a tender melody spread over the surface of various harmonies in a progression, each one leading to the next. Shona turned and looked all around trying to catch the origin, the source of this gentle melodic, yet complex song. Then she stood still and closed her eyes to allow the sound to more deeply penetrate her senses and she wondered if this was the sound that had entranced Taijaur when they first came to the portal. It seemed that this was the same song that she had learned long ago from the arachnid weavers, or something very similar to it. She opened her eyes and saw the vibrations of the song blowing with the wind—moving through each fiber of the web throughout the entire chamber.

The song lulled her into an almost trance-like state, where it seemed that the wind was generated from the fibers of the web which was also the source of light, movement and sound, even the whispering voices. For a brief fleeting moment, she saw herself inside a fractal crystal, as if this entire chamber had transformed, once again, into a huge scintillating geode. This was the same image that she had seen before—the sparkling shining facets of a giant crystal lattice throughout the room. She was ensconced in the earth's innermost sanctuary, blessed to behold a vision of the interactions between elemental fibers that glistened and undulated into a pattern of connections, forming a network of conduits that feed the essence of life. And then just as it had happened before, as quickly as the image came, it vanished and the room converted back to black shiny rock filled with massive amounts of web and dust.

The bubble around her burst and she felt the wind biting into her skin as she turned and started back towards Saba. Although the voices were gone, absorbed into the melody of the song, the evil was still swirling all around her as the beasts and demons once again charged into her. She batted them away as before, staring straight ahead, not seeing them and feeling no concern for the damage she caused as she crushed, stomped and pulverized any and every thing that stood in her way. They stopped at the edge of the stream and did not follow her into the water. When she reached the other side, she lifted the healer-woman as if she was weightless, placing her down into the stream. Saba's whole body except for her head was immersed in water. Her head lolled back on the hard rocks of the bank. The pieces of web that had hardened and slightly calcified around her body began to loosen and float free in the water. Shona noticed for the first time that the whole bottom of the stream bed was inexplicably filled with the same black rocks and scintillating web design that was throughout this chamber. She stooped down in front of Saba, the water covering her up to her chest. She placed the tips of her fingers at strategic points on the Saba's forehead, temples and at the back of her neck. She went inside of Saba's sentiale and sought to strengthen and augment her pathways, the same way she had tried with the people in the scenes.

Saba opened her eyes, and with no sound or movement, she looked straight into Shona's eyes, piercing her through the center of her soul. Shona was shocked by the electrified energy that began to flow from Saba into and through every dimension of her being and throughout the water and up and down the walls of the chamber. Electrical charges radiated through the darkness, crackling from end to end on the interconnected lines that traversed their bodies and the walls, the floor, the ceiling, the water.

Shona gasped, with a sharp intake of breath as she felt intense storms of energized particles moving around and through her body. She was outside of herself—the cavern all around her became part of her consciousness, her senses. Every sight, sound, feeling, sensation was amplified, and flowing through her. It was too intense to hold, too much to bear. She could hear, feel the water molecules flowing, the atoms breaking their bonds and slipping, sliding into union with the next atom and then the next. She felt, heard the rocks, the molten lava inside the earth. She felt the whole of this world—the grass, the trees, the sky, the wind—all waking up, coming alive inside of her.

A steady stream of electrons and hot electrically charged gas billowed around her like solar wind driven by magnetic forces from the core of her being. Flowing hot plasma and superheated gases in an electrified state were dragging and pushing her internal magnetism. She watched gas and dust drifting together all around her, swirling into a sphere. The universe was coming into existence with nebula, stars, galaxies forming, planets colliding, forces pulling. The universe was living, dying, and being born again and again and again—expanding, contracting as if breathing in and out; matter coalescing and then dispersing over and over. Her body exploded into pure light; then the weight of her physical matter drew back in upon itself. The energy was bombarding her senses, galvanizing within her cells and molecules. She felt the universe's deep reservoirs of energy and power latent within the human spirit. The energy was expanding the boundaries of her sentiale into the physical reality of surface perceptions.

She could smell it, taste it, touch it—the energy, the wind, the light, the song. The song. It was here all along, through all the living, dying and being— the song. All matter in the universe was coming together in the notes and harmony of this song. She saw all words, all images, movement, action, numbers, equations flowing through the universe leading only to this song. The melody, the harmony was moving from sound waves into particles and waves of light, radiation. And then she knew, felt within the core of her being, that it is this song that pervades and holds together the dimensional reality of the universe. She could see, feel, hear—this song, this energy, this light flowing out, into the world, into the land, into the people. All other perceptual reality faded from her awareness, as she felt the song coming through her and from her. And finally in the end—there was nothing but the song.

Slowly her mind, her sense of reality came back into the physical existence of the cavern, where she found herself sitting in the water, on the opposite side of the stream from Saba, who appeared to be sleeping peacefully. Shona stood up calm, sedate, trance-like, moving slowly in the water, causing enormous pools of energy to awaken with every slight movement. The charges died down into a continual stream of minute ripples under her skin, as Shona reached Saba and lifted her limp unconscious body out of the water and laid her back on the stream bank.

She looked up and saw two spectral images moving near the tunnel, coming from behind the boulder. It was Mala and another woman, both appearing as vague figures wrapped in fog and a soft glowing light. The other woman, the one that Shona did not know, started walking, drifting toward the stream while Mala stayed behind near the entryway. Neither of the women looked at Shona or seemed to be aware of her presence. The woman bent down next to Saba and as soon as she touched her, the soft light spread from the woman's body and enveloped the healer-woman. Shona stood back and watched as the woman helped Saba to slowly rise to her feet, and began pulling her along. With the healer-woman leaning heavily on and into the woman, they walked back to the tunnel passageway where Mala still waited. It was strange watching the corporeal body of Saba being half-carried by a spectral image of light and shadow. The fog and light intensified for only a moment and then swallowed all three women as they walked, drifted into the tunnel disappearing behind the boulder.

Shona was now completely alone. She looked all around, listening, feeling. All the bodies, all the people—they were all gone. Even the voices were still. Only the sound of the running water echoed through the chamber. She crossed back through the stream for the last time, heading towards the tunnel on the opposite side of the cavern. Just before she entered the passageway, she saw something gleaming on the ground near where she had stood hiding from the first wave of terror that had come through the tunnel.

She picked it up and saw that it was the crystal that Taijaur had given to her. She had forgotten all about it and she had no memory of having dropped it. She felt its warmth in her hand and she suddenly recalled her mission, her purpose in coming to this place. She tucked the stone into her waist belt and turned around, saying with deference, yet in a strong commanding tone to the walls, to the ceiling, to the water, "Where is the power source, the prism, the fractal stone that will re-set the balance of power in the world?"

Older Female: *"You are standing within this world's eye."*

Shona looked all around and up and down, "Where? I don't see it."

As she was speaking the whole room started trembling and shaking as if a shudder went through the earth. Loose rock and dust spilled all around her and she had to duck to avoid being hit as she reached out and held onto the wall nearest her to keep from falling. She could hear a voice calling to her. It was Taijaur. She heard his voice in her mind and in the air all around her. It took all of her powers of concentration to block out Taijaur's desperate beckoning.

The voice of the older female responded to her questions as if nothing was happening. *"It is everywhere, just as it is in your world. All around you, everywhere that you look, everywhere that you can be."*

Shona searched with her eyes above, down all around as the room continued to shiver and quake. "Do you mean this spider's web? Or maybe this rock, this dust, these particles?"

Older Female: *"Yes, the web, the dust, the particles—all of it. But don't assume that any of it belongs to the arachnids. They, like you, are only a vessel for the substance and intent of this existence."*

Shona: "But how can anyone access power from a web?"

Older Female: *"Dust, web, stone; past, present, future—it is all the same. Do you possess the key to access the power?"*

Shona: "What key? I was told no physical object was needed; that, I alone could serve as the catalyst. Where can I find a key?"

Older Female: *"The key, the catalyst for the energy source is within you; within the collective god-consciousness of all of you.*

Shona: "Do you mean within the Ocan collective consciousness?"

Older Female: *"No, not just the Ocan—all of you, all of your kind, all of the people within your realm of existence. The only energy source that you—and each/all of you—must repair, harness and control is your own. This is the power that must be channeled into the world to affect the earth's balance of power. The giving, the receiving creates and maintains the balance of life. The key is the giving and the receiving; the giving, the receiving...*

The voice droned on repeating the same thing over and over—*the giving, the receiving, the giving, the receiving...*

The quivers in the earth had momentarily ceased but loose dirt and rock were still spilling and showering all around. Shona began walking through the passageway which was pitch black and the rocks on the wall would not illuminate no matter how she touched them with her hands or her mind. She took out the crystal, and held it up in front of her as she walked with its faint light leading the way. Taijaur's voice was growing more frantic. He seemed to be somewhere far from her—calling her, pulling her from a distant void. She reached a fork where the passageway branched off into two separate tunnels. She thought that the portal was in the left tunnel but she wasn't sure. She listened intently to the signal that Taijaur transmitted and decided to take this path to the left where she was almost certain the portal was located. When she reached the end of the passageway she was at a dead end and she had to go back, retracing her steps. Her sentiale contact with Taijaur was now sporadic and unclear like a radio transmission filled with static and breaking up from point to point. She tried calling out to him but the cave started rumbling again and all she heard was the shaking of the earth. The light from the crystal was weak and beginning to fade.

Her growing sense of apprehension forced her legs and feet to move faster, until she found herself running blindly in the darkness. She had only gone a few yards when she ran smack into the side of a boulder or a rock wall and she fell back bouncing hard onto the ground. She was momentarily stunned and she thought that she must have hit her head harder than she realized as she incredulously felt the wall or the boulder or whatever she had run into, reaching out and pulling her up to her feet, inquiring in a deep voice, "Are you okay?"

Her physical and emotional senses recognized Taijaur before her muddled thoughts could discern his reality. An overwhelming feeling of relief and gratitude flooded through her, and she sunk into his arms, his body as he held and bolstered her up.

Shona: "Taijaur, what's happening? Why couldn't I find the portal? It should have been in that tunnel."

Taijaur: "Come on, we don't have much time." He held her hand and pulled her along behind him. The cool air blowing through the tunnel passageway helped to revive her as they walked down long twisting tunnels, groping their way blindly through the dark endless passageways.

Taijaur: "The portal you came through shifted and closed. I thought that it was emerging into life but I was mistaken. It was actually in the final phase of its cycle. When I couldn't pull you back in time, I had no choice but to come through before it closed completely. I couldn't hold it open any longer."

There was a loud groan in the earth as the walls and ground began shaking once again.

Shona: "Is this an earthquake? Is this cave collapsing?"

Taijaur: "I think that these are just minor tremors. The portals have become unstable and they are shifting. There are other gateways to our world located in this cave and we have to find one in order to get out of here."

They walked hurriedly, sometimes running until they finally reached a point where Taijaur stopped and said, "There it is. This is another portal."

Shona could see a faint rainbow of light rising and falling in a small area on the wall in front of them. But this was not like the crawlway where there was a discernible opening close to the ground. This light spectrum was high up on the wall almost chest-level and there was only solid rock, with not even a pinhole of an opening.

Taijaur: "I don't know where we will come out or end up, but this may be our only chance to get out of here.

Shona: "But Taijaur, there is no actual opening. This is a solid rock wall."

There was another loud groan within the earth and they both stumbled as the earth shook.

Taijaur: "Trust me Shona, the opening is here. Do not be concerned with its size. The opening will adjust to your dimensions. Our time is running out, so please just do exactly as I say. Stand back over there," he pointed to the far wall near the tunnel that they had just come through. "And when I call to you run as fast as you can towards and through whatever speck of light that you see. I will only be able to hold it open for a limited amount of time, so you must move faster than you ever have in your life."

She backed up hesitantly. Taijaur closed his eyes and placed his hands around the perimeter of the moving colors on the thick rock wall. In the darkness she could not make out his shape or form. Then from the location where Taijaur had stood, a sudden ball of red fire ignited. She thought that this must be the opening and prepared herself for Taijaur's signal. She peered closer and saw that the ball of fire was a thin sheet of rock surrounding molten liquid earth. Wild winds started whipping through the tunnel into the area where they stood. The ball of fire moved and covered the entire wall swallowing the undulating spectrum of colors. Shona stood paralyzed with fascination as the surface of the whole wall appeared to be moving in waves. Without realizing that she spoke, Shona shouted, "Taijaur, the walls, the ground—they're moving. The air is changing. This place—is alive!!".

She heard a scratched raking sound of a voice burnt and raw, "Now, Shona, run. Now!!".

In the middle of the liquefied rock was a bright white light the size of a fist. She closed her eyes and ran, diving headlong into the center of this rock of fire. All sensation ceased, awareness sucked her down as she was pushed into a floating oblivion. From deep within its molten center, she felt the earth move drawing her into its hidden core.

24. Something Inside

Morning sunrise on a misty isle, with gentle cool rain and the waves of the ocean washing on and all around. Warm, steamy air rising from the earth with thunder and lightening in the distance, gently disrupting the quiet darkness. The hard ground smells clean, after the rain. She nears consciousness and feels him, lying next to her. Her body shivers with the touch, the smell of this man—a smell, a touch so open and completely alive, after the rain. She opened her eyes slowly, reluctantly and the sun, barely perceptible in the gray sky, intruded upon her consciousness, bringing her abruptly and fully into the day. She pulled herself out of his arms and sat up, looking around, trying to recall who, what, where—something? A storm? No, a fire, an explosion. She looked all around.

Shona: "Where are we?"

He sat up next to her. "Don't worry, we're safe now Shona. We're back in our own dimensional reality, in the physical world."

Shona: "No, I mean where is this place? Are we on the mainland?"

Taijaur: "We are where we intended to be—on the largest atoll close to the island."

Shona: "How did we get here?"

Taijaur: "The passageway through which we were finally able to exit put us closer to our destination. We walked, most of the night across the isthmus from the peninsula to get here. Don't you remember?"

Shona: "I just remember you telling me to run and then everything was black. And then, then, I woke up. Here. With you."

Taijaur: "It's no wonder that you don't recall; you were in a daze most of the way, and I half-carried you the majority of the time."

Shona: "Taijaur, what happened in there? How did we get out?"

Taijaur: "I'm not sure. At the end, there was some power greater than my own that helped to pull us through. Once we made it to the other side, I wanted to get away from that place as fast as possible. So I continued walking through the night to reach this atoll."

Taijaur stared at Shona who was uncharacteristically quiet as she looked all around, peering up at the sky and out into the unnaturally calm waters of the sea where bare ripples of waves broke the surface. He took her by the hand and pulled her to her feet, saying, "Come on, if we get started now we can make it to the island before nightfall. We can eat when we get to the island or when we find a campsite for the night.

From here, we will be able to walk most of the way to the island's shore. On this side of the lagoon, a little ways up this beach, there is another isthmus leading from this atoll to the island. I believe that it stretches all the way to the northwest shore. But even if it does not fully connect the two lands, we can still follow the spit for as far as it will go and then swim the rest of the way.

I wonder how long these hidden land bridges have existed and if the Ocan people in their exodus from the mainland could have also traveled this route."

He had hoped that he could draw her out, into another of their never-ending, long-winded discussions. But Shona made no reply, allowing herself to be led by the hand along the beach as she continued searching the sky and the terrain of this secluded seashore, watching the birds, the crabs and all the moving forms of life that she could see. Fog and mist seemed to rise from the ground and the sky was covered with dark oddly-shaped clouds that partially hid the sun which cast a preternatural white light all around. The incessant rumbling of distant thunder seemed to shake the air and the ground beneath them. The whole scene felt surreal as they made their way to and then along the narrow sandbar that stretched into the distance. It was if the atoll had been created from a spiraling disk of sand and rock with two arms or appendages having spun off in opposite directions—one toward the mainland, the other leading to the island

They walked in silence for quite a while and then finally she spoke. "There is something not right here. It feels strange. And look at the animals in the water. There are masses of them breaking surf, all swimming further out to sea. Look—see the dolphins and rays; there are so many of them. They seem to be heading in mass away from the island, away from this area. And where are the seabirds? There were great numbers of them just an hour ago, all flying away from the atoll. But now the sky is so empty. Even the crabs on the beach were moving frantically in mass out into the sea."

Taijaur: "They're fine Shona. They are probably just seeking shelter before the storm hits. We're almost home now. There is nothing to worry about. You're safe."

He studied her profile as they walked, waiting, in vain, for her to speak again and perhaps volunteer on her own what he wanted to know. When her silence continued, he could no longer resist the urge to ask, "Shona, in the end what happened to Saba?

She was startled. "How did you know that she was in there?"

Taijaur: "In the beginning, I saw what you saw, felt what you felt. The sentiale connection was sporadic and towards the end, everything went black. But for a significant portion of your time there, I was able to follow you intermittently."

Shona: "Mala was in there also. Mala and another woman. The other woman was the one who pulled Saba away."

Taijaur: "I would guess that the other woman was Olana. She is the only one who has the power. But who ever she was, I hope that she knew enough about that place to have a sentiale anchor to hold her steady and bring her back to the world we know."

Shona: "I think that your grandmother is okay, Taijaur. But I failed the purpose of our mission. I did not find the energy source."

Taijaur: "But you did find the energy source Shona. You found Saba."

Shona: "Taijaur, I know that your grandmother is a great healer, but surely you are not suggesting that she is the power source that we sought?"

Taijaur: "I am saying that Saba, as well as all those who are of saba-spirit, embodies one aspect of the source of power that is necessary for the world to sustain itself. You found and you were able to access one of the most powerful sources of energy on Earth—saba-energy. Saba always said that the flow of saba-energy is the essential life substance that allows the universe to renew itself over time. She said that healing power is the energy that sustains all aspects of existence—our minds, our bodies, our souls and most importantly the sentiale connections that make us whole."

Shona: "But there was no special stone, no rock. I am not the catalyst, after all."

Taijaur: "You are, indeed, the catalyst. Wasn't the transfer of energy with Saba successful?"

Shona stopped walking and gazed wide-eyed at Taijaur. "How did you know about that? Have you known all along that this transfer would take place? Did you know before I went in there?"

Taijaur: "I didn't know. But once I realized that Saba was in there, I suspected that you both were being led to that place for a reason. It is possible that your sentiale may have been reaching out to and connecting with Saba's spirit long before we came to the in-between. Or maybe a force reached out to both you and Saba, connecting your sentiale to one another.

I am only now beginning to suspect what this journey through the in-between is really all about; and what it actually means to 're-set the balance of energy'. All of my life, I have heard Saba speak of the essential nature of saba-energy and how it is needed in the continuity and perpetuity of life. And only now I can begin to understand more fully what she meant. For it seems that the injera of all existence may be stimulated at its core by saba-energy. And it is this perpetual transfer of saba-energy that helps to re-set the balance of power in the world.

Saba-energy, as it manifests in the lives of our people, connects us to the healing energy of the universe. No human or any life form can function in its absence. This is our primary defense against evil, against negative and destructive forces. The source of this power lives within us all. But healing energy must be transmitted to each new generation through the ages in order for spiritual transformation to be re-born into the world. Perhaps this is why the saba are also our Keepers of the Faith. The true task of a saba must be to transmit this force to others in a way that all life and spirituality on earth can evolve and be cultivated over time."

Shona: "But what if that was all just a hallucination? What if all that happened in the in-between was really only some kind of waking dream, an illusion? After all, we have to consider that Saba was the only person there to validate what I saw and what I experienced. And she was not fully conscious, if, indeed, she was actually there and not just another figment of my imagination."

Taijaur: "The experiences that come to us through the sentiale pathways can sometimes appear as if they are shrouded in the veils of a dream world. I don't doubt the 'realness' of any thing or any person that you experienced in the in-between. However, it is the message that you received that is most important part of your experiences there; the message and the knowledge that it conveys are all that matter.

In the end, all of our beliefs and the basis of our faith may turn out to be fantasy delusions. Nonetheless, they still function to fulfill a powerful human need to believe. This need to believe fuels the energy that we need to persevere in this realm. It is only the energy of belief and faith that can be transformed into action. All innovations, inventions and much of what becomes reality are conceived in the dreams that sustain us. The perceived realness of the in-between or any of our sentiale dream states does not matter. What matters is that our experiences, real or imagined lead us to a greater understanding and awareness of what life and living can become."

Shona: "I guess you are right. Mala once said that—at the root of all of our experiences in life there are the stories that we believe in—either the stories given to us by our religions, societies and governments; or the stories that we create for ourselves. Perhaps the most important stories are those told to us by the messages that the Earth and the universe reveal. We carry the stories of the universe within our beings, even though they may be hidden or whispered too softly to be heard. These are the stories that must convey the meaning behind the causes of who and what we are."

Taijaur: "Perhaps part of the challenge in life is deciding which stories we will listen to and allow to guide our lives. But it seems that the story, the knowledge, the message of belief that comes by way of energy transfer has to be the most profound story that we can strive to capture. I believe that the transfer of energy that you awakened with Saba was the beginning of what it takes to re-set the balance of energy in this world; in order to allow the Gift to be more fully felt and acknowledged as a part of our daily waking reality."

Shona: "But Taijaur, it was Saba, not me, who initiated and controlled the energy transfer. When it initially began, I thought that I was controlling the process; that the changes were happening through me. I thought that I was the one feeding the energy and making it expand, but it was Saba's energy that fed me. It latched on to me and made me feel and know—in ways that I did not know were possible, things that I did not know were possible.

At first, inside the Saba's mind, she seemed to be in a deep empty hole; a place absent of feeling or thought. It felt like when I was inside of that soldier; that young man who begged me to help him die. But this time, with Saba, was different, because in the middle of this void, this absolute darkness, there suddenly appeared a tiny, almost imperceptible spark, no bigger than a grain of sand. It was through this speck of light that I was able to go inside of her will to live and the energy began to grow and multiply. It was like a flow of ions expanding in all directions and then coming together to form fibers that stretched to establish a network, a pattern of connecting particles and waves of sound and light. Through this multi-layered structure our sentiale fused and our individual willpower became one.

The phenomenal part of all of this was that, through the Saba's thoughts, I came to know that this same tiny speck of energy or power exists within all of us. I realized that this is what I was seeing when I tried to go inside of the sentiale of the people in those nightmarish scenes. Every living entity on this Earth has something inside that is stronger than any external circumstance. No matter how much loss, injustice, devastation or despair that we experience in life, there will always be something inside of us stronger and more powerful than any negative reality that we encounter; stronger and more powerful than any of the situations and conditions in which we struggle to survive and to make sense of."

Taijaur: "Maybe in the end, that is what will endure, that is what will be left over from all that is and will ever be—a minute grain of energy that contains the will to live, the need to be. A will, a need so strong that it can grow from a point of near nothingness and expand beyond any known boundaries. This must be the Gift at its most basic and fundamental level."

Shona: "The feeling of being there, going through that transformation—it was almost too overwhelming, too intense. I felt close to bursting as this tiny piece of energy grew and pushed me past all limitations of body or mind. It pushed away all the damage, all the hurt, pain, guilt and wrongdoing. None of it mattered, none of it even existed when the light reached its full intensity.

Saba's will or need to live, to exist, initiated a transfer of energy. It is truly amazing to think that a personal transformation so profound can come from an almost microscopic piece of dust. It is hard to comprehend how something so small could be so powerful.

This transfer of energy has to be the most fundamental part of giving and receiving our gifts on this Earth. And it all comes to us by way of an interconnected web that underlies the structure of all our realities in this universe.

I watched, felt and became a part of the dust that expanded into fibers which, in turn formed an intricate web. This web was the medium through which the transfer of energy occurred, as the fibers of this web acted as a conduit for the transfer of energy. This is the web that connects us to each other and through which we receive the most profound gift that the Creator has bestowed upon the Earth."

Taijaur: "But Shona, this web, these fibers that you speak of—this must be the realm of the sentiale and the sentiale pathways which lie within the heart of injera. These vibrational patterns of existence must be made of injera. For surely, there is a web, a reticulum of microcosmic and macrocosmic need— needs of humans, needs of the Earth, needs of the universe—that connects us to each other, and to the fabric of this existence. We can only know true need-fulfillment by traveling through the sentiale pathways that lie within the heart of injera."

Shona: "It seems so sad to realize that many, if not most, of us spend our lives trapped, struggling and stuck in a web that was only meant to connect us and provide for our fulfillment."

Shona, hesitated and looked away from Taijaur as she said, "Another thing Taijaur—Om made a statement that was similar to what those voices, those in-between entities conveyed. They said that the in-between could only reveal and reflect back what was inside of those who enter the portals. If only Saba and I were in that room, then all those horrible, ghoulish episodes of evil had to come from one or both of us.

It is hard to even think about all the things that I did, all the inhuman feelings and desires that came to me. What if all that, that stuff is here inside of me all of the time, just waiting for the right moment or the right stimulus to be released? It is overwhelming to think of all the horrible things that I did—all the malevolent feelings that arose within me. Is that truly who and what I am?"

Taijaur: "It may take years, if ever, to fully understand and interpret all that transpired in that realm. And I don't have all the answers Shona, but I think those experiences convey the depths of horror, inhumanity and evil that can be generated within the human soul; the many forms of evil that result from unfulfilled need. I believe that as the catalyst for the transfer of energy, it was necessary for you to act as a filter for and a sentinel against the negative predatory energy that seeks to gain dominance within the human race.

But the evil could only feed on your fear. Once your fear was gone, then it could not harm you. Your fear is what allows negative energy to have power over you. The energy of that place was tearing down your defenses and your need for defense. I believe that you had to wade through that mire until you were able to reach an understanding of the necessity of the Gift in your life. I believe that your fear of negative realities had to be stripped away in order for your pathways to open to receive the Gift.

No matter how much we struggle against evil, we will never know a release from its terror until we allow the Gift to manifest within our spirits and guide the actions that we take. Only through the power of the Gift are we able to accept and deal with the impact of evil."

Shona: "But as long as distorted unfulfilled needs exist, there will be evil in the world; there will always be those who violently pursue their own distorted need-fulfillment, with destruction, hatred, and ignorance as their only guides."

Taijaur: "Oh, make no mistake—no matter what we do or how well we live our lives—evil will come, it will be here—this we know for sure. I have come to realize that this time period in which the human race exists on this planet coincides with a time in the universe's cycle of development when evil is a part of the nature of the world. Evil is a distorted form of the necessary destructive energy of the universe. Negative energy is required to maintain the balance in life and in the cosmos. It is a counter force that makes us stronger in our battle against it, and it helps to maintain equilibrium between alternating flows of different types of energy, thus ensuring our evolution and development.

However, the negative predatory form of energy that manifests as human evil is a distorted form of negative energy that is created as a byproduct of unfulfilled needs. It is an unnatural extreme form of chaos that results from a disconnect with the sacred. Rather than acting as a counter-force to fuel our development, it deters our growth and possibly, potentially ensures our extinction

Evil requires a self-centered, unintelligent immaturity. A spiritually mature person, like a mature universe, cannot tolerate the energy that it takes to sustain evil."

Shona: "But it is not always so simple to identify evil. Most people believe that their own enemies are evil, while their enemies believe the same about them."

Taijaur: "This is true. However, there are still some acts that are so heinous and malicious that they are classified as 'evil', no matter who commits them and no matter what reason or justification can be offered in their defense. In my opinion, conscious sentient predation—the unprovoked, intentional and violent harm, abuse and murder of any life form is the most readily identifiable form of evil that exists.

I think that, in the final analysis, there is an inherent need within all existence, for life to unfold in accordance with reason, logic and harmony. And more than anything else, evil is irrational; it is illogical. It does not fit within the universal reason and harmony that lies at the heart of the universe and makes up the underlying structure of its fabric. This universal reason and harmony is embedded in our souls and instinctively we understand that all our aspirations in life are leading to this place of rational ubiquitous synchronization in human relationships and in our interactions with the natural world.

We have an innate need to see the world within this harmonious framework and we subsequently experience cognitive dissonance when life presents itself in ways that contradict our expectation of harmony and reason."

Shona: "But I believe that, no matter how disconcerting reality may be, we must accept life as we find it; learn to love life in its roughest, rawest and messiest forms."

Taijaur: "I agree—rough, raw and messy, but this does not mean that we should ever accept evil. I believe that, no matter what happens, we must never stop believing in, fighting for, or lose sight of the harmony and reason that will one day annihilate the intent of evil in the world. This is the vision and the belief that will help transform the spirit of the human race to move in synch with the energy of the evolving universe.

The Earth is transforming, all life is developing and moving to higher and higher states of existence, higher states of knowing. So although the energy that brings about evil is a part of the nature of the world that we know at this time in history—there will be no place for evil in a fully mature universe. This is the energy that must be put in check in order for the world to transform."

Shona: "But still no matter how hard we strive for harmony, we will never escape the strife and discord of existing in a world of competing demands for need-fulfillment."

Taijaur: "Yet we can rise above the pain, the suffering and the petty nonsense that is created as a result of this competition. We can learn to cooperate and strive to create equitable systems that take into account the needs of all entities of life.

Despite the pervasive negative forces that can be generated from within the psyche of humankind, there will always exist deep reservoirs of power and energy latent within the human spirit and within the spirit of the Earth. This is why we must honor and continuously strive to make ourselves worthy of the Gift. The Gift gives us the power to go beyond the impact of evil, beyond the impact of sorrow, adversity, hatred, loneliness, fear. The land and the spirit of the land gives all terrestrial inhabitants the power to feel connected, loved and fulfilled. It gives us the power to reach inside another person to help strengthen and reaffirm their connection with life, their connection with the sacred."

Shona: "Then truly, it must be the Gift that leads us to the final stage of injera, in the sense of purpose, reason and cause; in the sense of contributing to the evolution of the spirit of man. It is as you said Taijaur—we are all healers. That is what we do with and for one another. We help each other to heal. We help one another to survive, to grow, to re-align our internal structures with the intent of the universe."

Taijaur: "The central issue of life on earth is how to transform need into power—power to truly live our lives, power to reach our potential as beings of wisdom, strength and compassion."

Shona: "Then the real quest in life is not to find one's purpose, but to learn how to receive the Gift and through this, all other gifts are possible. Only then can need be transformed into power. As we become true beings of power, then perhaps we can begin to create a world free of the weak unfulfilled needs that manifest in the form of evil and malice."

Taijaur: "Yes, perhaps we will then have the power to control our perceptions and work in harmony with the natural realm. We can achieve an awareness of how to move forward within life's truer intent, towards the continual evolution of the universe."

Shona: "Perhaps, in the end, this is what must endure—the power that living gives; the power to allow the spirit of God to be seen and heard through our lives and the way that we live. This spirit, this energy of Creation must endure beyond all else."

They both fell silent as they looked up and realized that they had reached the end of the isthmus with the open sea between them and the shoreline of the island which was visible in the distance. The mist and clouds had lifted and they stood staring in awe at the beauty and majesty of their island's lofty mountain peaks and the rugged precipitous cliffs of the western shore escarpment. They were stimulated and emotionally overwhelmed to the extent that, for a moment, they could not move.

Shona surfaced first, sighing deeply and then saying aloud, "It looks like we will have to swim the rest of the way."

Taijaur: "It should take us less than an hour. We can then walk along the coast up to the path that leads through the mountains down into the valley where our villages lie. It may take about three days to reach the mountain pass and another few days to make it through the mountains. With this shorter more direct route through the northern mountains, we should arrive back in the Ocanmain before the end of the week. We can at least start part of the way up the coast before nightfall and make camp somewhere in the caves along the shore."

Their water-proof packs were buoyant enough to float behind them as they towed them along secured with thin strips of fabric that each had tied to an ankle. Diving into the cold ocean waves, they both quickly realized that the surface water had been deceptively calm as they struggled against the strong underwater currents. Shona was determined to keep pace with Taijaur but she fell behind when mid-way through she stopped because she thought that she heard the loud screech of a bird of prey. For a few minutes she tread water turning in circles, searching the empty sky. This was indeed puzzling, because she was absolutely certain that she had heard the unmistakable cry of a carnivorous bird just above her head. Taijaur slowed down to allow her time to catch up and they continued on, finally dragging out of the water almost two hours later than what he had estimated.

They lie exhausted on a small patch of sand, side by side breathing hard for a few moments before rising to start on their path along the edge of the shallow surf. Just as they began trudging forth, Shona heard, for the second time, a loud screeching cry like some kind of bird of prey flying directly overhead. But when she looked up, the sky was still empty. Inexplicably, she began to feel a suffocating oppressive feeling like she was back there, underground, in that other world. Taijaur had continued walking in front of her, with his head slightly bowed, seemingly lost in thought, totally oblivious to the sounds of the raptor and the heavy sense of dread that permeated the air.

He turned to speak to her, "Shona, I——," and then finally noticing that she had not kept abreast and seeing the worried look on her face, he stopped and reached out to her, peering at her with concern. "What's wrong? Are you okay?"

Shona moved towards him clutching his arm and taking a few deep breaths as she responded, "I'm fine; just a little tired, I suppose. But did you see or hear a bird flying overhead just now, some kind of giant hawk or some other type of bird of prey?"

"Where?" shielding his eyes from the sun and looking up, "I don't see anything."

Shona also glanced once more at the empty sky. "I guess it is gone now."

Taijaur: "That's strange to have a bird of prey this far from the mainland, near the island and over the open sea."

Shona: "And you didn't hear anything?"

Taijaur: "No, nothing."

Still peering into the sky, Shona said quietly, "It seems almost like a sign or an omen of some kind, doesn't it?"

Taijaur studied Shona closely. "Are you sure that you are okay?" He looked back up at the sky. "We have to remember, Shona that not every strange occurrence portends disaster. Some things happen just because."

Near the edge of the forest she noticed a whole group of small reclusive animals that were usually hidden away running wildly out in the open day. She opened her mouth to bring to Taijaur's attention this further example of how abnormally the animals were behaving and then she decided to say nothing. She steadied herself and released her hold on his arm.

Shona: "I'm okay. What were you about to say before?" The light of the day was still strong, even though the sun was beginning to set as they started their trek again. Taijaur kept his eyes on the ground ahead of them as he responded, "Shona, there is one more thing; another dimension of the Gift that I must share with you before we go back to the settlements. It is really just one more way of understanding the Gift. I should have told you before, but I wanted you to understand the other dimensions and aspects of the Gift that are just as important as this final facet."

Shona: "What is it?"

Taijaur: "Well, it's something you already know; it is actually as you guessed, as you conjectured, but it is not as negative as it may seem. It is what you have been saying all along and in so many words, what I was also trying to convey."

Shona: "Taijaur, just say what it is."

Taijaur: "To a certain extent, you were correct about some of the things that you said about the Ocan people. Many of our people have come to believe that they—we, all Ocan—are a separate species from the other humans that populate the earth. They believe that the land—the power of the land—has developed something inside of our molecular structure that has allowed us to evolve into a different, more advanced type of being. They believe that our evolution is leading us to transcend the petty boundaries of human existence and transform more fully into beings of power. They believe that the present humans are like the Neanderthals and other prototypical form of homo sapiens that once existed. They believe that what we now know as the human species will soon become extinct; either destroying themselves or finding themselves no longer suitable to the earth's changing habitats."

Shona: "What?!!?? What about all that we have discussed today? I thought you said—"

Taijaur: "I know what I said. But think about it, you said it yourself—over 99 per cent of all the species that have inhabited this planet have become extinct. Why would the human species—above all other life forms—be immune to this consequence and reality of earthly existence? Thousands of new species are discovered each year. While many have existed for millennia, most are newly evolved species that have come into existence partially as a result of the changing environment, the changing climate. Why would humans be the only life form to escape the evolution of this world? Each species' allotted space is only theirs for a finite period of time."

She shook her head slowly from side to side, "Just when I think that the answer to the Ocan-enigma is finally in my grasp, some other morsel of information shifts my understanding back to zero. It must be the Aka who believe this, surely not those of the Ocan-main; surely not all Ocan believe this."

Taijaur: "For the most part, this is an accepted fact of most Ocan and Aka alike. It is this 'fact' that underlies the conflict between the two groups and compels us to compete against one another. Which ever group is first to unlock the key to controlling the portals, will hold the power when the new world becomes a reality."

Shona: "Taijaur, do you realize what you are saying? This warped belief runs counter to all that we have just discussed, all that we have agreed comes to us as a result of receiving the Gift."

Taijaur: "I know that it seems that way, Shona. But whether or not you believe that the time of the humans is drawing to a close, there is still no denying that there is something inside of the Ocan people that makes us fundamentally different from other humans who populate this sphere. The changes in our genotype leave little similarity between the Ocan and most other humans who are infected by the virus. However, there are many Ocan, like Alor and like your mother and her parents before her who do not believe that our differences necessarily make us a separate species."

Shona: "How is it possible that a separate species could have developed in so short a geologic time as two centuries?"

Taijaur: "The energy of the island has accelerated our rate of evolution."

Shona: "Is this, this theory something that was recently concocted?'"

Taijaur: "No, there is much in the Founders' Creed that supports this perspective. It is certain that the founders of the Ocan community deliberately and intentionally set out to change who we are on a genetic basis. However, the founders never exactly specified that we would become a separate species—just a fundamentally changed/altered/modified type of being. The rest has been inferred. One significant implication of this dimension of the Gift is that some of our people—the Elders in particular—or at least those presently serving on the council—contend that, as a result of our changed genotype, our destiny should not involve going back into the world to help rid the plague from the nations of the world.

They believe that we have only to wait until the humans destroy themselves or until they are destroyed by the earth. They point to the fact that increasingly many humans can only procreate through artificial means and they believe that this may be only one of many signs indicating the inevitable demise of this species. They further point to what they believe to be irrefutable evidence that supports the notion that, in a short while, the humans will no longer be able to adapt to an environment that they have so arrogantly, ignorantly and detrimentally altered. They believe that our real Gift is our ability to survive and outlast the time of the humans on the Earth; that we, the Ocan, are evolution's next step toward a truer expression of humankind, and perhaps the last hope for the survival of some vestige of what was once the human species."

They had stopped walking and Shona stood facing Taijaur, staring with her mouth and eyes wide open. They had wandered a little ways from the shore, closer to the edge of the forest.

Taijaur: "This is also one of the main reasons for the necessity of our group isolation and the reason that we don't, we don't—"

Shona: "Don't what? Don't mix your blood with the blood of other humans? Don't create hybrids like me?"

Taijaur: "Yes, this is the reason that miscegenation is forbidden."

Taijaur sighed heavily before continuing, "And it is also for this reason that the Elders want to see you returned to the Ocan. They believe that we cannot risk anyone knowing of our existence before the time has come for us to go back into the world and assume our place as the rightful inheritors of the Earth."

Shona: "Is that what you believe, Taijaur—that we, or rather the Ocan are some supremely different type of terrestrial being?" And then in a small sad tone of resignation and innocent curiosity, she asked, "Is this why you brought me back Taijaur—to deliver me to your elders?"

"Shona, I—"

Taijaur was interrupted by a sudden deafening noise and jolting movement that made them both instinctively turn to look up in the direction of the Ocan northern mountain range. Before they had time to move or react in any way, they felt-heard a thunderous explosion and saw the largest of the northern Ocan mountains disappear in a dark cloud of smoke. The ocean waves were building and crashing in a wild uproar as the earth moved beneath their feet. They were pushed and lifted into the air, falling forcefully into and against one another. When they landed, Taijaur managed to pull Shona and himself to a nearby tree, and he grabbed hold of it with Shona in his arms. She embraced him tightly even though she was wedged firmly between the tree and his body. He held on to the tree with all of his strength as other smaller trees swept by them, torn and uprooted by the fierce ocean waves that crashed all around them.

Something inside the earth had violently pushed dark billowing clouds of hot pumice and gas out of the largest northern mountain, high up into the air.

The brutal force and combustion of internal matter and energy then spewed and shot out of the mountain liquid fire and molten rock. Within moments the ash and dust blacked out the sky, obliterating the day. Taijaur and Shona stood immobile in the sudden darkness, their sentiale churning with the silent screams of thousands of living beings. In the midst of the tumultuous sounds and the trembling earth and sea, Taijaur heard Shona's choked, deep fervent whisper, "My God!! My God!!".

Epilogue

All there ever was—the wind, the dust, and the webs we weave.

Proof